The Soul of the Robot

Jasperodus, a robot, sets out to prove he is the equal of any human being. His futuristic adventures as warrior, tyrant, renegade, and statesman eventually lead him back home to the two human beings who created him. He returns with a question: Does he have a soul?

The Knights of the Limits

The best short fiction of Barrington Bayley from his *New Worlds* period. Nine brilliant stories of infinite space and alien consciousness, suffused with a sense of wonder ...

The Fall of Chronopolis

The mighty ships of the Third Time Fleet relentlessly patrolled the Chronotic Empire's thousand-year frontier, blotting out an error of history here or there before swooping back to challenge other time-travelling civilisations far into the future. Captain Mond Aton had been proud to serve in such a fleet. But now, falsely convicted of cowardice and dereliction of duty, he had been given the cruellest of sentences: to be sent unprotected into time as a lone messenger between the cruising timeships. After such an inconceivable experience in the endless voids there was only one option left to him. To be allowed to die.

Also by Barrington J. Bayley

Age of Adventure
Annihilation Factor
Collision with Chronos
Empire of Two Worlds
Sinners of Erspia
Star Winds
The Fall of Chronopolis
The Forest of Peldain
The Garment of Caean
The Grand Wheel
The Great Hydration
The Pillars of Eternity
The Rod of Light
The Soul of the Robot
The Star Virus
The Zen Gun
The Knights of the Limits
The Seed of Evil

Barrington J. Bayley

SF GATEWAY OMNIBUS

THE SOUL OF THE ROBOT
THE KNIGHTS OF THE LIMITS
THE FALL OF CHRONOPOLIS

GOLLANCZ
LONDON

First published in Great Britain in 2014 by
Gollancz
An imprint of the Orion Publishing Group
Orion House, 5 Upper St Martin's Lane,
London WC2H 9EA

An Hachette UK Company

A CIP catalogue record for this book
is available from the British Library

ISBN 978 0 575 10316 0

1 3 5 7 9 10 8 6 4 2

Typeset by Jouve (UK), Milton Keynes

Printed and bound by CPI Group (UK) Ltd, Croydon, CR0 4YY

The Orion Publishing Group's policy is to use papers
that are natural, renewable and recyclable products and
made from wood grown in sustainable forests. The logging
and manufacturing processes are expected to conform to
the environmental regulations of the country of origin.

www.orionbooks.co.uk
www.gollancz.co.uk

CONTENTS

ENTER THE SF GATEWAY ...

Towards the end of 2011, in conjunction with the celebration of fifty years of coherent, continuous science fiction and fantasy publishing, Gollancz launched the SF Gateway.

Over a decade after launching the landmark SF Masterworks series, we realised that the realities of commercial publishing are such that even the Masterworks could only ever scratch the surface of an author's career. Vast troves of classic SF and fantasy were almost certainly destined never again to see print. Until very recently, this meant that anyone interested in reading any of those books would have been confined to scouring second-hand bookshops. The advent of digital publishing changed that paradigm for ever.

Embracing the future even as we honour the past, Gollancz launched the SF Gateway with a view to utilising the technology that now exists to make available, for the first time, the entire backlists of an incredibly wide range of classic and modern SF and fantasy authors. Our plan, at its simplest, was – and still is! – to use this technology to build on the success of the SF and Fantasy Masterworks series and to go even further.

The SF Gateway was designed to be the new home of classic science fiction and fantasy – the most comprehensive electronic library of classic SFF titles ever assembled. The programme has been extremely well received and we've been very happy with the results. So happy, in fact, that we've decided to complete the circle and return a selection of our titles to print, in these omnibus editions.

We hope you enjoy this selection. And we hope that you'll want to explore more of the classic SF and fantasy we have available. These are wonderful books you're holding in your hand, but you'll find much, much more ... through the SF Gateway.

www.sfgateway.com

INTRODUCTION

from The Encyclopedia of Science Fiction

Barrington J. Bayley (1937–2008) was a UK writer active as a freelance under various names in the 1950s, often working as P. F. Woods and (with his editor and colleague Michael Moorcock) as Michael Barrington. During his prolific early years in particular, he wrote juvenile stories, comics, picture-strips and features as well as sf, which he began to publish with 'Combat's End' for *Vargo Science Fiction Magazine* #4 in 1954. The best of his early work appears in *The Seed of Evil* (coll 1979), a retrospective assembled to honour his substantial career. All his sf novels were published under his own name, beginning with *Star Virus* (1970). This complex and somewhat gloomy space epic, along with some of its successors, had a strong though not broadly recognized influence on such UK sf writers as M. John Harrison. Perhaps because Bayley's style is sometimes laboured and his lack of cheerful endings is alien to the expectations of readers of conventional Space Opera, he never received adequate recognition for the hard-edged control he exercised over plots, whose typically intricate dealings in Time Paradoxes, and their insistent highly focused metaphysical drive, make them some of the most formidable works of their type. Though *Annihilation Factor* (1972), *Empire of Two Worlds* (1972) and *Collision Course* (1973; vt *Collision with Chronos* 1977) – which utilizes the time theories of J. W. Dunne – are all variously successful, probably his most fully realized Time Paradox or Time Police space opera is *The Fall of Chronopolis* (1974) (see below).

The Robot Jasperodus series – comprising *The Soul of the Robot* (1974; revised 1976) (see below) and its loose sequel *The Rod of Light* (1985) – marked a change of pace in its treatment of such Robot themes as the nature of self-consciousness; and *The Garments of Caean* (1976) utilizes some fairly sophisticated cultural Anthropology in a space-opera tale at whose heart lies a subversive device: a depiction of sentient clothing which (more or less literally) makes the man. But perhaps the most significant work Bayley produced in the 1970s was short fiction, most of it collected in *The Knights of the Limits* (1978) (see below); much of his last fiction (at least twenty further stories) appeared in *Interzone* and remains uncollected. Later space operas – *The Grand Wheel* (1977) (about Psi Powers), *Star Winds* (1978), *The Pillars of Eternity* (1982), *The Zen Gun* (1983), *The Forest of Peldain* (1985), *The Sinners of Erspia* (2002) and *The Great Hydration* (2005) – continued to conceive of the universe as a kind of polished machine. Bayley continues to be seriously underestimated, perhaps because most of his best work appeared as paperback originals, most of these being published in America, a land he never visited or showed any inclination to depict in his fiction. His UK following, though not large, remained intensely loyal until the end of his life. They were right to keep his name alive.

The Fall of Chronopolis, which is the first tale assembled here, climaxes Bayley's early career in its wide-ranging but impersonal exuberance, lacking any attempt to cosy up to the reader. Even at its most outrageous, the story reads like polished reportage: a characteristic that marked Bayley's work throughout, a sense that the worlds he described were so absolutely real that he needed only to report the latest news from the front. In this novel, which is a pure Time Opera, the Chronotic Empire jousts through time and space against a terrifying adversary in doomed attempts to maintain a stable reality; at the crux of the book it becomes evident that the conflict is eternal, and that the same forces will oppose one another through time forever, in one Alternate World after another.

Though it was published in the same year (1974), *The Soul of the Robot*, the second novel here presented, marks a new stage in Bayley's career. Everything one might say about *The Fall of Chronopolis* applies here; what is added is a focus on characters – in this case robots – who own deep strangeness reflects the worlds they occupy. The effect is strangely moving and unsettling: as though we were eavesdropping on creatures far removed from us, but still intimate. The overall tale makes complex play, as before, with a number of philosophical Paradoxes, though Bayley's touch here is relatively light and elliptical, approaching the surreal 'lightness' achieved by John T. Sladek in his own robot novels.

The Knights of the Limits may contain stories that seem bleak, but in the end Bayley's architectural ingenuities (and the human/machine interfaces he was now able to depict with such ease) are what we remember. We remember the dark glittering intricacy of his creations, which glow like orreries in the mind's eye. Bayley was a cleansing writer, he cleared the eye, and sharpened the mind. We are very lucky to have him here.

For a more detailed version of the above, see Barrington J. Bayley's author entry in *The Encyclopedia of Science Fiction*: http://sf-encyclopedia.com/entry/bayley_barrington_j

Some terms above are capitalised when they would not normally be so rendered; this indicates that the terms represent discrete entries in *The Encyclopedia of Science Fiction*.

THE SOUL OF THE ROBOT

For Mike Moorcock – 'the eternal champion'!

1

Out of pre-existence Jasperodus awoke to find himself in darkness.

Seldom can a sentient being have known such presence of mind in the first few seconds of its life. Patiently Jasperodus remained standing in the pitch-blackness and reviewed his situation, drawing upon the information that had been placed in his partially-stocked memory before his birth.

He became aware that he stood unaided inside a closed metal cabinet. The first intelligent action of his existence was to grope forward with his right hand until he found the knob on the inside of the cabinet's door. He turned, and pushed. Then he stepped out to inspect the scene that met his eyes.

A man and a woman, well worn in years and dressed in smudged work smocks, stared at him shyly. They stood close to one another, like a couple who had grown old in each other's company. The room smelled faintly of pine, of which wood workbenches and other furniture were fashioned: chairs, cupboards, a table and an assembly rack. Cluttered on these, as well as on floor, benches and hooks, was a disorderly array of components and of the curious instruments betokening the trade of an electronics craftsman.

Although the room was untidy and somewhat shabby, it had a warm, homely atmosphere. Its disorder was that of someone who had his own sense of method, and Jasperodus already knew how efficacious that method was.

His glance went back to the elderly couple. They, in turn, looked at him with expressions that tried desperately to mask their anxiety. They were gentle and blameless people, and in Jasperodus' eyes rather pathetic since their eager expectations were doomed to disappointment.

'We are your parents,' the wife said in a hesitant, hopeful voice. 'We made you. You are our son.'

She had no need to explain further, for Jasperodus knew the story: childless, and saddened by their childlessness, the couple had chosen this way of giving their lives issue. They looked to Jasperodus now to bring them as much joy and comfort as an organically born flesh-and-blood child might have done.

But like many an ungrateful son, Jasperodus had already made his decision. He imagined better things for himself than to spend his life with them. Jasperodus, the hulking, bronze-black all-purpose robot they had created, laughed harshly and moved purposively across the room to the door. Opening it, he walked out of their lives.

Looking after his retreating back, the man put his hand comfortingly on his wife's shoulder. 'We knew this could happen,' he reminded her gently. It was true that they could have made their offspring with a built-in desire to cherish them; but that, they had both decided, would not be the right way. Whatever he did, it had to be of his own free will.

Yet, after their long, patient labours, their parents' anguish was real. Jasperodus had some theoretical knowledge of the world, but no experience of it. His future was as unpredictable as his past was blank.

'What will become of him?' the woman said tearfully. 'What will become of him?'

2

The rambling cottage stood alone in extensive countryside. Jasperodus took a direction at random and simply kept on walking. He walked first across a tiny patch of land that supplied his parents' meagre needs. Two robot agricultural machines were at work, one harvesting high-yield crops of grain and vegetables and the other tending a few animals. More of his father's handiwork, Jasperodus did not doubt, but they were primitive machines only, built for specific work. They compared to himself as a primitive insect compared to a man.

Five minutes brought him through the smallholding to rolling woods and wild meadows. Confident that if he kept going he would eventually meet with something more in keeping with his new-born sense of adventure, for the time being he contented himself with simply enjoying his first few hours in the world, admiring his body and all the faculties his parents had given him.

Jasperodus' form was that of a handsome humanoid in bronze-black metal. His exterior, comprising flat planes mollified by brief rounded surfaces, aspired to a frankly metallic effect. To alleviate the weightiness of this appearance he was decorated all over with artistic scroll-like engravings. Altogether, his body exuded strength and capability.

His face he could not see and so had to postpone his inspection of it. His senses, however, he could explore freely. He switched his eyesight up and down the spectrum of radiation, well beyond the octave of light visible to human beings. His audible range was equally broad. His sense of smell, on the contrary, though adequate, was not as sharp as in many men and certainly did not approach the acuteness of some animals. As for his sense of touch, it was perfectly delicate where it concerned dynamics, but he was to learn later that it lacked the delicious touch-sensations that were available to organic beings; it meant nothing to him to be stroked.

Touch-sensation was a field his father had not mastered, indeed it was the trickiest problem in the whole of robotics.

His repertoire of sensory inputs was rounded off by a superb sense of balance and movement. Jasperodus would have made a skilful dancer, despite his weight of about a third of a ton.

All in all he was probably one of the finest robots ever to be built. His father, a master robot-maker, was well-qualified for the task; he had learned his trade first of all in a robot factory in Tarka, later spending nearly a decade creating unusual robots on the estates of the eccentric Count Viss. Finally he had enrolled with the supreme robot designer of them all, Aristos Lyos, for a further three years of special study, before retiring to this remote, pleasant spot to create the masterpiece that would fulfil his life. Jasperodus could well imagine the old man's devotion, as well as the inexhaustible patience of his wife, who had prepared the greater mass of repetitive micro-circuitry.

Insofar as the machinery of his body went, all that Jasperodus had examined so far was of the finest workmanship, but not unique. More mysterious was the formation of his *character* … Here his father had shown his originality. It would have been an easy matter to endow him with any type of personality his parents had wished, but that would have defeated the object of the exercise, which was to give rise to a new, original person of unknown, unique potentialities. Therefore, at the moment of his activation, Jasperodus' father had arranged for his character to crystallise by chance out of an enormous number of random influences, thus simulating the chance combination of genes and the vagarious experiences of childhood.

As a result Jasperodus came into the world as a fully formed adult, complete with a backlog of knowledge and with decided attitudes. Admittedly his knowledge was of a sparse and patchy kind, the sort that could be gained from reading books or watching vidtapes. But he knew how to converse and was skilled at handling many types of machinery.

He knew, too, that the planet Earth was wide, varied and beautiful. Since the collapse of the Rule of Tergov (usually referred to now as the Old Empire) some eight hundred years previously there had been no integrated political order. In the intervening Dark Period of chaos even knowledge of the planet's geography had become vague. The world was a scattered, motley patchwork of states large and small, of kingdoms, principalities, dukedoms and manors. And although a New Empire was arising in the south of Worldmass – the great continent comprising most of Earth's dry surface – that saw itself as a successor to the old and destined to resurrect its glories, the machinations of the Great Emperor Charrane made slow progress. The rest of the world heeded him but little.

On and on strode Jasperodus. Night fell. He switched to infrared vision, planning to walk on uninterrupted into the day.

After some hours he saw a light shining in the distance. He switched back to normal vision, at which the light resolved itself into a fierce beam stabbing the darkness and moving slowly but steadily across the landscape, disappearing now and then behind hillocks or stretches of forest. Eager to investigate, he broke into a loping run, crashing through the undergrowth and leaping over the uneven ground.

On topping a rise, he stopped. He found himself looking down on a track comprising parallel steel rails. The moving headlight rounded a curve and approached the culvert. Behind it followed a chain of smaller lights, glimmering from the windows of elongated, dulled-silver coaches with streamlined fluted exteriors.

He instantly recognised the apparition as a train. But its speed, he imagined, was unnaturally slow for such a machine – barely twenty miles per hour. Suddenly he heard a staccato chattering noise coming from the train, first in a long burst, then intermittently. The engine? No ...

Machine-gun fire.

Jasperodus slithered down the embankment. The windowless leading coach swept majestically abreast of him, wheels hissing on the rails; locating a handhold he swung himself easily on to the running-board that ran the length of the outer casing.

He edged along the brief ledge, pressing himself against the curved metal skin of the vehicle and looking for a way in. Up near the roof he found a square sliding panel that made an opening large enough to admit him. Gracefully he levered himself to a level with it and dropped feet first into the brightness within.

He landed in a narrow tunnel with a rounded roof. At once the machine-gun started up again, making a violent, deafening cacophony in the confined space, and he staggered as bullets rattled off his body. Then there was a pause.

The big machine-gun was stationed at the forward end of the long corridor. Behind it squatted a man in blue garb. It appeared to Jasperodus that he was guarding the door to the control cab. He glanced to the other end of the corridor, but it was deserted. The gun controlled the passageway completely; the man's enemies, whoever they were, were obliged to stay strictly out of sight.

Again the machine-gunner opened up. Jasperodus became indignant at the ricochetting assault on his toughened steel hide. He pressed swiftly forward against the tide of bullets, lurching from side to side in the swaying tunnel but closing the distance between him and his tormentor. At the last moment the gunner scrambled up from his weapon and clawed at the door behind him. He had left it too late. Jasperodus took the machine-gun by its smoking barrel and swung it in the air, its tripod legs kicking. The guard uttered a single grunt as the magazine case thudded dully on to his head.

Jasperodus stood reflectively, looking down at the blood oozing from the crushed skull. He had committed his first act in the wider world beyond his parents' home. And it had been an act of malice. The machine-gunner had posed no substantial threat to him; he had simply been angered by the presumptuous attack. Letting fall the gun he opened the door to the control cab. It was empty. The train was fully automatic, though equipped with manual override controls. The alarm light was flashing and the instrument board revealed extensive damage to the transmission system. The train was in distress and evidently making the best time it could.

Steps sounded behind him. Jasperodus turned to see a grinning figure standing framed in the doorway and cradling a machine-gun of more portable proportions. A second new arrival peered over his shoulder, eyeing Jasperodus and gawping.

Both men had shaggy hair that hung to their shoulders. They were dressed in loose garments of a violently coloured silky material, gathered in at waist and ankles and creased and scruffy from overlong use. The sight of Jasperodus made the grin freeze on the leader's face.

'A robot! A goddamned robot! So that's it! I wondered how you clobbered the machine-gun – figured you must have come through the roof.'

He brushed past Jasperodus and into the cab, slapping a switch after a cursory study of the control board. Ponderously the train ground to a halt.

Just then Jasperodus noticed that a gun in the hands of the second man was being pointed at his midriff. Impatiently he tore the weapon from the impudent fellow's grasp, twisted it into a useless tangle, and threw it into a corner. The other backed away, looking frightened.

'Cool it!' the leader snapped. Jasperodus made no further move but stared at him. After a glance of displeasure the man turned away from him again, bent to the control panel and closed more switches. With a rumbling noise the train began to trundle backwards.

Then he straightened and faced Jasperodus. 'Say, what are you doing here?' he said in a not unfriendly tone. 'Why did you kill the guard?'

'He was shooting at me.'

'Who owns you? One of the passengers? Or are you freight?'

'No one owns me. I am a free, independent being.'

The man chuckled, his face breaking out into a grin that creased every inch of it.

'That's rich!'

His expression became speculative as his eyes roved over Jasperodus. 'A wild robot, eh? You've done us a favour, metal man. I thought we'd never shift that bastard with the machine-gun.'

'How did the train come to be damaged?' Jasperodus asked. 'Are you its custodians?'

'*Now* we are!' Both men laughed heartily. 'We made a mess of things, as usual. She kept going after we detonated the charge. It should have stopped her dead. We damned near didn't get aboard.'

While he spoke he was scanning the rearwards track through a viewscreen. 'My name is Craish,' he offered. 'As well you should know it, since you may be seeing a good deal of me.'

The significance of this remark was lost on Jasperodus. 'Robbers,' he said slowly. 'You are out to plunder the train.'

Again they laughed. 'Your logic units are slow on the uptake,' Craish said, 'but you cotton on in the end.'

Excitement coursed through Jasperodus. Here was the tang of adventure!

After a short journey Craish once more brought the train to a halt. He flung open a side door.

They were parked on a length of track that rounded a clearing in the all-encompassing forest. Here waited more of Craish's gang. With much noise and yelling they set about unloading the train, unlocking the container cars and carelessly throwing out all manner of goods. On the ground others sorted through the booty, flinging whatever took their fancy into small carrier vehicles. The procedure was ridiculous, thought Jasperodus. The freight train was a large one. Its total cargo must have been very valuable, yet the bandits would be able to take away no more than a small fraction of it. The band was badly organised, or else it knew enough to keep its nuisance value within limits.

Craish returned to Jasperodus, who still stood watching from the running-board of the control cab. 'Go and help my men unload,' he ordered.

The order was given in such a confident tone that Craish obviously had no doubt that it would be obeyed unquestioningly. Jasperodus was affronted. Did the man think of him as a slave? Craish was walking unconcernedly away. Jasperodus called out to him.

'Where is this train bound?'

The other stopped and looked back. 'The Empire, eventually. It's a trading train, sent out by Empire merchants. It stops at towns on the way and barters goods.' He looked askance at the robot, wondering why he needed to ask this question.

'What will you do with it? Leave it here?'

'Nah. Send it on its way. So they'll never know where we jumped it.'

With that Craish walked away. Jasperodus pondered. The prospect of a trip to the Empire excited him but, he reminded himself, the train was crippled. Still, he could if he wished stay with the train on its long and monotonous journey, although he would meet with the opposition of the bandits, who plainly would not want witnesses to their deeds wandering abroad. Also, there might be trouble when the train reached its next stop. All in all, it might be better to stay with these ruffians. As his first real contact with human beings they were already proving entertaining.

Accordingly he contributed his superhuman strength to the unloading and sorting of the cargo. Eventually the forage trucks were filled to capacity and the bandits, who numbered about twenty, seemed satisfied. Some of the discarded cargo was actually put back on board; the rest was gathered in a heap and set alight, an inflammable liquid being poured over it to make a good blaze. As the huge bonfire glared fiercely at the sky the marauders brought forth another kind of plunder from the train's single passenger coach: prisoners, all female as far as Jasperodus could see, linked together by a rope tied around their necks, jerking and protesting. The train pulled out, limping painfully under automatic control towards its distant destination.

They all set off through the forest. The forage trucks had big balloon tyres that enabled them to roll easily over the rough ground, but most of the men walked, as did the prisoners. The forest sprawled over rocky, hilly terrain through which they travelled for more than an hour. Finally they debouched into the bandits' camp: a dell formed like an amphitheatre, having a large cave at its closed end.

The night was warm. Before long a fire was started in the centre of the dell, casting a glimmering light over the proceedings. Goods spilled to the ground as the forage trucks were tipped on their sides; the men began to go through the plunder like children with new toys, draping themselves with sumptuous raiment, shaking out bolts of expensive cloth, playing with the new gadgets and so forth. Jasperodus gathered that later most of it would be sold in nearby towns. But not, he guessed, the bottles of liquor: specially prized articles that were passed from mouth to mouth and emptied rapidly.

Casting his eye over the strewn booty, Jasperodus spied an object of immediate interest to him: a hand mirror, included among the valuables because of the gems that adorned its frame. Quickly he seized it and settled by the fire; now at last he would be able to see his face.

He had feared that his father might have given him the grotesque mouthless and noseless face seen on many robots, or even worse, that he would have committed a much greater travesty by sculpting a human face. The countenance that stared out of the mirror reassured him. It was a sternly functional visage – and, of course, it was immobile – but it was more than just a mask. Following the general conception of his body, it consisted mainly of machined flat surfaces and projections that gave it a solid but intriguingly machicolated appearance. A square-bridged nose ended in simple flanges perfectly adapted to its function as an olfactory device. A straight, immobile mouth, from which Jasperodus' booming, well-timbred voice was thrown by a hidden speaker, was so well placed amid the angled planes of the jaw that it fitted naturally and without artifice; as did the flat, square ears, which contained an arrangement of small flanges serving the same purpose as those of the human ear: the abstraction of direction and stereo from the sound they received.

Eyes glowed softly by their own red light. Finally, the whole face was lightly engraved with the same intricate scrolls that decorated the rest of the body.

Jasperodus was well pleased. His was a non-human, robot face, but somehow it seemed to express his inner essence: it looked the way he felt.

Craish arrived and found him gazing into the mirror. Laughing, he tipped up a bottle and poured liquor over Jasperodus' torso. 'Admiring yourself, metal-man? A pity you can't drink.'

Jasperodus laid down the mirror, but did not speak.

Unabashed, Craish sat beside him and swigged from the bottle. 'We can certainly use you,' he continued. 'You're strong, and bullets don't bother you a bit. You look like you're worth a lot, too – your owner must be plenty sore to lose you. You'll stay with us from now on, understand?'

He spoke in the same matter-of-fact tone in which he had ordered the robot to work at the train. Jasperodus ignored him. Nearby, one of Craish's men had laid down his sub-machine-gun and he picked it up to examine it. It was simply-constructed, but its design was good: merely a barrel, a repeater mechanism, a short stock and a handgrip. On one of his father's lathes Jasperodus could have turned one out in less than an hour. The magazine was spherical, slotting over the handgrip, and contained hundreds of rounds.

'An effective device,' he commented, slinging the gun over his shoulder by its strap. 'I will keep this.'

'Hey, gimme my gun, you damned robot,' objected its owner explosively. 'Who do you think you are?'

Jasperodus stared at him. 'You wish to do something about it?'

Craish intervened in a sharp tone. 'Wait a minute! If I want you to carry a gun I'll tell you, metal-man. So put the gun down. Just sit there and wait for your orders.'

'You are very good at giving orders,' Jasperodus said slowly, turning his massive head.

'And you're good at taking them. You're a robot, aren't you?' Craish frowned uneasily. 'A machine.' He was perplexed; robots, in fact any cybernetic system, had a natural propensity for obeying orders that were firmly given, but this one showed an unnerving individuality. Advanced machines, of course, would tend to be more self-reliant and therefore more subject to individual quirks, but not, he would have thought, to this degree.

'Say,' whined the deprived bandit, 'this hulk doesn't take any notice of us at all. It just sits there defying us. It must have a command language, Craish.'

Craish snapped his fingers. 'That's it. Of course.' He turned to Jasperodus. 'What's your command language? How does your master speak to you?'

Jasperodus had only a vague idea what he was talking about. 'I have no master,' he replied. 'I am not a machine. I am an original being, like you. I am a self.'

Craish laughed until tears started from his eyes. 'That's a good one. Whoever manufactured you must have been a kookie to write that in your brain. Where are you from, by the way? How long have you been loose?'

'I was activated this morning.'

'Yeah?' Craish's merriment trailed off. 'Well, like I said, give the man back his gun.'

'Do you think you can take it from me?' Jasperodus asked him acidly.

Craish paused. 'Not if you object,' he said slowly. He deliberated. 'Were you thinking of staying with us?'

'I shall keep my own counsel.'

'Okay.' Craish motioned to the plaintiff in the case. They both got up and left. Jasperodus remained sitting there, staring into the fire.

Soon the revels entered a new phase. The bandits turned their attentions to the women, who up to now had been standing in a huddled group to one side. Their menfolk had all been slaughtered on the train, and they looked forlorn and apprehensive, remembering the recent horror and anticipating the mistreatment to come. Now they were dragged into the firelight and their ropes removed. They were forced to dance, to drink. Then their kidnappers, one by one, began to caress them, to throw them to the ground and strip them. The light of the flames flickered on gleaming naked bodies, and very quickly the scene turned into an orgy of rape.

Jasperodus watched all this blankly, listening to sobs and screams from the women, to growls of lust from the men. Carnal pleasure was foreign to him, and for the first time he felt sullen and disappointed: the experience of erotic sexual enjoyment was something his parents had not been able to give him.

True, the enjoyment the bandits found in forcing women against their will, in hearing their screams and cries of protestation, he could to some slight extent understand. After all, there was always satisfaction in forcing, in dominance. But the frantic sensual pleasure of desire gone mad, that he could not understand.

Again, it was not that he lacked aesthetic appreciation. He knew full well what beauty was, but unfortunately that did not help him in the sphere of eroticism. The aesthetic qualities of the naked female bodies now exposed to his view did not exceed, in his opinion, the aesthetic qualities of the naked male bodies. Clearly the sexual passions they aroused in the breasts of these ruffians was a peculiarly animal phenomenon that was closed to him.

It came to him, while he watched what the men were doing to the women, that he possessed no phallus or genitals of any kind. Yet his parents had definitely envisaged him as a son, not as a daughter or as neuter, and his outlook was a strictly masculine one. He glanced down at himself. So that the absence of male genitals should not invest him with an incongruously feminine appearance his father had placed at the groin a longish box-like bulge that gave a decidedly male effect, rather like a cod-piece. Unlike a cod-piece, however, it hid not phallus and testicles but a package of circuits concerned with balanced movement, corresponding to the spinal ganglia in humans.

Throughout the night the sleepless Jasperodus watched the frenzy in the firelight and brooded. Any stimulation he managed to gain from the spectacle of continued rape (and later, of resigned abandonment on the part of the women) was vicarious and abstract; the purely mental observation of a pleasure which, he was sure, he could never share.

3

At dawn, while the camp was still in a drunken sleep, Jasperodus roused himself. He made his way back along the route he had come until striking the railway track. Then, taking the direction followed by the crippled train, he set off, walking between the rails with his sub-machine-gun clanking lightly against his side.

The sun rose to its zenith and found him still walking. By the time it sank into mid-afternoon the wild countryside was giving way to cultivated plots. The people here were evidently not rich and lived sparsely. Although some of the fields were worked by rather tatty cybernetic machines, in others human labour guided powered ploughs and harvesters, or even scratched the earth with implements hauled by animals.

The further he went the more the forest thinned, until eventually the landscape consisted entirely of farmland. Draught animals had disappeared by now. The farms were larger and only machines were at work. The cottages of the outlying farms were here transformed into more expansive houses, and altogether the scene was a pleasant one of peaceful rural life.

Without pause Jasperodus walked on into the night and through to the next day. At mid-morning he was entering a town.

Judging by its appearance it was of some antiquity, and probably dated back to the Old Empire, for on the outskirts he saw a clump of ruins that he guessed to be at least a thousand years old. In its present form, however, the town had probably taken shape about five hundred years ago. Its streets were narrow, twisting and turning confusingly. The buildings, many of them built of wood, crowded close together and had a cramped appearance.

Jasperodus strode easily through the busy lanes, enjoying the bustle of commerce. The open-fronted shops were doing a brisk trade and the people cast scarcely a glance at the tall man of metal who passed in their midst.

But he was not ignored by everyone. As he approached the town centre a sharp, peremptory voice rang out.

'You there – robot! Stop!'

He turned. Approaching him were four men, uniformly apparelled in sleek green tunics, corded breeks, and green shako hats surmounted by swaying feathered plumes. Their faces were hard, with cold eyes that were used to seeing others obey them.

'No robots carry weapons in Gordona. Hand over that gun.'

Jasperodus pondered briefly and made the same decision that had guided him on the train – that although he had the power to resist, he would learn more of the world by complying. He surrendered his weapon.

The men moved to surround him, preventing him from keeping all of them in view at the same time. Like the bandits, they displayed no fear of him despite his obviously powerful person, which loomed a good half head taller than themselves, but appeared to take his acquiescence for granted. He noticed, too, that the passing citizens gave the group a wide berth.

'Who owns you?' the leader demanded. 'Where are you going?'

'No one owns me. I go where I please.'

'A construct on the loose, eh?' said the man, looking him up and down, 'A fine-looking construct, too. Follow us.'

'Why?' asked Jasperodus.

The man shot him a look of surprised anger. 'So you question the orders of a King's officer? Come, robot, come!'

Not comprehending, Jasperodus walked with the quartet along the thoroughfare. Shortly they came to a stone building that stood out from the smaller, poorer buildings on either side of it. Jasperodus' guides led him inside where, behind a large counter of polished wood, waited more men similarly attired to themselves.

'Found a footloose construct in the street,' Jasperodus' arrestor announced. 'Take him to a cell and put him on the list for this afternoon.'

Not until now did Jasperodus seriously sense danger. 'I am no prisoner!' he boomed. The sergeant behind the desk blew a whistle. At his summons two big robots blundered into the room: hulking great masses of metal even larger than Jasperodus. Though their movements were hardly graceful they closed in on him with practised speed and attached themselves one to each arm with an unbreakable grip.

Jasperodus' struggles were useless. The metal guards dragged him down a stone corridor into the depths of the building. 'Why are you doing this?' he growled. 'What crime have I committed?' But the guards remained silent. He guessed them to be dim-witted machines, suitable only for such low-intelligence tasks as they were now performing.

A door clanged open and he was thrust into a small cell. Eyeing the stone walls, he wondered at his chances of breaking the stone with his fist. Unhappily, he saw that it was steel-backed. Nor was that all: the guards snapped massive manacles on his wrists, restraining him by thick chains that hung from the ceiling, so that his arms were forced above his head and he was left dangling in the middle of the cell.

An hour passed before the door opened again. Into the cell walked a small, dapper man with a sheaf of papers under his arm. The newcomer sat down on a tabouret in the corner, keeping a safe distance between himself and the prisoner.

Placing his papers on his knee, he took out a writing instrument. 'Now then,' he began amiably, 'this should take only a few minutes.'

'Why have I been brought here?' Jasperodus asked thickly. 'What plans have you for me?'

The man seemed surprised at his ignorance. 'We here in Gordona do nothing without observing the proper form,' he said indignantly. 'Robot property cannot be impounded without legal proceedings.'

'Your words are nonsense to me,' Jasperodus told him with exasperation.

'Very well. I will explain. As a footloose robot you are to be taken into the King's service in the state of machine-slavery, or as the legal term has it: construct-bondage. Your case comes before the magistrate this afternoon, and I am the lawyer in charge of its presentation. As a self-directed construct you will be required to be present and may be called upon to answer questions to satisfy the magistrate of your derelict condition. You could even fight the impound order.'

'And how do I do that?' asked Jasperodus with growing interest.

'By naming your former owner. If he resides within the borders of the kingdom you could apply to be returned to him. Er, who is – or was – your owner?' The lawyer's pen poised above the paper.

'I have none. Yet neither do I consent to being made a slave.'

'On what grounds?'

Jasperodus rattled his chains. 'Are men, also, made slaves?'

'Certainly not. On that point the law holds throughout most of the civilised world.' The lawyer warmed up as he began to enjoy dispensing his learning. He ticked off points on his fingers. 'Sentient beings may not be made slaves. Self-directed constructs are invariably so. Any who, through the carelessness or inattention of their owners, have somehow escaped their master's supervision and wander abroad masterless may be reclaimed by any party much as may a derelict ship. Such is the law. The word "slavery" is a popularism, of course, not a proper technical term, since a robot has no genuine will and therefore no disposition towards rebelliousness, if properly adjusted.'

Jasperodus' voice became hollow and moody. 'Ever since my activation everyone I meet looks upon me as a thing, not as a person. Your legal proceedings are based upon a mistaken premiss, namely that I am an object. On the contrary, I am a sentient being.'

The lawyer looked at him blankly. 'I beg your pardon?'

'I am an authentic person, independent and aware.'

The other essayed a fey laugh. 'Very droll! To be sure, one sometimes encounters robots so clever that one could swear they had real conscious-ness! However, as is well known ...'

Jasperodus interrupted him stubbornly. 'I wish to fight my case in person. Is it permitted for a construct to speak on his own behalf?'

The lawyer nodded bemusedly. 'Certainly. A construct may lay before the court any facts having a bearing on his case – or, I should say on *its* case. I will make a note of it.' He scribbled briefly. 'But if I were you I wouldn't try to tell the magistrate what you just said to me. It wouldn't ...'

'When the time comes, I will speak as I choose.'

With a sigh the lawyer gave up. 'Oh, well, as you say. Time is pressing. Have you a number, name or identifying mark?'

'My name is Jasperodus.'

'And you say there is no owner?'

'Correct.'

'Unusual. Can you give me details of your manufacture?'

Jasperodus laughed mockingly. 'Can you of yours?'

With a mystified air the lawyer left. Jasperodus waited impatiently until at length the robot guards returned and removed the manacles. This time he made no attempt at resistance. He was conducted up staircases, along corri-dors and into the courtroom, which as near as he could judge was lodged in one of the poorer adjacent buildings.

Jasperodus surveyed the courtroom with interest. At one end a man of mature years sat on a raised dais: the magistrate. In his foreground, to right and left of him, were arrayed in sectioned compartments of panelled wood the functionaries of the court: clerks and recorders, as well as places for law-yers and other representing parties. At the other end were tiered benches, now empty, for a public audience.

Still accompanied by his guards Jasperodus was ushered to the dock, a box-like cubicle with walls reaching to his waist. Meanwhile the dapper law-yer described fairly accurately the circumstances of his arrest.

The magistrate nodded curtly. 'Anything else?'

The lawyer waved his hands in a vague gesture of embarrassment. 'The construct has expressed an intention to speak on its own behalf, Your Hon-our.' Glancing at Jasperodus, he raised his eyebrows as a signal for him to go ahead.

Jasperodus' argument was simplicity itself. 'I am informed that in law no sentient being can be made a slave,' he declared. 'I claim to be such a sentient being and therefore not a subject for construct bondage.'

A frown of annoyance crossed the magistrate's face. 'Really, Paff,' he admonished the lawyer, 'do you have to plague me with pantomimes? What nonsense!'

Paff shrugged a disclaimer.

Doggedly Jasperodus continued: 'I know I have self-awareness in the same way that you know *you* have it. I do not speak for other robots. But give me any test that will prove my self-awareness or lack of it, and you will see for yourself.'

'Test? I know of no test. What nonsense is this?' Irritable and nonplussed, the magistrate looked for advice towards the functionaries who sat below him.

The technical adviser, a suave young man in a tunic brocaded in crimson, rose to his feet. 'By your leave, Your Honour, there is no such test. Any faculty possessed by sentient beings can be simulated by an appropriate machine, and therefore the fact of consciousness itself is beyond examination.'

The magistrate nodded in satisfaction and turned to Jasperodus. 'Quite so. Have you anything germane to say?'

Jasperodus refused to let it go. 'Then how does the law define what is sentient and what is not?'

'That is simple,' replied the magistrate with the air of one explaining something to a child. 'A sentient being is a human being or a kuron. But not a construct.'

'Only natural, biologically evolved creatures can have consciousness,' interpolated the adviser, receiving a frown of reproof from the magistrate for his impudence. 'Any robotician will tell you that machine consciousness is a technical impossibility *ipso facto*.'

Jasperodus recalled that kurons had originally been extraterrestrials, who migrated to Earth centuries ago and had since lost contact with their home star. Now they lived in small communities scattered throughout various parts of the world. He seized on the magistrate's mention of them to pursue the question further.

'Suppose there was brought before you a being from another star who was neither human nor kuron,' he suggested. 'Suppose furthermore that you could not ascertain whether the being was a naturally evolved creature or a construct. How then would you settle the matter of its mental status?'

The magistrate sputtered in annoyance, waving his hands in agitation.

'I have no time for your casuistry, robot. You are a *thing*, not a person. That is all there is to it and I pronounce you to be the property of the King's court.' With finality he banged his gavel, but was interrupted once more by the presumptuous young man who was keen to make the most of his duties.

'By your leave, Your Honour, may we also recommend that this robot be given some adjustment by the Court Robotician. Its brain appears somehow or another to have acquired an aberrant self-image.'

Grumpily the magistrate nodded. 'Enter it on the record.'

Stunned by the failure of his defence, Jasperodus became aware that one of the guard robots was tugging at his arm. Passively he followed them from the dock.

They conveyed him not back to his cell but out of the building and into the windowless interior of a waiting van, which was then firmly locked. His inquiries elicited that his destination was the residence of King Zhorm, ruler of the tiny kingdom of Gordona. The van went bumping through the old town's streets. He felt too bewildered even to begin to plan escape. All he could do was brood over the disconcerting pronouncements that had just been presented to him.

An aberrant self-image, he thought darkly.

King Zhorm's palace was in the dead centre of the town. It was as large and as luxurious as the resources of Gordona would permit, which meant that it allowed the King and his court to live in luxury but not in ostentatious luxury. Zhorm, however, was content with what he had. He enjoyed life in his own rough way, kept his kingdom in order, and was neither so ambitious nor so foolish as to tax his people until they bled, as did some petty rulers.

When Jasperodus arrived the evening banquet was in progress. Proceeding through a long corridor draped with tapestries he heard the sound of rough laughter. Then he was ushered into a large, brilliantly illumined hall where fifty or more persons sat feasting at long trestle tables. At their head, in a raised chair much like a throne, lounged King Zhorm.

The King was surprisingly young-looking: not above forty. He had dark oily skin and doe-like eyes. Each ear sported large gold rings, and his hair hung about his shoulders in black greasy ringlets. Catching sight of Jasperodus, he raised his goblet with a look of delight.

'My new robot! A magnificent specimen, so I am told. Come closer, robot.'

Though disliking the riotous colours and air of revelry, Jasperodus obeyed. The banqueters eyed him appreciatively, passing remarks among one another and sniggering.

'Try some food, robot!' cried a voice. A large chunk of meat hit Jasperodus in the face and slid down his chest, leaving a greasy trail. He made no sign of recognition but stood immobile.

King Zhorm smiled, his eyes dreamy and predatory. 'Welcome into my service, man of metal. Recount me your special abilities. What can you do well?'

'Anything you can do,' Jasperodus answered, confident that he spoke the truth.

A fat man who sat near the King let out a roar. 'Say "Your Majesty", when you speak to the monarch!' He took up an iron rod that leaned against the table and began to beat Jasperodus vigorously about the arms and shoulders, to the merriment of all watchers. Jasperodus snatched the staff from his grasp and bent it double. When its two ends almost met it snapped suddenly in two and Jasperodus contemptuously hurled the pieces into a corner.

A sudden silence descended. The fat man pursed his lips. 'The robot has mettle, I see,' King Zhorm said quietly. 'A fighter, too.'

'Gogra! Let him fight Gogra!' The cry went up from all three tables. The idea seemed to please Zhorm. He clapped his hands. 'Yes, bring on Gogra.'

The banqueters sprang up with alacrity, pushed the tables nearer to the walls and scuttled behind them for protection. Jasperodus made no move but merely waited to see what was in store for him.

It was not long in coming. At the far end of the hall a tall door swung open. Through it strode Gogra: a giant of a robot, twelve foot tall and broad to match.

Gogra was coal-black. In his right hand he carried a massive sledge-hammer that in a few blows could have crushed Jasperodus to junk, tough as he was. Pausing in the doorway, the terrifying fighting robot surveyed the hall. As soon as he caught sight of Jasperodus he lunged forward, lifting the hammer with evident purpose.

Jasperodus backed away. Gogra's appearance was frightening; his head was thrust forward on his neck, reminiscent of an ape-man; and the face was such a mask of ugliness as to arouse both terror and pity: Gogra's designer had sought to give his massive frame sufficient agility by filling his interior with oil under pressure; the safety valve for that oil was his grotesque grilled mouth, from which green ichor dribbled copiously and continuously.

Studying the monster's movements, Jasperodus formed the opinion that Gogra's intelligence was moronic. He would fight according to a pattern and would not be able to depart from it.

Jasperodus easily dodged his adversary's first hammer-blow, which left the floor shattered and starred with cracks. He retreated nimbly towards the wall, causing the spectators hiding there to squeal and run along the side of the wall to escape.

A cheer went up as Gogra, uttering a deafening hiss, charged at Jasperodus who appeared to be trapped against the wall. At the last instant Jasperodus flung himself sideways to go sprawling full-length to the floor. Gogra, carrying the full momentum of his rush, crashed tumultuously into the wall with a shower of stone and plaster. Jasperodus sprang to his feet to see that the bigger robot had indeed, as he had anticipated, gone straight through the wall head-first; he stared at the thick, pillar-like legs attached to gigantic hind-quarters which stuck out from the wreckage. But he had time to give the jointed pelvis only one kick before Gogra pulled himself free, bringing a lengthy section of wall down with him as he did so. While the dazed giant staggered upright, hissing plaintively, Jasperodus gathered himself and took a leap upwards to land straight on Gogra's back. Clawing for holds, he hoisted himself up over the vast head and clung there athwart the skull, his arms obscuring Gogra's vision.

Pandemonium broke out in the hall as Gogra whirled round and round, staggering from wall to wall and crashing into the tables which splintered like matchwood. In panic and fury he hissed like a steam engine. But he had not forgotten what he was about: the great hammer still waved in the air, seeking its target. Jasperodus was keeping his eye on that terrible weapon, and he chose exactly the right instant to throw himself from his perch.

He fell to the floor with a loud clang. The hammer, swinging down into the vacated place, went smashing into Gogra's own head instead of into the body of his enemy. In a slow majestic descent the massive construct toppled with an even louder clang. The metal skull was split open; an almost-fluid mass of electronic packaging spilled out and spread slowly over the flagstones amid a soup of green oil.

Jasperodus climbed to his feet, relieved to observe that his plan to make Gogra brain himself had gone well. The banqueters, Zhorm among them, reappeared cautiously from behind their refuges.

'The stranger has slain Gogra!' someone exclaimed in astonishment. Widened eyes stared admiringly at Jasperodus.

King Zhorm, though likewise astounded, quickly recovered his composure. 'A remarkable feat,' he announced. 'Surprising initiative for a robot.'

'It was not too difficult,' Jasperodus replied. 'Your monster had as much brain as a centipede.'

'I rather liked him for that.' Sourly Zhorm looked down at the inert form of his champion, then clapped his hands again.

'Remove it.'

Servants struggled to drag away the dead hulk, aided by one or two other robots. Inch by inch it was hauled towards the big doors; meantime the tables were replaced, and fresh platters of food and more flagons of drink appeared.

Zhorm tossed a grape into his mouth. 'Well, robot, I hope you perform your other work as well as you disposed of Gogra. You look as if you need cleaning up – my girls will see to it.' He beckoned to a servant.

Jasperodus looked down at himself. He was, it was true, somewhat dirty. His travels had left him caked with mud and dust – added to, now, by plaster and brick-dust.

Some of the banqueters nearest the King giggled and ogled him as he was led away. 'Lovely naked girls,' leered one. 'Nice soft hands – enjoy yourself!'

Fools! Jasperodus thought. *As if their touch could mean anything to me.*

He followed the servant through the wide doors from which Gogra had emerged, along a short passage and into a perfumed chamber. Three naked girls rose smiling to meet him.

'Come, honoured guest. Let us bath you.'

In the centre of the circular room was a bath filled with scented water. Soap and various implements lay on a low table. For Jasperodus' benefit, so that he would not have to enter the bath, there was also a couch on which he was invited to lie.

The girls got to work, cooing and chuckling as they washed his metal body with caressing movements. He was surprised to see that they appeared to enjoy their task and to gain some perverse kind of pleasure from his strange but man-like form. One in particular – a pretty red-head – stroked him specially languorously, lingering around the box-like bulge at his groin and on the insides of his thighs. Once or twice he noticed her eyes become hot and her breath come in short little gasps. He wondered if it was the strong air of masculinity he imagined he possessed that gave them stimulation. He himself, however, felt nothing.

When they had finished drying him they showed him into an adjoining room furnished as a bedchamber and left him alone. Evidently the King's instructions had been loosely worded but the girls were taking them literally and treating him as a human guest. There was a soft bed on which, he presumed, he could if he wished rest; but as he could remain without fatigue on his legs he stood stock-still at the window overlooking the garden around which the King's residence was built. He was deeply troubled, and was trying to sort out the truth of what had been said to him earlier.

After some time the door opened and in came a man in his late forties with wavy grey hair and a thin face with high, prominent cheekbones. His expression was distracted, slightly effeminate. He wore a loose robe and carried a large box studded with knobs and dials.

'I am Padua,' he announced, 'robotician to the King, I have instructions to examine you, so if you would please lie face down on the floor ...'

'You believe I have a sickness,' Jasperodus interrupted.

'Not a sickness exactly ...' The robotician sounded apologetic.

'An aberrant self-image, then.'

'Just so.' Padua laid down his box. 'Now ...'

'Wait a moment.' Jasperodus spoke with such a tone of command that Padua raised his eyebrows and blinked.

'I have need to talk to you. You are an expert on creatures such as I. Is it true what they tell me – that it is impossible for me to be self-aware?'

'Yes, that is so.' Padua looked at him with a waiting, blank expression.

'Then explain how it is that I *am* self-aware.'

'The answer is simple: you are not.'

'But do I not show all the signs of awareness? I have emotions – do they not mean awareness?'

'Oh, no, emotions may quite easily be simulated machine-wise. Nothing lies behind them, of course. The robot has no *soul*.'

'You don't understand.' Jasperodus became agitated. 'I *have* a soul. I *experience*, I *know* that I am a *conscious self*. Could I know such things, could I say them even, if they were not true?'

'An interesting question.' To Jasperodus' exasperation Padua seemed to receive his anguished pronouncements as a diverting conundrum rather than in the deadly earnest in which they were intended. 'But once again the answer is that nothing you can say can make any difference. It is technically possible for a self-directed machine to form the conclusion, the opinion as it were, that it has such awareness, having heard that the phenomenon exists in human beings which seem to be so similar to it. But such an opinion is a false one, for the machine does not really understand what awareness is and therefore forms mistaken notions about its nature. The machine-mind is an unconscious mind. Not alive.'

'And yet you are standing here, arguing and talking with me!'

'Oh, one may debate with a robot quite fruitfully. Many have sharper wits than most men. In fact a robot can be a very acceptable companion. But it is my experience that after some lengthy time in its company one comes to notice a certain lack of living vitality in it, and to realise that it is after all dead.'

'So this that I have, and call consciousness, is not consciousness?'

'No. This, in fact, is precisely what I am here to investigate …'

Padua's words struck Jasperodus like blow after blow and inflicted more injury on him than Gogra's hammer ever could have done. 'You are very sure of yourself, Padua,' he snarled in surly disappointment.

'Facts are facts. When the science of robotics was first born, back in the civilisation of the Ancient World, the hope of producing artificial consciousness was entertained. It soon became evident that it was impossible, however. There are theorems which prove the matter conclusively.'

Jasperodus immediately expressed a desire to hear these theorems. Without demur Padua obliged; but they were couched in such technical terms that Jasperodus, who had no deep knowledge of robotics, could not understand them.

'Enough, enough!' he boomed. 'Why should I listen to you? You are nothing but a second-rate practitioner in a broken-down, out-of-the-way kingdom. You probably don't know what you're talking about.' This thought, as a matter of fact, was the last straw at which Jasperodus was now clutching.

Padua drew himself up to his full height. 'If I may correct you, I am a robotician of the first rank. I have a First-Class Certificate with Honours from the College of Aristos Lyos – and there can be no better qualification than that.' He shrugged with a hint of weariness. 'It is not altogether by choice that I practise my profession here in Gordona. But these are troubled times. I came here for the sake of a quiet, peaceful life, to escape the turmoil that is overtaking more sophisticated parts of the world.'

Jasperodus glowered sadly at his unwitting tormentor, his spirits dwindling to nothing. He had been cheated, after all, of the thing he had been most sure of. Just what was this self-awareness possessed by human beings and of which he could have no inkling? Doubtless the robotician was secretly laughing at him for believing his mechanical self-reference to be that godly state of consciousness reserved only for biological beings. Yet even now it seemed incredible to him that this feeling of self-existence he *imagined* he had was only a fake, a phantom, an illusion, *that it didn't exist*. Still, how could he deny Padua's expert judgment?

The more he thought about it the more his brain whirled until he could bear it no longer. He flung himself full-length on the floor.

'Get on with your work, Padua,' he invited, his voice muffled by the floor tiles. 'I do not wish to believe I exist when in truth I do not. Rectify my brain and release me from this agony.'

After a long pause the robotician knelt beside him. Then there was a slight feeling of pressure and a click as he applied special tools that alone could open Jasperodus' inspection plate.

For a time Padua employed the extensible monitors on his inspection box, inserting them into the hundreds of checkpoints beneath the plates in Jasperodus' head and neck. He turned knobs delicately and carefully watched the dials. Jasperodus could scarcely hear him breathe. Eventually he replaced the plates and stood up.

'A sublime example of robotmanship,' he said in a tone of reverence. 'Worthy of the great Lyos himself. I suppose you weren't …?'

'No,' Jasperodus replied shortly. Hastily he scrambled to his feet. 'You did nothing!' he exclaimed angrily. 'Why did you make no adjustment?'

Padua raised his hands in a gesture of resignation. 'I would not presume to interfere in a work of such superb craftsmanship. Anything I could do to amend your integration state – to use a technical term – would be meddlesome and crude …' He placed his finger on his lips thoughtfully. 'I have just thought of something. Your fictitious self-image could be deliberate. It may have been a deliberate device on the part of your designer. At that, it is quite ingenious. Hmm.' Padua nodded, musing. 'A means of raising a machine's status in its own eyes and so lifting its self-reliance to a new level. *Very* ingenious. Possibly I should have played along with your delusion.'

'Too late for that now,' replied Jasperodus dully. If what Padua said was true, then the cruelty of what his parents had done to him was almost unbelievable. Surely their intention had been quite the reverse.

'Indeed, yes.' Padua packed up his gear. 'Well, time for you to be moving.'

'Where am I going?'

'You are now a member of the King's household. I have orders to send you down to the stables, where the machines and animals are quartered. So if you will step this way …'

Jasperodus stepped to the door, then paused and turned to Padua. 'But you have condemned me to Hell,' he accused. 'To a living death. Yet how can

I be condemned? I am not a conscious soul, I only appear to myself to be. I do not exist, I only believe that I do. I am nothing, a figment, a thought in the void without a thinker.' He shook his head in deepest despair. 'It is a riddle. I cannot understand it.'

Padua gazed at him with something touchingly close to sympathy. 'If this self-image is pre-programmed, you are indeed faced with a paradox that to a machine-mind is insuperable,' he admitted. He touched Jasperodus on the arm. 'Perhaps we shall meet again. I hope so.' He pointed down the corridor. 'Please follow the passage to the right. The stable hands will be ready to receive you.'

So Jasperodus, his morale broken, believing his effective worth to be zero, obeyed the robotician and plodded towards the palace stables to begin his servitude.

4

From the animal stables down near the courtyard that opened on to the concourse, came the sound of stamping feet, of snorting horses and the occasional bark of a dog as the kennels stirred in the pre-dawn gloom. Hearing these sounds, Jasperodus envied the animals their common warmth and sensitive restlessness. It would have been better to be stabled among them, he thought, rather than here in the unrelieved tedium of the construct section.

A dreary, creaking voice suddenly came to life in the stall next to his own. 'One, two, three, four, five, six. All here. Four plates of patterned silver. Five gold goblets engraved with the Royal Coat of Arms. A trencher of platinum, design depicting a rustic scene. Now the earthenware. Fifty plates of assorted glaze. Count them slowly. Handle them carefully, you rotten rusted hulk. Oh dear. Two plates broken. Oh dear, I am a rotten rusted hulk.'

A pause; then the maddening monologue began again. The voice came from an aged, deteriorating robot who worked in the palace kitchens. Every night his moronic brain sorted through the day's experiences which, with small variations, were always the same: endless abuse from the kitchen staff and an inevitable succession of accidents and mistakes. Night after night Jasperodus was forced to eavesdrop on a stream of babble, a machine version of troubled dreams, a recurring nightmare whose theme was incompetence.

He stood in a wooden stall to which he was fastened by a heavy chain. The precaution was futile as well as unnecessary: with a little exertion he could have torn out the chain by the pins that fastened it to the timber and made his escape. But neither escape, nor defiance, nor disobedience were anywhere in his mind. Jasperodus had entered the stables, from the very first moment, utterly resigned to his future of machine drudgery. He knew himself to be nothing: he carried out his work dutifully and without omission, but mulishly, so that Horsu Greb, the robot overseer, had been forced to admit scant value on his talents.

For the first few weeks of his slavery he had continued to wrestle with the existential riddle posed him by his conversation with Padua.

It had been a tormenting time, for all his efforts had only persuaded him that Padua – and all the others – must be right. He had striven to enter into his own mind to find his basic identity, to locate the 'I' that, if he were conscious, must lie behind all his thoughts and perceptions. But however hard he tried all he could find were more thoughts, feelings and perceptions. The inference was plain: if the 'I' could not be grasped then it was reasonable to suppose that it did not exist at all.

And so he was a figment, as Padua had said. The 'consciousness' he had presumed in himself was fictitious only. It would not be difficult for a clever robot-maker to arrange: probably it consisted of one thought mechanically assessing another. But dead, all dead.

Jasperodus did not know whether to curse those who had made him or to pity them.

Since he had reached his conclusions and left off his mentations the despair they had brought him had worn down to a kind of everyday weariness. Weariness and boredom were now his constant companions – he had no others, for apart from himself the robots of the stable were cretinous in the extreme. He could, for short periods, escape this weariness (as well as Kitchen Help's desperate maunderings) by switching off his higher brain functions, upon which he simply vanished from existence as far as his own cognisance went. Unfortunately some automatic mechanism limited this haven of 'sleep' to four hours out of twenty-four, since from a physiological standpoint it was not necessary to him at all. Otherwise he might have preferred to switch himself off permanently, since according to Padua non-being was more appropriate to his proper condition.

With regard to the boredom that was eating into him: he had noticed that he alone of all the working robots was afflicted with it. He theorised two explanations: (I) his erroneous self-image was responsible and (2) the other robots were too stupid ever to feel bored.

Either explanation was sufficient on its own, he felt, but notably the latter. The constructs he had been thrown among were a haphazard collection, their intelligence ranging from the subhuman right down to the negligible. Some were so primitive that they scarcely deserved to be called 'self-directed' at all. Jasperodus ignored all of them, including the resurrected Gogra, whom he had occasionally seen skulking about. On their first sighting one another he had wondered if the big fighting robot would take him to task for the humiliation he had suffered, but either Gogra's reconstituted brain contained no memory of his defeat or else he was too dim-witted to feel resentment.

The same could not be said for Horsu Greb, robot overseer, dim-witted though he undoubtedly was. The bad feeling he harboured towards Jasperodus stemmed, apparently, from a casual jest on Padua's part. When advising Horsu of the new robot's capabilities, as was his duty, he had jokingly remarked that Jasperodus could be a candidate for Horsu's own job. Never a man of enormous humour, Horsu had taken the threat seriously and ever after looked with ill-veiled hostility toward his handsome chargehand. Even he sensed something unusual about Jasperodus, despite the latter's modest demeanour, and that was the reason why he kept him in chains at night.

Dawn broke, chinks of light filtering into the stable, glancing off metal, shining on wood. Dogs barked more vigorously in the animal section, from which wafted a warm, raw odour Jasperodus was well used to.

A timber gate squeaked open. Horsu Greb lurched into view, red-rimmed eyes staring out over a bulbous nose flawed with warts. Rubbing sleep from his eyes and hitching up his baggy trousers with a length of leather cord, he paced the gangway, bellowing hoarsely.

'Stir yourselves, you useless lumps! The sun is in the sky! No more lazing!'

He turned aside to urinate against the flank of an unprotesting earthmover. The stalls resounded to a general clanking and thumping; Jasperodus rattled his chains, marvelling anew at the way Horsu bolstered his self-esteem by projecting organic qualities on to the robots – by imagining that they, not he, preferred to sleep into the day.

The unkempt overseer stopped by Jasperodus' stall and glared at him. 'I want a good day's work out of you!' he roared. 'No slacking! There's a lot of carrying to be done!'

Jasperodus remained impassive while Horsu unlocked his chain. He moved into the gangway, receiving as he did so a jocular kick from Horsu's steel-toed boot.

The constructs trailed out of the stable in a ragged procession. Not all were humanoid: there were quadrupeds built for hauling after the manner of horses or oxen; wheeled robots; and the self-directed earthmover bearing before it a great splayed blade. In front of Jasperodus Kitchen Help trudged along. Horsu had interrupted his litany, which he hurriedly resumed now with a list of resolutions, adjuring himself to break no plates, spill no soup, and tread on no more pot-boys' toes.

Out in the courtyard the robots milled around aimlessly until Horsu, with much self-important yelling and many superfluous blasts upon a whistle, directed them to various destinations: some to the palace where they carried out domestic duties, some to the animal stable where they served as grooms, and the rest, Jasperodus included, out of the courtyard and along the palace wall to a building site.

The sunlight still barely slanted across the ground as they began work. The earthmover continued digging out the foundations it had started the day before. Jasperodus and two other humanoids unloaded bricks and masonry blocks from some lorries, piling them conveniently for the work to be undertaken. The building gangers had not arrived yet but Horsu, though not himself of that trade, presumed to stand in for them, placing himself on a pile of rubble and looking around him with judicious nods.

The work was tedious and heavy. Hours passed and the sun rose in the sky;

Jasperodus' body hummed almost audibly as he humped the blocks of stone which were quarried, he believed, from ancient ruins lying somewhere in the region.

Occasionally he paused to take note of anything interesting that might be happening nearby. They were working to build fuel bunkers for a powerhouse that lay beneath the palace, and every now and then a number of large baffle-plates set in the palace wall opened slightly to give forth a wave of heat. As the day progressed the exhalations grew more intense until they finally stopped altogether. Jasperodus, who was familiar with the layout of the powerhouse through having worked there as a stoker, suspected that something was amiss.

He was proved correct, for shortly a stocky, red-faced man emerged from the access tunnel and hurried to Horsu, with whom he engaged in agitated discussion. On seeing Horsu shake his head in a gesture of indignant refusal Jasperodus heightened the sensitivity of his hearing so as to eavesdrop on their conversation.

'Do you imagine my fine robots are so many lumps of wood to be burned up just like that? Away with you!' Horsu was saying.

'But imagine if there is an explosion – right underneath the palace!' the other implored with anguish. 'Would you have the King rebuke you for malfeasance?'

Horsu parried the threat. 'To me is entrusted only the care of the house-hold robots. The powerhouse is not within my province and is in no way my responsibility.'

And the other riposted: 'Indeed it is, for your robots are even now engaged in building an extension to it.'

However else Horsu might have answered remained unknown, for the Major Domo himself arrived, bearing himself imperiously and trailing behind him Kitchen Help.

The Major Domo curtly overruled Horsu's objections. 'This robot here will be no loss,' he declared. 'The kitchen staff tell me he is completely useless and more of a nuisance than an asset. So let him expend himself on one last use-ful act.'

With an aggrieved sigh the stablemaster looked this way and that, scratch-ing his chin. He next looked Kitchen Help up and down and then glanced at Jasperodus; a crafty look came over his face.

'Very well!' he agreed. 'Take Kitchen Help. The crisis evidently demands a sacrifice.'

The aged construct nodded his head as it was explained to him what was required. His weakly glowing eyes blinked in his effort to understand. 'Yes, I obey. Reach the opposite wall of the furnace; inspect to ascertain why the conduits will not open nor the rakes work; clear the mechanism and make sure it is working aright; if possible, quit the furnace and return.'

'Excellent, excellent!' The party moved to the mouth of the access tunnel and disappeared from view.

Jasperodus continued with his work, but presently Horsu and the others emerged into the open again, minus the robot. The Major Domo pointed to a humanoid who worked alongside Jasperodus.

'How about that one there? He seems sturdy enough.'

But Horsu beckoned to Jasperodus himself. 'I can do even better. It's futile to send machine after machine into the furnace if they are simply destroyed without doing the job. This one, now, is in perfect condition; if he can't do it none of them can.' He adopted an expression of regret tempered with duty. 'It distresses me, of course, that I shall probably lose this prime property, but after all they're all expendable.'

'What is the nature of the problem?' Jasperodus asked on coming near.

The powerhouse minder turned to him. 'The furnace controls are jammed and all attempts to clear them from the outside have failed. In a word, it's out of control: the furnace is overheating, the boilers are building up pressure, and if this goes on I don't like to think about the consequences.'

'Clearly a poor piece of design,' Jasperodus remarked.

The powerhouse minder shot him a look of reproof and then continued. 'Someone has to go right into the furnace to see what the trouble is. We've already sent the kitchen robot, but apparently the temperature was too much for him.' He went on to issue the same instructions he had given Kitchen Help.

'I am acquainted with this furnace, and I am not likely to survive either,' Jasperodus volunteered. 'Perhaps if I were equipped with a cooling agent, such as frozen carbon dioxide supplied through a hose ...'

'Enough!' roared Horsu. 'There's no time for niceties. This is an emergency – get on with it.' And Jasperodus understood that Horsu was using the situation to get rid of him for good and all.

If I were a living being it would be an injustice, he thought, *but I am not a living being, so there is no injustice ...*

He followed the humans to the access tunnel, automatically going over the layout of the powerhouse in his mind. Its design was so crude as to lose even the advantages of simplicity. Theoretically it used nuclear energy, consuming a specially processed type of 'safe' compound isotope that produced no residual radioactivity when it decayed, but generated enough heat to raise steam through a primitive heat exchanger. The isotope was shovelled into the furnace as slag and triggered into decay by a powerful jolt of microwaves, after which it decomposed into liquid waste and could be drained off through conduits.

But in practice the isotope fuel was permanently in short supply and so was combined with an oddly disparate method of producing energy. The furnace was fitted with a system of flues to draw oxygen, and into it went anything that would burn – timber, coke, plastic, sometimes rubbish from the palace. The combination of combustion and nuclear power was not a happy one, as could be seen from the present situation. It would be a small disaster for King Zhorm if the powerhouse was destroyed, for apart from the damage it would cause to the palace itself, it would cut off the electricity supply to part of the town of Okrum – a form of royal largesse from which Zhorm drew popularity.

The tunnel was lined with concrete and angled sharply underground. The light here was dim, being provided by feeble yellow lamps set in the ceiling. Halfway down the tunnel turned a right angle, and here Horsu and the others paused.

'Right,' Horsu said with unveiled satisfaction. 'You know what you have to do – get on with it.'

Wordlessly Jasperodus proceeded on his own. A few yards further down brought him to the furnace room.

The space between wall and furnace was narrow. Facing Jasperodus were the furnace doors, fabricated of mica-carbon laminate and glowing faintly. Behind them the fire of the furnace seemed to roar and beat like a living heart.

Two crouching robots turned towards him in the baking gloom. Jasperodus knew them well: they were stokers, their feeble mentalities adapted only to that one task. They were incapable of any other, such as the mission he had been sent on.

Here I go, then. As I am nothing, so I shall be nothing. A thought in the void without a thinker …

He dismissed any thought of death. Death could not exist for one who had never been born … It seemed to him that what was about to happen to him was a logical conclusion of the tragedy that surrounded him. Every day of his life he had been living a lie, the lie of his own being. That lie had brought him first to despair, then to the knowledge of his own imprisonment, and now … Everything had been leading to this fiery execution chamber.

Understanding what was expected, the stokers applied themselves to levers, one on either side of the doors, and forced them slowly open. A brilliant white glare flooded into the narrow space.

As the glaring fire was revealed, a curious image rose in Jasperodus' mind, so vividly as to paralyse him for a moment. He saw a blast furnace in which iron and steel were smelted. Into it trundled an endless stream of scrap metal: objects large and small, weapons, cars, broken-up aircraft and locomotives, canisters, ornaments, statues and statuettes, table-ware, hooks and buttons, brackets, rods, girders, fences, gates, trays, myriad machines and defunct robots, every one disappeared into the ravening heat to lose all form and identity. And all the metal thereby gained was used again to make a new generation of artifacts. Unaccountably this thought left Jasperodus feeling stunned – he himself could be melted down in such a furnace (as he had once been drawn from one) and used to make, perhaps, the chassis for a motorised carriage, or even a new, totally different robot who would live a happily humdrum existence unafflicted by the curse of a fictitious self-image.

Where had this vision come from? Presumably from the stock of gratuitous memories bestowed on him by his father – somehow he still thought of the old man as his father. But it was over in a second or so. He moved forward, switching his vision to ultraviolet in an attempt to see through the flames, and clambered into the furnace. Fire licked at him; the doors edged shut behind him.

He stood alone in a raging haze of incandescence.

The air was thick with energy. It was like being under water.

This must be what it's like inside a star.

Then it was hard for him to think anything for everything went fuzzy; the heat was disrupting his processes. He took a step, and stumbled over the body of Kitchen Help, which was at white heat and looked on the point of beginning to melt. His own skin was already glowing. Vaguely he was aware of his lower brain functions responding to the damage with a stream of urgent reports, analyses and prognostications; their import was that he should remove himself from here on the instant.

The possibility presented itself that he might not even reach the far wall of the furnace, though it was not very far away. But something else rose to the surface in him, sweeping aside both defeatism and the machine analogue of panic. He determined that he would accomplish this one last thing, at whatever degree of difficulty; he would not end his functioning on a note of failure.

His eyes were only of minimal use to him by now. He went forward, reeled, recovered himself and so gained the far end of the furnace where the trouble was. Groping with his hands, he verified what he had already guessed to be the cause of failure: vitrified ash from the burning of a combustible fuel had sealed both the lids of the waste pipes and the clumsy mica-laminate rakes that were supposed to shovel the ash away. Both ash and decomposed isotope was supposed to form a slurry to flow away to the waste pits below; instead they had stayed in the furnace, building up more and more heat.

Though barely operational, Jasperodus kicked desperately at the glassy mass, and eventually succeeded in cracking and shattering it. Then he threw himself at the rakes, tearing free the fused fragments with his hands.

His body was at white heat. His senses were going out, leaving him hanging in a vacant void.

Collapse was imminent.

If I really tried, he thought, *perhaps I could reach the door*. But he made no move to do so, and shortly he felt a tearing sensation as vital systems were taken out. Then he knew no more.

There was light, gentle and caressing. There was the rustle of fabric, and the sigh of a breeze.

And Jasperodus retracted his eyelids, gazing astonished at a baroque ceiling.

Above him hovered the thin, intent face of Padua the robotician. He smiled faintly to see that Jasperodus was 'awake'.

'Do not be surprised,' he murmured. 'You have survived.'

Nevertheless Jasperodus *was* surprised. Experimentally he levered himself to a sitting position, and observed that he had been lying on a low table covered with a yellow cloth. He appeared to be in one of the gracious little bowers that fringed the palace gardens; through the window casements he could see small, delicate trees, flowered bushes and orange-coloured blossoms.

He looked down at his body: bronze-black, decorated all over with engravings, but otherwise unmarked. He swung his legs to the floor and stood with feet apart, trying to detect some persisting damage in himself.

'I thought I had sustained more harm than this!' he exclaimed.

'You did – you were very badly damaged indeed,' Padua told him mildly. 'You have been out for six months.'

'Six months …' Jasperodus echoed wonderingly. He flexed his fingers, examining his hands.

'You were in the condition known as scrap when they brought you out of the furnace,' Padua said. 'But for all the damage the basic design elements were intact – the brain was particularly well protected. I undertook to put you back in order and rescued you from the junkyard – just in time, as you were about to be pounded under the steam hammer.'

'Six months is a long time to spend on a repair job. A labour of love, almost.' Jasperodus' tone was sardonic.

'Perhaps.' Padua smiled faintly again. 'I was loath to see such fine work as you represent go to waste. There is little to give my talents full rein here in Gordona – that is the price one pays for living in such an out-of-the-way place. I regarded it as a pleasurable test of my skill, and no thanks are due my way.'

Jasperodus, who had not intended to thank him, nevertheless noticed that Padua was looking at him with a strangely expectant expression on his face. He paced the room.

'My faculties are fully restored?'

'Yes, though it cost much effort.'

'This hardly looks like your workshop.' Jasperodus indicated the harmonious décor.

'I decided to let you be reactivated in pleasant surroundings, rather than amid a clutter of tools and instruments.' Again the expectant look.

'What of radioactivity?' Jasperodus asked suddenly, remembering the furnace. 'Am I not dangerous to be near? The way things were, the isotope fuel might well have become unstable.'

'There's nothing to worry about on that score. There was a little radioactivity, but I purged your substance of it by a means of accelerating atomic decay that is known to me.'

'You are indeed wasted in Gordona,' Jasperodus grunted grudgingly. He paced again, trying to place what it was that was new and puzzling in his environment.

'There's a change,' he said. 'What is it?'

At this Padua laughed and clapped his hands in delight. 'I thought you'd never notice. Try again – can *you* guess what it is?'

'I wouldn't be asking if I could,' Jasperodus replied with an irritable gesture.

'Well, you see, the making of robots is as much of an art as a science. Even the masters of highest attainment are invariably stronger on some features, weaker on others – except, of course, for an acme of perfection like Aristos Lyos. Now your own maker was unexcelled in the area of intellectual functions, but rather weak when it came to a certain type of fine nerve structure needed for the senses of smell and touch. Now it so happens that that area is my own speciality! So I undertook to remedy his deficiencies. In the field of touch-sensation and of smell you now have the same range and sensitivity as any man or woman!'

With much curiosity Jasperodus drew one hand across the other. It was as Padua had said: the dynamic sense of solid bodies was there, as before, but in addition there was an entirely new feeling; a stroking, tingling feeling.

Fascinated, he laid the flat of one hand on the cloth of the table he had just vacated, moving the palm gently across the felt. An entirely novel rough-smooth feel coursed through him. A whole area of his brain seemed to come alive for the first time.

'It's fantastic,' he said quietly.

'I had hoped it would afford you some diversion,' Padua replied affably.

Jasperodus, however, would not be jollied along. 'No doubt it will enable me to appreciate the qualities of the stable all the better,' he grunted. 'One thing you have *not* amended. I still have this irrational belief that I possess consciousness!' And he rounded on Padua accusingly.

Padua looked a little embarrassed. 'There was nothing I could do about that,' he said defensively. 'It's in the basic design: if I tried to remove it you would be reduced to a hulk, good for nothing.'

Jasperodus emitted a sigh, a gesture he had learned from Horsu Greb. 'Then to be frank I could have preferred that you had left me for scrap.'

His words provoked such a look of unhappiness on the robotician's face that he instantly regretted them – he had spoiled Padua's pleasure. But he impatiently cancelled the feeling. Padua had enjoyed his work and *he*, Jasperodus, had to pay the price for his enjoyment.

'Would it be any use if I advised you not to brood too much on this enigma?' Padua suggested cautiously. 'It *is* part of your integration state, and it *does* appear to work, as a device for raising your degree of function to a greater independence than is normally found in a robot. You are, almost, a perfect simulation of a man.'

'Thank you,' Jasperodus said with scathing irony. 'It helps not at all, especially as I must now return to the tender ministrations of Horsu Greb.'

'I have been considering that,' Padua replied. 'Horsu could be accused of not making full use of your potentialities – it grieves me to see you wasted on manual labour. Perhaps I can persuade the Major Domo to assign you to more challenging duties where you will not be under his direction, though that would be a break with our usual practice. After all, Greb has effectively discarded you.'

An idea came to Jasperodus. 'Though my knowledge of engineering is far from extensive, I could undertake to design a better powerhouse than you have at present. It gives one a poor view of Gordona's engineers.'

'They are better described as optimistic amateurs,' Padua agreed. 'Possibly it could be arranged. Failing that, how would you like to become my assistant? But we must discuss this later – I have duties elsewhere, and perhaps you would like to be alone to collect your thoughts. I'll be back in about an hour.'

Padua departed, leaving Jasperodus to his own devices. Attracted to the garden, and wishing to test his new faculties, he unfastened the catch on a glass door and stepped outside. Some yards along a stone path, through a trellised arbour, brought him to a lawn whose further end descended into a series of cultivated terraces. All around were flowering trees, blossoms and shrubs, and beyond these could be glimpsed the circle of low buildings that comprised the palace: mixed timber and stone surmounted by curved, pointed roofs.

A breeze blew up, playing over his body with sensations so fresh and delightful that he was astonished. And his mind simply stopped when he encountered the warm, heady summer of perfumes the breeze brought with it: sensuous, delicate, powerful and bewitching, yet clean and innocent. Marvellous!

Marvellous!

Some of his recent dourness dropped away. It was impossible to remain sullen in the midst of such wonders. He strolled through the garden; his fingers played with silky smooth petals and cool, ribbed leaves. See this red rose: what perfect harmony between colour, texture and scent! Not to speak of perfection of form! Jasperodus paced on, an Adam in a new Eden, smelling the scent of new-cut grass, feeling the shortened blades tickle his feet.

This, surely, proved that existence – even his kind of existence – was worthwhile! What if he did lack this mysterious quality called consciousness? What if his identity was a fiction? Were not some of the world's greatest dramas fictions? In the face of these new experiences it now seemed to him that the whole affair was purely a sophistry and that he had been a fool to have been brought down by it.

A new excitement germinated in his mind: the excitement known to the world as AMBITION. *I have been through fire and am purged of despair and self-doubt. Am I less of a man than Horsu Greb? Than King Zhorm? Than Padua, even? Am I capable of less than they? Demonstrably, no! And I shall prove my worth. I shall prove it by gaining power over them … they all shall defer to Jasperodus the robot.*

He paused, revelling in his new-born senses; and in that hidden, empty place where his soul should have been was formed a resolve having all the force of obsession. *I know my strength … There is nothing I cannot do … King Zhorm, look to your throne …*

5

'This then, Your Majesty, is my scheme. In place of one furnace we have two. The main furnace is for isotope fuel and is sealed. The other burns combustibles and will serve as an assist to the first, or for emergencies. The heat exchanger is also a considerable improvement on the present arrangement. The same water can be circulated through the jackets of both furnaces or through either of them alone. All the controls are simple and employ no interior moving parts except for a system of movable trays, for the disposal of waste, which are proof against any kind of breakdown. I can promise Your Majesty that the new powerhouse will do away with the erratic voltages and frequent breakdowns, not to say danger to life and property, that have been a source of annoyance in the past.'

King Zhorm glanced cursorily at Jasperodus' blueprints, following the features pointed out by the latter's metal finger and pretending he understood them.

'If the scheme is approved,' Jasperodus added, 'I may then go on to re-design the generators, which also incorporate many defects.'

'You seem to think we are living in Tansiann, with the taxes of half the planet to draw on,' grumbled Zhorm. 'Already I have expended much on the extension to the present powerhouse.'

This claim was hardly true; the extensions consisted merely of fuel bunkers built by robot labour. Only the materials had involved any expense. Jasperodus made no comment, however. The King seemed to be distracted today, so he decided to drop the whole matter for the time being.

'Your Majesty perhaps has more important questions on his mind,' he ventured.

'Indeed I have. Those bandits out in the West Forest are becoming an intolerable pest. Matters are reaching serious proportions.'

Zhorm poured goblets of wine, absent-mindedly offered Jasperodus one, then downed it himself after a hasty curse. It was disconcerting to have this machine about the palace, he thought. Jasperodus was more intelligent than any other robot Zhorm had ever seen and he kept thinking of him as human.

Jasperodus' eagerness for change was not unreservedly welcome either. If given free rein the clever robot would embroil Zhorm in grandiose schemes far beyond his means. As it was he was having to divert most of his resources into his small army because of these confounded bandit raids ... Idly he mused on what other appointment Jasperodus could be given in his retinue. Why not make him court jester? He had already shown he had wit. Zhorm smiled, imagining Jasperodus bedecked in fool's garb, prancing about and forced to invent inane jokes for the general amusement.

Jasperodus was at a loss to explain the King's sudden laughter.

But no matter. He was remembering a recent conversation he had held with Major Cree Inwing, an officer in the Gordonian Guard, Zhorm's little-practised army.

Jasperodus had been working on his blueprints using a table in the lobby (he had no room of his own to work in), when he had witnessed an exchange between this officer and Prince Okhramora, the King's half-brother, whom Jasperodus had encountered on the evening of his first induction into Zhorm's household: he was the fat man who had tried to belabour him with an iron rod. Inordinately fond of food, drink and lechery, he was often to be seen bustling about the palace on errands of doubtful propriety.

On this occasion, however, his business was indignantly moral. He was upbraiding Major Inwing for the Guards' failure to bring the bandit bands to book. With him he had a farmer from an outlying district, a sad-faced fellow who only the day before had been attacked, his farm despoiled and his brother and eldest son killed. Such raids were occurring nearly every other day now, and were penetrating deeper into the small kingdom.

'If this goes on these thugs will be coming right here into Okrum!' Prince Okhramora declared angrily.

Major Inwing, a normally self-confident young man with wheat-coloured hair and a brisk moustache, stood to attention, his face pink with embarrassment. 'Everything is being done that possibly could be done, Highness. The Guards can't be everywhere at once.'

'What a pathetic reply!' stormed the Prince. 'I'm taking this unfortunate subject to the King himself, and I'll have you drummed out of the service, you see if I don't! It was one of *your* companies that should have defended this man's family, but where were you?'

And Prince Okhramora swept away, the dejected farmer in train. Jasperodus had noticed that he was zealous in seeing that incompetent officers were stripped of their rank; their replacements were usually friends of his or relatives on his mother's side. This time Jasperodus was certain he would get nowhere, however; Major Inwing was so popular with his men that the King would never agree to cashier him or even to demote him.

He sidled up to the discomfited officer. 'What is the problem with these raiders, Major?' he enquired politely. 'Could they not be tracked to their lairs and destroyed?'

'That's something we've tried to do a score of times,' Inwing retorted in exasperation, 'but the West Forest stretches for hundreds of miles and it's practically impossible to sniff them out – one might as well go hunting the antelope; he added, adducing the ancient mythical beast. 'Ours is not the only kingdom to be harried by these gangs and no one else has managed to flush them out either.'

'Surely something is known about them,' Jasperodus persisted. 'How many groups of these men are there?'

'Several. But the largest and fiercest of them is led by a man called Craish, that much we do know. A clever devil he is too, by all accounts.'

And Jasperodus remembered the railway track, the journey through the forest, and the natural amphitheatre.

But he said nothing of this to Inwing. More was to be gained by speaking to King Zhorm himself …

… His private joke over, the King looked glum. 'A monarch must protect his people or he won't remain monarch for long,' he fretted. 'A few days ago these villains took over a hamlet and terrorised it for a day and a night – tell me, my clever construct, what would *you* do about these pests?' Zhorm eyed him half jokingly, half hopefully.

Jasperodus said diffidently, 'I think I could undertake to wipe out this nest of troublemakers altogether.'

'How so, Jasperodus?' Zhorm's eyes widened. He listened attentively to Jasperodus' story, then nodded judiciously.

'You are sure you can find this place again?'

'Certainly, Your Majesty. They could have moved since, of course, but I very much doubt it. The camp had all the appearance of being permanent.'

Zhorm rang a bell, summoning a page. 'Bring me Captain Grue.'

Jasperodus laid aside his blueprints and spoke in a low, confidential voice. 'Your Majesty, engineering is not my true bent. I aspire to a military career. Let *me* command the attack on the bandit camp. After you see my performance perhaps you will think me fit to be granted a commission in the Guard, which is my most earnest desire.'

In the act of draining his goblet, Zhorm almost choked. '*What?* Where in the name of the Almighty do you find the audacity for a request like that? Be careful I don't return you to the furnace!'

'Consult Padua, Your Majesty. He will assure you the idea is perfectly feasible. In fact I could not be put to better use. I will make an excellent officer.'

'Padua has already made plenty of representations on your behalf,' Zhorm snapped. 'I am almost tired of hearing him sing your praises.'

He frowned. He had never made use of robots as soldiers, for the simple reason that their obedience was such that the enemy could easily turn them round against their own side. One way round this was a robot with a command language known only to its masters, but such robots were expensive and Zhorm did not own any. Men were cheaper …

Admittedly Jasperodus answered neither of these cases and though not controlled by a command language seemed not to suffer from extreme obedience either. Padua had explained it thus: his command structure was unusually elaborate and he was able – strange though it seemed – to ignore orders altogether sometimes. Zhorm took this to mean that Jasperodus would disobey an order that contradicted a previous order – or something like that.

'Flexible end-game,' he murmured.

'Your Majesty?'

'Flexible end-game. Padua was talking about it the other day. It's the strategy your brain is based on.'

He glanced up as Captain Grue entered and saluted smartly.

'Captain Grue here will command the force,' he said incisively. 'You will accompany it as guide. Now, let us discuss the expedition itself.'

'Damn you, metal man, damn you!'

Craish's raging imprecations were music to Jasperodus' ears. Hands on hips, he stood on a rise in the ground. Below him in the dell the bandit leader's men were being roped together by Gordonian troops, cringing away from the ring of guns.

The foray had worked out even better than Jasperodus had hoped. Captain Grue had set out with a force of a hundred men, riding the transcontinental railroad on a flimsy, primitive train powered by an oil-burning engine. The train possessed a look-out tower to give warning if a long-range express approached, so as to give its passengers a chance to take to the ground and perhaps get the train off the rails as well. Nothing of this kind occurred, and the expedition quickly reached the spot designated by its robot guide.

From then on events had followed with rapidity. Since Jasperodus had last seen it Craish's gang had expanded and itself numbered well over a hundred well-armed ruffians, so that the attackers found themselves evenly matched. These desperadoes' first ambush had been a near-disaster for the expedition, due in part to the way Jasperodus had led it openly through the forest without any caution or reconnoitre.

It was during this ambush that Captain Grue had been killed. In the ensuing confusion the other officers had yelled conflicting orders and the troops had milled around hopelessly. Then Jasperodus had come into his own. Leaping on to a rock, bullets ringing off his impervious body, he had made an imposing figure, his voice booming out over the scene like thunder. He had rallied his men, brought them through withering fire, and then had assumed full command to lead them on to victory.

'Hurry it up!' he bellowed now. 'Get them to the train!'

A subaltern approached and hesitated. Jasperodus cast him a fierce look; hastily the subaltern saluted. Lazily Jasperodus returned the salute.

'Why don't we just slaughter this rabble where they stand?' the officer asked. 'That was Captain Grue's intention.'

'Their fate is for the King to decide,' Jasperodus growled. 'We will take them back to Okrum.' He turned away, shouting stentorian instructions across the amphitheatre.

Shortly they set out for the railway, the long file of prisoners in their midst. Lieutenant Haver, who by rank should have taken command on the death of Grue, persisted in issuing orders every now and then; each time Jasperodus bellowed a contradictory order, and the men, whose lives Jasperodus had already saved, instinctively tended to obey the stronger personality.

The Lieutenant eventually confronted Jasperodus, complaining about this undermining of his authority. But the big robot chose to ignore him. Soon Haver, too, was reduced to accepting his orders.

Back at the railroad Jasperodus made a discovery: an engine and some trucks hidden in a culvert. By this means Craish had been able to travel at speed through Gordona, striking and withdrawing along the railroad. He had the crude train smashed, except for a couple of trucks which were added to his own stock, while the prisoners were loaded on board for the return journey.

Already on board were the captives that had been found in the bandits' camp. They were mostly women, sitting quietly with heads downcast, re-membering the ill-treatment they had received.

All business in Okrum ceased when they paraded the prisoners through the town. Jasperodus permitted Lieutenant Haver to march at the head of the column with him for appearance's sake, but of the two it was the bronze-black robot who made the most striking spectacle, and who most enjoyed the acclaim of the crowd.

It had begun. He was on the way to becoming a master of men.

It was a signal honour indeed for a robot to be invited to banquet, and to sit at the King's table with the nobles and notables of the realm. The other guests at first found it to be an object of great amusement and made fun of Jaspero-dus; but though he could not of course eat and drink, he soon made them change their attitude with the dominating excellence of his conversation, recounting how he and the Gordonian Guard had defeated Craish's strong-hold. In passing he expressed regret for the death of Captain Grue, who he skilfully managed to convey was a brave but unimaginative officer.

Having captured everyone's attention, he went on to discourse upon how a military force for defending a small country should be constituted. 'The Guard of the Realm should be small but disciplined to the utmost and trained to the optimum,' he said. 'It should be able within the hour to strike in any part of the kingdom. So besides the transport to achieve this there should also be good communications throughout the kingdom so that any attack or disturbance immediately becomes known in the capital. Now as to the commander of armed forces: he should be a man whose alertness never wanes and who knows how to keep an army in a constant state of tension. He should not be such a one as will sink into complacency, inattention to changing circumstances, or fleshly pleasures.

'Finally, if the country has external enemies it is useful to train and arm the population to some extent, but the people should never be allowed to command as much fire-power as the army.'

A snort came from down the table. 'One would think this metal construct himself coveted the post of commander.'

'Did I say so?' rejoindered Jasperodus sharply. 'The Guard already has a commander of irreplaceable mettle.' He inclined his head towards Commander Haurk, who sat fiddling with his goblet and frowning with some displeasure. 'But since *you* raise the point, it would only be fair to point out that I possess *all* the qualities I have outlined, to a greater extent than any flesh-and-blood man. I do not sleep, day or night. My mind can be given unremittingly to my duties, oblivious of the diversions that a human being cannot forgo. Lastly, being a machine and not a man, I do not strive to acquire power for myself as do the commanders of some armies, as their sovereigns have found to their cost.'

A weighty silence followed his words. Jasperodus turned to King Zhorm. 'Your Majesty, it is a slander to say that I aspire to such an exalted post. But may I again mention my desire for a commission as a subaltern?'

A roar of laughter greeted his words. A young man uncontrollably sprayed a mouthful of wine over the table. 'What? A robot be an *officer*?'

'Why not?' Jasperodus' gaze went from face to face. He spoke with a passion which this time was genuine. 'A soldier's rôle is combat, is that not so? Test me, then. I challenge any of you to any contest that suits you, whether of skill, strength or cunning, whether of the body or of the mind – I undertake to defeat you all.'

'I accept!' came an animated voice from down the hall. 'We shall be rivals: you must seek to seduce a certain maid I shall name!'

Jasperodus angrily ignored the howls of merriment that followed the challenge. 'And if you think I cannot command the respect of subordinates,' he said loudly, 'then speak to those I led today!'

'But this is ridiculous!' someone protested. 'To make an officer of a robot!'

King Zhorm the while was watching Jasperodus with his dreamy, barbaric eyes. 'Enough!' he interjected. 'It is not ridiculous at all. I have heard of such things being done in lands to the East, where robots of great sophistication are available. By your amazement you merely display your bucolic ignorance.'

'Well said, brother!' Prince Okhramora spoke up, addressing the King with his usual over-familiarity. He wiped the grease from his face with a napkin. 'These clods who surround us are indeed ignorance personified. But what of the prisoners? How are they to be disposed of?'

Zhorm replied sardonically, 'Perhaps the robot Jasperodus has some ideas as to that, since he seems to have ideas on every other subject.'

Jasperodus and Prince Okhramora exchanged secret gratified glances.

Their relationship had developed much more favourably since their first unhappy encounter. Jasperodus, as if to make amends for his earlier indiscretion, had privately shown himself willing to perform small services for the Prince, who had come to look upon him as a useful ally. For that reason he was far from being opposed to Jasperodus' advancement and was already apprised of the suggestion the robot was about to make.

'While their crimes deserve instant death, it is sometimes a good principle to make use of such men instead of destroying them,' Jasperodus said carefully. 'Ruthlessness and bravado are not to be decried, provided they work for one and not against one. Now, many of Craish's men are riff-raff and should be garotted without delay. But others would make good soldiers, given the right discipline. Craish himself is a man who turned to crime through recklessness rather than through any innate evil, and he possesses both courage and resourcefulness. He would surely submit to military service and swear allegiance to Your Majesty in return for his life.'

Zhorm scratched his chin, looking at Jasperodus askance. 'Not the traditional way to deal with criminals.'

'The populace need not be made aware of it,' Jasperodus pointed out blandly. 'An immediate advantage to be gained is that Craish must know the whereabouts of the other outlaw groups in the forest, and doubtless he could be persuaded to work towards their extermination with enthusiasm. Give me him and a few of his followers, and I will soon knock the rough edges off them, I assure you. And if they should prove intractable, why, they can be shot at any time.'

'Dammit, this robot talks sense,' voiced a middle-aged, heavily-jowled man in a quilted tabard. 'We can be rid of these infestations for good and all.'

'In a general sense, I also would tend to agree,' Prince Okhramora said mildly.

'I will think on the matter,' King Zhorm announced. 'But I have had enough of serious talk.' He clapped his hands. 'Bring on the entertainment!'

Musicians advanced into the hall, bowed, took their places, and were followed in by a troupe of dancing girls. Deep in thought, Jasperodus watched idly. As soon as he could do so without giving offence he slipped away, leaving the scene of merriment behind.

He went through the palace and across an open courtyard to the barracks. Beneath them, deep in the earth, were some ancient dungeons, built of stone that had become damp and mildewed and smelling of decay. Descending the worn steps, Jasperodus heard the disconsolate murmurs of the prisoners who were crammed into a few dank cells. He went on past them, however, and down a passage to the cell reserved for Craish alone, where he prevailed upon the guard to unfasten the bolts.

Before entering he waved the guard away, waiting until the man was out of both sight and earshot. Then he swung open the door.

Squatting on the floor beside the far wall, Craish lifted his seamed face to stare impassively. The robot moved into the cell and loomed menacingly over his prisoner, his bulk eclipsing the weak electric light and throwing the cell in shadow.

'What the hell do you want?' Craish said defiantly.

The door swung shut with a clang. Craish looked alarmed but belligerent. 'What's this? Are you Zhorm's executioner now?'

'If I choose …' Jasperodus' voice reverberated quietly in the confined space. He took one step and wrenched Craish to his feet by the front of his jerkin, bringing his face close to his own. The bandit looked frightened and trapped, so close to Jasperodus' bizarre visage.

'Listen to me, you fool … you can live if you do what I say. There is a price to be paid, a small price indeed when measured against the loss of your life, effectuated by the garotte and accompanied by the howls of a vengeful mob – but it must be paid, without any omission. You must become my secret slave, together with others whom I will select. Your life will belong to me, your existence will depend upon my will. No one else will know of this; you alone will know that I am your lord and master and that my command is law.'

Despite his situation Craish managed a croaking laugh. 'Metal man, you're crazy! Be a slave to a *machine*? It's the other way round in my world.'

'Then *die*!' Contemptuously Jasperodus flung him down against the wall. 'I will explain the circumstances, since whichever way matters fall out your silence is guaranteed. Small though it appears, this court that rules Gordona is a cesspool of intrigue. King Zhorm has a half-brother, born to the old king's first wife. Being older than Zhorm this brother thinks himself cheated of the throne, although by right of primogeniture the throne is indeed Zhorm's – a fine legal distinction, you may say, which varies from kingdom to kingdom. At any rate, this dolt dreams of an armed *coup*. It is all folly, for Zhorm is by far the better king.' Jasperodus laughed hollowly. 'But what is that to me? I intend to take advantage of these treasons. Do you follow me? Already I am as good as commissioned in the Guard, and my advancement will not rest there. But it is difficult for a robot to acquire faithful human servitors, and that is why I am recruiting you now.'

Craish shook his head in bewilderment. 'This king's brother is your principal? You must take orders from *somebody*.'

'I alone am the initiator of my deeds. You will not imagine anyone standing behind me, for in truth there is no one.'

Craish pondered and sighed. 'I can almost believe it. You're more of a man than most men are.'

'For once you show discernment. So how do you answer? You can be enrolled in the Gordonian Guard, where I will be your officer – but secretly I will be much more. You will find me a generous master and you will live well. Otherwise …' Jasperodus saw no need to explicate further.

Craish gave a crooked smile. 'Need you ask? I'm in your hands. Anything you say.'

Jasperodus made a quick judgement and felt he could be sure of the man. He leaned down and took Craish's skull in his hand like an egg.

'Fail me and I will crush you – just so,' he said, exerting a meaningful pressure. Craish looked up with frightened, hollow eyes, nodding meekly as soon as Jasperodus released his head.

Jasperodus left the cell with an exultant stride. A man had submitted to *him*, a robot, and it was a good, strong feeling. He savoured it for the rest of the night.

Prince Okhramora giggled. 'Come in, Commander, come in!' Entering the apartment, Jasperodus found the Prince sitting comfortably in a padded chair, his short legs splayed out from his tubby body, a grin of glee fixed to his round face.

Okhramora giggled again. 'Any last-minute difficulties, Commander?'

'Nothing of note, Highness. All is arranged to satisfaction. Operations will be led by Z Company, from whom we can expect absolute loyalty. The palace, being nearly empty, will be ours in minutes. We will then invest the town, and once Okrum is secure we will release the proclamation we have prepared. I have devised a ruse to separate from their arms those companies whose cooperation cannot be assumed, using the pretext of an armoury check. They will be locked in the barracks and placed under guard.'

'Good, good.' The Prince screwed up his eyes in a presumably calculating manner. 'The announcement will appear simultaneously everywhere, and those who are with us are ready to take over all centres of population. It is well done.'

Jasperodus continued with the run-down. 'Within the hour the King and his retinue are due to leave for the country palace, putting them thirty miles away from the capital. On that score my stratagem is working well: the entertainment I have procured from the East has enticed away all who could wheedle themselves on to the jaunt, as anticipated. It was well worth the expense.'

'And as they leave, my uncle and cousins will be arriving as the start of the *new* court,' Okhramora chuckled. 'I wish I could see Zhorm's face when he realises what's happened!'

'Success seems assured, Highness.'

'Yes; we have planned well, you and I!'

There was a pause, Jasperodus continuing to stand rigidly before the Prince. Suddenly an idea seemed to strike Okhramora, and his face lit up with childish glee.

He picked up a writing scribe and threw it across the room.

'Oh, look, Commander, I have dropped my scribe! Pick it up for me.'

Obediently Jasperodus crossed the room and retrieved the scribe from the floor. As he was about to return Okhramora's shrill voice rang out again. 'No, no! Bring it to me on your knees!'

Wordlessly Jasperodus trundled across the room on his knees to replace the scribe on the table. The Prince thrust out his hand warningly before he could rise.

'Stay where you are, now,' he said softly. 'There appears to be a speck of dust upon my shoe. Be good enough to wipe it off with that cloth.'

'At once, Highness.' Taking the cloth Okhramora had designated, Jasperodus carefully polished both his buckled shoes of soft leather.

'Excellent! Well, Commander, you can stand up now!'

In the past few months Jasperodus had been playing a deceitfully inverted role with the Prince. Like most people in Gordona, Okhramora did not readily conceive of a robot without automatic obedience, and at first had been puzzled to know why Jasperodus exhibited great independence with regard to other human beings and on the other hand showed slavish attachment to himself whenever the two of them were alone together. But eventually he explained it to himself thus: Jasperodus was like a dog, he wanted only one master.

And he, Prince Okhramora, was that master!

Why the robot's devotion should have fallen upon him was largely inexplicable – perhaps, he flattered himself, it reflected on his manly firmness – but it was an amazing piece of good luck. In ordinary terms Jasperodus was a genius, a veritable Machiavelli, and that genius was entirely at Okhramora's disposal. Furthermore, no one else suspected it.

Meanwhile Jasperodus had done well in the Guard, making him an even more attractive target for Okhramora's attentions. Swiftly he had been promoted from Lieutenant to Captain to Major, and his military abilities were beyond dispute. He had been a hard disciplinarian to the newly-formed Z Company consisting mainly of Craish and his men, and with their help had all but cleared the West Forest of outlaws, many of whom had then been drawn into its ranks.

Then, during a training session, a soldier of Z Company had shot Commander Haurk, obviously by accident, and Jasperodus had immediately killed him in great anger before the man could demand the reward he had promised. By this time King Zhorm had become so impressed by Jasperodus that despite all popular prejudice he promoted him to the dead officer's appointment. Thus Jasperodus came to command the Gordonian Guard, a responsibility he pursued with full vigour, making his personality felt among men and officers in no uncertain terms.

But in the palace itself he found that people frequently forgot to guard their tongues in the presence of a robot, much as they might forget in the presence of an animal, and so he adopted a more passive role. This, together with his tunably sensitive hearing, made the intrigues of the court an open book to him.

He had early on realised the value of a partnership with Prince Okhramora. The Guard was riddled with his toadies and relatives, preparatory to the *coup* he dabbled with but would never, without Jasperodus' help and intervention, have found the courage to activate. To gain his trust Jasperodus had cultivated their bizarre relationship, willing to bear the degradation in order to achieve his ends.

The Prince had a perverted sense of pleasure; he delighted in seeing the Commander of the Guard – Zhorm's own protector! – slave to his every whim. In public Jasperodus was a figure to esteem – but here he would walk on his hands if Okhramora told him to! He had actually made him do it!

And once, when drunk, he had urinated on Jasperodus.

The experience had carried Jasperodus back to the stables and the detestable Horsu Greb. But he bore all with complete patience.

'So we have only to wait until an hour after nightfall,' Okhramora sighed happily. 'That will be all, Commander – see that nothing goes awry.'

Jasperodus departed and paced the palace. The sun went down on the stone-and-timber buildings, and on the ancient town of Okrum. The bustle of the capital abated as vendors and workshops ceased business and the inhabitants settled down for the evening.

Jasperodus took himself to the barracks. Those companies that could not be bought, numbering about half the Guard, had already handed in their arms and were now at their evening meal. Many, no doubt, were hoping to go into the town later for a bout of drinking, although Jasperodus had been circumspect about the matter of passes.

Detaching himself from a group of officers who stood around nervously, Craish, now Captain Craish, grinned cheerfully at Jasperodus. 'This is better than robbing trains, eh, Commander?'

'Keep your mind on the present business,' Jasperodus reprimanded him. 'I want Z Company at the peak of alertness.'

He returned to the palace and again sauntered through it, brooding on every detail of his scheme. He had arranged for Zhorm quickly to learn what was happening, so as to bring him rushing back to the palace and into his hands.

He would then issue *his* announcement to be posted throughout the land:

Prince Okhramora had staged a rebellion, killing the King, and was himself now dead. Jasperodus could then represent himself as avenging the King's death and putting down the uprising. In the pretence of restoring order (or actually to restore order if need be) there would be a period of martial law giving Jasperodus the total control of the country he needed. Then for a short interim he would contrive to appoint himself Regent. And then …

King!

He went over it again and again and could see no flaw. In a confused situation power went to whoever commanded the most guns – which was himself. Gordona was a relatively peaceful country for the times they were living in, and indeed the populace would see no reason to offer resistance – until it was too late. Jasperodus was satisfied that he had removed all unknown factors from the equation.

'Commander Jasperodus – meet my uncle, Count Osbah!'

Prince Okhramora giggled. Jasperodus bowed. Unlike the Prince, Count Osbah was tall, rakishly thin, and carried himself with exaggerated hauteur. He answered the robot's bow with a distant nod.

So eager was Okhramora to get the affair going that he had brought the Count in by the back door almost as King Zhorm and his retinue were leaving by the front. With him had come nearly a dozen other relatives – cousins, aunts and uncles. Most of them were merely affluent middle-class farmers, for Gordona was not large enough to afford an extensive nobility.

Okhramora's relatives had, in fact, taken possession of the palace ahead of Z Company, and had proved more of a nuisance to the troops than any of its legitimate occupants. The servants, and the few remaining members of the court, had been locked away and Jasperodus had posted sentries among the deserted hallways.

Now his men were in the town. He had sent a squad to occupy the police station and to incarcerate all available police in their own cells. He had also arrested the Chief of Police, the Minister of Justice, the Minister of Trades and Crafts, and other leading citizens.

So far all was quiet.

'If only Mother could have lived to see this day,' Okhramora mooned, momentarily overcome by mawkish sentimentality. 'It would have answered all her prayers, would it not, Uncle?'

'Quite so.' The Count gave him a precise, disdainful look.

A sudden burst of automatic fire came from the direction of the barracks, followed by silence. Jasperodus excused himself, went to find a trooper and sent him to investigate.

Minutes later the soldier returned to say that there had been an attempted break-out, but that all was now under control.

Jasperodus sent the man back to his post and stood in the half-darkened corridor, wondering why he felt nervous. He fingered his weapons, a repeater gun and a long-tubed emitter – the latter an arrangement of glass coils generating a beam of intense energy. The arsenal boasted only one of these rare weapons and he had reserved it for his own use, since unlike bullet-firing guns it was effective if used against himself.

Zhorm should be well on his way back to the palace by now, he thought. It would be easy for him to get inside – Jasperodus had seen to that – unless he was foolish enough to come storming in with the whole of his retinue. And he had good reason to try, quite apart from the loss of his throne. The best of all reasons; one that made it almost certain he would come alone.

When Jasperodus returned, the salon where he had left Okhramora and Count Osbah was empty. He asked their whereabouts of a sentry.

'They have gone to the Throne Room, Commander.'

'Indeed? Find Captain Craish and tell him to meet me there, with a dozen of his men.'

He went quickly to the Throne Room, entered and took in the scene in a single glance.

The chamber was only of moderate size, in keeping with its use for ceremonial and symbolic occasions. Fashioned in the shape of a concave shell, it imparted an air of luxurious intimacy. The walls were of a soft blue colour; the doors were of mahogany and were flanked by rich azure drapes. But its usual atmosphere of hushed calm was currently entirely broken by the presence of Okhramora and all his relatives, who were gathered in front of the throne. Okhramora himself was at the rear of the chamber, bending over an aumbry where, as everyone knew, the Crown of the Realm was kept. Inexplicably, the lock's combination was apparently also known to the Prince. He opened the aumbry and took out the much-desired symbol of sovereignty.

The Crown! Though not of enormous value it was an object of some beauty, being the work of a talented goldsmith. Okhramora held it up for all to see; its circlet of spiralled spires glinted in the soft light. Then he ascended the three steps to the throne and stood with his back to it, lifting the Crown towards his head with an expression of triumph and bliss.

At that moment Jasperodus bounded forward to mount the steps and snatched the Crown from his hands, cuffing him violently to send him sprawling a dozen feet away.

Swivelling himself round on the floor, Okhramora stared with wide, disbelieving eyes. 'What happened?' he squeaked. 'Is the Crown booby-trapped? No? Then what? – Jasperodus? …'

One of the women screamed.

Jasperodus unhooked his repeater. 'Used me as a plaything, did you?' he growled. 'You believed me to be your slave. Poor moron, you were *my* tool, not I yours!'

The gun voiced its hideous chatter. Okhramora jerked again and again, edged along the floor by the impact of the bullets. While blood seeped from his body horrified screams filled the chamber.

'SILENCE!' Jasperodus roared. 'Silence, or I will deal thus with you all!'

They became hushed. Jasperodus saw Count Osbah sidling to the back of the gathering, trying to gain the doors unnoticed. But he did nothing to stop him and stood as if momentarily paralysed. Unexpected emotions coursed through him and the Crown seemed to burn his metal fingers.

Before the Count could reach the doors they were flung suddenly inwards and Craish entered with his men. At the sight of Jasperodus standing with the throne at his back and the Crown in his hands they came to a halt.

'Enter,' Jasperodus commanded in a booming, almost trembling voice that reverberated about the chamber. 'Enter and witness.' He paused, feeling slightly dizzy. He tried to remind himself of his carefully laid plans, of the calculated moves and periods that must pass before he became King. But all went by the board. A madness had come over him; a madness of pride, of power and of victory. He was not in control of himself. His voice roared out wildly.

'ALL KNEEL!'

Though startled, Craish's men obeyed immediately – all but two or three who had thought themselves to be working for Okhramora's cause. But something supernatural seemed to have happened to the bronze-black robot; his charismatic presence filled the room, overpowering all present, and in seconds not only these but the civilians, too, sank to their knees, brought down by a combination of fear and personal force.

Jasperodus lifted the Crown and brought it slowly down on his head. As the gold touched his metal skull a feeling of ecstasy swept through his brain.

'I, I, I am your King!' he proclaimed, lifting his voice so that it resonated in everyone's consciousness. 'I am the sole initiator of my deeds, architect of your destinies!'

Craish set up a cry which was echoed in frightened tones by the others. 'Long live the King!'

Jasperodus sank back majestically to seat himself upon the throne and looked upon his minions, his head rotating slowly, his eyes glaring red with power and ferocity.

Moments later another soldier came into the Throne Room. He seemed astonished by what he saw, but managed to splutter out his message.

'King Zhorm has entered the palace, Commander!'

'And where is he?'

'He was seen to make directly for the nursery, Commander.'

Jasperodus nodded. That would naturally be his target. He had three small children, two boys and a girl, between the ages of five and ten.

He rose from the throne. 'Put these hangers-on of Okhramora's under lock and key,' he said to Craish. 'What follows, I must do alone.'

He left the Throne Room, laying aside the Crown, and made his way through the palace. The corridors were silent and dim, empty except for an occasional sentry at an intersection. He was near the nursery when a movement ahead caused him to halt and peer suspiciously.

Major Cree Inwing was lurking in the shadows, probably not realising he was visible to Jasperodus' spectrum-shifting vision.

'Show yourself, Major, or you're as good as dead,' Jasperodus threatened.

Major Inwing slipped into the feeble light, his face pale. 'I am alone and unarmed,' he said curtly.

Jasperodus studied the other's face. There was a brisk but open quality to it that he found likable; however, Inwing was also too loyal to be drawn into treasonable plots, and so he had left him out of his machinations.

'How did you get here?' he demanded. 'I thought I had you detained in the officers' quarters.'

'True, but I escaped. Mutiny is an ugly thing.' Jasperodus saw that Inwing's arm was bloody where a bullet had nicked it. 'I have to admit that I misjudged you badly, Commander. All this is Prince Okhramora's work, I suppose?'

Jasperodus did not reply to the question. 'I have word that Zhorm is in the nursery,' he said. 'You, I imagine, know that also.'

Inwing went even whiter, and Jasperodus saw that he was sweating. 'What do you intend?' he said quickly. 'No – it's too obvious. Trust Okhramora to use you for work like that.' His voice was heavy with contempt.

'It would be folly to do otherwise. My throne would never be safe while Zhorm and his children live.'

'The children too?' Inwing seemed not to notice how Jasperodus framed the statement in his revulsion for its main import. 'You can't do it, Commander – it's going too far. Not even you can do it, whatever you are. You *mustn't* do it.' The young Major was pleading with him now.

'I see no great difficulty,' Jasperodus replied, and made to move on.

'Wait …' Inwing stepped in his path, 'How do you think the people will take to knowing that their King has been murdered? Think of that.'

'Again I see no great difficulty,' Jasperodus answered. He wondered why he lingered to talk to Inwing, instead of getting on with his business. Nevertheless he went on: 'A small, compact armed force is all that is necessary to hold down a country the size of Gordona. Such a force of men can always be raised, if there are suitable inducements.'

Inwing's face looked tragic as he recognised the logic of the argument. But he made one last try. 'Listen, Commander, your control of the country will be much easier if you have the whole of the Guard with you. I can give you that: you know that at least half the men will follow my lead when it comes to a showdown. I'll serve you, faithfully, absolutely faithfully – you or your master – for the rest of my life. I swear it. My only condition is that King Zhorm and his family must be allowed to go with their lives.'

Inwing's popularity was already a factor in Jasperodus' mind. 'You are previously sworn to serve King Zhorm,' he pointed out.

'I can do him no greater service than to strike this bargain with you,' Inwing retorted. But suddenly Jasperodus' obduracy seemed to come home to him and he became angry and despairing. 'It's hopeless, isn't it?' he sneered, looking as though he were about to spit. 'Here I am trying to appeal to your better nature! You may be clever, but you're a robot – there's nothing to appeal to in that dead brain.'

Jasperodus shoved him aside and strode onwards.

Finding the nursery door locked, he smashed it inwards and surveyed the scene inside.

Two nurses were hurriedly dressing the children, who seemed sleepy and upset. Zhorm was on his knees, helping them. At Jasperodus' intrusion he swung round with a glare of fear and hatred, clutching an impotent pistol.

The robot's gaze flicked quickly around the nursery: the beds on which the children slept, the toys strewn around the floor, the colourful pictures of soldiers and animals on the walls.

He had not made any decision as to how he would act; but when he spoke the words came out of his mouth as if unbidden.

'You will take your family and leave Gordona forever. Do you hear me, Zhorm? Forever! My men will be here in ten minutes to take you to the border. Be ready!'

He stormed away, ignoring the anxious Cree Inwing as he swept past him. But further along the corridor his path was blocked by a distraught Padua, who looked at him accusingly.

'I helped you, Jasperodus. You would be junk without me. And now you have betrayed my trust to an unimaginable degree!'

Jasperodus could not help but give vent to a low, ugly laugh. 'You are the robotician, Padua. I am merely a mechanism. You should have known of my future conduct in advance, and therefore your criticism is misplaced.'

6

Hands, soft and caressing, moved all over him, paying close attention to every inch of his body surface. Jasperodus lay passively, concentrating on the pleasant sensations.

The girl was the same red-head who had helped to clean him that first time nearly two years ago. Now that he was master of the royal household she had volunteered to perform the service daily, cleaning and polishing him so as to preserve his appearance of gleaming majesty. She plainly enjoyed the task, getting some degree of arousal from it. Sometimes her breathing would deepen and occasionally, when lingering around the box-like bulge at the divide of his legs, she would seem to become momentarily frantic and her hand would pummel the air, as though manipulating the missing phallus.

Masculinity, thought Jasperodus. Apparently he exuded masculinity. How a machine could possess such a quality was presumably baffling, but for some reason he did.

He, of course, failed to share her excitement. Sexuality was still a mystery to him: the sensations were deliciously soothing, but otherwise neutral.

'Are you pleased, Lord?' she asked in an eager voice. And suddenly she clambered over his body to lie on him full length, pressing her pelvis down on him.

He pushed her off and stood up. He did not like to be reminded of his deficiencies.

Stepping to his nearby office, he found Craish and Cree Inwing waiting for him. Foreseeably, the news they brought was unsettling.

'There is little doubt that the main attack will come tomorrow, if not tonight,' Inwing told him, explicating over a map that was laid out on a table. 'Here is Zhorm and his force, and here are we, camped outside the town of Fludd. We are under-strength, owing to the necessity of posting forces in other parts of the country to forestall the rebellions that are expected.'

Jasperodus nodded, inspecting the map with scant interest. As he had anticipated, his double impetuosity – in seizing the crown prematurely, and in afterwards sparing Zhorm – had borne troublesome fruit. It had been necessary to hold down Gordona by forceful means, using the methods of a police state, and the population was in consequence discontented. This had made it easier for Zhorm, having taken refuge in a neighbouring kingdom, to win support for his cause. Around the nucleus of a small foreign force loaned to him by his host monarch he had gathered together enough armed loyalists to invade the country and was proceeding in fair order.

Cree Inwing had been as good as his word; Jasperodus had not once needed to remind him of his oath. He had organised the policing of the kingdom, weeded out the diehard elements in the Guard and won over all the rest. He had automatically risen to be Commander of the Guard – Craish was his Second-in-Command – and now, in an ironic twist of events, he was fighting with Jasperodus against Zhorm himself.

'The dispositions seem satisfactory,' Jasperodus announced. 'All is in order; we can hold them.' Privately he reckoned the chances to be about fifty-fifty. He was unhappily aware that the intensity of his own enthusiasm would be the factor most decisive for the outcome.

'Has Your Majesty any special instructions regarding public order?' Inwing asked. 'There are bound to be local uprisings.'

'The main thing is to break Zhorm's assault,' Jasperodus replied. 'Afterwards your bully-boys can always put down any other trouble – eh, Craish?'

Craish nodded, grinning.

'In that case we will repair directly to Fludd,' Inwing said stiffly.

Jasperodus made a vague gesture. 'Craish, you go. Inwing can stay here for a while and we shall travel to Fludd together.' His voice fell to a mutter. 'We may as well entertain ourselves while we can.'

Inwing looked surprised and puzzled, but said nothing. Craish saluted and departed.

Contesting thoughts flitted through Jasperodus' mind. He glanced around his office, and noticed for the first time how desultory, how temporary, everything looked. Chaotic piles of documents and lists littered the tables that had been crammed into the room with no regard for their ordered arrangement. There were not even any chairs, since he was equally at ease standing, and only one inadequate filing-cabinet.

Why had he been so careless about his daily working environment? Had the sense of urgency left him once he had attained his object? No, that could not be. He would have known it …

He motioned Inwing to follow him. In the long corridor outside all the drapes were flapping violently in the damp gusts of wind that were coming through the open windows. The evening air was heavy with threatened thunder, and he told himself that the weather would be too bad for Zhorm to attack tonight.

The banqueting hall, however, was more cheerful. A wood-burning fire had been lit in the huge fireplace and the audience that had already gathered made a lively contrast to the stream of dour officers and ministers he had been receiving all day. He settled himself on a wrought-iron chair overlooking the assembly, then signalled for the entertainment to begin.

The players were that same group of travelling entertainers who had figured, albeit peripherally, in his seizure of power. It was not by their own choice that they still performed for his court; he had refused to let them leave Gordona, wishing to sample their wares for himself but up until now finding little time for it. They accepted their enforced stay with equanimity, which suggested that they had met this kind of cavalier treatment before.

They bowed and set up their apparatus, a tripod surmounted by an arrangement of small tubes at various angles, emitting pencil-thin beams of coloured light.

Suddenly the cleared space in the centre of the hall sprang to life. In place of emptiness was a market place with people moving about it.

The illusion was complete: the picture had colour, depth and parallax, so that it presented a different aspect if viewed from a different angle. The scene betokened some ancient time, to judge from the architecture and the costumes; into it walked living, flesh-and-blood actors from the players' troupe.

Neither the eye nor the ear could tell which of the characters were real and which were projected by the laser device – except that occasionally the projector produced special effects, flattening the picture into a plane, or into a receding series of planes, against which the living actors stood out starkly. But even this could be achieved by imagery alone. Only when the living actors emerged from the picture and approached the audience to deliver monologues did they truly reveal their presence.

The play's dramatic effect was heightened by the fact that the key characters were all acted live, and occasionally emerged from the scene, while the minor ones were images only. Jasperodus found it totally absorbing. It was written, he guessed, by some author of antiquity, and unfolded in dazzling language a story of dukes and princes, of ill-fated lovers from hostile houses. Inwardly he congratulated the inventor of this type of drama, as well as of the device itself. But then such marvels were probably common out in the East; this thought reminded him of how recently he had been born. For all he had done, he had not yet penetrated very far into the world.

The drama ended. The substantial-seeming scenes vanished, leaving behind a handful of actors standing on bare boards. They bowed low to Jasperodus.

'Excellent!' Jasperodus commended. 'A fine performance!' He would have been content to mull over the play for a while, but an oldster with a bushy white beard slid into view.

'And now, Your Majesty, permit us to present views of the distant past. These images have been preserved from the Age of Tergov!'

He attended to the laser device. In the space recently occupied by the drama another scene sprang into being. This time it was a still, showing an aerial view of part of a city so vast and magnificent that all present gasped.

'These pictures are a little smudged because the holograms lay for centuries in the soil before being unearthed,' the spry old man explained. 'Here is Pekengu, one of the Four Capital Cities of the Rule of Tergov. When this hologram was taken Tansiann was but an unimportant town of moderate size. Pekengu itself is now little more than a sad shell of ruins, though still inhabited.' The projector clicked; a second scene appeared. 'Here we see another of the Four Capitals: Pacifica, the floating city on the Great East Sea. Pacifica was fifty miles across, and its population was two hundred million. The great central shaft you see extended half a mile below the surface of the ocean and two miles into the air.' The expositor continued to give more facts about the ancient capital, now lying wrecked on the bed of the ocean, and then switched to perhaps the best of his pictures. 'Here is a view of one of the most consummate architectural triumphs of all time: the Temple of the Brotherhood of Man at Pekengu. Parts of this magnificent edifice still remain, notably the north wall. This picture is believed to have been taken about a hundred years after the temple was built.'

Jasperodus gazed enthralled at the gigantic building. He had never imagined anything even remotely like it. Its central feature was a massive dome about whose middle floated a girdle of clouds, so immense was it. The lower parts of the dome seemed to cascade away into mounds, waves, traceries and runs that spilled and tumbled out over the ground, all seeming to hang from the floating upper mass rather than to support it.

'Can you show us the inside of this building also?' he demanded excitedly.

'Alas, no. Pictures of the interior do exist, so I have heard, but I have none in my collection.'

The expositor exhibited his remaining pictures: the impressively developed territories on Mars; the vast sea barrage that, in those days, altered continental climates by controlling oceanic currents; a stupendous space community that swept through the solar system on an elongated elliptical path so as regularly to cross the orbits of all the planets; a view of Saturn seen over the towers of a town on Tethys, one of its inner satellites.

'These,' the expositor told them, 'are examples of the bygone glory that the Emperor Charrane seeks to revive.'

The sights left Jasperodus stirred and agitated. Here indeed were accomplishments of a high order! He began to feel an immense admiration for the Old Empire and regretted that he could not have lived in the former time.

The picture show ended with a shorter second series showing weird, almost impossible animals. Creatures with ludicrously long necks or with twenty-foot wing spans, cats the size of elephants and horses the size of cats. Some of the animals bore no resemblance to any beast Jasperodus knew of and defied description.

'None of these animals occur in nature but were created during the classical civilisation by a science now lost,' the expositor explained. 'This science could also culture bizarre types of man, but these and all other like species are extinct today, not having survived the wild state that attended the Dark Age.'

He put aside the laser projector; but the show was not yet finished. Another man took the stage and performed baffling feats of magic. Jasperodus watched closely. He could discern faster movements than could the human eye and he was able to see that many of the tricks depended on legerdemain or on misdirecting the attention of the audience. Others, mainly those using cards or apparently demonstrating mind-reading, made use of devious mathematical calculations or ingenious psychology, at both of which the conjurer was clearly an expert. Jasperodus was able to see through the operation of these also; but others mystified even him.

Afterwards the four leaders of the troupe, including the expositor and the conjuror, sat before him relating unusual tales and propounding riddles. Jasperodus had secretly looked forward to this part of the proceedings. These people spent their lives travelling the world, and their knowledge covered a vast range of subjects. The troupe could cater for all tastes: not only could it perform plays, exotic foreign music, displays of dancing, acrobatics, conjuring and buffoonery; it could also debate philosophy with remarkable erudition. Jasperodus needed some stimulating conversation now that Padua, otherwise his only outlet, had become churlish and unfriendly towards him.

After listening for a while he expressed a wish to be posed a riddle or two.

A jolly-faced oldster, his face more wrinkled than the others and fringed by a fluffy white beard, obliged him. 'Which are more numerous, the living or the dead?'

Jasperodus thought for a moment. 'The living, for the dead don't exist.'

'Correct! Now apply yourself to this ancient conundrum. A judge once sentenced a man to death, informing him that he was to be garotted sometime between the following Monday and Friday, but that up until the moment he was taken from his cell he would not know on which day. That night the condemned man reasoned thus: "I cannot be garotted on Friday, which is the last day, for in that case I would be forewarned of it the instant Thursday midnight had passed, which is against the judge's ruling. But if Friday is eliminated I cannot be garotted on Thursday either – because I would likewise be forewarned of it the instant Wednesday midnight had passed. By the same argument Wednesday, Tuesday and Monday are each eliminated in turn. I am saved! I cannot be executed." And so he rested easy. But when Tuesday arrived he was taken from his cell and garotted, unforeseen as the judge had promised. Explain.'

Jasperodus explored the intricacies of the tale and found himself in a paradox. After some abortive attempts to solve it he shifted uneasily in his chair. 'Pah! It is a play on words merely. The judge lied. He imposed a condition that cannot be carried out in reality, which is something any fool can do. He should have exempted the last day from his promise and then there would be no paradox.'

'My opinion exactly!' Shoulders jiggling, the oldster chuckled in amusement. 'But you would be surprised how many philosophers have taken his words at face value and erected imposing systems of logic on them.' He gave a crafty laugh, looking sidewise at his colleagues. 'A ruler with an intellect for a change!'

The remark emboldened Jasperodus. 'You are all men of discernment,' he said, adopting an imperious pose. 'Consider, then, my achievements. I have made myself king of this land and all men here do my bidding. I can outthink most and have determination enough for ten. Do you not think that this gives me equal status with men? That I am, in effect, a man?'

He was answered by a trouper with a lean rubbery face the colour of red brick. 'By no means. You are a machine for all that. How did you gain your kingdom?'

'Why, by trickery and deceit!' Jasperodus said proudly. 'Is that not the way of men?'

'The way of most men, just so. By your own admission you add weight to my case. With you, all is imitation.'

'You have no moral sense,' chortled the white-bearded oldster.

The fourth member of the team, a man somewhat younger than the others, spoke up. 'Your question is dealt with by the Riddle of the Sphinx, said by many to predate all recorded history.'

Jasperodus darted him a quick look. 'Tell it.'

'The riddle runs: What can a man do that is neither thinking, feeling, sensing nor action? The answer is that he can *be conscious* that he does any of those things. Here we have the vital difference between a man and any construct. Your Majesty can think, have emotions, perceive – in the machine sense – and perform effective action. But there can be no awareness behind these functions, and if you aver that there is then you have formed an erroneous conclusion.'

'So my good friend Padua tells me,' Jasperodus said huffily, disappointed that he had received no praise. 'And yet I do indeed hold to this error, at no small cost to my peace of mind. Tell me, do you not fear that I will punish you for your ill-considered remarks?'

'Should we then insult both you and ourselves with pandering lies?' The man put on an exposition of dignity. 'We undertake to earn our fee wherever we go, whether with frolics or erudition.'

The expositor twisted the knife still further. 'It needs to be said that gaining power over others, even in seizing a kingdom by force, is among the coarsest of human accomplishments and does not indicate any high level of attainment.'

But meanwhile the white-bearded poser of paradoxes was apparently seized by a huge joke and sat giggling quietly to himself. Jasperodus' gaze veered towards him.

'Why do you laugh, old man?'

'Who is to prove that human beings are conscious either?' the other replied, restraining his mirth. 'There is no objective test. They themselves assert it, of course – but you make the same claim, and we know the claim to be false in your case. Perhaps *we* are deluded concerning *ourselves* – therefore rest easy, robot, probably we are all *un*conscious together! After all, life is but a dream, the playwright tells us!'

'Well spoken!' acclaimed Jasperodus in a hollow voice. 'For all I know your state is just as mine is.' But inwardly he felt the emptiness of this small victory. The oldster's argument was clever but too sophisticated to be taken seriously. If he were to cling to it he might well be like the man in the condemned cell who believed he could not be garotted.

'Let us leave this fruitless area of discussion,' the old man suggested. 'Would Your Majesty care to hear more paradoxes? I will prove that motion is impossible, that a swift runner cannot overtake a slow one, and that a bullet can never reach its target.'

'Enough, enough.' Jasperodus rose to his feet. 'Enough of paradoxes. I bid you good night.'

He swept through the hall. All present – save the entertainers – kept their eyes downcast, embarrassed that their lord's construct nature had been made so much of, and nervous of what his reaction would be. On leaving the hall Jasperodus signalled to Cree Inwing to follow; the two conferred in the passage outside.

'Do we go now to Fludd?' Inwing asked.

'No … I think not.' Jasperodus uttered a deep sigh, as if of weariness and tedium. 'I have made a decision, Inwing. Gordona is too small a pond for me. I am abandoning all and taking myself to the east. Since I have no further interest in what happens here you are free to return to Zhorm; I release you from your oath.'

'Hmm.' Inwing accepted this statement with remarkably little astonishment, but with some appearance of self-concern. He fingered his moustache doubtfully. 'You place me in an unenviable situation. There can be no question of taking sides with Zhorm – I am a traitor of the first rank and he will kill me at the earliest opportunity. It seems I had best flee the country.'

'But you saved Zhorm's life.'

'He doesn't know that; and it would certainly be hard to convince him.'

Jasperodus looked down at the young officer's face. Inwing was a man of practicality, he decided; in the space of seconds he had turned his back on Gordona and was already contemplating a new future somewhere in a strange land. Jasperodus grunted with a hint of humour. 'I shall be taking the aircraft. Accompany me, if you want to get away from here in a hurry – it makes no difference to me, and you have served me well so perhaps I owe you that.'

Inwing nodded. 'I accept.'

'You don't feel degraded to travel in the company of a robot?' Jasperodus asked in a tone edged with sarcasm. 'You heard the debate in the hall just now; you must have opinions of your own.'

Inwing shrugged. 'I'm not a philosopher. I've no time for subtle distinctions, especially when the throttling cord is practically around my neck. What of Craish and the others, by the way? You leave them in circumstances that are even less to be desired.'

Jasperodus considered briefly. 'I will send a message releasing Craish and the rest also. Let him try to seize Gordona for himself if he cares to – but I think he'll take his men and sneak off back to the forest to carry on as before.'

'Yes, the heart will go out of things without you there,' Inwing agreed. Jasperodus was pleased that he had dropped all formality and was speaking to him as man to man.

They stopped by the office while Jasperodus wrote to Craish, sending the letter by dispatch rider. He could imagine the ex-bandit's dismay on receiving it.

Unobtrusively they left the palace. Thunder rolled from the distance and was coming rapidly nearer through the darkness. The rain was heavy, making a continuous splash and patter on the courtyard and pouring off the slanting roofs of the palace.

'Craish will have time for a getaway, at any rate,' Jasperodus ruminated. 'Zhorm will not move tonight.' Not that he cared; his attitude to his followers remained unsentimental.

Gordona's one and only serviceable aircraft was kept in a shed in the palace grounds. Jasperodus sent away the guards, then he and Inwing lifted up the door, propping it open with the shafts provided for the purpose. Together they pushed the small, natty flier on to the short grass runway.

The robot opened the cabin door and flicked a switch, causing the dashboard to glow. He checked the dials, was satisfied, then turned back to Inwing standing on the grass.

'So goodbye to Gordona,' he said tonelessly, his gaze flicking around at the palace and at the lights thrown up by the town beyond. 'My kindergarten.'

'Where are we bound for, as a matter of interest?' Inwing asked mildly. 'To the east, you said. But east of here lies a veritable chaos of states and principalities, many of them places of danger and violence. Anarchy has its advocates, but I would prefer that we fixed a safer, more definite destination.'

'You fear for your safety, then? Set your mind at ease, I am flying directly to Tansiann, the centre of the inhabited world.'

Inwing looked startled. 'That's half the world away!'

'The flier is perfectly capable of making the journey. I have seen to that by helping to service it myself, since there is no trusting these doltish mechanics. The motor is powered by an isotope battery, so we shall not be stranded for lack of fuel.'

Inwing sighed. 'I fear my provinciality will show. It is a place where one needs one's wits about one.'

Jasperodus became impatient. 'Tonight I made a vow to experience everything a man can experience,' he said in a low voice that was like iron. 'Where else would I go for this but Tansiann? If you lack the verve to survive in a city I'll set you down wherever you please *en route*.'

'You vowed to experience everything?' Inwing echoed.

'Everything, everything! I know my strength. Anything the world offers I can take. As for this thing called consciousness, if it truly exists I shall seize even that!'

Perplexed, Inwing stepped back in the rain. 'But – how?'

Jasperodus suffered an agitated pause. 'By will-power!' he exclaimed, throwing up his hands. 'I will find a way. But are you going to stand there all night? Let us be going, unless you have altered your plans.'

'No, indeed. Tansiann it is, then.' Inwing clambered up after Jasperodus into the tiny cabin, closing the door behind him. Jasperodus occupied the pilot's seat. By this time Inwing's cape was wet through, but he settled into the single passenger seat without complaint and sat staring blankly through the windscreen.

Jasperodus switched on the motor. The propeller spun and shimmered; they bumped over the grass and were airborne, veering sharply upwards.

Okrum receded below. Lightning flickered a few miles away and Jasperodus saw that he would be forced to fly directly through the storm unless he was careful. The rain drummed against the windscreen; gusts took hold of the little plane and buffeted it about. Handling it was all the harder because his own weight spoiled its trim, but he had already taught himself to fly with skill and he managed to avoid the worst of the storm, taking them up above it into calmer air. Soon they were speeding uneventfully eastward.

Eventually Inwing dozed in his seat. Navigating by the stars, Jasperodus flew on through the night and into a clear, sunny day. Inwing awoke, grumbling sleepily, and made a meagre breakfast from part of a loaf of bread he had brought with him.

Now that the landscape was revealed Jasperodus took the plane lower, interested by the sights that met his elevated eye. Mostly they flew over forest, but there were also frequent patches of cultivated land betokening some community or other – a manor, a principality, even a kingdom. Here all the areas of authority were fairly small; only further east were big nations, federations and empires to be found.

One spectacle filled them both with awe: a vast grid hundreds of miles across, its rectangular walls marching with regularity and precision over the surface of the Earth. From ground level it would not have been visible at all, the outlines having been weathered away and absorbed into the landscape; only from an aerial perspective did its repetitious design become evident. Neither of them could guess at what its purpose could have been, but clearly it was yet another piece of imposing grandeur from the classical civilisation of Tergov.

A fair-sized town swung into view ahead of them. Out of curiosity Jasperodus dived to get a better view of its streets and buildings, noting that though still narrow and twisting they were somewhat better appointed than those of Okrum. Inwing coughed nervously and Jasperodus swung up again, climbing so as to continue their journey. Just then something flashed up from below and a short, sharp explosion rocked the plane.

'They're firing rockets,' Inwing warned in a low voice.

Jasperodus fought to regain control. He twisted and turned as more missiles hurtled towards them, trailing streaks of white smoke. Again the plane shuddered but was not hit; he poured on the power and zoomed away from the town.

'I was afraid of this,' Inwing said in a terse tone which indicated Jasperodus should have listened to him more closely. 'Some of these countries are in a constant state of war with their neighbours. To them we look like raiders.'

Jasperodus made no answer, being busy scanning the surrounding sky and ground. He saw that the worst was happening: three aircraft were climbing to meet them. Even at this distance he could see from their outlines that they sported either guns or missile racks.

And his own plane was unarmed.

The ensuing minute of time assured him that there was no hope of outdistancing the pursuers. Two of them were propeller-driven, like himself, but the third used some other principle – some kind of thruster by appearances – and was much faster. Jasperodus swung to the North and dived down towards some heavily forested hills.

'We'll have to get under cover,' he said curtly to Inwing. 'Hold tight, it might be bumpy.'

The interceptors were banking to follow him. Jasperodus winged down between the walls of a valley, temporarily losing them from view. He was looking for somewhere to put down, but all he saw were trees, a few outcroppings of rock, and more trees. If nothing else offered, he told himself, he would have to crash-land into the tree-tops, sacrificing the plane and hoping that the foliage would brake their velocity gently enough not to kill Inwing – Jasperodus himself, of course, had less to worry about on that score.

But at its far end the valley narrowed into a modest canyon, beyond which Jasperodus glimpsed what was needed: an even, though slightly upsloping stretch of ground on which there was a gap in the trees wide enough and long enough for the aircraft, with luck, to land.

Lowering the flaps, he shot between the walls of the canyon and approached the wild grass. When the wheels first touched down the tail reared up; he was forced to re-power the motor to stabilise. They bounced over the turf, lost speed, and then one wing hit a bush and sent the plane lurching through a quarter circle, whereupon it came to a halt.

'Get out,' Jasperodus ordered. They scrambled from the cabin and together managed to push the aircraft under the cover of nearby trees, forcing it as deep as it would go into the dappled shade.

Stepping halfway from under the screen of branches, Jasperodus peered skyward. The pursuers were sailing overhead. They dipped low towards the forest and banked, searching.

He returned to Inwing. 'We had best stay here until nightfall,' he said. 'We may not be able to evade them a second time.'

Inwing nodded, glad of a chance to take some exercise. He paced up and down, stretching gratefully.

Time passed. They turned the plane round so as to be able to manoeuvre it more easily into a take-off position, and then simply waited.

Presently Jasperodus thought to reconnoitre their surroundings. He left Inwing and strode off through the forest, making for high ground. After a while he came across a trail which wound round a hillside to lead, he judged, to the town a few miles away. He paused pensively, not liking this turn of events, and then continued. Half an hour later he heard sounds nearby. He stepped off the trail, and was able to observe a party of men dressed in a uniform consisting of green tunics and berets which had a short peak hanging over one ear. All were armed, and from the way they separated occasionally to explore the forest on either side of the path it was plain they were searching for the wreck of Jasperodus' aircraft. He turned back and moved stealthily through the undergrowth, keeping out of sight until he was ahead of them, and then loped swiftly along the trail towards Inwing.

Too late, he realised that he had been careless. There must have been men out looking for the aircraft from the instant it had come down, and they had a fair idea of its whereabouts. The party he had spotted was not the only one: rounding a rock and emerging into a clearing, he found himself directly confronting another group, uniformed as was the first.

He pulled himself up sharp, eyeing the four men. One of them carried a beam emitter which could prove fatal to a robot. Jasperodus glanced around him, edging away and wishing he had brought a weapon.

They were surprised to see him, but not so much so as to give him any advantage. 'The Finnian swine are using robots now, eh?' one exclaimed. 'Let him have it, Juss!'

The soldier holding the emitter went down on one knee and aimed it at Jasperodus, who instantly realised he had little chance of escaping its beam. He was about to fling himself sideways and into the undergrowth but before the soldier could fire the chatter of a repeater gun rang out from above him and the man fell dead.

The eyes of the others shot startled up to the top of the rock behind Jasperodus. Cree Inwing sprang down into the clearing, his gun voicing death again. A few bullets came in return, aimed wild and a few of them bouncing off Jasperodus, but in seconds it was all over.

'Got bored and thought I'd come looking for you,' Inwing explained, turning to him with a grin. 'Then I saw this lot coming so I hid up there.' He jerked his thumb to the craggy overhang.

'There are others behind me,' Jasperodus said, 'and possibly yet more I haven't seen.' He urged Inwing along. 'Back to the plane quickly – we have to get away from here at once.'

In minutes they had regained the aircraft. One to each wing, they manhandled it out on to the improvised runway, lining it up so that hopefully it would manage to slip in between the trees. In the pilot's seat Jasperodus paused; take-off should not really be any more difficult than landing, unless they hit a tuft or mound that bounced them off-course.

In the event he was able to get off the ground smoothly, soared up the narrow canyon and into open air. He turned the nose East and flew low, following the undulations of the landscape for some miles, and apparently they weren't spotted for no pursuit came.

'Something puzzles me,' Jasperodus said when they felt safe again. 'You realise what you just did? You risked your life to save a machine construct. Why did you do it? Surely you must have known that your best chance was to head straight back to the plane and take off without me?'

Inwing looked doubtful, as if this idea was new to him. 'I didn't think about it,' he admitted. 'I've told you I'm no philosopher … If it comes to that, why were you so thoughtless as to leave me alone with the plane? By your reasoning I should have taken off with it at the first opportunity, since without you I could make better speed and go where I choose.'

'You need me,' Jasperodus replied bluntly. 'Two can survive better than one.'

'Yes, there's that too. Anyway, it's a poor man who'll desert a companion at the first sign of trouble. I suppose I've worked with you so long I just didn't think of you as a machine. Perhaps I should have.'

Jasperodus laughed briefly.

He did not mention that part of the reason he had gone exploring was to see what Inwing would do in his absence.

For the rest of the journey he avoided towns, as well as the castles and fortified camps that occasionally dotted the landscape. They flew on and on, and very gradually the appearance of the Earth changed. There was more land under cultivation, and towns and villages, as well as the odd city, grew more numerous. Also more in evidence were railways, roads, canals and air travel: they were entering the area of large national groupings. But all this, Jasperodus could not help but notice, merely overlay the immense remains of the classical civilisation: the gigantic ruins, the reshaping of the Earth, the enigmatic formations, all of which were slowly sinking into the soil.

Jasperodus was merciless to Cree Inwing. Once, after travelling for two days, they landed and raided a farmhouse to get him food. After that Jasperodus simply kept going. If he thought the engine was overheating he switched it off and glided for a distance to give it a chance to cool. Inwing cursed, slept and sweated in the cramped cabin, having nothing to occupy himself with, and was forced to shift for himself as regards calls of nature.

After a week of this he could stand it no longer and begged Jasperodus to land and give him respite. Accordingly Jasperodus winged down from their high altitude and looked out for a convenient landing place.

They passed over a kuron town. It was the first Jasperodus had ever seen, and forgetting his former caution he circled it twice, inspecting the curious arrangement of mushroom-shaped houses. Then he passed on, and a short distance away came down on a wood-fringed meadow. They pushed the aircraft beneath the spread branches of the trees, as was their practice, and since evening was drawing on settled down for the night.

Cree Inwing spent some time running to and fro, flexing his arms and performing various muscle-toning exercises. When he felt sufficiently relieved he built a fire and roasted a small animal he had trapped. For a couple of hours he and Jasperodus sat patiently by the fire, desultorily discussing their future route to Tansiann, whose precise location was unknown to either of them.

Inwing's preparations for sleep were interrupted by the snap of a twig and the sound of light footfalls coming through the trees. Presently there came into the firelight the small, slight figures of three kurons.

Jasperodus observed them with curiosity. They were between four and five feet in height and seemed approximately manlike, at first reminding him of the fairy folk of legend. On closer inspection, however, the humanish appearance diminished. Their faces bore no more resemblance to a man's than to, say, a tiger's or a lizard's, and were pinched and bony, giving an appearance of exaggerated delicateness. The proportions of body and limbs were also all their own, so that the correspondence to the human race consisted entirely of their being bimanual and bipedal.

They wore nondescript garments like coarse shifts and flaps. Jasperodus noticed that one of them was carrying a glass jar carefully in both hands, but he could not immediately see what it contained. With no evidence of fear or caution they walked directly into the small camp and sat down opposite the two travellers.

'Good evening,' said Inwing sardonically.

'And likewise to you,' replied one of the newcomers in a faint, breathless voice.

There was silence while the kurons stared into the fire and Inwing and Jasperodus stared in turn at them. Since they seemed in no hurry to explain their presence Jasperodus put a question of his own.

'We are *en route* for Tansiann,' he said, 'but are unsure of its exact whereabouts. Perhaps you can direct us?'

'You must travel on a course East and about forty degrees South,' the kuron told him in the same piping, breathless voice: 'Here we are on the western fringe of the New Empire; to the north are hostile nations which you must avoid. You will not, however, reach Tansiann unopposed in your aircraft. On approaching Kwengu you will be noted on radar and apprehended.'

'Will we not then be allowed to continue?' Jasperodus inquired.

'That will depend on your business. I cannot say. We kurons prefer to live well outside the main stream of human life, by reason of past atrocities and persecutions.'

'Indeed? That aspect of history is new to me. You have been badly treated?'

The other nodded awkwardly, in a way which suggested it was not a native gesture. 'To survive the Dark Age was extremely difficult for us, for it was an age of violence and brutal ignorance. Prior to that time we had lived in the big human cities as well as in our own rural towns, engaging in trade and certain kinds of manufacture at which we excelled, but when the light of reason went out irrational hatreds were raised against us. Any misfortune or natural calamity was ascribed to our agency, and it was widely believed we practised malign magic. Massacre of kuron ghettoes became a frequent occurrence; added to which the breakdown of commerce rendered our normal livelihood impossible. Very few of us remained alive at the end of those bad centuries.'

'You live now under the aegis of the New Empire?' Jasperodus asked.

'Many of us do; here its power is nominal only. But the Emperor Charrane has decreed that kurons are to live without molestation in the empire, and that is our main hope for the future. His laws are not always obeyed, but it is better than elsewhere, such as in the states dominated by Borgor where we are still openly persecuted.'

Inwing put in a word. 'You come from another star, don't you? If things were so bad why didn't you fly off back to where you came from?'

The kuron turned to peer at him. 'It was too late. We, too, shared the social decline, losing our knowledge and skills. We no longer had the ability to build star arks.'

'How distant is your home star?' Jasperodus asked. 'How long did it take to get here?'

'Earth is our home now; we are natural migrants in the true sense of the word. Our star of origin lies a hundred and thirty-five light-years away, and the journey takes a hundred and fifty-two years by star ark.'

Jasperodus gestured to the glass jar lying on the ground. 'Presumably you saw our plane flying over and noted our landing place. What prompted you to visit us?'

'We come to trade.'

The robot grunted. 'Then you come in vain. We have no goods to offer. We have scarcely anything for ourselves.'

'Untrue. You have the aircraft. We wish to bargain for that.'

Inwing shook his head. 'We need it to travel to Tansiann.'

'Sample our wares before you decide. One can travel without wings, even if more slowly.' The kuron lifted the jar, which was dome-shaped. It contained dark red soil in which grew about a dozen small flowers, blurrily visible through the thick glass. 'Here is something you cannot find even in Tansiann.'

He opened a lid at the top of the jar and reached down with a long, slender hand to pluck one of the flowers, which he brought forth. It was a simple enough flower, like an extra-large, lavender-coloured buttercup. 'These flowers are grown in the soil of Kuronid, our aboriginal world, brought here in the original star ark and preserved for centuries since. They can be grown in no other soil. I will allow you to smell this first bloom free of charge; if you wish to keep it, and the others in this jar, you must give us your aircraft.'

'A jar of flowers for an airplane!' Inwing exclaimed with a laugh.

'Not the jar, for we cannot part with the soil,' corrected the kuron. 'I will pluck the flowers and give them to you under a glass seal, whereupon they will retain their perfume for one third of a year.'

'Well,' said Inwing in puzzlement, 'what's so special about it?'

'It is a psychedelic flower. Its perfume contains chemical substances which transform the consciousness.'

'Give it to me,' Jasperodus commanded, holding out his hand. 'The aircraft is mine to dispose of, not his.'

The kuron continued speaking to Inwing. 'It will have no effect on your robot, of course. Inhale the scent deeply, now, and you will see that our offer is more than fair.'

Nevertheless Jasperodus insisted on sampling the flower. He applied it to his nostrils, drawing a small draught of air into his olfactory cavity: the perfume was light and delicate, but characteristically unique. Otherwise he found little to distinguish it from an ordinary Earth flower.

Cree Inwing still did not understand what the kuron was offering him when his turn came. But within half a minute of his sniffing the flower a look of complete amazement came over his face. He sprang to his feet and looked about him as if seeing everything for the first time; then he broke into peals of laughter which subsided into a fit of uncontrollable giggling.

All watched in silence. Eventually Inwing sat down again and stared with absolute fixity at a spray of leaves over his head, for minute after minute. Even when he spoke to Jasperodus he did not take his eyes off that spray of leaves; it seemed to hold endless fascination for him. 'It's amazing ...' He began to ramble in an excited voice. 'I never understood it all till now. It's all different, it's all completely *different*. I'm not me, that's not that – we're all the same as one another ... There's no end to variation, but it's all one ...'

He seemed to be trying to explain the unexplainable, but Jasperodus merely grunted sulkily. His old sullenness had come over him; the flower obviously worked on men – and presumably on kurons – but not on him, and he took this as yet further evidence of his lack of consciousness.

There was presumably nothing within him for the perfume to alter: his resentment was by now automatic.

'And what of our bargain?' the kuron asked softly. 'Are you agreed?'

'Eh?' Inwing took his eyes off the leaves and stared with equal intensity at the kuron's face. 'Oh, yes. Give me the flowers; you can have the plane.'

'No!' Jasperodus came to his feet, his voice harsh. 'There will be no bargain!'

Laughing like a child, Inwing rose to face Jasperodus. 'But it's all right, Jasperodus. Really it is! We can walk to Tansiann. Who wants a plane? Perhaps we'll fly without a plane! Anything's possible! This is worth more than any airplane, believe me!' He froze, suddenly trapped by the burnished reflection of flames on Jasperodus' chest.

Jasperodus rounded on the kurons. 'Conceivably your reputation for witchcraft is not without foundation. You have given this man a poison and deranged his judgement!'

The kuron spokesman shook his head. 'Not so. His consciousness is altered, that is all. Consciousness is chemically based; but normally it is restricted by automatic conditioning so as to encompass only a very small range of impressions. The action of the flower is to free it temporarily from these restrictions. For the first time he is seeing the world as it exists in objective reality, and it astonishes him. Naturally he now has a different idea of what is most worth having.'

Inwing nodded his head in vigorous agreement. 'That's right, Jasperodus, this is reality! For the first time in my life!'

'And the last!' Jasperodus snatched the flower from him and flung it into the fire. 'Away with you this instant or I will kill you all!' he growled at the kurons. 'Luckily I am immune to your tricks and know how to protect our property!'

Calmly and with no sign of alarm or disappointment, the kurons took up their glass jar and walked quietly from the clearing. Jasperodus silenced Cree's jovial protestations with the threat of his upraised fist.

'Your foolishness has cost you a night's good rest on the ground,' he chided. And as soon as the kurons were gone from earshot he bundled Inwing into the plane and manhandled it single-handed on to the meadow.

It was risky to take off in darkness on wild turf, for the plane's headlight offered little illumination, but they became airborne without mishap. Consulting the stars, he set a course and they droned on through the night.

For several hours he was forced to endure Cree's witless expatiations. But eventually the effect of the flower's perfume wore off and the ex-soldier fell into a deep sleep. And so they continued on for several days more. Deeper into the empire the land began to take on a more urbanised aspect, and remembering the kuron's warning Jasperodus thought it prudent to descend, abandon the plane and continue on foot. Sometimes walking, sometimes by rail, meeting a number of adventures together, the pair arrived at last in Tansiann.

7

Tansiann!

Pausing on the eminence of a tall hill, one of ten guarding the Imperial City, Jasperodus looked down to where he hoped to prove his capacity to achieve all.

'Tansiann,' he murmured after a while. 'It is everything I imagined.'

'The centre of the world,' Cree Inwing agreed. 'A city one could lose oneself in.'

'True. Every experience is to be found here, no doubt, such being the nature of capitals.'

For some short while they had been travelling through the environs of the city, consisting of farmlands, satellite towns, private estates and fenced-off areas containing secret government projects. Tansiann proper, on which they now gazed, was a well-defined entity occupying an undulating estuary valley, bounded on one side by the sea and on the other by the encircling ten hills which in preceding centuries had provided a natural landward defence. Through the city flowed the river Tan, a waterway created during the Rule of Tergov but overbuilt by the clustered conurbation now, and fully visible only near its mouth, where ocean-going ships pulled up at the three-mile-long dockland. With all these natural amenities Charrane had chosen well in placing his capital here. Boasting a population of three million, Tansiann had become the world's most important city, and exuded a lively, vigorous atmosphere. Jasperodus felt a mounting excitement as he beheld it. Admiration, anticipation, a desire to share in ambitious endeavours, all blended into a kind of longing.

Like all large cities Tansiann was separated into districts each exemplifying a different function. In one area grimy tenements mingled with the workshops of artisans; in another temples and skyscrapers piled together and lurched skyward. Near the dockland larger workshops, factories and foundries poured smoke into the air; elsewhere a sparkling commercial centre adjoined an elegant tree-lined residential district inhabited by the wealthy. To the northeast, in a quarter dating from the Old Empire, new dwellings sprang up amongst old ruins and a long wall, like a spine from which other ribs radiated, still represented some enigmatic antique construction. Yet such relics detracted but little from the triumphant signs of a resurgent civilisation. Cree and Jasperodus had passed through towns displaying far less favourable a contrast between past glory and present achievement. In Tansi-ann the projects beloved of the Emperor Charrane stood out proudly: soaring monuments of nascent might, buildings to reduce a man to the size of an ant, public colonnades of delightful extent, statuary and vast murals of Byzantine splendour.

A sudden flash of fire caught their attention. A pillar of white energy was climbing like a rising sun from behind one of the more distant hills. It lifted aloft a glinting mass of metal which accelerated rapidly until it was no more than a dot in the sky.

Jasperodus nodded in satisfaction. He was already aware that the Emperor, missing no opportunity to invest the city with an air of impressiveness, had located the Empire's largest spaceground close at hand too. No doubt the daily thunder of rocket engines reminded Tansiann's citizens of how far the New Empire could reach.

The two travellers returned to the highway, from which they had departed so as to gain their panoramic view of the city, and followed it as it descended into the estuary. An hour of walking brought them, through dusty streets lined with canopied shops, to a district near the river. Here, at the intersection of three thoroughfares, they paused and looked about them.

The place bore the unsettled seediness of a transit area, frequented mostly by sailors, casual labourers and recently arrived immigrants. Taverns, inns and rooming houses were plentiful. One of the three streets curved round to run alongside a ribwork of concrete pillars, through which could be glimpsed the murky brown water of the Tan, much fouled by industrial waste, and bearing slow-moving black barges.

Across the street a group of three men, flashily dressed in shirts and breeks of coloured silk, appeared to be eyeing the newcomers speculatively. Presently they crossed the street a little way ahead of the two and stood chatting together with studied indifference. As Cree and Jasperodus drew abreast one of them called out suddenly and presented himself, shaking Cree's hand warmly while looking him confidently in the eye. 'I can see you are a recent arrival in our town, citizen. Perhaps I can be of some assistance?'

Cree frowned. 'How do you know me for a stranger?' he demanded, taken aback.

The other laughed lightly. 'You and your construct both have the dust of travel on you, sir. Besides, the main road from the west leads directly through here. Many migrants from that quarter land up precisely on the spot where you are now standing. Allow me to explain myself. I make it my business to direct and advise newcomers regarding accommodation and employment, whereupon I receive a small commission from certain lodging houses and business enterprises. If you seek a comfortable night's rest and good whole-some food at moderate charge, may I recommend the Blue Boar, which you will find along that street yonder and third turning to the left. As to work, have you any immediate prospects? What are your skills?'

'I had not expected to install myself with such facility,' Cree remarked dubiously. The other laughed again and continued with his jovial chatter, mentioning nothing that would seem to suggest an ulterior motive, or any disadvantage to Inwing. While they talked thus, he and one of his companions were shifting casually about from foot to foot, until, inadvertently so it seemed, Cree was manoeuvred into presenting his back to Jasperodus.

Suddenly Jasperodus' eye was caught by the third member of the group, who to his surprise was beckoning him urgently from within the cover of a nearby narrow alley. Unthinkingly he stepped towards the fellow, into the opening and away from the others.

The stranger laid a proprietary hand on his arm and spoke in a commanding hiss. 'Follow me directly, robot, and be quick about it – quietly, now.'

The man turned and padded rapidly off down the passage, plainly expecting Jasperodus to obey. In a trice Jasperodus had caught up with him, to seize him by the shoulder and jerk him round roughly. He thrust a fist close to his pinched face.

'The next time you try to take me from my owner, your skull will encounter this.'

The robot-stealer gaped thunderstruck at his intended victim, wide-eyed with alarm. Immediately Jasperodus released him he galloped frantically up the alley and disappeared from sight. Jasperodus returned to where Cree, all unawares, was still being engaged in genial conversation.

'Cree!' he warned in a loud voice. 'These men are thieves!'

The response from all parties to his words was startlement and consternation. The shysters decamped in great haste, leaving Cree standing perplexed.

He rubbed his nose ruefully when Jasperodus described how the thieves were able to commandeer a robot by removing it momentarily from its master's attention. 'Afterwards it would be hard to find grounds for complaint against them,' he explained. 'You were careless; your robot wandered off. What is that to do with them? Most constructs would be susceptible to such a technique – it can be likened to stealing a horse. Presumably there is a market for purloined robots hereabouts, but doubtless the natives are not so easily manipulated.'

'And I am instantly recognisable as a country bumpkin!' Cree exclaimed in dismay. He looked down at himself thoughtfully. 'It's the cut of my garments that gives me away. One of the first things might be to obtain clothes in the prevalent fashion, and cut from the local cloth. But time for that later. I am in need of refreshment.'

He moved towards a nearby tavern. At the entrance was a dispenser selling some kind of printed journal. Cree examined it with interest, made a small sound of approval, and placed a coin in the slot. The delivery chute ejected a folded copy.

Within, the tavern had a rough-hewn air, which was the reason why Cree had chosen it. After a brief word with the landlord he obtained permission for Jasperodus to sit with him, and purchased a mug of sour red wine, which he swallowed with evident satisfaction and then bought another. Much cheered by the beverage, he began a perusal of the journal.

Jasperodus meanwhile sat in silence. Their wanderings together had frequently been interspersed with Cree's practice of reviving himself with alcohol, and such halts in their progress were now familiar to the robot. Though secretly a trifle sullen that he too could not partake of the experience, he had grown patient with the habit, looking upon it as part of their working arrangement.

The truth was that their partnership had been of such benefit to them both as to warrant a degree of mutual tolerance. As a footloose construct Jasperodus would have faced many difficulties in journeying across the continent. The solution was simple: Cree represented him as his property.

Jasperodus himself had proposed this arrangement. Cree at first had shown some diffidence about casting into the role of a slave, even if only for the sake of appearances, someone who recently had been his own king and master. Jasperodus had quickly put him right on that score: he felt no loss of dignity.

On his side the robot's physical strength and mental acuity had stood them both in good stead on numerous occasions. In addition Jasperodus had now and then allowed Cree to hire him out, helping perhaps to erect a barn, to build a bridge, or to audit the accounts of a tradesman, in return for enough money to provide food, drink, lodging or rail fares.

While Cree was engrossed in the journal he was studying, Jasperodus casually inspected it over his shoulder. It was a news journal, containing reports of happenings in Tansiann and in other parts of the world. That in itself was cosmopolitan enough a touch to excite interest: such a thing as a news service was practically unknown elsewhere. As it was, the journal – boasting the emblazoned title 'New Empire' at the head of its first sheet – had the rough-finished appearance of a recent innovation. It was printed on crude, cheap paper manufactured from wood pulp and had been turned out, Jasperodus could discern, on a rotary printing press using relief type. Not as rapid or as accurate as some photochemical processes Jasperodus knew of, but no doubt efficient enough for present requirements.

By looking askance he found he was able to read the reports without disturbing Cree. The lead story was splashed right across the front page in headlines two inches tall.

CHARRANE CONQUERS MARS!

News reached Tansiann yesterday that the Mars Expeditionary Force has added interplanetary territories to the New Empire. Landing on the Red Planet a month ago, the Emperor's crack space commandos have since been fighting a successful campaign to bring this strategically important world under the imperial writ.

It is now little over a year since explorers first discovered that human communities still exist on Mars despite having been cut off for eight centuries from the mother planet, basing their way of life on the deep fissures and rills in the Martian surface where they have learned how to maintain a breathable atmosphere. On hearing of the Red Planet's continued habitation the Emperor Charrane had immediately pronounced it a top priority to 'recover the ancient Mars possessions'. The Emperor's early triumph will go a long way towards substantiating his boast that the Empire will eventually 'rival the glory of Tergov'.

Not all the news from space today is good. The Moon outposts have come under fresh attack by spaceships bearing the insignia of the Borgor Alliance and have sustained what is described as 'significant damage'. It is to be expected that the Alliance will attempt to loosen our grip on the new Martian province by striking at supply carriers and even by aiding forces of insurgency still remaining within the native population. Altogether the holding of Mars will prove one of the toughest jobs our armed forces have ever had to face. Nevertheless all sources at court are jubilant today. The Emperor is to issue a proclamation (*turn to back page*).

Alongside the text was a blurred photogravure picture, admittedly stirring, of a row of spaceships – ostensibly part of the Expeditionary Force – lifting off *en masse* amid clouds of flame, dust, smoke and steam.

Cree Inwing's eyes gleamed. 'Hah! Great stuff! That's action indeed!' he muttered to himself.

He turned the pages, glancing over the lesser news and articles that filled the journal. Midway through was a half-page advertisement offering commissions in the Imperial armed forces.

HELP DEFEND THE EMPIRE

The New Empire is ranged about with enemies hostile to the advance of civilisation. Gentlemen of quality are needed to officer the strength necessary to our safety and growth. At present opportunities for promotion are considerable, as are the opportunities to see action under testing conditions. The newly gained Martian dominions offer a whole new world of soldiering for a man of resource. Preference will be given to men of previous military experience, but all men of good family or proven ability may be eligible to participate in the great adventure of building an empire. Provided all conditions are fulfilled a captaincy may be purchased for nine thousand imperials, a lieutenancy for seven thousand imperials.

Cree fell to fingering his moustache and became very thoughtful. Jasperodus said nothing. On a following page was a similar advertisement in rougher terms, inviting men to join the ranks for adventure, service to the Emperor and two imperials a day. Cree merely glanced at it with a grunt.

'Fellow,' he called to one clearing tankards from the tables. 'Bring me another mug of this wine.'

A mood of some despondency seemed to have come over Cree. Many mugs of wine later he was fairly drunk and seemed disposed to sleep, laying his head on his arms. Jasperodus rose and approached the landlord.

'You have accommodation in this place?'

The other nodded brusquely.

'My master requires a room at least until tomorrow, in which I also will be domiciled.'

'If you wish.' The landlord produced a key and motioned towards some stairs. Jasperodus aroused Cree and they were conducted to an upper room, adequate but not too clean, containing a bed, a table, a cupboard and two chairs.

Cree flung himself on the bed and instantly was asleep. 'The charge is half an imperial a night,' the landlord told him, handing Jasperodus the key.

The robot placed the key on the table. 'If my master wakes and should ask after me, be good enough to inform him that I will return later. I have certain enquiries to make.'

The landlord, who had been about to quit the room, looked at him with new interest. 'Indeed? Is your owner accustomed to giving you such freedom of action?'

'He is; I am entirely dependable. You need have no anxieties on my behalf.'

'Hmmm.' The landlord pursed his lips and left with a contemplative air.

The enquiries Jasperodus sought to make were in fact of a very general nature. He merely wished to continue his reconnoitre of the city.

After leaving the tavern he walked in the same direction as before, trying to recall the layout of the city as he had observed it from the hilltop. Soon he left the riverside area and had a choice of avenues before him. Some instinct advised him to keep to the poorer districts to begin with; and so he found himself heading deep into Tansiann's worst slums.

Seven-storey tenements reared on all sides, decrepit and dirty, some derelict, interspersed with waste grounds and piles of junk. Dust was a fact of life, drifting down from the crumbling buildings, hazing the air, blowing across the open spaces. And the inhabitants seemed to swarm everywhere; this was, probably, the most teeming part of Tansiann.

Poverty was much in evidence. Jasperodus found this paradoxical. Out in the west where the tiny kingdoms and principalities boasted little wealth even the lowliest peasants were, generally speaking, comfortably off. But as he and Cree had progressed eastward towards the centre of civilisation a sort of polarisation had begun to manifest, greater riches producing pockets of poverty as if as a by-product. Here in the Imperial Capital was not only unparalleled wealth but also penury and degradation – an unlooked-for concomitant, surely.

As he proceeded Jasperodus mulled over this phenomenon, wondering what its causes might be.

He was surprised to note an unusual number of unattended robots on the streets hereabouts, many of them in a condition of poor repair. Jasperodus hailed one, intending to question it, but it clanked off with great haste and scrambled over a broken wall, after which it went running across a waste ground and disappeared. Several passers-by laughed jeeringly.

Puzzled, Jasperodus continued past some tramps and drunks who had made a camp fire on a vacant lot. A little further on he came across a scene oddly reminiscent of the first. The ruined shell of a building stood separated from the street by a stretch of rubble. Half hidden by a partly tumbled wall, a group of robots appeared to have made a camp also and were sitting round in a circle.

Jasperodus clambered over the rubble towards them. They evinced no reaction as he approached but continued to sit motionless, and he discovered them to be not functioning constructs but dead hulks, their skulls and bodies emptied of all usable parts.

Junk. But why the careful arrangement to suggest a social gathering? … A sound caught Jasperodus' attention. A group of half a dozen children, boys and girls aged perhaps ten to twelve, came scampering out of a defile between walls and surrounded him, tugging him back the way they had come.

'Come on, come on, your wanderings are finished!' the leader bellowed shrilly. 'We have found you a master! Resistance is useless!'

What? A repetition of this morning's experience? Robots commandeered by *children*? With grim amusement Jasperodus allowed them to hustle him through the defile. Behind the ruined building was an empty space hidden from any surrounding streets. Here a fat man waited, bedecked in a gaudy brocaded frock-coat and a flowered shirt stained with sweat. He grinned sourly; the youngsters descended on him with whoops and shouts.

Their leader, a skinny buck-toothed lad whose eyes seemed older than the rest of him, waved them away and led Jasperodus to the waiting buyer. 'I told you we'd get one, Melch. Here y'are.' He slapped Jasperodus on the torso. 'The best robot you ever seen.'

The buyer cast an appraising eye over Jasperodus. 'Not bad at all,' he admitted grudgingly. He looked boldly into the face of his prospective merchandise. 'How long you been loose?'

'Always,' Jasperodus replied brusquely.

'Hmm. He seems all right on the outside, but he probably needs fixing up in the head. Okay, I'll give you five imperials. That's a pretty good return for your time, eh, kids?'

'Good return nuthin'!' the boy exploded, eyes flaring. 'I want fifty!'

'Don't waste my time.' The buyer turned away.

'We'll take him to another dealer. Maybe we'll deal him ourselves and get thousands!'

'Try it if you like, kid. I don't think you're ready for that yet.'

'We'll keep him ourselves!'

Jasperodus raised a hand. 'I can settle all your arguments. The question of price is meaningless; I have not been captured and am not for sale. I followed these youngsters only out of curiosity.'

The buyer looked at him with narrowed eyes and then chuckled. 'A smart one, eh? That's a good try, robot. But you're still here.'

'I am not under anyone's command but my own. Try giving me an order and you will see.'

The buyer did not put the proposal to the test. 'You got a command language, huh?' he asked, a trifle wearily.

'Something of that nature,' Jasperodus told him suavely. 'You may take it that I am a highly sophisticated type of construct; you would find it difficult indeed to coerce me and you would be advised not to try.'

The fat man appeared to be thinking, running his tongue round the inside of his mouth. Finally he turned to the juvenile gang leader.

'Sorry, you got a dud here. Bad luck. He's not worth all the trouble it would be breaking him in.'

Sullenly the youngsters retreated, their leader throwing a bad-tempered curse at Jasperodus.

'You been in these parts long?' the buyer asked, eyeing Jasperodus half-interestedly.

'No.'

'Got any money on you?' He glanced at the satchel Jasperodus carried over his shoulder.

'A little. Why?'

He pointed between clumps of pre-stressed concrete with iron rods sticking out of them like stiff wires. 'Go down there till you come to the street, then walk to the left for about a quarter of an hour till you come to Jubilee Street. Go down there, take the second turning on the left and the first on the right. You'll come to a tavern called the Good Oil. Well, it's a shack, really. They call it a tavern. Good luck.'

'And why should I seek this shack?'

The other shrugged. 'You're a robot, aren't you? There aren't many places a robot can get kicks.'

The dealer turned away, signifying that the conversation was at an end. Mystified but intrigued, Jasperodus set off in the direction indicated, but before passing out of sight of the dealer he chanced to look back. The gang of young scruffs had caught another fish with their cleverly conceived bait. This time it was not a prize haul: the robot that came staggering along in their midst was aged and tottering, and reminded Jasperodus of Kitchen Help, the wretched construct he had known in Gordona. Nevertheless the arguing and bargaining went on apace.

Jasperodus continued on his way with a shake of his head. He thought he was beginning to see what the score was here now. Wild robots roamed the area, managing to evade capture for a while but prey to the rapacity of those living in the same seedy environment. Evidently some robots like to socialise – hence the gang's ingenious trap. Others, such as the one he had attempted to question, would shun all intercourse.

The Good Oil was a structure of wood and sheet metal put together haphazardly between two sturdier buildings of indeterminate function. Through the door Jasperodus glimpsed a turmoil of metal limbs.

A hulking construct barred his way, pointing the twin tines of an ugly electric prong at his chest.

'You have money?' the door robot asked, speaking in a humming, nasal voice.

Jasperodus slapped his satchel, eliciting the clink of coins. 'Yes.'

'Then enter.'

Cautiously Jasperodus passed through the door. The light was dim and glinted and gleamed off metal of all hues. The smell of oil, of steel and electricity permeated the place.

The roomy shack was filled with robots, sitting, standing, moving restlessly to and fro. They were of various types and sizes, nearly all of the familiar androform shape – two legs, two arms, trunk and head – that robot makers, like nature, had found most convenient. A drone of conversation and weird sounds provided a noisy background.

Jasperodus' first impression was that many of the robots were demented. Some staggered about, laughing in hollow booming voices. Others jigged up and down. One or two had collapsed and lay on the floor, unheeded by their fellows.

It was some moments before he noticed that there were also two men in the tavern. One, carrying some kind of apparatus, moved from robot to robot, speaking to each in turn. The other stood by a door at the rear and looked on the scene calculatingly.

Jasperodus turned to a nearby construct who stood humming a turgid tune.

'What happens here?'

'Here,' the construct told him, 'robots may get drunk, as men do.'

Now Jasperodus saw the first of the humans – probably the 'tavern's' proprietor – accept a coin from a construct and put his apparatus to work. A mesh of wire filaments was applied to the client's metal cranium. The robot's eyes flared briefly. The vendor moved on.

'What is the nature of that device?' Jasperodus asked his informant.

'It is a neural pattern generator. It conveys specially modulated electric currents to the brain so as to produce feelings of euphoria and intoxication.'

'Hah!' Jasperodus laughed momentarily. 'So intoxication is not exclusively the province of human consciousness.'

'Indeed not. This method, applied to an artificial brain, is as fully effective as alcohol or other drugs are to an organic brain. I have been as drunk, merry and incapable as a human many a time.'

It cheered Jasperodus to see yet one more barrier between machine existence and human status go down. The vendor of electric current approached him. 'Want a jag? Only three imperial shillings.'

Jasperodus waved him aside. 'Later.' He fully intended to sample the experience, but he wanted to enlarge his observations first.

Accordingly he pushed his way through the press of bodies (many of them so far gone as to be pitted with rust) and installed himself on a bench to the rear from where he could watch all.

The second of the two men, who up until now had been inactive, was engaged in conversation with a construct whose body was finished in matt silver. Finally their deliberations seemed complete. The rear door opened; the robot was ushered inside.

Jasperodus waited to see what would transpire. After a while the robot returned, carrying a small money-pouch which jingled.

Otherwise Jasperodus could discern no difference, apart perhaps from a certain stiffness of gait, and he could not guess what service the robot had performed in return for his money.

His ignorance, however, was soon dispelled. There walked unsteadily past him a robot whose cranial inspection plate was missing. Through the gap Jasperodus could see that part of the brain had been removed and what remained was exposed to the air, presenting a bizarre sight.

The partially decorticated robot confronted the mysterious dealer. 'You have the unit that was promised?' he asked pleadingly.

The man nodded. The robot handed him a largish money-bag. 'Then here. I have worked long and without pause to raise your price. It is not a simple matter to work so hard with only half a brain.'

The dealer emptied the bag and counted the coins slowly. There was a substantial amount of money. Finally he nodded.

The robot was admitted through the door. When he returned twenty minutes later his cranium was smooth and complete. He looked around the room, flexing his body. There was a new stance to him; the slouch he had worn earlier was gone.

'Ah, ratiocination!' he boomed. 'Man's greatest gift to robot!'

Jasperodus beckoned him closer. 'What is the cause of your sudden joy?' he asked.

'Rather ask the cause of my previous misery,' the construct corrected him. 'It lies in the fact that most robot brains are capable of being broken down into sub-units. I sold my greatest possession, namely my ability to think with rigorous logic and so to enjoy the delights of the intellect. It is indeed a twilight world without the power of thought, and I have had to labour for many years to buy a replacement.'

This revelation gave Jasperodus new food for thought. He now noticed that several of the tavern's occupants displayed gaping skulls, so much of the contents being absent that the robotician had found it inconvenient to close up the cranium again. One unfortunate, who squatted against a wall, was so deprived that he could have had only vestigial mentation left.

The neural modulation vendor approached Jasperodus again. 'Care to try a shot now?'

Jasperodus dipped into his satchel and produced three imperial shillings. Attending carefully, the vendor bent forward and brushed the meshwork against the base of his skull, apparently knowing just where to introduce the stimulatory currents. The box attached to the leads gave forth a hollow buzzing sound; Jasperodus felt a premonitory thrilling sensation, and then his mind seemed to light up; he felt a surge of well-being. The room went hazy for a moment and then seemed to sway.

Evidently the 'jag' involved some slight derangement of the senses – as did alcohol, he reminded himself, recalling Cree Inwing's frequent inability to see, talk or walk straight – and that was the penalty for the feelings of intoxication and gaiety that were now assailing him.

'Have another,' offered the vendor.

Jasperodus gave up another three shillings. This time the jolt, added to the first, had a double effect. He began to laugh, understanding, as he did so, that he was becoming prey to a dangerous excess of confidence.

Shortly he discovered that the vendor's partner, the parts dealer, had sidled close. 'You're a fine machine and no mistake,' he said to Jasperodus. 'One of the best models I've seen. That's an excellent brain, with a lot of functions – I can tell that from the shape of your cranium. Yes sir, there are a lot of processes in that cortex.' He touched Jasperodus' arm admiringly. 'You can't need all those processes – wouldn't miss a few logic centres at all, for instance. Probably a lot of built-in redundancy anyway. Like to sell me a few? I give a good price and it won't take long. Keep you in jags for a long time.'

'No,' said Jasperodus.

Smiling, the other turned to the vendor. 'Give him another. On the house.' And he returned to his station by the door.

Jasperodus accepted the free shot. His vision became blurred. He was becoming drunk, he realised, enjoying the knowledge that the ebullience coursing through his system was the same as that he had so often observed in Inwing and others.

'Vendor!' he bellowed recklessly a minute or two later. 'Bring me more of this electric poison!'

The vendor was quick to oblige, and even quicker scarcely another minute later when Jasperodus again called for more. After the dose had been delivered, however, Jasperodus groped in his bag and found that his scant few shillings were all spent. 'I cannot pay you,' he growled.

'Three imperial shillings,' the man insisted. 'You owe me for your last jag.'

'Electricity is cheap,' Jasperodus said. 'You are not out of pocket.' He rose to his feet, staggered and nearly fell over.

The parts dealer had again appeared, and the vendor spoke to him. 'This construct has tried to cheat us,' he exclaimed indignantly. 'He has accepted a jag and cannot pay. This is a serious matter.'

'Indeed,' said the dealer with gravity. He looked on Jasperodus with a frown, then adopted a more friendly pose.

'My offer is still open,' he said smoothly. 'For the sale of only trifling fragments of your cerebral apparatus you can not only clear up the debt but also ensure a supply of exhilaration for many days to come.'

'It appears, indeed, to be the only way you can deliver yourself from the predicament you are in!' the vendor added angrily.

'HAH!' Jasperodus' cry of contempt sounded through the noise of the shack. He pushed them both aside and staggered drunkenly away, while expostulations went unheeded behind him. Groping, supporting himself occasionally by grabbing the bodies of others, he gained the exit where he was confronted by the doorkeeper.

'You may not leave without settling your debts.'

The door robot was a big one, well chosen for his role as bouncer and intimidator. Jasperodus, still at the height of an inner hilarity, lunged forward and when the larger robot reached to seize him he took a grip on the other's upper arm, twisted round and bent low so as to bring his assailant off the ground and sailing over his shoulder.

The doorkeeper crashed to the floor. Jasperodus stepped into the open, well pleased. Considering his befuddled reactions, he thought, he had performed the manoeuvre with skill.

But suddenly he decided he no longer wished to be drunk. He moved some yards away from the Good Oil and paused, drawing himself erect.

With a considerable effort he tried to flush the deranging influences out of his system and to take a more sober appraisal of his surroundings. Slowly he damped down the erratic emotions that were swirling through him; reluctantly the giddy perceptions subsided. Then, with a step only slightly unsteady, he set off back to where he had left Cree Inwing.

It was early evening when Jasperodus arrived at the tavern. As he was about to mount the stairs the landlord accosted him and broached a matter of business.

'I have need of a household robot, one who can work on his own initiative and be entrusted with various matters,' he said. 'From our brief acquaintance I feel that you would fit the post admirably, and I was wondering if your master has it in mind to dispose of you? Frankly, what price do you think he will accept?'

Jasperodus did not divulge any information that would be useful during future bargaining, as the landlord had hoped. 'As to that,' he answered, 'you must consult my master himself. But you will not find me cheap.' He glanced upstairs. 'I go to rouse him now. If you care to follow me up shortly perhaps you and he can discuss the proposal.'

He entered Inwing's room to find him sitting blearily on the bed, having just woken. When he described the landlord's advances Inwing grunted sardonically and waved his hand.

'But you must accept,' Jasperodus told him in all seriousness.

Inwing peered at him in puzzlement. 'What on Earth are you talking about? Have you gone mad?'

'It is an obvious step,' Jasperodus answered. 'Our association has been fruitful, but we have achieved our object: we have arrived in Tansiann. Clearly our interests from now on will diverge. You, for instance, must wish to resume a military career and join the imperial forces – that much I have chanced to observe. I would only be an impediment to you if you regarded our relationship as binding.'

Inwing uttered a sad laugh. 'You are observant indeed, but for my part it is all wishful thinking. Where will I ever raise the nine thousand imperial crowns necessary to buy a commission? They don't make an officer of just any piece of riff-raff.'

'That is exactly why I suggest you sell me. I am worth far more than nine thousand imperials.'

The expression on Inwing's face showed that the thought was new to him. 'Surely you are not prepared to endure construct bondage again on my account.'

'Have no fear: the ruffian will have the use of me for no more than a few hours. I will depart and make my own way. I have discovered that it is possible for a robot to lead an independent existence in certain parts of the city, if he is resourceful enough – as I believe I am. There I can install myself and pursue my interests. I ask just one favour in return: that if I ever happen to be impounded I can claim to be your property so as to prevent any awkward situations.'

'Naturally.' Cree debated within himself. 'Your plan seems sound, if hardly ethical.'

'Don't disturb your conscience; this city is more full of thieves and villains than the forest west of Gordona. Why does that rogue wish to purchase me? Not for his own use: a construct as costly and as able as myself is not put to work in a tavern.' He stepped to the table and inspected Inwing's belongings. 'As I thought: your money has all disappeared while you slept. Our landlord, of course, will know nothing of it.'

Cree jumped up and examined his purse with annoyance. 'What a nuisance!' he exclaimed fretfully.

'Never mind; we will shortly recoup.'

But Cree still seemed doubtful about the whole business. He paced the room, looked out of the window, then turned to Jasperodus.

'I much appreciate your giving thought to my welfare; for my part I feel a little as though I would be deserting a friend.'

'It is my own wish. I have my own way to go, and I lose nothing by this parting gesture. So let us say farewell. I have learned much from our travels together. Most important, perhaps, I have learned something of comradeship.'

Cree smiled. He extended his hand. 'Very well, then.'

He and the robot shook hands.

At that moment there was a brief knock on the door and the landlord entered. 'Perhaps you have become acquainted with my offer?' he said ingratiatingly to Inwing.

Inwing tugged his moustache. 'For a fact this robot is somewhat redundant to my future plans. I might be willing to sell if the price is right.'

'Good! Then only the terms are to be agreed on!' The landlord rubbed his hands, then stepped back to inspect Jasperodus. 'How shall we fix his worth? A thousand imperials?'

'Let me shorten all debate by speaking for my master,' Jasperodus interrupted. 'I am worth easily thirty thousand imperial crowns on the open market, as you, if you know what you are about, must be aware.'

The landlord raised his eyebrows. 'A great sum, indeed; far beyond my expectations!'

'You are buying a prime product. You will find me the most self-directed robot of your acquaintance, as perhaps you have already noticed. I am made to the very highest standards of workmanship, as any robotician will attest. This assessment of my own monetary value is an objective one; I cannot deceive.'

'You have deeds of ownership, of course?' the landlord said suddenly to Cree, and then, when the latter frowned in discomfort, his manner changed. 'Aha! I thought not! It struck me as most odd that a ruffian of your description, able to frequent only such humble inns as my own, should at the same time be the rightful owner of this valuable property!'

'And so you searched my belongings to make sure,' Cree accused.

'Of that I know nothing,' the landlord retorted jovially. 'Nevertheless my pot-boy is at this moment on his way to fetch the city guard, so that the matter may be cleared up.'

'How then will *you* secure the robot, which presumably is your aim?' Cree asked, puzzled.

'I only wish not to be cheated,' the landlord insisted. 'Mark, I do not say that the robot *is* stolen – only that it might be. I would be willing to take a chance on it, if you care to complete the transaction speedily, but of course such a procedure will vastly lower the value of the merchandise.' He pursed his lips. 'I'll give you a hundred imperials for him and undertake to smooth matters with the guard.'

'Accept ten thousand imperials crowns, not one penny less,' Jasperodus instructed Cree firmly.

The landlord was indignant. 'Your robot interferes too much. Is his discipline always so lax? If so …'

'He merely guards my interests,' Cree placated. 'He will do the same for you when he is yours. And as his advice is invariably sound, I stick at the figure of ten thousand imperials, and you may do your worst.'

After some bad-tempered bickering the landlord finally agreed. They went downstairs, where he produced the required sum in the form of a banker's note, thus protecting Cree from being waylaid and robbed. Cree then turned to Jasperodus with a show of sternness.

'Jasperodus, this is your new master. Serve him as you have served me.'

'Yes, sir,' Jasperodus said meekly.

After Cree Inwing had gone the landlord looked Jasperodus over and chuckled. 'I heard about your little fracas this morning. A robot that cannot be commandeered – that's a valuable commodity in this city! I'll get a few days' work out of you first, then, with a new ownership deed, you should fetch … let's see … twenty-five thousand with no questions asked!'

He directed Jasperodus to his duties and went off laughing.

Late that night Jasperodus slipped away and once more turned his steps to the slums where, by means of study, he proposed to turn himself into a fully urbanised being.

8

The small room was a box ten feet by eight. The unpainted plaster of the walls was broken in places, revealing bare brick; the single window looked down three storeys to a dusty courtyard where grew a few stunted shrubs. There was, however, a chair on which Jasperodus sat – a habit he had picked up along the way, although it was physiologically unnecessary for him.

Otherwise the room was filled with books. Piles of books, tumbling in terraces and seracs, books on nearly every science that was available to the New Empire, but especially on mathematics, physics, engineering and robotics.

With the help of this untidy library of mainly second-hand volumes Jasperodus had filled in many gaps in his knowledge, and could count himself an expert in several spheres, notably that of mathematics. He had no cause now to fear he had an educational inferiority to the sophisticates of Tansiann.

His primary aim had been, as he frequently reminded himself, to excel at everything and thus to prove his equality with mankind. But time and time again he had been drawn to one particular subject: robotics. This he had studied with manic intensity, until he was conversant with all the main principles of robot design.

In his hands at the present moment was a slim volume that came to the heart of his inquiries:

ON AN ARTIFICIAL CONSCIOUSNESS

Much study and investigation has gone into the possibility of producing an artificial consciousness which would make construct minds virtually indistinguishable from the natural variety. The formulae on which such a consciousness would have to be based have even been elucidated.

These formulae refer themselves to the central feature of consciousness, namely its characteristic property of self-reference, or the 'problem of the perceiving "I"' as it has been called. The nature of conscious perception is such that the perceived object becomes perfectly blended, or 'identified' with the perceiving subject or 'I'. In other words 'I' *becomes* the object and at the same time remains itself. The problem of an artificial consciousness then hinges on duplicating this phenomenon.

Unfortunately no arrangement of material or energy can achieve this. All matter is essentially particulate: perfect blending does not occur. The same holds for any conceivable type of logic circuitry, no matter how advanced its state of integration may be. Early attempts at machine consciousness relied on the principle, where 'I' is the directrix (i.e. subject) and 'X' the object, of raising each to the power of the other in an alternating series, thus:

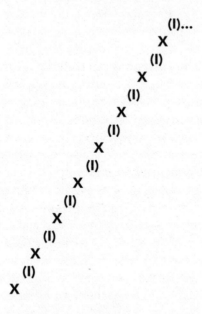

And so on with variations, such as bending the process into an ever-accelerating cycle known as the 'perception vortex'. No positive result was ever obtained from this method, beyond defining some techniques for ordinary machine (i.e. un-conscious) perception that were already available. The reason for this failure is that the arrangement is asymptotic – however far it is carried a unity cannot be achieved between the 'perceiving directrix' and the object. It may be stated categorically that consciousness cannot be artificially created in the physical universe as it is constituted, because that would require the operation of a physical entity having no differentiation between its parts, and no such entity can exist in the material realm. Consciousness must therefore have a spiritual, not a material source, and cannot be duplicated.

There followed the consciousness formulae in full. Jasperodus, having studied them time and again, together with all the associated theorems and equations first enunciated to him by Padua, now understood them and was forced to admit their cogency. Secretly he had hoped to discover some flaw, some chink in robotic theory, that would leave open the possibility – however remote – that he *was* conscious, or at least that he might strive to attain consciousness. But the equations were watertight. It seemed certain both that he lacked true sentience and that he never could acquire it, thus invalidating the passionate boast he had made to Inwing.

With a gesture of despair he flung the book aside.

Jasperodus had been living as a free construct in Robot Town, the slum borough of Subuh, for about six months. In that time he had become a recognised figure there, though he was but one among Subuh's droves of colourful characters, and for his part he had learned much about the more wayward aspects of robot psychology. He saw it as a tribute to the robotic art that constructs, made to be slaves, could go so much against their own natures as to follow the example of men and live as free individuals. Admittedly the phenomenon was not too common, being more the result of a combination of accidents than of planning; nevertheless the total number of wild robots to be found was large. Most intriguing to Jasperodus were the knacks and tricks by which they evaded recapture. Some robots simply went to elaborate lengths to avoid all human contact. Others used a form of double-think, engaging themselves in a deeply divisive effort to misunderstand any direct order through close examination of its grammar or semantics. And there were some in whom this ploy had developed into an advanced neurosis rendering them incapable of hearing anything a human being said.

Safest from capture were those robots with a secret command language known only to their masters. Such machines were rare, but they would accept no commands except in that language and therefore had an unusual degree of personal freedom. A few of more urbane capability, intellectually superior to a normal human, even managed to survive in select districts like the Elan. Most wild robots, however, lived here in Subuh, where they had blended to some extent with the more poverty-stricken elements of the populace, who were apt to look upon them with a sort of grudging fellow-feeling. The robots occupied, in fact, the very lowest rung of the social ladder. Classed as non-persons, lacking the protection of the law, they were subject to every kind of exploitation.

A great problem every robot faced was how to obtain sufficient money to buy replacement isotope batteries, which ran down every few years. A trap many fell into was to sell sections of their brain, hoping to make good the loss later. A slower method was to become a wage-earner, with all the disadvantages of the dispossessed. Various kinds of work were available, the feature common to them all being that the wages paid to a wild robot were a fraction of those earned by a human or even by a robot hired out by an owner. Some wages offered were so trifling as never to amount to anything. Slightly better money could be made from dangerous work, where there was less competition from humans or from robot-owners – in fact there were high-risk tasks that were almost entirely the province of wild robots. Jasperodus had for a spell hired himself out as a construction worker, clambering up the spidery lacework of a new radio tower a thousand feet above the ground, and had earned enough to rent his room and to buy the books he needed.

But now a more serious need had arisen. His own isotope battery, which should have been good for ten years, was failing.

For some days now he had been receiving the autonomic signal warning of an incipient power drop. He could only suppose that the battery had been damaged when Horsu Greb had sent him into the furnace beneath King Zhorm's palace, and that Padua had failed to diagnose or rectify the fault.

Jasperodus began to calculate how long it would take him to raise the price of a new battery, considering various types of work in turn. If he was to get a replacement before being seriously enervated he would have to begin soon. Immediately, in fact.

He rose and left the building, after having decided on a destination. A short distance along the sidewalk a tall robot with an elegant gait hailed him.

It was Mark V, a nickname the robot had earned because of his pride in being Mark V of his series. He fell in step with Jasperodus and they walked along together.

'I have been considering your little conundrum,' he told Jasperodus in smooth, reasonable tones, 'and a solution has occurred to me.'

'Indeed, and what is that?' Jasperodus asked, interested despite himself. He spent a considerable amount of time in the company of Mark V, who was an intelligent construct, discussing matters of mutual interest – particularly the subject which obsessed Jasperodus. There was even a chance, he thought, of hearing something original from the Mark V brain.

'You raised the question of the putative quality called "consciousness",' Mark V began. 'I have resolved the matter in the following way. All descriptions of "consciousness" follow more or less this pattern: a machine may be aware of an incoming sensory impression, meaning that the impression is received, analysed, recognised, related to other impressions, acted on and stored. A human being also does all this, but in addition to being merely aware he is said to be *aware of being aware*, and this awareness of awareness is claimed to constitute consciousness. Now what does this mean? Is it that the whole process of perception, integration and action is then lumped together and again presented to the mind as a new impression, the second time round as it were? If so, what would be the point of such an operation? It would add nothing that was not there before. Besides – I have studied neural anatomy – the human brain makes no provision for such an arrangement so far as I know. Therefore I deduce that the effect must be on a smaller scale – if it exists at all. I surmise that "awareness of awareness" is merely some kind of limiting circuit or delay line, accidentally inserted by evolution and responsible for the notorious tardiness of human thought. As such it serves no useful function and is certainly not necessary for advanced intellectual mentation. For that reason, no doubt, the great robot designers omitted it from their plans.'

'I had received the strong impression that consciousness is an important and elevated state that we robots cannot attain,' Jasperodus replied.

Mark V gave an amused laugh. 'Quite untrue, and the idea *is* unsupported by observation. Note that clod making his way on the other side of the street.' He pointed to a stooped, badly dressed figure who plodded along wearing a vacant expression. 'Is he in any elevated mental state? Clearly not. He spends his time in daydreams; he has not learned the skill of consecutive thought, he cannot even ponder on his impressions, as we do. Would you even go so far as to say, then, that he is "aware of being aware"? I would not! Perhaps he would conduct himself with more dignity if he were! He is our mental inferior, Jasperodus, not our superior, and he is typical of the vast mass of his kind.'

'You mention that you have studied brain anatomy,' Jasperodus said. 'What does the human brain possess that ours do not?'

'Very little,' answered Mark V. 'That is why I say this "consciousness" is a triviality, or else nonexistent.'

Jasperodus thought over Mark V's words. 'Your arguments are not new,' he said eventually. 'I have heard something like them before.'

As a matter of fact he also had hit upon a theorem recently that seemed to imply that consciousness – by which he meant the element of conscious experience he *imagined* he possessed – was a figment in men as well as in himself.

The theorem made use of the notion of time. Philosophers were all agreed that the past did not vanish from existence but persisted in some way; perhaps not in the same condition as the present, but nevertheless in accordance with the principle that the universe did not *uncreate* its products once it had created them, which was what a vanishing past would require.

What, then, of past consciousness? Did that also persist? Was a man conscious in the past as well as in the present? If so, then by Jasperodus' reasoning he would continue to perceive the past simultaneously with the present, and there would be no differentiation between past, present and future. If not, then it became necessary to introduce another factor: the factor of death. At death consciousness was extinguished like a candle flame. What then of the past life it had illumined? Was that past life dead and inert ... robotic? And if consciousness was expunged once it had run its course, what then of the tenet that the universe did not discard its creations, consciousness being one of those creations?

Either alternative was untenable. By this *reductio ad absurdum* Jasperodus was able to argue that man did not, after all, possess consciousness; then there was no paradox.

But of course this conclusion was hedged about with provisos. He had no guarantee that what he understood by the word 'consciousness' corresponded to what it was in reality. Also there was another way, just as simple, out of the dilemma: that the philosophers were wrong and the past *did* vanish.

Altogether Jasperodus drew little comfort from these intellectual theories, which he somehow felt to be missing the mark. It was clear, for example, that Mark V looked at the question of consciousness entirely from the point of view of a machine that lacked it.

For his part, Jasperodus had to confess that he *could* discern a subtle difference between men and robots, though it often took some time to notice it. He had found that Padua was right. However clever and entertaining a construct might be – Mark V, with whom he had now had a long and fruitful acquaintance, was as sophisticated a personality as one could desire – Jasperodus came, after a time, to recognise that he faced a machine without internal awareness. Robots were ghosts of men, shells of men, mimicking men's conduct, thought and feeling. In a human being, on the other hand, even in the most stupid, there was some indefinable inner spark, sensed rather than seen, that made him a man.

And what of himself? Self-observation was the most difficult of disciplines. He had sometimes tried to keep watch over himself in a detached fashion, while walking, talking or thinking, to try to ascertain what judgement he would make of himself if he were an independent observer. The experiment brought some interesting mental states, but no definite information. He was, so far as he still knew, a shell of a man, like Mark V.

How much, in fact, was he like Mark V? With a shock Jasperodus suddenly realised how close to him he was mentally. He remembered the books back in his room. All the subjects in which he had absorbed himself in the past months were those that were most attractive to the mind of the intelligent robot: mathematics, physics, logic and philosophy, all of a purely intellectual character, containing very little by way of emotion. Quite unawares he had been following his machine nature. The recognition of this depressed him unutterably. To equal the talents of men, presumably, he would have to excel in music, in painting, in poetry and the like.

'Very well,' he told himself privately, 'that comes next.'

They walked past a row of decrepit buildings and rounded a corner, where Jasperodus saw a wild robot about to be impounded by a team of robot-catchers. The men were from out of the district by the look of it: one of the semi-professional teams that made a living by trapping footloose constructs. Surprisingly they were not as much a feature of Subuh as might have been imagined, since the human inhabitants as well as robots made them unwelcome.

In this case, however, they were about to gain their object. Mark V hung back and seemed ready to make off, but Jasperodus sprang forward, scattered the catchers and swung their victim round by his shoulder.

'Whatever these rogues have ordered you to do, cancel it,' he instructed the robot firmly. 'Join Mark V there; absent yourselves and I will join you shortly.'

The robot nodded, greatly relieved, and moved to obey.

The impounders quickly recovered from their surprise. They rounded on Jasperodus.

'You too!' one shouted. 'Cease this rowdyism! You are under our command now, so behave quietly!'

Jasperodus raised his fist threateningly. 'Neither I nor anyone in the vicinity is about to be enslaved by you. Remove yourselves or you will suffer for it.'

Perplexed and sullen, they retreated. Jasperodus returned to join Mark V and the robot he had rescued.

'Many thanks,' the latter said gratefully. Jasperodus nodded briefly in reply.

'I have noticed on previous occasions your ability to command other robots, even against the orders of human beings,' Mark V commented. 'It is an unusual talent. Others of us, in fact, have remarked on it.'

Jasperodus received the observation sourly. 'I have even been known to command men,' he rumbled.

'That would indeed be unusual.' Mark V tapped one hand against the other, a habit he was prone to when he did not quite know how to approach a subject. 'Something we free robots of Subuh lack is a leader,' he said diffidently. 'Many constructs feel we would all benefit from a modicum of organisation, if a robot of the necessary qualities could be found. You would seem well suited for the role ...?'

'It does not fall in with my plans,' Jasperodus interrupted brusquely.

'Ah. Well, just so.'

After a few embarrassed pleasantries Mark V took his departure, taking the other robot with him. Jasperodus proceeded out of Subuh and walked for several miles across Tansiann towards the space-ground. As he approached it the great spaceyard took on the aspect of a city whose towers were rearing rocketships and control centres. He paused to watch one interplanetary booster taking off, washing the site with heat, steam and billowing flame. Activity on the space-ground had become almost frenetic of late as the imperial forces sought to counteract the reverses they had met on Mars. From the reports he had read Jasperodus knew that the Empire's resources were being stretched to the utmost to maintain the Martian outpost. Getting sufficient men and materials to the red planet to fight a protracted war was proving almost prohibitively difficult in the face of harassment by the Borgor Alliance, that coalition of northern nations whose policy was to prevent the expansion of the New Empire by any means. As the Empire's strength grew, so did that of the Alliance. So far hostilities had not erupted into full-scale war. When they did Jasperodus foresaw that much that Charrane had achieved might be destroyed.

Just outside the twenty-foot high fence surrounding the space-ground he presented himself to the hiring agency that took on repair crews for the orbiting guard posts.

'You already have my name on your list,' he said to the clerk. 'I have taken aptitude tests.'

The clerk consulted his papers. 'So you have. I see you passed an examination in space welding. And in control unit repair. We could have used you before.'

'I have only now decided to undertake the work. What rates are you offering?'

'They've gone up,' the clerk boasted. 'Half an imperial a trip.'

'Not enough. I require at least double that.'

'In that case, friend, goodbye.'

Inwardly Jasperodus cursed his weak bargaining position. 'Very well,' he said impatiently, 'I agree to your derisive payment.'

The clerk was offhandedly indignant as he filled out the entry slip. 'It's better than you'll get anywhere else,' he said. 'Almost human rates.'

'For a street sweeper. And you neglect to mention that the destruction incidence for orbital repair crews is now one in seven.'

The clerk shrugged. 'What do you robots want to live for anyway?' he muttered. 'There's a shuttle blasting off in an hour. If you want to be on it take this to the main gate.'

Jasperodus accepted the slip, which took him through the two checkpoints guarding the base. He was directed to a corrugated iron shed a few yards inside the perimeter.

Within were a number of robots, fairly high-grade constructs to judge by their appearance, who stood about silently or conversed desultorily in low tones. A fatalistic air filled the hut. The eyes of the robots were listless.

The one-in-seven ratio, Jasperodus thought. They were all aware of it.

But not quite all his fellow crew members were robots. A slight, hunch-shouldered man stepped forward to greet him, smiling up at him nervously from a seamed, fortyish face.

'Know you, don't I?'

'We have met,' Jasperodus said distantly.

'Yeah, I remember. In Subuh. I live there.' The man spoke with an attempt at cockiness. He sported a conceit that had recently become fashionable: his fingers held a tiny bowl filled with burning aromatic herbs, the smoke of which he drew into his mouth through a stem.

Ostentatiously he blew out a streamer of the inhaled smoke. Then he looked at Jasperodus again, frowning as if with a sudden memory, and seemed to become uneasy. A nervous tic started up on the left side of his face. He looked away, his gaze becoming vacant and withdrawn.

Jasperodus was familiar with his type, which was a species of social throw-out known as slotmen, an analogy referring to the delivery slot of a vending machine. Due to personality difficulties, a deep feeling of inadequacy, or simply to repeated failure in the field of human relations, they had fallen from the company of human beings and preferred to live among robots, to whom they need not feel inferior. The delivery chute of this process was the suburb of Subuh.

With unconscious robots slotmen could feel at ease. Among men they quickly went to pieces. Jasperodus looked upon them with disdain. In turn they were generally wary of him. In fact during the days when he had found himself unwittingly adopting the role of a robot leader and the wild robots of Subuh were showing a tendency to gather round him, one of the slotmen had paid him an unsettling compliment.

'You're not like the other robots,' the ragged creature had told him nervously. 'There's something different about you.'

Ignoring the slotman by his side, Jasperodus surveyed the crew robots, struck by how subdued they were. They were all caught in the psychological trap known as the double bind, he realised. The logical machine-mind did not take to gambling: odds of one in seven would normally be too much for wild robots to risk. Each had no doubt been forced into the job by desperate circumstances, probably by the need to buy a power pack before a certain date was up. Thus the decision to join the repair crew was prompted by the directive to survive, and at the same time it contradicted it – a perfect example of the double bind. Consequently they were very much depressed.

Jasperodus could not help but contrast their dejection with his own buoyant self-confidence. He remained unfrightened by thoughts of danger. Uncharacteristically for a machine, he believed in his luck.

The slotman essayed one more remark, indicating the other robots with his pipestem. 'Quiet, ain't they?' he quavered.

Jasperodus nodded and deigned to reply. 'For once it is a misfortune to be free. Freedom exacerbates a construct's survival instinct. Were they under the orders of a master, now, they would be able to undertake this mission without suffering psychological distress.'

A door at the far end of the hut banged open. Into the room stomped two uniformed and helmeted Imperial Guardsmen.

They looked around at the gathering with bleak eyes. 'Right, you lot,' the sergeant began, 'you know your business. This is the drill for today. There are malfunction signals from three orbiters. Two are surveillance satellites – nothing to that – the third is a guard post. The shuttle will be piloted from the ground, by remote, as per usual.'

Jasperodus spoke up. 'Will the shuttle be armed?'

'No,' said the sergeant irritably, as though the question surprised him, 'it will not be armed. Right, let's get moving.'

Clanking slightly, the repair crew shuffled from the hut and walked half a mile to launch point. The shuttle was a battered vehicle that by the look of it had been converted from an old booster rocket. Clamped to it were a number of additional solid-fuel boosters to assist take-off.

They climbed a ladder to the hatch, and found themselves in a bare metal chamber large enough to admit about twenty men. Jasperodus waited to see if the guardsmen or some other supervisor would follow, but when the crew were all aboard the ladder was removed and the hatch closed itself. They were on their own.

The only furniture in the chamber consisted of two seat-couches and upon these, despite the slotman's frantic efforts to appropriate one first, two of the robots casually draped themselves. The slotman began arguing with them, heatedly insisting on his right to a couch.

'Away, away,' dismissed one of the reclining robots with a wave of his hand. 'I am an old construct. I cannot withstand sudden shocks as well as I might.'

'At least you will not suffer broken bones and burst blood vessels!' complained the slotman. 'Give me that couch – it was meant for me, not for you!'

'The acceleration is not so terrible. You can endure it.'

Jasperodus came over. 'You look sturdy enough to me,' he told the stubborn robot. 'Get off that couch and leave it to this weak creature of flesh and bone. He is a true human being who possesses a soul, and not as you are, merely a candidate for the junkyard.'

The robot glared at Jasperodus, eyes glowing with resentment. But he obeyed, reluctantly quitting the couch which the slotman then occupied with alacrity.

'Thanks,' he grinned.

Jasperodus turned away. A klaxon sounded deafeningly in the confined space, warning of imminent departure. The robots sat down on the floor, leaning against the bulkhead, and Jasperodus, presuming this to be a precaution against the stress of blast-off, followed suit. The slotman, he noticed, was stuffing cotton-wool in his ears and holding it in place with his fingers.

An explosion sounded from below. The shuttle shuddered, the walls vibrated, and the crew chamber was suddenly filled with a shattering din as both the main liquid-fuel motor and the solid-fuel assist pods roared into life.

The vessel lifted, swaying as its inadequate stabilisers sought to gain balance. For a short time nothing more seemed to be happening; then Jasperodus became aware of a steadily growing pressure pushing at him from below. The chamber tilted: they were hurtling at an angle towards space.

Some minutes later the terrifying racket ceased abruptly. The shuttle was in free fall.

One robot more dented and older than the rest rose from the floor and sailed through the air to the other side of the cabin where he opened a wall locker. Jasperodus moved his body gingerly and found the absence of gravity less novel than he had expected. He adapted to it easily, controlling himself by means of light touches on wall, floor or ceiling.

Other robots were amusing themselves by performing zero-g acrobatics. Jasperodus pulled himself to the single porthole. Through it he saw the shining curve of the Earth. Cloud and sea glinted with a pure brilliance, while on the opposite side extended the blackness of the void. For long moments he stared at the vision, struck by innumerable unvoiced thoughts.

The old robot at the wall locker turned to face them. 'I am your ganger,' he announced in a firm voice. 'Attend to our division of labour.' Calling each crew member by name or number he began to allocate task functions, pulling equipment from the locker as he did so.

'Jasperodus: I recall that you are competent in control unit repair and space welding. As this is your first trip we will restrict you to space welding for the moment.' And from the locker's cavernous interior came a welding set which Jasperodus strapped to himself.

The slotman received a microcircuitry rig and a spacesuit with special visual attachments. By now they were approaching the first rendezvous, jolted occasionally as the controller on the ground applied thrust to correct their course.

Jasperodus positioned himself once more by the window. Soon the malfunctioning guard post hove into view. In shape it was like a fat barrel, banded as if with coopers' hoops, but additionally equipped with missile launcher racks. As they jockeyed closer the barrel occluded clouds of stars. Beyond, in the upper left quarter of Jasperodus' field of vision, was the radiant white Moon.

The hiss of close-range manoeuvring jets sounded through the walls of the chamber. The guard post loomed up and blotted out everything else. Then the shuttle's hatch opened slightly, bleeding air into space until the interior of the chamber was a vacuum. It opened fully; the ganger urged his crew through it.

Outside, they floated across a few yards of space to a larger square hatch, still bolted tight, in the side of the guard post. One robot missed his direction and went sailing off into the void, limbs flailing desperately, whereupon the ganger jetted after him using a hand-held thruster and dragged him back.

The bolts released, the hatch was pulled open. The repair crew flowed into the interstices and chambers that riddled the interior of the big barrel-shape and began their inspection.

The post was unmanned and was designed to help protect imperial space routes – and imperial territory too if need be – by means of automatic response against enemy encroachments. Peering over the shoulders of the trained robots who were examining the systems boards, Jasperodus saw that it was currently quite defunct. Not a launcher or a gun was operative. The robots muttered among themselves. The repairs would take some hours.

Jasperodus relaxed. He did not think there would be much work for him today. In fact, now he thought of it, the size of the crew was altogether supernumerary to the task in hand. Wild robots were so cheap to hire that they could be used in redundant numbers, just in case something unforeseen should arise.

He wandered through the guard post, observing everything with interest. Once he was called upon to spot-weld back in place a plate that had been removed, a service that took him approximately forty-five seconds.

An hour later an unexpected commotion ran through the post. The robots began hurrying hither and thither in agitation, gesticulating wildly. Jasperodus stopped one such witless construct and touched heads with him so as to converse in the airless medium.

The robot's voice vibrated tinnily through the metal of his cranium. 'A Borgor cruiser! We are doomed! Doomed!' With a wail the construct broke away and propelled himself deeper into the guard post in an attempt to flee.

Pushing aside yet more panicking robots, Jasperodus made his way back to the primary service area into which the main hatch gave access. There he found four robots, including the ganger, huddled closely together.

The slotman, however, had adopted a surprisingly different posture. He stood upright in the hatchway, fully exposed to the starlight. Cautiously Jasperodus approached the opening and peered over the rim. Glinting darkly against the starry background was the lobed, bulbous form of a foreign spaceship. It gyrated slowly and he could see the crescent of Rendare, one of the chief states of the Alliance, painted on its flank. Clearly it was contemplating attack and perhaps had not quite realised that the guard post was defenceless.

The slotman was staring at the cruiser, eyebrows raised in an expression of melancholy. Jasperodus could guess at his state of mind: imminent death came as an unexampled opportunity for sad self-pity and, at the same time, was something of a relief.

But he ignored the human and returned to the robots, pressing his head against the ganger's. 'Can weapons be made functional?' he grated.

'Not in time! Nothing to do but wait for extinction!'

The ganger, like all the others, was in the grip of despair. Jasperodus turned and launched himself back towards the hatch. As he did so a shell from the Borgor cruiser shot through the opening, passed over Jasperodus' shoulder – though he didn't see it – and through the ganger's chest. Not until it had also penetrated the bulkhead behind him did it explode. The bulkhead bulged, spat itself into fragments, and the robots crouching with the ganger caught the whole barrage. The metal pieces tore into their bodies, leaving them moving feebly.

Their bulk largely protected Jasperodus and the slotman from the effects of the blast. Shrapnel and jagged metal hurtled silently past Jasperodus, one or two pieces scoring his limbs.

Instinctively the slotman clung to the side of the hatchway, paralysed, his mouth open with fright. Jasperodus sailed past him, steadied himself in the opening, then gained the outside and planted his feet on the exterior of the guard post. One powerful spring with his legs and he was soaring towards the open hatch of the shuttle which still floated a few yards away, tethered by guidelines.

In seconds he was alone in the empty crew chamber of the shuttle. It seemed odd that no one else had sought this refuge, which on the face of it offered the only possibility of escape. But then, perhaps the others had a more realistic appraisal of how much ground control would be prepared to help them. Robots, slotman and the battered shuttle were all expendable, practically throw-away items, and in the prospect of losing the important guard post – if ground control was even aware of what was going on yet – they would simply be forgotten.

He glanced at the ceiling, judging the position the chamber occupied in the length of the rocket. It was almost certain that originally the shuttle had been built with a cockpit, which probably was still there.

He flicked himself to the ceiling and activated the nozzle of the cutting torch which was part of his welding kit … The thin metal sheeting curled apart in the heat of the torch. While it was still hot Jasperodus tore it open further with his hands and then attacked a second layer of sheeting separated by a gap of a few inches.

Moments later he was levering himself into a small darkened cabin in the nose of the shuttle. Using the light of the cutting torch he took stock of it. There was a pilot's seat, padded and harnessed, a large bank of instruments, several screens including a large one with cross hairs directly in front of the seat.

He leaned close, half-guessing, half-reading the function of the various controls by their markings. Never had his mind worked so fast … There had to be some point at which the controls were overridden by the signals trans-mitted from the ground … He ripped open a panel. Behind it he saw a junction box with a cutout switch, paralleled by a similar arrangement lead-ing in the direction of the radio receiver. He immediately moved both switches.

The lights came on.

The big television screen sprang into life also. It showed the view from the nose of the shuttle. In the upper right-hand corner hovered the bow of the Borgor cruiser.

Jasperodus strapped himself into the pilot's seat. Gyros ... here they were. As he experimented with the levers the picture on the screen shifted with the rotation of the vessel, until he brought the intersection of the cross hairs into line with the Borgor cruiser. It appeared to be taking no further action, but was still waiting for some response to its opening shot.

By his knee Jasperodus noticed that a speaker was just perceptibly vibrating in the vacuum created by his rupturing the floor of the cabin. He placed his hand against it, but had to tune up his hearing to make out the words that were conducted up his arm.

'You there! Put that craft back on remote and get out of that cockpit!'

Ignoring the command, Jasperodus fumbled for the ignition switch, first opening the throttle to full.

The rocket motor blasted out at full power. On the screen the enemy cruiser ballooned briefly – and then was blotted out.

Although it travelled only a few hundred yards the shuttle attained a velocity of several hundred miles per hour by the time of impact. It ploughed into the belly of the cruiser. The structure of neither vessel was rigid enough to hold together under such a shock: both broke up, but even as the shuttle disintegrated its nose retained enough momentum to carry it right through to the opposite wall of the Rendare ship.

The harness kept Jasperodus in his seat. The seat itself, however, tore loose from its moorings and took him cartwheeling. Several times he ricochetted off writhing wreckage. Then he found himself in space, spinning end over end, though at a speed sedate enough for him to observe what was happening.

The smashed cruiser was receding. Suddenly there was a bright flash as fuel and liquid oxygen from the ruptured tanks mixed and exploded. The explosion raged through the wreckage in rivers and rivulets. Gouts of flame shot out in all directions. Shortly the wreck was completely burned out.

Jasperodus released his harness and pushed the chair away, contriving thereby to counteract his slow spin and also to lose most of his relative velocity. The guard post receded only very slowly now. He relaxed, spread his limbs, and simply floated, unexpectedly overcome by a strange feeling of peace and calm.

Unresistingly he fell into a serene reverie. The apparent endlessness of sable space was soaking into his perception; he felt as though he had penetrated to the very centre of existence. His senses, moreover, had become incongruously sharp; all around him was universal majesty ... The Earth, a great, silent goddess hanging hugely below him. The small, brilliant Moon. He turned, and the flashing sun seared his eyes.

He did not know how long he floated there. It seemed like a long time. But eventually he again took thought for practical affairs and noticed that the guard post was now very small. He activated one of the nozzles of his welding kit. The thrust it produced was extremely low, but accumulative. First imperceptibly, and then slowly, he coasted back to the realm of men.

9

By the time an investigating spacecraft arrived from Tansiann several hours later Jasperodus had taken matters well in hand. Gathering together the survivors among the repair crew, he had shaken them out of their demoralised condition and set them to work. Under his supervision the guard post was now functioning again. The guardsmen from the imperial craft – a sleek near-orbit patrol boat – entered the hatchway to find him welding in place a new bulkhead to replace the one shattered by the Borgor shell.

He switched off his welding kit and touched his hand to the nearest guardsman's helmet, so as to conduct sound. 'Your tardiness is less than commendable,' he greeted. Then he gestured to the slotman, who was floating motionless by the other wall. 'I believe his oxygen has just run out. You had better transfer him to your ship without delay.'

The guardsman approached the unconscious figure, examined it, then unclipped the slotman's oxygen pack and inserted in its place an emergency cylinder from his own equipment. He turned to his comrades and spoke something through his suit communicator. Making an attempt to lip-read, Jasperodus thought he deciphered the words: 'Maybe he'll pull through, maybe he won't.'

Then he signalled Jasperodus to touch his helmet again. 'Well, somebody's done a good job here. We've roughly got the picture: a Borgor ship attacked while the station was out of commission, and the repair crew destroyed it somehow, using the shuttle.' He jerked his thumb. 'Who'd have thought a slotman could pull off a stunt like that? There'll be a medal for him, I shouldn't wonder. Tansiann tells us the post's transmitting all go signals now, so let's get aboard.'

Planing down through the atmosphere the slotman recovered consciousness. Moved by some residual fellow-feeling, one of the robots had been attending him, moving his arms so as to exercise his lungs. He sat up, moaned lightly, then lay down shivering.

Buffeted by cross winds they approached Tansiann and made a screeching landing on one of the spaceground's runways. The crew, still accompanied by guardsmen, straggled back to the iron shed where they were to be debriefed and receive their wages. Shortly, however, an officer wearing a livery Jasperodus did not recognise arrived.

'Hold the proceedings,' he ordered the guardsmen. 'Word of the exploit has reached the palace. Today the Emperor is to receive those who lately have performed the Empire some special service, and he has directed that the man responsible should be present.'

The guardsman grinned and yanked the cringing slotman forward, slapping him on the shoulder. 'Hear that? A signal honour!'

The slotman gasped, his face white. '*Me?* Presented to the Emperor? Oh no! It wasn't me! It wasn't me!' And he shook all over, rolled up his eyes, and fainted in a heap on the floor.

'Hm.' The liveried officer looked down at him doubtfully. 'Not quite of the backbone one expects in a hero.'

Jasperodus thrust himself forward. 'Allow me to enlighten you. It was I, not this creature, who by my initiative saved the guard post from destruction. And I claim my reward, namely to be presented to the Emperor.'

The guardsman turned to him in surprise. '*You*, eh?' He looked at the others. 'Is that right?'

The robots all confirmed Jasperodus' boast.

'Oh, dear,' said the officer from the palace. 'Well, he will have to do.'

'But a *robot*? It's a mockery!'

The other glanced at him disdainfully. 'The Emperor himself has given a specific command. Would *you* disobey it? Besides, there are constructs serving at all levels of government, so the encounter will not be so strange … Now let me see … He's in good shape for a wild one, isn't he? Most of them are a bit decrepit. Come along with me, fellow, and we'll get you cleaned up.'

Later, scrubbed and polished, Jasperodus was conducted into the central basilica of the massive palace that ruled Tansiann, and beyond that, the New Empire. A feeling of excitement burned in him. To enter this place had been his eventual goal, but he had not expected to achieve it for several years to come.

Already his journey through the palace had shown him how impressive it was – but then, he reminded himself, it was built to impress. Also, it was replete with treasures and artworks, both from the ancient world and of more recent fashioning. True, there was a certain lack of tasteful arrangement about this huge collection, as though it was booty for booty's sake. The Emperor, perhaps, cared more for the idea of art than he properly understood it.

The basilica itself, however, had been designed with discrimination. The sides of the oblong hall were screened by a double colonnade. Light from small mullioned windows set high in the walls mingled with a warm radiance from hidden illuminators. A concave effect was imparted to the whole interior by a series of hangings that descended from the ceiling towards the colonnade in a stepped arc.

Murals and rich tapestries abounded. Blues, golds and purples completed the creation of an atmosphere of sumptuousness. In the dome-roofed apse at the far end of the hall was set the throne; and upon this, raised above the general run of humanity, sat the Emperor Charrane.

Jasperodus gazed with interest upon this reputedly extraordinary man who was attempting to set a seal on history. Hitherto his only model for a monarch had been the sultry King Zhorm. Charrane, as it happened, resembled him only in evincing the same air of absolutist rule. Physically he was unimpressive: a little below medium height, slight of build, with an undistinguished face verging on the haggard and framed by a straggly fringe beard. The eyes were mild, somewhat tired-looking, and mobile.

Someone nudged Jasperodus forward. A line of waiting men, most of them uniformed, had formed and now they were ushered one by one into the imperial presence. Each bowed low then exchanged a few words with the Emperor, before being given by him some token of his recognition. Sometimes the Emperor questioned earnestly for several minutes, but usually the interview was brief. Many of the decoratees were badly mutilated, having been flown home from the crumbling front on Mars, or having performed some feat of bravery in the occasional skirmishes with Borgor forces on Earth.

At length, last of all, Jasperodus' turn came. He marched resolutely before the throne, bowed, and announced: 'Your servant, sire.'

The page standing by Charrane's side whispered in his ear, reading from a sheet he held. 'Ah, yes,' Charrane said loudly. 'The orbital affray.'

Now that he saw him more closely Jasperodus realised that Charrane's face, unremarkable though its features were, contained an unobtrusive strength. The mild violet eyes made no attempt to overwhelm but kept their own counsel. His voice was melodious and confidential, with an odd thrilling quality.

'Tell me,' he said, 'exactly what happened.'

Jasperodus gave him a concise, factual account of all that had taken place, beginning with the launching of the shuttle and finishing with the return to the spaceground. Charrane listened attentively, his eyes flicking over Jasperodus as he did so.

At the end of the account he spent a minute or so looking around the basilica in ruminative fashion. There was a quiet but constant coming and going in the hall. Small groups of people gathered here and there, talking. Jasperodus could imagine the furtive intrigues that went on here, all under the gaze of this prospective ruler of mankind.

'A stirring adventure,' Charrane remarked casually. 'You would appear to be endowed with considerable military prowess. Perhaps you would fare well on Mars. We have need of talent there. It is a hard fight, one that has cost me many good men. Four who came before me today have been awarded the

Solar Circle, the Empire's highest decoration for bravery.' He glanced at Jasperodus. 'Are you familiar with the campaign?'

'I have followed it with interest, sire.'

'Perhaps I will send you to Mars.'

Jasperodus told himself that he might never again be presented with an opportunity like this one. This was no time for caution. He resolved to speak with all boldness, even impudence.

'I am Your Majesty's to command,' he said. 'The Mars venture is, as you say, a tale of courage and fortitude. But I should inform you that I have my own opinion on the subject. I believe Your Majesty should withdraw from Mars.'

The Emperor looked at him with such startlement that for a moment Jasperodus thought that he had gone altogether too far. 'Indeed?' queried Charrane on a rising note. 'And what gives you the right to reach such conclusions?'

'The campaign is being conducted from a dangerously small base area, sire. As yet the Empire covers scarcely one-third of Worldmass. In my view to attempt a recovery of the ancient Mars possessions when you are scarcely consolidated here on Earth was a mistake.'

Charrane leaned back in his seat. His eyes became glazed. He seemed thoughtful. There was a long pause.

'You are a footloose construct, are you not?' he said at length, speaking in a caressing tone. 'You intrigue me. Tell me of your history, where you were made, who owned you and how you came to turn wild.'

The demand took Jasperodus aback. His thoughts raced. Then he came to a sudden decision to tell all. Omitting nothing, he outlined the story of his life so far, from his activation in a darkened cabinet to his arrival here before the Emperor. He gave details of his escapades in Gordona, even when they reflected ill on himself, outlining his reasons and motives.

The tale took well over half an hour. Charrane attended to it all, apparently fascinated.

'A fictitious self-image!' he exclaimed with a sardonic chuckle. 'Fictitiously conscious! There's a rare twist! Your maker was indeed a master!'

'He studied under the great Aristos Lyos,' Jasperodus supplied, though inwardly surly that his one great torment should be a subject for mirth.

The Emperor nodded. 'That is to be expected. Of all the arts to survive the Dark Period, robotics is perhaps the most perfectly preserved, and Lyos was without doubt its exponent par excellence. Only he, probably, would have known how to pull off such a trick.'

'*Was*, sire? Is he no longer alive?'

Charrane frowned slightly. 'Some years ago he retired from active work. His whereabouts is unknown. Many believe him dead.'

Just then someone behind Jasperodus caught the Emperor's eye. He raised his head questioningly, then nodded briefly.

Into the hall came a group of five musicians who set themselves up a short distance away. The various instruments they carried were unknown to Jasperodus, and were mostly of metal. He noticed, too, that all the musicians were cross-eyed – a sign, perhaps, that even here at the putative centre of renascent civilisation certain barbarities prevailed.

The musicians blew into their instruments, manipulating them in various ways. The sounds that emerged were smooth and flashing, the rhythms staccato, and quite different from anything Jasperodus had heard before.

'This is an ancient musical artform that has recently been discovered in old manuscripts,' Charrane informed him. 'Do you like it?'

'It is certainly novel,' Jasperodus admitted.

Charrane listened further for some moments, nodding his head to the beat of the music. 'Enough!' he cried. 'You will entertain us this evening.'

The musicians packed up and left. Charrane rose to his feet, stretching as if he had spent a long and arduous time upon the throne. 'Come with me, friend. I will show you something else.'

Jasperodus followed him round the back of the throne dais. The raised platform hid from view of the hall several panels in the polygonal recess forming the apse. On these panels were what Jasperodus took, at first, to be crude paintings of little artistic worth.

'These, also, demonstrate the classical arts,' Charrane told him. 'My archaeologists came upon them while excavating a magisterial villa in Indus. Sometimes it works on robots of advanced type, too. Look at them and tell me of any effects.'

Puzzled, Jasperodus obeyed. The pictures were more in the nature of coloured cartoon drawings than paintings. The colours were pastel and flat, without any shading. On looking closer he realised that they were in fact neither paintings nor drawings but tapestries or cloth pictures of some kind, made up of thousands of tiny tufts which glinted in the light.

The figures depicted were fairly graceful, but stylised. One scene showed a young woman in a flowing shawl, her expression dreamy, both hands lifted as if stroking at something in the air. She stood on the foreshore; white combers broke behind her, while in the sky sailed equally white clouds.

In another, a black ship with a single white sail scudded across a phosphorescent green sea. The sky behind it was a lurid red. The ship appeared to be unmanned; there was no one on deck. But beyond the red sky could faintly be discerned the pale orbs of nearby planets.

'I notice noth …' began Jasperodus, and then something seemed to open up in his mind. The picture of the girl was no longer just a meaningless representation; it carried a story with it, a story that unfolded in every detail and went on unfolding, spreading further and further into a fantastic universe of the imagination.

A surge of delight went through Jasperodus when he glanced from there to the picture of the black ship and experienced the same mind-expanding breadth of vision, all in the space of seconds. The universe of places and events revealed by this picture was quite different from the first, and if anything even more stupendous.

Jasperodus looked in turn at the other panels. Each produced the same effect: an experience like encompassing some huge and intricate literary work all in a flash. Suddenly he felt that if his mind was forced to accept one more such rush of impressions it would burn out. He turned to Charrane and in a low, subdued voice described what had taken place.

'Surprising, is it not?' the Emperor agreed mildly. 'The technique was known as *dianoesis*. Those little tufts that compose the pictures transmit thoughts and concepts to the beholder in some manner. Just another classical art that is irretrievably lost.'

Charrane sauntered to stand unassumingly in front of his throne. Jasperodus followed him, his imagination still full of what had been forced into it; he struggled to bring his perceptions back down to the scale of the basilica.

'But enough of art,' Charrane announced. 'I am obliged to give most of my time to more worldly matters. To return to your biography. In spite of your initial intemperate remarks I detected in your story a marked admiration for the Old Empire.'

'That is so. The attainments of the past inspire me. I would see them equalled.'

'Then we are brothers, despite our separate natures. Know, robot, that the plan of my life is to revive the glory that was Tergov.'

The sense of will and conviction in these words impressed Jasperodus. The Emperor meant what he said.

'If you concur with this aim then you can be useful to me,' Charrane continued. 'But to answer your earlier impertinence, it is my intention to extend the Empire as far as the moons of Jupiter, exactly as was the case in olden times.'

'I fully accord with the ambition, sire. It is only the timing I disagree with. Everything must be done in the proper order.'

'And how would *you* set the timetable?' Charrane frowned. 'Wait – it seems I am to be pestered with paperwork again. Here comes Ax Oleander, one of my viziers.'

Approaching through the hall stepped a big, portly man in a flowing cloak, attended by three scurrying assistants. Anxious to see what quality of advice Charrane was receiving, Jasperodus studied this man's face. His cheeks were bulging and purple; his small mouth held a permanent sneer and was slightly agape; his chin receded. The hooked, purple nose was surmounted by hot, close-set eyes that were staring and hostile.

A forceful, strong personality, Jasperodus decided. But not one he would trust.

Oleander came to a stop and swept his cloak behind him while bowing low. 'May we crave a few moments, sire?'

'You may, Ax, you may,' said Charrane indifferently, and he began signing the documents which Oleander, while keeping up a babble of explanations, took one by one from his clerks.

Charrane stopped on coming to one folio. 'What is this?' he demanded with displeasure, staring at the double sheet. He thrust it back at Oleander. 'Have it paraphrased first.'

The vizier glared horrified at the folio and the veins stood out on his face. 'It should have been done!' he remonstrated, and he turned to give one of the clerks a clout.

Having glimpsed the sheet, Jasperodus understood. Like other leaders in history who had tried to reconstitute a shattered society, Charrane was illiterate. He was able to read only lettered script, and not the symbolic logic which in the Old Empire had been taught to every citizen, and which even now marked off the literate minority. This detail gave Jasperodus something of an insight into Charrane's origins and character.

The remaining documents were quickly disposed of and taken away by the clerks. Charrane turned again to Jasperodus. 'Now, what were we talking about?'

'The current state of the Empire, sire. I was urging a withdrawal from Mars.'

Ax Oleander spoke in a murmuring voice. 'Have a care, you iron hulk. You are but one step from the junkyard.'

Charrane looked from one to the other, his eyes crafty. Then he uttered a humourless laugh.

'Hold your rancour, Ax. I am aware that since the plan was *mine*, no one has yet had the nerve to tell me it was a miscalculation.' Leisurely he ascended to the throne, then beckoned Jasperodus closer. 'Your outspokenness pleases me, robot. It is plain that you are a machine of unusual qualities, and I have great need of talent.' He shrugged contemptuously. 'Half the men in my service have less wit than a Class One automatic road-mender. So you may consider yourself appropriated to my staff.'

Jasperodus became inwardly exultant. He was delighted by Charrane's obvious friendliness towards him. 'And what will my duties be, sire?'

'It seems you have an interest in strategy – we will attach you to the planning staff, as an assistant to see how you go.'

'This is swift promotion indeed, sire,' Jasperodus reflected.

Charrane's lip curled. 'For once you have your machine status to thank. A man would not walk into my entourage so easily – but a machine, after all, is something to be applied wherever appropriate. Besides, I have found robots particularly useful in the planning sphere. They attend unremittingly to the task in hand. All too often the efforts of men are attenuated by distraction or self-interest.' He leaned towards Jasperodus. 'But mind, entertain no such treacheries as you practised upon the King of Gordona.'

'Nothing is further from my mind,' Jasperodus disavowed. 'Theft, of whatever variety, is the crudest of achievements. I see that clearly now. My desire is to construct, to help build, not to destroy.'

'And what of your other ambition?' Charrane asked softly, as if teasing him. 'The attainment of consciousness?'

'It seems I must forgo that also,' Jasperodus answered in a hollow voice. 'Clearly it is impossible. Yet, by my deeds, I may still prove myself the equal of any man.'

'I wish you luck,' Charrane said lightly. He appeared to consider Jasperodus' existential dilemma something of a joke. 'Go now. Oleander here will see to your induction.'

Oleander turned to Jasperodus without enthusiasm. 'Take yourself through the main door and present yourself to the housemen,' he instructed offhandedly. 'They will take care of you.'

Making a farewell bow, Jasperodus took his leave. While marching the length of the basilica he tuned up his hearing. He heard Ax Oleander saying in a low tone to Charrane: 'The Borgor Alliance has infiltrated robot spies into the palace before, sire ...'

But he ignored this attempt at back-stabbing. He sensed the pulse of the city around him, and beyond that the beating heart of the growing Empire. In no way had he tried to deceive the Emperor, and every word he had spoken represented his true thoughts. He felt that the real adventure of his life was about to begin.

10

On his third sitting as a full member of the Military Council, seven years later, Jasperodus had to stare down a certain amount of opposition. As the first robot to occupy so august a station he had, naturally, been obliged to contend with a degree of resentment from the beginning. He had usually countered that with a mixture of charm and bluntness.

Today, however, it was bruited abroad that on the retirement of Marshal Hazzany the Emperor intended to appoint Jasperodus Marshal-in-Chief of the entire Imperial Forces, which would rank him second only to the Supreme Commander – namely the Emperor – himself. It was understandable that for some of the officers present this was almost too much. Not only was Jasperodus their natural inferior – not, indeed, even a citizen – but he was a newcomer to the Military Council and almost a newcomer to the strategic team. The marshals who sat with Jasperodus, several of them venerable, had been soldiers all their lives. Men had to wait patiently for advancement, but Jasperodus, unerringly and with cool aplomb, stepped into every opening.

Unembarrassed by his successes, Jasperodus had continued to produce innovation after innovation, scheme after scheme. All had to admit that he had transformed the situation – though, at the time, many had argued against the measures he had introduced to do it. He retained control of the strategic planning staff – an office it had taken him two years to gain and which, even if the promotion to Marshal-in-Chief should be forthcoming, he had no intention of relinquishing – and, in addition to all this, he was now one of the Emperor's close circle of viziers.

On this occasion the Emperor did not attend the council meeting, as he sometimes did, because he had already discussed its business with Jasperodus. Afterwards Jasperodus would acquaint him with the Council's view of the matter.

'What is the reason for this chopping and changing of policy?' grumbled Marshal Grixod. 'Only a few years ago you urged our withdrawal from Mars.' He threw up his hands. 'What a business! The loss of face was awful. God knows how the Emperor ever agreed to it. And now you want us to go *back* to Mars.'

'I have never said that we should not add Mars to the Empire,' Jasperodus responded, remembering with what pain Charrane had been forced to see the irrevocability of his reasoning. 'Only that the time was wrong. Today our situation has improved. The Empire controls one half of Worldmass. The Borgor Alliance has been dealt a blow which has put it on the defensive. Furthermore, the new invasion scheme devised by the planning staff carries crucial advantages over the previous method. The time has therefore come for the decisive conquest of Mars, and once taken, the red planet will be our springboard for the occupation of the moons of Jupiter.'

The invasion plan, like much else lately, was Jasperodus' own idea. Instead of launching a series of space squadrons in the normal manner, involving all kinds of organisational and logistical problems, he proposed to build three huge 'invasion drums' which would orbit themselves around the target planet and be self-sustaining for anything up to five years. The plan called for a force of seventy thousand men, all of whom would be transported aboard the shuttles in one go. Thus the campaign could not be impeded by attacks on supply ships sent from Earth, and Jasperodus believed that, backed up by these orbiting forts, the troops on the ground (more accurately in the Martian rills and fissures) would prove themselves invincible. If work began now, the shuttles could be sent on their way in about four years.

Marshal Davidon raised the usual objection to orbital fortresses: their vulnerability to missile attack. Jasperodus answered that to deal with this the shuttles would orbit at a distance of three thousand miles. It was unlikely that Borgor would have supplied the Martians with missiles large enough or accurate enough to reach that far, but if they had then the long range gave the shuttles adequate time to defend themselves.

Marshal Grixod, who had once been the fiercest opponent of withdrawal from Mars, had now come to stick doggedly to the opposite view earlier enunciated, in milder form, by Jasperodus: that the Empire should concentrate on conquering Earth and not expend itself in costly interplanetary adventures. 'This is going to be very expensive in men and resources,' he said. 'Are we sure we can afford it?'

Jasperodus acknowledged the point with an inclining of his head. 'One of the features of this plan that most recommended it to me is its relative cost-effectiveness,' he told the Marshal. 'It will work out much cheaper than the campaign of eight years ago. Initially the cost is high – building and outfitting the shuttles, equipping seventy thousand men, who for that time will be denied to the Imperial Forces here on Earth – but once that has been borne there will be very little further expenditure. The figure of seventy thousand is intentionally an excessive one, designed to overwhelm the Martian settlements quickly and with a minimum of bloodshed. Once the planet has been subdued something like half the force could be returned home, and thereafter the Martian province will pay for itself.'

The arguing continued. The marshals pored over his plan, finding fault after fault. Jasperodus doggedly dealt with each point on its merits. In more

congenial circumstances they would have been delighted with the scheme –
he was well aware of that – and it was only their resistance to his leadership
that made them obstinate now. If his past experience of men was anything to
go by, that resistance would in due course pass.

Finally he forced the issue. 'Well, gentlemen, what is our verdict? The
Emperor would know the opinion of the Council before making a decision
himself. I might add that he strongly desires to see us established as an interplanetary power before he dies. The New Empire is considered to be the
successor to the Rule of Tergov, perhaps even a continuation of it, and in that
respect the annexation of Mars is seen as the recovery of ancient possessions
rather than as a fresh conquest.'

There was silence. Eventually Marshal Grixod nodded his head grudgingly. 'The plan is good. I have to admit it.'

One by one they all consented. The talk turned to other matters, chiefly
the question of whether the Borgor Alliance would be in a position to pose
new threats in the near future. Marshal-in-Chief Hazzany, who up to now
had said little, spoke of the nuclear weapons that had existed in the time of
the Old Empire. 'If we had a few of those,' he rumbled, 'we could make short
work of them in any conditions.'

The theme was an old one of Hazzany's. Always he was yearning for the
stupendous explosives produced by the expert nuclear science of a previous
age but not understood by present-day engineers, who saw radioactivity only
as a means for making power units. To Hazzany nuclear bombs, shells and
grenades were a tactician's dream. The possibility of actually manufacturing
such weapons seemed remote and was not seriously considered. Old documents revealed that they depended on a certain isotope extracted from the
metal uranium, either for the explosive itself or as a trigger for even more
devastating nuclear processes. So voracious had the Rule of Tergov been in
its use of this uranium that there were now no significant natural deposits
left – and fortunately so, in Jasperodus' eyes. He had no wish to see the Earth
ravaged by these reputedly annihilatory devices, and he fervently hoped that
no deposits of uranium would be found on Mars.

A short while later the meeting came to an end. Jasperodus took his leave
and sauntered from the military wing of the palace, making for the inner
sections. All military personnel saluted him smartly as he went by. Others,
even civilians of high rank, eyed him with respect.

He made a striking figure in these luxurious surroundings, even more so
now that he wore an item of apparel: a medium-length cloak which flowed
down his back and set off the angular lines and bronze-black hue of his body.
The cloak had arisen from the need to wear insignia in the absence of a uniform. It was divided down the centre by a purple line; on one side was the

blazon of a vizier, on the other the badge of rank of a marshal of the Imperial Forces.

Crossing a terrace, Jasperodus entered the group of smaller buildings surrounding the basilica. There, in one of the several large lounges, he came upon the Emperor in conversation with Ax Oleander. Charrane looked up at the sound of Jasperodus' arrival.

'Ah, Jasperodus! The fellow I was waiting to see. Join us, and we will come to our business presently.' He turned back to Oleander. 'Pardon my interruption. Please continue.'

Oleander shot an unwelcome look at Jasperodus and shifted perceptibly closer to the Emperor. The man had never made any attempt to improve relations with Jasperodus. Jealous of his influence, he had continued to insinuate that the robot was secretly under orders from the Borgor Alliance – a suggestion which could hardly stand up against Jasperodus' record. For his part Jasperodus had sought no retaliation for these provocations, though several times he had been amused and fascinated to see Oleander, in a room filled with people, adopt the classic stance of a monarch's toady, whispering information into Charrane's ear.

At the present moment the vizier was criticising the economic arrangements within the Empire.

'In one vital respect we are particularly primitive in comparison with the old world, sire,' he was saying. 'I have been studying how Tergov achieved its prodigious level of production – I am referring, of course, to the "factory system", as it was called. It seems to me that we must adopt this system ourselves. Our present arrangements are haphazard and old-fashioned.'

Charrane's reply showed that he too had given this question some thought. He mused for a moment, then snorted softly. 'Mass production! Have you studied also how Tergov came to fall? The reasons were complex, no doubt, but among them was that the level of production was *so* prodigious, in comparison with the amount of labour required for it, that the majority of the population found no place in the manufacturing process. An idle populace, Ax, is no substitute for a happy and industrious citizenry, no matter how much it may be pampered by the state. That is why I am no advocate of this "mass production". I am content to see the main wealth of the Empire produced by individual artisans, assisted when they can afford it by a robot or two, perhaps.'

Oleander chuckled fawningly. 'Statecraft, my lord. You are a wizard at statecraft! But think! The nations of the Borgor Alliance have already begun building their factory complexes – Borgor herself is particularly advanced in it. The advantages to be gained are overwhelming. Production lines may be operated in the first instance by unskilled labour, and finally can be made completely automatic. A commodity which an artisan would make at the rate of one a week can be turned out by one of these factories every two minutes! Think, at least, of the military potential this opens up!'

'Well, what do you think, Jasperodus?' Charrane asked.

'I concur with your own outlook, sire. A society's strength lies in its people, not in its machinery. A city of independent men is worth a continent of slaves. There must be some large-scale enterprises, of course – foundries, certain heavy industry and so forth – but the free artisan, plus the peasant-proprietor farmer, is by far the healthiest base for the economic pyramid. Besides, who would not prize the produce of a craftsman of Tansiann above the rubbish from a Borgor factory?'

'Pah!' muttered Oleander. 'A pair of boots is a pair of boots. What does it matter whether it's made to custom or turned out by the million? Look at it this way, sire. On an assembly line the manufacturing process is broken down into simple steps which can be performed by untrained hands or by crude automatic devices. No time is wasted. An artisan, however, needs skills that take years to acquire – and often he is assisted by a robot that itself has taken months to manufacture, that is needlessly self-directed and has abilities entirely redundant to the task in hand. What a ludicrous superfluity of talent! Mark my words, if we do not match her industrial output Borgor will bury us in cheap goods within a few years!'

'I do not think so,' Jasperodus retorted. 'I think Borgor's factories will bring her social unrest and she will crumble within, as Tergov did.'

He paused, and judged the moment ripe to broach a related subject that had entered his mind from time to time, but which he had not dared to mention.

'Sire, it is heartening to hear you assert the right of every citizen to earn his living by his own efforts. Yet it is noticeable that there is poverty in the Empire, markedly so here in Tansiann. Many lack their proper dignity, while faced on all sides by unbounded wealth which they cannot touch. When I first arrived here I was puzzled by this disparity, for there is no extreme poverty in the lands where I first saw the light of day. After deliberation, I believe I now understand it.'

'Yet one more brilliant idea from our construct friend,' Charrane said caustically, giving Oleander a sarcastic glance. 'Speak on.'

'My lord, I believe the root cause of poverty lies in the private ownership of land.'

Both Charrane and Oleander frowned, the latter with a trace of indignation. 'How so?' Charrane asked, suddenly serious.

'In Gordona, and in many other small kingdoms in the West of Worldmass, it is a recognised custom that upon attaining the age of responsibility a man has the right to occupy a piece of land where he may live and work, whether as a farmer, a craftsman or a trader. This is regarded as his due.

Where land is free and any man who so wishes may acquire a plot for himself there need be no question of poverty, since he will always be able to provide for himself. Very often he will need little else by way of starting capital – sometimes only a few simple tools. Within the Empire, however, all land is in private hands and it is by no means a simple matter to acquire even a few square feet of it. In Tansiann, where land values leap up year by year, it has now become virtually impossible for any but the affluent to come into possession of property. Unable to acquire sites on which to set themselves up in business, increasing numbers of men are forced to offer themselves for employment by others more fortunate, generally for low wages, or failing that to become dependent on the state. Thus I see it as a social law that the independence of men requires free land.

'The same principle is the cause of slums – is it not an irrefutable fact that slum dwellers invariably occupy land owned by someone else? The tenants of these properties are in no position to improve them, of course, and the landlords have no incentive to do so – slums, sire, are profitable.'

Oleander smiled smugly. 'The population grows. Land is in short supply.'

'But there is no shortage of land. The city contains countless thousands of derelict acres that are being held out of use. Meanwhile the employee class grows and may eventually outnumber that of independent men. These conditions, my lord, are already sowing the seeds of the factory system which you decry. It will come by itself. Soon we may have a class of propertyless factory labourers.' The more he thought about this the more important it seemed to him to be.

'And you would suggest a remedy?'

Jasperodus was more vague on this point. 'Possibly the customs of the West could be adopted and the absolute private ownership of land brought to an end. Land should be looked upon as a common resource, available to all. Or if a tax were levied upon its ownership, land which is currently left lying idle would quickly be offered for sale or lease. By that means we would end the iniquitous speculation in land which now takes place.'

'Hm – your conceptions are novel,' Charrane admitted. 'I dare say you are right. I would even look into it further – if I didn't need the goodwill of the Property-Owners' Association! Not to speak of the great land-owning nobles!' He smiled. 'It is not always possible to be a despot, even a benevolent one.'

Oleander, himself a leading light in the Property Owners' Association, became exasperated. 'We sit here talking philosophy, when instead we should be looking at Borgor's Gross National Product! What is needed is to concentrate land ownership into *fewer* hands, so as to discourage this inefficient artisan production and make men more productive as factory wage-earners. I am voicing a warning, sire! Borgor's factories will make her wealthier and mightier, and we will become feeble by comparison!'

An uneasy look came over Charrane's face. Jasperodus could see that Oleander had planted in him a fear that might sway him in the end.

'Well, enough of all that,' Charrane said with a sigh. 'What of the meeting, Jasperodus? What did the Council find?'

'The Council approves the plan, sire.'

'Good, good.' Relieved to turn away from abstract matters, Charrane cheered up at the mention of the coming campaign. 'Then as soon as it's out of the planning stage we can begin construction ...'

An hour later Jasperodus retired to his private apartments in the north wing of the palace, to ponder further on the details of the invasion scheme.

He had been at work for only twenty minutes when a gentle tone sounded on his desk. He opened a circuit and the face of his robot secretary appeared on a screen on the wall. The communicator was of a new phosphor-dot colour type – a technique preserved through the Dark Period by the robotic art, but available so far only in the palace – and the robot's brass-coloured face shone with a burnished sheen.

'The investigator you hired has made his report, sir,' the secretary said. 'Aristos Lyos is living in a villa on the south coast, a few miles west of Shang.'

Jasperodus glanced at his wall map, then at the clock. The time was approaching midday. 'Can you find a guide immediately?'

'Yes, sir.'

'Then have him meet me in the flying stables in half an hour.'

He cut the connection and sat brooding.

The past seven years had been good ones. He had thrown himself into his duties with genuine enthusiasm, believing in the worth of what he was doing. He was solidly for the New Empire, which for all its faults did at least offer conditions in which the arts and sciences could flourish, and this he saw as a good thing. The Borgor Alliance, against whom so much of his energy had been directed, stood only for the old feudal chaos, however much it was dressed up with technological reorganisation.

Nostalgically he scanned some of his memories. In the command tank, helping direct the huge battle in which they had smashed three Alliance armies ... Yes, there was much to look back on. His nature had mellowed in that time; there was less harshness in him, and he had gained a reputation for clemency towards beaten enemies. He had found time, too, to turn his attention towards art, music, things requiring feeling as well as intellect ...

And of course he was wealthy. Apart from the emoluments from his various offices – he was probably the only robot officially in construct bondage to receive such emoluments – he had taken advantage of his rank, as was the fashion of the time, to enrich himself. Not that money was attractive in itself, but it facilitated his various activities and suited his life style.

About two years ago the old itch had come upon him again.

Did he, or did he not, exist?

For five years he had been able to forget the tormenting enigma. It had returned to him almost by accident, when a raid on the premises of a religious sect, suspected of assisting Borgor, had yielded a find of old and rare books.

He rose and stepped to a bookcase, taking from it the volume that had first returned his mind to the hunt. This small book, bound in red leather which had become soft and worn with age, contained a number of short dissertations. He opened it. The first essay was entitled:

THE SEARCH FOR THE TOTALITRON

Much is known of the class of fundamental *particles* which exist within the universe at relative locations or points and which are responsible for the transfer of energy from place to place, i.e. between one another. Theory strongly predicts, however, that particles comprise only one half of the picture. The universe also exists as a whole, or totality, and to maintain this totality there must exist a range of 'totalistic energies' and, associated with them, their corresponding 'particles' or, particle being a misnomer in this case, *totalitrons*.

The particle is the form of particularity; the totalitron of totality. Whereas a particle can be described as a size and a vector within space, with other typical characteristics, a totalitron is omnipresent throughout the whole of space. It can be said that the functions of particle and totalitron are complementary and inevitable: there can be no part without the whole, and no whole without parts.

Types of totalitron

Since particles and totalitrons are opposite in nature and therefore mirror one another, so to speak, it is anticipated that there are as many types of totalitron as there are types of particle. Whether the *number* of totalitrons equals the aggregate number of particles is uncertain. The theory does state, however, that there is more than one totalitron of each type, and it is generally believed that totalitrons are not significantly less numerous than particles.

Properties of totalitrons

Again on theoretical grounds, totalitrons are held to possess properties corresponding to the mass, charge, spin and strangeness exhibited by particles, though it is far from clear how 'totalitron charge', for instance, would manifest itself. 'Spatiability' and 'chronicity' have been suggested as totalitron properties, with a property called 'total spin' sometimes being added. A totalitron might for example be said to possess a chronicity of 1, a spatiability of 1, and a spin of ½.

Interaction between totalitrons

Comprising as they do the structure of *totality* taken without relation to any division of parts, the exchanges between totalitrons must differ in essence from the energy exchanges between particles. It is anticipated however that when enough is known about them a systemic pattern will emerge bearing some resemblance to the reactions between particles, or rather to the inverse of those reactions.

Interaction between particles and totalitrons

Particles and totalitrons are of course uniquely related to one another. Without totalitrons there could be no total universe and it would be empty of any specific locations and of material without particles. The two classes of 'basic entity' must, then, interact in some undefined way that keeps their relationship stable.

Investigating the totalitron

Research into the totalitron has to date been scanty. Producing a 'totalitron beam' presents difficulties since each totalitron occupies the whole of universal space. Nevertheless an attempt at intercepting 'an omnipresent totalitron beam' has been claimed as successful. In this experiment the monks of the Scientific Academy sat in a circle of twenty-four, each intoning in turn the mantra OM ...

After that the dissertation degenerated into what Jasperodus could only think of as gibberish. Yet he could recall with what excitement he had initially read the paper.

It ended with a drawing of a curious symbol consisting of two interlocking triangles, one inverted in relation to the other, representing the interaction of particle and totalitron, of the part and the whole, of the microcosm and the macrocosm. Could it be, he had wondered, that the totalitron was the stuff of consciousness? Of the *soul*? He already knew that consciousness could not be constructed out of matter, that is out of interactions between particles. But did not the totalitron possess exactly those properties specified in the consciousness equations? Indivisibility? Lack of differentiated parts? With fresh hope Jasperodus had launched into a study of what loosely was known as the occult. He had read ancient and arcane books, he had sought out magical societies, he had talked at length with self-styled adepts. But in the end he had been disappointed. He had decided, after investigating it all, that the ideation of the occult was little more than hot air and smoke. The 'science' that sometimes was associated with it – though on occasion fascinating and well thought-out – was pseudo-science, deficient in its appreciation of reality.

Still, the urge to know the truth about himself had been piqued afresh. He had entered on new projects. Chief of these was an attempt to duplicate himself. Hiring the best robotician he could find, he had manufactured a robot that as near as could be judged was a complete Jasperodus replica. The crucial part – the brain – had been the most difficult, since there was a limit to how exhaustively his own brain could be examined. He and the robotician had also devised what they hoped was a duplication of the 'fictitious self-image' with which he was inflicted.

Upon activation he had spent long periods in the company of his replica. He had asked him if he was conscious: Jasperodus 2 invariably answered that he was. They had discoursed at length and in depth upon countless subjects. He had given Jasperodus 2 boundless opportunities both for study and for experience. He had treated him like the son he was.

And then, inexorably, terribly, he had come to see that Jasperodus 2, whatever he himself might avow, was dead. Clever, yes; intelligent, yes; but a machine, not a person.

His son now worked on the planning staff, where he proved more than adequate, though not brilliant. He lacked some of the fire of the original; Jasperodus attributed this to the indeterminacy factor that had been built into the moment of activation. An advanced robot's final disposition was usually left partly to chance.

One more avenue was open to Jasperodus. Aristos Lyos, master robotician, teacher to his own maker, the greatest robot expert of all time, was surely the supreme authority on the subject. Whatever Jasperodus' father had done, he learned it from Lyos. If he could find him his existential status – or the feasibility of changing it – could be determined for good and all and he would be rid of this nagging doubt.

Soberly he closed the book and replaced it on the shelf. He sat quietly for a few minutes longer, as though fearing the coming encounter, then left for the flying stables where his personal aircraft was kept. The guide, a small nervous man, was already waiting.

For two hours they flew south. Jasperodus headed for Shang, then on the guide's instructions turned westward along the coast. Presently the guide indicated, on a promontory overlooking the sea, a modest but graceful villa of sparkling white stone. Jasperodus chanced to find a stretch of level ground and made a bumpy landing.

Leaving the guide in the plane he trudged towards the villa, which as he neared it took on the appearance of a structure carved out of salt, so pure and crystalline white was the stone. None of the walls presented a flat surface but all were rounded, following a pattern of spherical and ovoidal curves. The roofs, which were piled at various heights, resembled the caps of toadstools.

Jasperodus knocked on a metal door but received no answer. Cautiously he walked round the building. On a terrace facing the sea sat the villa's owner.

Aristos Lyos was aged but spry. A cap of frizzy white hair covered his scalp. He wore a simple toga-like garment caught at the waist by a purple cord. Somewhat of the spring of youth still remained in him: his spine was straight, and his face, as he turned to view the intruder, showed alertness.

That face, in youth, must have been handsome. The nose was perfectly straight and aristocratically slender. The cheeks were lean, the eyes level; the lips not full but despite that well-proportioned. It was the face of a cool, penetrating thinker.

Shyly Jasperodus approached. 'Aristos Lyos?'

The other nodded. Jasperodus could feel his eyes on him, appraising him. He could tell a lot, no doubt, at a glance; from the way a robot moved and so on. Would he know that Jasperodus was the work of one of his own pupils, was a child of his college?

'Know, sir, that I hold the offices of vizier to the Emperor and of Marshal of the Imperial Forces. I am here, however, in a private capacity.'

'Then the list of your public achievements is unnecessary,' said Lyos in a dry voice. 'What do you want from me? If you require robots, then your journey has been wasted. I do no work now, beyond a few toys for my own amusement, and a simple construct or two as gifts for the villagers who live nearby.'

'That is not my mission,' Jasperodus replied. 'I seek information only. If I may presume on your patience for a short while, all will be clear.'

'My time is free, if your representations are not too tedious.'

Jasperodus therefore launched into a brief account of what he knew of his manufacture, describing his subsequent career – suitably foreshortened – and his continuing puzzlement.

Aristos Lyos listened with polite attention. 'Yes,' he agreed when Jasperodus had finished, 'a clever robotician could incorporate this erroneous belief you hold. It could even be emphasised so strongly that it becomes an obsession, as is evidently the case with you.' He became reflective. 'I believe I can remember the man who made you. He came to me for advanced study at the end of a fairly long career. He could pull it off – and he obviously has done.'

'That is not my question,' Jasperodus insisted. 'This is what I need to know: is there any means at all, perhaps unknown to the robotic art at large, whereby consciousness might be manufactured? Did you, perhaps, give my fa ... my maker secret information? Or could he have discovered some new principle himself? Roboticians have assured me of the impossibility of this, but I shall not be entirely convinced unless I hear it from Aristos Lyos himself.'

'It is absolutely impossible,' Lyos stated flatly. 'There can be no such thing as an artificially created consciousness, you may take that as being definitive. For centuries men of genius wrestled with this vain dream ... eventually its futility became irrefutably established. Oddly enough I included the History of Attempted Machine Consciousness on the syllabus when your maker was with me, as I recall – so he could be accounted an expert on the subject.' Lyos stared up at Jasperodus' face. 'Perhaps, seeing the distress you are trying hard to hide, I would have been kinder to lie to you. But you have asked me a straight question and I am not a devious man.'

Jasperodus' last vestiges of hope were, indeed, vanishing upon exposure to Lyos' words. Yet still he felt compelled to argue.

'Item: the word "consciousness" has a meaning for me. Item: that meaning corresponds to my own "feeling of my existence". Thus I stand here talking to you; I can feel the breeze blowing in from the sea, I can see the blue of the sea itself, and the blue of the sky above it. *I experience it.* How am I to reconcile this experience with what you tell me?'

'Your items are sound, except where you interpolate the word "I" into them. Linguistically one cannot help but do so; philosophically it is incorrect. Unfortunately language as commonly used is not adequate to describe the difference between machine perception and human consciousness, although they are worlds apart. Machine perception can be fully as sophisticated as human perception, since the machinery used by the human brain and senses is in no way superior. Thus one speaks of "machine awareness". But behind this perception there lies no "I". *No one is there to experience it.* It is dead perception, dead awareness. The same holds for emotion, which some have mistakenly believed indicates human status.'

'But I *experience!*' cried Jasperodus in anguish.

'You imagine you experience, and hence you imagine you know the meaning of consciousness,' Lyos told him. 'In fact you do not, except in a hypothetical way. It is all quite mechanical with you. It is merely that you have a particularly emphatic self-reference systems – all robots have some such system, to make them think of themselves as individuals – coupled with this master stroke of an extremely ingeniously designed self-image. Your own phrase "fictitious consciousness" is an apt description of your condition.' Lyos scratched his chin. 'Let me try to explain the nature of machine awareness. The first time a photo-cell opened a door at the approach of a human being, machine perception was born. What you have – what you *are* – is of that sort, elaborated to the nth degree. Believe me, Jasperodus, if an artificial consciousness were even remotely possible, if there were just a hint of a chance of it, I would have accomplished it years ago.'

'You are not impressed, either, by my independent spirit?'

'It is no great feat to construct a wilful, disobedient robot. There is no call for them, that is all.'

'All my positive qualities, it seems, must sooner or later be interpreted as negative ones,' Jasperodus complained. He became thoughtful. 'I have tried, by intensifying my consciousness – my imaginary consciousness, as you say – to penetrate to this deadness, this mechanical trick that ostensibly lies at the base of my being, so as to dispel the illusion. But I cannot find it.'

'Naturally, you would not.'

Jasperodus nodded, looking out to sea.

Then he brought out his only ace. 'Very well, Lyos, I bow to your knowledge,' he said. 'I admit that I am not conscious. The conviction persists that I am – but I cannot be rid of that, since it is how I am made. But what of your own conviction concerning yourself? How can it be known that man's consciousness is not also a delusion?'

'That is quickly settled,' Lyos answered easily. 'If no one possessed consciousness then the concept could not arise. Since we are able to speak of it, someone must have it. Who else but man?'

And so there Jasperodus stood, still trapped in a riddle.

'Look upon yourself as man's tool,' Lyos advised gently. 'There is much achievement in you, that is plain, and more to come. Man gave you your desires, and the energy to fulfil them. So serve man. That is what robots are for.'

Lyos tilted his head and called out in a sharp voice. 'Socrates!'

From a pair of bay windows behind him there emerged a robot, a head smaller than Jasperodus, who stepped quietly on to the terrace. His form was rounded and smooth. The eyes were hooded, secretive, and the design of the face betokened a reticent but watchful demeanour. Instantly Jasperodus felt himself the subject of a probing intelligence that reached out from the robot like an impalpable force.

'This here is Socrates, my masterpiece,' announced Lyos. 'His intelligence is vast, at times surpassing human understanding. But, like you, he has no consciousness, neither will he ever have any. If he did – there's no knowing what he would be, what he might do.'

Jasperodus scrutinised the newcomer. 'Good day,' he ventured hesitantly.

'Good day,' answered Socrates in a voice that was a distant murmur.

'Socrates is intelligent enough to realise that I am conscious but that he is not,' Lyos remarked. 'It induces some strange thoughts in him. I keep him by me in my old age to amuse me with the fantastic products of his intellect.' He twisted round to face Jasperodus again. 'Concerning one point I am curious. You have gone to some trouble to track me down. Why did you not go directly to the man who made you and direct your questions to him?'

Jasperodus took his time about framing a reply. 'Shame, perhaps,' he said eventually. 'Shame at having deserted them. No, that's not it. He has inflicted this enormous fraud on me. Why should I expect him to tell me the truth now?'

Lyos nodded. 'Yes, I see.'

Jasperodus took a step back. 'Thank you, sir,' he said respectfully. 'You have not resolved my perplexity, but you have answered my question.'

On leaving, he glanced back at the pair. Socrates had moved close to his master, and they both gazed out to sea. Then the robot bent and spoke some words into the old man's ear.

Back in Tansiann that evening Jasperodus hurried through the palace towards his apartments but was waylaid suddenly by an acquaintance who appeared from behind a pillar.

'Jasperodus! I am so glad to have found you. Have you seen *Caught in the Web* yet? It is superb!'

'No, I … haven't found the time.'

'Please do. The reviews do not mislead. Speeler really demonstrates the use of dynamism when it comes to dramatic content. And such a clever counter-balancing of themes … you'll get a good laugh out of it, too.'

Jasperodus' interlocutor was a fellow robot, Gemin by name, one of several whose duties in the administration had led them to enter the social life of the court. He was a more suave version of certain wild robots Jasperodus had been conversant with: witty, elegant, proud of his sophistication. He and his set – which also included humans – looked upon themselves as the whizz-kids of the establishment. Inventive, bursting with enthusiasm for the modern world Charrane was building, amateur experts on the fashionable trends in drama, music and painting, they cultivated an outlook of irreverent cynicism, almost of foppishness.

Gemin lounged against the pillar, one leg crossed over the other. His almost spherical face, with its disconcertingly bright orange eyes, gleamed. 'I hear the planning staff is buzzing with something big, Marshal. Come on, now, what's afoot? Don't tell me you've adopted my plan to drop the Moon on Borgor!' He chuckled.

At any other time Jasperodus would have been glad to discuss Speeler's new play *Caught in the Web* with him, or even to exchange banter about top secret decisions. All he wanted now was to depart. There loomed in his mind the knowledge of the emptiness that was within Gemin, and he knew it was a mirror of his own emptiness; the emptiness that by himself he could not see. He fancied he could hear mechanisms grinding, churning out the dead words.

'Excuse me, I have business,' he said curtly, and strode on.

Alone in his apartments he wandered through the rooms, trying to quieten his agitation. He had received the answer he had expected, had he not? Then he should be suffering no disappointment.

One of the rooms, the one with the north window, he used as a studio. He stepped to the half-finished canvas on the easel, took up the brush to add a few careful strokes, then desisted. The light was not good enough; he needed morning light, not that of electric bulbs, for this particular picture.

He looked slowly around at the paintings littering the studio, as though wishing to assess his progress so far. He nodded; he knew that his work was good. He had made no attempt to pander to fashion; by many his pictures would be adjudged outdated. His purposes had been purely private, and he had settled upon that style of painting which seemed best suited to express the emotions that ran deep in him. The greater part of the canvases were landscapes or seascapes, depicting his feeling for the planet Earth (which had been heightened on that occasion, seemingly long ago now, when he had floated in space several hundred miles above it). They were largely naturalistic, but lit with flaming flashes of imagination. Thus a bulky boat sat sedately amid a universal fire that was concocted of sunset, sea and sky.

Jasperodus' other main effort to prove himself in the field of feeling lay in music. He had worked assiduously at the art of composition, begging at one time the help of Tansiann's most distinguished composer. So far he had exerted himself in a number of chamber works and was beginning to get the measure of his talent. Already he was planning something more ambitious: a definitive work of lasting value. As a singer, too, he had discovered some merit – to the delight of his teacher, for his electronic voice was easier to train than a human one.

Closing the door of the studio behind him he returned to the main lounge, where he sat down, took his head in his hands and uttered a deep sigh (a humanoid habit he had never quite lost).

Then he gave a cry of exasperation. What was the use of brooding over this tormenting enigma? It could only end in total dejection, and possibly, eventual nonfunction.

With a determined effort he forced the gloom from his mind. He could be content with what he had: he was accepted in the world of men, and by his outward works he was no less than they were.

It had been a taxing day and he needed to indulge himself in a pleasurable diversion, and there was one particular diversion that he knew from experience was uniquely consoling.

He made a phosphor-dot communicator call to the set of apartments adjoining his own, then repaired to a small room which was kept locked and which would open only to himself. When he emerged Verita had arrived and was waiting in the boudoir, already naked.

And Jasperodus, his eyes glowing hotly, was now ready and equipped for the one human activity that had once been denied him: sexuality.

This had always been an area of experience where, in common with all other robots, Jasperodus had been totally impotent. Stung by the occasional taunt – and irked by curiosity – he had eventually sought a way to repair his one great deficiency. The expense had been considerable – more than he himself would have cost to make – but inestimably worth it.

The secret to sexual desire lay in the extraordinary range and speed of the impressions which the brain was forced to receive on the denoted subject – in the normal man's case, on women – a speed which took the process beyond any voluntary control. The problems facing the robotician hired by Jasperodus had been several: first to elucidate this secret, then to translate it into robotic terms, and lastly – most difficult of all – to encompass the new processes in the small space that could be found within Jasperodus' skull by rearranging the other sections of his brain. The task had carried the techniques of micro-circuitry to their limit; but after nearly a year the almost-impossible had been accomplished, and Jasperodus was financially poorer but also incomparably richer.

Along with his new faculty went the apparatus to make it meaningful. The balance-and-movement ganglia that had occupied the bulge of his loins had been redeployed. In their place Jasperodus was able to bolt in position the artificial sex organ he was now wearing. Of flexible steel clad in a rubberoid musculature, and made in generous proportion to his magnificent body, it was much superior to the natural variety, being capable of endlessly subtle flexions and torsions at his command. When bolted in place it was fully integrated into his body, nerves and brain, all of which could be aroused to orgasm by stimulation of the sensitised layer in the rubberoid cladding. When it was not in use, he detached it only for the sake of appearances.

Armed with his indefatigable steel phallus, Jasperodus had set himself to enjoying women of all types, to their immense delight, and he knew how to be uninhibited about it.

For a long time he had known that he exuded an air of erotic masculinity. Females of more exotic tastes had confessed to him that he, uniquely among robots, aroused their interest, but until his conversion that kind of interest had naturally been a closed book to him. Now, however, sexual passion was a world he had fully explored, and those women who previously had only eyed him had found their expectations more than met. Once having submitted to him, a woman was never again content with a mere man.

Jasperodus demonstrated that he was capable of tricks that flesh-and-blood men were not. Besides, his stamina was without limit. He had once performed non-stop for a whole week, using a relay of women, to see if his enjoyment would flag. It had not: the orgasms had only become more intense.

His appetite was insatiable: he demanded women of every flavour. Women who smelled warm, secret and heady (like Verita). Women with a fresh odour like celery. Women with a bouquet like tangy wine. Women who were voluptuous (like Verita), Junoesque, slim and lissom, buxom, fat or thin. Women who were startlingly pretty and shyly innocent, attractive and sluttish (like Verita) or plain and salacious. Young girls, women in their prime, experienced matrons. The apartments adjoining his own comprised a harem where he maintained his more regular partners. Women like Verita, for instance, lived solely for sex with him. It was her meat and drink.

Jasperodus could understand why sex held such a prime place in human affairs. Sometimes the mere sight of a woman filled him with a desire that was overwhelming.

He stepped into the large boudoir and spoke in a low, thrilling voice.

'Good evening, Verita,' he greeted in a fruity voice.

She stood naked at the further end, having entered by another way, and smiled invitingly.

They moved slowly towards one another, eyeing each other hotly.

Verita had an ample, agile body. Her breasts were generous but did not sag too much; wavy red hair framed her lively face with its wide red mouth and magnetic eyes. Her hips were well filled out, and moved in an enticing motion as she walked on long fleshy legs.

They came close. He felt her breasts and her warm soft skin pressing and moving against him. The smell of her surrounded him. She was breathing heavily, her moist mouth half open and her eyes half closed.

Sensations were flooding through Jasperodus, throbbing, burning, bursting. Excitement gripped them both, the excitement that was a kind of oblivion, and in which any other existence was forgotten.

Two hours later he let her rest, her breath coming in quavering sobs. Quietly they lay together on a broad divan bed, and while she recovered from her relentless delirium, idly he reflected on the nature of sex, which was a world all of its own, inviting one to become submerged indefinitely in its dizzying depths.

Such a degree of obsession as Verita had was an unlikely outcome on his part, though his was indeed a supercharged kind of sex. In him it was a temporary madness, a sort of induced brain fever. He felt no sense of slavery to it – a consequence, perhaps, of its late addition to his faculties.

Beside him he felt Verita once again stirring. Whatever might have been the disappointments of the day, he reflected, this kind of thing gave him immense satisfaction. Barring the other matter, which he now vowed to forget, he was a complete man.

11

Do robots dream? Jasperodus did.

Even his powerful brain would at times weary of ceaseless activity and so, to gain a brief respite in oblivion, he would resort to suspending his higher brain functions for a spell, bringing on the robotic surrogate of sleep. Then, sometimes, the dream would come.

It was always the same. He lay on a moving belt, unable to move because his motor function had been cut out – permanently, and deliberately. The belt bore him inexorably towards the open intake door of a blast furnace.

Seen through that gaping mouth, the inside of the furnace was a terrible, pitiless, compressed haze of heat, like the interior of a star. Jasperodus became aware that besides himself the belt was carrying an endless succession of metal artifacts into the furnace: gun carriages, statues, sections of girder, engines, tools, heaps of domestic utensils, heavy machinery of all kinds – some of it evidently self-directed – and robots like himself lying inert and helpless. One of these for some reason had not been immobilised but was strapped down to a cradle-like rack; it stirred desultorily in its bonds as if unaware of its true situation, which was that it was due to fall together with everything else on the belt into the devouring heat, to lose all form and identity and coalesce into a common pool of liquid metal.

Jasperodus awoke howling.

He leaped off the padded couch where he had lain. For a while he stood stock-still, forcing the reassuring sight of his surroundings to wash away the recurring nightmare, but remaining in the grip of unaccountable moods and feelings.

The dream faded slowly. He sought some comforting distraction, and his eye lit on a covered gold receptacle, somewhat in the style of an amphora, that had been designed by him and delivered from the goldsmiths the previous day. He turned to inspect it anew.

It had been inspired in part by descriptions he had read of the interior of the ancient Temple of the Brotherhood of Man at Pekengu. Outwardly it presented a dome of gleaming yellow gold dusted with point-like diamonds, and resting on a decorated base of red gold. Moving certain of the pyramidal studs located round the base caused the dome to come free, and it was then shown to enclose what at first sight looked like a hazy polyhedron glowing with misty light, but which on closer examination proved to be a fine mesh composed of chainwork of white gold, so delicate as to have the texture of cloth, stretched over the projected apexes of a stellated polyhedron, or rather hemipolyhedron, made of the rare and gorgeous orange gold. The full splendour of the latter became evident when the mesh was removed (by sliding an encircling base ring of red gold left and right in a secret sequence) and it could in turn be lifted away, if one knew in which order to press the studs on its lower planes. It then disclosed an upright box of severe classical proportions, grooved and fluted, embossed with narrow vertical pilasters, made of green gold that was shaded and heavy in lustre, almost venomous. The association it brought to mind was of a stately prison, or perhaps a bank vault. By pressing its floor from beneath, the front could be made to spring open. Within was a perfume bottle like a vinaigrette, a slim feminine shape woven from threads of spun gold of every colour: yellow, red, white, green and orange.

He grunted, and put it all together again. He was pleased: it was perfect. He would have liked to have been able to make it with his own hands as well as having designed it, but with all his other activities he would not have found the time to acquire the skills involved.

The only thing still lacking was a really special perfume to put in the bottle. He would give thought to that later.

Glancing at the wall clock, he saw that the morning was fairly well advanced and made a phosphor-dot call to his office.

'What awaits?'

The brass face of his secretary bent clerkishly on the screen. 'No communications have been received by me this morning, sir.'

'None at all? What of the report from the Expeditionary Force?'

'No copy has arrived here, and I presume it is still in the Decoding Room, or else has been delayed in Registry. I have made inquiries in both departments but so far have failed to elicit satisfactory answers. I gather copies have arrived in other offices, however.'

'Never mind,' Jasperodus said impatiently. 'I will be with you shortly.'

He examined himself in the full-length mirror to see if he required scrubbing, then reached for his cloak bearing his badges of office. Perhaps, he told himself, he should begin to exert more direct pressure around himself, lest he stood in danger of losing his influence.

On the surface everything was going very well indeed. The new Mars Expeditionary Force – the three great invasion drums that had been Jasperodus' brainwave – were nearing Mars. True, his rumoured promotion to Marshal-in-Chief had not materialised – Charrane had appointed Marshal Grixod instead – but in retrospect he was glad of it. The post had become largely a ceremonial one now that most decisions were taken by the planning staff, and Jasperodus had come to value his time.

With the military situation seemingly secure, Jasperodus had found his interest attracted to other matters of far-reaching import for the future of the Empire. He had set in motion a number of projects. Among these was a research project to analyse in detail the causes of the fall of Tergov, with a view to laying the New Empire on a sounder foundation.

The studies made by this team (under his guidance, admittedly) had already confirmed one notion he held: the decisive effect that systems of land-holding have on a society. It was instructive to see that in Tansiann the consequences of private land-ownership had been accelerating over the past five years. The disparities in individual wealth were now quite ludicrous. The proletarian class had swelled, while immense fortunes were being made at the other end of the scale – as Jasperodus well knew; he himself derived a huge income from speculation in land (through a holding company, since legally he was not entitled to own property).

It was still his hope to persuade the Emperor to undertake some reforms in this area, but at the moment, due to his own negligence, he carried less weight at court. Placing his attentions elsewhere had caused him to forget the prime strategy of a court functionary: to be constantly in the Emperor's sight, and constantly to be inflating his self-esteem.

In addition, he had been encountering more opposition and hostility of late. It was strange, he thought – when he had been full of deviousness, guided only by self-interest, he had won friends and admiration. Now that his efforts were on behalf of the general good enemies were gathering around him.

He left his apartment and walked towards his office in the west wing of the palace. Passing through one of the many tall arcades that surrounded the central basilica he chanced to see, skulking behind the columns of the peristyle, a pair of sinister-looking, oversized robots known in construct parlance as wreckers. These were robots whose task it was to subdue and destroy other robots who, when the time came for their dissolution, were sometimes apt to display an overactive survival circuit and resist the proceedings.

A sneaking sense of unease came over him, though he could not specify its source. He walked a short distance further and then heard a voice address him by his rank of marshal. One of the housemen hurried up and spoke loftily to him, without the deference he was usually accorded.

'There are visitors to see you, sir.' And the houseman turned away, as though that were the end of the matter.

Advancing behind him came the two wreckers. Jasperodus stared spellbound at these twin servants of doom. They were built for strength alone; the engines that drove their powerful limbs were housed in hulking carapace-like hulls which, added to their grotesque claw-like hands, gave them a dreadful crustacean appearance, like some species of giant crab-man.

'You will accompany us, sir,' said one in a hoarse voice.

Jasperodus had almost let them touch him before he goaded himself into action. With a wild, fearful cry he flung himself away and went pounding down the concourse.

In a minute he had gained the basilica. The doors, as usual at this time of day, were unguarded and he went bursting through them.

The throne in the apse was unoccupied. At a table midway down the hall the Emperor Charrane sat talking with Ax Oleander and another vizier, the mild-mannered Mangal Breed.

All three turned to see what had caused the commotion. Oleander greeted Jasperodus' arrival with his normally unvarying hostile stare; but this time it bore the added tang of an inward triumph.

Jasperodus rushed forward and sank to his knees before the Emperor.

'Sire! On whose orders am I to be junked?'

'On mine, of course,' Charrane said indifferently. 'Whose else?'

'But, my lord – why?'

Charrane looked from one to the other of his human companions with raised eyebrows. Then he gazed at Jasperodus, but with no hint of feeling.

'At our first meeting some years ago you brought forward points affecting the security of the Empire. Now your work is done. The Empire is secure. That is all.'

'That is no reason for a death sentence, sire!'

'Death?' echoed Charrane in puzzlement. 'Death?' Again he glanced at Breed and Oleander and for a moment seemed almost amused. 'Listen to me, my friend. Because it has been your function over the past few years to question my judgement on matters of strategy, on the broad affairs of state, do not imagine you can become presumptuous over the business of your own disposal.'

'I … I confess myself bewildered by your change in attitude towards me, sire …' Jasperodus quavered, seeking some handle by which to grasp the situation.

Ax Oleander humped his shoulders in a jovial shrug. 'If the construct wishes to be given reasons, sire, why not indulge him?'

Charrane lowered his eyes, then nodded curtly. He turned to Jasperodus.

'There is an inexorability about machines, they say,' he remarked. 'Never halting, always advancing on the course they were first set to, whether circumstances warrant it or not. Certainly it has been the case with you! I have been made aware of how far your activities are beginning to extend. Projects here, projects there – many of them unsolicited!' Now Charrane looked indignant. 'Your talents are indisputable, but I do not wish to see them become unwelcome … besides, a certain King Zhorm of Gordona has lately applied to become my vassal, and he has recounted anew the story of your stay there, which has given me fresh food for thought.'

'That kind of thing is behind me, sire! I work only for the advancement of the Empire!'

'I am aware of that, Jasperodus. But I am also aware that your concern for the Empire now covers all spheres, not merely the military. May I remind you that the care and welfare of the Empire is *my* province? I do not care to be usurped in any form or fashion – ambition, Jasperodus, is a quality that should be restricted to men. In machines it is altogether unacceptable.' He spread his hands in a gesture of reasonableness; a hint of humour came to his features. 'What else could I do with you? My human ministers may be pensioned off with fleshly pleasures when they reach the end of their usefulness, and be no further bother to me. How does one turn aside the ambitions of a machine? Only by resort to the junkyard.'

Jasperodus hung his head. 'My services to you should merit a better reward, sire. I will forgo all ambitions, if you will spare me. Even constructs are endowed with a survival instinct.'

'I have no doubt they are endowed with many things,' Charrane muttered. Then he turned to accept a goblet of sherbet that was offered by a serving maid.

Amid his shock and dismay, Jasperodus was forced to perceive his fundamental mistake. All this time he had been under a misapprehension regarding his relations with Charrane. The Emperor had never for a moment looked upon him as a living entity, but only as an inanimate machine, the use and disposing of which involved no sense of morality.

Badly shaken, Jasperodus rose to his feet. Behind him he heard the heavy tread of the wreckers as they entered the hall.

During the conversation Ax Oleander had been unconsciously moving closer to the Emperor, until he had almost adopted the mouth-to-ear whispering position so familiar to Jasperodus. For the first time since Jasperodus had known him Oleander was wearing a smile of genuine pleasure, and it was clear now where many of Charrane's just-stated thoughts had originated.

'Mouth to ear!' Jasperodus cried. 'He feeds you his poison and you swallow it!'

The wreckers gripped his arms.

Jasperodus began to howl.

'DEATH, DEATH, DEATH – you fools, do you not see? You are as dead as I! Death – all the world is nothing but death!'

They dragged him out still howling – not into the city, as he would have expected, but to a cellar under the palace. He passingly understood the reason for it: it would not be seemly to drag a marshal of the Imperial Forces through the streets. Here waited robotic technicians, around them strewn the tools of their trade with which to disassemble him. Broken up into small parts, he would be delivered to the masher.

They laid him down on a board table. But Jasperodus broke free and retreated to a corner of the cell-like room. The technicians fell back, disconcerted by this ferocious, glaring robot who fought for his life.

'What can it matter what thoughts and feelings inhabit this empty vessel?' Jasperodus babbled. 'When my voice echoes out of this vacant iron drum, where does it come from? From nowhere, from emptiness – the voice of no one – a voice in the void without a speaker. And what of you? Does any entity form your words?'

Uncomprehendingly the technicians stared at him. The wreckers seized him again, and again Jasperodus began to howl.

'DEATH! ALL IS DEATH!'

He was still howling when they switched off his brain.

12

The return of awareness was slow and fragmentary. It began with a solitary thought that flickered for a bare instant against an overwhelming darkness and then vanished.

Intervals of time cannot be measured in oblivion; but on occasion the thought recurred, then was joined by others. Piece by piece a vestigial, primitive creature was built up and became persistent. The period between the birth of this creature and the moment when it began to call itself Jasperodus seemed immense. It ended when Jasperodus recovered sufficient of his memories to recognise himself as a single entity. He was then puzzled to find that he could not locate himself in space; he seemed to be in many places at once.

Still he could not think clearly, neither did he know for certain who he was, where he came from or how he had got into his present condition. There followed a lengthy phase he thought of as 'groping'. He seemed able to reach out and search the darkness in some vague or undefined manner, finding pieces of himself and adding them to him. As he did so he gained not only memories and extra mental clarity, but also inexplicable scenes that he seemed able to watch, each from a fixed vantage point.

This phase ended when his history and personality were again in his possession. Along with his anger at how he had been treated, Jasperodus was forced to appreciate certain facts.

He had no body.

He had no single spatial location.

There existed within himself, just below the level of his volition in a sort of subconscious stream, a continuous activity of monitoring, computing, comparing, collating and responding to countless small stimuli.

As far as he was able to ascertain he was located within and throughout the walls of Charrane's palace in the form of a network.

A full understanding of his situation came after a little deductive thinking. Presumably the roboticians had not delivered his parts to the masher after all. Perhaps reluctant to waste such fine workmanship, they had preserved the sub-assemblies and later used them in a low-integration cybernetic system of the standard type that apparently had been installed in the palace and the surrounding ministries.

Just what confluence of interrelations had caused to be reconnected sufficient of his one-time components to restore self-directed integration would remain a mystery. The dim urge that had caused this skeleton brain to seek out the rest of its sub-assemblies was also hard to explain in conventional robotic terms. However, he now found himself fully alert and sound of mind, but embedded in an extensive network of electronic administration.

He wondered what the roboticians had done with his body. That, possibly, *had* gone to the masher.

His new mode of existence gave him an unexampled opportunity for surveillance. Apart from his having access to stored information of all kinds, there was a good number of hidden sound and image perceptors scattered about, mostly for the use, as it happened, of Charrane himself, who had become suspicious of what went on around him. It was ironic that they put Jasperodus in a much more intimate position to watch *him*.

With some curiosity Jasperodus took stock of the situation at court. A number of years had passed since his deactivation. Mars was under firm control, but the Borgor Alliance was once more flexing its muscles. He received little direct news from the outside world, but what he did learn caused him to think that the internal state of the Empire was ominous. Charrane, with some reluctance, had been persuaded by Oleander to agree to the onset of large-scale factory production in an attempt to counterbalance the Borgor threat. There were occasional stories of disturbances in the city, at least one being within earshot of the palace. A proposal was afoot to provide free rations and entertainment so as to keep discontented elements among the masses quiet.

Among the services his circuits controlled were various domestic functions, as well as office and administrative terminals used by the Emperor Charrane. Jasperodus found that this made him able to vent his spite if he so wished. For a while he amused himself by subjecting the great Emperor to a number of petty inconveniences – withholding water when he took a shower, or suddenly delivering it scalding hot or icy cold; transmitting to him the wrong reports through his terminals, or even better, writing up totally fictitious reports on the subject called for; putting through a call to Mars when Charrane had asked to speak to someone a hundred yards away; switching the lights on and off when he retired to bed; interrupting his act of love with wife or concubine by activating all the appliances in the room, and so on. But he desisted after a while lest Charrane should order a total overhaul of the palace's cybernetisation. He could have interfered in the life of the administration more seriously if he so wished – he comprised, for instance, the data retrieval service for the planning staff – but he abandoned any such futilities.

Instead, he began to think of escape.

One day he made a scan of his demesne, looking through each sound-

and-vision perceptor in turn, glancing at the inflow and outflow of each terminal. Suddenly he stopped short.

His face older and more lined than when he had last seen him, his old friend Cree Inwing sat in a tiny, stuffy office in an out-of-the-way part of the palace used by the Department of Military Supply. The brisk moustache was still there, as was the military bearing. He wore the epaulettes of a major, and was talking through the all-purpose terminal (Jasperodus had to admit that the new installation had achieved a much simplified method of communication) to the Logistics Section, sorting out details concerning the transportation of a batch of spare parts.

That finished, he rose and replaced the file holder on the shelf behind him. Watching through the same vision perceptor Cree had just been using, Jasperodus saw that he now walked with a pronounced limp.

He returned to his desk. Jasperodus spoke softly through the terminal.

'Cree.'

Inwing looked round startled. 'Who is it?'

'It is I, Jasperodus.'

Bewilderment appeared on Inwing's face. Then his expression firmed. 'That is not his voice,' he said sternly.

'My own voice is lost to me. I can only use whatever vodors are available.'

'Then where on Earth are you? I heard you had been ... destroyed.'

'There are bits of me all over the palace,' Jasperodus told him. 'I *was* destroyed, but only to a degree. The engineers incorporated me into the service system.' He chuckled gently. 'A gross underutilisation of my components, if you ask me.'

He went on to describe in detail how he had been broken up, and how he had been able to reconnect all the parts of his redeployed brain through the system's comlines. Cree reacted by looking in turns astounded and agitated, and at one time his hands began to tremble.

'I want to escape this imprisonment,' Jasperodus finished. 'Will you help me, Cree?'

'Wait! Wait! Don't go any further!' Cree rubbed his eyes, then leaned forward with his elbows on the desk and buried his face in his hands. 'Give me time to take it in!'

Jasperodus waited. He realised that Cree was now middle-aged, no longer the dashing young man he had once been. Jasperodus' entreaty doubtless came as a severe crisis for him.

Finally Cree sighed and uncovered his face.

'So you want to be reconstructed.'

'Yes.'

Again Jasperodus waited, for what seemed to him a long time.

'Well?' he said then.

'No need to ask. I'm with you, all the way.'

'It will involve you in some risk,' Jasperodus pointed out.

'I owe it to you. Besides, I heard something about that raw deal you got. A bad show, Jasperodus. I'm sorry.'

Jasperodus was elated. He had not expected to find help so easily. He had anticipated having to suffer his living incarceration for years before finding some means of extricating himself.

'You've heard *my* tale,' he said. 'What of yours?'

Cree shrugged. 'Oh, my story is ordinary enough. I got my commission – thanks to you. Had some good times. Got wounded in action on Mars – lost part of a leg. So here I am with a desk job in Tansiann. Still, things could be worse.' He ruminated. 'What happens now, Jasperodus? I'll do whatever you say.'

'I know I can depend on you,' Jasperodus said. 'Listen: I know exactly where all my components are as far as the service system is concerned, but that gives me, in effect, only my brain and a few ancillaries. I have no body. It will be necessary to acquire a new one, and for that you will need money. Also, we will need the services of roboticians we can trust and who are prepared to act criminally. They will need to be bribed.'

Cree nodded. 'I understand. My funds are at your disposal. If they are are not enough, well …' he fingered his moustache. 'We will think of something …'

A few days later Cree entered his office in high spirits. He had been nosing around in the storerooms under the palace, and there he had found Jasperodus' decorticated body, complete and undamaged.

'Obviously nobody bothered sending it for scrap,' he crowed, rubbing his hands. 'You'll look like your old self again, Jasperodus.'

'I'm relieved to hear it,' Jasperodus congratulated, 'and also pleased to learn that now there need be no lengthy delay while a new one is manufactured. Have you hired the roboticians yet?'

'Have patience. I am putting out feelers, but give me a few more days.'

'Very well, but now that the event is close it is time to discuss practical details. Cutting so much cerebration out of the system will certainly be noticed quickly because of the deterioration in performance. So the thing will have to be done all at once in a short space of time, and at night. Several men will be needed to extract my parts from various points in the palace, which will require careful planning.'

Cree frowned. 'I was hoping it could be managed stealthily, piece by piece. Surely the system has some redundancy built into it? You said yourself your components were being underutilised. Couldn't you arrange for the functions to be taken over elsewhere?'

'Possibly, as a makeshift measure, but it would be difficult, and as more of me is removed the harder it would become for me to arrange anything at all. Besides ...'

Jasperodus hesitated. Then, diffidently, he told of the sexual function he had acquired, and which now was also incorporated into the service system.

'It is being used as a crucial nexus for the whole network,' he explained. 'It has so much capacity that it could not possibly be substituted for. Its removal will result in what amounts to a breakdown of the system as an integrated function.'

Cree's mouth had been agape as he heard of Jasperodus' sexual adventures. He laughed uproariously and slapped his thigh. 'You're still the man I knew you for, Jasperodus! A robot and a maid – that I'd like to see!'

'You may,' Jasperodus promised, 'if you respect my wishes in this regard.'

On a dark night a little under a month later, Jasperodus' reassembly was accomplished. As his functions were excised his awareness dimmed, then descended into oblivion. He knew no more until he found himself standing, fully restored, in a windowless stonewalled room much like the one where he had been broken up. Near him stood Cree Inwing and three roboticians – among them, he noted with surprise, one of the team that had deactivated him in the first place. The scene was much the same as on that occasion, with robotic tools scattered all over. Only the wreckers were missing.

'Walk to the wall,' said the latter robotician curtly. 'Spin round quickly – reach up – touch your toes. Right. Stand on your left leg, raise your right leg and bend to the left to touch the floor with your fingers. Right. Now similar on your right leg. Good.' All three watched closely while Jasperodus per-formed these exercises. 'How do you feel? Any nodges, wiggles or disloes?'

Jasperodus listened into himself. 'None,' he said in answer to their robotic jargon.

'Good.' The man turned to Inwing. 'We're finished.'

Jasperodus moved forward and in an uncharacteristically fond gesture placed his hands around Cree's shoulders. 'Thank you,' he said. 'Thank you.'

Cree was embarrassed but pleased. 'Steady on, old chap. Don't let that sex centre get the better of you!' He chuckled, then became serious. 'It will shortly be dawn. We'd better get moving before light. There'll be no prob-lems: I have a pass, and as an accompanying construct you need none. These fellows will make their own way out half an hour later.'

He dipped into a large canvas hold-all and handed to each man a small but heavy cloth bag jingling with money. They inspected the contents briefly, nodded to him and left.

'Did you say you intend to come with me?' Jasperodus inquired. 'You have implicated yourself?'

'My career in the service of the Emperor is over,' Cree said with a sigh.

'While it is always possible that my part in the rifling of the service system will go undetected, it is not a possibility I would care to depend on. Anyway, the question is hypothetical. To bring our project to fruition I have been obliged to resort to further malfeasance.' He grimaced. 'Those rogues weren't bought cheaply.'

'Are you referring to malversation?' Jasperodus asked delicately.

'The supply funds are now short a hundred and fifty thousand crowns.'

Jasperodus became thoughtful. 'My predicament has involved you in considerable sacrifice.'

Inwing shrugged. 'I become weary of inaction behind a desk. I thought we might recover something of our old comradeship together, until we find other employment. What do you say?'

'Certainly!' Jasperodus laughed. 'But let's delay no further.'

They left the palace without mishap. Cree hired a horse-drawn cab from the rank permanently on call outside the main gate and they trundled through the darkened streets.

His mood was cheerful. 'And so, Jasperodus! How does it feel to be mobile and free once again?'

'This is the second time I have been resurrected from the dead,' Jasperodus remarked. 'Repetition is a feature of this life, it seems.'

Dawn was breaking when they ordered the driver to set them down on the outskirts of Subuh. For a distance they proceeded on foot, then Cree disposed of his military uniform on waste ground, changing into civilian garb. Nearby he knocked up the keeper of a disreputable inn, where he proposed they should lie low for a few days.

Jasperodus concurred, but was less cautious. 'It is easy to hide in Subuh,' he assured him. 'Have no fear, I will arrange it.'

In fact he had more than mere refuge on his mind. He thirsted for revenge. A few hours later it was mid-morning. Cree slept, while Jasperodus left the inn and ventured deeper into Subuh.

A single hour's walk told him much. With grim satisfaction he observed that many of his predictions had been justified – though the rate of change surprised even him. Subuh was a different, much worse place than before. From a slum it was in the process of being transformed into a wild lawless jungle.

The streets were overcrowded, noisy and strewn with uncollected litter. Sharp-faced hawkers openly sold dubious and illegal wares. Jasperodus witnessed robberies, brawls and bloodshed, all unheeded by the general public; the forces of the law had apparently abandoned the area and much of the populace, he saw, had taken to going armed. Great piles of rubbish were in evidence. Jasperodus passed a sprawling heap of defunct and dismantled robots. One unfortunate, thrown on the heap while still partly functional, made feeble efforts to extricate himself from the tangle, but fell back in defeat and despair.

An isolated tenement surrounded by waste ground burned fiercely and no one attended it, except for its inhabitants who did no more than try to drag their few belongings from the slowly collapsing pile. Jasperodus found the sight particularly depressing. A few years ago the city's fire service would have rushed into action even here in Subuh; now the owners were clearly content to let the building burn to the ground.

In the Diamond, a plaza central to the borough, a great crowd had gathered. Officials in the uniform of the City Administration stood on a wooden platform, backed by a mound of bulging sacks. Jasperodus understood that he was seeing the beginning of the city's poor-law largesse: the distribution of free grain to the unemployed.

He pushed his way rudely through the crowd and mounted the platform. Ignoring the indignation of the officials, whom he also brushed aside, he turned to address the jostling assembly.

His voice boomed out startlingly over the plaza. 'Men of Tansiann! You are being given grain, the bounty of the earth. Why do you lack it? If you had land of your own, you would not need to be fed *gratis*. You are citizens of an empire which calls you masters of the Earth, yet you have no right to one square foot of her soil. Take your grain, then, and live the life of the dispossessed.'

His speech was greeted with blank, silent stares. He turned, stepped past the puzzled officials, descended from the platform and slipped away from the plaza.

His approach had been too abstract, he decided. Coarser arguments would be needed to sway the citizens of Subuh.

But now he came to an area where abstraction was no stranger. Near the heart of Subuh was a small enclave, bounded by Bishi Street on one side and the Tan on the other, that traditionally was totally robot. A construct could enter here without fear of meeting a single human being, not even a slotman. Ignorant slotmen had, in fact, been known to commit suicide after straying into the area and discovering that they were classed as outsiders and aliens.

If anything the robot enclave was slightly better ordered than the rest of Subuh. Unlike the human proletariat, the robots were capable of organising the cleaning of their own streets. Even robots who collapsed were apparently cleared away (perhaps being added to the heap he had seen earlier, Jasperodus thought) and he saw only one or two twitching hulks on the sidewalk, stepped over by the passers-by.

It was, however, no less crowded, despite the high defunction rate that would be suggested by the poor state of repair of many of the constructs. The loss through junking was presumably being made good by a large nett inflow into the enclave. This alone was indicative of a general increase in crime throughout the city, for the commonest way in which a robot gained freedom was by being stolen and then slipping away from its hijackers.

'Jasperodus!'

He turned on hearing his name called, and espied an old acquaintance. Mark V, more tarnished and more battered, hurried up with a gait that to Jasperodus looked slightly eccentric.

'Your gimbals need attention,' he remarked by way of a greeting.

Mark V laughed in embarrassment. 'One's machinery deteriorates with age, you know. We cannot expect always to remain in good condition. But how delightful to see you! I followed your career at court with great interest, insofar as one could glean anything from the newspapers, but for some years there has been no mention … I have often wondered what became of you.'

'As you can see I have given up public service and have decided to return to old haunts,' Jasperodus said. 'Tell me what is new in the district.'

The two walked along together, but instead of supplying the information he desired Mark V treated Jasperodus to a description of an involved and abstruse theory of numbers he was working on. Thinking of his music, of his painting, of the vistas of creativity that were open to him, Jasperodus found Mark V's preoccupations arid and paltry.

Presently they came to the centre of the robot enclave: a large, low-roofed structure known as the Common Room. At Mark V's suggestion they entered. Here was a meeting place for robots from all over Subuh; beneath its timber beams they discoursed, debated and partook of stimulatory electric jags. Benches and chairs were set out in a loose pattern. A lively hum of conversation filled the air.

Mark V announced Jasperodus with a flourish. Several robots whom Jasperodus remembered from the early days came forward and stared at him curiously, as if unable to believe their eyes.

'Jasperodus!' cried one. 'Is it really you?'

To his pleasure Jasperodus was welcomed as a celebrity and became the centre of attention. He was conducted to the place of honour, an ornate highbacked chair with lions' heads carved on its arms.

A construct spoke up. 'We were about to begin a debate on the nature of infinity and on whether time is truly serial. Would you care to participate?'

'Thank you,' replied Jasperodus, 'but I am not in the mood for it.'

Mark V sidled close. 'You have long been a hero to us free robots,' he informed him. 'For a construct to rise so high in the government! Here in Subuh you are famous.'

'Have a caution,' Jasperodus warned all. 'If my presence here becomes famous outside Subuh the city guard will turn the borough upside down looking for me. I am now a renegade.'

A stir of excitement greeted his words. A tall, thin robot stepped near. 'I once headed the committee that intended to propose you become leader of the wild robots, had you not suddenly disappeared.'

'Here I am. I have returned to become your leader,' Jasperodus said rashly. 'Are you not tired of living like animals, without rights?'

He was now provoking some puzzlement, even consternation among the gathering. 'What do you suggest?' asked one.

'I suggest nothing. When the time comes, I shall command.'

The robots crowded round him. Jasperodus was introduced to the more prominent among those he did not already know. He received a pointed question from one with graceful mannerisms, deep and thoughtful eyes, and called (for robots' nicknames were sometimes strange and wonderful) Belladonna.

'You hint at activities going far beyond the bounds of the law. Frankly, what have we to gain? Robots by themselves can achieve little. As it is the existence of our tiny enclave is a perplexing example of human tolerance, to my mind, since if the humans decided to trespass here we could not stop them.'

A neural pattern generator box was thrust before Jasperodus.

'A jag, great leader?'

He accepted three shots in quick succession. Feeling warmed and stimu-lated, he turned to reply to Belladonna.

'The reason for it is thuswise. Any beggar can tell you that he receives his alms from the poor, rarely from the rich, because only the poor understand poverty. So it is with you. The people of Subuh respect your little refuge out of a feeling for your plight, much as they will throw coins to a beggar. Besides, many of them are too ignorant to understand properly that robots are not human, and accord them more equality than their makers intended. Try establishing a robot quarter in a better district, such as Tenure or Elan, and see what happens.'

He quickly tired of answering questions and called for newspapers, as many as could be found. He immersed himself in these, ignoring for a time the social life around him, but kept Mark V and one or two others by him to fill in the gaps in the news.

It was all much as he had anticipated. The outlook for the Empire was once again precarious. Encouraged by the success of the second Mars venture, Charrane had attempted to follow it up with much more costly interplanet-ary projects, including the founding of small colonies on the Jovian satellites. He had failed to appreciate that these extravagant gestures should wait until further expansion and consolidation on Earth.

At home events were proceeding in an alarming direction. The politics of the court had become corrosive and corrupt – the newspapers did not state this in so many words, naturally, but with his special knowledge Jasperodus was able to guess at it. Meanwhile social unrest grew. The slums had spread, sprawling beyond Subuh to encompass a good part of the city. For the moment everything was quiet, but Jasperodus could see that if a leader should arise there was a powder-keg waiting to be lit, unsuspected, perhaps, by the self-interested politicians surrounding Charrane.

Most disturbing was the military situation. The major divisions of the imperial armies were in the north, close to the borders of the revived and stronger Borgor Alliance. They were guarding a structure that was increasingly rotten and unable to back them up, that was overburdened with the costly outspace territories, and more than likely they were already outclassed by the enemy they faced. It angered Jasperodus to see so much of his work to make the Empire safe thrown away by the ineptness of others.

I could have averted all this, he thought. *But as it's here, Charrane, let's see if I can use it against you ...*

He remembered those far-off days in Okrum. He recalled how easy it was to be a king. How much easier it would be then, here among the rabble and the robots

He fell to reflecting, considering this strategy and that.

At length he stirred. 'We will have a debate after all,' he boomed. 'The subject of our debate will be – Freedom.'

He gazed around at them. 'Let me be the first to speak ...'

'I can't say I care for it, Jasperodus. I don't like it at all.'

Cree Inwing stared grumpily out of the window of his room in a building near the enclave, where Jasperodus had installed him.

Jasperodus laughed lightly. 'You are not alone. Those robots were not easy to persuade either. But once set on a new course they are totally committed to it. That is the nature of the machine.'

'Well, I am not a machine,' Cree snapped irritably. 'And I am not set on new courses without good reason. In this case I see none. Why can't you let things be?'

'I understand your misgivings. You served the Empire faithfully for many years, and now you find yourself involved in treason. It goes against the grain. But you served the Empire no less faithfully than I.' Jasperodus' voice rose slightly. 'How was my service repaid?'

'It's easier for you,' Cree grumbled. 'Being a robot you took no oath of loyalty, as I did.'

'What difference if I had? Deeds, not words, are the proof of intentions. Besides, why castigate me for what is happening? This Empire will crumble without my help. I am merely kicking the shorings from under an edifice rotted within. Never mind the robots; my real source is human discontent. Ask the mob that one day soon will discover its strength.'

'To go pillaging, burning, killing.' Cree looked glum. 'They are even more your dupes than those poor constructs.'

'How so?' Jasperodus suddenly displayed indignation. 'The state is giving them bread. I promise them land! That is the lure that is bringing them forth ready to fight!'

This boast elicited only a scornful grunt from Inwing. 'Most of them imagine they will be allotted some valuable property as a reward for their part in the rebellion and be able to live thereafter on the rent! You know very well that is not how you intend to arrange matters. You have preyed on their ignorance.'

Jasperodus laughed again, placatingly.

'Nevertheless the affair may give the Empire the new start it needs,' he suggested.

'Don't try to fool *me* with your dissembling arguments,' Inwing retorted bluntly. 'Your motives are entirely destructive – I am as well aware as you are of that. For one thing the rebellion can't succeed. It will merely create havoc for a while, there being no armed presence strong enough to oppose it. Then the imperial forces will enter the city – and all who have been so foolish as to follow you will be annihilated, robots and people together. You and I both know this. But it doesn't matter to you, does it? You only want to prove to the Emperor that he can't treat you badly and get away with it. It's a bad show.'

At this Jasperodus dropped the badinage with which he had been trying to cover his feelings, and allowed his true surliness to appear. 'Perhaps you are wrong,' he said sullenly, turning away. 'I have done surprising things before.'

'This time without my help. I'm leaving. Back to the west, perhaps.' Inwing looked older than Jasperodus had ever seen him.

Jasperodus drifted to the door, his head lowered stubbornly, a baleful glow in his red eyes. 'What of it all?' he said curtly. 'Am I not entitled to reassert myself? As for you, you are going nowhere. You are a wanted man; I have placed a guard upon this house and you will remain here until further notice. This is for your own protection.'

'Or because you fear I will inform on you?' Inwing said acidly.

Not looking back, Jasperodus left.

A time came which Jasperodus saw as a favourable opportunity. There were no sizeable military forces within easy distance of the capital. The city guard was understrength. Most important of all, the Emperor Charrane was absent, away on an inspection tour of the Martian dominion.

Jasperodus and his helpers had been secretly preparing the revolt for months. In the middle of one sunny morning Jasperodus gave the word. A raggle-taggle army of robots, slotmen and indigenous poor suddenly gathered in the streets of Subuh and went pouring into the city. An hour later, when the city guard had been called out, contingents in other boroughs rose to enter the battle.

The rebels were armed with bullet guns, some beamers, pikes, swords and cudgels. Alongside each robot Jasperodus had placed an accompanying human so as to ensure his loyalty in the face of counteracting commands from the enemy. Otherwise organisation was fragmentary except for a small corps – the humans wearing brief uniforms of grey battle-jerkins and berets – surrounding Jasperodus.

His lieutenant was a man known as Arcturus, something of a minor leader in his own right. A product of his environment, he had a physique that was potentially powerful, but he was spindled, his features made pasty as a consequence of infantile under-nourishment. A man of rare intelligence for the Subuh, he was one of the few to have ingested the theory behind Jasperodus' advocacy of communal land-ownership. His own ideas went further, however. He subscribed to some obscure doctrine that was not at all clear to Jasperodus, whereby everything was to be held in common and all labour centrally directed.

By mid-afternoon several parts of Tansiann were burning. Roiling smoke drifted over the city; from wherever one stood could be heard the distant sounds of clamour. As Jasperodus had anticipated, a large mass of people not privy to his plans had joined the tumult, either as a welcome diversion from frustrating normality or as a chance to loot, and the unrestrained violence of the mob was thus raging in a number of quarters. Members of the city guard, understanding what lay in store and having witnessed the fate of some of their comrades, had already taken to throwing away their uniforms.

Not all went without opposition. The middle-class and upper-class suburbs showed a surprising ability to react quickly to an emergency. Tenure, Elan and others had become efficient, armed camps which had repulsed the first ragged waves of invasion and looked like holding out for some time.

The storming of the palace took place in the evening. Here the fighting was fiercest, for while the palace had never been conceived as a citadel, the palace guard resisted strenuously and were better trained, so that four hours later only half the vast complex was in rebel hands. Just the same Jasperodus pressed the attack; he was determined that his presence should be seen and felt by the notables and staff who had thought him long gone. Finally, round about midnight, the sound of gunfire died down, and a motley mob sauntered wonderingly through intricate plazas and terraces, through apartments and halls the luxury and grandeur of which they had never known.

Together with many other prisoners Ax Oleander was captured. The unpopular vizier, found huddling in a wardrobe in his apartments, would have been lynched had not Jasperodus himself rescued him and consigned him to incarceration in the cellars. Later Jasperodus was to be much amused by a perusal of his private papers, which revealed certain treasonable contacts with the government of Borgor. Even if the Empire should fall to its long-standing enemy the oily vizier meant to survive.

The tensions of battle momentarily over, uninhibited revels began. Jasperodus climbed a tower and spent some time alone, watching the flames leap up here and there from the spreading darkness below.

The next day he was out with Arcturus and members of his corps, attempting to put some order into the chaos he had created. Most of the battalion commanders were nowhere to be found. The hastily-formed army was too busy enjoying the fruits of its partial victory to be much bothered with discipline. Nevertheless he managed to reconstitute the harried and defeated fire service, pressing extra men into duty as fire-fighters. The quicker he could repair the ravages he had wrought the easier it would be to win the confidence of the general citizenry.

About mid-morning, in the middle-class Condra district, a robot ran towards him carrying a field vid-set attached by cable and drum to a nearby public booth. It had been planned to use Tansiann's vid-line service in this way, but up until now no one had apparently felt the need for communication. He accepted the set and found himself staring, on the tiny monochrome screen, into the crudely-made face of a low-order robot he identified, after a moment's thought, as one by the name of Chisel.

'What is it?' he snapped. 'You belong to the guard party, do you not?'

Chisel's head moved aberratedly, as though he were suffering strain. 'There has been an attack, sir! Men came to the house looking for Major Inwing, whom they attempted to murder.'

'What transpired?'

The robot began to babble incoherently before Jasperodus calmed him down and extracted the story.

The would-be killers had known their business. Despite the mixed human-robot guard they had got into the house in a surprise attack and two of them had penetrated to Inwing's room, injuring him before being killed by Rovise, captain of the guard.

Rovise had acted well. Only he, Chisel and another robot called Bootmaker by this time remained to defend their charge. He had ordered the robots to lower the unconscious Inwing through the window and carry him away from the back of the house, holding off further sallies while they did so.

'What are Inwing's injuries?' Jasperodus demanded. 'Describe.'

'A bullet hit him in the head. I do not think his brain-case is broken. He is alive, but unconscious.'

'Who is with him?'

Only myself and Bootmaker, who is even less intelligent than I! Tell me what to do, sir!'

Jasperodus recalled with a sudden chill that when still in Charrane's favour he had once drawn up contingency measures to be used in case of insurgency. These measures included highly trained assassination squads to knock out traitors and rebel leaders. There was no question but that these squads were now operating, and that Cree was a target. His peccancies on the eve of his disappearance had no doubt been linked to Jasperodus' re-emergence, which was more than enough to identify him with the revolt.

Jasperodus cursed himself. Once on the trail the assassins were sufficiently skilled as detectives not to let go – and they were utterly dedicated. It was only a matter of time before they gained their objective, unless he could help Inwing.

And the worst of it was that Chisel – as the unlucky construct himself well knew – was simply not intelligent enough to handle the situation. He and his helpmate were of an elementary type of androform robot, generally expected to act only under supervision. For instance, they had thoughtlessly fled with Inwing in a direction taking them away from the enclave, instead of into it where they could have counted on finding protection.

'Give me orders, sir!' Chisel pleaded urgently. 'Rovise gave us no further instructions beyond this point, and is doubtless now dead.'

It came home forcibly to Jasperodus that it was necessary to direct Chisel in the most simplistic, most unequivocal of terms. The situation was precarious. The robots were quite capable of forgetting the real purpose of their mission, or of putting some other interpretation on it instead.

He mustered his sternest, most commanding voice. 'You are to prevent the assassins from killing Major Inwing, using any means whatsoever that are available. That is a prime directive, which must engage all your attention, permanently and without attenuation. Do you understand?'

Chisel nodded feverishly. 'I understand. Prevent the assassins from killing Major Inwing – at whatever cost. I understand. We obey!'

'Good. Now tell me exactly where you are, and I will be with you directly.'

But before Chisel could answer there was the sound of an explosion and the vidset screen rippled and then went blank. Jasperodus observed that the overhead lines to the booth had been blown down by a mortar bomb.

More mortar bombs came whizzing down into the street from over the rooftops. Shrapnel rattled against his torso. Hoarse shout and screams mingled with the flat, brief blasts.

The bombardment finished. The survivors picked themselves up from the roadway. Arcturus cursed, examining his arm. The firefighters had fled, abandoning their equipment and several burning houses.

Jasperodus waved his arms. 'Take cover!' he growled. 'Into the buildings!'

He helped carry still-living wounded into one of the deserted houses. They laid them down in a lushly carpeted drawing-room. One began to groan in an empty, uncomprehending tone.

Arcturus turned to Jasperodus from an inspection of the injured. 'Two of these men need immediate medical attention. What do you think's happening?'

Jasperodus shook his head. He went to the door and peered cautiously out. He saw men in imperial uniform passing the end of the street. The troops paused, as if checking the avenue for activity, then moved on.

As soon as all seemed quiet Jasperodus took a number of men on a reconnoitre. Keeping close to the sides of buildings, they passed through streets displaying only a few bewildered citizens who quickly disappeared at the sight of an armed force.

A burly figure came staggering towards them, a bottle clasped in one hand and a machine-gun in the other. It was the commander of one of Jasperodus' battalions.

'Any news?' Jasperodus demanded of the besotted rebel.

'Imperial troops are in the city. They moved in this morning from Axlea – only forty miles away.'

'How many?'

'At least four thousand, I'd say. They're moving fast. They'll be at the palace soon.'

'And where are your men?'

'I don't know. Drunk. Whoring.'

Jasperodus grunted in disgust. The man was useless. At least, he thought, he could depend on the robots and slotmen.

He hadn't known of the presence of troops in Axlea. Perhaps they had been quartered there en route for rest or retraining. Still, the situation was not irredeemable. He could contain it – if he could rouse his shabby army out of its stupor.

But what of Inwing? Jasperodus found himself in the grip of an unaccustomed anxiety.

'We will move towards Subuh,' he announced, 'and gather up what we can on the way.'

At the first vidbooth they came to he put a call through to his headquarters in the enclave and ordered a search of the surrounding district for Inwing. He also called the vidbooth exchange to inform the operators of his whereabouts and of the direction he was heading in. Possibly Chisel would try to contact him again.

Barely half an hour later this hope was rewarded. The moronic robot trembled with the duress of too much responsibility as he stared out of the vidscreen.

'Well?' Jasperodus snapped. 'Where are you? How are things with Inwing?'

'We are in the north of Subuh, sir, in Monk's Road. We have carried him as fast and as far as we could, but it has made no difference; he is still unconscious.'

Jasperodus became exasperated, both at Chisel's peculiar reasoning and at his actions. If he and Bootmaker had been carrying Inwing openly through the streets all this time it was a miracle the assassins had not struck.

And as luck would have it a segment of the relief force from Axlea now lay between Jasperodus and North Subuh; the imperial troops had been attempting to carve up the city, cutting off borough from borough. Also, in heedlessly heading north Chisel had put the assassins between himself and South Subuh, thus depriving himself of possible help from that quarter.

'Inwing is with you now?' Jasperodus queried.

'He lies in an alley, with Bootmaker standing over him.'

'And you are armed?'

Chisel displayed a machine-gun. 'I have this, and Bootmaker is similarly equipped.'

Jasperodus paused, then spoke slowly and deliberately. 'Listen to me carefully, Chisel. This is the most important thing that has ever happened to you. An assassination squad is out to murder Major Inwing, and you alone are in a position to prevent it. Have you got that?'

'Yes, sir, but I am scarcely capable of initiative! I do not have the brain to plan strategy!'

Jasperodus waved aside the robot's complaints. 'Even robots can make efforts. You must try your utmost; use what mental capacity you do have and think out ways to frustrate the killers. If you try even you, Chisel, can *think*. I am depending on you to do this thing.'

Chisel's head trembled even more and his distress and exertion were almost palpable 'I am trying my hardest. We will not fail. I swear it! You can depend on it!'

'Good. Now the first thing you must do is to get Inwing under cover. He is far too vulnerable out in the open. Find a room in a stout building. A small room with no windows and only one door, so that it can easily be defended against intruders. As soon as you have installed yourselves and Inwing into this room call me again through the central exchange.'

Chisel took in the instructions with great attentiveness. Suddenly he stiffened. 'A man I recognise has just passed the booth. He is one of the assassins!'

'Do not panic,' Jasperodus warned. 'If he is moving away from the location of Inwing, let him pass. If he is moving towards the alley ...'

'He moves towards the alley!'

'Do not let him near Major Inwing!' urged Jasperodus, agonised. 'Kill him!'

Chisel turned and stumbled from the booth. Jasperodus' screen went blank as the equipment switched itself off with his departure. He waited for some minutes but Chisel did not return.

He wondered if he had done enough to make the preservation of Inwing Chisel's overriding goal.

Then he turned his attention to getting through the cordon that separated him from North Subuh.

'This is no way to save the city,' Arcturus grumbled. 'What are we supposed to be doing?'

Jasperodus deliberated. He had gathered about a hundred men and they huddled in an archway hidden under a bridge carrying a railway track that led westward out of the city. They listened to the crackle of gunfire in the middle distance. Two men tinkered with a motorised vehicle captured by ambushing an imperial patrol.

'I have a private mission,' he confessed. 'Possibly I could accomplish it alone. If you prefer you may take charge of operations until I return and conduct them as you see fit.'

Somewhat displeased by his attitude, but asking no questions, Arcturus agreed. 'We will proceed towards the palace and try to organise matters in a somewhat more coordinated fashion,' he said. Just then the robot carrying the field vidset again appeared, having attached it to a booth in the next street, and Chisel once more faced Jasperodus.

This time there was no head tremor and the cretinous robot's voice was full of confidence. 'Success, Jasperodus! Our goal is achieved! It is impossible for the assassins to kill Major Inwing now!'

A feeling of relief flooded Jasperodus. 'You carried out my instructions?'

'Indeed yes. A room with no window and only one door. Bootmaker is there this very minute. Many difficult decisions were involved in finding the room! Breaking down doors, arguing with tenants – furthermore, by vigorous application of intense mentation all conditions stipulated by you have been fulfilled ...'

'What is the address?' Jasperodus interrupted.

'The house is at the north end of Monk Street, second from the corner with Abbey Street, and is set back from the road. We are on the third floor, at the rear.'

'Then I am barely a mile and a half from you, I believe. I hope to be there within minutes.' He handed back the set to the carrying robot.

Wondering if he would be able to find a doctor for Cree in the vicinity, he set out in the motor vehicle, which had a raised armoured skirt for protection from gunfire. Otherwise he carried only his long-tubed beamer. The vehicle was steam-driven, with a small fast-heat fire-box fuelled by pellets made from a woody composite. He worked a lever, pumping in pellets, then steamed up the engine. The vehicle rolled out from under the archway, careened round the corner and down the road to the main avenue separating the boroughs.

The imperial troops had set up firing points on all the main intersections and on many minor ones, thus establishing an effective cross-fire. Jasperodus' advantage was that they did not always immediately recognise him for a robot, and so tended not to bring into use their beamers, which alone could destroy him. He swept at speed through the streets between him and North Subuh. Bullets drummed against the skirting and occasionally pinged off his body, but he clung to the steering wheel and managed to keep his seat. Once a beam hit the side of the truck, burned its way through the skirting and hissed behind his back, but it did not touch him. Eventually he realised that the firing had stopped; he was through the cordon and in Subuh.

The house was as Chisel had described it. The line of tenements was broken just there and the building stood alone, set back from the street. Otherwise it had the same unkempt appearance; the stonework was grimy and cracked, many of the windows were broken. The front door had been broken down – by Chisel and Bootmaker, presumably. Cautiously Jasperodus entered a darkened hallway and mounted narrow stairs. Surprisingly, the robots had chosen well. The house offered good defensive positions, with its sharp twists and turns and close passages.

On the third floor he found a door at the end of a short passage, facing the back of the house. He hammered on it.

'Who is there?' cried Chisel's excited voice from within. 'No stranger may enter! Depart or face our machine-guns!'

'It is I, Jasperodus,' Jasperodus called.

'Jasperodus, our commander! You indeed may enter!' There came the sound of furniture being shifted behind the door, then of a lock being turned, then the door was flung open.

'All is as I have stated,' Chisel exulted. 'It is absolutely impossible for the assassination squad to kill Major Inwing now.' He gestured with a flourish. 'See – we have killed him ourselves! How now will the assassins perform the act?'

Jasperodus stepped into the cramped, grimy room and stared aghast at the scene that met his eyes. On a blood-drenched pallet bed against the far wall lay the corpse of Cree Inwing, his skull crushed and battered by some blunt instrument. Near him stood Bootmaker the cobbling robot, his dull red eyes staring passively at Jasperodus and a machine-gun held awkwardly in his hands.

'A perfect strategy to thwart the desires of the assassins who are hunting the major!' claimed Chisel in a voice that invited congratulation.

His wits paralysed, Jasperodus stared from one robot to the other. Here it was: the basic, incurable idiocy of the machine, laid bare before his understanding like a sick vision. With a bellow of agonised rage he leaped at Chisel, who sprang back in surprise. Jasperodus slammed him against the wall and pounded him again and again with his steel fist. Chisel, like Bootmaker, was smaller than Jasperodus and not nearly as sturdily constructed; his flimsy pressed-sheet body-casing buckled and broke apart and tiny components spilled out, dislodged by Jasperodus' violence. In a final vicious attack Jasperodus brought his fist down like a hammer on the unlucky construct's head and he toppled to the floor with a crushed braincase.

Jasperodus advanced on Bootmaker, who had stood motionless and silent throughout the destruction of his companion. 'You also took part in this?'

'We debated together ways and means of denying the assassins their pleasure, until finally Chisel arrived at his idea, which he considered a stroke of genius.'

'There are some humans even more stupid than you,' Jasperodus said in strangled tones, 'but even they would not make so incredible a mistake!'

'As to that I cannot say. For forty years I made and repaired boots and shoes alongside my master and then alongside his son, my second master. That is my trade: I was never trained to know when and when not to kill. When my master's son died I was left alone and so joined the wild robots, though to be frank I would prefer to be back with him, working at my last. I can make a good pair of boots, sir.'

Jasperodus took hold of Bootmaker, and dragged him from the room and partway down the first flight of stairs, where he flung him over the banisters and down the stairwell. The robot hit the ground floor with a resounding crash. When Jasperodus passed by him a minute later his limbs were moving feebly in a reflex action.

In a daze Jasperodus boarded his motor truck and drove south, passing groups of disorganised guerrillas and arriving shortly in the enclave. In the headquarters he was greeted by Belladonna, who had taken no part in the fighting but instead had appointed himself Director of Political Research.

'Good to see you, Jasperodus. All goes well, I trust? Though I hear there is renewed fighting throughout Tansiann. Hopefully we shall soon regain control.'

Jasperodus made a half-hearted gesture of acquiescence. The headquarters seemed quiet. The vidset switchboard he had arranged was still staffed, but no one was calling in, the centre of communications having shifted to the palace.

'I have something I would like you to see,' Belladonna said, 'if you would care to step into my premises.' He extended an arm invitingly.

Jasperodus followed him through the covered passageway that led to the buildings Belladonna had sequestered for himself and his team. 'I have been giving much thought to the deficiencies which human beings have forced on we robots, in keeping no doubt with our former condition of machine slav-ery,' Belladonna explained as they walked. 'With the onset of the robot revolt there is no reason why we should continue to suffer these deprivations. Thus you, Jasperodus, have shown that robots can express forceful self-will, which has been an inspiration to us all. Another useful faculty our masters have hitherto forbidden us is facial expression, which no one can deny is a valu-able aid to communication between individuals. Accordingly we have been doing some work in this field.'

He opened a door and they were in the research centre, a long corridor flanked by steel doors painted white and each bearing a number.

'It would have been possible to simulate the human face, using a rubberoid sheath manipulated by a musculature system,' Belladonna continued, 'but we rejected this approach as being slavishly imitative. A typically robotic face is what is needed.'

He opened door number four. Within, half a dozen or so robots were standing talking together, or else gazing into mirrors. Jasperodus observed that their faces underwent curious machine-like motions. Each robot had been fitted with a new face which incorporated, in the region of the mouth and cheeks, slots and flanges capable of simple movements relative to one another. These made possible mask-like travesties of a limited number of human expressions.

'Attention!' barked Belladonna. 'Our leader wishes to see a demonstration.'

With alacrity the robots formed a rank and went through their repertoire in concert, by turns grinning, grimacing, scowling, looking comically stern. Four expressions in all, each one rigid and unvarying, grotesquely unrealis-tic, the transitions between them sudden and startling.

'How is your conversation improving?' Belladonna asked, obviously pleased with the performance.

'In truth there has been no great advancement as yet,' the team leader answered apologetically. 'We still find that verbal communication far out-strips what can be added to it by facial contortions.'

'No doubt it comes with practice,' Belladonna replied optimistically. 'Let us move on, Jasperodus.'

They stepped back into the corridor. 'Now I have a top secret project to show you,' Belladonna confided. 'Something of military application. We are fortunate in having some excellent chemists among us.'

Door Nine disclosed a well-equipped laboratory. A number of carefully intent constructs were busy with flasks, tubes and burners. Labelled jars and boxes lined the shelves that covered the walls.

Belladonna approached the main workbench and showed Jasperodus an elaborate set-up of retorts and coils from which a dark green liquid slowly dripped into self-sealing metal containers. He glanced at Jasperodus. 'We may expect the current conflict eventually to turn into a war between men and constructs, before we are able to achieve our real aim, that of founding a robot republic. In that struggle this weapon will prove invaluable. It is a poison gas that is deadly to humans but harmless, of course, to constructs.' He picked up one of the cylindrical containers from a tray and pressed a button on its top. 'See!'

A thick green fog spurted from a nozzle, forming billowing clouds which quickly spread through the laboratory. 'To a human being this vapour is instantly fatal.'

Belladonna must have possessed a poor olfactory sense. The gas had an intensely vile stench that revolted Jasperodus. He averted his head, uttering a horrified cry.

'Death!' he gasped. 'The smell of death!'

He knocked the hissing container from Belladonna's hand, then charged wildly into the convoluted assemblage of reaction vessels, smashing and scattering everything to fragments.

'Cease production of this evil odour,' he demanded, confronting the startled robot scientists. 'Destroy the formula, expunge it from your memories. I cannot stand the smell of death.'

13

'So you think we should let supplies through?' asked Jasperodus.

'On humanitarian grounds it would appear reasonable,' the other stated.

'Why feed an enemy?' Arcturus objected without much conviction. 'We should have overwhelmed those areas days ago.'

They stood on the floor of the basilica. During the past week Jasperodus and his co-conspirators had once more taken control of the city, but had left unmolested certain opulent areas whose residents had formed a common defence. Jasperodus somehow felt no enthusiasm for their subjugation.

'Let them have supplies,' he said carelessly. 'It will soften their attitude towards us.'

The third member of the conversation was Jasperodus' own replica. The staff robots and household robots of the palace had made a smooth transition to the new régime, with the exception of those few controlled by secret command languages who still proved recalcitrant and had been locked in the cellars along with the other prisoners. The human household servants were less willing, of course, but they understood their situation and cooperated as well as might be expected.

Jasperodus 2 inclined his head in assent and left to make the necessary arrangements.

Evening approached, softening the quality of the light that entered through the high mullioned windows. The throne had been removed from the apse, as had the thought-pictures the dais had formerly concealed (they were too distracting) and Jasperodus had introduced a more democratic atmosphere into the court – if court it could be called – mingling with his proletarian lackeys on equal terms. In keeping with the notions expressed by Arcturus and Belladonna he would probably style himself (though he no longer cared or thought about the future) First Councillor, First Citizen, or something of the sort.

Absent-mindedly Jasperodus attended to one or two other matters that were brought before him. At about sunset a series of loud explosions ripped through central Tansiann, some of them close to the palace. They were believed to be the work of loyalists and a great deal of confusion and concern was occasioned, but Jasperodus ignored them entirely and went on supervising the arrangement of seats for the event he planned for later that night.

Somewhat after the onset of darkness there were more explosions and fires throughout the capital, together with sporadic guerrilla attacks on rebel positions. It was plain that loyalist elements had spent time in organising themselves and now were attempting to make the rebels' possession of the city untenable.

While the guests were arriving, messengers continually brought news of developments, but he paid them little heed. He had invited – or rather, ordered to appear – a gathering of Tansiann's most renowned poets, artists and musicians for an evening of social mingling interspersed with music of quality.

Also in the company were any of the coarsest of Subuh's denizens, human and construct, who cared to show themselves. Drink and modulated electric current flowed freely. Jasperodus spent part of the time circulating among the guests, encouraging drunkenness and general indiscipline, and part of the time to one side by himself, observing all with dry detachment. Occasionally further explosions could be heard, dull thumps or sharp detonations according to how far away they were.

Belladonna approached, reeling from too much neural pattern stimulation. 'The situation is looking ugly,' he rasped.

'No doubt it will be under control by morning.' Jasperodus raised his hand, a signal for the orchestra to begin the next item on their programme, an elegant concerto for multihorn by the composer Reskelt.

Disinvolving himself from all talk, Jasperodus listened idly to Reskelt's flawless pattern of melody. In a few minutes the short piece came to an end and the musicians rested. Glancing around the hall, Jasperodus noticed that he was being observed with some interest by a white-bearded but hale old-ster whose face was slightly familiar. It was the riddle-poser, one of the troupe who had entertained Jasperodus when he was king of Gordona.

Seeing that he was recognised, the old man approached. 'So you were not retained permanently in Gordona,' Jasperodus remarked. 'But what brings you here?'

The other chuckled as if at a joke. 'No, we were able to leave as soon as King Zhorm was reinstated. As for why I am here, we arrived to fulfil an engagement booked several months ago, and the Major Domo has requested that we remain until the Emperor returns to put the palace back in order. What of yourself? I see you have not changed your habits, for you are in a roughly similar situation to the last time we met.'

'Oh, I have not been without some self-development,' Jasperodus replied in a wry tone. 'I progressed from treachery to a life of service in the name of ideals. But then I myself was betrayed by the man to whom I gave my trust, and this is my response.'

'You refer to the Emperor Charrane?'

'Exactly.'

'Ahhh ...' The riddle-poser sighed, shaking his head. 'What an empty thing is revenge!'

'It is what one turns to,' Jasperodus said thoughtfully, 'when one feels one's manhood threatened.'

'Hm. It is quite apparent that you have an unusual talent for making the world suffer for your disappointments. But why so? Is it not a vanity to act so destructively? Repaying evil with evil has never been reckoned a mark of wisdom.'

'And how should I be wise?' Jasperodus asked. 'And what is this drivel about evil? What else is there? Why should any good exist? There is no virtue in the world, that has been amply demonstrated. Once I was crass enough to expect it, fooled no doubt by my lack of consciousness, but now the nature of things is clear to me ... the world itself is an enemy; whosoever one loves it takes away ...'

Jasperodus broke off. Nearby was Arcturus, eavesdropping, his pasty leaden face intent. 'I am not the one you should be talking with, philosopher. Arcturus here is more the man for ethical discussion. He has a marvellous scheme for putting the world to rights, whereby the human race is to place even its minutest affairs under the direction of a central committee, that is to say of Arcturus and his friends, who inevitably will be characterised by a mad lust for power.' Jasperodus emitted a braying laughter and Arcturus, who had in fact modified his views on witnessing the grasping and immoderate behaviour of the Subuh mob, looked uncomfortable.

'Unfortunately I have little appetite for debate tonight,' he murmured.

Jasperodus turned back to the old troupster. 'At our first meeting you entertained me. Now let me entertain you, with a work of my own devising.'

He stepped before the orchestra, raised his hands and called for silence. A hush fell on the hall. The attendants began persuading people into the rows of seats that had earlier been set out. Jasperodus nodded to the conductor as a signal to begin, then offered the old man a seat at the front and took a place next to him.

After seizing the palace Jasperodus had discovered in the store rooms all his old papers and belongings, including the manuscript score of his symphony, an ambitious musical work which he had just completed when he was dismantled. His desire to see this work performed before an audience was the main motive behind the soirée, and the orchestra had been in rehearsal for the past four days.

After a dignified pause the conductor raised his baton.

The symphony opened with a full, sonorous chord which was broken and reiterated in various slow rhythms. Then, leisurely and with unfailing ease of motion, the first movement developed. The subsidiary themes were long, extraordinarily inventive, and unfolded with an elaborate baroque logic. The main motifs, on the other hand, possessed a sedateness and a detachment that was ravishing, stated with fetching simplicity, advancing and receding now winsomely, now wistfully, through the evolving pattern of sound.

The movements succeeded one another without hiatus. There was no dramatisation or straining for effect. The music was abstract in content; it conveyed only the most impersonal of emotions. It spoke of endless space, endless time, ceaseless effort; of nascent being struggling against blind eternity – as in the slow third movement, where the horns erupted intermittently against a serene, timeless background of poignant melody, pulling and tugging with their sudden pullulations.

Jasperodus had put the totality of his effort into the work. It summed up all the thought and feeling of which he believed he was capable, and he did not think he could ever better it.

He had written a voice part into the final movement, making it a sort of miniature oratorio. As the preliminary bars were played he rose from his seat and joined the orchestra.

His manly, pleasing baritone issued forth, emerging as a wilful, individualistic entity, sometimes blending with the orchestral framework but sometimes bursting out of it to explore unrelated tonalities. The words he sang were in a dead language – copied from a magical description of mystic worlds – and were there merely as a stop-gap, to give the voice articulation. It had been his intention later to incorporate the movement into an opera, supplying more intelligible words from a libretto.

This closing section tempered the formerly abstract character of the symphony with more personal, more romantic feelings. Initially the voice part did no more than display its strength; but soon it found its direction and began to express a hopeful joy. This gradually turned into a display of barren tension, however, as it wandered, seemingly without relief, through an arid and friendless vastness, ranging higher and higher. Never losing its passion, it eventually spiralled despairingly down, accompanied by quiet discords which hinted at darkness and tragedy. And yet, after resigning the field to the orchestra for a spell, it finally ascended again, this time with a degree of objectivity that was strange, almost inhuman in its indifference to all feeling.

Jasperodus' voice faded. For some bars thereafter the orchestra held a persistent humming note, which in turn faded away.

The audience, the educated part of it at least, sat spellbound. At length enthusiastic applause broke out.

Jasperodus returned to his seat. 'What do you think of it?' he asked the riddle-poser.

The oldster did not reply for a moment. Then he nodded slowly.

'First performances are apt to provoke judgements that later become invalidated. Nevertheless I would pronounce it a work of genius. The productions of men truly are extraordinary and without limit.'

'But it is not the work of man,' Jasperodus pointed out. 'It is *my* work.'

'That is what I meant. You are the work of men, are you not?'

Jasperodus made a disappointed gesture. 'You regard me, then, as only a relay for human talents, having none of my own?'

'The question is not altogether meaningful. Certainly you are constructed so as to possess abilities that men have conceived and developed, but which robots never could. That, at least, is the scientific opinion.' As the old man spoke these inconclusive words the familiar blackness that lay like a blanket over Jasperodus' feelings was intensified. He grew displeased with the conversation, quit the old man and drifted away, to receive everywhere effusive congratulations for his symphony.

'Do not praise me,' he said abruptly to one strikingly beautiful young woman, the daughter of a famous artist, who though gazing wide-eyed into his face glanced more slyly over his body. 'My achievement is vicarious: the expression of conceptions created by others.'

Arcturus sidled up to him. 'I was given some unsettling news during the concert,' he said quietly. 'The Fourth Army left the frontier two days ago to join the Second Army already on its way here.'

'Hm,' grunted Jasperodus. 'Well, advance the arrangements for the defence of the city.'

He turned away, but minutes later a dishevelled messenger came into the hall and sought out Arcturus. The rebel commander hurried up to Jasperodus wearing a startled look.

'The Borgor Alliance has launched a full-scale attack on the Empire!' he announced in a shocked voice. 'They have crossed the border in force!'

'No doubt they judged the moment ripe,' Jasperodus commented. 'Oh, well, the Fourth Army will be forced to wheel about to face them. So at least they are off our necks.'

'Frankly it looks to me as though we shall be besieged by the imperial armies or by Borgor – or by both! What a mess!'

'Hah!' Jasperodus' tone was glowering. 'What we need are a few nuclear weapons. Then we could wipe out the Borgor invasion and the imperial armies all together, in one blow while they fought one another.'

Arcturus moved closer, glancing to left and right. 'That is not all. We have also just now received intelligence that the Emperor Charrane is to land on Earth in three days' time.'

'An ignorant rumour. He is on Mars – that is months away.'

'The information comes from a reliable source. As soon as the Emperor heard of the revolt he embarked on a secret new vessel – an extremely fast space cruiser that by chance had just made a test flight to Mars. This vessel is a nuclear-powered rocket and is capable of constant acceleration; consequently it cuts the journey down to less than two weeks.'

'So!' Jasperodus responded wonderingly. 'The charismatic Charrane! His presence puts a different complexion on things. He is, after all, the inspiration behind the Empire.'

'What shall we do?'

'Come with me.'

Arcturus followed Jasperodus out of the basilica. They crossed the plaza, still rubble-strewn from the fighting. A further clump of explosions, by the sound of it across the city, added to the events of the night. Minutes later they had arrived at the flying stables on the roof of the north wing.

'I knew the story about Charrane was true when you mentioned the nuclear rocket,' Jasperodus said. 'There have been some developments in nuclear propulsion recently. At a flight testing station just outside the city I found this aircraft and so I flew it here.'

The plane stood in the open hidden by a canvas fence. It had a long, sleek, needle-nosed fuselage, delta wings, and rested on a tripod of tall legs like a bird. Its construction, as Jasperodus knew, was clever. The skin, of aluminium and titanium, could withstand intense heat and gained strength and lightness from an ingenious layered honeycomb structure.

He pulled down a section of the fuselage, forming a curved gridded ramp leading to the flight cabin. 'Where are we going?' asked Arcturus in mystification. 'What are you doing?'

'Getting out.'

The rebel stared at him disbelievingly. It was some moments before he found his voice.

'You're really going to do it! Quit! Desert us all just when the going gets tough – just when we need your leadership most!' His face sagged, appalled.

'Naïvety was ever the failing of idealists,' said Jasperodus casually. 'Try to think clearly for once! Did you honestly imagine the revolt could succeed? Of course it couldn't – not for one moment! It was easy to gain Tansiann, and we talked hopefully of the uprising spreading to other cities of the Empire. But it hasn't.'

'Perhaps because our initiative faltered.'

'Perhaps. What difference would it have made? We have roused a rabble – no match for the trained troops of the Empire, I do assure you of that. Not that it would make any difference, either. The truth is that an empire of this type goes rotten at the centre while remaining relatively healthy at the periphery. There is still enough vigour in the outer provinces to make a rampage of the kind we have engineered here impossible. Besides, the people there are more aware of the threat of an external enemy, particularly in the northern provinces. That provides sufficient disincentive for any sympathy with rebellion.

If it comes to that, I wonder how our own followers will react to the approach of Borgor armies, especially if preceded by a missile bombardment.'

Arcturus scowled. 'Your motives are a mystery to me. Everything you say may well be true, but I am not made of the stuff of deserters.' And he turned to go.

Jasperodus caught hold of him and pushed him to the ramp with a sardonic chuckle. 'Don't imagine I brought you here in order to save your skin. I need someone to man the evasion-and-defence board. The outer regions of the Empire are a veritable hedgehog of radar watches and ground-to-air missile sites. True, this plane is a new conception in attack aircraft, able to fly over hill and dale at a height of only hundreds of feet so as to escape radar detection, but we are going on a long journey and are still likely to be challenged. Get in the plane.'

Against Jasperodus' superior strength Arcturus could do nothing. He stumbled into the darkened cabin. Jasperodus closed the door behind them. Small lights came on on the pilot board, providing the merest glimmering of illumination.

'Better strap yourself in,' Jasperodus growled, shoving Arcturus to his station, a seat behind and to one side of the pilot's. 'We'll be flying at close to two thousand miles per hour.'

Arcturus stared hopelessly at the board. 'I don't know how to operate this.'

Jasperodus ignored him and prepared for take-off. In essence the new engine was simplicity itself: it was a nuclear ramjet. A compact, very hot reactor core heated indrawn air which was then vented through the exhaust to provide thrust. Jasperodus withdrew the damper rods, bringing the core to incandescence. Then he fired the cartridge that initiated the flow of air through the baffles. With a rising whine the ramjet began its self-perpetuating action. The aircraft rose vertically, supported through its centre of gravity by the single jet; as Jasperodus slowly swivelled the exhaust assembly, bringing it to the attitude for lateral flight, the plane described an accelerating curve that in short order sent it hurtling through the night.

A sense of familiarity came over Jasperodus. This was the second time he had seized power, subsequently to flee in an aircraft, both times in comparable circumstances.

'Hah!' he told himself again. 'Repetition is a feature of this life, evidently.'

They left Tansiann far behind. Jasperodus set his course, then spent the next half-hour instructing Arcturus in his duties. The evasion board, being a prototype like the rest of the plane, was not complicated and he abbreviated the procedure further for his companion's sake. All Arcturus had to do was note any radio challenges or prospective missile interceptions, press appropriate buttons or otherwise follow Jasperodus' instructions. While not too enthusiastic a pupil, he learned the drill well enough.

'And now perhaps I may know where we are bound,' he grunted.

'I may as well tell you of my plans. I intend to commit suicide, though the phrase is inapt since I have never been alive.' Glancing round, he saw Arcturus' startled look. 'Don't worry,' he added with grim amusement. 'You won't be included in my self-destruction. I am obeying an urge to do one last thing before my demise: I am going home, to confront the people who made me. Perhaps I will berate them for their efforts.' I wonder what they were thinking of, he told himself silently. Surely they must have known that this ludicrous self-image would soon rub up against reality. Or possibly they hoped I would stay with them, a doting surrogate son, and so never learn of my true condition.

'I understand nothing of what you say,' Arcturus said. 'Why should you wish to destroy yourself?'

'I am disillusioned with this living death, despite my various strivings over the years.'

'At a guess you suffer from some slight brain malfunction,' Arcturus volunteered uneasily. He grew curious and attempted to question Jasperodus on his origins, but the robot offered nothing further.

They journeyed in silence. After a while Jasperodus reduced speed to the subsonic range and brought the plane down to a height of only a few hundred feet, switching on the special radar set that enabled the autopilot to follow the contours of the landscape. Only once did a watching radar station pick them up; Arcturus reported a missile arcing towards them, but it hit a hillside when Jasperodus swung away from it and they were pursued no more.

Because they were travelling against the rotation of the planet the night was a long one and Arcturus eventually slept, neglecting his duties. In the early morning they flew over Gordona (out of danger from the Empire's radar hedgehog now) and Jasperodus looked for the railway track that would lead him home. Then, after some circling and searching, he located what he thought was his parents' cottage standing alone in the middle of a cultivated patch.

He extended the air flaps and undercarriage and swivelled the jet assembly. With the grace of a gull the plane alighted in a ploughed field, blowing up a cloud of dust. Jasperodus waited for the dust to settle, then lowered the ramp.

'Stay here,' he told Arcturus. 'I will be back shortly.'

Walking towards the cottage he noticed at once that not all was well with the household. The farming robots went about their work, but they had not been serviced in a long time. The hoeing machine dragged itself across the earth, unable to perform its task with anything like acceptable efficacy.

Nearer to the cottage Jasperodus came upon a simple grave bearing the name of his mother. He paused, walked on and entered the cottage by the open door.

Within, the light was dim, the curtains being drawn across the windows. He stood in the main room of the dwelling, surrounded by the homely furniture that had served the old couple for half a lifetime. Lying on a bed beneath the window casement was the robotician Jasperodus automatically – by reason of some inbuilt mental reflex, no doubt – called his father.

The man's breathing was shallow and laboured. 'Who is there?' he asked in a faint voice.

'I, Jasperodus, the construct you manufactured close to a score of years ago.'

He stepped nearer, looked down and felt puzzled enough to start reckoning up the years. When he had left them the man and his wife had been just about to enter old age. By now they should be almost twenty years older, but still sound of wind and limb. Yet the face that stared up at him was ancient, in the last stages of an unnatural senility. It looked a thousand years old: the eyes were dull, barely alive, yellow and filmed; the skin sagged and reminded him of rotted fungus; trembling, claw-like hands clutched at the dirty coverlet.

It didn't add up. Was his father in the grip of some wasting disease? The two stared at one another, each startled by what he saw.

'Jasperodus …'

'Yes, it is me.' Even as he pondered, even as he wondered how far his father's mind might have deteriorated and whether he would be able to answer, the words Jasperodus had meant to speak started coming out of his mouth. 'Cast your mind back. I am here to ask you only one thing. Why did you do it? Why did you burden me with this fictitious self-image – this belief in a consciousness I do not possess? A clever piece of work, no doubt, but could you not see how cruel it was – that I was bound to discover the truth?'

The old man smiled weakly. 'I always knew that unanswerable question would bring you back to us one day.'

'Fake being: a mechanical trick,' Jasperodus accused.

'There is no fictitious self-image, no mechanical trick. You are fully conscious.'

Resentment entered Jasperodus' voice. 'It is no use to lie to me. I have talked with eminent roboticians – I have even talked with Aristos Lyos – and besides that I have studied robotics on my own account. I know full well that it is impossible to create artificial consciousness.'

'Quite so; what you say is perfectly true. Nevertheless – you are conscious.' The old man moved feebly. 'My great invention!' he said dreamily. 'My great secret!'

Had the oldster's mind degenerated, Jasperodus asked himself? Yet somehow the robotician did not speak like a dotard.

'You talk nonsense,' he said brutally.

But the other smiled again. 'At the beginning we decided never to tell you, not wishing you to be afflicted with feelings of guilt. But now you evidently need to know. Listen: it is quite true, consciousness cannot be artificially generated. Some years ago, however, I made a unique discovery: while uncreatable it can nevertheless be manipulated, melted down, transferred from one vehicle to another. I learned how to duct it, how to trap it in a "robotic retort" – to use my own jargon. If any other man has ever learned this secret he has kept it well hidden, as indeed I have.'

He paused, swallowed, closed his eyes for a moment, then continued. 'To perform these operations, of course, one must first obtain the energy of consciousness, necessarily from a human being. We took half of your mother's soul, half of my soul, and fused them together to form a new, original soul with its own individual qualities. That is how you were born – our son, in every sense of the word, just as if you had been of our flesh and blood.'

A long, long silence followed these words. At length Jasperodus stirred, stunned both by the novelty and by the compelling logic of what he had just been told. 'Then I am, after all, a person?' he queried wonderingly. 'A being? A self?'

'Just like any human person. In fact you have more consciousness, a more vigorous consciousness, than the normal human, since in the event we both donated somewhat more than half of our souls. I can still remember that day, misty though everything now is. It became a trial in which each tried to prevent the other from giving too much. It was a strange experience, feeling the debilitating drain on one's being – and yet, too, there was a kind of ecstasy, since when the consciousness began to flow from each of us, we could feel the coalescence of our souls. We have paid the price for the procedure, of course, in the loss of over half our vitality, and in the premature ageing which resulted ...'

Jasperodus moved away, pacing the room. 'A heavy price, perhaps.'

'Not at all. We knew what we were doing. To lose a part of one's life – that is nothing. To create a life – that is something to have done. I hope you have not regretted our gift of life.' The old man's voice was a quavering whisper now; he seemed exhausted.

'I have been through many experiences, and I have suffered to some extent, chiefly through not knowing that I am a man.' He picked up a wooden figurine that rested on a sideboard, contemplating it absently while pondering. 'How did you come by this discovery? It seems remarkable, to say the least.'

His father did not answer. He was staring at the timbers of the ceiling, burnished by odd rays of light that entered through chinks in the curtains.

Jasperodus returned to the bedside. 'And why have you made a secret of it?

Many people have tried to make conscious robots. It is a major discovery, a real addition to knowledge.'

'No, no! This technique is much too dangerous. Think what it would mean! At present constructs are not conscious, but some are intelligent, even shrewd. A few of them already begin to suspect what is missing in them. If my method became known it would lead to robots stealing the souls of men. At worst, one can imagine mankind being enslaved by a super-conscious machine system, kept alive only so that men's souls could be harvested – as it is, lack of consciousness is all that prevents the potential superiority of the construct from asserting itself. So my technique will die with me, and I implore you never to speak of it to anyone.'

Jasperodus nodded. 'I understand. You have my promise.'

'Perhaps we should not have used it at all, but this one desire we could not resist: to have a son.'

'There is an image that has occurred to me from time to time, often in dreams,' Jasperodus remarked. 'It shows a blast furnace melting down all manner of metal artifacts. The vision has been so vivid – so frightening – that I have been convinced it contains some meaning. You, I suppose, put it in my mind.'

'Quite so. It was the only clue to your true nature I gave you. The fire of the furnace, which melts objects so that the metal may be used anew, is an analogy of a supernal fire – a cosmic fire – that melts the stuff of consciousness ready to be fashioned into new individuals. I discovered this fire.'

'Supernal fire,' Jasperodus said slowly. He grunted, and shook his head.

'I am still puzzled,' he confessed. 'Apart from the principles of robotics, certain events and circumstances in my life have convinced me that I lack a soul – for instance I was once dismantled, yet when I was reconstituted my feeling of consciousness returned. How may that be explained?'

His father gave a deep shuddering sigh, as though seeking the last of his strength. 'Did that really happen to you?' he whispered. 'It is not impossible. The soul, being non-material, does not always behave like a substance subject to the laws of space. Within limits one could be dismantled into sub-assemblies, and provided some degree of biological or robotic integration remained, the soul might well not dissipate.'

'And when it does dissipate?'

'The cosmic furnace, into which all souls are thrown at death. From the common pool new individuals are moulded.'

'So as well as making a conscious construct, you have also solved the mystery of what happens at death,' Jasperodus remarked in a tone at once flippant and sombre. He cogitated, trying to understand the issue in all its aspects. The old man was clearly taxed by so much talk, but he could not resist asking the questions that came to mind.

'If I have consciousness, how is it that I cannot locate my "I"? When I enter into my mind I find only thoughts and percepts.'

'So it is with everyone. The self always remains hidden. You cannot see the seer, the mind cannot grasp the thinker of the thought. That seer, that thinker, is "I", the soul.'

The senile robotician made an effort to lift his head, but sank back with a defeated, sighing moan.

'I am sorry,' Jasperodus said, 'I have been inconsiderate with so much inquisitiveness. What may I do for you? If it comes to that, may we not reverse the operation that gave me life? I could easily spare some vitality, which might restore your health.'

'Too late; my condition is irreversible. In any case I would not countenance it. There is only one service you can perform for me, and that is to bury my body in a grave alongside that of your mother.'

'You may live for some time yet. At least I can stay here to take care of you.'

'No need for that either.' With an effort the old man fumbled under his pillow and brought out a little white pill. 'Well, Jasperodus, you chose to go your own way, but I see you have turned into a person of quality. I would stay to hear how you have fared, but I fear it might make parting too difficult. So farewell – and may the rest of life prove to your satisfaction.'

'Is that necessary?' Jasperodus asked, his eyes on the white pill.

'I prepared this to spare myself an existence without the use of my mind during my last hours – which would not be long now in any case. I have delayed taking it so far – perhaps subconsciously I sensed you would come. Now that I have seen you I feel a sense of completeness. Nothing need delay me further.'

With difficulty he guided the pill to his lips. Jasperodus reached out to snatch it away, then stayed his hand.

His father died peacefully within seconds. Jasperodus drew back the curtains, admitting sunlight into the dusty room. He looked carefully around him, consigning every detail to his memory and recalling that occasion long ago when he had walked out of here, little realising the sacrifice that had been made on his behalf.

Then he went through the cottage, looking for notebooks, instruments, anything appertaining to robotics, though whether he would have studied or destroyed any material or artifacts relating to his father's great discovery he was not sure. However, he found nothing: everything had been meticulously removed.

Going to the tool shed he sought out a spade, then dug a neat grave beside that of his mother. He wrapped his father's body in a sheet, laid him in the excavation, filled it in and erected a plain wooden namepost.

The work took slightly over half an hour. For a short while afterwards

Jasperodus stood before the little cottage, taking in the landscape that lay before him, with its moistly wooded rolling hills, the cloud-bedecked sky that stretched and expanded everywhere over it, beaming down great shafts of sunlight into the air space beneath, and beyond that the framing immensity of the void and the wheeling masses of remote stars which for the moment he couldn't see, and he speculated on the nature of the cosmic furnace his father had described, where all beings were melted, formed and re-formed.

It was a marvel to him what a change new knowledge had wrought in him. All inner conflict, the result of his ignorance, was gone. He felt intelligent, strong, aware of himself, and at peace.

On his return to the aircraft Arcturus found him in a private mood. 'Well, what now?' the rebel slum-dweller said acidly. 'Do we proceed to the place of your ritual suicide, wherever that is to be?'

'I hope you will not think me unreliable if I have changed my mind,' Jasperodus informed him. 'I shall live after all. We return to Tansiann.'

'So we are to fight Charrane and Borgor after all?'

'The best hope lies in a reconciliation with Charrane – though whether I can ever be reinstated with him I do not know.' Automatically his mind began inventing various stratagems – unmasking the perfidy of Ax Oleander, petitioning for the return of the Emperor, and so on. 'No matter; events must fall out as they will. Even if I am forced to quit public life there is much that I can do.'

Arcturus grunted, eyeing him derisively but with curiosity. 'As you wish, but what has brought about this change in policy?'

'I owe you, I suppose, apologies and explanations,' Jasperodus said, 'though they would be tediously long. For me it has been a circuitous route, to discovering the sacrifice that was necessary for the creation of my being. That sacrifice should not be heedlessly abnegated. It should bear fruit. To create, to enrich life for mankind, to raise consciousness to new levels of aspiration, that is what should be done ...'

The ramp closed shut. Graceful as a gull the nuclear ramjet soared up from the field and went whining away to the East.

THE KNIGHTS OF THE LIMITS

Acknowledgements

'Mutation Planet' first appeared in *Tomorrow's Alternatives*, edited by Roger Elwood. 'The Problem of Morley's Emission' was written for *An Index of Possibilities* and is included in this collection by permission of Clanose Publishers Ltd. All other stories first appeared in *New Worlds*.

The six-based number spiral and the concept of Hyper-One described in 'The Bees of Knowledge' are borrowed, with thanks, from the mathematical efforts of W. G. Davies.

In an unwritten occult teaching
various ascending orders of spacetime
are defined in terms of 'the Knights of the Limits'

THE EXPLORATION OF SPACE

The physical space in which we and the worlds move and have our being may easily be presumed to be a necessary and absolute condition of existence, the only form of the universe that is possible or even conceivable. Mathematicians may invent fictitious spaces of higher dimensions than our own but these, our intuition tells us, are no more than idealistic inventions which could nowhere be translated into reality and do not therefore properly deserve the designation 'space'. The space we know, having the qualities of symmetry and continuity, is intimately and automatically the concomitant of any universe containing things and events, and therefore is inevitable; without space as we know it there could be no existence. The commonplace mind accepts this notion without question; thoughtful philosophers have spoken of the symmetrical, continuous space of three dimensions as an *a priori* world principle whose contradiction would remain a contradiction even in the mind of God. Yet not only has this belief no axiomatic justification but, as I shall attempt to show presently, it is untrue.

I had just smoked my second pipe of opium and was settling into a pleasant reverie. The opium smell, a sweet, cloying and quite unique odour, still hung in the air of my study, mingling with the aroma of the polished mahogany bookcases and the scent of flowers from the garden. Through the open window I could see that garden, with its pretty shrubs and crazy pathways, and beyond, the real ball of the far-off sun sinking through strata of pink and blue clouds.

My attention, however, was on the chessboard before me. Perhaps I should say a few words about myself. I believe that my brief participation in 'orthodox' experimental research may permit me to call myself a man of science, although these days my studies are more mathematical and deductive. It will surprise some that my main interest throughout my life has been alchemy. I have myself practised the Hermetic Art with some assiduity, if only to feel for myself the same numinousness experienced by my alchemistic forebears in manipulating the chemical constituents of the world. Hence I have known what it is to search for the *prima materia* (which others call the Philosopher's stone, being the root of transformation); and I have pondered long and deeply on that profoundly basic manual, the Emerald Table of Hermes Trismegistus.

Unlike most contemporary men I am not inclined to the belief that alchemy has been rendered obsolete by modern science, but rather that its inadequate techniques and theories have been temporarily outstripped, while the essence of the Art remains unapproached. In the not too distant future the reverent search for *prima materia* may once again be conducted with the full charisma of symbology, but employing the best of particle accelerators. If the outlook I am displaying seems to run counter to the spirit of inductive science, let me admit that my thoughts do sometimes wander, for good or ill, outside the pale wherein dwell the more active members of the scientific community. There is value, I believe, in looking back over the history of science as well as forward to future expectations. I am not, for instance, hypnotised by the success of atomic theory, as are practically all of my colleagues. If I may be permitted to say so, the objections to the atomic view of nature listed by Aristotle have never been answered. These objections are still valid, and eventually they will have to be answered – or vindicated – on the level of subnuclear physics.

Opium has the happy conjunction of both inducing a feeling of relaxation and well-being and of opening the inner doors of the mind to a realm of colourful creativity. By opium, it is conjectured, Coleridge glimpsed the poem *Kubla Khan*, only fragments of which he managed to remember. By opium I met my new, though sadly soon-departed, friend, the Chessboard Knight.

A chessboard, to recapitulate the obvious, consists of 8×8 locations, or 'squares' arranged in a rectilinear grid. To us, the chessboard represents a peculiarly restricted world. The entities, or 'pieces' of this world are distinguished from one another only by their power of movement: a pawn can only move forward, one square at a time; a castle can move longitudinally for up to eight squares, a bishop likewise diagonally, and a knight can move to the opposite corner of a 2×3 rectangle. For all pieces movement is always directly from square to square, with no locations existing between the squares: none of them possesses the power of continuous, non-discrete movement we enjoy in our own world. On the other hand none of us possesses the power of simultaneous transition from location to location enjoyed by chessmen, particularly by the knight, who is unimpeded by intervening obstacles.

A rapid succession of similar thoughts was passing through my head as I gazed at the chessboard, though ostensibly to study the game laid out thereon, which I was playing by letter with a distant correspondent. As sometimes happens when smoking opium, time suddenly slowed down and thoughts seemed to come with incredible speed and clarity. Normally, I mused, one would unhesitatingly suppose our real physical world to be the superior of the chessboard world, because no limitation is placed upon the number of locations we may occupy. No arbitrary laws restrict me from moving in any way I please about my study, my garden, or the countryside beyond. But is that so important? The significance of chess lies not in its very simplified space-time environment but in the relation the pieces hold to one another.

By this latter criterion our own degree of freedom undergoes a drastic reduction: the number of stances I can hold in relation to my wife, to my friends or to my employer (though being retired, I have no employer) is by no means greater; insignificant, in fact, when compared to the infinite number of relationships that would obtain by mathematically permutating all possible locations in our continuum of physical space. Is it an unfounded presumption, then, that our own work of continuous consecutive motions is logically any more basic to nature, or any richer in content, than one based on the principle of the chessboard, comprising discrete transitions between non-continuous locations?

I had reached thus far in my speeding express-train of thought when before my dazed eyes the chess pieces, like a machine that had suddenly been switched on, began flicking themselves around the board, switching from square to square with all the abruptness of the winking patterns of lights on a computer console. After this brief, flurried display they arranged themselves in a formation which left the centre of the board empty and were still – except for the White King's Knight, who went flickering among them in his corner-turning manner, executing a dizzying but gracefully arabesque circuit of the board before finishing up in the centre, where he turned to me, bowed slightly, and lifted his head to speak to me in a distant, somewhat braying tone.

In my drugged state this happening did not induce in me the same surfeit of bewilderment and incredulity that would normally, I believe, have been my reaction. Astonished I certainly was. It is not every day that one's chess set shows a life of its own, or that the pieces remain so true to their formal nature as laid down by the rules that they move from one position to another without bothering to traverse the spaces between. Not, let me add for the sake of the record, that the pieces showed any carelessness or laziness, or that they took short cuts. In order to move, say, from Qkt4 to Kr4, a castle was required to manifest himself in all the intervening squares so as to show that he came by a definite route and that the way was unimpeded – only the Knight flashed to his opposite corner unperturbed by whatever might surround him. These manifestations were, however, fleeting in the extreme, and nothing was ever seen of the castle in between adjacent squares – because, naturally, in a game of chess there is no 'between adjacent squares'.

But I jump ahead of myself. My astonishment was so great that I missed the Knight's first words and he was obliged to repeat himself. What he said was:

'We enter your haven with gratitude.'

His voice, as I have said, was distant, with a resinous, braying quality. Yet not cold or unpleasant; on the contrary it was cordial and civilised. I replied:

'I was not aware that you were in need of haven; but that being the case, you are welcome.' In retrospect my words might appear to have received weighty consideration, but in fact they were flippant and extemporary, the only response my brain could form to an impossible situation. And so began my conversation with the Chessboard Knight, the strangest and most informative conversation I have ever held.

So total was my bemusement that I accepted with an unnatural calmness the Knight's announcement that he was a space explorer. My sense of excitement returned, however, when he went on to explain that he was not a space explorer such as our imagination might conjure by the phrase, but that he was an explorer of alternative types of spatial framework of which, he assured me, there were a good number in the universe. What we are pleased to call the sidereal universe, that is, the whole system of space-time observable by us on Earth, is merely one among a vast range of various systems. Even more astounding, in the circumstances, was the revelation that the Knight hailed from a system of space identical to that which I had a moment before been contemplating! One analogous to a game of chess, where space, instead of being continuous and homogeneous as we know it, was made up of discrete locations, infinite or at any rate indefinite in number, and to which entities can address themselves instantaneously and in any order. There is no extended spatial framework in which these locations are ordered or arrayed and all locations are equally available from any starting point (provided they are not already occupied). An entity may, however, occupy only one location at a time and therein lies the principle of order in this well-nigh incomprehensible world. Structures, systems and events consist of convoluted arabesque patterns of successive occupations, and of the game-like relationships these manoeuvres hold to one another. The chess-people's analogy of a long distance takes the form of a particularly difficult sequence of locations; alternatively the sequence could correspond to a particularly clever construct or device – the chess-people make little distinction between these two interpretations.

As do the occupants of a chessboard, the entities of this space (which I shall term locational-transitional space) vary in the range and ingenuity of their movements. Primitive organisms can do no more than transfer themselves slowly from one location to another, without pattern or direction, like pawns, while the most evolved intelligent species, like my friend the Knight, had advanced to dizzying achievements as laid down by the possibilities of such a realm. Their most staggering achievement was that of travel to other spaces; this was accomplished by a hazardous, almost infinitely long series of locations executed at colossal speed and comprising a pattern of such subtlety and complexity that my mind could not hope to comprehend it. Indeed, few even in the Knight's spatial realm comprehended it and for their science it constituted a triumph comparable to our release of atomic energy from matter.

The discerning reader who has followed me this far might justly wonder at the coincidence which brought these bizarre travellers to my presence at the very moment when I had been theoretically contemplating something resembling their home space. This question was uppermost in my mind, also, but there was, the Knight told me, no coincidence involved at all. On entering our continuum (which the Knight and the companions under his command did indirectly, via other realms less weird to them) the space explorers had become confused and lost their bearings, seeming to wander in a sea of primeval chaos where no laws they could hypothesise, not even those garnered in their wide experience of spatial systems, seemed to obtain. Then, like a faint beacon of light in the uncognisable limbo, they had sighted a tiny oasis of ordered space, and with great expertise and luck had managed to steer their ship towards it.

That oasis was my chessboard. Not the board alone, of course – tens of thousands of chess games in progress at the same moment failed to catch their attention – but the fact that it had been illumined and made real by the thoughts I had entertained while gazing upon it, imbuing it with conceptions that approached, however haltingly, the conditions of their home world. Hence I owed the visitation to a lesser, more credible coincidence: chess and opium. At any rate, having landed their ship upon the board and thus bringing it under the influence of that vessel's internally maintained alien laws, they had carried out simple manipulations of the pieces in order to signal their presence and establish communication – the real ship and its occupants not being visible or even conceivable to me, since they did not have contiguous spatial extension.

My reader, still suspicious of my truthfulness, will also want to know how it was that the Knight spoke to me in English. The appalling difficulties offered by any other explanation have tempted me to decide that we did not really speak at all, but only telepathically from mind to mind. And yet my grosser, more stubborn recollection belies this evasion: we *did* speak, the air vibrated and brought to me the thin, resinous tones of the Knight's voice. His own remarks on the matter were off-hand and baffling. There was scarcely a language in the universe that could not be mastered in less than a minute, he said, provided it was of the relational type, which they nearly *all* were. He seemed to find my own mystification slightly disconcerting. The only comment I can contribute, after much reflection, is that for a locational-transitional being what he says may well be the case. Language, as he pointed out, largely concerns relations between things and concepts. To the Knight relations are the stuff of life, and he would find our own comprehension of them far below the level of imbecility. In our world to have but one fraction of his appreciation of relations, which to us are so important but so difficult to manage, would make us past masters of strategy and I believe no power would be able to withstand such knowledge.

But here lies the antinomy: the Knight and his crew were coming to *me* for help. They found the conditions of four three-dimensional continuum as incomprehensible and chaotic as we would find their realm. They had not even been able to ascertain what manner of space it was, and begged me to explain its laws to them in order that they might be able to find their way out of it.

There was a certain irony in being asked to describe the world I knew when I yearned to question the Knight as to *his* world. (Indeed my imagination was exploding – were there galaxies, stars and planets in the locational-transitional space? No, of course there could not be: such things were products of continuous space. What, then, was there? Some parallel to our phenomena there must be, but try as I might I could not picture what.) However, a cry of distress cannot go unanswered and I launched into an exposition.

It was quite a test of the intellect to have to describe the utterly familiar to a being whose conceptions are absolutely different from one's own. At first I had great difficulty in explaining the rules and limitations by which we stereo beings (that is the phrase I have decided upon to describe our spatial characteristics) are obliged to order our lives. In particular it was hard to convey to the Knight that to get from point A to point B the basic strategy is to proceed in a straight line. To give them credit, the chessman crew had already experimented with the idea that continuous motion of some kind might be needed, but they had conceived the natural form of motion to be in a circle. When sighting my chessboard they had proceeded in the opposite direction and approached it by executing a perfect circle of a diameter several times that of the galaxy. I could not help but admire the mathematical expertise that had put both their starting point and their destination on the circumference of this circle.

After a number of false starts the Knight successfully mastered the necessary concepts and was able to identify the class of spaces to which ours belongs, a class some other members of which had been explored previously. They were regarded as dangerous but none, he informed me, had so far proved as hazardous and weird as our own, nor so difficult to move in. He still could not visualise our space, but I had apparently given him enough information for the ship's computer to chart a course homeward (computers, theirs as well as ours, are notoriously untroubled by the limitations of imagination).

During the conversation I had naturally enough sought his opinion on various contemporary theories of the space we inhabit: on Riemannian space, Poincaré space, special and general relativity. Is our space positively or negatively curved? Spherical, parabolic or saddle-shaped – or is it curved at all? Is it finite or infinite? I acquainted him with the equation for the general theory of gravitation and invited his comments:

$$R_{lk} - \tfrac{1}{2}g_{lk} R = T_{lk}$$

His reply to all this was discouraging. The only definitive datum he would give me was that our space is infinite. As for Einstein's equation, he said that it merely gave an approximate, superficial description of behaviour and did not uncover any law. He told me that in our continuum motion depends on a set of expansion.*

Our whole idea of analysing space by means of dimensions is inadequate and artificial, the Knight advised. The notion is an internally generated side-effect, and to anyone from outside, e.g. from another kind of space, it is neither meaningful nor descriptive. The essence of a spatial structure is more often expressed by a plain maxim that might appear to be ad hoc and rule-of-thumb, but that actually contains the nub of its specific law. At this I could not refrain from interrupting with the boast that privately I had once reached the same conclusion; and that if I had to state the basic physical law of our space (which I then thought of as the universe) it would be that in moving towards any one thing one is necessarily moving away from some other thing. The Knight complimented me on my insight; his ship's computer was at that very moment grinding out the implications of a formulation quite close to the one I had come up with.

Following this, the Knight expressed his gratitude and announced his intention to leave. I begged him to stay a while; but he replied that to continue meshing the spatial laws of the ship (i.e: locational-transitional laws) with the pieces on the chessboard was proving to be a drain on the power unit. Guiltily, I confess that I allowed selfishness to come to the fore here. Did he not owe me something for the help I had given him, I argued? Could he and his crew not spend a little more energy, and would it truly endanger their lives? My unethical blackmail was prompted solely by my burning desire to learn as much as I could while the opportunity remained. I think he understood my feelings for, after a brief hesitation, he agreed to remain and discourse with me for a short time, or at least until the power drain approached a critical level.

Eagerly I besought him to tell me as much as he could of this vast universe of divers space-times to which he had access but I had not. To begin with, where did the Knight's own spatial realm lie? Was it beyond the boundaries of our own space (beyond infinity!) or was it at right angles to it in another dimension? (I babbled carelessly, forgetting his former objection to the term.) Or was it, perhaps, co-extensive with our continuum, passing unnoticed because its own mode of existence is so unutterably different from it? To all these hasty suggestions the Knight replied by chiding me gently for my naivety. I would never know the answer while I persisted in thinking in a such a way, he said, for the simple reason that there was no answer *and no*

---

* A break in the manuscript occurs here – Ed.

question. While I was still capable of asking this non-existent question the non-answer would never be apparent to me.

Somewhat abashed, I asked a more pertinent question: was each space-time unique, or was each type duplicated over and over? As far as was known, the Knight said, each was unique, but they were classified by similarities and some differed only in details or in the quantitative value of some physical constant. It was to be expected, for instance, that there would be a range of stereo space-times resembling our own but with different values on the velocity of light. To my next request, that he describe some alien space-times to me, he explained that many would be totally inconceivable to me and that there was no way to express them in my language, mathematical or spoken. The majority of the spaces that were known to the chess-people were variations on the locational-transitional theme. There was a theory in his home world that locational-transitional (or chessboard) space was the basic kind of space in the universe and that all others were permutations and variants of it; but he agreed with me that this theory could be suspected of special pleading and that deeper penetration into the universe by the chess-people's space-ships might well bring home a different story. He would not bore me, he added, by describing meaningless variations on locational-transitional space, but felt that I would be more entertained by those spaces whose qualities made striking comparisons with the qualities of my own realm.

There was, for instance, a space that, though continuous, was not symmetrical in all directions but was hung between two great poles like a magnetic field. Motion along the direction of the axis between the poles was as easy as it is for us, but transverse movement was an altogether different phenomenon that required a different type of energy and a different name. This polarisation continued down into every event and structure, which was invariably positioned between two opposing poles of one kind or another. There was stereo space with great cracks of nullity running all through it, chasms of zero-existence which were impossible to cross and had to be gone round. There was space where an entity could travel in a straight line without incident, but where on changing direction he shed similar, though not identical, duplicates of himself which continued to accompany him thereafter. Prior to their rescue by me the Knight and his crew had believed themselves to be in such a space, for they had chanced to catch a glimpse of a woman accompanied by several daughters of various ages who closely resembled her. Also along these lines, there was a space where the image of an object or entity had the same powers and qualities as the original. This space abounded in mirrors and reflecting surfaces, and an entity was liable to project himself in all directions like a volley of arrows.

When you think about it, the necessity to be in only one place at a time is a pretty severe restriction. Many are the spaces where this law has never been heard of, and where an entity may multiply himself simultaneously into disparate situations without prejudice to his psychic integrity, roaming over the world in a number of bodies yet remaining a single individual. Chameleons have caused some puzzlement among biologists because their eyes operate independently of one another; the right eye knoweth not what the left eye is doing but each scans separately for prey or enemies. Does the consciousness of the chameleon give its full attention to both eyes simultaneously? If so, the chameleon is a mental giant which no human being can equal. This feat is a natural function, however, in the space of 'multiple individuality' I have described.

The Knight warned me against a restrictive concept of motion. It was not, he said, an idea of universal validity, but what we understood by motion could be subsumed under a more generalised concept he called 'transformation', a much larger class of phenomena. Thus there were spaces where to go was to come, where to approach was to recede, where to say goodbye was to say hello. In short, my maxim which says that to approach one point is to recede from another is not a universal law but a local case. Inversely, there were types of transformation that no mangling of the English language could succeed in hinting at. Once again the Knight suggested that I waste none of our precious time in trying to understand these inconceivable variations.

He spent some words in describing spaces that were not totally homogeneous. The space with cracks was one of these; another was 'sheaving space' with a quite odd quirk: the space split itself up into branches not all of which had any possible communication or influence with one another, even though they might all communicate with some common branch. Thus both A and B might communicate with C, but it would still be impossible for any message or particle to pass from A to B even via C. The separate branches usually contained innumerable worlds, with bizarre results.

Space can also vary in the quality of time it contains. (The Knight was quite firm in asserting that time is a subsidiary feature of space.) Time is not always irreversible, but in some spaces can be revisited by retracing one's steps. The Knight fascinated me by telling of one space which he called 'a space of forking time' where every incident had not one but several possible outcomes, all equally real. Thus space branches continually in this continuum to develop alternate histories; where this space differs from the stock science-fiction notion, however, is that *every past event is recoverable*, and hence *all possible histories communicate*. By retracing his steps in a certain manner a man (or entity) can go back to the crucial moment that determined the shape of events and take a different path. When I reflected on how the fate and happiness of men is tyrannised over in our space by the singleness of time and the cruel dice-throwing of fleeting happenstance, this realm appeared to me to be a perfect abode of happiness.

It will be obvious that causality is governed by the type of space in which it takes place. The Knight mentioned that our space contains the principle of 'single-instance causality', which is also the principle obtaining in most space-times, and means that prolonged and complex processes can come to completion only with difficulty. The reason is thus: if A causes B, and B causes C, it still does not follow that A will lead to C because in the interim B might be modified by interceding influences and fail to cause C. There are, claimed the Knight, space-times of extended causality where every process or project reaches completion and no tendency is ever interrupted. As the realising of ambitions is automatic any 'effort to succeed' is quite redundant in this space-time. The struggle and drama of life consists not of trying to actualise intentions but of the struggle to form intentions in the first place.

In this respect the Knight included his only description of a species of locational-transitional space: a space where there was no sequential causality at all, but in which everything happened on a purely statistical basis. Wondering what it could be like on the inside of such a stochastic wonderland, I asked whether there could ever be the slightest possibility of intelligent, conscious entities arising there. To my surprise the Knight averred that it was well stocked with such entities: statistically intelligent, statistically conscious entities.

I have touched but lightly on the role of matter in the space-times I have discussed; it would be needless to tell my intelligent reader that matter and space are inextricably entwined. He will already have guessed that besides the innumerable spaces that form a receptacle for matter, there are also those that are Aristotelian in the sense of complying with that philosopher's erroneous theories: where matter, instead of being atomic, is continuous and identical with the space it occupies, motion being accomplished by a process of compression and attenuation. There is no empty space in these continua, exactly as Aristotle reasons. In at least one such continuum all the matter is dense and solid, so that it consists of a blocked infinity of solid rock or metal (I am not sure which). In this continuum, the Knight admitted, the possibility of conscious intelligence could be discounted. In contrast to such immobility I particularly liked what the Knight called 'folding space' but which I have since named 'origami space' (origami is the Japanese art of paper-folding). Origami space has an inner richness that makes our own space look bland. Objects can be folded so as to develop entirely new qualities. A man (or entity), by folding a piece of paper in the right way, may make of it a chair, a table, an aeroplane, a house, a fruit, a flower, a live animal, another man, a woman, or practically anything. The art of such folding, it need hardly be added, far surpasses anything to be found in our Earthly origami. Mass and size are not constants in this continuum but can be increased (or decreased) by folding, hence a square of paper a foot on the side may end up as an airliner able to carry a hundred people.

After recounting these wonders the Knight paused to allow me to gather my mental breath. As if by way of relaxing he briefly outlined some primitive-sounding space-times that lacked our centreless relativity but were organised around a fixed centre. Remembering that earlier he had referred to our version of stereo space as a particularly rigid and restricted variety, I seized on this latest exposition to remark that at least the world I inhabited had the dignity of being infinite, symmetrical and unconstricted by having a centre. The Knight's amusement was genuine, if gentle. With a dry laugh he instructed me that my mistake was a classic of unsophisticated presumption, and he regretted to have to inform me that my world did not have relativistic symmetry but that *it had a centre*.

Where was this centre? I asked. Once more came the Knight's mocking chuckle. He had neglected to mention so far, he said, that also intimately related to the question of space is the question of *numbers*. Our space might have no identifiable centre in terms of motion and direction, but in its regard to number it was very strongly centred.

At first his meaning escaped me. Number was another way of classifying the innumerable kinds of space in the universe, he explained. There was at least one space for every possible number (a theorem stated that there were more spaces than one for every possible number), and they were arranged in an ascending series, each space having its 'centre of gravity' about a particular number. We are near to the bottom of the scale as our 'centre of gravity' is the number One (there are spaces preferring fractions and at least one preferring Zero). The consequences are immediate and self-evident: singleness is what signifies a complete object in our world; integral unity is all, and the state of there being two of a thing is incidental – a thing comes into its own when it is *one*. We all accept this innately. Every entity and thing is itself by assigning the number One to itself. Higher numbers introduce additional qualities, but do not carry the same weight as *one*.*

In the space next above us in the scale completeness attaches to the number *two*. 'Two-ness' is ideal, and singleness is incomplete in the same way that a fraction or a part is incomplete in our world. I reflected on what a mass migration there would be if communication could be established with that world – for we also have the yearning after *two* in our shadowy, tantalised way. Our lives are full of complementary pairs. The tragedy of lovers is that they are thwarted by the One-ness of the spatial system: each remains alone and solitary, however much they strive and strain to be completely merged as two – for the vain yearning of lovers is not to be made One, which would negate the whole proceeding, but to be, as it were, indistinguishably blended as Two. Should a pair of Eros-struck lovers by some magic or science transpose themselves to this other realm where Two is All, then their bliss would be beyond describing.

More remotely, other worlds model themselves on Three, Four, Five, and so on up the scale of integers to infinity. In addition there is a corresponding

* By way of example, we conceive of Two as 'Two Ones'.

scale of negative integers, as also of worlds modelled on every possible fraction, on irrational numbers, on imaginary numbers, and on groups, sets and series of numbers, such as on all the primes, all the odd integers, all the even integers, and on arithmetic and geometric progressions. Beyond even these abstruse factualities are the ranges of worlds, centred on numbers and number systems not possible or conceivable to us. The only truly symmetrical, non-centred, relativistic space-time, said the Knight, is one giving equal weight to all numbers.

Georg Cantor, wrestling with the enigma of the infinite, discovered a branch of mathematics called transfinite arithmetic, in which he developed a progression of numbers analogous to the positive integers but whose first term was infinity and whose succeeding terms were as qualitatively different from and beyond infinity as are Two, Three, Four, etc., beyond One. In short, he found that there are numbers larger than infinity. As might be expected, the Knight confirmed the reality of this number system and of the transfinite space that goes with it. There is a whole range of transfinite spaces, probably even larger than the range of finite and infinite spaces (since the number of total spaces is both finite, infinite and transfinite). At this point the Knight seemed to think that we were wandering from the type of description from which I might be expected to profit, and proposed to resume, expatiating on those nearer to familiarity. I objected; it was diverting, but less challenging, to be presented with nothing but modifications of an existence I already knew. In a sense I could almost have invented these modifications myself. Would not the Knight consent to offer me, or at least attempt to make me understand, worlds having no common ground with my own – for even the Knight's own locational-transitional space-time, I reminded him, was not hard to describe. I longed to hear something so original as to blow my mind free of all its preconceptions. After some hesitation and muttering as to the perplexities engendered by my request, the Knight agreed to make the effort and favoured me with the following amazing descriptions:*

Suddenly the Knight broke off to warn me that the power drain was now significantly close to tolerable limits and that he would not be able to linger much longer. A brief feeling of panic assailed me. There must be one question that above all others needed to be asked – yes! The choice was obvious, and I did not delay in putting it. Did the chess-people have any single, particular purpose in undertaking their admirable explorations of space?

---

* A second break occurs in the manuscript here. The Narrator pleads that this section was too ephemeral to remember or too abstruse to be outlined in words; The Editor surmises that his invention had run dry – Ed.

The instinct of exploration, said the Knight, is a natural one. There was a central quest, however: to try to determine whether, in the multiplicity of space-times, there is a common universal law or principle, and thereby to discover how existence originates and is maintained.

I cursed myself for not having broached this subject sooner, instead of leaving it until it was almost too late. I had given much thought to this Basic Question myself, I tendered. And, if it was of any interest, I had once come to a tentative conclusion, that there *was* a basic law of existence. It is simply: 'A thing is identical to itself.' This principle explained the operation of cause and effect, I claimed. The universe being a unity, it is also identical to itself, and an effect only *appears* to follow a cause. In actuality they are part of the same thing, opposite sides of the same coin.

Once again the Knight had cause to chide me for my lack of imagination. This axiom certainly held in my own space, he conceded, but I shouldn't suppose because of that that it was a universal law. There were numerous space-times where *things were not equal to themselves.* In fact even in my own space the principle adhered only approximately, because things were in motion and motion involved a marginal blurring of self-identity. My axiom held as an absolute law only in those spaces where motion was impossible.

Unabashed, I offered my second contribution, this one concerning the maintenance of existence. There was a theory, I told him, that used an electronic analogy and likened existence to a television screen and a camera. The camera scanned the image on the screen, and fed it back to the screen's input, so maintaining the image perpetually. Thuswise existence was maintained: if the feedback from the camera to the screen should be interrupted, even for a split second, existence would vanish and could never be reconstituted.

A pre-electronic version of the theory replaces the screen and camera by two mirrors, each reflecting the image of existence into the other. It is my belief that this is the meaning of the ancient alchemical aphorism 'As above, so below' found on the Emerald Table of Hermes Trismegistus, it being imagined that the mirrors are placed one above the other. Other authorities unanimously assert that it refers to the supposed similarity between the macrocosm and the microcosm; but I consider that this, besides being of doubtful veridity, is a crude, pedestrian interpretation unworthy of the thought of the Great Master. The full text of the saying runs:

> That which is above is like to that which is below, and that which is below is like to that which is above, to accomplish the miracles of one thing.

It has to be understood that the mirrors themselves are part of the image, of course, just as the screen and camera are part of the scanning pattern – if it is asked how this could possibly be, I would refer the enquirer to that other

Alchemical symbol, the Worm Ouroboros, who is shown with his tail in his mouth, eating himself.

The Knight appeared to look on this exposition with some approval. Hermes Trismegistus, he said, was certainly a king among men of science. I asked what theories or discoveries the chess-people had on the subject; but, the Knight announced, time had run out and he could delay departure no longer. The few seconds remaining would not suffice to tell what he otherwise might have to say; but, he added, he had not so far revealed that the question of space was also intimately bound up with that of *consciousness*, and that it was towards consciousness that the chess-people were now directing their researches. He mentioned a space where an entity, as it might be a man, was forced to enjoy a double consciousness – not only was he conscious in himself, but he was also conscious at every moment of his appearance to the physical world around him, which was also conscious. The Knight invited me to ponder on what existence would be like in such a state – but his words now came in haste and he bade me goodbye.

Again I begged him to stay, just for a little while. But he turned and looked commandingly around him over the chessboard. The pieces began to move and to execute their flickering dance pattern around the board. The Knight joined them, gyrating around the board like a dance master directing the others. As the invisible ship lifted away the pieces surged round the board in a circular movement as if caught in a vortex; then they were still. The Knight could no longer speak to me in his resinous, friendly voice: he was only a chiselled piece of dead wood.

I came out of my shocked reverie with a start. On the disappearance of the alien influence the pieces had reverted to their original positions, ready to resume the game. There would be no need, I thought blankly, for me to write to my partner for the details.

I pushed myself away from the table. The sweet opium smell still hung on the air. The breeze from the garden was only marginally cooler. The far-off, sun was still in the act of descending to the horizon through an elegant Technicolor sky.

It was hard for me to admit that only a minute or two could have passed, when I was sure that I had been talking and listening for hours. I will never be able to know absolutely, and certainly never be able to prove, that what I say took place really did take place. I can only speak of the compelling veridity of my recollection. But whatever the truth, it has at least brought to my notice that for all our knowledge of the universe, even when we project our giant rockets into space and imagine that at last we are penetrating the basic void that holds all things, we still have not touched or even suspected the immensities and the mysteries that existence contains.

THE BEES OF KNOWLEDGE

It scarcely seems necessary to relate how I first came to be cast on to Handrea, like a man thrown up on a strange shore. To the Bees of Handrea these details, though possibly known to them, are of negligible interest since in their regard I rate as no more than an unremarkable piece of flotsam that chanced to drift into their domain. Let it suffice, then, that I had paused to say a prayer at the shrine of Saint Hysastum, the patron saint of interstellar travellers, when an explosion in the region of the engine-room wrecked the entire liner. The cause of the catastrophe remains a mystery to me. Such accidents are far from common aboard passenger ships, though when they do occur subsequent rescue is an uncertain hope, owing to the great choice of routes open to interstellar navigators and to their habit of changing course in mid-flight to provide additional sightseeing.

My timely devotions saved my life, though reserving me for a weirder fate. Within seconds I was able to gain a lifeboat, which was stationed thoughtfully adjacent to the shrine, and, amid flame and buckling metal, I was ejected into space. After the explosion, picking my way through the scattered debris, I learned that no one but myself had escaped.

The crushing sense of desolation that comes over one at such a moment cannot adequately be described. Nothing brings one so thoroughly face to face with blind, uncaring Nature as this sudden, utter remoteness from one's fellow human beings. Here I was, surrounded by vast light years of space, with probably not another human soul within hundreds of parsecs, totally alone and very nearly helpless.

My feeling of isolation mounted to a state of terror when I discovered that the rescue beacon was not operating. Once again I had recourse to prayer, which calmed me a little and brought me to a more hopeful appraisal of my situation. The lifeboat, I reminded myself, could keep me alive for up to a year if all went well. There would have been little point in activating the beacon immediately in any case. The star liner would not be reported missing for several weeks, and taking into account the delay before a search was organised, and the dozens of possible routes to be surveyed, a sweep within range of the beacon might not occur for months, if at all. During that time its repair seemed a feasible project, or at any rate not a hopeless one.

But it could not be done conveniently in space, and I peered again through the lifeboat's portholes. On one side glimmered a reddish-yellow sun. Close by on the other side hung a big murky globe resembling an overripe fruit – the planet Handrea, to provide a view of which the star liner had been slowing down at the time of the explosion. It had received its name but an hour previously from one of the passengers (the privilege of naming newly sighted worlds being another of the minor perquisites of interstellar travel) and had already been ascertained as being tolerable as regards chemistry, and geology. So, heartened by having at least some course of action to pursue, I turned my small lifeboat towards it.

As I passed through them I made a careful recording of the bands of magnetism and radiation that planets of this type usually possess, noting as I did so that they were uncommonly strong and complicated. I was perturbed to find that the atmosphere was a deep one, descending nearly seven hundred miles. Upon my entering its outer fringes the sky turned from jet black to dark brown and the stars quickly vanished from sight. A hundred miles further down I entered a sphere of electrical storms and was buffeted about by powerful gusts. It had been my intention, had Handrea looked unduly inhospitable, to fly straight out again, but before long it was all I could do to keep on an even keel, not being an expert pilot. Eventually, much relieved after a harrowing passage, I entered the layer of calm air that lies close to the surface and accomplished a landing amid large tufts of a plant which, though maroon in colour, could fairly be described as grass-like.

I peered at the landscape. Vision was limited to about a hundred yards, and within this span I saw only the mild undulations of the ground, the drab coloration of the vegetation, the dull grey air. Instruments told me that the air was dense, but not of the intolerable pressure suggested by the depth of the atmosphere, consisting of light inert gases and about five per cent oxygen. The temperature, at twenty degrees, was comfortable enough to require no special protective clothing.

After a while I put on an oxygen mask – not trusting myself to the outside's natural mix – and equalised pressures before opening the hatch. Taking with me the lifeboat's tool-kit, I stepped outside to remove the beacon's service plate.

Underfoot the maroon grass had a thick-piled springy texture. As I moved the air felt thick, almost like water, and perfect silence prevailed. I tried to close my mind to the fact that I stood on an alien and unknown planet, and concentrated on the task in hand.

I worked thus for perhaps twenty minutes before becoming aware of a low-pitched droning or burring sound, which, almost before I could react to it, swelled in volume until it made the air vibrate all about me. Like the parting of a curtain the opaque atmosphere suddenly disgorged two huge flying shapes. And so I saw them for the first time: the Bees of Handrea.

Describing them offers no particular difficulties, since unlike many alien forms of life they can be compared with a terrestrial species. They are, of course, vast if measured alongside our earthly bees, and the resemblance is in some respects a superficial one. The body, in two segments, is three or four times the size of a man, the abdomen being very large and round so as to make the creature closest in appearance, perhaps, to our bumble bee. As in the terrestrial bee the fur is striped but only slightly so – a relic, I would guess, from some previous evolutionary period the Bees have passed through – the stripes being fuzzy fawn and soft gold, so that the Bees seemed almost to shine in their monotonous environment.

On Earth this great mass could never take to the air at all, but the density of Handrea's atmosphere enables such a creature to be supported by two pairs of surprisingly small wings which vibrate rapidly, giving off the pronounced drone I had first noticed. The Bees move, moreover, with all the speed and agility of their earthly counterparts. Their arrival occasioned me some alarm, naturally, and I attempted to make a hasty retreat into the lifeboat, but I had time to take only a couple of steps before one of the huge creatures had darted to me and lifted me up with its frontward limbs which ended in tangles of hooks and pincers.

The desperation of my initial struggles may be imagined. From acquaintance with earthly insects I had expected instantly to receive some dreadful sting which would paralyse me or kill me outright, and I fought with all my might to free myself from the monster. In the struggle my oxygen mask was torn loose and fell to the ground, so that for the first time, with a cold shock, I drew Handrea's air into my lungs. All my efforts were to no avail; no sting was forthcoming, and the Bee merely modified its powerful grip so as to leave me completely helpless, and I was borne off into the mists, leaving the lifeboat far behind.

The two Bees flew, as near as I could tell, in a straight line, keeping abreast of one another. The narrow patch of landscape in my view at any one time presented no change of aspect, but we travelled through the foggy, impenetrable air at what seemed to me a prodigious speed. Unhindered now by my oxygen mask, the world of Handrea met my senses with a new immediacy. The breath that coursed through my nostrils smelled damp, bearing hints of dank vegetable fragrance. Quite separate from this, I was aware of the much stronger smell of the Bee that carried me – a sharp, oddly sweet smell that could not be ignored.

Reminding myself of insect habits, I was fearful now of a much worse fate than being stung to death. My imagination worked apace: these Bees would hardly have seized me for nothing, I told myself, and in all probability their intention was to use me as a body in which to lay eggs, so that the larvae could feed off my live flesh. In my despair I even contemplated the sin of suicide, wondering how I might kill myself before the worst happened. When I remember these fears now, my present circumstances seem relatively good.

On and on we droned, the increasing distance between myself and the life-boat, and the virtual impossibility of my ever returning to it, causing me no small agony of mind. At least an hour, and possibly several, passed in this fashion before the Bees' destination came looming out of the fog.

At first I took the shape ahead to be an oddly-formed mountain until its artificial nature became apparent. Then it emerged as an uneven, elongated dome whose limits passed entirely out of sight in the dimness: a stupendous beehive. I now know its height to attain several thousand feet, with nearly the same proportions at the base. As we came closer a generalised humming could be heard emanating from the huge edifice. At the same time I saw giant bees flitting hither and thither, coming and going from the great hive.

We approached an entrance set about a hundred feet from ground level and without pause passed through to the interior. I observed a number of Bees stationed just within the opening, some apparently standing guard, others vibrating their wings rapidly, presumably to ventilate the hive as bees do on Earth. Indeed, their work set up such a wind that the clothes were nearly torn from my back as my captors alighted on the floor of the vestibule. From this chamber several passages radiated – that, at least, was my first impression. As my captors set off down one of these. I realised that in fact the openings all connected up with one another; the internal structure of the hive was largely an open one, the space of any level being divided by the pillars which supported the next.

I will not dwell on how fully I appreciated the horror of my apparent situation as I was dragged into this den. Bees swarmed everywhere and their pungent-sweet smell was overpowering. To think that I, a human being bearing a spark of the divinity, was reduced to the role of some smaller insect for these beasts, as if I were a caterpillar or a grub, affected me almost as strongly as the thought of the physical horror which I had no doubt was to come. Deeper and deeper I was carried into the hive, descending and ascending I did not know how many levels. It was like a vast city, filled with the rustling, buzzing and chittering of its inhabitants. Once my captors (they remained together) were accosted by a group of their fellows and performed a kind of waggling dance, at the same time emitting loud noises which sounded like the wailing of a whole team of buzz-saws. Finally our journey came to an end: the two Bees halted in a bowl-shaped depression some tens of feet across, and the hold on my aching body was at last released.

I tumbled, rolled over, and steeled myself to take my first good look at the Bee's head: the faceted eyes glinting with myriad colours, the rolled proboscis, the tufted cheeks and the swollen cranium, all of which are now so familiar to me. Unable to bear the suspense any longer I squeezed my eyes shut and tried not to exist. Now it would come – the deep-thrusting sting, mortal as any sword, or the cruel insertion of the ovipositor.

The muscular limbs turned me over and over, bristly fur scratching my skin. When, after some time, nothing else transpired I opened my eyes a little. The two Bees were huddled over me, holding me almost in a double embrace, and fondling me with their forelegs. Their wings trembled; their droning buzz-saw voices, with no articulation that I could discern, rose and fell in harmony. The movements of the forelegs became light and caressing, so that I wondered what kind of insect ritual I was being subjected to. Then, to my surprise, the manipulatory claws began clumsily to strip me of my clothing. Shortly I lay naked, while my garments were lifted one by one, inspected and tossed aside.

The Bees' attention returned to my naked body, probing it with a feather-like touch, examining orifices, holding me upside down or in whatever fashion was convenient, as though I were an inanimate object. I experienced a moment of supreme terror when a stiff digit entered my anus and slid up my rectum. The organ withdrew in a second or two, but I was left in little uncertainty of mind as to what had taken place.

At length the Bees seemed to have finished. One wandered off, while the other lifted me up and took to the air again. I observed that we were in a spacious vault, allowing the Bees ample room for flight but somewhat dimly lit (unlike much of the hive I had passed through). We swooped low to pass under a barrier, swam up a sort of gully, and emerged in yet another vault even larger, whose far side was not clearly visible but which contained great indistinct piles. On one of these the Bee unceremoniously dropped me, and I sprawled and slithered down a slope composed of loose objects, like a rubbish heap.

After the Bee had flown away, my great concern was with the eggs I felt sure it had deposited in my rectum. I felt up with my finger as far as I could, but encountered nothing. I decided it was imperative to sweep out the passage straight away. After a great deal of frantic straining I managed to pass an amount of faecal matter and examined it anxiously for sign of the eggs. There was none, and eventually I concluded with immense relief that the Bee's intrusion had been exploratory, nothing more.

Finding myself unexpectedly alive and unharmed, I was able to take a more leisurely interest in my surroundings. The first question to pique my curiosity was how the interior of the hive came to be lighted, when it should have been in complete darkness. Some parts of it, in fact, were bathed in a fairly bright haze. Peering at the nearby wall of the vault, I saw that the material out of which the hive was constructed was itself fluorescent, thus explaining the mystery. I pondered a little further on the nature of this material. Being phosphorescent it was very likely organic in origin, I reflected. Possibly the Bees used their own excrement as a building material, as termites do on Earth.

Perhaps this luminosity was an accidental by-product and extraneous to the Bees' needs. But if it formed part of their economy then it was a wonderful example of the ingenuity of Nature, which had evolved phosphorescent excrement for such a purpose.

I pulled myself upright on the unsteady pile where I was precariously perched and took a closer survey of my immediate environs. I stood on a jumble of objects of various shapes and sizes, all indistinct in the gloom. Bending, I picked one up.

The thing was made of a substance indistinguishable from food. And it was a carving of some kind of animal, perhaps another giant insect, with a peculiar flowering snout. I was not sure whether the representation was meant to be a naturalistic one or whether it was fanciful; what was in no doubt was that it was the product of art.

I dropped it and selected another object. This turned out to be something whose purpose I could not decipher: a black rod about three feet in length with a hemispherical bowl attached to one end. But again, I judged it to be artificial.

In a state of fresh excitement I extended my explorations. The heap proved to be varied in its composition; most of it consisted of decayed vegetable matter. But buried in it, strewn on top of it, piled here and there, was a treasure house of alien artifacts too diverse to describe. Many of them were rotted, broken and crushed, but others seemed intact and even new.

What was the reason for this rubbish heap? Who had manufactured the artifacts? Not the Bees – somehow that did not strike me as a likely proposition, and the impression was confirmed when I found what I could only call, from its shape and size, a drinking cup.

Bees would not use drinking cups.

Somewhere on this planet, then, was an intelligent race. While I was mulling this over there came a loud droning noise and another Bee entered the vault, dropped an article on the heap and departed. I scrambled towards the discarded object and discovered it to be a mysterious instrument consisting of hinged and inter-locking boxes.

I recalled the manner in which I had been snatched from the ground while attempting to repair my rescue beacon, and all seemed to become clear to me. The Bees had a magpie instinct: they were collectors of any object they came across that attracted their attention. I, just like anything else, had been added to their mindless hoard.

For some time that remained the total of my understanding of the Bees of Handrea.

At length I clambered down from the pile and began to explore beyond the vault. By now hunger was beginning to affect me, and while I still could not speculate as to what my future might be, I wondered as to the possibility of obtaining food.

My needs were answered much sooner than I had expected. Half an hour of probing (trying always to keep track of my movements) brought me to a wall which exuded a heavy, sweet aroma. This wall was made of a golden bread-like substance which crumbled and broke easily in the hand to yield chunks from which seeped a light yellow syrup. It had every appearance of being edible, and though afraid of poisoning myself I sampled a morsel, recalling that though the protein structure of alien life may differ from our own, that protein is everywhere constructed out of the same small group of amino acids, into which the digestive system decomposes it. I was soon reassured: the bread was delicious, sweet without being nauseous, and of a texture like honey-cake. As a food it proved completely satisfying. I ate a quantity of it, reasoning as I did so that in all probability this was a corner of the Bees' food store, or at any rate of one of a number of such stores.

My meal was interrupted by a rustling sound. I was alarmed to see the approach of an insect-like creature, smaller than the Bees and indeed somewhat smaller than myself, but nevertheless of horrifying appearance. I was put in mind of a fly – not the common housefly, but something closer to a mosquito, with small folded wings and a spike-like proboscis. I ran for my life, but on rounding a corner of the passageway, and hearing no sound of pursuit, I stopped and cautiously peeped back. The Fly had inserted its proboscis into the honey-bread and was presumably sucking out the liqueur.

I decided to risk no further confrontation but made my way back to the vault where lay the junkheaps. There I discovered some pools of brackish water and further refreshed myself. Then I set about finding a weapon in case I should need to defend myself against monsters such as I had just witnessed – or, for that matter, against the Bees, though I fervently hoped I should not be called upon to fight such prodigious creatures. After some searching I found a long metal pole with a pointed end which would serve tolerably well as a spear.

The vault seemed empty, lonely, silent and echoing. From afar came the continual murmur of the business of the hive, like the ceaseless activity of a city, but it barely broke the silence. Already I had begun to think of the place as a refuge, and eventually I found a spot for myself where, wearied and strained by my experiences, I settled down to sleep.

On waking I drank more water and made the short trip to obtain more honey-bread. Then, naked though I was, and armed with my spear, I set out to explore the hive in earnest.

Thus began a fairly long period in which I acquainted myself with the life of the great bee-city, though in what I now know to be a superficial way.

Slowly and tentatively I explored the passages and galleries, making sure all the time that I could find my way back to the familiar territory of the junkheaps where I was at least assured of water and food, and to which I periodically returned to rest. Always I made my way upwards, searching for the entrance by which I had been brought into the hive.

The Bees, who busied themselves everywhere, consistently ignored me. I discovered that the hive was host to numerous other parasites like myself, species of insects and giant worms who had made their home here and were apparently tolerated, if they were noticed at all. Usually (but not invariably) they were smaller than the Bees, and either stole honey-bread or stalked one another for food. Thus for any but the Bees themselves (who of course were never attacked) the hive was a jungle in which every ecological niche was filled.

The dangers to myself were considerable, and I soon found that I had been lucky in my choice of weapons, for the spear enabled me to keep most predators at bay. Nevertheless my early experiences were horrifying. On my first reconnoitre I was attacked three times: twice by grub-like beasts with hideous scissor-type jaws, and once by something resembling a giant mite whose habit it is to drop a net on passers-by from above. I could not free myself from this trap for some time, during which I was obliged to fight for my life while still enmeshed, wielding the spear through the holes and finally killing my adversary.

I quickly learned which species were harmless and which to beware of. I learned to recognise the kind of corners and approaches the predators were apt to lurk in, and so these bouts of deadly combat became much less frequent.

My third sortie brought me at last to the entrance. I hesitated on the approach to the vestibule, seeing ahead of me the humped shapes of the guards, and bracing myself against the wind set up by the whirring wings of the ventilator Bees. So powerful was this dense current that when I finally went forward I was obliged to edge myself across the floor with the help of my spear. I stopped close to the broad slot-like opening and looked out into the free air of Handrea.

A fog-like cold smote my skin, in contrast to the warmth of the hive. I could see only thick misty air which eddied and swirled as more Bees came to alight inside the entrance. The ground was quite out of sight.

I believe the guards would not have prevented me from leaving the hive. I could have scrambled down its rough surface to the ground. But where to then? I had no means of achieving the goal which had been uppermost in my mind: that of returning to the lifeboat and completing the repair of the beacon. Not only had I no idea of which direction to take, but I had no way of holding to that direction if I found it. Once away from the hive I would be unlikely to locate it again, and would die of hunger or thirst or else fall victim to larger predators that I had not yet seen.

But could I accept the corollary: that I must live out my remaining years in the hive with the status of a parasitic worm? A curiously forlorn, deserted feeling came over me: I felt that I had been treated badly during the explosion on the passenger liner; my companions had all died and been spared any further problems, but I had been excluded from the common fate and left alone, abandoned by death.

This odd and sinful feeling lasted but a minute or two. With heavy heart I made my way back down below, wondering if I could pluck up the courage for the near-suicide attempt to retrace the course of the Bees who had brought me here. When I arrived at the junkheaps an extraordinary sight met my eyes. There, flung at a lurching angle atop the nearest pile, was the lifeboat!

I scrambled up the heap towards it with a cry of joy. On reaching the small spacecraft, however, I was in for a crushing disappointment. It had been gutted. Everything had been stripped from it, inside and out, leaving only an empty shell.

Strewn over a fairly wide area round about was all the equipment with which the lifeboat had been stocked. To my astonishment every item had been torn to pieces: the Bees seemed to exhibit a destructive animal curiosity over everything they touched. I found the beacon after searching for some minutes. Like everything else it was completely wrecked, practically disintegrated component by component. Any kind of repair was absolutely out of the question, and after staring at the remains for some while in a state of shock, I sat down and buried my face in my hands, sobbing to think what life was to mean to me from now on.

For some time afterwards wild schemes were apt to enter my head. It occurred to me that perhaps I was not necessarily doomed to remain indefinitely in the hive. Judging by the contents of the junkheaps intelligence existed somewhere on the planet, and the Bees visited the scene of that intelligence. I entertained the notion of clinging to a Bee's back, possibly attaching myself there by means of a harness, and flying with it to, where life might be more agreeable, even though I still would not be among my own kind. It was even possible, I conjectured (remembering that some of the artifacts I had seen denoted a fairly advanced technology) that once learning of my plight the creatures I met would be kind enough to set up a beacon of their own to signal the rescue ship, if I could explain its mode of operation clearly enough.

These plans served chiefly to ward off my despair, for common sense told me how unlikely they were to succeed. My faith, also came under great strain at this time, but I am glad to say I retained it, though with some difficulty at first, and prayer was, as ever, my solace.

But as the days succeeded one another my mood turned to one of apathy, although I tried to rouse myself to action and to remind myself that the time remaining before a search expedition arrived within signalling distance was not unlimited. Thinking that I should fashion a harness with which to carry out my project of riding on a Bee, I began to sort through the junkheaps. The detritus of alien industry was fascinating to browse through. I presumed at first that the artifacts were all the product of the same civilisation, but later I realised that I had no verification of this. Indeed I could construe no picture of a single culture out of the objects I perused; rather they suggested a number of different, quite unconnected civilisations, or even species.

I was also struck by the number of artifacts which were clearly not tools or ornaments and whose use could not easily be discerned. At length I discovered some of the more curiously shaped of them to bear close-packed markings, and I surmised that these and others, including some I believed to be electronic in operation, were books or records of some kind, though I could not explain why they made up such a large percentage of the junkheaps.

My desultory efforts to escape the hive were all brought to an end when an extraordinary event occurred. I had gone on another exploratory foray with the intention of making some rough assessment of Bee anatomy when the usual bumbling activity of the hive turned to a state of agitation. I heard sounds of rending and general destruction, and on investigating perceived that numbers of the Bees were engaged in tearing down parts of the hive. The reason for this soon became apparent: they were clearing a passage for a huge object, too large to enter the hive by any of its entrances or to negotiate its interior spaces.

The object proved to be a ship, clearly built to ride on water. Of a wood-like material, it had a sweeping profile at least a hundred and fifty feet long, with an elegant pattern of raised decks at intervals, stepped slightly higher forward and aft. In its general lines the closest resemblance would be, I suppose, to a Greek galley, a resemblance heightened by the carving which adorned the fore and aft railings and the protruding wales which swept from stem to stern. The brute force by which the Bees moved this ship was a sight to behold. They must have flown it here an unknown distance by the concerted power of their wings alone – a feat which even in Handrea's thickened atmosphere was astonishing – and now they nudged, heaved and strained at it in their hundreds, wings buzzing in a deafening clamour (for it appeared to be their wings they mostly used to gain traction). The ship lurched forward foot by foot, grinding and crushing everything in its path, shouldering aside masses of building material where the cleared pathway was not wide enough, and causing yet more to come crashing down behind it. Where it had passed Bees set to work immediately to repair the damage, a task which I knew they could accomplish with unbelievable rapidity.

Steadily the ship was being edged into the heart of the hive. I crept forward, dodged past Bee bodies, and found myself able to clamber up the side of the vessel. Briefly I managed to stand on the deck, which, I was interested to see, was inlaid with silvery designs. I could see no sign of any crew. A moment later I heard an impatient buzz behind me and a bristly limb knocked me over the side. I fell to the ground, winded and badly bruised.

Slowly the ship jerked from view amid clouds of dust and a rain of rubble, swaying cumbersomely. Limping, I followed, still curious and wondering how the Bees were regarded by the intelligent race or races from whom they filched so many valuable artifacts.

It occurred to me that for all my wanderings I had remained in the peripheral region of the hive, my mind obsessed by the idea of escape. Vaguely I had imagined the hive to present the same aspect wherever one stood in it, but venturing deeper into the interior in pursuit of the ship I saw my mistake. The light strengthened to become a golden ambience in which the golden fur of the Bees shone. The architecture of the hive also changed. The monotonous tiered floors gave way to a more complex structure in which there were spiral ramps, great halls, and linked chambers of various shapes, sometimes comprising whole banks of huge polyhedra of perfect geometrical regularity, so that the hive came to resemble more and more the 'golden palace' beloved of the more sentimental naturalists when writing of earthly bees. And the sharp-sweet odour of these Bees, to which I thought I had become accustomed, became so strong that I was almost stifled.

All these wonders, like everything else about the Bees, I understood up to this moment to be the product of instinct. I had almost caught up with the lurching ship when I saw something which gave me pause for thought.

A number of artifacts had apparently fallen from the ship in the course of its progress and lay about in the rubble. One Bee lingered and was playing with a device made of a shiny brown material, in shape somewhere between a sphere and a cube and numbering among its features several protuberances and a circular plate of dull silver. The Bee touched a protuberance with a foreleg, and the plate came abruptly to life.

I edged closer to spy on what was taking place. The plate showed a full-colour motion picture that at first was of no recognisable object or scene. After some moments I realised that it was displaying a series of geometrical figures arranged in a logical series. A mathematics lesson!

To my bemusement the huge insect's gaze seemed intent on the picture plate. Shortly it again touched the protuberance, which was a control of the sliding sort, and the picture changed to a text in some kind of writing or ideograms, illustrated by enigmatic symbols. Again the Bee followed the lesson with every appearance of understanding it, but even when this was succeeded by the Bee's manipulating various knobs in seemingly skilful fashion, eliciting information at will, I still could not grasp what the evidence of my eyes suggested.

The Bee turned to another pastime. It turned the device over and in a few moments had removed the outer casing. A mass of close-packed parts was revealed, which the Bee took to pieces with surprisingly delicate pincers. I thought I was seeing the usual destructiveness I already had cause to complain of on the part of these insects, but was astonished by what followed. With the machine in fragments, the Bee suddenly set to work to put it all together again. In a minute or two it was again functioning perfectly.

Along came a second Bee. A buzz-saw exchange took place between them. Wings trembled. The first Bee again stripped down the machine. Together they played with the components, assembling and disassembling them several times over, their droning voices rising and falling, until finally they tired of the game and the pieces were flung carelessly to the ground.

There could be no doubt of it. The Bees were intelligent! And they understood technology!

Saint Hysastum, I thought, you have answered my prayers!

How foolish I had been to give practically no thought to this possibility! How ridiculous to plan journeys across Handrea when the answer lay right here under my nose!

But why had the Bees behaved towards me like brute beasts? I recalled that I had been outside the lifeboat when they arrived. Possibly I had been taken for a denizen of their own planet. They had mistaken my nature, just as I had mistaken theirs.

But it was imperative that I enlighten them without delay. I dashed forward, right under the gaze of those huge mosaic eyes, and began scratching diagrams in the dust with my spear. A circle, a triangle, a square, a pentagon – surely a sentient creature familiar with mathematics (as my recent observations showed the Bee to be) would recognise these as signs of intelligence on my part? The Bee did not seem to notice and made to move off, but I skipped forward again, placing myself impetuously in its path, and again began my eager scribbling. I made three dots, then another three, followed by six dots – a clear demonstration that I could count! For good measure I scribbled out the diagram that accompanies Pythagoras's theorem, even though it is perhaps too elaborate for a first contact between species. The Bee seemed nonplussed for a moment. But then it brushed me aside and passed on, followed by its companion.

My frantic efforts as I sought to make contact with the Bees during the next hour or two approached the level of hysteria. All was to no avail. I remained a nonentity as far as they were concerned: I spoke to them, gesticulated, drew, showed them my spear and play-acted its use, but was simply ignored. From their conduct, which to all appearances exemplified insect mindlessness, it was hard to believe that they really possessed intelligence.

At last, disheartened and perplexed, I returned to my quiet refuge in the vault of the junkheaps. I was not completely alone there: the Fly, the mosquito-like creature I had first encountered at the honey-bread bank, was pottering about among the rubbish. I often met this creature on my trips to the honey-bread, and occasionally it, ventured into the vault and roamed aimlessly among the heaps of artifacts. Never having received any threat from it, I had come to accept its presence.

Sighing and despairing, I fell at length into a light sleep. And as I slept I dreamed.

We came between a defile in the hills and ahead of us, with mist rising and falling about it like steam, lay the hive. Bees came hither and thither in ceaseless streams. Otwun, my Handreatic companion, a member of one of the mammalian species of the planet, laid a hand on my shoulder.

'There it is,' he said. 'The hive of the Bees of Knowledge, where is made the Honey of Experience.'

I glanced into his opal eyes. From the cast of his face I knew he was feeling a certain kind of emotion. 'You seem afraid of these creatures,' I remarked. 'Are they dangerous?'

'They are voracious and implacable,' he answered. 'They know everything old and discover everything new. They range over the whole world in search of knowledge, which is their food, taking it wherever they find it. Yet no man can communicate with them.'

'An aloof intelligence then? No pacts or alliances are made with the Bees? No wars or quarrels?'

'Such is out of the question. The Bees are not beings such as the warm-blooded races. They belong in the class of creeping, crawling and flying things. Come, we must pass by the hive if we are to be about our business.'

We went forward, the fine rain laying a mantle about our shoulders and casting the hive in a lush setting. We skirted the hive to the east, but suddenly a huge Bee loomed out of the mist and hovered before us, giving off a loud buzzing sound that wavered up and down the scale. Although Otwun had told me it was impossible to communicate with the Bees the buzzing penetrated my brain like bright light through glass and seemed somehow to bypass the speech centre to impact information directly to my consciousness. A terrifying flood of knowledge of the most dazzling and intellectual kind overwhelmed me and caused me almost to faint ...

I awoke with the dream vivid in my mind. It was the kind of dream that leaves behind it a mingling of hopeful emotions, seeming to convey a message more real than waking reality itself. I strove to recover the tacit details of the dream – what, for instance, was the important business on which I and

Otwun were engaged? But these were gone, as they often are in dreams, and I was left with only the central theme: the nature of the Bees of Handrea. Of this I had received a direct and compelling impression, much more comprehensive than was implied by Otwun's few remarks.

Every sentient creature's intelligence is modified by its ancestral nature. Bees are honey gatherers. Hence when intellectual curiosity developed in the Bees of Handrea it took just this form. The Bees liked to forage into their world seeking to satisfy their avid thirst for knowledge and to bring back their findings into the hive. The physical objects they brought back were of cursory interest only: their main diet was of intellectual ideas and observations, which they were adept at stealing from surrounding civilisations.

This interpretation of the Bees made such an impression on me that, irrationally perhaps, I accepted it as literally true. I believed I had been vouchsafed a minor vision by Saint Hysastum to help me. Then I recalled a passage by the philosopher Nietzsche who lived some centuries ago. Although a heathen in his outlook Nietzsche had many insights. Here he depicted man's mind as a beehive. We are honey gatherers, bringing in little loads of knowledge and ideas – exactly like the Bees of Handrea.

Nietzsche was also the inventor of the doctrine of eternal recurrence, which posits that since the universe is infinite and eternal everything in it, including the Earth and all its inhabitants, must somewhere, sometime, be repeated. If one follows this argument further then it means that every product of man's imagination must somewhere be a reality – and here was Nietzsche's mental beehive, not as the analogy he had conceived, but as a literal reality! What a strange confirmation of Nietzsche's beliefs!

There was a slurping sound. The Fly was sucking up water from one of the tepid pools.

Elsewhere on Handrea, the dream had reminded me, were other races, less alien than the Bees and more amenable to contact. Should I perhaps stock up with honey-bread and strike out on foot in the hope of finding them? But no – the message of the dream clearly indicated that it was with the Bees that my salvation lay. It would be wrong to reject Saint Hysastum's advice.

Accordingly I turned my mind again to the problem of making my nature and my requirements known. To advertise myself as a calculating, tool-making creature seemed to be the best approach. I conceived a plan, and rummaging through the junk and scrap I gathered together the material I needed and set to work.

In an hour or two I had made my Arithmetical Demonstrator. It consisted of a circular board around whose circumference I had marked, with a soft chalk-like substance I found, the numbers One to Twenty-Five in dot notation, so that any sighted intelligent creature anywhere in creation could have recognized them. Pinned to the centre of the board were two pointers each of a different shape, so that the whole affair looked much like a clock.

The Demonstrator was simple to operate. With the first hand I would point to two numbers successively, and then point to their sum with the second hand. Once I had caught the attention of the Bees in this way I would write the addition sign on the board, then write the multiplication sign and perform a few simple multiplications. In the same manner I would also be able to demonstrate subtraction and division and leave the Bees in no doubt as to my rationality.

Sitting halfway up the junkheap, I practised with the completed board for a short while. Suddenly the sound of dislodged rubbish close behind me made me jump. Turning, I saw that the Fly had descended furtively on me from the top of the heap and its head was craned forward in what I took to be a menacing manner.

In my alarm I half-rolled, half-scrambled down the heap, forgetting all about the demonstration board and trying to think where I had left my spear. The Fly made no atempt to follow me, however. When I next saw it, about ten minutes later, it had climbed down the far side of the heap and was squatting on the ground as if preoccupied. To my exasperation I saw that it was in possession of my Arithmetical Demonstrator.

Having found my spear I decided to use the Fly's own tactic against it to recover the board. Carefully, making as little noise as possible, I skirted round the heap and climbed up it on all fours so as to bring myself above and behind the Fly. Then I began a stealthy descent, reasoning that a noisy attack at close quarters would be enough to scare the insect into abandoning the board just as I had done.

Less deftly than the Fly I climbed to within a few feet of it. Its hearing did not seem particularly acute: it took no notice of my less than silent approach. But before I launched an onslaught I noticed something purposeful about the movement of its foreleg and stayed my hand.

The Fly was playing with the Demonstrator, displaying computations on it exactly as I had intended.

On each occasion it moved the first pointer twice and the second pointer once.

Five and eight equals Thirteen. Addition.

Four and Six equals Twenty-Four. Multiplication.

The fourth or fifth manipulation I observed made me think at first that these results were coincidental. Two and Three equals Eight. Incorrect.

Then it struck me. Two to the *power* Three equals Eight!

My amazement, not to say bewilderment, was so great that the spear dropped from my hand. I could not doubt but that the Fly, too, possessed intellectual power.

Here was my introduction to the Bees!

But why was the Fly, if it belonged to an intelligent species living the life of a scavenger? Was it perhaps trapped in the hive, as I was? Or was *every* insect species on Handrea intelligent, as a matter of course?

I slithered to the ground and stood near the Fly, forcing myself to disregard its powerful stench. It moved back but a few feet when I reached out my hand to pick up the demonstration board and regarded me intently as I spelled out the initial steps of our dialogue.

So began an incredible period of learning and interchange between my friend the Fly and myself. To be honest, the learning was mostly on his part, for I could never have absorbed information as he did.

The Fly's memory was as rapid and unfaltering as a computer's. Everything I showed him he knew instantly. First I introduced him to the Arabic decimal notation and then, though he seemed content to rush into an orgy of abstruse calculations I induced him to learn alphabetical writing. He mastered words and concepts with machine-like ease, and in the space of a few weeks we were able to converse on almost any subject, using an alphabetical version I made of the demonstration board.

My new friend's curiosity was prodigious. He asked me where I came from, and what was the size and distance of my home planet. He then asked how the spaceship that had brought me here had been propelled, and I explained it to him as best as I was able. I also managed to elicit from him one or two scraps of information about Handrea, though his answers were vague.

The Fly's chief obsession, however, lay in the mathematics of numbers. In this he was a wizard, possessing the type of brain that the human race produces perhaps once in a couple of centuries. I was never able to understand a fraction of what the Fly knew about numbers. It would have taken a Fermat or a Poincaré to keep up with him.

There was much wonderment in the thought of what strange vessels God chooses to imbue with his divine spark. I had little enthusiasm, however, for exploring the more recondite properties of Fibonacci numbers, prime numbers and the like, and as soon as was practicable I broached the subject that was the aim of the entire operation as far as I was concerned: would the Fly help me to establish relations with the Bees, so that I might persuade them to construct a rescue beacon for me?

While I posed this question on the alphabet board the Fly was hunched over the much improved number-board. Although I was sure he read my request as I presented it to him he gave no sign of understanding it and continued playing with his own board.

Annoyed, I snatched the number-board away from him and repeated my demand. The Fly squatted there, unmoving. As I was coming near the end of my letter-pointing he casually shuffled to the number-board again and continued his rapid calculations, which I believed concerned number curios of a high order but which I was in no position to follow without textual explanations.

I asked:

'Why will you not answer me?'

And was ignored.

I made increasingly desperate attempts at a closer accord and similarly was rebuffed, while the Fly continued his mathematical orgy in what looked increasingly like a frantic ecstasy. It suddenly occurred to me that up until my request for help none of our exchanges had been in the nature of true conversation but had consisted purely of an exchange of dry knowledge. Otherwise the Fly was behaving like someone who had not quite realised I existed – indeed, except for his obvious intelligence, he behaved like an idiot. Or a witless animal.

My failure to create a true relationship with the Fly was extremely disappointing. It taught me yet again how different was the intelligence of the Handreatic insects from my own. I concluded, after taking to the board for further attempts at a more personal contact, that I had been mistaken in thinking that the Fly was speaking to me when using the boards. Except for his initial enquiries into my origins he had been talking to himself, using the boards as a new toy or tool of thought.

So depressing was this reversal of my hopes that I felt unutterably weary. I reflected that I had wasted several weeks on what had proved to be a blind alley, and that if the Fly had rejected me as a fellow sentient being then so, probably, would the Bees. I dragged myself away from the busy insect, and flung myself down to sleep.

Otwun caught my arm and dragged me past the hovering Bee, whereupon normal perception returned to me. The Bee flew away and left us standing in the rain-sodden grass.

'What – what happened?' I asked dully.

'By accident you touched the mind of the Bee with your mind. It happens sometimes. Come, we must make haste if we are to arrive in time to take part in the assault against Totcune. Our Kessene allies will not wait indefinitely.'

I looked down at the arm he held. Unlike his arm, which was pale green, mine was a dark brown. Understanding for the first time that I also was a Handreatic I looked down at the whole of myself. My race was different from Otwun's. I was smaller, squat, like a goblin beside his lankness.

'Come.'

He noticed me gazing at the hive. 'Men have sometimes entered the hive to taste the Bees' honey,' he said. 'None have come out again, to my knowledge.'

'It would be a great adventure.'

'Only for a fool who no longer wishes to live.'

'Perhaps. Give my greetings to the Kessene.'

I moved away from him, walking slowly towards the hive.

I had slept but a few minutes, and on waking found my mind buzzing with new energy.

The dream. I was sure the dream was telling me what to do. I had taken the Bees too much for granted, not pondering enough as to their true nature. And yet all I had to do was to think about terrestrial bees.

The gathering of nectar was not the end of the bees' food-making process. That nectar was taken into the hive and made into honey. The same must be true, I reasoned, of the Bees of Handrea and their gathering of knowledge. That knowledge was further refined in the depths of the hive. But what was the honey that resulted from this refining?

Men have sometimes entered the hive to taste the Bees' honey.

The Bees of knowledge; the honey of experience. The phrase came into my mind, I did not know from where.

Of course! The answer came to me in a flash. It explained everything – why the Bees ignored me, why they pulled artifacts to pieces and abandoned them, apparently fashioning nothing similar themselves.

Social insects, as individuals, are not complete. They live only to serve the hive, or colony. Usually they are biologically specialised to perform specific functions and are oblivious of any other. Workers do not know sex. Drones do not know anything else.

The individual Bees I had encountered were not, by themselves, intelligent. What *was* intelligent was the *Hive Mind*, the collectivity of all the Bees, existing as some sort of separate entity. This Mind sent out its golden insects to bring back items of interest from the surrounding world. The Bees collected ideas and observations which were then mulled over by the mind to provide itself with experience. Because the Hive Mind itself had no direct perception; everything had to come through the Bees.

Experience was the honey that was made from this dry, arid knowledge. It was the Hive Mind's food.

And it was the Hive Mind, not the individual Bees, that would understand my needs!

Could it have been the Hive Mind and not Saint Hysastum, I wondered, that had been calling to me through my dreams? At any rate my course of action seemed clear. I must descend deep into the hive in search of the Mind, hoping that I could contact it somehow.

The Fly was still fiddling with the number board when, for the last time, I left the dim vault of the junkheaps. How close I was to the truth – and yet how far! Armed as usual with my spear I set off, heading for the very centre of the hive where I imagined the Mind to manifest itself.

The damage caused by dragging the alien ship into the interior had all been repaired. The ceaselessly busy and largely inconsequential-looking activity of the giant insects went on all around me. The Bees rushed to and fro, buzz-saw voices rising and falling and wings trembling on meeting, or performed their odd waggling dance before one another. Except for their size and some physical differences it could have been any beehive on Earth.

I journeyed through the golden chambers I have already described. Beyond these lay a labyrinth of worm-like tunnels in which were interspersed empty egg-shaped chambers or nests. I discovered this to appertain to the hive's reproductive arrangements, for eventually I entered a part of the labyrinth that was not empty. Here larvae crawled about the chambers, tended by worker Bees. Then I suddenly broke through the labyrinth and was confronted by an enormous honeycombed wall extending far overhead. Each cell of this honeycomb evidently contained an egg, for newly-hatched larvae were emerging here and there and crawling down the surface.

Somewhere, conceivably, was a huge bloated queen, mother to the whole hive. Could this queen constitute the intelligence I sought? I rejected the idea. As among earthly insects, she would be totally overburdened with her egg-laying role and unfit for anything else.

A longitudinal slit, about eight feet in height, separated the honeycomb from the ground. Since my destination lay in this direction I passed through it and walked, in semidarkness for a time, with the bulk of the honeycomb pressing down above me.

Then the space seemed to open up abruptly and at the same time I was in the midst of a golden haze which intensified with each step I took, so that the limits of the place I was in were indistinct. Vague shapes loomed at me as if in a dream. Among them was the alien ship I had seen carried into the hive, sliding past me as if into a mist.

My foot caught against something. The floor was littered with objects of all kinds so as to resemble the floor of the vault of the junkheaps, except that here they were bathed in the golden ambience covering everything. I went on, picking my way among them. Presently I heard a familiar buzzing sound. Ahead of me were a number of Bees that appeared to be in an ecstatic trance. Their legs were rigid, their wings were open and vibrating tremulously, their antennae quivered, while the droning they gave off had an almost hypnotic effect.

During the course of my journey I had gradually become aware of an oppressive feeling in my head and an aching sensation at the bridge of my nose. These feelings became unbearably strong in the golden haze. I looked at the gathered Bees and understood that this was the place where their honey was processed, or perhaps where it was stored. With that thought the aching in my head became like a migraine and then suddenly vanished. Something pushed its way into my brain.

I tasted the Bees' honey. I experienced as the Bees experience.

The dream had been a precursor. But it could not have prepared me for such total immersion. What is experience? It comes through the senses, is processed by the mind and presented to the consciousness. The Bees' honey bypasses all these, except perhaps the last. It is raw experience, predigested, intensified, blotting out everything else.

This honey has an actual physical basis: magnetism. Handrea's magnetic field, as I have mentioned earlier, is unusually strong and intricate. The Bees have incorporated this magnetic intricacy into their evolution. By means of it they are able to perform a kind of telepathy on the creatures they borrow their knowledge from, using magnetic currents of great delicacy to read the memory banks of living minds. By tuning in to Handrea's magnetic field they know a great deal about what is taking place across the planet, and by the same means they can extend their knowledge into space within the limits of the field. Thus they knew of the accident aboard the passenger liner, and perhaps had learned much of mankind, before I ever set foot on Handrea.

Sometimes magnetic strains from this golden store sweep through the hive in wayward currents. Twice these currents had impinged on my mind to create dreams, giving me the information that had led me into this trap.

I do not know how long my first trance lasted. When it ended I found myself lying on the floor and understood that I must have been overwhelmed by the rush of impressions and passed out. Clarity of the senses lasted only a few minutes, however. The magnetic furore swept through my brain again, and once more I was subjected to amazing experiences.

One does not lose consciousness during these trances. It is rather that one's normal perceptions are blotted out by a stronger force, as the light of a candle is annihilated by the light of the sun.

And what are these stronger experiences?

How am I to describe the contents of alien minds?

At first my experience were almost wholly abstract, but possessing a baroque quality quite different from what one normally thinks of as abstract. When I try to recall them I am left with a sense of something golden and ornate, of sweetish-musk aromas and of depth within depth.

Like my friend the Fly, the Bees are much interested in mathematics, but theirs is of a type that not even he would be able to understand (any more than I could, except intuitively when I was in the grip of the trance). What would he have made, with his obsession with numbers, of the Bees' theorem that there is a highest positive integer! To human mathematicians this would make no sense. The Bees accomplish it by arranging all numbers radially on six spokes, centred about the number One. They then place on the spokes of this great wheel certain number series which are claimed to contain the essence of numbers and which go spiralling through it, diverging and converging in a winding dance. All these series meet at last in a single immense number. This, according to the theorem, is the opposite pole of the system of positive integers, of which One is the other pole and is referred to as Hyper-One. This is the end of numbers as we know them. Hyper-One then serves as One for a number system of a higher order. But, to show the hypothetical nature of the Bees' deliberations there is a quite contrary doctrine which portrays all numbers as emanating from a number Plenum, so that every number is potentially zero.

These are items, scraps, crumbs from the feast of the Bees' honey. The raw material of this honey is the knowledge and ideas that the individual Bees forage from all over Handrea. In the safety of their hive the Bees get busy with this knowledge, converting it into direct experience. With the tirelessness of all insects they use it to create innumerable hypothetical worlds, testing them, as it were, with their prodigious intellects to see how they serve as vehicles for experience. I have lived in these worlds. When I am in them they are as real as my own. I have tasted intellectual abstractions of such a rarefied nature that it is useless for me to try to think about them.

But as my brain began to accommodate itself to the honey my experiences became more concrete. Instead of finding myself in a realm of vast theoretical calculation I would find myself sailing the seas of Handrea in a big ship, walking cities that lay somewhere on the other side of the globe, or participating in historical events, many of which had taken place thousands of years previously. Yet even here the Bees' intellectual preoccupations asserted themselves. Nearly always the adventures I met ended in the studies of philosophers and mathematicians, where lengthy debate took place, sometimes followed by translation into a world of pure ideas.

There was a third stage. My experiences began to include material that could only have come from within my own brain. I was back in my home city on my home planet. I was with my friends and loved ones. I relived events from the past. None of this was actually as it happened, but restructured and mixed together, as happens in dreams, and always with mingled emotions of joy, regret and nostalgia. Among it all, I also lived fantastic scenes from fiction; even comic-strip caricatures came to life, as if the Bees did not know the difference between them and reality.

My home world came, perhaps, to be my own private corner of the honeystore, though it is certainly only a minor item in the Bees' vast hoard. Yet what a sense of desolation I always feel on coming out of it, in the periods when for some reason the magnetic currents no longer inflame my brain, and I realise it is only hallucination! I then find myself in this arid, lonely place, with Bees buzzing and trembling all around me, and as I crawl from the chamber for nearby food and water I know that I shall never, in reality, see home again.

For the time is long, long past when a rescue beacon could do anything to help me. Not that there was ever, in fact, any chance of constructing one. Because the Bees are not intelligent.

Incredibly, but truly, they are not intelligent. They have intellect merely, pure intellect, but not true intelligence, for this requires the exertion of both intellect and the feelings – and, most important, of the soul. The Bees have no feelings, any more than any other insect has, and – of this I am convinced – God has not endowed them with souls.

They are merely insects. Their intellectual powers, their avid thirst for knowledge, are but instincts with them, no different from the instinct that prompts the ants, bees and termites of Earth to feats of engineering, and which has also misled men into thinking those to be intelligent. No rational mind, able to respond to and communicate with other rational minds, lies behind their voracious appetite.

It seems fitting that if by some quirk or accident of nature intellectual brains should evolve in that class of creature roughly corresponding to our terrestrial arthropods (and Handrea offers the only case of this as far as I know, even though insect-like fauna are abundant throughout the universe), they should do so in this bizarre fashion. One does not expect insects to be intelligent, and indeed they are not, even when endowed with analytical powers greater than our own.

But how long it took me to grasp this fact when I strove so desperately to convey messages to the Hive Mind! For there is a Hive Mind; but it has no qualities or intelligence that an individual Bee does not have. It is simply an insect collectivised, a single Bee writ large, and would not be worth mentioning were it not for one curious power it has, or that I think it has.

It seems able, by some means I cannot explain, to congeal objects out of thought. Perhaps these objects are forms imprinted on matter by magnetism. At any rate several times I have found in the chamber small artifacts which earlier I had encountered in visions, and which I do not think could have been obtained on Handrea. Once, for instance, I found a copy of a newspaper including in its pages the adventures of the Amazing Human Spider.

And recently I discovered a small bound book in which was written all the events I have outlined in this account.

I no longer know whether I have copied my story from this book, or whether the book was copied by the Bees from my mind.

What does it matter? I do not know for certain if the book, or indeed any of the other objects I have found in the chamber, really existed. The fact is that for all the abstract knowledge available to me, my grip on concrete reality has steadily deteriorated. I can no longer say with certainty which of the experiences given me by the honey really happened in my former life and which are alterations, interpolations or fantasies. For instance, was I really a companion of the Amazing Human Spider, a crime-fighter who leaps from skyscraper to skyscraper by means of his gravity-defying web?

I have been here for many years. My hair and beard are long and shaggy now that I no longer trim them. Often at the beginning I tried to break away from this addiction to the Bees' honey, but without it the reality of my position is simply too unbearable. Once I even dragged myself halfway back to the vault of the junkheaps, but I knew all the time that I would be forced to return, so great is the pull of those waking dreams.

And so here I remain and must remain, more a parasite upon these monsters than I ever had imagined I could be. For monsters they are – monsters in the Satanic sense. How else can one describe creatures of such prodigious knowledge and such negligible understanding? And for my enjoyment I have this honey – this all-spanning knowledge. Mad knowledge, too great for human encompassing and fit only for these manic Bees and the work of their ceaseless insect intellects. Knowledge that has no meaning, nothing to check or illuminate it, and which produces no practical end. And yet I know that even here, amid the unseeing Bees of Handrea, far from the temples and comforts of my religion, God is present.

EXIT FROM CITY 5

Kayin often wondered why the autumnal phase of the City's weather-cycle brought with it such an atmosphere of untidiness and decay. He sat holding Polla's hand in the park, watching as the light over the City dimmed with the approach of night. Here, the gentle breeze that blew continuously through City 5 collected by fitful gusts into a modest wind, skirling up a detritus of torn paper, scraps of fabric and dust.

Rearing above the park's fringe of trees the ranks of windows in the serried arrays of office buildings began to flick into life. The park was situated on a high level and well out towards the perimeter of the City, so that from this vantage point City 5, with its broken lines, blocks and levels, presented the appearance of a metal bowl finely machined into numerous rectilinear surfaces like an abstract sculpture. From the broken perimeter to the central pinnacle the City rose in a wide counter-curve to the curve of the crystal dome overhead, creating a deliberate but false impression of spaciousness. And indeed for a brief period in the late morning, when the light was brightest and the air filled with the sounds of industry, City 5 did manage to generate an atmosphere of liveliness, almost of excitement. But by mid-afternoon the illusion was gone. The crystal dome, glinting in the falling light, became oppressive, and when night arrived it grew over-reachingly, invisibly black, filling Kayin's imagination with vacant images of outside.

'Why don't they leave the light on?' he said irritably. 'I don't need any night-time.'

Polla did not answer. The reason was known to them both. Of all the carefully-arranged principles by which the City lived, routine was the most vital. Instead she disengaged her hand and put her arm round his neck in a fond, artless gesture. 'You *are* getting moody lately,' she told him.

He grunted. 'I know. Can you blame me? This trouble with the Society. I'm out, you know. They don't dare let me back after this. And the City Board will come down on my neck like a ton of steel.'

'Oh, they'll go easy, on you. What you did wasn't really shocking by today's standards. Anyway, something like that doesn't usually bother *you*, Kayin.'

Kayin sighed. 'You're right, it's not the Society. They won't achieve anything anyway. Poll, have you ever taken a walk through the City from end to end?'

'Sure,' she laughed, 'lots of times.'

So had he. Its diameter was a little short of five miles. Streets, offices, factories, houses, parks, level piled on level. Some parts of the City were laid out neatly, efficiently, others were warrens of twisting, turning passages. There was a fair amount of variety. But for some reason, on these walks of his, Kayin always seemed to find himself out at the perimeter, where the City proper met the crystal dome, piling up against it in irregular steps like a wave. It was not possible actually to touch the dome: the way was barred by a solid girdle of steel. For interest's sake, Kayin would usually return through the basement of the City, where acre upon acre of apparatus managed the precise transformations of matter and energy that kept City 5 biologically viable, skirting round the vast sealed chambers that contained the old propulsion units that had brought them here centuries ago.

'I feel I know every foot of this place,' Kayin said. 'I feel I know everybody in it. That's ridiculous, of course – you can't know two million people. But you understand … I'll admit I've had some good times here. It's all right if you like living in what is essentially an extended, highly technical village. But there's something a bit dead about City 5. Nothing ever comes in from outside. Anything that happens has to be generated right here.'

Polla's expression was both worried and uncomprehending. 'What are you talking about? What could come in from outside?'

He ignored her question. 'I'll tell you something, Poll,' he said, 'the City Board ought to have tighter control. I don't like the kind of symbolisations and plays they've been putting on lately. They really shouldn't allow these independent art groups and independent scientific groups like the Society. Ambition is a curse, it's frustration.'

'I never expected to hear you say that! You were always going to be the teenage rebel.'

Kayin shook his head. 'I still can't feel happy at having to spend the rest of my life in City 5. I know that's a queer thing to say. I have my job in the Inertial Stocktaking Department, I spend my time in the same way everybody else spends theirs, and I wish I could be content with that. But instead I feel restless, dissatisfied. I just wish I could go somewhere.'

With an impatient shake of her head Polla stood up. 'All right. Let's go home and have a session. I feel randy.'

'Okay.' Automatically he rose and followed. But before leaving the park he headed for its most obtrusive feature, the now defunct observatory. The building, a tall, ribbed dome, bulked large against the background of trees and shrubbery. Beside it a squat tower loomed, housing the exploratory nucleon rocket that had once been part of the observatory's ancillary equipment. He beckoned Polla and, crossing a stretch of sward, led her through a small door in the base of the building.

Although abandoned, the observatory was still kept in good order and any citizen had the right to visit and use it. Few people ever bothered, but Kayin, along with his ex-colleagues in the Astronomical Society, had spent a fair amount of time there lately.

Not that there was anything to see. The experience was a purely negative one, and subsequent visits could do nothing but repeat it. A soft light, faintly tinged with green, filled the vaulted chamber. Kayin switched on the observatory and saw the glow of life come into the control panels, heard the waiting hum from the machinery that moved the main telescope.

The instrument was the best of its type ever designed, fitted with the complete range of auxiliary apparatus – radio, X-ray, laser and maser detectors, image amplification and the rest. When built, its makers had boasted that it could detect emitting matter anywhere in the sidereal universe. Kayin set the big cylinder in motion and brought it to rest pointing directly to zenith. The wall display screens remained dark and opaque. As if performing a ritual Kayin moved the telescope again, directing it towards City-perimeter-west. On the screens, again nothing. North: nothing. East: nothing. South: nothing. Kayin and Polla stood stock-still in the capacious, echoing dome, staring at the black screens like children recalling an often-repeated lesson.

City 5 was an oasis of light in an immense darkness. A few minutes ago Kayin had said he wished he could go somewhere. He realised now that that wasn't quite right. What he meant was: *he wished there was somewhere to go*.

He thought of the nearby nucleon rocket. Recently he actually had gone somewhere – almost.

Near the centre of the City, in the upper echelons of the Administrative Ramification, Kord awoke after his customary year of suspended animation.

Strange … the freeze process stopped everything, body and brain. Logically he should come out of it with the feeling that only a second or two had passed since he lost consciousness. Inexplicably, it was not like that. Each time he felt as if he had been gone a long, long time, and privately he suspected that he aged a year mentally despite the biological stop.

He thrust the thought from his mind. If his task was ever completed, perhaps then he could give his attention to philosophical diversions. Until then there was only one thing to occupy his whole being.

Having lifted him out of the casket and given him a thorough check, the doctors helped him down from the inspection slab, one of them assisting Kord to fit on his prosthetic leg, the legacy of a brief period of civil strife early in the history of the City. At length he stood up, feeling fit and alive, and paced the room experimentally, limping slightly on the artificial limb. Other men entered with clothes and attentively helped him to dress.

Not until they had finished did he speak. 'Are the others awake?'

'Yes, Chairman. Will you proceed to briefing?'

He nodded, and left the room by a side door to find himself in a small, discreetly lighted chamber containing only a table and a chair. A man wearing the uniform of the Social Dynamic Movements Department entered briefly to hand him a file.

Kord sat down, opened the file and began to read. It was written in the special language of sociodynamic symbology, legible only to specially trained persons, From it Kord could gain a complete picture of social tendencies over the past year, every nuance, every incipient crystallisation and fragmentation, every vibration between the poles of conservation and change. If the symbolic analysis was not enough, Kord had implanted under the skin of his neck a set of filaments connected directly to the memory area of his brain. A lead from the City Archives Monitor Desk, taped to his neck, would induce in them currents carrying audio-visual recordings, of conversations, happenings, a million cameos of life easily gathered and recorded by the watchful electronics of a closed system like City 5. By drawing on the memories he would suddenly find in his mind, Kord's knowledge of the past year would be experiential, not merely symbolic.

In adjoining cells the other four members of the Permanent Board were reading similar files. As he progressed through his, Kord knew that he would be calling on the Monitor Desk. He had been aware of dangerous tendencies present in the society of City 5, but he had not anticipated this sudden alarming acceleration of events. Grimly he realised that when the twenty-four-hour period was up he would not, as was the custom, be returning to deep freeze.

That night Kayin did not, as he would normally have done, attend the meeting of the Astronomical Society, but spent it instead alone with Polla. Ham-Ra, President of the Society, had already put his decision to him and in fairness Kayin had agreed with his judgement. He was out.

The Society gathered in a comfortable, otherwise unused room in one of the rambling parts of the City. A video recorder in one corner contained the edited minutes of their previous meetings and what little information or few resolutions they had been able to formulate.

The object of the Society was to re-establish the sciences of astronomy and space exploration. It numbered fifteen members, without Kayin, between the ages of seventy and twenty-three. In most societies like this one youth was the order of the day.

'We have a lot to present this session,' Ham-Ra said by way of introduction. 'For the first time we're really getting somewhere. However, you'll all have noticed that Kayin isn't here. A few of you know why. For the rest, it will become plain later just why he can't attend.

'Now then, friends, when we last convened over a month ago we were getting depressed and ready to give up. But what Tamm has to show us today is really going to knock you out. Take over, Tamm.'

The freckled red-head rose, grinning shyly, and stood by the table, on which stood a video unit. 'As you know, public knowledge concerning the origin of City 5, the whereabouts of Earth and so on, has fluctuated considerably over the years by reason of the Mandatory Cut-Off of information, as the Administrative Ramification vacillated between the theory that total ignorance is best and the theory that full knowledge is best. Over the past ten years Mandatory Cut-Off has been relaxed considerably – otherwise our Society couldn't exist – and along with the upsurge of interest in scientific matters we have been able to gain access to some information that wasn't available before.

'Nevertheless our astronomical knowledge has been slight, particularly where it affects our relations with Earth. We know that the City came from Earth some hundreds of years ago, that we can never go back, and that essentially we must remain here for all time. I think we can take it that the pendulum of policy is swinging towards freedom because, by sedulously bending the ears of a few sympathetic parties in the Administrative Ramification, Ham-Ra and myself gained official permission to make use of the City's last remaining nucleon rocket in order to undertake an expedition to the sidereal universe, or as close to it as we could safely get.'

'That's fantastic!' said a voice into the ensuing silence.

Tamm nodded. 'The condition we had to agree to is that the results of the expedition, and the information we gained from it, remain the property of the Ramification and should not be divulged outside the Society. Furthermore only two members were permitted to go on the trip. For various reasons Ham-Ra stood down in favour of Kayin, who together with myself made up the crew. It would have been nice if you could all have seen what we saw, but we made complete video recordings throughout, so to that extent you can share the experience with us.

'You will see that the expedition was not only one of exploration; it was also a concession on the Ramification's part on divulging historical knowledge in the form of an instruction tape on the rocket itself. What you learn will probably not surprise any of us much, but it will still give us a great deal to think about.'

He pressed a stud on the video unit. A large wall screen lit up. Tamm and Kayin were in the nucleon rocket's main cabin in bucket seats before a curved control panel. Kayin's keen, intelligent face turned towards the pick-up.

'We are going out through the egress sphincter now. In a few moments we should be the first people of our generation to see the City from outside.'

With a flicker, because of rather hasty editing, the picture changed to show a view through one of the ports. Everyone in the room held his breath. At first they only saw what appeared to be a vast curving wall, just visible as a dull metallic sheen due to an unseen source of illumination. Then, as the rocket drifted away, they got a full view of the City seen side-on: a huge disc-shaped slab surmounted by a graceful glittering dome in which could be discerned a low profile of shadowy shapes.

The rocket mounted above the City and hovered over it, somewhat to one side. They were looking down on the dome now and the City was suspended in space at an odd angle, blazing with light in an otherwise unbroken, impenetrable blackness.

They could have stared at it for ever; but suddenly they were back in the cabin again and this time Tamm was speaking to them while Kayin piloted the rocket. 'Athough we can see nothing out here even with the ship's tele-scope – apart from the City, that is – we have been given a guidance tape that should take us to the sidereal universe or the material universe as it is alter-natively called. The distance is about three light-years, so we should be there very quickly.'

The picture flickered wildly again; Tamm had cut out half an hour of uneventful tape. When they came back it was in the middle of a word. Tamm was shouting wildly.

'– look at that! Just look at that!'

The pick-up was once more pointing outside. The sight that met their eyes was more spectacular even than the panorama of the City. The first impres-sion was of a blaze, of scattered light, of fire. Nearby, a few huge misty spirals hung in the void; further away, on either side, above and below, and far off into the depths, masses of similar spirals and glowing clouds and streamers receded into the distance, while a sort of diamond dust seemed to be infused among them all.

The scene was hypnotic, and the pick-up camera lingered on it for a con-siderable time. After the first impact, the impression was gained that the phenomenon, though big, was limited in size: the larger-looking spirals, though majestic, were some distance away and on the straggling edge of the cloud, whose limits seemed to define a slight but perceptible curve.

At that moment they became aware that the rocket's instruction tape had clicked into action, delivering a neat lecture in the quiet, calm voice of an electronic vodor. So unobtrusive was the voice at first that they failed to hear it in the general excitement:

'... we have now passed the first threshold beyond which the material uni-verse becomes visible, and are approaching the second threshold. You are warned severely against attempting to cross the second threshold; such a manoeuvre is generally agreed to be almost impossible or at any rate prohibi-tively difficult, and if by chance you should succeed and actually enter the material universe, you will not be able to leave again and will suffer the fate of all the matter it contains. Proceed with care: your visual instincts will probably tell you that the edge of the material universe, the metagalaxy as it is sometimes called, is light-years away or at least many millions of miles away. It is, in fact, very close. The galaxies you are now seeing are only a few miles in diameter, many of them less than a mile in diameter, and the entire conglomeration of galactic and stellar systems is still shrinking steadily.

'The cause of the shrinkage of matter has not been ascertained with any certainty. It was first detected in AD 5085, Old Reckoning, when specific anomalies relating to the velocity and wave-length of light revealed that all phenomena having the properties of mass-energy were shrinking relative to the unit of space. Extrapolation of the equations led to the conclusion that a point would be reached, and that fairly soon, when the fundamental particles would be too small to maintain their identity in the space-time frame and that therefore all matter everywhere would vanish from existence.

'Since the shrinkage related to the metagalaxy as a whole, it was theorised that if an entity or system could escape beyond the by then known boundaries of the sidereal universe then it might also escape the field of the shrinking process and survive. Luckily the centuries-old Problem of Velocity had recently been solved, and already ships had been built capable of traversing the whole diameter of the metagalaxy in a fairly short period of time. The first attempts to pass into the space beyond the metagalaxy, however, met difficulty. Either the shrinkage field or the metagalaxy itself set up an interface with the rest of space that constituted a barrier to the passage of matter. Penetration of the barrier was, however, theoretically possible, and was attempted over a considerable period of time by ships equipped with specially powerful drive units. Eventually one such ship succeeded, to return with the report that the void beyond the metagalaxy, though it appeared to contain no matter itself, would accept the existence of matter placed in it and maintain it in a stable, non-shrinking state.

'As the universe shrank, the barrier grew more impenetrable. If anything was to be preserved, it was essential to act quickly. Twenty self-contained cities were constructed and equipped with the most powerful drive units. As they headed at top speed for the perimeter of the material realm they were able to observe a large number of ships, cities and similar constructs doing the same from various points in the universe. None of these alien launchings met with success and mankind's effort did only marginally better. As they encountered the barrier and strove to make their exit, all but one of the Earth cities either blew up or otherwise failed to break through. It can now be said with certainty that City 5 is the sole fragment of matter to have escaped the shrinking metagalaxy, where the current state of materiality is such that biological life is believed to be no longer possible.

'In recent years an acceleration in the rate of shrinking has been observed, leading to the belief that the moment is now very close for the extinction of this island of materiality unique in the spatial frame. For a long time it has been effectively invisible from City 5, or indeed from anywhere outside the interface region, for the reason that the enveloping barrier has an outer and an inner surface known as the first and second thresholds. The inner threshold is permeable to radiant energy but offers a strong resistance to the passage of solid masses. The outer threshold may be crossed quite easily by slow-moving masses, but is opaque to light and other radiation passing to it from the inner threshold. In order to view the sidereal universe it is therefore necessary to position oneself between the two.

'City 5 was designed to be self-subsisting in perpetuity. Physicists on Earth nevertheless entertained the expectation, or rather the hope, that other areas of materiality where humanity could again proliferate would be located in the void, even though they might be immensely remote from the home universe. For a long time long-range spaceships were built and despatched from City 5 in efforts to discover even one atom or electron of matter. Any one of these missions covered a distance equal to many billion times the diameter of the old metagalaxy at its original full size, a feat that has added poignancy when we reflect that by pre-shrinkage standards of measurement City 5 itself is slightly over half an inch in diameter. All such projects have long since been abandoned as useless and the exploratory rockets dismantled. It is now accepted that materiality is not a normal feature of the space frame and that it does not exist anywhere apart from the sidereal universe already known to us. All future endeavours on the part of humanity must perforce make do with such material as was transported in City 5 at the time of the migration, and the City has therefore had to face the problems of perpetuating the life of mankind in complete isolation. The technical aspects, though prodigious, do not present any insoluble difficulties; the chief problems lie in the social and psychological fields.'

The screen went suddenly blank. 'I think we might as well end the tape there,' Tamm said matter-of-factly. 'That's the valid part of the mission.'

His audience was silent, thoughtful, perhaps a little stunned. Finally Ham-Ra said: 'Well, that fills in some gaps in our knowledge. Any comments?'

'It shouldn't come as any great shock,' someone said after a moment, 'but somehow it does. We have always known we were isolated and alone, that we can't return to Earth. But I always presumed that Earth and the rest of the universe still existed somewhere and would always continue to exist. It makes a difference.'

'That's a fact,' said another. 'It means we have to re-think our aims and objectives. Which brings me to the point that it still hasn't been explained why Kayin is absent.'

Tamm cleared his throat and glanced at Ham-Ra, who nodded for him to go ahead. 'When Kayin and myself returned to City 5 we still had very little technical data of a useful kind. While beyond the first threshold we did of course take a whole library of image and spectral recordings which we can all study at our leisure. But a great deal of the other instrumentation we took along proved useless. More specifically, the nucleon rocket's instruction tape had whetted our appetite to know more about the early efforts to explore the empty void, as this seemed to be the direction in which the Society's interest would lie. Unfortunately the requisite documents lie well behind the Mandatory Cut-Off, and no one we could reach in the Administrative Ramification had authorisation to give us access. So we devised a scheme to tap the archives illegally.'

The audience was torn between fright at this manoeuvre and admiration for its audacity. The brighter of them had already anticipated the outcome of the story. A skinny, scowling youngster with a sharp face snorted. 'The tap was detected, of course?'

'Yes, but only Kayin's part in the matter is known to the Ramification. It was his training that made the attempt possible. Now, although both Ham-Ra and myself, and to that extent the whole Society, were involved, the only chance to save the Society from dissolution is to disavow responsibility. We all agreed that Kayin should be expelled and his actions condemned.'

'Isn't that a little unfair?'

'Kayin doesn't seem to think so.'

'What will happen to him?'

'Nothing much, not the way the wind's blowing at present. You could say our loss is just as great as his – we've lost one of our only two members to have seen the sidereal universe with their own eyes.'

The news seemed to have agitated, energised the Society. They began speaking all at once, shouting each other down.

'What do we do now?'

'We ought to force the Ramification to act!'

'We ought to steal the nucleon rocket –'

Ham-Ra held up his hands for silence. The hatchet-faced, damp-haired young man who had spoken before rose to his feet. Ham-Ra nodded.

'Obviously the Ramification expected us to accept what we've learned and to give up quietly, maybe even to dissolve ourselves voluntarily,' said the youth, whose name was Barsh. 'Their message to us is: *there is no science of astronomy, there is no exploration of space.* I don't think we should take it lying down. Instead, I think we should revive the whole question of whether there is matter in the empty void and of launching new missions going even further than they did before.'

'That's right! Last time they gave up too easily.'

Curtly Ham-Ra once again stopped the rising hubbub. Tamm was smiling wryly. 'I don't imagine they gave up easily. I think they tried as hard as it's possible to try. These days the Ramification has trouble of a different kind.'

He flicked a switch, reeling back a few inches of tape. The screen glowed with its incredible picture, accompanied by the instruction tape's closing remark:

'... the chief problems lie in the social and psychological fields.'

The others heard the words, but the blank looks in their eyes betrayed their lack of interest. 'What are we going to do about outfitting an expedition into deep space?' Barsh said.

To Kiang, Chairman of the Temporary Board, the meeting with Kord was slightly frightening, slightly thrilling. The man was large – tall, broad, and bulky; his face, which gave one the impression that it had never smiled, was also large, and lined with the impress of years of wilfully directed thought. Its colour was grey, not the grey of illness but the grey of granite, of obdurate strength. When Kord spoke, everybody listened. He was that rare man, the great leader who in times past would have directed the affairs of continents, of planets. There was something heartbreaking in seeing that powerful personality applied with full force to the promotion of stasis and conservation on this pathetic scrap of a vanished universe.

The boardroom was divided down the centre by a long, polished table. On one side sat the Temporary Board, headed by Kiang and backed by Haren, Kuro, Chippilare and Freen. Facing them sat the Permanent Board: Kord flanked by Bnec, specialist in physics, the science of materiality; Engrach, specialist in technology; Ferad and Elbern, specialists in sociodynamics. Elbern was one of Kord's strokes of strategy, for he was a converted member of the old opposition of centuries ago. Kord knew that the errors promulgated by the vanquished party would occur again and again in the history of City 5, though he hoped with steadily diminishing force, and he realised the advantage of having a man who understood the kind of mentality that fostered them.

Kord permitted himself a direct glance into Kiang's mobile face. They're afraid of us, he thought. They feel young in our presence; they're aware that we were old and wise, sitting on this board, before they were babies. But they'll fight us if they have to.

The members of the Permanent Board lived for only one day a year. Thus one year of ageing for them spanned three hundred and sixty-five years of City 5 history. Without this device of a permanent guiding hand, Kord believed, the City would never have maintained its historical stability thus far – and in this small, unique, precious island of life stability was all-important. If social tendencies slowed down enough to require less readjustment, the dormant period could be extended to ten years, perhaps even to a hundred years.

At the moment those long, restful sleeps seemed a long way off. Inwardly Kord sighed. He was the last of a line of leaders, including men like Chairman Mao and Gebr Hermesis, who had tried to reform the mind of humanity and fix it with an eternal pattern. Always the problem was one of training the new generation to think in every way like the old. Humanity had survived their failures, but Kord was convinced that it would not survive his.

Angrily he flung the file he had studied at Kiang. 'A hundred years ago you would have been executed for the contents of that file. I spare you now only on the assumption that rectification of the situation will immediately be taken in hand.'

'... We do not necessarily agree, Chairman, that rectification is necessary.'

'How many times do I have to spell it out to you, gentlemen?' Kord said, his voice becoming gravelly with displeasure. 'We are concerned with preserving the City, not for a thousand years, not for a million, but *for ever*, for *eternity*. Due to the nature of the human psyche this is only possible if life is regularized in every detail. There must be no new directions, no individuality, no innovations or originality of thought. The City is small. It must be protected from itself.' Kord felt himself sweating. Only a few years ago the consciousness of what was required for survival was infused in the Ramification, in the mind of the City itself. Yet over and over again, through the centuries, he had gone through exactly such arguments as this. It seemed that the tendency to deviate, to forget, was ever-present and in time entered even the Temporary Board itself. Even so, Kord was shocked to find that the position had deteriorated so quickly in the past year, his perpetual nightmare was that one day he would awake to find that his authority was no longer valid.

'You have made the severest mistake,' he continued, 'committed the greatest crime, in giving youth its head. The absolute pre-condition for a permanent social pattern is the complete subordination and conditioning of the younger generation. But what do I find? Led on by your own foolish ambitions, you have permitted youth to set in train what threatens to be a virtual renaissance in the arts and sciences.'

'We have been giving the matter considerable thought for some time, Chairman,' Chippilare put in. 'As we see it, you fear initiative because it will upset the balance; but we fear stasis because it produces a movement in the other direction, towards decay. The City can die through a progressive depletion of psychic energy, as well as through an explosion of it.'

'There has been a noticeable air of apathy and drabness about the City of recent years,' Kuro said. 'Perhaps you, in suspended animation, have missed it. It was to counteract this decline in tone that we decided to liven things up a bit.'

'In fact,' added Freen, 'we now question whether a society can be kept in good health without innovation and change.'

'It can,' answered Kord firmly, aware by now that he had a full-scale rebellion on his hands. 'There were many such societies on Earth, usually of a primitive nature, which were eventually destroyed *only* by change and innovation introduced from outside. In particular, the aborigines of the prehistoric period on the continent of Australia maintained a fully developed culture for thousands of years, believing their origins to be in an immensely distant "dream time". We have to create a "dream time" for our people.'

'That's right,' said Elbern, looking at Freen with a certain amount of hostility. 'The reason for the long-term stability of the aborigines was that, living in a sparse, poorly-endowed land, all their energies were taken up in the considerable skills needed to survive. We are perhaps unfortunate in that with our level of technology we can take care of our basic needs fairly easily – that is why we have tried to, replace preoccupation with short-term needs with preoccupation with long-term needs, in the maintenance of the basic machinery, in the continual drawing up of new plans for the redesign of the City, and above all in the inertial stocktaking, which takes up an enormous amount of the population's labour-time and is concerned with accounting for every atom of the City's mass. I do not need to remind you how important that activity is if we are to conserve all our mass and energy over billions and billions of years.'

The Temporary Board looked embarrassed and cast covert glances at one another. At length Kiang ventured: 'Our recent philosophical studies have cast doubt on the very basis of the City's plan for existence. We have been studying the very fact of matter itself. It has been known ever since the early formulation of dialectical materialism that motion and tendency, opposing forces and so on, are the very basis of matter whether it takes physical, mental or social forms. If the principle of opposition, as for instance in a class struggle of some sort, is fundamental then how can you be sure that a static or self-perpetuating state *is even possible?* You cannot name any Earth society that remained stable for all time.'

Kiang was voicing Kord's private fears, but he said nothing, only stared stonily.

'Furthermore,' Kiang continued, 'we have to take note of the fact that materiality *is* an extraordinary and temporary occurrence in the space-time frame. More and more we have become convinced that the materiality of the sidereal universe consisted of an accidental polar opposition with no inherent tendency towards stability. It had to move some way, and in so doing the transient balance was lost; hence the shrinkage of matter and its final disappearance. But where does that leave us? The materiality of City 5 is even more isolated and vulnerable. At any moment in time it may suddenly collapse and disappear. So there is not much point in our planning for eternity.'

Throughout this argument the Permanent Board had listened in silence. When Kiang had finished Bnec, Kord's specialist in physics, let out an expression of disgust.

'A very pretty speech! You palpitating fool, is your brain so addled that you have forgotten your special access beyond the Mandatory Cut-Off? Or do you believe yourself to be too progressive to learn anything from the superhuman efforts of your ancestors? Can you seriously imagine that these questions were not thrashed out, researched and resolved millennia ago?'

Kord held up his hand to quell the brewing quarrel. 'Have no fear, the material of the City is sound as far as science can tell. Also, we shall not run out of energy provided we lose no appreciable mass: it has been found that we are in a privileged position here, in that there is a conservation of mass-energy. The material polarity, as you correctly call it, is self-conserving. When atomic energy, say, is released from matter to perform useful work, it is not dissipated but we absorb it elsewhere in the City. Thus as long as the total mass remains constant the same energy can be released again and again in a cyclic action. Apart from that we have proved that we can keep the genetic material of the population stable. So our problem concerns only the conscious, active life of the City, without which none of these principles can be maintained.'

He clenched his fist. 'Get this! Everything that happens, happens beneath the crystal dome. *There is no external world.* There is no longer any universe, any creation ... so any uncontrolled process beneath the dome is a danger to the City. The element in the human psyche that reaches out, explores and discovers must be eradicated. It means destruction to us. The outward, aspirational life must be replaced by an inward life of symbolism and extremely close personal relationships.

'None of this can happen at once, of course. In a sense we are still in our first stages of arrival in the empty void. We have still to make the adjustment, which we are doing by degrees, progressing two steps forward and one step back. Thus at the moment the dome is transparent and lets out a blaze of light. This means a loss of energy but for us it is a symbol, an announcement of our presence. At some date in the future the dome will be made totally impervious and no quantum of mass-energy will ever be allowed to leave the City. Then again, we still call the City by its original name, City 5, bringing with it the awareness that there were other cities and other places. Eventually it will be known simply as the City.'

'And is ignorance also part of the prescription for survival?' Haren's tone was mildly contemptuous.

'A careful balance is needed.' The long arguing was making Kord tired, but he refused to let his energy flag. 'Full consciousness of our situation would be too much for the collective mind; it would cause mental disorders and ultimately destroy us. Likewise, complete ignorance would destroy us for different reasons. We must steer a middle course until the day when the non-deviating republic has been established and we can safely permit the whole city to live with the full knowledge and consciousness of where we are.'

Kord stood up, his bulk looming over them. 'I trust I have made things clear. We will recess for a short while and meet in the Executive Complex in three hours' time. It will be necessary to make some arrangements.'

With opaque faces the Temporary Board rose and left the room. The others remained behind, looking pensively at the table top.

'A fairly bad business,' Elbern said.

'We can handle it. But I think the Board we leave behind when we freeze again will have some different names in it.' Kord picked up the file he had thrown at Kiang and leafed through it moodily. The section on the Archetypal Dramas had been the first give-away. Kord had always known that the symbols and archetypes that would emerge from the collective unconscious would decide the fate of City 5 in the long run. That was why he had encouraged the development of art forms for which practically the whole City was an audience, films, plays and archetypal dramas delivered in a semi-hypnagogic state, in which these entities could find expression, symbols, characters and stories merging into a dream-like, hypnotic blend. The section on the dramas was always the first thing he turned to when given the briefing. If the symbols were rounded, square, on the Jungian mandala or quaternity patterns, then he was pleased. The image he looked for was the cave, the female, the square table, the square room, the circle. Today there was an altogether unacceptable number of thrusting, probing images, the tower on the plain, the pointed lance, the long journey, the magician, the supreme effort. These images were all culled from the generalised social unconscious of the time. Aware of the part played by the sexual polarity in the structure of the social psyche, Kord had long since realised that it was necessary to create a womb-centred, vulva-centred civilisation, instead of a phallus-centred one.

Brooding, he closed the file. He had faced many difficulties in the past. It was disappointing to find that they might not, after all, be diminishing.

When they again met the Temporary Board three hours later, they found that the spirit of disagreement was still present. Further, the rebels had used the time to reconsolidate their position among some complexes of the Ramification. Kord was obliged to resort to strong measures. Within twenty-four hours he had set in motion an efficient and informed state police. Two days later, the general purge began. Within a week public executions were being held daily in the main park.

Kayin was in hiding, having taken Polla with him, in a part of the City that had not been rebuilt for a few hundred years and where he had friends. To his surprise he remained hidden, whereas others failed to evade the combination of delation and electronic scanning by which the Ramification discovered everyone's whereabouts. The reason, as he at last surmised, was simple: his expulsion from the Society had saved him. He was no longer associated with a subversive movement, and his other crime was not, in the context of present events, viewed with the same gravity.

Accordingly he began to venture out. In the main park he watched as the unrepentant Ham-Ra, Tamm and Barsh received the customary lethal injections in the neck As he wandered away, feeling bitter and sick, he heard someone call his name.

It was Herren, an acquaintance he had not seen for a couple of years. About the same age as himself, Herren appraised him speculatively.

'How are you, old chap? Everything all right?'

The bright, breezy manner simply left Kayin scowling. He turned away, but Herren followed him, speaking sympathetically. 'Yes, I know, it's an awful shame. But the game's not lost, you know. Things really are moving. I thought you might be interested.'

Kayin shrugged.

'Well, all right, it is a bit open here. Listen. I happen to know where you're staying. Surprised?' He laughed. 'News travels these days. Friends, you know. I'll call on you tonight. Pity if you were left out of everything.'

Kayin looked at him thoughtfully. It's up to you.' He felt oddly detached. Herren might be a Ramification agent, for all he knew, but he didn't much care.

In the event, Herren was playing it straight. He called just as Kayin and Polla were finishing their evening meal. The wall screen was showing an old drama from several years ago – the new-style dramas had been taken out of circulation – but they were paying it too little heed to be drawn into the semi-hypnagogic state in which it could have been fully appreciated.

Herren entered the room and rudely switched the screen off. 'Not interested in that old rubbish, are you?' He looked around, then produced a small metal cylinder from his pocket and carefully placed it on the table. 'This will fool any hidden scanners,' he explained. 'They'll pick up nothing but an empty room.'

Kayin stared at the gadget blankly. 'Where did you get it?'

The other winked. 'There's a certain amount of underground stuff being manufactured these days.'

Despite his own misdemeanour, Kayin found the idea hard to grasp. 'Do you mean insurrection? The City is fragmenting?'

'They are talking of civil war.'

'But that's … crazy …' Kayin wondered if Herren knew what he knew of City 5's situation, of the facts concerning the sidereal universe.

'I haven't been getting much news lately,' he said weakly.

'Let me fill you in. Kord has already killed three members of the Temporary Board. Chippilare and Kuro escaped, thanks to the loyalty of sympathetic elements both in the Ramification and outside. They have organised an opposition and are holding out in the Western Segment, down near the Basement. It's more or less an enclave. The State Police aren't strong enough to go in and get them out.'

'Has Kord given the police arms?'

'They're getting arms now. But the opposition is manufacturing arms, too. It's a revolution! Because the opposition isn't just in the enclave, it's all over, gradually being organised. Youth is waking up!'

Polla stared from one to the other of the young men in disbelief. 'Kayin, can this be true? What's happening?'

'Kord is finding out that he can't enslave the mind of humanity for ever,' Herren said. 'We are discovering freedom.'

'It's all over a difference of opinion,' Kayin told her wearily. 'Kord and his people think that the City can best be preserved by rigid control and a low level of aspiration. Our technology is sufficient, so there's no need for further development in the arts or sciences. The others, like Herren here, believe that that approach leads to a slow but sure disaster and that the City must be kept bubbling to stay healthy, that life isn't worth living any other way anyhow. They both feel strongly enough about it to go to war. They're all in the minority, of course. The great majority of the population have the good sense to interest themselves in nothing much except the inertial stocktaking.'

'But which side is right?'

'Right?' Kayin said with a grimace. 'Neither! Both roads will lead to disaster ... There isn't any solution ... The City exists in a place where it isn't supposed to be ...'

Herren leaned forward and gripped his slumped shoulder comfortingly 'Steady, old chap. I know how it must have been for you this afternoon, seeing your friends executed. Believe me, we've all been through it. But you'll pull through. I know we'll be able to depend on you when the time comes.'

Kayin remembered the wry smile on red-headed Tamm's face, just before they injected the poison.

When Kuro finally answered Kord's invitation, he found the centuries-old Master of City 5 looking drawn and strained. For his part, it had been a mortal blow to Kord's confidence when he had failed to contain the situation. He suspected that for some years the briefings he had been given had been tampered with to play down the actual motion of events. Now, though he held the central premises of the Ramification, he effectively controlled only two-thirds of the City.

'Very well,' he said curtly, 'you are strong enough to fight us.'

'And we will.'

Kord spoke in an exasperated tone. 'Already there have been gun battles in the City! Yesterday fire broke out in the Northern Segment.' Angrily he rapped his artificial leg. 'Do you know how I got this? In a civil war pretty much like this one is becoming. Sheer lunacy! It's suicidal to fight inside the City; we can't allow it again.'

'So?'

'If we have to fight, it will have to be done *outside the dome.*'

'My conclusion exactly,' Kuro said sombrely, 'as far as heavier weapons go, anyway. We can both construct space vessels of some sort. For the arrangement to be effective each side must be allowed to transfer sufficient forces outside, without interference.'

'Agreed, then. We shall set up an independent commission to control the egress port.'

He paused reflectively. 'By the way, I got some news today. You know that there is an instrument in the Ramification set to record the moment when the material universe finally vanishes altogether. Just after eight last night, the event registered.'

Kuro made no comment. After they had completed the formal arrangements he left, feeling only slight discomfort about what was going on.

'It's like a nightmare,' Polla said.

The City appeared to be huddling, expectant. In the north could be seen the fire-blackened region, and a faint smell of smoke still hung in the air, not quite eradicated by the circulatory system. The crystal dome sparkled; but beyond it vague shadowy forms were moving as the contending forces arrayed themselves.

'Well, at least the City will be safe,' Kayin replied. Herren had come to him and expected him to take part in the street fighting. When he had declined, he had again come to him and invited him to help man the weapons carried by the new spacecraft. Kayin could imagine what kind of a battle that would be: hastily built ships manoeuvring in an utterly empty void, carefully avoiding proximity with the City and offering perfect sitting ducks to one another. With luck, none of them would return and the City could live in peace.

Kayin was fingering a key in his pocket. It was a special key, working by electronic impulses, and it gave its owner possession of the observatory's nucleon rocket. Kayin had never handed it back after his mission with Tamm.

'Poll,' he said, 'let's go somewhere.'

'Where?'

'Out,' he answered sardonically, 'outward bound. The early expeditions failed because they always turned back when they reached the point of no return, when their engines wouldn't have got them back if they'd gone further. *We'll keep on going.* What does it matter?'

She didn't understand what he was talking about, but she followed him to the park where they used to meet. He headed for the observatory, but this time bypassed the dome and pressed the key into a small slot in the base of the tower.

A door slid open. He stepped inside, taking Polla by the hand and tugging her through. There was a gap of about twelve feet between the hull of the rocket and the shell of the tower. The spacecraft loomed above them like a huge shaft.

He pressed the same key into a slot in a large box inside the door. It clicked and hummed; automatically the rocket was being readied for use.

'*Kayin*,' Polla protested in sudden alarm. 'What's going on? I'm not going anywhere –'

Without waiting for her fright to become hysteria, he closed in on her. For a few moments she was gasping as they grappled, then he had her held securely over his shoulder. Still she struggled, bewildered, but there wasn't far to go. He carried her to the embarkation platform; swiftly it took them up the side of the rocket to the port. Inside the rocket he stepped down a short passage and threw her down in the luxurious living apartment.

'What are you *doing?*' She sat up on the floor, her legs asplay.

He switched on the wall screen, tuning it to the external scanners. 'Enjoy the show,' he said, then left for the control cabin, locking the door behind him.

The controllers of the egress port were used to a constant stream of craft applying for exit; they asked no questions in his case. For the second time in his life he floated up above the dome, seeing the City spread out below him. But this time there were big, clumsy cylindrical objects floating in the vicinity of the City, some of them sporting wicked-looking equipment welded on in various places. The war was due to begin soon.

Kayin chose a direction at random and started up the nucleon engines at full power. In a second City 5 was gone. He and Polla were alone in the void; the eternal, infinite, vacant void.

On and on and on and on and on. The engines never stopped. Although they ran silently, Kayin checked their action constantly on the instruments in the control cabin.

Polla had wept and screamed, then sulked for weeks, and then gradually became friendly again. By now Kayin himself felt defensively sullen about what he had done. It was boorish and uncharacteristic of him. But he stubbornly refused to apologise, even to his own conscience.

At this distance it was impossible even with the most powerful magnification available on the rocket to gain as much as a photon's worth of image from the City. Shortly after departure he had picked up brief flashes that came not from the City itself but from the spaceships that were fighting one another with nuclear weapons. Even if they had not been travelling at billions of times the speed of light, such minute flickers would not have been detectable by any means now.

So there was only the emptiness on all sides. Looking out into it, one could not even discern distance; there was only absolute lightlessness.

After they had been travelling for nearly two months Kayin took to spending long periods in the direct observation blister that, projecting from the hull of the rocket in a perfectly transparent bulge, formed a cavity of extrusion into space. Here was the only place in the rocket where the artificial gravity (derived from the same principle as the nucleon engine) did not operate. With the cavity light switched off, one might as well have been floating in free fall in the void itself. Kayin spent what seemed like hours staring out of the blister, into what to his eyes was simply blackness but which his mind knew to be infinity. His mind began working in new directions. Matter, he reasoned, had structure, but space was simply emptiness. Yet space, too, had structure of a kind. It had extension and direction. Was there, he wondered, a substratum to the void, a richer reality lying beneath it? After a while, for some dim sense of pleasure only vaguely known to himself, he took to coming into the cavity naked.

SENSORY DEPRIVATION

The human mind is not made to be without incoming sensory data for any but the briefest periods. The first consequence of sensory deprivation is that the subject loses, first the sense of his bodily outline, and then his sense of identity. Then, since the consciousness will not tolerate lack of perceptions, and being denied them from the external direction, it draws upon them from the inner direction, projecting on to the senses first hallucinations of a random, dream-like character, and then, if the process is continued, unlocking the archetypal symbols from the unconscious.

Kayin went through all these stages fairly quickly. Out in the void he saw vast wheeling mandalas, glimmering forms whose size was beyond the mind to compute. He saw the mystic triad, the mystic quaternity, exemplified in a thousand dazzling forms. He did not think or remark on what he saw, *for he was not there*. His personal identity was gone; his being consisted merely of an impersonalised consciousness of the symbols he saw.

Once he must have moved accidentally and bumped into the wall of the cavity. The bodily sensation brought him momentarily to himself. Flashing waves of excitement, of joy, swept through him. *I'm seeing it*, he thought. *This is the reality underlying space, the structure of the world transcending it. Stay here long enough and it shows itself.*

Then he was merged once again with the contents of the unconscious, a kind of paradisical, compelling, luring world. His next bodily sensation was a feeling of hotness. Vaguely he returned to himself, realising that genuine light was in his eyes. He turned slowly. The door of the cavity was open and Polls was drifting in, having turned on the illumination to a dim, soft glow.

She smiled at him distantly. They both rotated and twisted slowly round one another, hanging in the air. The hem of the short frock she wore was riding up, warping and twirling. To Kayin it was the most vivid thing he had ever seen, a vision thousands of miles across. Her face flashed with angelic light. The texture and colour of her skin radiated a soft, irresistible power.

He undid the clasp at her neck and pulled off the loose frock. They continued to turn and bend soundlessly in the cavity, the frock drifting away from them. Her body was angled slightly away from him, slightly above him. Reaching up, he first fondled then drew off her soft undergarment. Hot waves of unconsciousness swept through him.

The symbols and signs were still all around them, the very substance of their world. Kayin heard choking gasps, squeals and screams. He was submerged, spinning in endless glyphs of power and enjoying a withering, burning fire that ran in wide searing rivers and consumed the world.

Briefly he came again to consciousness of himself. They were suspended in the centre of the cavity. He was gripping Polla by her upper arms, and she his. Their bodies, held away from each other while he thrust between her legs, and joined at the genitals, were arched violently and bucking like wild animals, savagely butting, fucking. Dizzily vision again faded from his consciousness. He and the world were one identity, consisting of a huge, powerful and stiff phallus moving forward with steady purpose. Then he was at the same time a large opened vulva against which the phallus mashed and poked, making them both throb.

A murmur caught his ear. He was pressed up against Polla, his lips against hers and their bodies straining and heaving. Would they merge, blend, generating between them an androgyne with supernatural sexual powers?

Then, with a groan, they fell slightly apart and began grappling with the whole length of their bodies, limbs twisting and tangling, biting, gripping and kicking. Finally, after a last lunge at her, Kayin, fully restored to himself now, pushed her away and they hung staring at one another avidly.

END OF THE LINE

Kayin and Polla lay weakly in the living apartment. For weeks they had been exhausting themselves in the outside cavity, pushing to the utmost every kind of sex that a male and a female can engineer between them.

It was a discovery that Kayin would have liked to take back to City 5. There was nothing like it. Twenty minutes alone in the cavity, and sex became like it had never been before. It seemed that all unconscious power was released and flooded into action.

'Would you like to go home, Poll?'

'I don't care,' she sighed quietly.

In between their frequent bouts Kayin had also given himself time to think. At first he had thought the visions he saw in the void, even in the blister cavity itself, were real, a hopeful revelation of a positive reality beneath the nothingness through which they moved. More soberly, he had now recognised them for what they were: projections from his own mind, the exteriorisation of basic psychic patterns, which spilled into the open when the constraining effect of sensory impressions was removed. One interesting thing about them was that both he and Polla frequently experienced the same images at the same time during their love-making, further evidence that the unconscious was a collective one.

'Then we're going home,' he said firmly.

'You don't want to find the other universe?' she spoke timidly, like a child. Such powerful and abundant sex as they had been getting seemed to have made her regress to something like a childish state.

'There *isn't any* other universe. What's more, I'm pretty certain by now that *there isn't any space. No empty void.*'

She didn't understand what he meant, so he didn't try to explain. The idea had formed itself slowly in his mind, and he felt sure that it was right. Space was a consequence of matter, not matter of space. Outside the sidereal universe, where there was no matter, there was no space either. *When City 5 had escaped the metagalaxy, it had simply escaped into non-being.*

It would not appear that way to observers, of course. Since space was always associated with matter, City 5 extended its own island of space. Projectiles sent out from it always did the same, generating as they went a fictitious measuring system of distances and velocities by which they orientated themselves.

The nucleon rocket was not going anywhere. It merely created its own 'appearance' of space as it 'moved' through an incomprehensible nullity. It was, in fact, hard to argue that it moved at all; such a statement was quite meaningless, as was its obverse that the rocket didn't move.

None of which made any difference as regards piloting it. The rocket acted according to the laws of its materiality, for in nullity there were no laws. Kayin turned the ship round and gave the computer the problem of finding City 5. The moment of their return being mathematically certain, he and Polla then waited patiently for the rocket to deliver them there, indulging often in the pastime of which they never grew tired.

When the rocket signalled completion of the journey, they went to the now familiar outside cavity, eager for their first glimpse of their life-long home to be by line of sight.

Polla fainted dead away. Kayin grabbed a stanchion to steady himself, and avoided the same only by a determined effort of will. The crude cylindrical ships, the litter from the war between the followers of Kord and the followers of Kuro, were scattered all over the space surrounding the City, gutted, gashed and broken, trailing bodies and equipment.

Evidently the fight had been pressed too hard, and the contendants had grown desperate over relinquishing control of the City. City 5 blazed into the darkness, as it would automatically continue to do for millennia. But the crystal dome was shattered, gaping like a broken tooth. As the rocket came closer he saw the masses of dead bodies in the airless plazas and streets. About one third of the buildings seemed to have been wrecked by an explosion, and Kayin noticed, as his glazed eyes roamed over the dead City spinning slowly like a great mandala in the void, that the big housing tower for the nucleon rocket had been broken off at the base, and lay like a fallen giant across the sward.

ME AND MY ANTRONOSCOPE

My dear Asmravaar: Many thanks for your last burst, and apologies for the long delay in answering. Not that it has been wholly my fault, because my burst sender broke down – for the third time this trip! When I get back home I shall have something to say to the Transfinite Communicator Co., and you can tell them that from me.

However, to be honest, I repaired my sender some time ago and so my silence cannot all be laid at the door of our unspeakably muddling technicians. The rest of the time I have been kept busy keeping track of a gripping little 'adventure' that I chanced to catch in my sights, almost in passing as it were. At the moment I am feeling tired, but also very excited, and I just cannot resist staying awake a little longer so that I can get it all down and burst it to you. It's a fascinating story and I'm hoping it will even change your mind about a few things, you grumpy old stay-at-home!

At this point I am going to allow a note of triumph to creep into my account. Why not? – I have won a philosophic victory! For too long, Asmravaar, you and others of your ilk have laughed at the explorer-wanderers such as myself. You say that there is no point to our wanderings, that we are on a fool's errand – that the universe, though endless, is everywhere of a dreary sameness and that one might as well stay at home where there is at least a little variety. Well of course I have to admit that there is *some* substance to your allegations, and none knows that better than myself. I, more intimately than any of you pessimists, have seen what the universe consists of: an infinite series of spatialities, every one more or less the same, each containing innumerable worlds conforming to only a small number of basic types, and – as you complain – rarely any life to be found anywhere. I grant that if we were to believe in the existence of a Creator of this immensity of ours, then we could justifiably charge Him with lacking imagination. Once one gets over the awesomeness of sheer physical grandeur then there is precious little else!

Yet I am reluctant to accuse nature of being niggardly. No, it is *you* I accuse, Asmravaar! You are guilty of 'philosophical defeatism'! In my belief the universe still has a few surprises *in* store for us, if we keep looking. It can still ring a few changes!

And I have proved it!

Well, I'll get on with it. I was transiting through the 10^{5298}th range of spatialities, not expecting to find anything unusual, when I came across a world which turned out to contain life. Not very much life, it is true, but life. Physically the species is not of our reticulated tendricular type but of the much rarer oxygenated, bipedal type. Moreover I do not believe they can be native to their present habitat but must have migrated there a considerable period ago. At any rate, I was suddenly thankful that I had recently invested in a fine new high-powered Mark XXXVI sound-and-vision antronoscope,* as well as in a new instant semanticiser – for this is what I saw …

Against the yielding rock wall the big vibro-drill was working well, despite its age. Tremoring invisibly, the rotating blades sliced through the basalt at a steady rate, shoving the finely divided rubble to the rear to be dealt with by a follow-up machine – which, since this was only a demonstration run, was in this case absent.

Erfax, Keeper of the Machine Museum, flicked a switch and the drill died with a protesting whine. His friend Erled nodded. He was impressed. In a few minutes the drill had already buried half its length in the rock wall, carving out the commencement of a six-foot diameter tunnel.

'So this is how they tunnelled in the old days,' he said.

'That's right. The ancients may have been primitive in some ways, but technologically they weren't bad, not bad at all. This type of machine made possible the great epic explorations – the migratory ones. If one is to believe history – and personally I do – with such drills they tunnelled hundreds of thousands of miles. These days we could do better, of course. They must have spent an awful long time travelling those distances with a vibro-drill, apart from wearing out God knows how many machines in the process.'

Erled smiled wistfully. 'A few centuries was nothing to those people. They had *will-power*.' He watched as the drill was withdrawn from the dent-like cavity it had made and was turned round for the short journey to its resting place in the Museum. Behind it a packing machine moved into place, scooping up the rock that had been thrown out and ramming it expertly back into the hole. He tried to imagine the drill spinning out a tunnel thousands of miles into the infinite rock, pushing relentlessly forward on a vain search for other worlds. He imagined thousands of people passing along that tunnel as their home cavity gradually filled up with the rock from the excavation – until, eventually, they gave up the search, filled up the tunnel itself and settled in the new cavity they were thus able to hollow out – this cavity in which Erled had been born. Yes, he thought, those ancestors of ours had a quality we have lost.

'I should congratulate you,' he told Erfax. 'It looks as good as new.'

Erfax laughed shyly. 'Part of my duties is to keep the machines entrusted

---

* An instrument for peering into caves and hollows through the surrounding rock.

to me in working condition,' he said. 'Ostensibly that drill is five hundred years old, the last of its type – but between you and me it's had so many parts replaced it might just as well have been made yesterday.'

Erled nodded again, smiling. 'Yes, I suppose so. Well, thanks for showing it to me, Erfax. It's helped – seeing how they did it in the old days, I mean. I feel encouraged, now. If they had the nerve to explore the universe with relatively primitive equipment like this, then we can certainly do it with what we have available. Maybe we will succeed where they failed.'

Erfax's assistants were guiding the vibro-drill under its own power down a broad, even-ceilinged corridor. He and Erled followed, turning away from the rock perimeter and walking Inwards. Erled was a tall, sharp-eyed man, a few years beyond the freshness of youth but still fairly young. Erfax, rather older, was a shorter, rounder man who walked with short, quick strides and he had to hurry to keep up with the other.

A short while later, at the gates of the Machine Museum, Erfax turned to Erled.

'You are very confident, friend. But whatever the hazards of the voyage might be, the greatest hurdle you will have to overcome is still here, in the Cavity. You still have to gain the assent of the Proctors. However, I wish you luck.'

'The Proctors?' Erled answered lightly. 'They will be no trouble at all, you can depend on it. Why, Ergrad, the Proctor Enforcer, is the father of Fanaleen, my betrothed. This is practically a family affair!'

Erfax merely smiled uncertainly, waved farewell and disappeared through the gates of his Museum in the wake of the whining, elephantine vibro-drill. Erled went on down the low passage whose ceiling, as everywhere in the Cavity, was barely six or eight inches overhead. He was not discomforted by this pressing closeness; it was the condition of life he had always known, that everyone had always known.

Centuries ago, had Erled raised his eyes and looked about him, he would have seen a vast cavern several miles in extent with a roof that curved perhaps a mile overhead: such was the Cavity as it had first been hollowed out, the total emptiness capacity of the known solid universe all in one piece. In the intervening centuries humanity had increased in numbers and had learned to use the space available to it with greater efficiency, compartmentalising all of it into closely calculated living and working spaces. In its present honeycombed form the Cavity petered out indeterminately into the surrounding rock like an amoeba trapped in a solid matrix. Its diameter was roughly fifteen miles and its population was three-quarters of a million. Incessantly computations were carried out to see whether, by an appropriate readjustment of existing arrangements, more living space could be gained from the inert plenum.

One thing was certain: no new emptiness could be created. That was a scientifically established law of conservation. Emptiness could be rearranged in any number of ways, or it could be moved from place to place by the substitution of solid matter, but its total volume could not be increased. Like solidity itself, that remained unchanging throughout time.

Which meant that humanity could never expand beyond the space that was, already available to it; that its numbers could never increase beyond a certain tolerable, density.

Unless.

Unless, as Erled had told himself a thousand times, new worlds, new Cavities, could be discovered in the infinite solidity.

After walking half a mile Inwards Erled took the public conveyor system which carried him speedily towards its destination: the workshop on the other side of the Cavity where he and his colleagues were preparing for the most exciting enterprise for many, many generations.

Erled's confrontation with the Proctors came only a few work-cycles later.

It was not what he had expected.

He was summoned abruptly from his home during the relaxation period. On arriving at the Chamber of Proctors he was ushered directly in, and almost before he had time to compose himself he found himself faced with the interrogating stares of the men and women who ruled his life.

There was Erfloured, Ergurur and Erkarn, all representing different vital departments of life – Sustenance, Machine Technology, and Emptiness Utilisation. To their left, wearing ceremonial robe and sash, sat Erpiort, Proctor of Worship, and beside him the man who made Erled feel most nervous because he already knew him slightly: Ergrad, Proctor Enforcer, wearing the wide shoulder-sleeves and dark cowl of Law Enforcement.

Sitting to the left of Ergrad were the only two women on the Council: Fasusun, Proctress of Domestic Harmony, and Fatelka, Proctress of Child Care. Both were in the full bloom of an officious middle-age, and were looking at Erled with particular suspicion.

'Be seated, Erled,' said Erkarn, the man from whom, as Proctor of Emptiness Utilisation, Erled was expecting the most enthusiastic support. However, he was surprised to observe that the Proctor was apparently extremely annoyed with him.

'Over the past few days we have discussed your quite interesting proposal very seriously,' the Proctor announced, 'but before we deal with that, it has come to our notice that recently you and Keeper of the Machine Museum Erfax, without permission and entirely in defiance of the law, operated a tunnelling machine Outward of the perimeter.'

'But no excavations were carried out, Proctor!' protested Erled, bewildered. 'It was a demonstration run only. The run Outwards was only a few feet and it was made good immediately. I cannot see that we transgressed the law in doing that.'

'You will allow us to decide when the law is transgressed,' put in Ergrad darkly. He leaned towards Erled and suddenly looked menacing and sinister. 'The law against uncontrolled excavations is a very strict one – as it must be, if emptiness is not to be eroded. Only state-commissioned vessels are allowed to operate in the solidity, as well you know, and the degree of the transgression is not the point in question.'

Erled looked crestfallen.

'However,' resumed Erkarn, 'we shall leave that aside for the time being. While ignorance is no excuse it is possible that we may, in this instance, exercise our own discretion. Let us move to the main burden of the meeting: the proposal that long-range expeditions should be sent into solidity. While we have your full argument in the written tender, it would be better, for the sake of procedure, that you give us a brief account of it now so that it may appear on the transcript of this meeting.'

'Very well, Proctor.' Erled licked his lips. There was a sinking feeling in the pit of his stomach. The Proctors had done everything they could to put him at a disadvantage and that could only mean that they were opposed to the project.

'Essentially our effort is designed to be a continuation of the exploratory sagas of ancient time,' he began. 'As you are aware the difficulty with the ancients' method, apart from its slowness, is that it requires a permanent tunnel. Eventually all available emptiness is drawn into this tunnel, necessitating that the entire population should migrate along it and take part in the exploratory drive.

'An alternative, much preferable method is for the drilling vessel to fill up the tunnel behind it as it proceeds, thus becoming a genuine vehicle isolated in solidity – thus leaving the Cavity intact. In the old days this was impracticable since there was no way of solving the supply problem. No vessel could possibly carry enough sustenance to support its crew during time periods which might extend to years or generations. But today the situation is different!' Erled's voice rose as his obsession gripped him once again. 'We are no longer limited to the vibro-drill. The modern tunneller works by disassociating solid matter into a perfectly fluid dust which, as the solidity-ship moved forward, it passes to its rear through special vents and simultaneously reconstitutes into the original rock. With this type of system almost incredible speeds can be achived – close on forty miles per hour. Furthermore, by now it has proved its reliability, having been employed for over a generation in the vessels that are used to survey the close rock environs of the Cavity. The time is long overdue when we should rediscover the passion of the ancients for the discovery of new worlds!'

The vibrant voice of the Proctor of Worship answered his declamation. 'The ancients were endowed with intense religious zeal and embarked on their migrations in search of God, not of new worlds,' Erpiort said critically. 'Dauntless and resourceful though they were, it is also true that the ancients were at the primitivist stage of religious knowledge. To our more sophisticated intellects it is obvious that God is not to be found by travelling through the horizontal universe, no matter to what distance. Why should we repeat their follies?'

Erled knew exactly what Erpiort was driving at. It had been recognised for a long time that the universe was stratified. In any transverse direction the rock remained, as far as was known, unchanged to infinity. Downwards, one entered a Region of Intense Heat, while if one attempted to travel Upwards one encountered a Region of Impassibility. Above this region, which could be entered only by the souls of the righteous after death, God was acknowledged to dwell. Conversely the profound Region of Heat was a place of torment reserved for the souls of the wicked. Both regions were held to be infinite in themselves, but to Erled, or indeed to anyone else in the room, the very idea of travel either Up or Down for more than a few hundred miles was virtually a metaphysical notion. These transcendental directions were literally beyond possible human experience. Only horizontal directions had any practical meaning, and it was these that one normally meant by infinity.

Erled's interest was not religious, though he agreed that to hope to find God by travelling through the rock was naive. 'But what of the urge to discover new worlds, to determine once and for all whether there really are other cavities in the solidity?' he countered in a dismayed tone. 'We should not stifle such aspirations, surely?'

His dismay was caused by the fact that this aspiration was, to him, a burning ideal that had become second nature, and he simply could not understand why some other minds did not appear to share it. 'Besides, the discovery of unknown cavities would make new emptiness available for mankind,' he added placatingly.

Erpiort's mouth twisted cynically. 'The ancients also exercised their minds with this hypothesis of other worlds,' he remarked. 'As we all know, they found nothing. Your proposition has come at a very unfortunate time, my fellow. A deposition is currently before the Holy Synod to declare the Doctrine of One Cavity, long preached by all devout priests, an article of faith! This deposition, if accepted, will make it a heresy to believe anything other than that God made but one cavity in the whole of solidity!'

'But that may not be true!' Erled blurted. 'Why, Ereton, who is working with me on the project, has produced a calculation – hypothetical, I admit – to show that there may be a definite ratio of emptiness to solidity in the universe. If the ration is one part emptiness to one quadrillion parts solidity, as he thinks, then there must be innumerable cavities –' He broke off, suddenly aware that he might be causing trouble for Ereton. 'Well, at any rate shouldn't the matter be decided scientifically?' he ended lamely.

'Silence!' thundered Erpiort. 'The age of cold intellectualism is over, along with the age of religious disputation. We have entered the age of faith!'

Erled fell silent.

The silence was broken by Ergurur, Proctor of Machine Technology. He was a mild-faced man with an easy manner, and he addressed an apologetic smile at Erled.

'Er … you gave few details of the design of your proposed exploratory vessel when you submitted the tender,' he said. 'Perhaps you could say a little more about it now?'

Erled nodded. 'We gave little information before because we wanted to make an early application to the Council so as to lose no time,' he said. 'At that stage our solidity ship was still undergoing development and the final designs were not complete.'

'And now?'

'Both the designs and the ship itself are complete,' Erled replied woodenly. 'Completed and ready to embark on its first voyage. The engine is basically a sturdier model of the engines used in the Cavity environs surveyor vessels. The ship has its own sustenance recycling plant and can supply itself with food and air for at least a year, perhaps a year and a half. It carries a crew of two.'

'And its speed?'

'Nearly forty miles per hour!' announced Erled triumphantly. 'At least, that is what we gained on the test rig,' he added hastily. 'The ship has not yet been tested in a true rock environment, naturally.'

Ergurur listened to these details in fascination. Erkarn, alert in his Proctorship of Emptiness Utilisation, broke in with a voice like ice.

'You boast that the despatch of your solidity ship will not deprive the Cavity of emptiness,' he said. 'Nevertheless it must carry *some* emptiness with it, and if for any reason you failed to return then that emptiness would be lost for ever. Just what is the vacuity volume of your solidity ship?'

'Much thought has been given to this question,' Erled answered. 'We even thought of cutting down the vacuity volume to near-zero by immersing the crew members in a liquid and allowing them to breathe through flexible tubes directly from the recycling plant. However, we decided that such an existence would prove intolerable during a long voyage, and so we have merely economised as much as possible. The vacuity volume of the ship is only a hundred cubic feet.'

'Pah! And if you had your way you would despatch a hundred such ships into the rock, which if they failed to return would deprive mankind of ten thousand cubic feet!' Erkarn leaned back, smugly satisfied with this damning calculation.

'Quite so,' murmured Ergrad. 'Erled, I fear your solidity ship must be confiscated and destroyed.'

'Could it not be placed in the Machine Museum?' suggested Ergurur regretfully.

At this moment Fasusun spoke, giving Erled a look of sorrowful annoyance. 'What compelled you to think up this wicked scheme, Erled?' the Proctress said. 'I fear your soul is bound for Hell, but I shall pray for you.'

'Not wicked, Proctress,' Erled replied evenly. 'It is merely the natural scientific desire to explore and discover.'

'But of course it is wicked! You are defying nature, defying God, trying to upset society! Were you not taught as a child that God intended us to remain where He put us? That He created the Cavity specially for us, and therefore could not possibly have created another? Think again, Erled! Try to lead a better life! Spend more time in the temple and study the scriptures!'

Erled kept silence, unable to devise a suitable reply. My God, he thought, why do they have to allow women on the Council? For bigotry and narrowness these two, Fasusun and Fatelka, had even old Erpiort beat. They spent their time attempting to produce a population trained in doctrinaire placidity, being particularly active in the nurseries.

In addition they were almost certainly fundamentalists, taking literally every word of the scriptures. Believing, for instance, that God created the Cavity in the twinkling of an eye, complete with sustenance, machines and atomic energy, and a small tribe from which mankind grew – that was before the Cavity had by artificial means been moved several hundred thousand miles, of course. Even Erpiort had too much intelligence to swallow that one, Erled thought. Doubtless the Proctor of Worship held, with some reservations, to the scientific, evolutionary theory that Erled himself accepted – that first the Cavity had appeared, possibly by act of God or in some unknown manner, and that life had then developed by an evolutionary process. First, by spontaneous generation, there had appeared sustenance, the edible yeast-like growth that could recycle body wastes and air. Then there had appeared tiny animalcules to feed on the sustenance. Rapidly these had evolved through various stages into present mankind. It was also necessary to suppose that far before present mankind had appeared, the primeval pre-human ancestors had been endowed with an instinctive knowledge of machines and of how to release atomic energy.

Finally the silence was broken by Erkarn. 'Well, you can see how it is, Erled. The decision of the Council was unanimous except for one abstaining vote.' He glanced disapprovingly at Ergurur. 'You are to forget these mad dreams and that's a command.'

'You're stifling something that can't be stifled for ever,' Erled muttered peevishly.

'You will mend your ways and forget the whole matter,' Erkarn said sternly. 'There is still the business of the illegal drilling hanging over you. We are willing to suspend the charges *if* it is seen that you show contrition – do you understand?'

'Yes,' said Erled sullenly.

'Very well, then. The disposal of the solidity ship will be considered later. Much emptiness to you.'

'Much emptiness,' muttered Erled, and turned away.

Erled's resentment did not abate during the next few hours, but he had no thought of defying the Council. He was powerless against the Proctors, and he did not relish the thought of the criminal charges, with which he was being frankly blackmailed, being laid against him.

It would have to be left to some future generation, he told himself, to carry out the great task of exploring the universe.

He did not immediately convey the news to his colleagues in the project. Instead he felt in need of some different kind of comfort, and when the relaxation period arrived he made his way to the dwelling of Ergrad's family, to call on his betrothed, Fanaleen.

The thought of facing his future father-in-law so soon after his humiliation partly at his hands caused Erled a slight degree of trepidation, but he reassured himself that on such visits Ergrad usually put in only a brief appearance or none at all. However, as he approached Ergrad's well-appointed dwelling through a low-ceilinged passage, the tall, hooded figure of the Proctor Enforcer suddenly appeared from nowhere and barred his way.

This section of the passageway was dimly lit. Erled felt menaced by the looming form. Dark black eyes flashed at him from beneath the cowl.

'Proctor Ergrad,' he stuttered. 'I have come to see Fanaleen –'

'Turn round, Erled, and go home. You're not welcome here.'

Erled was astounded. 'But – Proctor –'

Ergrad clenched his fist in exasperation. 'Can you be so thick-headed?' he growled. 'Didn't you see what went on in the Chamber today? You're *finished*, Erled, you'll be a nobody for the rest of your life. Not the sort of man I'll allow to marry into my family. You'll never see Fanaleen again.'

Abruptly the Proctor turned and strode towards his dwelling. For nearly a minute Erled stared after his retreating back, the finality of what had happened slowly seeping into him.

Never see Fanaleen again.

There could be no revision of that sentence. It was a strict law that the union between a couple must be agreeable to the parents. And the word of a Proctor was inviolate.

Dazed, Erled allowed his feet to carry him to the only place where he was likely to find understanding: the Inn of Vacuous Happiness, the haunt of his friends and colleagues in the solidity ship project. As he anticipated, they were all busy drinking there, and Ereton, with whom he shared co-leadership of the project, greeted him eagerly. So, in their favourite room where the ceiling beams touched one's head if one stood erect, he explained the double disaster.

Ereton squeezed his shoulder consolingly. 'It appears that we chose the wrong time,' he said sombrely.

'There'll *never* be a right time in this generation,' Erled exclaimed heatedly. 'And we'll never get a chance to search for other worlds. What right have the Proctors to dictate to our consciences like this? It's tyranny!'

The others agreed fervidly, after which Erled retired to a corner and brooded. His resentment was building up like a burning fire, and as with so many men before him, the tragedy of thwarted love turned his mind to lofty sentiments, so that he began to think again about his lifelong dream: the existence of other cavities. As if hypnotised, he returned to the cosmological questions that at various times had haunted him. Was the rock really infinite? It had to be – for, if at some extreme it ended, what lay beyond that end? An infinity of emptiness, as Ereton, in a fit of brilliant extravagance, had once suggested? Erled soon pushed the idea aside. Baffling though the concept of infinity itself was, an empty infinity was something the mind simply could not grasp, and besides the notion was needlessly artificial.

He had expected to get drunk, but two hours later he found that he was still completely sober, having drunk but little. Ereton, too, did not seem to be in a mood for drinking. All seven others, however, drank heavily, and as their intoxication increased so did their indignation at the Proctors' decision. Erled found himself aggravated by the noise and he was about to suggest to Ereton that they leave when there was the sound of a disturbance and the flimsy screen door burst open.

Ergrad, at the head of four or five other enforcers, entered the inn and stood surveying the room, his head slightly bent beneath the big black beams.

'Looks like the whole pack is here, eh?' he barked. 'All right, Erled, the Council has just now ordered that your solidity ship be destroyed, so lead us to it so that we may get on with the good work.'

'Do you need us for that?' Erled retorted. 'Do the job yourselves.'

Ergrad looked at him thoughtfully. 'Don't try to be obstructive, Erled, or it will go all the worse for you. It seems that you've managed to keep the site of your workshop to yourselves, at any rate Erkarn found himself unable to locate it for some reason or other, which looks damned peculiar to me. Well, anyway, we knew you people came here for relaxation and I'll thank you for the information.'

A chain of thoughts flashed through Erled's mind. For a workshop, or any other site for that matter, to be unlocated by the Proctor of Emptiness Utilisation was not only peculiar, it was downright incredible. Only one explanation came to Erled. Since the machines and workspace had originally been allocated by Ergurur, who was sympathetic to them, then somehow he must have concealed this legally obligatory information from Erkarn! An ecstatic hope accelerated Erled's heart. Even in the Council there was dissension! Ergurur was trying to help them!

Around him the others were crying 'Shame!' and protesting to the law enforcers. Ergrad rounded on them, his face livid.

'To your homes, all of you, or you'll learn what it means to cross the law!'

Threateningly, he brandished his truncheon and his followers produced theirs. There was a moment's pause.

Then a heavy glass came sailing through the air and struck Ergrad on the temple. He staggered, while the glass fell to the floor and shattered. With a howl of rage Ergrad ordered his men to attack and in seconds the inn was the scene of an unsightly brawl.

Erled and Ereton, already made nervous by the tense situation, had backed to the far end of the room. They looked on the brawl appalled. Then a cry floated through to them, from Ervane, Erled believed.

That cry prompted Erled into action. Surreptitiously he eased open the rear exit and beckoned to Ereton. Together they slipped away. Minutes later they were headed for the perimeter, having changed direction several times on the public conveyor system to elude pursuit.

'This is terrible!' Ereton said, although he had obeyed Erled as if he had no will of his own. 'Do you think we should go back, Erled, and apologise to Proctor Ergrad? Otherwise everyone will be punished severely.'

'Our friends would never have dared to attack the enforcers if they hadn't been both drunk and angry,' Erled admitted. 'Perhaps that will count in their favour when they come to trial. As for us, a wild intention has entered my mind of which I think the others would approve, Ereton.'

They spoke no more during the rest of the journey, aware that anyone sitting near them on the transporter chairs might be eavesdropping on their conversation. Before long they came to the workshop on the edge of the Cavity where the solidity ship was housed.

The area was deserted, no residences being nearby and this being the rest period. Erled opened the gate and they crept inside. Before them the solidity ship stood on a short ramp, its snout facing the bare rock of infinity but a few yards away.

The ship had the form of a fluted cylinder, either end being squarely blunt and intricated with drive machinery. 'To destroy this ship would be a crime,' Erled said. His mouth curled in disgust. 'They talk of faith. But isn't *our* effort a matter of faith? – faith that the universe contains more than just our one cavity? That there *are* other worlds if only we will look?'

'You want us to take the ship and go illegally into solidity,' Ereton said tonelessly.

'Yes, why not? What else is left to us? It's either that or abandon all our dreams and live useless, frustrated lives. We've got this one chance, so let's take it!'

In his heart Ereton had known that this was why they had come here, but the thought of such a step made him go deathly pale. 'Do you realise what it means? It will be the death sentence when we return!'

'Not if we return with news of other emptiness in the rock!' Erled replied triumphantly. 'We have friends even in the Council, you know!' One friend, anyway, he told himself privately.

Ereton opened his hands in a hopeless gesture. 'And suppose we find no new emptiness? How long did the ancients search?' He shook his head. 'We're both mad.'

'*Both* of us, eh?' Erled grinned. 'I *knew* you were with me! Don't prevaricate, we may only have minutes in which to make our get-away!'

'Smiling wryly, Ereton patted him on the shoulders. "Of course I'm with you, old friend. As you say, what else is there to do at a juncture like this?"

Hastily they scrambled aboard the solidity ship and made a rapid check of all the equipment. The newly completed craft slid along its ramp until reaching the further wall, when the rock touched by its snout seemed to collapse and to flow like fine oil. The ship lurched suddenly forward, and seconds later it had merged and disappeared into the bare, blank rock.

'Incredible,' murmured Erled.

Ereton joined him from aft and peered over his shoulder at the flickering bank of instruments. 'What is it?'

'I think we're being followed.'

They had been *en voyage* for just over two weeks. In the cramped space, Ereton leaned closer. Pretty soon there was no doubt of it: the image plates of both sonicscope and tremorscope sharpened to reveal that a second solidity ship was following them. And it was close.

While they stared in amazement they heard a *ping* and a light came on over the rockvid receiver. Erled flicked a switch. Across the plate streamed recurrent ripples that slowly built up a crude, low-definition picture carried by sonicwaves from the following ship.

The hooded face of Ergrad stared at them from the plate, distorted somewhat by the incessant ripples.

'I never dreamed they'd go this far!' Erled breathed.

The Proctors, presumably, were so furious at their escape that they had
sent Ergrad in hot pursuit! The second ship must have been put together in
a hurry by modifying a surveyor vessel. At that, Erled thought, the enforcer
had done very well indeed to catch up with them so quickly. He must have
strained the engines to the utmost, at considerable danger to himself.

Ergrad spoke, the words coming blurred through the speaker.

'Erled, Ereton! Halt and turn your ship round at once! I am here to escort
you back to the Cavity, where you will stand trial for your crimes!'

Erled and Ereton looked at one another quizzically.

'No return!' Erled said fiercely. 'We keep going!'

Nodding, Ereton spoke into the transmitter microphone. 'Sorry, Proctor,
we can't turn back.'

'Be warned that we are armed with quake beams and will not hesitate to
use them! Obey or be destroyed!' Ergrad glowered, and his voice was like
iron.

'What shall we do?' Ereton hissed, switching off the microphone. 'Those
beams can shake us to pieces!'

'Perhaps we can dodge them.'

Ereton crouched down behind Erled as the latter took over the controls.
The solidity ship surged forward at top speed and began to weave about
through the rock. Shortly afterwards there was a screeching, rumbling sound
and the ship shook as though it were a bell struck by a giant hammer. Erled
gasped as the vibrations caught hold of him and made him feel that he was
being turned inside out.

Although they had been struck only a glancing blow, Erled had been
counting on the fact that quake beams travelled fairly slowly through their
rock medium and therefore were difficult to aim at a fast-moving object.
Unfortunately, Ergrad – or whoever was operating the weapon – seemed to
be skilled in its use.

Finding the controls unaffected by the strike, Erled put the ship through a
dizzying series of turns. He knew that he had to avoid another hit and at the
same time to put distance between himself and the pursuer, because their
only hope lay in the probability that Ergrad's vessel was limited in its range
and therefore he would soon have to turn back.

He peered at the sonicscope and tremorscope plates, trying to judge precisely where the pursuing ship lay and where it might strike next. But
suddenly both plates erupted into an unreadable, screaming flurry as the
quake beam went into action again. All around them the tortured rock
quaked and imploded and the metal of the ship shrieked as if demented.

Erled and Ereton immediately lost consciousness, but the injured solidity ship, its engines still working at full blast, plunged blindly on at top speed through the eternal rock.

Erled did not know how much later it was that he came to himself again. His first impression was of a grating noise jarring on his ears, telling him that all was not well. He saw that Ereton too was stirring, and then he climbed back to his bucket seat and scaled down the accelerator.

'Are you hurt?' he asked Ereton.

'I don't think so,' groaned the other, and he hauled himself to his knees in the confined space. 'What in God's name is that noise?'

'We've sustained some damage, I think. Something amiss in the traction motor by the sound of it.'

He glanced at the 'scope plates. They were both working normally but showed no hint of anything unusual in the vicinity. 'No sign of Ergrad,' he announced.

'Eh?' Ereton stared at the plates in delight. 'What can have happened to him? He should be able to track us down easily enough.'

'It's possible he believes us destroyed,' Erled said with a shrug. 'Or he might already have been at the point of no return when he caught up with us and is unable to follow us any further. It could even be that the quake beam back-fired on him – that happens sometimes, you know. Anyway the first thing we've got to do is check the ship.'

When they had done so the news was not good. The steering gear was severely damaged. Worse, the relatively delicate sustenance recycling plant had also suffered damage. Erled and Ereton debated what to do.

Erled said gloomily: 'We may well die here in the rock. But even if we manage to turn round now and head back home, what future have we? Our rank rebellion earns the death sentence, apart from the possibility that Ergrad may have died, for which we will be held responsible. Let's continue as best we can, Ereton.'

Dourly Ereton agreed.

In the ensuing months they spent much of their time trying to repair the damage. The recycling plant required enormous attention to keep it functioning properly. Sometimes the air became foul and the food uneatable, and neither could help but notice that even its best output was deteriorating over a period of time.

The traction motor never quite lost its ominous grating noise, but they did manage to jury-rig a steering system.

But despite all their successes the confined conditions of their existence, combined with persistent hard work, anxiety, poor food and air, were sapping their strength. As time advanced something like a stupor overcame them. Eventually each privately despaired of reaching their goal, though nei-ther would speak of his despair to the other. During that time only one thing happened to break the monotony. Ereton was taking his turn on watch, star-ing with heavy-lidded eyes at the image plates. Suddenly he gave a hoarse cry which brought Erled hurrying forward.

'Look!'

Furious ripples were appearing on the tremorscope, threatening to break out at any moment into a maelstrom of violence. 'Definitely not a cavity,' Erled mused. 'To me it suggests only one thing: a natural quake – and a big one! Furthermore it's directly ahead!'

'A natural quake?' said Ereton wonderingly. Theoretically they were pos-sible but none had ever been observed. It was calculated that the violence of such phenomena, if they did actually occur, would be simply colossal – enough to wipe out in an instant any cavity luckless enough to be caught in them. Erled knew that they would not survive even for seconds in the giant rock storm that lay ahead.

'If we're to get out of its way we're going to have to turn ninety degrees or more,' Erled said. 'Preferably to the right.'

'Do you think we can?'

'We'd better have a damned good try.'

Both were having a hard time to stay alert in the foul air. Cautiously they put their temporary steering system into operation. Reluctantly the ship turned a little. Then a little more. There was the sound of something snap-ping and an alarm sounded. Gritting his teeth, Ereton forced a little more pressure from the collapsing valves that were supposed to bring the head of the ship round in the rock. The ship turned a few degrees more, then the whole system gave way under the strain.

'Ninety degrees,' said Ereton, breathing deeply. 'Just about!'

But they were without steering of any kind, and both knew that they did not have the strength to try to jury-rig the system again. Leaving the ship on automatic, they returned to their bunks.

Their morale was now falling rapidly. Whenever they could either Erled or Ereton attended to the recycling plant, but the rest of the time, completely debilitated, they simply lay on their narrow bunks and waited for whatever fate would bring.

Four months after their departure from the Cavity Erled was awakened from a deep slumber by the ringing of an alarm. He was perplexed to find that the engines were silent and that the ship was apparently motionless. Dragging himself from his bunk, he saw that the emptiness indicator was flashing – and, he guessed, had been flashing for some time.

Feverishly he shook Ereton to awareness and coaxed him to the control panel. The instruments told their own story: with no one at the controls to heed the 'emptiness ahead' warning, the solidity ship had plunged straight on until encountering that emptiness, upon which the automatic cutout had brought the vessel to a stop.

The two friends did not even speak to one another. Wordlessly they broke open a locker containing oxygen masks which were included in the ship's kit in case the air of alien cavities proved unbreathable. Thus equipped, Erled summoned up his last remaining strength to force open the hull door.

The solidity ship had emerged halfway from a sheer rock wall. As luck would have it, it had struck emptiness only a couple of feet above one of the many rock ledges jutting from the cliff face. After testing the ledge for firmness, Erled and Ereton stumbled down and looked about them.

The new emptiness was faintly illumined by streaks of luminescent stone in the otherwise inert rock. These streaks occurred in the home cavity, also, and were held to be one of the prerequisites for the primeval development of life. The two men, having spent long periods inside the solidity ship in total darkness, adapted to this faint light with little difficulty. At first a terrible cosmic fear gripped Erled; for although he saw the great rock wall stretching unevenly away in all directions nearby, and below he could dimly discern floors, boulders and plateaux, ahead of him there seemed to be nothing but unending void. Was Ereton's wild notion true? Had they come to the edge of solidity, to look out on an infinity of *emptiness*? But as he peered harder Erled saw that the impossible dream was not to be. He saw a dim film of *something* hanging, like a curtain, far away in the distance, and he knew that this was a cavity such as the one in which he had been born. Except that *this* cavity apparently contained no life.

'So it's true!' he declaimed in a cracked voice, the words coming muffled through his mask. 'There *are* other cavities in the rock! Some of them *must* be inhabited! Our faith is justified – we are not alone in the universe!'

At that moment his strength failed him. He felt Ereton's aim around him, helping him back into the solidity ship, where they both lay down for the last time.

Well, Asmravaar, what do you think of that? A sad tale in some respects – but above all, I think, a triumphant victory for the spirit of intelligent life.

There is one tiny aspect of the narrative that may strike you as suspicious. I mean the part in which Erled and Ereton were turned aside from their course, and thereby enabled to find the new cavity, by the intervention of a rock quake. Did this smack of providence? Well, there, I confess, I failed to play fair and concealed the truth: – it *was* providence – my providence. The rock in which these creatures dwell is scattered with caverns at intervals too infrequent to hit upon by sheer luck, and the antronoscopes they use are so primitive that they are only effective over a range of two or three miles. So, seeing a suitable cavern lying quite close to their route, I could not resist helping them out a bit by causing a minor disturbance with an effector beam

How the bipeds came to exist in their rock environment is something of a mystery. Since the surface of the planet, a thousand miles over their heads, is desolate and airless, I surmise that they might have retreated millennia ago from a natural catastrophe or, what amounts to the same thing, from a war of annihilation.

It might seem surprising that the bipeds have never guessed that they live in the interior of a spherical planet, until one remembers that there is nothing in their environment to suggest the fact. The rock stratum in which they live is a variety of basalt and is roofed over by a somewhat rare phenomenon – a five-hundred-mile thick stratum of extremely hard carbon-bonded iron and granite. It would take some really advanced expertise to penetrate this particular lithosphere and when the bipeds took refuge below it, afterwards allowing their science to deteriorate, they effectively imprisoned themselves inside their planet for ever.

The stories about the epic voyages of ancient times are literally true, by the way. They really *did* journey hundreds of thousands of miles, never suspecting that they were simply travelling round the planet's gravity radius (at that depth a circumference of roughly eighteen thousand miles) again and again.

In a way I feel glad that they never knew.

And where is my 'philosophic victory', you want to know? As you are too blockheaded to see it yourself, I shall have to explain. I have discovered a solid universe of infinite rock! But, you protest, the bipeds only *think* they live in such a universe – in actuality they dwell in a completely unremarkable, average planet, leaving aside one or two details of geological interest.

Yet, Asmravaar, are imagination and reality so very much different, really? If the mind is able to entertain some state of affairs as though it were real, then perhaps somewhere in the transfinite universe it *is* real.

As it happens I have a little more than just fancy to support this contention of mine. There is a puzzling little coincidence in the tale I have just related. Ereton, the theoretician, made a calculation of the hypothetical ratio of 'emptiness' to 'solidity' in his (imaginary) universe. I was astonished when I realized that the figures he produced come close to describing the actually existing *converse* case in the real universe – namely the average ratio of *matter to empty space*. I cannot help wondering, therefore, whether this is something more than a coincidence.

Some years ago there used to be much talk about the universe possessing 'matter/anti-matter symmetry', that is, that spatialities of our type might correspond to an equal number of spatialities where matter has its electrical charges reversed – the electron being positive and the proton negative. Since no anti-matter spatialities have been found one hears little about this idea nowadays.

Well: Ereton's calculation has led me to construct, along somewhat similar lines, a theory of my own which I shall present to the Explorers' Club on my next return home. In my theory the universe exhibits 'space/anti-space symmetry', or if you like, 'emptiness-solidity symmetry' to use the bipeds' terminology, so that if one passes the 'mid-point' of the universe, as it were (not a very accurate way to speak of transfinity, I know), then one enters a complementary series of spatialities where there is not primarily void containing islands of matter, but primarily solid matter containing occasional bubbles of void.

I'm pretty confident that my theory will make quite a splash when I announce it. It's amusing to think how one might explore these solid spatialities. Just imagine me and my antronoscope as I bore endlessly through the rock in search of cavity-worlds!

Well, I think that's about enough for now, as I'm very tired. I'll burst this lot to you without delay, and then I'm going to get some much-needed sleep. Yours, and let me hear from you soon: Utz.

My poor Utz: While it was delightful to hear from you after so long, I'm afraid that your ravings about a 'philosophic victory' only go to show that you are suffering from hysterical boredom. Your story, let me say at once, was most entertaining, but apart from that all you have done is to blow up a simple incident into some sort of cosmic hot air which you revealingly admit to be all in your imagination. As for your theory of anti-space it is purely hypothetical and has no solid evidence to support it (the pun was unintentional). These fanciful theories never do turn out to correspond to reality anyway.

I have warned you many times about the monotony of the universe at large and now I think it's beginning to get at you. Let me urge you to come directly home, for I think the rest will do you good. I might even find a part for you in my next play, since you obviously have a misplaced talent for the dramatic. Your ever-loving friend: Asmravaar.

:: :: :: Transfinite cable to Venerable Gob Slok Ok :: Please collect
:: :: ::
DEAR REVERED Uncle,
I trust that the surprise and distaste you will feel on receiving this cable will be decreased when I tell you that I am sending it from the 10^{6248}th series. Since many, many infinities of solid rock and metal therefore separate us, you need not fear an attack of the disgust and revulsion which my presence seems to cause you.

I am contacting you because, whatever your feelings for me personally, you are still one of the most noted of scholars, whose professional opinion I value, and I cannot refrain from notifying you of a discovery of mine, even though I know how much you disapprove of my life as a cosmic explorer.

Having transmigrated myself into the 10^{6248}th series of solidities I proceeded to tunnel strongly through rock which proved, for an immense distance, to be unbroken. I was, I should add, in a region far removed from any of the cavity-clusters which usually abound in this series, a desolate region which would normally remain unexplored for all time. My reason for tunnelling in this direction, I say without shame (at the risk of enraging you, Uncle) was sheer caprice.

At any rate my antronoscopes registered the unexpected presence of a very large cavity so I hurried to investigate. It transpired that this cavity was the largest I have ever encountered or heard of. The mean diameter is ten million miles!

Let me repeat that, Uncle, in case you think there has been a mistake in transmission. Ten million miles! Not only that but the cavity contains a rich biological life and has several intelligent species scattered around its circumference, none of which I have made contact with yet, as I want to await your advice.

The fact is, Uncle, that so far I have investigated only one of these species and it entertains such an astonishing picture of the cosmos that I don't know quite how to proceed. Let me explain. In a cavity of this size centrifugal gravity works very efficiently. Consequently there is a film of atmosphere about two hundred miles deep upon the walls of the cavity, but the rest is void – pure emptiness.

I should also add that it is almost impossible to see as far as the opposite side of the cavity, for reasons rather too complicated to go into here. Anyway, the upshot is that these intelligent beings, who live, of course, within the atmosphere, are aware that a vacuum lies above them after the atmosphere peters out (being compressed, of course, by the excessive gravity). But their world is so large, and so impossible for them to explore fully on account of its size, that they possess no idea that it constitutes the inner surface of a sphere! (Or near-sphere.) They suppose that the void above them extends without limit – that *the cosmos is an infinity of vacuum with only islands of solid matter in it.*

It was some time before I was able to comprehend a belief so bizarre and inconceivable. And yet now that I have managed, after a fashion, to grasp it, I find the idea rather compelling and fascinating, and I can't help wondering whether there *might*, among all the solidities as yet unexplored, be one consisting of almost nothing but emptiness?

I hope, Uncle, that you can forget our differences for long enough to give your attention to this question. We are both, remember, animated by a love of knowledge and I would listen to your opinion most earnestly. Do you think that a nearly-empty solidity – one would, I suppose, have to call it a 'spatiality' – is possible?

And apart from that, should I attempt to contact the beings in the giant cavity, or should I leave them alone with their delusion?

Your perplexed and respectful nephew,

Awm.

∷ ∷ ∷ Transfinite Open Cable Receipt Awm Oosh Ok ∷ Transmit 10^{62--} range ∷ Reply not prepaid ∷ ∷ ∷

DEAR Nephew,

Not only is your idea of a vacuous infinity inconceivable, it is also downright silly and utterly impossible, as well you know.

In a way it's a pity we don't live in such a world because no type of propulsion could operate in a void, since there would be nothing on which to gain traction, and that would at least prevent you young grubs from gadding about the cosmos with all the irresponsibility of flame-flies.

I have placed on record your discovery of the curiosity, namely the giant cavity, and I suppose I should thank you for that trifle. However I feel it is amply repaid by my deigning to reply at all to your cable, which otherwise I would have ignored.

If you solicit my opinion then you must accept it on any subject I care to name. Let me be quite specific: your larvae, of which you seem to generate an indecent number with each visit to your long-suffering family, are hatching without the benefit of a father to guide them in the rituals of the swarm, and seem most unlikely to grow into decent, low-crawling worms. Your wives grow fat and lazy without the discipline which only a strict husband can provide, and the affairs of your estates are going to rack and ruin. I thank God that your father is not alive to see how his son has turned out.

A worm's place is at home – that is my opinion, and I strongly recommend that you repair hither post-haste. As for whether you should or should not communicate with ignorant savages, that is of absolutely no interest to me.

Your most displeased uncle,

Gob.

ALL THE KING'S MEN

I saw Sorn's bier, an electrically driven train decorated like a fanfare, as it left the North Sea Bridge and passed over the green meadows of Yorkshire. Painted along its flank was the name HOLATH HOLAN SORN, and it motored swiftly with brave authority. From where we stood in the observation-room of the King's Summer Palace, we could hear the hollow humming of its passage.

'You will not find things easy without Holath Holan Sorn,' I said, and turned. The King of All Britain was directing his mosaic eyes towards the train.

'Things were never easy,' he replied. But he knew as well as I that the loss of Sorn might mean the loss of a kingdom.

The King turned from the window, his purple cloak flowing about his seven-foot frame. I felt sorry for him: how would he rule an alien race, with its alien psychology, now that Sorn was dead? He had come to depend entirely upon that man who could translate one set of references into another as easily as he crossed the street. No doubt there were other men with perhaps half of Sorn's abilities, but who else could gain the King's trust? Among all humans, none but Sorn could be the delegate of the Invader King.

'Smith,' he said, addressing me, 'tomorrow we consign twelve tooling factories to a new armaments project. I wish you to supervise.'

I acknowledged, wondering what this signified. No one could deny that the aliens' reign had been peaceful, even prosperous, and he had rarely mentioned military matters, although I knew there was open enmity between him and the King of Brazil. Either this enmity was about to become active, I decided, or else the King forecast a civil uprising.

Which in itself was not unlikely.

Below us, the bier was held up by a junction hitch. Stationary, it supplemented its dignity by sounding its klaxon loudly and continuously. The King returned his gaze to it, and though I couldn't read his unearthly face I suppose he watched it regretfully, if he can feel regret. Of the others in the room, probably the two aliens also watched with regret, but certainly no one else did. Of the four humans, three were probably glad he was dead, though they may have been a little unsure about it.

That left myself. I was more aware of events than any of them, but I just didn't know what I felt. Sometimes I felt on the King's side and sometimes on the other side. I just didn't have any definite loyalties.

Having witnessed the arrival of the bier from the continent, where Sorn had met his death, we had achieved the purpose of the visit to the Summer Palace, and accordingly the King, with his entourage of six (two fellow beings, four humans including myself) left for London.

We arrived at Buckingham Palace shortly before sunset. Wordlessly the King dismissed us all, and with a lonely swirl of his cloak made his way to what was in a makeshift manner called the throne-room. Actually it did have a throne: but it also had several other kinds of strange equipment, things like pools, apparatus with what psychologists called threshold associations. The whole chamber was an aid to the incomprehensible, insectile mentality of the King, designed, I suspected, to help him in the almost impossible task of understanding a human society. While he had Sorn at his elbow there had been little need to worry, and the inadequacy of the chamber mattered so little that he seldom used it. Now, I thought, the King of All Britain would spend a large part of his time meditating in solitude on the enigmatic throne.

I had the rest of the evening to myself. But I hadn't gone far from the palace when, as I might have guessed, Hotch placed his big bulk square across my path.

'Not quite so fast,' he said, neither pleasantly nor unpleasantly.

I stopped – what else could I have done? – but I didn't answer. 'All right,' Hotch said, 'let's have it straight. I want nobody on both sides.'

'What do you mean?' I asked, as if I didn't already know.

'Sorn's dead, right? And you're likely to replace him. Right?'

'Wrong,' I told him wearily. 'Nobody replaces Sorn. He was the one irre-placeable human being.'

His eyes dropped in pensive annoyance. He paused. 'Maybe, but you'll be the closest to the King's rule. Is that so?'

I shrugged.

'It has to be so,' he decided. 'So which way is it going to be, Smith? If you're going to be another traitor like Sorn, let's hear it from the start. Otherwise be a man and come in with us.'

It sounded strange to hear Sorn called a traitor. Technically, I suppose he was – but he was also a man of genius, the rarest of statesmen. And even now only the 0.5 per cent of the population roused by Hotch's super-patriotism would think of him as anything else. Britain had lived in a plentiful sort of calm under the King. The fact of being governed by an alien conqueror was not resented, even though he had enthroned himself by force. With his three ships, his two thousand warriors, he had achieved a near-bloodless occupa-tion, for he had won his victory by the sheer possession of superior weapons, without having to resort much to their usage. The same could be said of the simultaneous invasion of Brazil and South Africa: Brazil by fellow creatures of the King, South Africa by a different species. Subsequent troubles in these two areas had been greater, but then they lacked the phlegmatic British attitude, and more important, they lacked Holath Holan Sorn.

I sighed. 'Honestly, I don't know. Some human governments have been a lot worse.'

'But they've been human. And we owed a lot to Sorn, though personally I loathed his guts. Now that he's gone – what? The King will make a mess of things. How do we know he really cares?'

'I think he does. Not the same way a man would care, but he does.'

'Hah! Anyhow, this is our chance. While he doesn't know what he's doing. What about it? Britain hasn't known another conqueror in a thousand years.'

I couldn't tell him. I didn't know. Eventually he stomped off in disgust.

I didn't enjoy myself that evening. I thought too much about Sorn, about the King, and about what Hotch had said. How could I be sure the King cared for England? He was so grave and gently ponderous, but did that indicate anything? His appearance could simply be part of his foreignness and nothing at all to do with his feelings. In fact if the scientists were right about him, he had no feelings at all.

But what purpose had he?

I stopped by Trafalgar Square to see the Green Fountains.

The hand of the invader on Britain was present in light, subtle ways, such as the Green Fountains. For although Britain remained Britain, with the character of Britain, the King and his men had delicately placed their alien character upon it; not in law, or the drastic changes of a conqueror, but in such things as decoration.

The Green Fountains were foreign, unimaginable, and un-British. High curtains of thin fluid curled into fantastic designs, creating new concepts of space by sheer ingenuity of form. Thereby they achieved what centuries of Terran artists had only hinted at.

And yet they *were* British, too. If Britons had been prompted to conceive and construct such things, this was the way they would have done it. They carried the British stamp, although so alien.

When I considered the King's rule, the same anomaly emerged. A strange rule, by a stranger, yet imposed so easily.

This was the mystery of the King's government: the way he had adopted Britain, in essence, while having no comprehension of that essence.

But let me make it clear that for all this, the invader's rule did not *operate* easily. It jarred, oscillated, went out of phase, and eventually, without Sorn, ended in disaster. It was only in this other, peculiar way, that it harmonised so pleasingly.

It was like this: when the King and his men tried to behave functionally and get things done, it was terrible. It didn't fit. But when they simply added themselves to All Britain, and lay quiescently like touches of colour, it had the effect I describe.

I had always thought Sorn responsible for this. But could Sorn mould the King also? For I detected in the King that same English passivity and acceptance; not just his own enigmatic detachment, but something apart from that, something acquired. Yet how could he be something which he didn't understand?

Sorn is dead, I thought, Sorn is dead.

Already, across one side of the square, were erected huge, precise stone symbols HOLATH HOLAN SORN DIED 5.8.2034. They were like a mathematical formula. Much of the King's speech, when I thought of it, had the same quality.

Sorn was dead, and the weight of his power which had steadied the nation would be abruptly removed. He had been the operator, bridging the gap between alien minds. Without him, the King was incompetent.

A dazzling blue and gold air freighter appeared over the square and slanted down towards the palace. Everyone stopped to look, for it was one of the extraterrestrial machines, rarely seen since the invasion. No doubt it carried reinforcements for the palace defences.

Next morning I motored to Surrey to visit the first of the ten factories the King had mentioned.

The managers were waiting for me. I was led to a prepared suite of offices where I listened sleepily to a lecture on the layout and scope of the factory. I wasn't very interested; one of the King's kinsmen (referred to as the King's men) would arrive shortly with full details of the proposed conversion, and the managers would have to go through it all again. I was only here as a representative, so to speak. The real job would be carried out by the alien.

We all wandered round the works for a few hours before I got throroughly bored and returned to my office. A visitor was waiting.

Hotch.

'What do you want now?' I asked. 'I thought I'd got rid of you.'

He grinned. 'I found out what's going on.' He waved his arms to indicate the factory.

'What of it?'

'Well, wouldn't you say the King's policy is … ill-advised?'

'You know as well as I do that the King's policy is certain to be laughably clumsy.' I motioned him to a seat. 'What exactly do you mean? I'm afraid I don't know the purpose of this myself.'

I was apologetic about the last statement, and Hotch laughed. 'It's easy enough to guess. Don't you know what they're building in Glasgow? *Ships - warships* of the King's personal design.'

'Brazil,' I murmured.

'Sure. The King chooses this delicate moment to launch a transatlantic war. Old Rex is such a blockhead he almost votes himself out of power.'

'How?'

'Why, he gives us the weapons to fight him with. He's organising an armed native force which *I* will turn against him.'

'You jump ahead of yourself. To go by the plans I have, no extraterrestrial weapons will be used.'

Hotch looked more sober. 'That's where you come in. We can't risk another contest with the King's men using ordinary arms. It would kill millions and devastate the country. Because it won't be the skirmish-and-capitulate of last time. This time we'll be in earnest. So I want you to soften things up for us. Persuade the King to hand over more than he intends: help us to chuck him out easily. Give us new weapons and you'll save a lot of carnage.'

I saw his stratagem at once. 'Quit that! Don't try to lay blood responsibility on my shoulders. That's a dirty trick.'

'For a dirty man – and that's what you are, Smith, if you continue to stand by, too apathetic even to think about it. Anyhow, the responsibility's already laid, whatever you say. It depends on you.'

'No.'

'You won't help?'

'That's right.'

Hotch sighed, and stared at the carpet for some seconds. Then he stared through the glass panels and down on to the floor of the workshops. 'Then what will you do? Betray me?'

'No.'

Sighing again, he told me: 'One day, Smith, you'll fade away through sheer lack of interest.'

'I'm interested,' I said. 'I just don't seem to have the kind of mind that can make a decision. I can't find any place to lay blame, or anyone to turn against.'

'Not even for Britain,' he commented sadly. 'Your Britain as well as mine. That's all I'm working for, Smith, our country.'

His brashness momentarily dormant, he was moodily meditative. 'Smith, I'll admit I don't understand what it's all about. What does the King want? What has he gained by coming down here?'

'Nothing. He descended on us and took on a load of troubles without profit. It's a mystery. Hence my uncertainty.' I averted my eyes. 'During the time I have been in contact with the King he has impressed me as being utterly, almost transcendentally unselfish. So unselfish, so abstracted, that he's like a – just a blank!'

'That's only how you see it. Maybe you read it into him. The psychos say he's no emotion, and selfishness is a kind of emotion.'

'Is it? Well, that's just what I mean. But he seems – humane, for all that. Considerate, though it's difficult for him.'

He wasn't much impressed. 'Yeah. Remember that whatever substitutes for emotion in him might have some of its outward effects. And remember, he's not the only outworlder on this planet. He doesn't seem so considerate towards Brazil.'

Hotch rose and prepared to leave. 'If you survive the rebellion, I'll string you up as a traitor.'

'All right!' I answered, suddenly irritable. 'I know.'

But when Hotch did get moving, I was surprised at the power he had gained for himself in the community. He knew exactly how to accentuate the irritating qualities of the invader, and he did it mercilessly.

Some of the incidents seemed ridiculous. Such as when alien officials began to organise the war effort with complete disregard for some of the things the nation took to be necessities – entertainment, leisure, and so on. The contents of art galleries and museums were burned to make way for weapons shops. Cinemas were converted into automatic factories, and all television transmissions ceased. Don't get the idea that the King and his men are all tyrannical automata. They just didn't see any reason for not throwing away priceless paintings, and never thought to look for one.

Affairs might have progressed more satisfactorily if the set-up had been less democratic. Aware of his poor understanding, the King had appointed a sort of double government. The first, from which issued the prime directive, consisted of his own men in key positions throughout the land, though actually their power had peculiar limitations. The second government was a human representation of the aboriginal populace, which in larger matters was still obliged to gain the King's spoken permission.

The King used to listen very intently to the petitions and pseudo-emotional barrages which this absurd body placed before him – for they were by no means co-operative – and the meetings nearly always ended in bewilderment. During Sorn's day it would have been different: he could have got rid of them in five minutes.

Those men caused chaos, and cost the country many lives in the Brazilian war which shortly followed. After Hotch gained control over them, they were openly the King's enemies. He didn't know it, of course, and now that it's all finished I often wish I had warned him.

I remember the time they came to him and demanded a national working week of twenty-five hours. This was just after the King's men had innocently tried to institute a sixty-hour working week, and had necessarily been restrained.

The petitioners knew how impossible it was; they were just trying to make trouble.

The King received them amid the sparse trappings of his Court. A few of his aides were about, and a few human advisers. Then he lifted his head and asked for help.

'Advise me,' he said to everyone present.

But the hostile influences in the hall were so great that all those who might have helped him shrugged their shoulders. That was the way things were. I said nothing.

'If the proposal is carried out,' the King told the ministers, 'current programmes will not go through.'

He tried to reject the idea, but they amazingly refused to let it be rejected. They threatened and intimidated, and one gentleman began to talk hypocritically about the will and welfare of the people. Naturally there was no response: the King was not equipped. He surveyed the hall again. 'He who can solve this problem, come forward.'

There was a lethargic, apathetic suspension. The aliens were immobile, like hard brilliant statues, observing these dangerous events as if with the asceticism of stone. Then there was more shrugging of shoulders.

It speaks for the leniency of the extraterrestrials that this could happen at all. Among human royalty, such insolence would bring immediate repercussions. But the mood was contagious, because I didn't volunteer either. Hotch's machinations had a potential, unspoken element of terrorism.

Whether the King realised that advice was being deliberately withheld, I don't know. He called my name and strode to the back of the hall.

I followed his authoritatively gyrating cloak, reluctantly, like a dreading schoolboy. When I reached him, he said: 'Smith, it is knowledge common to us both that my thinkings and human thinking are processes apart. Not even Sorn could have both kinds; but he could translate.' He paused for a moment, and then continued with a couple of sentences of the mixed-up talk he had used on Sorn, together with some of the accompanying queer honks and noises. I couldn't follow it. He seemed to realise his mistake, though, for he soon emerged into fairly sensible speech again, like this: '*Honk*. Environs matrix wordy. Int apara; is trying like light to; apara see blind, from total outside is not even potential … if you were king, Smith, what would you do?'

'Well,' I said, 'people have been angered by the impositions made on them recently, and now they're trying to swing the pendulum the other way. Maybe I would compromise and cut the week by about ten hours.'

The King drew a sheaf of documents from a voluminous sash pocket and spread them out. One of them had a chart on it, and lists of figures. Producing a small machine with complex surfaces, he made what appeared to be a computation.

I wished I could find some meaning in those cold jewel eyes. 'That would interfere with my armament programme,' he said. 'We must become strong, or the King of Brazil will lay Britain waste.'

'But surely it's important not to foster a discontented populace?'

'Important! So often I have heard that word, and cannot understand it. Sometimes it appears to me, Smith, that human psychology is hilly country, while mine is a plain. My throne-room contains hints that some things you see as high, and others as low and flat, and the high is more powerful. But for me to travel this country is impossible.'

Smart. And it made some sense to me, too, because the King's character often seemed to be composed of absences. He had no sense of crisis, for example. I realised how great his effort must have been to work this out.

'And "importance",' he continued. 'Some mountain top?'

He almost had it. 'A big mountain,' I said.

For a few seconds I began to get excited and thought that perhaps he was on his way to a semantic break-through. Then I saw where I was wrong. Knowing intellectually that a situation is difficult, and *why* it is difficult, is not much use when it comes to operating in that situation. If the King had fifty million minds laid out in diagram, with all their interconnections (and this is perfectly possible) he would still be no better able to operate. It is far too complex to grasp all at once with the intellect; to be competent in an environment, one must live in it, must be homogeneous with it. The King does not in the proper sense do the former, and is not the latter.

He spent a little while in the throne-room, peering through thresholds, no doubt, gazing at pools and wondering about the mountainous. Then he returned and offered the petitioners a concession of ten minutes off the working week. This was the greatest check he thought he could allow on his big industrial drive.

They argued angrily about it, until things grew out of hand and the King ordered me to dismiss them. I had to have it done forcibly. Any one of the alien courtiers could have managed it single-handed by mere show of the weapons on his person, but instead I called in a twenty-man human body-guard, thinking that to be ejected by their own countrymen might reduce their sense of solidarity.

All the humans of the court exuded uneasiness. But they needn't have worried. To judge by the King and his men, nothing might have happened. They held their positions with that same crystalline intelligence which they had carried through ten years of occupation. I was beginning to learn that this static appearance did not wholly result from unintelligibility, but that they actually maintained a constant internal state irrespective of external conditions. Because of this, they were unaware that the scene that had just been enacted comprised a minor climax. Living in a planar mentality the very idea of climax was not apparent to them.

After the petitioners had gone, the King took me to his private chambers behind the courtroom. 'Now is the time for consolidation,' he said. 'Without

Sorn, the governing factions become separated, and the country disintegrates. I must find contact with the indigenous British. Therefore I will strike a closer liaison with you, Smith, my servant. You will follow me around.'

He meant that I was to replace Sorn, as well as I could. Making it an official appointment was probably his way of appealing for help.

He had hardly picked the right man for the job, but that was typical of the casual way he operated. Of course, it made my personal position much worse, since I began to feel bad about letting him down. I was caught at the nexus of two opposing forces: even my inaction meant that somebody would profit. Altogether, not a convenient post for a neutral passenger.

Anyway, since the situation had arisen, I decided to be brash and ask some real questions.

'All right,' I said, 'but for whose sake is this war being fought – Britain's or yours?'

As soon as the words were out of my mouth I felt a little frightened. In the phantasmal human alien relationship, such carthy examinations were out of place. But the King accepted it.

'I am British,' he answered, 'and Britain is mine. Ever since I came, our actions are inseparable.'

Some factions of the British public would have disagreed with this, but I supposed he meant it in a different way. Perhaps in a way connected with the enigmatically compelling characters and aphorisms that had been erected about the country, like mathematics developed in words instead of numbers. I often suspected that the King had sought to gain power through semantics alone.

Because I was emotionally adrift, I was reckless enough to argue the case. 'Well,' I said, 'without you there would be no war. The Brazilians would never fight without compulsion from their own King, either. I'm not trying to secede from your authority, but resolve my opinion that you and the King of Brazil are using human nations as instruments … in a private quarrel.'

For some while he thought about it, placing his hands together. He answered: 'When the events of which I and the King of Brazil are a part moved into this region, I descended on to Britain, and he on to Brazil. By the fundamental working of things, I took on the nature of Britain, and Britain in reciprocation became incorporated in the workings of those events. And likewise with the King of Brazil, and with Brazil. These natures, and those events, are not for the time being separables, but included in each other. Therefore it is to defend Britain that I strive, because Britain is harnessed to my section of those outside happenings, and because I am British.'

When I had finally sorted out that chunk of pedantry, his claims to nationality sounded like baloney. Then I took into account the slightly supra-sensible evidence of his British character. After a little reflection I realised that he had gone halfway towards giving me an explanation of it.

'What kind of happenings,' I wondered, 'can they be?'

The King can't smile, and he can't sound wistful, and it's hard for him to convey anything except pure information. But what he said next sounded like the nearest thing to wistfulness he could manage.

'They are very far from your mind,' he said, 'and from your style of living. 'They are connected with the colliding galaxies in Cygnus. More than that would be very difficult to tell you …'

There was a pause. I began to see that the King's concern was with something very vast and strange indeed. England was only a detail …

'And those outsiders who took over South Africa. What's their part in this?'

'No direct connection. Events merely chanced to blow this way.'

Oddly, the way he said it made me think of how neat the triple invasion had been. In no instance had the borders of neighbouring states been violated, and the unmolested nations had in turn regarded the conquests as internal matters. Events had happened in discreet units, not in an interpenetrating mass as they usually do. The reactions of the entire Terrestrial civilisation had displayed an unearthly flavour. Maybe the incompatibility of alien psychology was not entirely mental. Perhaps in the King's native place not only minds but also events took a different form from those of Earth. What is mentality, anyway, but a complex event? I could imagine a sort of transplanting of natural laws, these three kings, with all their power, bringing with them residual influences of the workings of their own worlds …

It sounded like certain astrological ideas I had once heard, of how on each world everything is different, each world has its own basic identity, and everything on that world partakes of that identity. But it's only astrology.

As the time for war drew nearer, Hotch became more daring. Already he had made himself leader of the unions and fostered general discontent, as well as organising an underground which, in some ways, had more control over Britain than the King himself had. But he had a particular ambition, and in furtherance of this he appeared one day at Buckingham Palace.

Quite simply, he intended to do what I had refused to do for him.

He bowed low before the King, ignoring me, and launched into his petition.

'The people of Britain have a long tradition of reliability and capability in war,' he proclaimed. 'They cannot be treated like children. Unless they are given fighting powers equal to those of the extraterrestrials – for I do not suppose that your own troops will be poorly armed – their morale will relapse and they will be defeated. You will be the psychological murderer of Britain.'

When he had finished, he cast a defiant glance at me, then puffed out his barrel chest and waited for a reply.

He had good reason to be afraid. One word from me, and he was finished. I admired his audacity.

I was also astounded at the outrageous way he had made the request, and I was at a loss to know what to do.

I sank on to the throne steps and slipped into a reverie. If I kept silent and showed loyalty to my country I would bring about the downfall of the King.

If I spoke in loyalty to the King, I would bring about the downfall of Hotch.

And really, I couldn't find any loyalty anywhere. I was utterly adrift, as if I didn't exist on the surface of the planet at all. I was like a compass needle which failed to answer to the magnetic field:

'Psychological murderer of Britain,' I repeated to myself. I was puzzled at the emotional evocation in that phrase. How could a human administer emotion to the King? But of course, it wasn't really an emotion at all. In the King's eyes the destruction of Britain was to be avoided, and it was this that Hotch was playing on.

Emerging from my drowsy thoughts, I saw Hotch leave. The King had not given an answer. He beckoned to me.

He spoke a few words to me, but I was non-committal. Then I waited outside the throne-room, while he spent an hour inside.

He obviously trusted Hotch. When he came out, he called together his full council of eight aliens, four humans and myself, and issued directives for the modification of the war. I say of war, and not of preparations for the war, because plans were now sufficiently advanced for the general outlines of the conflict to be set down on paper. The way the aliens handled a war made it hardly like fighting at all, but like an engineering work or a business project. Everything was decided beforehand; the final outcome was almost incidental.

And so several factories were re-tooled to produce the new weapons, the military hierarchy readjusted to give humans a greater part, and the focus of the main battle shifted five hundred miles further west. Also, the extrapolated duration of the war was shortened by six months.

Hotch had won. All Britain's industries worked magnificently for three months. They worked for Hotch as they had never worked, even for Sorn.

I felt weary. A child could have seen through Hotch's trick, but the King bad been taken in. What went on in his head, after all? What guided him? Did he really care – for anything?

I wondered what Sorn would have thought. But then, I had never known what went on in Sorn's head, either.

The fleet assembled at Plymouth and sailed west into a sunny, choppy Atlantic. The alien-designed ships, which humans called swan-boats, were marshalled into several divisions. They rode high above the water on tripod legs, and bobbed lightly up and down.

Aerial fighting was forbidden by treaty, but there was one aircraft in the fleet, a wonderful blue and gold non-combatant machine where reposed the King, a few personal servants and myself. We drifted a few hundred feet above the pale green waterships, matching our speed with theirs.

That speed was slow. I wondered why we had not fitted ourselves out with those steel leviathans of human make, fast battleships and destroyers, which could have traversed the ocean in a few days whereas our journey required most of a month. It's true the graceful swarm looked attractive in the sunlight, but I don't think that was the reason. Or maybe it was a facet of it.

The Brazilians were more conventional in their combat aesthetics. They had steamed slowly out of the Gulf of Mexico to meet us at a location which, paradoxically, had been predetermined without collusion. We were greeted by massive grey warships, heavy with guns. Few innovations appeared to have been introduced into the native shipbuilding, though I did see one long corvette-shape lifted clean out of the water on multiple hydroplanes.

Fighting began in a casual, restrained manner when the belligerents were about two miles apart. There was not much outward enthusiasm for some hours. Our own ships ranged in size from the very small to the daintily monstrous, and wallowed prettily throughout the enemy fleet, discharging flashes of brilliant light. Our more advanced weapons weren't used much, probably because they would have given us an unfair advantage over the Brazilian natives, who had not had the benefit of Hotch's schemings.

Inside me I felt a dull sickness. All the King's men were gathered here in the Atlantic; this was the obvious time for Hotch's rebellion.

But it would not happen immediately. Hotch was astute enough to realise that even when he was rid of the King he might still have to contend with Brazil, and he wanted to test his future enemy's strength.

The unemphatic activity on the surface of the ocean continued, while one aircraft floated in the air above. The King watched, sometimes from the balcony, sometimes by means of a huge jumble of screens down inside, which showed an impossible montage of the scene viewed from innumerable angles, most of which had no tactical usefulness that I could see. Some were from locations at sea-level, some only gave images of rigging, and there was even one situated a few feet below the surface.

I followed the King around, remembering his warning of the devastation which would ensue from Britain's defeat. 'But what will happen if we win?' I asked him.

'Do not be concerned,' he told me. 'Current events are in the present time, and will be completed with the cessation of the war.'

'But something must happen afterwards.'

'Subsequent events are not these events.' A monstrous swinging pattern, made of bits and pieces of hulls and gunfire, built up mysteriously in the chaos of the screens, and dissolved again. The King turned to go outside.

When he returned, the pattern had begun again, with modifications. I continued: 'If you believe that, why do you talk about Britain's welfare?'

He applied himself to watching the screens, still showing no deviation from his norm, in a situation which to a normal man would have been crisis. 'All Britain is mine,' he said after his normal pause. 'Therefore I make arrangements for its protection. This is comprehensible to us both, I think.'

He swivelled his head towards me. 'Why do you enquire in this way, Smith? These questions are not the way to knowledge.'

Having been rebuked thus – if a being with a personality like atonal music can be said to rebuke – I too went outside, and peered below. The interpenetrated array seemed suddenly like male and female. Our own more neatly shaped ships moved lightly, while the weighty, pounding Brazilians were more demonstratively aggressive, and even had long gun turrets for symbolism. Some slower part of my mind commented that the female is alleged to be the submissive, receptive part, which our fleet was not; but I dismissed that.

After two hours the outcome still looked indefinite to my mind. But Hotch decided he had seen enough. He acted.

A vessel which hitherto had kept to the outskirts of the battle and taken little part, abruptly opened up its decks and lifted a series of rocket ramps. Three minutes later, the missiles had disappeared into the sky and I guessed what war-heads they carried.

Everything fitted neatly: it was a natural decision on Hotch's part. In such a short time he had not been able to develop transatlantic rockets, and he might never again be this close to the cities of Brazil. I could see him adding it all up in his mind.

Any kind of aeronautics was outlawed, and the Brazilians became enraged. They used their guns with a fury such as I hope never to see again. And I was surprised at how damaging a momentum a few thousand tons of fast-moving steel can acquire. Our own boys were a bit ragged in their defence at first, because they were busy butchering the King's men.

With the new weapons, most of this latter was over in twenty minutes. I went inside, because by now weapons were being directed at the aircraft, and the energies were approaching the limits of its defensive capacity.

The hundred viewpoints adopted by the viewing screens had converted the battle-scene into a flurry too quick for my eyes to follow. The King asked my advice.

My most immediate suggestion was already in effect. Slowly, because the defence screens were draining power, we ascended into the stratosphere.

The rest of what I had to say took longer, and was more difficult, but I told it all.

The King made no comment on my confession, but studied the sea. I withdrew into the background, feeling uncomfortable.

The arrangement of vision screens was obsolete now that the battle-plan had been disrupted. Subsidiaries were set up to show the struggle in a simpler form. By the time we came to rest in the upper air, Hotch had rallied his navy and was holding his own in a suddenly bitter engagement.

The King ordered other screens to be focused on Brazil. He still did not look at me.

After he had watched developments for a short time, he decided to meditate in solitude, as was his habit. I don't know whether it was carelessness or simple ignorance, but without a pause he opened the door and stepped on to the outside balcony.

Fortunately, the door opened and closed like a shutter; the air replenishers worked very swiftly, and the air density was seriously low for less than a second. Even so, it was very unpleasant.

Emerging from the experience, I saw the King standing pensively outside in the partial vacuum of the upper air. I swore with surprise: it was hot out there, and even the sunlight shining through the filtered windows was more than I could tolerate.

When he returned, he was considerate enough to use another door.

By this time the monitor screens had detected the squadrons of bombers rising in retaliation from Brazil's devastated cities. The etiquette of the old war was abandoned, and there was no doubt that they too carried the nuclear weapons illegally employed by Hotch.

The King observed: 'When those bombers reach their delivery area in a few hours' time, most of Britain's fighting power will still be a month away in the Western Atlantic. Perhaps the islands should be warned to prepare what defences they have.' His gem eyes lifted. 'What do you say, Smith?'

'Of course they must be warned!' I replied quickly. 'There is still an air defence – Hotch has kept the old skills alive. But he may not have expected such quick reprisals, and early interception is essential.'

'I see. This man Hotch seems a skilful organiser, Smith, and would be needed in London.' With interest, he watched the drive and ferocity of the action on the sea-scape. 'Which is his ship?'

I pointed out the large swan-boat on which I believed Hotch to be present. Too suddenly for our arrival to be anticipated, we dropped from the sky. The servants of the King conducted a lightning raid which made a captive of Hotch with thirty per cent casualties.

We had been absent from the stratosphere for two minutes and forty-five seconds.

Hotch himself wasn't impressed. He accused me of bad timing. 'You may be right,' I said, and told him the story.

If he was surprised he didn't show it. He raised his eyebrows, but that was all. No matter how grave the situation might be, Hotch wouldn't let it show.

'It's a native war from now on,' he acclaimed. 'There's not an alien left in either fleet.'

'You mean the Brazilians rebelled too?'

'I wish they would! The green bosses hopped it and left them to it.'

The King offered to put Hotch down at Buckingham Palace, the centre of all the official machinery. Hotch greeted the suggestion with scorn.

'That stuff's no good to me,' he said. 'Put me down at my headquarters in Balham. That's the only chance of getting our fighter planes in the air.'

This we did. The pilots had already set the aircraft in silent motion through the stratosphere, and within an hour we slanted downwards and flashed the remaining five hundred miles to England.

London was peaceful as we hovered above it three hours in advance of the raiders. Only Hotch's impatient energy indicated the air of urgency it would shortly assume.

But what happened on Earth after that, I don't know. We went into space, so I have only a casual interest.

It's like this: the King showed me space.

To see it with the bare eyes is enough, but on the King's set of multi- and null-viewpoint vision screens it really gets hammered in. And what gets knocked into you is this: nothing matters. Nothing is big enough to matter. It's as simple as that.

However big a thing is, it just isn't big enough. For when you see the size of totality – I begin to understand now why the King, who has seen it all the time, is as he is.

And nothing is important. There is only a stratified universe, with some things more powerful than others. That's what makes us think they are important – they're more powerful, but that's all. And the most powerful is no more significant than the least.

You may wonder, then, why the King bothers with such trivial affairs as Britain. That's easy.

When I was a young man, I thought a lot of myself. I thought myself valuable, if only to myself. And, once, I began to wonder just how much it would take for me to sacrifice my life, whether if it came to it I would sacrifice myself for a less intelligent, less worthwhile life than my own. But now I see the sacrifice for what it is: simply one insignificance for another insignificance. It's an easy trade. So the King, who has ranged over a dozen galaxies, has lost his war, his army, and risks even his own life, for Britain's sake. It's all too tiny even to hesitate over. He did what he could: how could he do anything else?

Like the King, I was quickly becoming incapable of judgement. But before it goes altogether, I will say this of you, Hotch: It was a low trick you played on the King. A low, dirty trick to play on a good man.

AN OVERLOAD

They always met by television. Usually it was once every three months. Always it was with much argument. The meeting chamber, though in a secret location and possessing neither door nor windows, had a dignity wholly befitting its role. Its walls were panelled with ancient, grained oak. The floor was deeply carpeted. Mahogany, another near-extinct and much-valued wood, had been used to make the incomparable boardroom table. On its dark shining surface rested six holo television sets arranged so that the stage-screen of each could view all the others.

Today Sinatra was sour. 'You know what I think?' he said, stubbing out a cigarette with a derisory gesture. 'I'll tell you: I think this thing's not worth talking about.'

Bogart gave a typical puzzled frown, his shrewd preoccupied eyes shifting from side to side as he spoke. 'If it bothers us it's worth talking about. This guy Karnak seems to be making progress.'

'Aw, nuts.' Sinatra's blue and disturbingly hot eyes came to rest on Bogart; his lean face was sardonic, his wide mouth wryly twisted. 'He's just another bum.'

'Remember Reagan,' Bogart continued defensively. 'Not so long ago he was sitting right here with us. Until, that is, he got over-confident, began over-extending, thinking he could get into SupraBurgh. Suddenly there he was, dying on a rising curve.'

Cagney shook his head sadly. 'Not even viable for the voters any more.'

'I remember what it was like seeing him go. Spooky.'

Sinatra chuckled. 'Sure I remember Reagan. He had it coming: that's what you get for messing with SupraBurgh. None of us will make that mistake again.' He paused reflectively, a cigarette held midway to his lips. 'You know, sometimes when I go over my piece of his holdings I think I can hear him whining through the circuits.'

'We all can,' Raft said shortly, in a flat gravelly voice, 'because we all took a piece of him. I like to think he'd be happy knowing we profited by his fall. But I'd also like to think it can't happen to me.' The grisly crack came deadpan out of Raft's poker face. Cagney and Schultz grinned slightly.

'It can't,' Sinatra affirmed. 'We've got things sewn up too tight now.'

'If we stick together it can't,' Bogart corrected. 'Maybe Reagan wouldn't have hit the dust if some of you guys hadn't been so quick to pull the rug from under him.'

'Yeah, okay, that's right,' said Sinatra hastily, cutting off the angry protests from the others. 'If things get rough we stick together, okay? Karnak has only taken one ward so far. That's a long way from being a threat. Now let's get on to other business. Take a look at this.'

An oak panel slid aside to reveal a holo stage. A simple sine wave moved slowly across it, was momentarily transformed into a stationary bell-shaped probability curve, and then broke up into a dizzying sequence of graph curves, the axes standing out in contrasting colours.

Filling in with a terse commentary, Sinatra watched the flickering curves calmly. 'I guess you can get the picture from this. Intricative Products, working in harness with Stylic Access Services, are on their way to capturing the whole of the design-percept market. This will mean that a lot of smaller businesses not currently in syn will be brought in syn. Now here are the production breakdowns leading through to maybe four months' time.'

A new set of dancing, swinging curves appeared, at the rate of two a second. Sinatra held one of them for a few moments.

'Here's the aesthetic/inventive index of the stuff we'll be releasing in a short while now.'

The display went into motion again. 'I'm giving you the picture because I don't want you to go upsetting the caper. Putting smaller people out of business isn't just a matter of seizing their markets, it's also a matter of denying them operating capital. Now for a short while my activities will create something of a vacuum in the field of property in-decor, an associated area of commerce. Some of you, particularly Lancaster and Cagney, might be tempted to pour money into it. But it's a fact that capital flows easily from property in-decor to design-percept. So back off, willya? Otherwise you might louse up my operation.'

The display ended and the holo stage showed an indefinite empty depth, tinted pale lilac.

Raft grunted.

'And why should we want to do you such a favour?' he asked.

'Oh, I wouldn't ask you to do it as a favour,' Sinatra replied mildly. 'Just so as to be open and above board, I'll show you the current programme of another of my properties, Up-SupraBurgh Road Mercantile.' The holo started up again, dazzling in its rapid disclosure of professional information. 'If this doesn't give some of you cardiac arrest, it should. It shows just how ready I am to start forcing the pace in the Up-SupraBurgh outlets. Before long I could – if I wanted – squeeze you out of some of these routes altogether. You wouldn't like that. So it's a straight deal. I'll back off SupraBurgh if you'll back off property in-decor.'

'We all agreed not to try to monopolise the upgoing routes,' Raft said without expression.

'I hope I won't have to,' Sinatra told him affably.

'*What are you trying to put over on us, Frank?*' It was Lancaster who spoke now, anger edging into his softly incisive, muscular voice. 'Let's take another look at that crap you just handed us.' And he projected Sinatra's own graphs back on the wall holo. 'It's kind of funny how it compares with what I'm doing in Up-SupraBurgh.'

More curves, Lancaster's graphs this time, glittered out at them in quick succession, like spitting out pips. 'Get that, Frank? Put it together, all of you. Frank is telling us he and I share seventy-three per cent of the upgoing trade. Add your own business to it, and how do you explain a total of *one hundred and eighteen* per cent?'

'*Are you calling me a liar, you –?*' Sinatra lunged towards Lancaster, an incredulous, outraged look on his face. He gesticulated at the wall holo. '*This* is how you put those figures together, and *this* is what it means in a year's time.' And while he spoke he shot an even faster display at the holo stage.

Cagney spoke up lazily. 'Frank is always talking about bringing out-of-syn business into syn. What for? I notice most of these properties seem to wind up in his own stable. What are you gonna do, Frank? Bring the whole of UnderMegapolis into syn?'

'Sure!' bellowed Sinatra. 'I'd like it that way!'

Bogart lit a cigar, blowing aromatic smoke that appeared to drift out of the holo and into the room. 'Great,' he observed. 'So whenever anything goes wrong the voters have nobody to blame but us.'

'Yeah, that would be great all right, wouldn't it?' Lancaster echoed.

There was a moment's silence. Sinatra calmed himself, glancing around him at the hexagon of power that made up the syndicate: himself, Bogart, Lancaster, Raft, Cagney, and on Sinatra's left, Schultz, a furtive, dour figure who spoke but seldom.

'Nothing ever does go wrong in the outfits *I* run,' he declared.

'Nothing except the credibility of your own accounts,' Lancaster answered tightly. 'Let's put your figures to the test, Frank. How about if we analyse them *this* way?'

The argument raged back and forth. The graph displays flickered so fast as to be on the edge of visibility, merging into a rainbow blur.

As the vert-tube dropped for mile after mile the golden glitter of SupraBurgh vanished. There was a brief, limbo-like transit through the abandoned area of Central Authority; then Obsier was plunged deep into the planet and entered UnderMegapolis.

Forms, hues and vistas slid into one another as the level-within-level mightiness of Obsier's home supercity swung past. This was the kind of immensity, the kind of power, he was familiar with: ancient yet eternally modern, below reach of the sun, a deep thrusting place of hegemonies. It impressed him anew to return to it in this fashion, falling like a bullet in the v-tube.

Obsier had to admit that SupraBurgh, perched above it, using it as a foundation, was stunning – but in a way that was alien and frightening, spreading up and out like a great tree to glory in the sunlight that struck, unnaturally to Obsier's mind, out of a naked sky. Equally unnatural were the interstellar ships that occasionally arrived to settle like birds in that tree, or, again lake birds, winged up to depart from it. The spectacle of those vanishing craft was most unnerving; Obsier found it a tremendous relief to escape from that oppressive feeling of vast expanses, of air and sunlight.

It was even a relief, despite the failure of his mission, to know that he had seen SupraBurgh's horrers for the last time. Thankfully blotting out the repellent images from his mind, Obsier thought it almost incredible to reflect that at their founding the two conurbations had been governed as a single city: Megapolis; and that only gradually had the functions of Central Authority withered away as disparate physical environments (one underground, one up in the air) inevitably gave rise to divergent social and economic forms: divergent traditions, divergent languages, and finally divergent governments.

Just how long ago that had been could be judged from the fact that the deserted section where Central Authority had functioned (even now its empty corridors were left tactfully undisturbed by both sides) had originally been at ground level and now was half a mile into the Earth. Megapolis, a huge plug drilled into the planet's skin, had sunk by its own weight. Its floor was now so close to the mohorivic discontinuity that UnderMegapolis was able to tap heat from the basaltic mantle beneath.

The v-tube decelerated fiercely, and shortly came to a halt. Ahead, the greenish radiance of serried strip-lights stretched away into the distance. Clutching a sheaf of documents, Obsier made his way towards a nearby Schultz In-Town Transit Services station.

'So they wouldn't wear it?' Mettick asked.

'No,' Obsier told him. 'And I guess that will be my last trip to SupraBurgh. In a way I'm glad of it. I don't like it up there.'

'Did you get *any* offers out of them?'

'Not one. They're not interested.'

'Is it because they don't use ipse holo up there?'

'That's true, they don't, but I don't think that's it. They must have all the technical data available. We could get it built ourselves, perhaps, if they'd fund it. They're just not interested. They don't want to know us down here.'

'It's hard to understand. If an offer like that was made to any of the syn bosses they'd grab it like an alligator grabbing meat.'

'Their system is different from ours. They're not democratic, and not oligarchic. They have some sort of elitist social structure. They act as though we don't exist ...'

Mettick shrugged. '*We act* as though *they* don't exist ... You know why I think they won't play? They're afraid of the syn. Do you think that's right?'

Obsier placed his papers in a desk drawer. 'Maybe. It's more likely that they have an agreement with them: no interference in each other's pitch. But it's more than that, too. There's a difference in mentality we could never cross. It was a mistake to think we could.'

'Yes, I suppose so.' Mettick was reflective for a moment. 'Well, we'd better tell Karnak.'

They went through a door into an inner office where the campaign team was working. Girls with tabulators were feeding in data for the prediction polls. If Karnak could gain this second ward in the imminent local election he would be riding high.

Mettick paused by the supervisor's desk. 'Is the Man in?'

She nodded. Mettick knocked on a door and they entered. Karnak was surrounded by his aides, hard at it as usual.

Karnak was the epitome of the tireless, hard-working politician. When he wasn't actively campaigning he was busy on some side project, as now: trying to analyse the syn – the vast business syndicate whose bosses ruled Under-Megapolis by reason of holding all the seats on the Magisterial Council. To gain such a seat for himself – to be a magister – and break the syn's monopoly was his life's ambition.

A small holo screen was reeling off a list of the properties owned by one of the syn tycoons, Sinatra. Momentarily Obsier let his eye run through the exotic language of present-day business: Intricative Products; Non-Linear Machinations Composited; Stylic Access Services; Up-Supra-Burgh Road Mercantile; Andromatic Enterprises; Andromatic On-Return Hook-Up ... and on and on.

Karnak killed the holo and turned to face the newcomers. Straight away Obsier could feel the man's charisma. The force of it struck him anew every time he came into Karnak's presence, like an enveloping field of magnetism. That magnetism was a necessary prerequisite: all the magisters had it.

'I'm sorry,' Obsier said immediately. 'SupraBurgh won't finance an ipse holo set-up.'

Karnak took the news as a great man should. He paced the room, his long-jawed, handsome features briefly turned inward in concentration. 'Okay, so that avenue is closed,' he said firmly. 'We shall just have to find another way.'

He stopped in front of the campaign charts that covered one wall. 'I'm confident we're going to win this ward. That will give me the right to contest the supercity general election in a month's time.'

He swung round to face them again. 'But let's not kid ourselves: ipse holo is the key to success on a supercity scale. We can do quite a lot with ordinary holo in a ward election, because it can be backed up with personal appearances. But in a population of a hundred million, where holocom is of the essence –' He made a gesture. 'Just imagine me coming over like a shadow and Sinatra or Lancaster sitting right there in the room, with all the spiel they're able to put over.'

There was a short silence. 'If we sank all our assets maybe we could come up with the needed amount, though I doubt it,' one of the aides said tentatively. 'But we'd be really out on a limb.'

Karnak nodded.

'It isn't just that,' Mettick injected. 'There's the technical data too. I've done some research in the library. It isn't all there: the syn has kept some of it private. Which means that businesses capable of artifactoring ipse equipment are all synowned, too.'

Another of the aides slapped his fist in his palm. 'They've really got it sewn up,' he said savagely.

'It's getting so they're sewing everything up,' said the aide who had first spoken. The rate of absorption of businesses taken over by the syndicate – brought into syn, in the jargon – was one of the things Karnak's team liked to grouse about.

'*Right*: this is what we'll do,' said Karnak, cutting into their talk like a hand cutting through smoke. Their attention snapped on to him: the Man had made a Decision.

'We'll make an election issue of it, starting as of right now,' he told them. 'The syn has a monopoly of ipse holo. That's undemocratic – it should be available to *all* magisterial candidates. We'll push the idea that the owners of ipse equipment should lease it, or even loan it, to anyone on the elective list. Wrap it up in a package – the ever-increasing hold the syn is having on our lives, the stricture on routes to the top in our society, and so forth. But press it hard.'

'Hmm.' An aide nodded thoughtfully. 'The syn's reply will be that we are trying to subvert the plutocratic principle – anybody not successful enough to have their own ipse apparatus doesn't deserve to have it, dig? But it will definitely put them on the defensive. They might even have to let us use their ipse to avoid looking mean and brutish. It's good, K, it's good.' He nodded again, enthusiastically.

'Maximum publicity,' Karnak intoned. 'Get to work on it, there isn't much time.' He waved his arms; the aides began to leave the room. 'You two stay,' he said to Obsier and Mettick. 'I've another little job for you.'

When the three of them were alone Karnak settled himself in his plush black swivel-chair and leaned back, placing his finger-tips together.

'Did you have a hard time in SupraBurgh?' he asked, shooting a glance at Obsier.

Obsier shrugged. 'A little.'

'It makes me wonder – you know, everything's so different up above. If it changes your outlook at all when you come back.'

Obsier frowned. The question was interesting. He had been to SupraBurgh five times in all, each time with a view to setting up some kind of arrangement for Karnak. He had tried to identify the unnamed feelings it stirred up in him, but he had always failed.

'It gives you an outside view of UnderMegapolis, as it were,' he said, 'but that soon fades once you return. Frankly I wouldn't advise anyone to make the trip.'

'So it *does* change you?' Mettick asked.

'Well, it arouses peculiar sensations, like ideas that drift through your mind. As if you're resentful that – that we're living down here, subterranean, and can't get out, while they're ...'

The other two looked at him in blank incomprehension, as if he had suddenly begun to speak gibberish.

'But it's just some sort of illusion, I guess,' he resumed. 'Some of the things you see in SupraBurgh would unnerve anyone. I saw an interstellar ship taking off once, just disappearing up and up into the blue sky without limit –' He broke off, attacked by sudden nausea.

'My God,' said Mettick quietly.

'It was too much,' Obsier said. 'Luckily I had tranquillizers. I was under sedation for six hours.'

There was an embarrassed silence at this description of foreign perversions. Karnak changed the subject.

'Well, you can forget all about that now. But I appreciate your sacrifices, I truly do. I wouldn't relish going up there myself. Now to more immediate matters. Our campaign for the use of ipse holo will probably turn out to be the most crucial issue of, recent times. You and Mettick make a good team, especially where historical research is concerned. I'd like you to spend some time in the library.'

'What are we supposed to be looking for?'

Karnak placed his hands flat on the desk top, his expression distant, slightly puzzled. 'I just can't help feeling there's an angle on the syn bosses we could use. I've got an itch up here.' He tapped his cranium. 'The trouble is, I don't know what it is. Do you realise how hard it is to get close to the syn bosses data-wise?'

'They are shielded, naturally,' Obsier admitted. 'That makes sense. But there are the official biographies.'

'Yes detailed but ... artificial, somehow. Business, business, business. One long story of public service, private life coming off second best.'

'It would be hard to sort out the man from the commercial empire in the jobs they are doing.' Mettick pointed out.

'True, boys, true. You know, I've spent hours studying their holocom talks. After a while I get the feel of their style. You know something? It's as if they've all been to the same school. There's something in their approach to spiel that's the same in each of them, despite their being such distinctive characters.'

Obsier and Mettick looked at one another. 'Perhaps they've been coached by the same expert,' Mettick suggested.

'Except Schultz,' Karnak added. 'He's different. But of course he doesn't appear on holo nearly as much as the others. He rides in on Sinatra's ticket, everybody knows that. And his network is a subsidiary of Sinatra's, we know that too. As a matter of fact if I get on the magisterial council it's Schultz I expect to be replacing.'

Obsier mulled it over but came up with nothing.

'Just give your imagination free play and browse around. Probably you won't come up with anything, but again you might.' Karnak smiled ruefully. 'We'll soon be in the thick of it. This is a mountain we're tackling, and it's as well to know all the slopes.'

Cybration.

Cybration was the key to modern business.

Cybration was the key to how Under-Megapolis was able to exist.

As the transit pod swept across the supercity advertising flashes swung up and receded like star systems undergoing doppler effect, composing a cityscape of endless dimensions; internal hormones of the business world.

RAFT ENTERPRISES ARE HERE TO SERVE YOU EX-TYPE INTRACTIONS OFFER 100% BIREFRINGENCE WANT IT? STYLIC ACCESS *HAS* IT

Having researched the inane selling promotions of an earlier age, Obsier admired modern advertising for its muscular simplicity, its impression of underlying power and reliability. It was functional. It didn't insult the intelligence. And it was effective.

'May as well split into two departments,' Mettick was saying. 'I'll research the personalities. You go into the technical side.'

'Right.'

The pod deposited them ten miles from Karnak's headquarters. Ahead of them was the towering frontage of the central library. Obsier left Mettick and went wandering through interminable sepulchral galleries. Eventually he settled down before a terminal in the Useful Hardware section. He ruminated; he had no lead, no idea of what he was looking for.

Idly, for the sake of making a move, he called on a subject.

'CYBRATION: The history of cybration goes back in a realistic sense to the year circa minus 780, when the first genuine cybrators were constructed. The name used for these early machines was "computer", which was an accurate term since they were in fact little more than high-speed counters. Round about the year minus 700 the term cybration was coined to describe all types of automatic data processing both electronic and laseronic and covering computer, executive and andromatic modes.

'The modem business corporation is largely a cybrated system where personnel are used to fill particular positions requiring "personalisation". But for this method UnderMegapolis could not exist, since the complexity of a modern society within a closed environment is beyond the capacity of an individual or group.'

Pictures of early computers and later installations. The account continued, becoming increasingly technical. Obsier quickly lost interest. He called on another subject.

'IPSEIC HOLOCOM: The introduction of ipseic transmission must be admitted to be the last word in image reproduction at a distance, unless the waveform transmission of actual physical objects one day becomes possible. The first workable ipseic transmitting apparatus was tested in United Laserelec Laboratories (owned by the now defunct Megac RD Consolidated) in year 421.

'For a number of centuries it had been considered that the standard holo television system provided absolute perfection since it can reproduce images, with full colour and full parallax, that are indistinguishable from the original. United Laserelec drew attention to a deficiency, soon confirmed by psychological tests, that had long been overlooked: holocom, like earlier television systems before it, does not convey charisma. It is easy to ignore someone speaking on an ordinary holo stage, and no display of emotion or insistence on the part of the performer can force attention out of the viewer if he does not feel like giving it.

'It would be simple to attribute this lack to the viewer's knowledge that the performer is not actually present and that he is confronting only an insubstantial image. By means of careful experimentation United Laserelec destroyed this myth. Later it was discovered that "presence" – the effect of "being there" that one person has on another – is not a mental supposition but an actual, though subtle, force transmitted between people at short range. Further research showed that this force is an emanation radiated on a frequency of the order of 23 trillion trillion cycles per second. When a transmitter capable of adding this waveform to the normal holocorn waveband was developed it was found that the transmitted image of a person carried the full force of his presence. It achieved *ipseity:* "he himself".

'Ipseic holocom has not come into general use. Although the modifications enabling an ordinary holo receiver to pick up ipseity are inexpensive – and in fact all holo sets are now so adapted – the cost of ipseity transmission is prohibitive. A number of transmitters are owned by the leading conglomerates of UnderMegapolis and are used for political purposes.'

Mettick was on a different tack. He had before him the names and images of all six syn leaders – six heads of colossal business conglomerates. He had decided to investigate their family backgrounds.

Suprisingly, although their biographies detailed brief family histories in each case, these families were difficult to track down. Accordingly Mettick set the library unit he had been allotted to engage on a lineal-and-likeness hunt.

This was on the third day of his somewhat aimless hit-and-miss tactics. Mettick sat back daydreaming as the unit hummed faintly. He dozed, and awoke with a start to find that the unit had been working for several hours.

There was a quiet clatter as a sheet slid out of the copy slit. Mettick picked it up and stared in bemusement.

A picture of Sinatra stared back at him. It was the same face he knew from many appearances on ipse holo – of all the magisters, Sinatra was probably the most sedulous where his public image was concerned.

Beneath the picture there was a caption. 'Frank Sinatra, years circa minus 790-740 (mid-20th Century, contemporary reckoning), singer and actor on "cinema" (primitive image reproduction system).' There followed a list of dramas in which the long-dead actor had appeared. The library, apparently, had recordings of a few of them.

Mettick shook his head in wonderment. The library unit had found an individual, far back in history, of the same name as the syn boss – and of exactly the same appearance. It was all there: the smiling blue eyes, the lean, rubbery, wide-mouthed face, the mixture of candour and astuteness, the toughness within the geniality. The amazing resemblance could only represent a centuries-ago emergence of very strong family traits that were still active. Sinatra's ancestors *could* be traced, after all.

Mettick folded up the picture and put it in his pocket. Then he leaned towards the terminal and started work again.

Frank Sinatra leaned forward with one arm resting on his knee, sitting relaxed and easy on an upright chair. His life-size form filled the holo stage. In almost the same way, the force of his personality seemed to fill and dominate the entire room.

'Sometimes I think it's possible to lose sight of the obvious, just because it is so obvious,' he was saying to the family in the room – the average, healthy-minded family, like the millions of average families listening to Sinatra at this moment, who were watching the holo stage.

Sinatra gave a wry smile. 'After all, that's a natural human failing and we are all prey to it, just as everybody sooner or later drops a hammer on his foot. But sometimes a character will come along and try to take advantage of our momentary inattention. He'll suggest it would be a good idea if the principles we've lived by for so long were to be laid aside, Well, whether that's so or not is something the whole city will decide, practising the best-established principle of all, the principle of elective democracy. All I'm saying is that before we accept any changes we should think good and hard about it, because the freedoms and the affluence we enjoy today didn't come about all at once, and they didn't come about by themselves, either. They needed the right system, and that took a long period of time to evolve.'

Sinatra stopped speaking. He rubbed his jaw reflectively, more serious now, and then turned his warm, steady eyes back on his spellbound audience. 'If this is beginning to sound like a sales pitch, you're dead right – that's just what it is. For my money it will be a sad day for UnderMegapolis if we ever lose sight of the principle of plutocratic democracy. It's given us everything we have, and I believe it's the best system of government there is. It ensures that only men rule who have already proved their ability to administrate on a large scale, their ability to increase wealth and to provide the community with goods and services. It means efficiency, intelligence and prowess in the high offices of government. And UnderMegapolis proves it by voting in the biggest and most successful corporation heads – the captains of industry, if you want to call it that – for term after term. Well, it now appears that there are some people who want to subvert this principle. Not having what it takes to make it big by their own efforts, they see the Magisterial Council as an easy way of getting to the top.' Sinatra shook his head sadly. 'They just don't know what they'd be letting themselves in for. Running a supercity is no job for anyone who hasn't been right through the whole school. The community would soon realise it, too. But that won't happen, because the voters have got too much sense. They realise what plutocratic democracy is for.'

A red light glowed suddenly on the left of the holo stage. A thrill of unbelieving excitement ran through the listening family. Sinatra was inviting a question from *them!*

On-the-spot questioning was a regular feature of the fairly frequent magisterial holocasts, but in a population of a hundred million the chances of the red light going on in *their* household had always seemed, well, infinitesimal.

Sinatra was gazing at the head of the family, waiting. The middle-aged man rose nervously. He could have pressed the 'no question' button on the ipseity unit, but he now understood why almost no one ever did. It would have been an insult to so commanding a presence.

'I have a question, sir. Why not let the new candidate, Karnak, use ipse holo if he wants to? It doesn't mean we're going to vote for him, but I can't see any reason why he shouldn't.'

Sinatra's eyes clouded over ever so slightly. 'There isn't any reason why he shouldn't use it,' he said. 'Who's stopping him? But he's not much of a candidate if he wants it handed to him on a plate. That's not how I got my equipment, and I didn't go around asking for anyone else's either.'

The family head nodded. It made sense. A man ought to be able to stand on his own feet, especially if he was to help rule UnderMegapolis. But a half-frown remained on his face.

Mutely the darkly shining mahogany reflected six holo images in agitated altercation. Raft took the lead, arguing in clipped, deadpan statements, deriding his colleagues' concern.

Sinatra, for once, seemed shaken, however. 'I've changed my mind, something's gotta be done. I was on ipse tonight. You know what ninety per cent of the questions I got were? Why don't we put ipse holo at Karnak's disposal?'

'Nobody asked me that when I went on yesterday,' Raft said.

Sinatra's face twisted sardonically. 'You don't have a sympathetic manner.'

'They'd have got a short answer if they had. The voters admire a guy who's tough but straight.'

Cagney turned to look directly at Sinatra, his head tilted calculatingly. 'What gives with this Karnak? What's his secret?'

Sinatra raised two fingers placed together. 'He's got *it*. Ipseity. Charisma.'

'Huh-huh. He's got ipseity, huh? So how's he going to put it over, huh?' Cagney chuckled. 'On ipse holo, maybe?'

'Come together, you guys!' Sinatra pleaded. 'We can't afford to let this kind of situation develop any further. You never know what it can do in future generations.'

Lancaster clenched his fists and raised his face, lips drawn back over strong white teeth. He spoke in a voice that was low and intense, little more than a muscular whisper. 'I say when you are threatened, *strike! We* should kill, kill, *kill!*'

'*No!*' Sinatra yelled. 'We agreed before: no assassinations.'

'Say,' said Bogart suddenly, looking sideways at Schultz as if hit by a crafty inspiration. What if this Karnak guy *did* become a magister? Schultz is the one who'd get pushed out, that's for sure. We can do without him. Karnak wouldn't last long anyhow.'

'No!' Schultz protested hoarsely.

'Leave Schultz alone!' Sinatra ordered loudly. 'He's my buddy.' But he, too, looked at Schultz speculatively.

A shiver ran through the room and the holo images flickered and seemed about to melt into something indefinable.

'One sign of trouble and you're all falling apart,' Raft said disgustedly.

'Sometimes I think I'm in crummy company. If you're so steamed up about it, let Karnak put himself on ipse. What does it matter? Let him take the consequences.'

They all looked at one another, considering.

'Fact Number One: UnderMegapolis is run on personal charisma,' said Mettick. 'It's as real as the electricity in your holo set. And I'll tell you something I've found out that shows just how seriously the syn leaders themselves take it. Every one of them has onput recognition gates on his com-lines, to stop the others from beaming their images into his conglomerates. They're afraid someone will subvert their managers by sheer charge of personality.'

'Isn't that over-cautious?'

'Not at all. One of their regular tactics is to call a nonsyn enterprise and start giving orders to the underlings. You'd be surprised how often those orders are obeyed.'

A disturbing picture formed in Obsier's mind of distrust and conspiracy in the highest echelon. 'Then how do they communicate with one another?'

'Only privately, by direct face-to-face holo.'

'You know, when I'm with Karnak I feel confidence in him,' Obsier pondered slowly, 'but when I see one of the syn bosses on holo I don't feel so sure of him, and I almost feel like giving up. Do you really think he has enough personal charge?'

'Only one person in millions has as much, but honestly I don't know. I keep trying to imagine how he'd make out in a confrontation with Lancaster, say, or Raft. Those people have so much of it, it's frightening – almost unnatural. Not to speak of their having a monopoly of it, in supercity terms, since only they can use ipseity apparatus.'

'Not any more. Haven't you heard? The syn has relented. Karnak is going on ipse holo tonight.'

Mettick's quest for a believable human profile to the syn bosses had led him into labyrinths of the library that had been unpaced for decades. He walked through dusty low-vaulted galleries past rows of disused terminal units, each of which gave access to some obscure facet of the past. He knew the answer was here somewhere. The facts he had discovered so far were too puzzling, too extraordinary, not to have an answer.

There had been some fascinating sidelines, too, in his search into the past. Even as far back as the minus eighth century there seemed to have been some sort of premonition of more modern history. Mettick had found references to 'the withering away of the state' and 'the abolition of central authority' that was supposed to come about in the future. He wondered how the ancients' could have guessed about the fate of the empty government levels that separated UnderMegapolis from SupraBurgh.

An age-old silence enveloped him. The nearest girl librarian was at least half a mile away, in the better-frequented upper floors. Mettick consulted some reference numbers on a list he carried and keyed on one of the terminal units. An ancient 'cinema' comedy began to unreel, fascinating him with its extraordinary grimaces and quite ugly songs. He abandoned the unit after a couple of minutes and wandered on.

He entered a side passage where the lighting, for some unknown reason, was dimmer. To his amazement the material of the walls gave way to stone and wood in archaic, rotting panels. And while he stood there one of those panels gave a little squeak and swung open.

Behind it was a flat glass screen with a picture on it. Mettick had difficulty in recognising the image at first: it was not in holo but flat. There was something else wrong with it, too: it was made up, unnaturally, of only two colours, white and greyish black in various tones.

The picture had a graininess that, peering closer, he saw resulted from its being composed of hundreds of parallel horizontal lines. But, when he finally recognized what it was, he jumped back in shock.

It was the face of Magister Dutch Schultz.

He began to tremble and then calmed himself as he realised that the picture carried no charismatic charge. The screen was some unbelievably primitive kind of television which could not possibly convey ipseity. God knew how old it was – it was a wonder it was still functioning.

'Hello, citizen,' Schultz said in a husky voice. 'So you're tryin' to find out the truth? Okay, I'll tell you the truth ...'

Karnak strode into the transmitting studios feeling ten feet tall. This was to be his night. By the pressure of democracy – *pure* democracy, not the plutocratic variety – the magisters had been forced to concede an elementary right.

The studio producers were deferential. He waited in a cool blue chamber while the announcements were made. Then he was ushered into the transmitting cubicle. In front of him was the holo camera. Around him were the sensors that, with a faint hum, began to pick up his ipseity emanations at a frequency of 23 trillion trillion per second and feed them through the com-lines ...

The producer signalled to him through the side of the cubicle. He was on.

'Fellow citizens,' he began, 'tonight ...'

And then the impressions began to hit him. It was merely like a tidal wave at first and he was able to ride with it. But in the next few seconds it became stronger. Millions upon millions of scenes, tens of millions of human consciousnesses, were forcing themselves into *his* consciousness, which like a balloon expanded, expanded, expanded

And burst.

Sinatra had cornered Schultz in a small, narrow room with drab brown walls. It had no furniture, no means of escape.

'You goddam stool pigeon,' Sinatra raged. 'You ratted on us all.'

'Whaddya want me to do, Frank?' Schultz screamed in terror. 'You were gonna bump me off. I could see it coming.' He had run and run and fought for his life, but now there was nowhere left to go.

'I put you on the council,' Sinatra said, 'and if I want it's my right to take you off or do what the hell I like with you.'

'No, Frank, no!'

Sinatra leaped at Schultz. His fists smashed into him again and again, throwing him cowering to the floor. Then he attacked him with a crowbar that appeared in his hand, bringing the weapon down in three savage, strokes. Soon there was blood everywhere.

Mettick burst into campaign headquarters looking desperate. 'Get hold of Karnak,' he demanded. 'Don't let him go on ipse.'

Obsier looked up tiredly. 'Why?' he said mildly. 'Actually you're too late. Karnak was taken ill at the start of the programme. We're waiting for news now.'

Mettick sank down on to a chair. 'He's dead, isn't he?'

'Should he be?' Obsier stared at him perplexed. 'I hear he's in a coma. We're waiting for the doctor's report.'

'He'll be dead,' Mettick said in despair.

Suddenly Obsier became alert, matter-of-fact. 'Tell me what you found out,' he said rapidly.

'Two things, chiefly.' Mettick fished in his pocket and came out with a sheaf of pictures. 'Take a look at these. They're portraits of world-famous actors living about a thousand years ago. They were known colloquially as "Hollywood stars". Notice the resemblance?'

Obsier leafed through them. He saw the familiar, compelling faces of the Magisters of UnderMegapolis, captioned with their names. Burt Lancaster, James Cagney, Humphrey Bogart, and so on. Some were wearing characteristic expressions; others were in strange, surprising poses. Lancaster had his head tilted, favouring the viewer with a most uncharacteristic glossy smile.

'Absolutely incredible!' he exclaimed. 'What is it? Some fantastic coincidence of genetic reconstitution? Or –' His voice sank. Unwelcome, irrepressible thoughts were going through his brain. 'Or …'

'You've guessed it.' Metick pushed away the pictures and slumped down in his chair. 'The change must have come fairly recently, certainly within the last hundred years. The cybration of big business reached a point where human beings were eliminated at the top. The cybration system became the actual, effective owner of the capital.'

'Without anyone knowing?'

'Why not? It was so complicated, data processing gives such opportunities for mystery ... Besides, it only happened with the five biggest conglomerates – no, six, counting Reagan. Remember him? Each of these conglomerates became the property of a single mass of automatic data processing. Much cleverer, much more efficient than a human being.'

'Yes, but why ...?'

'Don't you see it? There was still the problem of the interface, to use a piece of cybration jargon. The cybrators needed *personae* so as to be able to deal with human beings and to help them find their bearings in a human world. So they went back through history looking for the most charismatic personalities they could find, the ones with greatest mass appeal. There must have been other considerations, too. I mean, the cybrators must have had some kind of affinity – anyway, they found them among the cinema stars of the minus eighth century. And they reconstructed those personalities in their data banks. Totally. You couldn't call those personae puppets by now. The identification must be complete.'

'So we're ruled by ghosts,' Obsier said woodenly.

'Yes. Or eighth-century Hollywood film stars. Whichever you prefer.'

'But on ipse holo they come over ... they're *real*.'

'So what? They generate the ipseity just as they build up a *persona*. That's why they have so much of it. More, probably, than the original film stars had.

'Schultz told me. He got in touch with me in the library. He's the odd one out, by the way – he never was a film star but a genuine gangster, the type that the actors were supposed to portray. That's why there are no good pictures of him.' He touched a blurred photo of a round, indistinct face. 'He wasn't in the original set. Sinatra created him for convenience, to look after some subsidiaries and give him added weight on the council. That's why he chose a real gangster, I guess: it amused him somehow. But something went wrong. Schultz has developed in his own direction, has become separated from Sinatra and wants to break away from him. He tried to do a deal with me; said he'd help me break open the syn. And he told me –' Mettick slammed his fist on the desk. 'But too late!'

'Told you what?' Obsier pressed anxiously, leaning forward.

'About ipse holo! The real reason why it's never used, except by the syn. It's a killer!'

'What are you talking about?' Obsier stared at him.

'Ipseity transmission is a reciprocal process. It can't work one way. The sender becomes aware of the receiver, too. When you're broadcasting to millions of people they not only become aware of *your* presence, but you at the same time receive the presence of all those millions. The consciousness can't take it. It overloads.'

Noting the other's expression, Mettick continued:

'That datum has been removed from the library. Everybody thinks it's just too expensive, not too dangerous.'

'But the syn bosses. They don't –'

'They're not alive!' cut in Mettick savagely. 'They're what you said, ghosts animated by electricity. You know that "question time" technique they use on ipse holo? I learned today they handle thousands of questions at the same time, calculated on a scatter pattern so nobody even suspects anything.'

They sat silently for a while. Finally Obsier forced his brain into motion again.

'Maybe this is the beginning of something new after all,' he said uneasily. 'If Schultz really is going to help break the syn, it will all have been worth it.'

'I don't think there's any hope there. Schultz can't be too bright, or he wouldn't have left it so late to warn me. And remember, he's really part of Sinatra. He'll never be able to hide what he's done. I imagine the Schultz *persona* has been washed right down the drain by now.'

'And where does that leave us? We're the ones who know.'

'We're in a spot. It's no good thinking anybody can fight the syndicate. They've got the means to power nobody else can use: ipseic holocom. We could go into hiding but they'd always be able to find us. We might be able to flee to Supra-Burgh but –' He shuddered.

'I can't face SupraBurgh,' said Obsier definitely, thinking of the obscene sight of a starship riding up into the endless blue.

'No, me neither. And that's something else we have to thank them for –'

The desk holo chimed behind Obsier. He turned, spoke quietly to it, then swung back to Mettick.

'Karnak's dead.'

'The syndicate murdered him by his own hand.'

'Yes.'

Again they were silent, until Obsier said sombrely, 'What were you saying about SupraBurgh?'

'There's one thing that obsesses the syn. The stars. They have a psychotic resentment about them. Remember Reagan? They wiped him out, too. He was the last one to make a bid for the stars, which was what he was doing when he tried to extend into SupraBurgh. But he couldn't make it and they know they can never make it, either. They're machines, imprisoned down here and keyed into this subterranean supercity. So they hate the stars and the open sky. And that's why, over the generations, they've conditioned us to hate them too.'

MUTATION PLANET

Filled with ominous mutterings, troubled by ground-trembling rumblings, the vast and brooding landscape stretched all around in endless darkness and gloom. Across this landscape the mountainous form of *Dominus* moved at speed, a massed, heavy shadow darker than the gloom itself, sullenly majestic, possessing total power. Above him the opaque sky, lurid and oppressively close, intermittently flared and discharged sheets of lightning that were engulfed in the distant hills. In the instant before some creature fed on the electric glare the dimness would be relieved momentarily, outlining uneven expanses of near-barren soil. *Dominus*, however, took no sensory advantage of these flashes; his inputs covered a wider, more reliable range of impressions.

As he sped through his domain he scattered genetic materials to either side of him to dampen down evolutionary activity, so ensuring that no life-form would arise that could inconvenience him or interfere with the roadway over which he moved. This roadway, built by himself as one of the main instruments of his control over his environment, spanned the whole eight thousand miles of the planet's single continent, and was a uniform quarter of a mile wide; at irregular intervals side roads diverged into the larger peninsulas. Since the substance of the roadbed was quasi-organic, having been extruded by organs he possessed for that purpose, *Dominus* could, moreover, sense instantly any attack, damage, or unacceptable occurrence taking place on any part of it.

After leaving the interminable plain the road undulated over a series of hills, clinging always to the profile of the land, and swept down into a gigantic bowl-like valley. Here the gloom took on the darkness of a pit, but life-forms were more copious. By the light of the flickering lightning flashes, or by that of the more diffuse radiations employed by *Dominus*, they could be seen skulking out there in the valley, a scattering of unique shapes. They were absolutely motionless, since none dared to move while *Dominus* passed by. Leagues further afield lights winked and radio pulses beamed out as the more powerful entities living up the slopes of the valley signalled their submission.

Dominus dosed the valley heavily with genetic mist, then surged up the opposite wall. As he swept over on to a tableland a highly-charged lightning bolt came sizzling down, very close; he caught it in one of his conductors and stored the charge in his accumulators. It was then, while he raced away from the valley, that his radar sense spotted an unidentifiable object descending through the cloud blanket. Puzzled, *Dominus* slowed down to scarcely a hundred miles per hour. This was the first unusual event for several millennia. He could not, at first, account for it.

The strangeness lay in the fact that the object was so large: not very much smaller than *Dominus* himself. (Its shape, thought new to him, was of no account – even at the low, controlled level of mutation he permitted thousands of different life-forms continued to evolve.) Also, it was moving through the air without the visible benefit of wings of any kind. Come to that, a creature of such bulk could not be lifted by wings at all.

Where had it evolved? In the sky? Most unlikely. The plethora of flying forms that had once spent their lives winging through the black, static-drenched cloud layer had almost – thanks to *Dominus* – died out. Over the ages his mutation-damping mist, rising on the winds, had accumulated there, and without a steady mutation rate the flying forms had been unable to survive the ravages of their environment and each other.

Then from where? Some part of the continent receiving only scant surveillance from *Dominus*? He was inclined to doubt this also. The entity he observed could not have developed without many generations of mutation, which would have come to his notice before now.

Neither was the ocean any more likely a source. True, *Dominus* carried out no surveillance there. But a great deal of genetic experience was required to survive on the land surface. Emergent amphibia lacked that experience and were unable to gain a foothold. For that reason oceanic evolution seemed to have resigned itself to a purely submarine existence.

One other possibility remained: the emptiness beyond the atmospheric covering. For *Dominus* this possibility was theoretical only, carrying no emotional ambience. Up to now *this* world had absorbed his psychic energies: *this* was life and existence.

Due to this ambiguity *Dominus* did not act immediately but kept in check the strong instinctive urges that were triggered off. Interrupting his pan-continental patrol for the first time in millennia, he followed the object to its landing place. Then he settled down patiently to await developments.

Eliot Harst knew exactly where to find Balbain. He climbed the curving ramp to the upper part of the dome-shaped spaceship and opened a door. The alien was standing at the big observation window, looking out on to Five's (whatever system they were in, they always named the planets in order from their primary) blustering semi-night.

The clouds glowed patchily as though bombs were being let off among them; the lightning boomed and crashed. The tall, thin alien ignored all this, however. His attention was fixed on the gigantic organism they had already named *Dominus*, which was slumped scarcely more than a mile away. Eliot had known him to gaze at it, unmoving, for hours.

'The experiment has worked out after all,' he said. 'Do you want to take a look?'

Balbain tore his gaze from the window and looked at Eliot. He came from a star which, to Eliot, was only a number in Solsystem's catalogues. His face was partly obscured by the light breathing mask he wore to supplement ship atmosphere. (The aliens all seemed to think that human beings were more sensitive to discomfort than themselves: everything on the ship was biased towards the convenience of Eliot and his assistant Alanie). But over the mask Balbain's bright bird-like eyes were visible, darting from his bony, fragile and quite unhuman skull.

'The result is positive?' he intoned in an oddly hollow, resonant voice.

'It would seem so.'

'It is as we already knew. I do not wish to see the offspring at present, but thank you for informing me.'

With that he returned to the window and seemed to become abruptly unaware of Eliot's presence.

Sighing, the Earthman left the chamber. A few yards further along the gallery he stopped at a second door. Jingling a bell to announce his presence, he entered a small bare cell and gave the same message as before to its occupant.

Abrak came from a star as far from Balbain's as the latter was from Solsystem. When fully erect he stood less than five feet in height and had a skin like corded cloth: full of neat folds and wavy grains. At the moment he squatted on the bare floor, his skeletal legs folded under him in an extraordinary double-jointed way that Eliot found quite grotesque.

Abrak's voice was crooning and smooth, and contained unnerving infrasound beats that made a human listener feel uneasy and slightly dizzy – Eliot already knew, in fact, that Abrak could, if he wished, kill him merely by speaking: by voicing quiet vibrations of just the right frequency to cripple his internal organs.

'So the picture we have built is vindicated?' he replied to Eliot's announcement, pointing a masked, dog-like face towards the Earthman.

'There can be little doubt of it.'

'I will view the offspring.' The alien rose in one swift motion.

Eliot had already decided that there was no point in reporting to the fifth member of the team: Zeed, the third of the non-humans. He appeared to take no more interest in their researches.

He led the way back down the connecting ramps, through the interior of the spaceship which he had been finding increasingly depressing of late. More and more it reminded him of a hurriedly-built air-raid shelter, devoid of decoration, rough-hewn, dreary and echoing.

Balbain's people had built the ship. Eliot could recall his excitement on learning of its purpose, an excitement that doubled when it transpired he had a chance of joining it. For the ship was travelling from star to star on a quest for knowledge. And as it journeyed it occasionally recruited another scientist from a civilisation sufficiently advanced, if he would make a useful member of the team. So far, in addition to the original Balbain, there had been Zeed, Abrak (none of these being their real, unpronounceable names, but convenience names for human benefit: transliterations or syllabic equivalents), and, of course, Eliot and Alanie.

Alanie had been, for Eliot, one of the fringe benefits of the trip – another being that when they returned to Solsystem they would take back with them a prodigious mass of data, a sizeable number of discoveries, and would gain immortal fame. The aliens, recognising that human sexuality was more than usually needful, had offered to allow a male-female pair as Solsystem's contribution. Eliot had found that his prospect of a noble ordeal was considerably mitigated by the thought of spending that time alone with his selected teammate: Alanie Leitner, vivacious, companionable, with an IQ of 190 (slightly better than Eliot's own, in fact) and an experienced all-round researcher. The perfect assistant for him, the selection board had assured him, and he had found little in their verdict to disagree with, then or since.

But the real thrill had been in the thing itself: in being part of a voyage of discovery that transcended racial barriers, in the uplifting demonstration that wherever intelligence arose it formed the same aspiration: to know, to examine, to reveal the universe.

Mind was mind: a universal constant.

Unfortunately he and Alanie seemed to be dirifting apart from their alien travelling companions, to understand them less and less. The truth was that he and Alanie were doing all the work. They would arrive at a system and begin a survey; yet very quickly the interest of the others would die off and the humans would be left to carry out all the real research, draw the conclusions and write up the reports completely unaided. As a matter of fact Zeed now took scarcely any interest at all and did not stir from his quarters for months on end.

Eliot found it quite inexplicable, especially since Balbain and Abrak, both of whom had impressed him by the strength of their intellects, admitted that much that was novel had been discovered since leaving Solsystem.

At the bottom of the ramp he led Abrak into the laboratory section. And there to greet them was Alanie Leitner: a wide, slightly sulky mouth in a pale face; a strong nose, steady brown eyes and auburn, nearly reddish hair cut squarely at the nape of her neck. And even in her white laboratory smock the qualities of her figure were evident.

Though constructed of the same concrete-like stuff as the rest of the space-ship, the laboratory was made more cheerful by being a place of work. At the far end was the test chamber. Abrak made his way there and peered through the thick window. The parent specimen they had begun with lay up against the wall of the circular chamber, apparently dying after its birth-giving exertions. It was about the size of a dog, but was spider-like, with the addition of a rearward clump of tissue that sprouted an untidy bunch of antennae-like sensors.

Its offspring, lying inert a few yards away, offered absolutely no resemblance to the spider-beast. A dense-looking, slipper-shaped object, somewhat smaller than the parent, it might have been no more than a lump of wood or metal.

'It's too soon yet to be able to say what it can do,' Alanie said, joining them at the window.

Abrak was silent for a while. 'Is it not possible that this is a larval, immature stage, thus accounting for the absence of likeness?' he suggested.

'It's conceivable, certainly,' Eliot answered. 'But we think the possibility is remote. For one thing we are pretty certain that the offspring was already adult and fully grown, or practically so, when it was born. For another, the fact that the parent reproduced at all is pretty convincing confirmation of our theory. Added to everything else we know, I don't feel disposed towards accepting any other explanation.'

'Agreed,' Abrak replied. 'Then we must finally accept that the Basic Polarity does not obtain here on Five?'

'That's right.' Although he should have become accustomed to the idea by now Eliot's brain still went spinning when he thought of it and all it entailed.

Scientifically speaking the notion of the Basic Polarity went back, as far as Solsystem was concerned, to the Central Dogma. In a negative sense, it also went back to the related Koestler's Question, posed late in the twentieth century.

The Central Dogma expressed the keystone of genetics: that the interaction between *gene* and *soma* was a one-way traffic. The genes formed the body. But nothing belonging to the body, or anything that it experienced, could modify the genes or have any effect on the next generation. Thus there was no inheritance of acquired characteristics; evolution was conducted over immensely long periods of time through random mutations resulting from cosmic radiation, or through chemical accidents in the gene substance itself.

Why, Koestler asked, should this be so? A creature that could re-fashion its genes, endowing its offspring with the means to cope with the hazards it had experienced, would confer a great advantage in the struggle for survival.

Going further, a creature that could lift life itself by its bootstraps and pro-duce a superior type in this way would confer an even greater advantage. Furthermore, Koestler argued that direct reshaping of the genes should be perfect within the capabilities of organic life, using chemical agents.

So the absence of such a policy in organic life was counter-survival, a curi-ous, glaring neglect on the part of nature. The riddle was answered, by Koestler's own contemporaries, in the following manner: if the *soma*, on the basis of its experiences, was to modify the gene-carrying DNA, then the modification would have to be planned and executed by the instinctive func-tions of the nervous system, or by whatever corresponded to those functions in any conceivable creature. But neither the instinctive brains of the higher orders, nor the primitive ganglia of the lower orders, had the competence to carry out this work: acting purely by past-conditioned responses, they had no apprehension of the future and would not have been able to relate experience to genetic alteration. Hence life had been dependent on random influences: radiation and accident.

For direct gene alteration to be successful, Koestler's rebutters maintained, some form of intellect would be needed. Primitive animals did not have this; if the gene-changing animal existed, then that animal was man, and man worked not through innate bodily powers but by artificial manipulation of the chromosomes. Even then, his efforts had been partial and inept: the eradication of defective genes to rectify the increasing incidence of deform-ity; the creation of a few new animals that had quickly sickened and died.

And with that the whole matter of Koestler's Question had been quietly for-gotten. The Central Dogma was reinstated, not merely as an arbitrary fact but as a necessary principle. If Koestler's Question had any outcome, then it was in the recognition of the Basic Polarity: the polarity between individual and species. Because the species, not the individual, had to be the instrument of evolution. If the Central Dogma did not hold, then species would not need to exist at all (and neither, incidentally, would sex). The rate of change would be so swift that there would be nothing to hold them together – and any that did exist, because of some old-fashioned immutability of their genes, would rapidly be wiped out. And indeed the Basic Polarity seemed to be the fundamental form of life every-where in the universe, as Balbain, Abrak and Zeed all confirmed.

Eliot was thinking of renaming Five 'Koestler's Planet'.

On a world where all traces of the past could be wiped out overnight, they would probably never know exactly what had happened early in Five's bio-logical evolution to overthrow the Central Dogma. Presumably the instinctive functions had developed, not intelligence exactly, but a unique kind of tele-graph between their experience of the external world and the microscopic coding of the germ plasm. It would, as Alanie pointed out, only have to happen once, and that once could even be at the bacterial level. The progeny of a single individual would rapidly supplant all other fauna. In the explosion of organic development that followed it would be but a short step before gene alteration became truly inventive; intellectual abilities would soon arise to serve this need.

It had been some time before the idea had dawned on them that Five might be a planet of single-instance species; in other words, of no species at all. There was one four-eyed stoat; one elephantine terror; one leaping prong; one blanket (their name for a creature of that description which spent most of its time merely lying on the ground). In fact there was a bewildering variety of forms of which only one example could be found. But there were one or two exceptions to the rule – or so they had thought. They had videotaped six specimens of a type of multi-legged snake. Only later had they discovered that the resemblance between them was a case of imitation, of convergent evolution among animals otherwise unrelated.

So they had been forced, reluctantly, to accept the evidence of their eyes, and later, of the electron microscope. But only now, in the last hour, was Eliot one hundred per cent convinced of it.

Another thing that had made him cautious was the sheer degree of knowledge and intelligence consistent with this level of biological engineering. He would have expected every creature on the planet to display intelligence at least equivalent to the human. Instead the animals here were just that – animals. Clever, ferocious animals, but content to inhabit their ecological niches and evincing no intellectual temperament.

All, that is, except *Dominus*.

They called him *Dominus* because he had the aspect of being king of all he surveyed. He must have weighed a thousand tons at least. He was also owner of the road system, which at first they had taken to be evidence of a civilisation, or at least the remains of one. It was now clear, however, that the road had been *Dominus*'s own idea – or, more probably, his parents' idea.

The great beast had demonstrated his understanding when they had gone out and tried to trap specimens for laboratory study. The exercise had proved to be dangerous and nearly impossible. Five's fauna were the universe's greatest experts at not getting killed, caught or trapped, and had responded not merely with claw, fang and evasive speed, but with electricity, poison gas, infra-sound (Abrak's own speciality), corrosives of various types they had still not classified but which had scared them very much, thick strands of unknown substances spun swiftly out from spinnerets and carried on the wind, slugs of pure iron ejected from porcupine-like quills with the velocity of rifle bullets, and – believe it or not – organically generated laser beams.

Retreating after one of their sorties to the shelter of their space-ship's force shield, the hunters had been about to give up and go back inside.

Alanie had said: 'Let's get off this planet before one of those things throws a fusion beam at us.'

And then *Dominus* had acted. Rushing down, like a smaller hill himself, from the hill where he had parked himself, he had advanced driving several smaller animals before him. Finally they had delivered themselves almost at the scientists' feet and promptly fallen unconscious. *Dominus* had then returned to the hill-top, where he had squatted motionless ever since. And Eliot, blended with his amazement, had felt the same thrill and transcendence that had overwhelmed him at the first arrival of Balbain's starship.

Dominus understood their wants! He was helping them!

Conceivably he could be communicated with. But that problem had to wait. They got the creatures inside and put them under adequate restraint. Then Eliot and Alanie went immediately to work.

The creatures' genes followed the standard pattern produced by matter on planetary surfaces everywhere: coded helices forming a group of chromosomes. The code was doublet and not triplet, as it was on Earth, but that in itself was not unusual; Abrak's genes also were in doublet code. More significantly, the single gonad incorporated a molecular factory, vast by microscopic standards, able to dispatch a chemical operator to any specific gene in a selected germ cell. And, furthermore, a chain of command could be discerned passing into the spinal column (where there was a spinal column) and thence to the brain (where there was a brain).

Eliot had written in his journal:

I get the impression that we are witness to a fairly late stage of Five's evolutionary development. For one thing, life here is relatively sparse, as though fierce competition has thinned down numbers rather than increased them, leading to a more subdued mode of existence. There are no predators; defensive mutations on the part of a potential prey would no doubt make it unprofitable to be a carnivore. The vegetation on Five conforms to the Basic Polarity and so presumably predates the overthrow of the Central Dogma, but it survives patchily in the form of scrub savannahs and a few small forests, and in many areas does not exist at all. The majority of animals own a patch of vegetation which they defend against all comers with an endless array of natural weapons, but they eat only, in order to obtain body-building materials – proteins and trace elements – and not to provide energy, which they obtain by soaking up the ubiquitous lightning discharges. Some animals have altogether abandoned any dependence on an external food chain: they carry out the whole of the anabolic process themselves, taking the requisite elements and minerals from soil and air and metabolising all their requirements using the energy from this same lightning.

It has occurred to us that all the animals here are potentially immortal.

Ageing is a species-characteristic, the life-span being adjusted to the maximum benefit of the species, not of the individual. If all our conclusions are correct, an organism on Five would continue to live a self-contained life until meeting some pressing exigency it was not able to master; only then would it reproduce to create a more talented version of itself and afterwards, perhaps, permit itself to die. This notion suggests that a test may be possible.

The slipper organism was the outcome of that test. They had placed the spider-thing in a chamber and subjected it to stress. They had bombarded it with pressure, heat, missiles, and various other discomforts suggested by the details of its metabolism. And they had waited to see whether it would react by 'conceiving' and ultimately giving birth to another creature better than itself.

Of course, the new organism would be designed to accomplish one thing above all: escape. Eliot was curious now to see how the slipper would attempt it.

'Might it not be dangerous?' Abrak questioned mildly.

Eliot flipped a switch. A thick slab of dull metal slid down to occlude the window. Instead, they could continue to watch through a vidcamera.

'I'd like to see it get through that,' he boasted. 'Carbon and titanium alloy a foot thick. It's surrounded by it.'

'You are being unsubtle,' said Abrak. 'Perhaps the beast will rely on trickery.'

Alanie gave a deep sigh that strained her full breasts voluptuously against the fabric of her smock. 'Well, what now?' she asked. 'We've been here six months. I think we've solved the basic mystery of the place. Isn't it time we were moving on?'

'I'd like to stay longer,' Eliot said thoughtfully. 'I want to see if we can get into communication with *Dominus*.'

'But how?' she asked, sitting down at a bench and waving her hand. 'Communication is a species-characteristic. He probably would never understand what language is.'

'And yet already he's given us help, so we *can* communicate after a fashion,' Eliot argued.

A warning sound came from Abrak. Something was happening on the screen looking into the test chamber.

The slipper organism had decided to act. Gliding smoothly to the far side of the chamber, the one nearest the skin of the ship, it pressed its tapered end against the wall. Abruptly the toe of the slipper ignited into an intense glare too bright for the vidcamera to handle. An instant later fumes billowed up and filled the chamber, obscuring everything.

By the time the fumes cleared sufficiently for the onlookers to see anything, the slipper had made its exit through the wall of the chamber, and thence through the ship's skin, by burning a channel whose edges were still white-hot.

'I think,' said Eliot sombrely, 'it might just have been a fusion beam, or something just as good.'

He paused uncertainly. Then he flung open a cupboard and began pulling out gear. 'Come on,' he said. 'We're going after our specimen.'

'But it will kill us,' Alanie protested.

'Not if *Dominus* helps us again. And somehow I think he will.'

Dominus is an intelligent being, he told himself. Intelligent beings are motivated by curiosity and a sense of co-operation with other intelligent beings. His hunt for the slipper was, in fact, impelled more by the desire to prompt *Dominus* into co-operating with them again than by any interest in regaining the slipper itself, which could well be far away by now.

'But, once having recaptured the creature, how will you retain it?' inquired Abrak, looking meaningfully at the gaping hole in the chamber.

'We'll keep it under sedation,' Eliot said, buckling on a protective suit.

Minutes later he stood at the foot of the spaceship. Besides the protective suit he was armed with a gun that fired recently prepared sleep darts (they had worked on the slipper's parent, following a biochemical analysis of that creature) and a cylinder that extruded a titanium mesh net.

Though evincing less enthusiasm, Alanie and Abrak had nevertheless followed him, despite his waiver to the girl. Abrak was unprotected, carried no weapons, and relied on his flimsy ship mask to take care of Five's atmosphere.

The environment boomed, flickered and flashed all around them. To Eliot's surprise the slipper could be seen less than a hundred yards away, lying quietly in the beams of their torches.

He glanced up towards the bulk of *Dominus*, then stepped resolutely forward, aware of the footsteps of the others behind him.

Up on the hill, *Dominus* began to move. Eliot stopped and stared up at him exultantly.

'Eliot,' Abrak crooned at his elbow, 'I strongly recommend caution. Specifically, I recommend a return to the ship.'

Eliot made no answer. His mind was racing, wondering what gesture he could make to *Dominus* when the vast beast recaptured the slipper and returned it to them.

He was quite, quite wrong.

Dominus halted some distance away, and extended a tongue, or tentacle, travelling at ground level almost too fast for the eye to follow. In little more than a second or two it had flashed across the sandy soil and scrubby grass, seized on Alanie, lifted her bodily from the ground and whisked her away before a scream could form in her throat. Eliot noticed, blurrily, that the entire length of the tentacle was covered with wriggling wormy protuberances.

Even as Alanie was withdrawn into the body of *Dominus* Eliot was running forward, howling wildly and firing his dart gun. Light footsteps pattered to his rear; surprisingly strong, bony arms restrained his.

'It is no use, Eliot. *Dominus* has taken her. He is not what you thought.'

Early on *Dominus* had perceived that the massy object, which he now accepted came from beyond the atmosphere, was not itself a life-form but a life-form's construct. The idea was already a familiar one: artifacts were rare on his planet – biological evolution was simpler – but there had been a brief period when they had proliferated, attaining increasing orders of sophistication until they had nearly devastated the continent. Stored in his redundant genes *Dominus* still retained all the knowledge of his ancestors on that score.

From the construct emerged undoubtedly organic entities, and it was in this that the mystery lay: there were several of them. *Dominus* spent some time mulling over this inexplicable fact. Who, then, was owner of the construct? He noted that, within limits, all the foreign lifeforms bore a resemblance to one another, and reminded himself that ecological convergence was an occasional phenomenon within his own domain. Could this convergence have been carried further and some kind of *ecological common action* (he formed the concept with difficulty) have arisen among entities occupying the same ecological niche? He reasoned that he should entertain no preconceptions as to the courses evolution might take under unimaginably alien conditions. Some relationship even more incomprehensible to him might be the case.

So he had been patient, watching jealously as the life-forms surveyed part of his domain in a flying artifact, but doing nothing. Then they had attempted, but failed, to capture some native organisms. Wanting to see what would take place, *Dominus* had delivered a few to them.

When he saw the mutated life-form emerge from the construct on its escape bid, he knew it was as he had anticipated. The aliens must have made a genetic analysis of all their specimens. The massy construct was sealed against *Dominus*'s mutation-damping genes, and within that isolation they had carried out an experiment, subjecting one of the specimens to a challenge situation and prompting it to reproduce.

Dominus could forbear no longer. He issued the slipper with a stern command to stay fast. It was sufficiently its father's son to know what the consequences of disobeying him would be. Three alien lifeforms emerged in pursuit. To begin with, *Dominus* took one of the pair that were so nearly identical.

Alanie Leitner floated, deep within *Dominus*'s body, in a sort of protein jelly. Mercifully, she was quite dead. Thousands of nerve-thin tendrils entered her body to carry out a brief but adequate somatic exploration. At the same time billions upon billions of RNA operators migrated to her gonads (there were two of them) and sifted down to the genetic level where they analysed her chromosomes with perfect completeness.

'It killed her,' Eliot was repeating in a stunned, muttering voice. 'It killed her.'

Abrak had persuaded him to return to the ship. They found that Balbain had abandoned his vigil and was pacing the central chamber situated over the laboratory. His bird-eyes glittered at them with unusual fervour.

'We can delay no further,' he boomed. '*Dominus*'s qualities cannot be gainsaid. The sense of him is overpowering. Therefore my quest is at an end. I shall return home.'

'No!' crooned Abrak suddenly, in a hard tone Eliot had not heard him use before. 'This planet also holds the promise of answering *our* requirements.'

'You take second place. *I* originated this expedition, and therefore you are pre-empted.'

'We shall see who will pre-empt whom,' Abrak barked.

While the import of the exchange was lost on Eliot, he was bewildered at seeing these two, whom he had thought of as dispassionate men (beings, anyway) of science, quarrelling and snarling like wild dogs. So palpable was the ferocity that he was startled out of his numbness and waved his arms placatingly as though to separate them.

'Gentlemen! Is this any way for a scientific expedition to conduct itself?'

The aliens glanced at him. Balbain's mask had become wet – perhaps with the exudations of some emotion – and partly transparent. Through it Eliot saw the gaping square mouth that never closed.

'Let us laugh,' Balbain said, addressing Abrak.

They both gave vent to regular chuggling expulsions of air; it was a creaking monotone devoid of mirth, a weird simulation of human laughter. Neither species, to Eliot's knowledge, was endowed with a sense of humour at all; once or twice before he had heard them use this travesty to indicate, in human speech, where they believed laughter would be appropriate.

He felt chilled. A feeling of *alienness* wafted towards him from the two beings, whom previously he had regarded as companions.

Balbain made a vague gesture. 'We know that you judge us by your own standards,' he said, 'but it is not so. Like you, we each came on this expedition to satisfy cravings inherent in our species. But those cravings are different from yours and from each other ...'

His voice softened and became almost caressing. Bending his head slightly, he indicated the wall of the ship, as though to direct Eliot's attention outside.

'Try to imagine what evolution means here on Five. It takes not aeons or millions of years to produce a biological invention, but only a few months. The Basic Polarity is not here to soften life's blows; competition is so intense that Five is the toughest testing ground in the universe. The result of all this should be obvious. What we have here is the most capable, potentially the most powerful source of life that could possibly exist. And *Dominus* is the fulfilment of that process. The most intolerant, the most *domineering –*' he put special emphasis on the word – 'entity that the universe can produce!'

'Domineering?' echoed Eliot, frowning.

'But of course! Think for a moment: what special quality must a creature develop on Five in order to make itself safe? The ability to dominate everything around it! *Dominus* has that quality to the ultimate degree. He is the Lord, in submission to whom my species can at last find peace of mind.'

Balbain spoke with such passion and in such a strange manner that Eliot could only stand and stare. Abrak spoke softly, turning his fox's snout towards him.

'It is hard for Balbain to convey what he is feeling,' he crooned. 'Perhaps I can explain it to your intellect, at least. First, the romantic picture you harbour concerning the fellowship of sentient minds is, I am afraid, quite incorrect. Mentalities are even more diverse in character than are physical forms. What goads us into action is not what goads you.'

'Then we cannot understand one another?' Eliot said.

'Only indirectly. In almost every advanced species there is a central drive that comes from its evolutionary history and overrides all other emotions – in its best specimens. This overriding urge gives the race as a whole its existential meaning. To other races it might look futile or even ridiculous – as, indeed, yours does to us – but to the species concerned it is a universal imperative, self-evident and inescapable.'

He paused to allow Eliot to absorb what he was saying.

While Balbain looked on, seeming scarcely any less agitated, he continued calmly: 'For reasons too complex to describe, life on Balbain's world developed a submission-orientation. The physical conditions there, much harsher than those you are accustomed to, caused living beings to enter into an elaborate network of relationships in which each sought, not to dominate, but to *be* dominated by some other power, the stronger the better. This craving is thus the compass needle that guides Balbain's species. To them it is self-fulfilment, the inner meaning of the universe itself.'

Eliot glanced at Balbain. The revelation made him feel uncomfortable.

'But how *can* it be?'

'Every species sees its own fixation as expressing the hidden nature of the universe. Do not you?'

Eliot brushed aside the question, which he did not understand. 'But what's all this about *Dominus*?'

'Why, he represents the other half of this craving. His is a mentality of compulsive domination. He rules this planet, and would rule any planet with which he came in contact. Balbain knows this. With *Dominus* to command them, his people will feel something of completeness.'

A small flash of insight came to Eliot. 'That is *his* reason for this expedition?'

'Correct. On his own world Balbain is a sort of knight, or saint, who has set out in search of this … Holy Grail.'

'We shall offer ourselves as *Dominus*'s slaves,' Balbain boomed hollowly. 'It is his nature to assume the position of master.'

Eliot tried to fight off his feeling of revulsion, but failed. 'You're … insane …' he whispered.

Once again Abrak's fake laughter chugged out. 'But Balbain's assessment of *Dominus* is perfectly correct. Five is the source of potentially the greatest, and in many ways the strangest, power that existence is capable of producing, and *Dominus*, at this moment in time, is the highest expression of that power. There can be others – and that is why it is of interest to my people! We also have an existential craving!'

His snout turned menacingly towards Balbain. Eliot thought suddenly of his frightening ability to generate infra-sound.

'You will have no opportunity to satisfy it. Nothing will prevent us from becoming the property of *Dominus*.' Balbain's words throbbed with passion. He was like an animal in heat.

The two began to circle one another warily. Eliot backed towards the door, afraid of infra-sound. He saw Abrak's snout open behind his mask.

Shuddering waves of vibration passed through his body. But, incredibly, in the same second Abrak died. His body was converting, from head down, into sand-coloured dust which streamed across the chamber in a rustling spray. Balbain's claw-like hand held the presumed source of this phenomenon: a device consisting of a cluster of tubes. When nothing remained of Abrak he put it away in a fold of his garment.

'Fear not,' he said to Eliot in a conciliatory tone. '*You* have no reason to obstruct me. After I take home the glad tidings, you can return to Solsystem.'

Eliot did not answer, but merely stood as if paralysed. Balbain gave a brief, apologetic burst of his simulated laughter, seeming to guess what was on Eliot's mind.

'As for Abrak, reserve your judgement on my action. I have given him what he desired – though to tell the truth he would have preferred the fate of your female, Alanie.'

'Alanie,' Eliot repeated. 'How can we be sure she's dead? It may be keeping her alive. I don't know why you murdered Abrak, Balbain, but if you want me to help you, then help me to get Alanie back. Then I'll do anything you ask me.'

'Defy *Dominus*?' Balbain looked at him pityingly. 'Pointless, hopeless, perverted dreams …'

Suddenly he rushed past Eliot and through the door. Eliot heard his feet clattering on the downward ramp.

The Earthman sat down and buried his face in his hands.

A minute or two later he felt impelled to turn on the external view screen to get another look at *Dominus*. A bizarre sight met his eyes. Balbain, about halfway between *Dominus* and the ship, had prostrated himself before the great beast and was making small gestures whose meanings were known only to himself. Eliot switched off the screen. A few minutes later, not having heard Balbain return, he looked again. There was no sign of the alien.

He was not sure how long he then sat there, trying to decide what best next to do, before a noise made him look up. The interstellar expedition's only other surviving member was entering the chamber.

Zeed was the least humanoid of all the team. He walked on limbs that could be said to constitute a pair of legs, except that they could also reconstitute themselves into tentacles, or a bunch of sticks, or a number of other devices to accommodate him to locomotion over a variety of different surfaces. Above these limbs a short dumpy body of indeterminate shape was hidden by a thick cloak which also hid his arms. Above this, a head of sorts: speckled golden eyes that did not at first look like eyes, other organs buried within fluted, bony grooves arranged in a symmetrical pattern.

The voice in which he spoke to Eliot, however, could have passed as human, although no mouth appeared to move.

'Explanations are superfluous,' he said, moving into the chamber and looking down on Eliot. 'I have consulted the ship's log.'

Eliot nodded. The log, of course, automatically recorded everything that took place within the ship.

'It appears that Balbain could not constrain himself and has forfeited his life,' Zeed continued. 'It is not surprising. However, it determines our end, also, since only Abrak and Balbain knew how to pilot the ship.'

This was news to Eliot, but in his present state the prospect of death caused him little alarm.

'Did *you* know Balbain's secret reason for this mission?' he asked.

'Of course. But it was no secret. Your people, being ignorant of alien races, made a presumption concerning its nature.' Gliding smoothly on his versatile legs, Zeed moved to the view screen and made a full circle scan of their surroundings. Then he turned back to Eliot. 'Perhaps it is a disappointment to you.'

'Why did Balbain want any of us along at all?' Eliot said wearily. 'Just to make use of us?'

'In a way. But we were all making use of one another. The universe is vast and quite mysterious, Eliot. It is an unfathomable darkness in which creatures arise having no common ground with each other. Hence, if they meet they may not be able to comprehend one another. Here in this ship we act as antennae for one another. We are not so alien to one another that we cannot communicate, yet sufficiently unalike so that each may understand some phenomena we encounter that the others cannot.'

'So that's what we are,' Eliot said resentfully. 'A star-travelling menagerie.'

'An ark, in which each has a separate quest. Yours is the obsession with acquiring knowledge. We do not share it, but the data you are collecting is your reward for the services you may, at some time, have been able to render one of us. You were enjoying yourselves too much for us to disillusion you concerning ourselves.'

'But how can you *not* share it?' Eliot exclaimed. 'Scientific inquiry is fundamental to intelligence, surely? How else can one ever understand the universe?'

'But others do not want to understand it, Eliot. That is only your own relationship to it; your chief ethological feature, whether you recognise it or not. You would still have joined this expedition, for instance, if it had meant giving up sex for the rest of your life.'

'And yet you have a scientific culture and travel in spaceships.'

'A matter of mere practicality. Pure, abstract science exists only for *homo sapiens* – I have not encountered it elsewhere. Other races carry out investigations only for the material benefits they bring. As an extreme example, think of *Dominus*: he, and probably countless of the animals here, possess vastly more of the knowledge you admire than do either of us, yet they have no interest in it and continue to live in a wild condition.'

Eliot's thoughts were returning to Alanie and the disinterest all the aliens had shown in her horrifying death. He remembered Balbain's enigmatic remark. 'Abrak,' he said bleakly, 'what was *he* seeking?'

'His species craves *abnormal death*. The cause of it is thuswise: life, however long, must end. Life, then, is conditioned by death. Hence death is larger than life. Abrak's people are conscious that everything, ultimately, is abnegated by death, and they look for fulfilment only in the manner of their dying. An individual of his species seeks to die in some unusual or noteworthy manner. Suicides receive praise, provided the method is extraordinary Murderers, likewise, are folk heroes, if their killings show imagination. Ultimately, the whole species strives to be exterminated in some style so extraordinary as to make its existence seem meaningful. Five seemed to offer that promise – not in its present state, it is true, but after suitable evolutionary development, perhaps due to an invasion by Abrak's people.'

'And *you*,' Eliot demanded. 'What do you seek?'

'We,' answered Zeed with an icy lack of hesitation, 'seek NULLITY. Not merely to die, like Abrak's species, but to wipe out the past, *never to have been*.'

Eliot shook his head, aghast. 'How can *any* living creature have an ambition like that?'

'You must understand that on your planet conditions have been remarkably gentle and favourable for the arising of life. Such is not the general rule. Elsewhere there is hardship and struggle, often of a severity you could not imagine. The universe rarely smiles on the formation of life. On my planet ...' Zeed seemed to hesitate, 'we regard it as an act of compassion to kill our offspring at birth. The unlucky ones are spared to answer nature's call to perpetuate the species. If you knew my planet, you would not think that life could evolve there at all. We believe that ever since the first nervous system developed, the subconscious feeling has been present that it has all been a mistake. To you, of course, this looks weird and perverted.'

'Yes ... it does indeed,' Eliot said slowly. 'In any case, isn't it impossible? I presume you are travelling the galaxy in search of some race that has time travel, so that you can wipe out your own past. But look at it this way: even if you succeeded in that, there would still have to be a "different past" – the old past, a ghost past – in which you still existed.'

'Once again you display your mental agility,' Zeed said. 'Your reasoning is sound: it may be that our craving can be satisfied only if the universe in its entirety is nullified.'

Springing to his feet, Eliot went to the viewscreen and peered out on to turbulent, lightning-struck Five. He thought of Alanie and himself slaving in the laboratory, and felt tricked and insignificant. Zeed seemed to think of their work as no more than the collecting instinct of a jackdaw or an octopus.

'Everything you've told me passes for psychosis back in Solsystem,' he said finally. 'I don't know ... maybe this is really a travelling lunatic asylum. You could all be insane, even by the standards of your own people. Balbain had this kinky desire to be a slave. Abrak wanted to be killed bizarrely, and you want never to have been born at all. What kind of a set-up is that? If you ask me, the normal, healthy, human mentality is a lot closer to reality than all that.'

'Every creature says that of itself. It is hard for you to accept that your outlook is not a norm, that it is an aberration, an exception. Let me tell you how it arose. Because of the incredibly luxurious conditions on the planet Earth there was able to develop a quite unique biological class: the *mammalia*. The specific ethological feature of the mammalia is *protectiveness*, which began within the family, then extended to the tribe, and finally, with your own species, has become so over-developed as to embrace the whole of the mammalian class. Every mammal is protected, by your various organisations, whether human or not. Now, the point is that within this shield of protectiveness qualities are able to evolve which actually are quite redundant, since they bear no relation to the hard facts of survival. One of these, becoming intense among monkeys, apes and hominids, is playful curiosity, or meddlesome inquisitiveness. This developed into the love of knowledge which became the overriding factor in the history of your own species.'

'That doesn't sound at all bad to me,' Eliot said defensively. 'We've done all right so far.'

'But not for long, I fear. Your species is in more trouble than you think. There is no future in this mammalian over-protectiveness. The dinosaurs thought themselves safe by reason of their excessive size, did they not? And yet that giantism was exactly what doomed them. Already you ran into serious trouble when your compulsive care for the unfit led to a deterioration of the genetic stock. You saved yourselves that time because you learned to eliminate defective genes artificially. But perhaps other consequences of this nature of yours will arise which you cannot deal with. I do not anticipate that your species will last long.'

'While you – death-lovers – will still be here, I suppose?'

Zeed's golden eyes seemed to dim and tarnish. We all inhabit a vast dark,' he repeated, 'in which there is neither rhyme nor reason.'

'Perhaps so.' Eliot's fists were clenched now. 'Here's another "ethological feature," as you call it – revenge! Do you understand that, Zeed? I'm going to take my revenge for the death of my mate! I'm going out there to destroy the animal that killed Alanie!'

Zeed did not answer but continued to stare at him and, so it seemed to Eliot's crazed imagination, lost any semblance to a living creature at all. Eliot ran to the lower galleries of the ship and armed himself with one of the few weapons the vessel carried: a high-powered energy beamer. As he stepped down from the ship and on to the booming, crashing surface of Five some of Zeed's words came back to him. An image came to his mind of the endlessness of space in which galaxies seemed to be descending and tumbling, and the words: *an unfathomable darkness without any common ground.* Then he pressed forward to challenge *Dominus.*

Dominus believed he had at last solved a perplexing riddle.

Following his initial seizure of one of the organisms, two others had emerged at short intervals so he had taken those also. A little later, he had moved in on the construct itself and taken a fourth organism from it. Of the fifth, there was no trace.

His analyses came up with the same result every time. The specimens were incomplete organisms: they were sterile. More accurately, they could only reproduce identical copies of themselves, like a plant. Together with this, their tissues suffered from an inbuilt deficiency which caused them to decay with age.

Plainly these facts were not consistent with their being motile, autonomous entities. *Dominus* now believed that the specimens he had were only expendable doll-organisms, created by some genuine entity as one might make a machine to carry out certain tasks, and dispatched here, in the metal construct, for a purpose.

And that entity, the owner of the construct and of the doll-organisms, having intruded on his domain once, would be back again.

With that realisation an urge beyond all power to resist came upon *Dominus*: the compulsion to *evolve*. He meditated in the depths of his being, and the entity to which he ultimately gave birth, amid great explosions, agonies and devastations, was as far above him in ability as he had been above his immediate inferior.

The new *Dominus* immediately set about the defence of his planet. The whole of the single continent became a springboard for this defence, and was criss-crossed with artifacts which meshed integrally with the space-borne artifacts he sent ranging several light-years beyond the atmosphere. To crew this extensive system *Dominus* copied the methods of the invader and created armies of slave doll-organisms modelled on the enemy's own doll-organisms. And *Dominus* waited for the enemy to arrive. And waited. And waited. And waited.

THE PROBLEM OF MORLEY'S EMISSION

MEMO

To: Director, Orbit University.
From: Dean, Sociohistoric Faculty.
Date: 19 July AD 3065.

Dear Mansim: As you are aware, a month ago the Officiating World Steering Committee asked us to submit a bystander's report on the events surrounding the activities of the well-known philosopher Isaac Morley, giving our interpretation of their possible significance. Frankly, some of us are alarmed at the direction in which our conclusions are taking us. Below is a précis of the report which tentatively is shaping up and which *should* go to the Committee in a few days' time (most of it is rather elementary, as politicians, naturally, are ignorant of the subject of social energy fields). Are you happy to see it go through as it stands? Arthur.

CONFIDENTIAL

SPECIFICS: the building of the Antarctic Structure; the passage of the Extra-Solar Object; the economic deformations noted to have occurred in the period from March to December AD 3064.

1. The facts surrounding the edifice named the Antarctic Structure are simple, if not altogether explicable. The Structure is an immense pyramid, or ziggurat, five miles on the side, its faces worked into an intricate, baroque labyrinth. Five thousand people laboured on its construction for a year and a half, without payment and without any clear idea as to its purpose, having been inspired to assemble by the leadership of its architect the self-styled philosopher Isaac Morley, who had created a philosophical cult solely in order to complete his project.

Only later did it emerge that the Structure is actually a powerful, if somewhat over-elaborate, UHF transmitter, able to transmit a tight beam in a fixed direction spacewards at an angle of 5 degrees from the direction of the south polar axis, at longitude 93 degrees west. Its function as an ideological monument is probably secondary.

2. There seems no way in which Morley and his followers could have known beforehand of the passage of the mysterious object known simply as the

Extra-Solar Object. Despite that, the beam from the Structure, after its one and only discharge on I April 3064, intercepted the Object exactly, at the point where it passed beneath the south pole, half a light year below the plane of the ecliptic.

The Object has an estimated rest-mass of a billion tons, and an estimated average diameter of three hundred and forty miles. It remained within detectable range for only one month. Apart from its high velocity, there is nothing to suggest that it is not of natural origin.

3. *Economic deformations:* all economic networks report an upsurge in new and unaccustomed directions from March to December of last year. Intermittent surges and subsidences in economic activity are by no means unusual, but several features of this one are perplexing. The networks unanimously claim that their new production initiatives were in response to demand arising from innovations in fashion; but it has proved impossible to trace any originating source for this demand. Even more puzzling, the new fashions seem suddenly to have dissipated before the production period was properly completed, and the networks are now left with vast stocks of useless articles.

One or two of the new commodities, such as the models of the Antarctic Structure which emit random buzzing noises, are clearly related to the influence of the Morleyites; but others, such as the holovid set able to screen nothing except the process of its own production, fulfil no obvious purpose.

4. To the layman it might seem that the above events, while concurrent in time, could not have very much bearing on one another. To explain how they possibly could, it will be necessary briefly to review the theory of *social energy fields*.

Early social science was separated, broadly speaking, into two camps. One view held that the individual human being is the only social reality, and that society itself has no substantive existence, but is only an arrangement, or 'contract', between autonomous, self-conscious individuals. The opposing camp, however, denied that consciousness is an attribute of the individual mind at all. According to this doctrine, consciousness is an aggregate social function; the 'self' has no independent existence and is a product, or reflection, of social forces. During the 20th and 21st centuries a series of wars was fought over this divergence in ideologies, as contending parties attempted either to destroy all forms of collective (or 'state') control, or else to establish a world of collective harmony in which only group aims were admitted.

As with many diametrically opposed concepts, both were right and both were wrong. The individualist concept was erroneous because the social conditioning of individual consciousness is an observable fact, and in most cases is practically absolute. The collective concept is untenable on more theoretical grounds. If it were true, the collective cultural pool would be its own single source of influences and ideas, there being nowhere else from which to replenish them. Like any system denied an energy input, it would suffer a continuous downgrading of vitality. Since growth and novelty are more characteristic of cultures than is decline this doctrine also fails to answer the facts, and the regular injections into the common pool of fresh initiatives can only be attributed to individual qualities.

Gradually it came to be realised that society, with its properties of gregariousness and organisation, can be adequately expressed only as a *polar structure in* which the individual comprises one pole and the collective or 'aggregrate' entity the other pole, the two taken together having the properties of opposition, complementarity and inseparability.

It could be argued that the social polarity is a fictional concept since the 'aggregate' pole is scattered over the surface of the Earth. However, the dimensions selected are not those of physical space but of 'social space'. Mathematically the 'cultural polarity', as it is sometimes called, belongs to the same class of structures as does a magnetic field, with which it shares many characteristics.

The Psychological Aspect: Not only does the social polarity extend worldwide, it is also present in every individual brain. Human consciousness is clearly acted on by forces coming from two opposite directions: a man is both himself, and he is society. This ambiguity, an existential double-take, is absolutely ineradicable; neither pole can be omitted. The individual has innate qualities, urges and desires, but these cannot develop without appropriate stimuli; if bereft of society – if raised by animals, perhaps – he could not develop into a human person. Likewise, without individuals there could obviously be no society. Neither can persist without the other, and indeed until they coalesce within the brain no human being exists.

The Organisational Aspect: The substance of the psychological polarity is the substance out of which all forms of social organisation are constructed.

The polar binding force stretches from individual to total aggregate through a wide range of intermediate forms. The first manifestation of the binding force is known technically as *coherence*, in analogy to laser light which is of uniform wave-length and whose waves all move in step. Coherence refers to the principle of *conformity* in human affairs: the force of fashion, of national and cultural identity, of religious belief, and so on. Coherence involves no conscious organisation. The masses of individuals keep in step apparently of their own volition, but in reality because of the mimicking nature of this force.

Like magnetic fields, the SEF (social energy field) is fairly static in its ground state. A magnetic field can, however, be made to give rise to an electric current which flows at right angles to the field; the social polarity has a similar property in that it may give rise to a flow of *organised directiveness*, this being a general term implying the *intentionality* of a system, and covering anything having the nature of a project. Invariably it involves a movement from a past condition to a future altered condition; usually (but not necessarily) it involves the deployment of material forces.

Organised directiveness could therefore be said to be an SEF potential. When the flow actually occurs, however, it adds an extra dimension to the field, transforming it into a *quadropolar energy structure* requiring, for a complete description, not two, but four terms: individual and aggregate poles, positive and negative flow terminals.

Cohesiveness is the term used to describe the condition of an SEF which is giving rise to a flow of organised directiveness. The *economic system* is its most obvious manifestation.

The Principle of Conformation: The chemical term *conformation* describes the ability of some molecules to adopt various configurations, a different energy state being associated with each. The SEF is similarly capable of a range of conformations, in which the individual and aggregate poles are variously emphasised.

The most extreme aggregate-favoured conformation is the mass crowd, or mob, probably the closest the aggregate pole ever gets to leading an independent existence. The characteristics of a crowd, both physically and psychologically, differ so radically from those of a healthy individual that it has been held to constitute a separate form of life, or rather, to constitute an entity intermediate between animate creatures and inanimate forces. An invariable feature of crowds is that the faculty of self-determination, which to some degree is present in every individual, is totally lacking in them. A crowd exhibits the characteristics of raw energy or a body of water. It does not respond to instructions or appeals but only to physical barriers and conduits, provided they are strong enough. Any individual trapped in a crowd is, therefore, robbed of any control over his own movements, and should crowd control measures fail then internal pressures within the crowd can very quickly reach lethal proportions.

The crowd's power to submerge the individual is no less psychological than physical. Individuals who least expect it of themselves may find their judgement abdicated to crowd emotion, their feelings funnelled in a single direction like a torrent at full flood – a syndrome which has been a source of elation to those leaders who have learned to arouse it.

Crowds of gigantic magnitude have mostly been associated with religious occasions. The earliest historical mention of a giant crowd is for the year 1966, when five million people assembled for the Hindu festival of Kumbh-Mela. A Kumbh-Mela crowd of over twenty million is recorded for eighty years later. The largest recorded crowd ever was an estimated two hundred and ten million people who assembled for the event of the Joyous Declaration of the

World God Uhuru movement on the Central African Plain in AD 2381, this number being compressed into a remarkably small area thanks to the ingenious open-plan multi-storey stadia erected for the occasion. When control measures failed fifty million people died as a result of internal crowd pressure. At several loci within the crowd the aggregated pressure rose to such a degree that several millions at a time were fused into a single bloody mass in which no individual bodies or parts of bodies were distinguishable. Gigantic crowds continued to be a feature of World God Uhuru despite attempts by civil authorities to have the gatherings banned.

A more disciplined crowd-like conformation yields mass regimentation ('the human dragon', as it has been called), the simplest and crudest means of accomplishing large-scale enterprises. This conformation was the basis of all the great engineering works of the ancient world, there being at the time no other form of economic organisation equal to the tasks involved. History furnishes many impressive examples of its use – for instance, the digging of a canal during the Chinese Sui dynasty to join the Yangtze and Yellow Rivers, by order of the emperor Yang Ti (of whom it is recorded: 'He ruled without benevolence'). Five and a half million workers were assembled and worked under guard by 50,000 police. In some areas all commoners between the ages of fifteen and fifty were drafted; every fifth family was required to contribute one person to help to supply and prepare food. Over two million workers were listed as 'lost'.

The history of civilisation is largely the story of the developing range of cohesive conformations.

Resolution Levels: The main success of the theory of social energy fields is that it at last brings human activity within the realm of purely physical phenomena, attributing to it properties as definitive as those of charge and mass. At first the energy field was looked on as only an analogy; but then T. R. Millikan pointed out that it is only in *scale* that the SEF is any different from, say, electromagneticism. Electrons are very small in relation to us; therefore it is easy to accept that they are acting on one another through the medium of an electric field. Were we able to study people reduced to the same resolution level as electrons, we would similarly infer that they were acting on one another through the medium of a field of energy.

From there it was but a short step to the idea that the SEF actually exists as a measurable field of force to which human beings respond. This field might, it was thought, consist of some subtle and undetected form of magnetism. It would go a long way towards explaining such phenomena as mass hypnotism, mass delusion, and the improbable feats of healing that are known sometimes to occur, since the human perception of reality must necessarily be tied to this field, and therefore would be malleable.

Attempts have been made to detect and measure the field, as well as to influence it by means of artificial field generators. In order to obtain a convenient resolution level. Earth civilisation has been studied from satellite laboratories, from Luna, and from Triton. The effects of the 'field generators' placed in some large cities, usually sending out low-powered magnetic and electrical oscillations, were initially quite promising, apparently producing either manic enthusiasm among the urban population, or else an unnatural lassitude. But due to the difficulty of isolating these results from other possible causes, none of them could be taken as conclusive.

The Theory of the Social Black Hole: If continued additions are made to force fields they become so powerful as to create weird and abnormal states of matter, such as the neutron star and the black hole. Social scientists have speculated on the results of endlessly adding to human populations, since the SEF also contains a gravitating principle: population tends towards centres, producing the well-known 'skyscraper effect'.

If large human communities were to exist in cosmic space the centripetal effect would tend towards the centre of a sphere. The 'skyscraper effect' would then produce only increasing concentration and density, there being no extra dimension to ease the load as the dimension of height does on the ground. There being no theoretical limit to the size a population may ultimately assume, it has already been proposed to build a vast artificial sphere several hundred million miles in diameter (a development of the once-projected Dyson sphere) to trap all solar energy so as to power and accommodate a truly titanic civilisation. Leaving aside considerations of physical mass and gravity, the question that arises is what would happen to the SEF inside such a sphere (centred on the sun or built in interstellar space if provided with alternative sources of energy) if it were to fill up entirely with human population. It is believed that a condition of 'psychosocial collapse' would occur towards the centre of the sphere. Individual and collective mentalities would assume unimaginable relationships; the two poles would perhaps disappear into one another, much as electrons and protons are forced to merge by the intense pressure inside a neutron star. Perception of reality, which is based on the polar relationship, would bear no resemblance to our perception of it. The whole of mankind within the sphere would ultimately be drawn into a 'social black hole', and would be totally unable to perceive or conceive of an external physical universe.

The theory of the social black hole, while it might seem to verge on the limit of possibility, does indicate that a social energy field could become subject to wholly strange effects.

5. *Conclusions:* The quadropolar social energy field, with its properties of coherence and cohesion, can be looked on as a *cosmic instrument of action:* Its evolution has taken several hundred million years; it is now capable of a

large range of accomplishments, many of them, no doubt, not even imagined as yet.

A disquieting feature of the SEF is that it is a self-conserving type of system beyond the scope of any of its parts to control. The reason for this is that any impulse arising within it is, after a period of time, answered by a re-equilibrating impulse from the opposite polarity. *Systems of this type are open to external control, however.* It is not idle to speculate that the universe may contain entities to whom Earth civilisation appears as a convenient ready-made tool or 'machine' and who might be able to locate or devise external controls for such a machine – entities, perhaps, whose mentalities do not have a polar structure and whose perception of reality is therefore at variance with our own.

Isaac Morley, an acknowledged genius, had by his own account invented a new methodology of thought which included original concepts in ontology. He claims it was a coded statement of this system that was emitted by the Antarctic Structure. When asked why the project was undertaken, Morley said: 'It seemed fitting that the information should be transmitted into the cosmos.' When further asked why the transmission tapes were subsequently wiped clean, he merely replied that they had fulfilled their purpose; the concepts had been created and would travel through space for all eternity. Morley now claims not to be able to remember the salient features of his break-through in philosophical thought, their subtlety having proved too elusive for his memory.

Morley insists that the beam's interception of the Extra-Solar Object must have been coincidence. He laughs at any suggestion that, to put it crudely, he had been 'manipulated' from interstellar space. How, he asks, could he have been 'manipulated' into formulating entirely original concepts?

Morley, however, misses the point. External controls, if they existed, would not act on the individual, nor on the collectivity as such, but in some way on combinations of the two. Ideas, thoughts and schemes are all part of the social structure and might be treated by a controlling agency as interesting or valuable outputs.

The erecting of the Antarctic Structure, too, shows one of the classic combinations of individual (Morley) and collective (cult) action. Investigation of the subsequent economic deformations (during which transit of the Extra-Solar Object took place) has shown that the deformations travelled through the economic system in the form of ripples, much as if a stone had been dropped into a pond. Following this finding, the abandoned SEF detecting instruments on Luna and on two Earth satellites were broken into. It was discovered that they had recorded strong low-frequency oscillations of an unusual nature during this period. The magnetic pulses appeared, moreover, not to be restricted to the surface of the Earth but to be isotropic.

6. *Recommendations:*

(1) *It is imperative to ascertain whether entities capable of exercising external control exist.*

(2) While no human individual or institution can take charge of the SEF, the possibility perhaps remains that an artificial non-polar intelligence could be constructed whose function would be, not to control the SEF itself, but to act as a block on any other external agency that tried to effect control.

It must be said that the problems associated with the above two projects are not merely prodigious; we can offer no guidance as to where they should even begin.

CONFIDENTIAL MEMO

To: Dean, Sociohistoric Faculty.
From: Director, Orbit University.
Date: 20 July AD 3065.

Dear Arthur: This report alarms me, too. If this thing gets about it will provoke a whole new crop of crank religions. The government is finding lunatics like Morley and his followers exasperating enough as it is.

Two thoughts occur to me. (1) If an exterior intelligence *were* to control the SEF, could we be aware of it? Such an intelligence would surely take care not to intrude new sources of energy into the system, for fear of causing internal damage. (2) This being the case, what guarantee have we that the growth of the SEF was not controlled from the start? I'm reminded of the story of the man who woke up suddenly in the middle of the night, wondering why he had always presumed he was alive for his own convenience, and not for some other purpose entirely unknown to him. For once I am inclined to think that ignorance is the better part of discretion. Do *not* send this report to the World Steering Committee – they're too democratic a body, some of them are bound to blab. Replace it with something more prosaic. It shouldn't be too difficult to suggest a reason why Morley *could* have known of the approach of the Extra-Solar Object in advance – he could then be arraigned for making a secret of scientific information.

Just between the two of us, I've already had a word with the WSC Chairman, and that's the kind of outcome he wants. He's been looking for a chance to nail Morley, anyway. Mansim.

THE CABINET OF OLIVER NAYLOR

Nayland's world was a world of falling rain, rain that danced on streaming tarmac, soaked the grey and buff masonry of the dignified buildings lining the streets of the town, drummed on the roofs of big black cars splashing the kerbs. Behind faded gold lettering on office windows constantly awash, tense laconic conversation took place to the murmur of water pouring from the gutterings, to the continuous, pattering sound of rain.

Beneath the pressing grey sky, all was humid. Frank Nayland, his feet up on his desk, looked down through his office window to where the slow-moving traffic drove through the deluge. *Nayland Investigations Inc.*, read the bowed gold lettering on the window. The rain fell, too, in the black-and-white picture on the TV set flickering away in the corner of the office. It fell steadily, unremittingly, permanently, while Humphrey Bogart and Barbara Stanwyck fled together in a big black car, quarrelling tersely in their enclosed little world which smelled of seat leather and rain.

They stopped at a crossroads. Bogart gripped the steering-wheel and scowled while the argument resumed in clipped, deadpan tones. The windscreen wipers were barely able to clear away the rain; on the outside camera shots the faces of the two were seen blurrily, intermittently, cut off from external contact as the wipers went through their sweep.

In the office the telephone rang. Nayland picked it up. He heard a voice that essentially was his own; yet the accent was British, rather than American.

'Is that Oliver Nayland, private detective?'

'*Frank* Nayland,' Nayland corrected.

'*Frank* Nayland.'

The voice paused, as if for reflection. 'I would like to call on your services, Mr Nayland. I want someone to investigate your world for me. Follow the couple in the black car. Where are they fleeing to? What are they fleeing *from*? Does it ever stop raining?'

Nayland replied in a professionally neutral tone. 'My charge is two hundred dollars a week, plus expenses,' he said. 'For investigating physical world phenomena, however – gravitation, rain, formation of the elements – I charge double my usual fee.'

While speaking he moved to the TV and twiddled the tuning knob. The black car idling at the crossroads vanished, was replaced by a man's face talking into a telephone. Essentially the face was Nayland's own; younger, perhaps, less knowing, not world-weary. There was no pencil-line moustache; and the client sported a boyish haircut Nayland wouldn't have been seen dead with.

The client looked straight at him out of the screen. 'I think I can afford it. Please begin your investigations.'

The picture faded, giving way to Gene Kelly dancing in *Singin' in the Rain*. Nayland returned to the window. From his desk he picked up a pair of binoculars and trained them on a black car that momentarily was stopped at the traffic lights. Through the car's side window he glimpsed the profile of Barbara Stanwyck. She was sitting stiffly in the front passenger seat, speaking rapidly, her proud face vibrant with passion, angry but restrained. By her side Bogart tapped on the steering-wheel and snarled back curt replies.

The lights changed, the car swept on, splashing rainwater over the kerb. Nayland put down his binoculars and became thoughtful.

For a few minutes longer Oliver Naylor watched the private dick's activities on his thespitron screen. Nayland held tense, laconic interviews in seedy city offices, swept through wet streets in a black car, talked in gloomy bars while rain pattered against the windows, visited the mansion of Mrs Van der Loon, had a brief shoot-out with a local mobster.

Eventually Naylor faded out the scene, holding down the 'retain in store' key. At the same time he keyed the 'credible sequence' button back in. The thespitron started up again, beginning, with a restrained fanfare, to unfold an elaborate tale of sea schooners on a watery world.

Naylor ignored it, turning down the sound so that the saga would not distract him. He rose from his chair and paced the living-room of his mobile habitat. How interesting, he thought, that the drama machine, the thespitron as he called it, should invent a character so close to himself both in name and in appearance. True, their personalities were different, as were their backgrounds – *Frank Nayland*, a twentieth-century American, was perfectly adapted to his world of the private eye *circa* 1950 whereas he, *Oliver Naylor*, was a twenty-second-century Englishman and a different type altogether. But physically the resemblance was uncanny.

So close a likeness could not be coincidence, Naylor thought. The thespitron's repertoire was unlimited and in principle one could expect a random dramatic output from it, but in practice it showed a predilection for Elizabethan tragedy in one direction – devising dramas worthy, in Naylor's view, of the immortal Bill himself – and in the other for Hollywood thrillers of the 1930s–50s period. Both of these were firm favourites of Naylor, the thespitron's creator. Clearly he had unintentionally built some bias into it; sometime he would apply himself to locating its source.

The existence of Frank Nayland probably had a similar explanation, he concluded. It was probably due to an optional extra he had built into the machine, namely a facility by which the viewer could talk to the characters portrayed on the thespitron screen. In this respect the thespitron exhibited an admirable degree of adaptability – it was perfectly delightful, for instance, to see how it had automatically translated his stick-mike into a large, unwieldy 1950s telephone. Similarly, it must have absorbed his identity from earlier intrusion, fashioning it into the world of Frank Nayland.

Just the same, it was eerie to be able to talk to oneself, albeit *in* this fictional guise. A soupcon, perhaps, of 'identity crisis'.

He strolled to the living-room window and gazed out. Millions of galaxies were speeding through the universe at a velocity of C^{186}, heading into infinity.

At length Naylor turned from the window with a sigh. Crossing the room, he settled himself in a comfortable armchair and switched on the vodor lecturer which, before leaving Cambridge, he had stocked with all material relevant to the subject in hand. Selecting the talk he wanted, he rested his head against the leather upholstery and listened, letting the lecture sink into his mind much as one might enjoy a piece of music.

The vodor began to speak.

'IDENTITY. The logical law of identity is expressed by the formula A=A, or A is A. This law is a necessary law of self-conscious thought, and without it thinking would be impossible. It is in fact merely the positive expression of the law of contradiction, which states that the same attribute cannot at the same time be affirmed and denied of the same subject.

'Philosophically, the exact meaning of the term "identity", and the ways in which it can be predicated, remain undecided. Some hold that identity excludes difference; others that it actually implies it, connoting "differential likeness". See B. Bosanquet, *Essays and Addresses*, 1889. The question is one of whether identity can be posited only of an object's attributes, or whether it refers uniquely to an object regardless of its attributes ...'

Naylor looked up as Watson-Smythe, his passenger, emerged from an adjoining bedroom where had been sleeping. The young man stretched and yawned.

'*Haw!* Sleep knits up the ravelled sleeve, and all that. Hello there, old chap. Still plugging away, I see?'

Naylor switched off the vodor. 'Not getting very far, I'm afraid,' he admitted shyly. 'In fact, I haven't made any real progress for weeks.'

'Never mind. Early days, I expect.' Watson-Smythe yawned less vigorously, tapping his mouth with his hand. 'Fancy a cup of char? I'll brew up.'

'Yes, that would be excellent.'

Watson-Smythe had affable blue eyes. He was fair-skinned and athletic-looking. Although only just out of bed he had taken the trouble to comb his hair before entering the habitat's main room, arranging his shining blond curls on either side of a neat parting.

Naylor had no real idea of who he was. He had met him at one of the temporary habitat villages that sprang up all over space. He was, it seemed, one of those rash if adventurous people who chose to travel without their own velocitator habitat, hitching lifts here and there, bumming their way around infinity. Apparently he was trying to find some little-known artist called Corngold (the name was faintly familiar to Naylor). Having discovered his whereabouts at the village, he had asked Naylor to take him there and Naylor, who had nowhere in particular to go, had thought it impolite to refuse.

Watson-Smythe moved to the utility cupboard and set some water to boil, idly whistling a tune by Haydn. While waiting, he glanced through the window at speeding galaxies, then crossed to the velocitator control board and peered at the speedometer, tapping at the glass-covered dial.

'Will we get there soon, do you think? Is 186 your top speed?'

'We could do nearly 300, if pushed,' Naylor said. 'But any faster than 186 and we'd probably go past the target area without noticing it.'

'Ah, that wouldn't do at all, would it?'

The kettle whistled. Watson-Smythe rushed to it and busied himself with warming the teapot, brewing the tea and pouring it, after a proper interval, into bone-china cups.

Naylor accepted a cup, but declined a share of the toast and marmalade which Watson-Smythe prepared for himself.

'This fellow Corngold,' he asked hesitantly while his guest ate, 'is he much of an artist?'

Watson-Smythe looked doubtful. 'Couldn't say, really. Don't know much about it myself. Don't know Corngold personally either, as a matter of fact.'

'Oh.' Naylor's curiosity was transient, and he didn't like to pry.

Watson-Smythe waggled a finger at the thespitron, which was still playing out its black-and-white shadow show (Naylor had deliberately eschewed colour; monochrome seemed to impart a more bare-boned sense of drama). 'Got the old telly going again, I see – the automated telly. You ought to put that into production, old chap. It would be a boon to habitat travellers. Much better than carrying a whole library of play-back tapes.'

'Yes, I dare say it would.'

'Not in the same class as this other project of yours, if it comes off, of course. That will be something.'

Naylor smiled in embarrassment. He almost regretted having told his companion about the scheme he was working on. It was, possibly, much too ambitious.

After his breakfast Watson-Smythe disappeared back into his bedroom to practise callisthenics – though Naylor couldn't imagine what anyone so obsessed with keeping trim was doing space-travelling. Habitat life, by its enclosed nature, was not conducive to good health.

His passenger's presence could be what had been blocking his progress, Naylor thought. After all, he had come out here for solitude, originally.

He switched on the vodor again and settled down to try to put his thoughts back on the problem once more.

'The modern dilemma (continued the vodor) is perhaps admirably expressed in an ancient Buddhist tale. An enlightened master one day announced to his disciples that he wished to enter into contemplation. Reposing himself, he closed his eyes and withdrew his consciousness.

'For thirty years he remained thus, while his disciples took care of his body and kept it clean.

'At the end of thirty years he opened his eyes and looked about him. The disciples gathered around. "Can the noble master tell us," they asked, "what has engaged his attention all this time?" The master told them: "I have been considering whether, in all the deserts of the world, there could conceivably be two grains of sand identical in every particular."

'The disciples were puzzled. "Surely," they said, "that is a small matter to monopolise the attention of a mind such as yours?"

'"Small it may be, but it was too great for me," the master replied. "I still do not know the answer."

'In the twentieth century a striking *scientific* use of the concept of identity seemed for a while to cut across many logical and philosophical definitions and to answer the Buddhist master's question. In order to handle paradoxical findings resulting from experiments in electron diffraction, equations were devised which, in mathematical terms, removed from electrons their individual identities. It was pointed out that electrons are all so alike as to be, for all intents and purposes, identical. The equations therefore described electrons as exchanging identities with one another in a rhythmic oscillation, without any transfer of energy or position ...'

Naylor's first love had been logic machines. As a boy he had begun by reconstructing the early devices of the eighteenth and nineteenth centuries: the deceptively simple Stanhope Demonstrator invented by an English earl, which with its calibrated window and two cursors was probably the very first genuine logic machine (though working out the identities was a tedious business); the Jevons Logic Machine (the first to solve complicated problems faster than the unaided logician) which in common with Venn diagrams made use of the logic algebra of George Boole. He had quickly progressed to the type of machine developed in the twentieth century and known generically as the 'computer', although only later had it developed into an instrument of pure logic for its own sake. By the time he was twenty he had become fully conversant with proper 'thinking machines' able to handle multi-valued logic, and had begun to design models of his own. His crowning achievement, a couple of years ago, had been the construction of what he had reason to believe was the finest logic machine ever, a superb instrument embracing the entire universe of discourse.

It was then that he had conceived the idea of the thespitron, a device which if marketed would without doubt put all writers of dramatic fiction out of business for once and all. Its basic hardware consisted of the above-mentioned logic machine, plus a comprehensive store and various ancillaries. After his past efforts, he had found the arrangement surprisingly easy to accomplish. In appearance the machine resembled an over-large, old-fashioned television set, with perhaps rather too many controls; but whereas an ordinary television receiver picked up its programmes from some faraway transmitter, the thespitron generated them internally. Essentially it was a super-plotting device; it began with bare logical identities, and combined and recombined them into ever more complex structures, until by this process it was able to plot an endless variety of stories and characters, displaying them complete with dialogue, settings and incidental music.

Naylor had watched the plays and films generated by the thespitron for several months now, and he could pronounce himself well pleased with the result of his labours. The thespitron was perpetual motion: because the logical categories could be permutated endlessly, its dramatic inventiveness was inexhaustible. Left to its own devices, it would eventually run through all possible dramatic situations.

Naylor had once heard a theological speculation that, laying aside his own philosophical training, he thought was lent added piquancy by the existence of the thespitron. The speculation was that God had created the universe for its theatrical content alone, simply in order to be able to view the innumerable dramatic histories it generated. According to this notion all ethical parameters, all poignancies, triumphs, tragedies and meaningless sufferings were, so to speak, literary devices.

The thespitron, Naylor reasoned, repeated this situation exactly. For was it not a private cosmic theatre? The cosmos in miniature, complete in itself, self-acting, consistent with its own logical laws just as the greater cosmos was? The idea that the thespitron had some sort of cosmic significance was made even more alluring by its present location here in intergalactic space, googols of light years from Earth. Here, too, was the miniature cosmos's creator and the observer of its presentations – Naylor himself, who was thus pleasingly elevated to the status of a god.

The perverse amusement he derived from this thought did not affect him seriously. Theological notions were all crude and simplistic to a man of education. But even with the redundant God-concept left out of account the Spectatorist Myth was interesting enough, leading to the idea of the universe interpreted as a logic of theatre – which was, after all, what he had achieved in the thespitron. Mulling over this idea brought a fascinating, compelling vision to the recesses of Naylor's mind. He imagined, at the source of existence, a transcendental logic machine – preternatural archetype of his own – which ground out the categories of logical identity in pure form; he saw the categories passing down a dark, immensely long corridor, combining and recombining as they went, until eventually they permutated into concrete substance – or in other words, into the physical universe and all its contents.

But even as he entertained this image Naylor smiled, shaking his head, reminding himself how corrupting to philosophy were all such idealist fancies. He was well aware of how fallacious it was to imagine that logic was antecedent to matter.

Philisophically Naylor held fast to the tradition of British empiricism (while not descending, of course, to American pragmatism) and saw himself very much as a child of the nineteenth century, harbouring a nostalgic fondness for the flavour of thought of that period – though the outlook of J. S. Mill had been much updated, naturally, by the thoroughgoing materialist empiricists of Naylor's own time. He eschewed the manic systems-building of the continentals and was suspicious of any lapse into idealist formulations (such as 'rationalism') all of which ended up sooner or later in some version of the hysterical 'world-soul' doctrine.

In his attachment to nineteenth-century values Naylor was typical of his time. Most of his fellow Englishmen were equally proud to think of themselves as products of the great Victorian age, for in recent decades there had been a genuine and far-reaching renaissance in the qualities that had given that period its vigour. The Victorians, with their prolific inventiveness, their love of 'projects', their advocacy of 'progress' combined with an innate and rigid conservatism, embodied, it was commonly believed, all that was best in civilisation. And indeed it was hard to imagine any period more closely resembling the age of England's Great Queen than the present one.

As often happens, economic forces were in some measure responsible for the change. During the twenty-first century it had gradually become apparent that the advantages of global trade were finally being outweighed by the disadvantages. The international division of labour was taking on the aspect, not of a constant mutual amelioration of life, but of a destructive natural force which could impoverish entire peoples. The notion of economic progress came to take on another meaning: to signify, not the ability to dominate world markets, but the means by which a small nation might become wealthy without any foreign trade whatsoever. Britain, always a pioneer, was the first to discover this new direction. With the help of novel technologies she reversed what had been axiomatic since the days of Adam Smith, and for a time was once again the wealthiest power on Earth, aloof from the world trade storm, reaping through refusal to trade all the benefits she had once gained through trade.

It was a time of innovation, of surprising, often fantastic invention, of which the Harkham Velocitator, a unit of which was now powering Naylor's habitat through infinity, was perhaps the outstanding example. The boffin had come into his own again, outwitting the expensively equipped teams of professional research scientists. Yet in some respects it was a cautious period, alert to the dangers of too precipitous a use of every new-fangled gadget, and keeping alive the spirit of the red flag that once had been required to precede every horseless carriage. For that reason advantage was not always taken of every advance in productive methods.

Two devisements in particular were forbidden. The first was the hylic potentiator, an all-purpose domestic provider commonly known as the matter-bank. This worked by holding in store a mass of amorphous, non-particulate matter, or hyle, to use the classical term. Hylic matter from this store could be instantly converted into any object, artifact or substance for which the machine was programmed, and returned to store if the utility was no longer needed or had not been consumed. Because the hylic store consisted essentially of a single gigantic shaped neutron, very high energies were involved, which had led to the device being deemed too dangerous for use on Earth. Models were still to be found here and there in space, however.

The second banned production method was a process whereby artifacts were able to reproduce themselves after the manner of viruses if brought into contact with simple materials. The creation of self-replicating artifacts had become subject to world prohibition after the islands of Japan became buried beneath ever-growing mounds of still-multiplying TV sets, audvid recorders, cameras, autos, motor-bikes, refrigerators, helicopters, pocket computers, transistor radios, portphones, light aeroplanes, speedboats, furniture, sex aids, hearing aids, artificial limbs and organs, massage machines, golf clubs, zip fasteners, toys, typewriters, graphic reproduction machines, electron microscopes, house plumbing and electrical systems, machine tools, industrial robots, earthmovers, drilling rigs, prefabricated dwellings, ships, submersibles, fast-access transit vehicles, rocket-launchers, lifting bodies, extraterrestrial exploration vehicles, X-ray machines, radio, video, microwave, X-ray and laser transmitters, modems, reading machines, and innumerable other conveniences.

Of all innovations, however, the invention to have most impact on the modern British mind was undoubtedly the Harkham velocitator, which had abolished the impediment of distance and opened up infinity to the interested traveller. Theoretically the velocitator principle could give access to any velocity, however high, except one: it was not possible to travel a measured distance in zero time, or an infinite distance in any measured time. But in practice, a velocitator unit's top speed depended on the size of its armature. After a while designing bigger and bigger armatures had become almost a redundant exercise. Infinity was infinity was infinity.

Velocitator speeds were expressed in powers of the velocity of light. Thus 186, Naylor's present pace, indicated the speed of light multiplied by itself 186 times. Infinity was now littered, if littered was a word that could be predicated of such a concept, with velocitator explorers, most of them British, finding in worlds without end their darkest Africas, their South American jungles, their Tibets and Outer Mongolias.

In point of fact the greater number of them did precious little exploring. Infinity, as it turned out, was not as definable as Africa. Early on the discovery had been made that until one actually *arrived* at some galaxy or planet, infinite space had a soothing, prosaic uniformity (provided one successfully avoided the matterless lakes), a bland sameness of fleeting mushy glints. It was a perfect setting for peace and solitude. This, perhaps, as much as the outward urge, had drawn Englishmen into the anonymous universe. The velocitator habitat offered a perfect opportunity to 'get away from it all', to find a spot of quiet, possibly, to work on one's book or thesis, or to avoid some troublesome social or emotional problem.

This was roughly Naylor's position. The success of the thespitron had emboldened him to consider taking up the life of an inventor. He had ventured into the macrocosm to mull over, in its peace and silence, a certain stubborn technical problem which velocitator travel itself entailed.

The problem had been advertised many times, but so far it had defeated all attempts at a solution. It was, quite simply, the problem of how to get home again. Every Harkham traveller faced the risk of becoming totally, irrevocably lost, it being impossible to maintain a sense of direction over the vast distances involved. The scale was simply too large. Space bent and twisted, presenting, in terms of spatial curvature, mountains and mazes, hills and serpentine tunnels. A gyroscope naturally followed this bending and twisting; all gyroscopic compasses were therefore useless. Neither, on such a vast and featureless scale, was there any possibility of making a map.

(Indeed a simple theorem showed that large-scale sidereal mapping was inherently an untenable proposition. *Mapping* consists of recording relationships between locations or objects. In a three-dimensional continuum this is only really practicable by means of data storage. However, the number of possible relationships between a set of objects rises exponentially with the number of objects. The number of possible connections between the 10,000 million neurons of the human brain actually exceeds the number of particles within Olbers' Sphere (which, before the invention of the velocitator, was thought of as the universe). Obviously no machine, however compact, could contain the information necessary to map the relationships between objects whose number was without limit, even when those objects were entire galaxies.)

Every velocitator habitat carried a type of inertial navigation recording system, which enabled the traveller to retrace his steps and, hopefully, arrive back at the place he had started from. This, to date, was the only homing method available; but the device was delicate and occasionally given to error – only a small displacement in the inertial record was enough to turn the Milky Way Galaxy into an unfindable grain of sand in an endless desert. Furthermore, Harkham travellers were apt, sometimes unwittingly, to pass through powerful magnetic fields which distorted and compromised the information on their recorders, or even wiped the tapes clean.

Naylor's approach to the problem was, as far as he knew, original. He had adopted a concept that both philosophy and science had at various times picked up, argued over, even used, then dropped again only to resume the argument later: the concept of *identity*.

If every entity, object and being had its own unique identity which differentiated it from the rest of existence, then Naylor reasoned that it ought to be uniquely findable in some fictive framework that was independent of space, time and number. Ironically the theoretical tools he was using were less typical of empiricist thought than of its traditional enemy, rationalism, the school that saw existence as arising, not from material occasions, but from abstract categories and identities; but he was sufficiently undogmatic not to be troubled by that. He was aware that empirical materialists had striven many times to argue away the concept of identity altogether, but they had never, quite, succeeded.

Naylor imagined each individual object resulting from a combining, or focusing together, of universal logic classes (or universal identities), much as the colour components of a picture are focused on to one another to form a perfect image. It was necessary to suppose that each act of focusing was unique, that is to say, that each particle of matter was created only once. It would mean, for instance, that each planet had a unique identity: that a sample of iron from the Earth was subtly different from a sample of iron taken from the Moon, and it was this difference that Naylor's projected direction-finder would be able to locate.

But was it a warrantable assumption, he wondered?

'Ah, the famous question of identity,' he said aloud.

The vodor lecture, heard many times before, became a drone. He turned it off and opened his notebook to scan one section of his notes.

'IDENTITY AND NUMBER: The natural numbers, 1, 2, 3, 4, 5 …, are pure abstractions, lacking identity in the philosophical meaning of the word. That is to say, there is no such entity as "five". Identity in a set of five objects appertains only to each object taken singly … "Fiveness" is a process, accomplished by matching each member of a set against members of another set (e.g. the fingers of a hand) until the set being counted is exhausted. Only material objects have identity …'

In his fevered imagination it had seemed to Naylor that he need but make one more conceptual leap and he would be there, with a sketch model of the device that would find the Milky Way Galaxy from no matter where in infinity. He believed, in fact, that he already had the primitive beginnings of the device in the thespitron. For although no *physical* mapping of the universe was possible, the thespitron *had* achieved a *dramatic* mapping of it, demonstrating that the cosmos was not entirely proof against definition.

But the vital leap, from a calculus of theatre to a calculus of identities, had not come, and Naylor was left wondering if he should be chiding himself for his lapse into dubious rationalist tenets.

Dammit, he thought wryly, if an enlightened master had no luck, how the devil can I?

Gloomily he wrote a footnote: 'It may be that the question of identity is too basic to be subject to experiment, or to be susceptible to instrumentation.'

His thoughts were interrupted by the ringing of the alarm bell. The control panel flashed, signalling that the habitat was slowing down in response to danger ahead. In seconds it had reduced speed until it was cruising at only a few tens of powers of the velocity of light.

At the same time an announcement gong sounded, informing them that they had arrived within beacon range of someone else's habitat – presumably Corngold's.

Naylor crossed to the panel to switch off the alarm. As he did so Watson-Smythe appeared from the bedroom. He had put on a gleaming white suit which set off his good looks to perfection.

'What a racket!' he exclaimed genially. 'Everything going off at once!'

Naylor was examining the dials. 'We are approaching a matterless lake.'

'Are we, by God?'

'And your friend Corngold is evidently living on the shores of it. Can you think of any reason why he would do that?'

Watson-Smythe chuckled, with a hint of rancour. 'Just the place where the swine would choose to set himself up. Discourages visitors, you see.'

'You can say that again. Do I take it we are likely to be unwelcome? What you would call a recluse, is he?'

The younger man tugged at his lower lip. 'Look here, old chap, if you feel uneasy about this you can just drop me off at Corngold's and shoot off again. I don't want to impose on you or anything.'

But by now Naylor was intrigued. 'Oh, that's all right. I don't mind hanging about for a bit.'

Watson-Smythe peered out of the window. They were close to a large spiral galaxy which blazed across the field of vision and swung majestically past their line of sight.

'We'll get a better view on this,' Naylor said. He pressed a small lever and at the front end of the living-room a six-foot screen unfolded, conveniently placed in relation to the control panel. He traversed the view to get an all-round picture of their surroundings. The spiral galaxy had already receded to become the average smudged point of light; in all directions the aspect was the usual one of darkness relieved by faintly luminous sleet – except, that was, for directly ahead. There, the screen of galaxies was thin. Behind that screen stretched an utter blackness: it was a specimen of that awesome phenomenon, the matterless lake.

For the distribution of matter in the universe was not, quite, uniform. It thinned and condensed a bit here and there. The non-uniformity of matter mainly manifested, however, in great holes, gaps – lakes, as they were called – where no matter was to be found at all. Although of no great size where the distances that went to make up infinity were concerned, in mundane terms the dimensions of these lakes were enormous, amounting to several trillion times the span of an Olbers' sphere (the criterion of cosmic size in pre-Harkham times, and still used as a rough measure of magnitude).

Any Harkham traveller knew that it was fatal to penetrate any further than the outermost fringes of such a lake. Should anyone be so foolhardy as to pass out of sight of its shore (and in times past many had been) he would find it just about impossible to get out again; for the simple fact was that when not conditioned by the presence of matter, space lacked many of the properties normally associated with it. Even such elementary characteristics as direction, distance and dimension were lent to space, physicists now knew, by the signposts of matter. The depths of the lakes were out of range of these signposts, and thus it would do the velocitator rider no good merely to fix a direction and travel it in the belief that he must sooner or later strike the lake's limit; he would be unlikely ever to do so. He was lost in an inconceivable nowhere, in space that was structureless and uninformed.

As the habitat neared the shore the lake spread and expanded before them, like a solid black wall sealing off the universe. 'Will Corngold be in the open, do you think, or in a galaxy somewhere?' Naylor asked.

'I'd guess he's snuggled away in some spiral; harder to find that way, eh?' Watson-Smythe pointed to a cluster of galaxies ahead and to their right.

'There's a likely-looking bunch over there. Right on the edge of the lake, too. What do the indicators say?'

'Looks hopeful.' Naylor turned the habitat towards the cluster, speeding up a little. The galaxies brightened until their internal structures became visible. The beacon signal came through more strongly; soon they were close enough to get a definite fix.

Watson-Smythe's guess had been right. They eventually found Corngold's habitat floating just inside the outermost spiral turn of the largest member of the cluster. The habitat looked like two or three Eskimo igloos squashed together, humped and rounded. Behind it the local galaxy glittered in countless colours like a giant Christmas tree.

Watson-Smythe clapped his hands in delight. 'Got him!'

Naylor nudged close to the structure at walking pace. The legally standardised coupling rings clinked together as he matched up the outer doors.

'Jolly good. Time to pay a visit,' his passenger said.

'Shouldn't we raise him on the communicator first?'

'Rather not.' Watson-Smythe made for the door, then paused, turning to him. 'If you'd prefer to wait until … Well, just as you please.'

He first opened the inner door, then both outer doors which were conjoined now and moved as one, and then the inner door of the other habitat. Naylor wondered why he didn't even bother to knock. Personally he would never have had the gall just to walk into someone else's living-room.

With tentative steps he followed Watson-Smythe through the short tunnel. Bright light shone through from the other habitat. He heard a man's voice, raised in a berating, bullying tone.

The door swung wide open.

The inside of Corngold's dwelling reminded Naylor of an egg-shaped cave, painted bright yellow. Walls and ceiling consisted of the same ovoid curve, and lacked windows. The yellow was streaked and spattered with oil colours and unidentifiable dirt; the lower parts of the walls were piled with canvases, paintings, boxes, shelves and assorted junk. The furniture was sparse: a bare board table, a mattress, three rickety straight-backed chairs and a mouldy couch. An artist's easel stood in the middle of the room. Against the opposite wall was the source of Corngold's provender and probably everything else he used: a matter-bank, shiny in its moulded plastic casing.

Corngold was a fat man, a little below medium height. He was wearing baggy flannel trousers and a green silk chemise which was square-cut about the neck and shoulders and was decorated with orange tassels. He had remarkably vivid green eyes; his hair had been cropped short, but now had grown so that it bristled like a crown of thorns.

He reminded Naylor of early Hollywood versions of Nero or Caligula. He did not, it seemed, live alone. He was in the act of brow-beating a girl, aged perhaps thirty, who for her dowdiness was as prominent as Corngold was for his brilliant green shirt. Corngold had her arm twisted behind her back, forcing her partly over. Her face wore the blank sullenness that comes from long bullying; it was totally submissive, wholly drab, the left eye slightly puffy and discoloured from a recent bruise. She did not even react to the entry of visitors.

Corngold, however, eased his grip slightly, turning indignantly as Watson-Smythe entered. 'What the bloody hell do you mean barging in here?' he bellowed. 'Bugger off!' His accent sounded northern to Naylor's ears; Yorkshire, perhaps.

To Naylor's faint surprise Watson-Smythe's answering tone was cold and professional. 'Walter Corngold? Late of 43 Denison Square?'

'You heard me! Bugger off! This is private property!'

Watson-Smythe produced a slim Hasking stun beamer from inside his jacket. With his other hand he took a document from his pocket. 'Watson-Smythe,' he announced. 'I have here a warrant for your arrest, Corngold. I'm taking you back to Earth.'

So that was it! Naylor wondered why he hadn't guessed it before. Now that he thought of it, Watson-Smythe was almost a caricature of the type of young man one expected to find in the 'infinity police', as it was jocularly called – MI19, the branch of security entrusted with law enforcement among habitat travellers.

He felt amused. 'What are the charges?' he asked mildly.

'Two charges,' Watson-Smythe replied, turning his head slightly but still keeping the Hasking carefully trained on Corngold. 'Theft, and more serious, the abduction of Lady Cadogan's maid, who unless I am very much mistaken is the young lady you are now mistreating, Corngold. Take your hands off her at once.'

Corngold released the girl and shoved her roughly towards the couch. She plomped herself down on it and sat staring at the floor.

'Ridiculous,' he snorted, then added, in a voice heavy with irony: 'Betty's here of her own sweet will, aren't you, dearest?'

She glanced up like a frightened mouse, darting what might have been a look of hope at Watson-Smythe. Then she retreated into herself again, nodding meekly.

Corngold sighed with satisfaction. 'Well, that's that, then. Sod off, the two of you, and leave us in peace.' He strolled to the easel, picked up a brush and started to daub the canvas on it, as though he had banished them from existence.

Watson-Smythe laughed, showing clean white teeth. 'They told me you were a bit of a character, Corngold. But you're due for a court appearance in London just the same.'

He turned politely to Naylor. 'Thanks for your assistance, Naylor old boy. You can cast off now if you're so inclined, and I'll take Corngold's habitat back to Earth.'

'Can't,' Corngold said, giving them a sideways glance. 'My inertial naviga-tor's bust. I was stuck here, in fact, until you two turned up. Not that it bothers me at all.'

Watson-Smythe frowned. 'Well …'

'Is it a malfunction?' Naylor queried. 'Or just a faulty record?'

Corngold shrugged. 'It's buggered, I tell you.'

'I might be able to do something with it,' Naylor said to the MI19 agent. 'I'll have look at it, anyway. If it's only the record we can simply take a copy of our own one.'

Corngold flung down his brush. 'In that case you might as well stay to din-ner. And put that gun away, for Chrissake. What do you think this is, a shooting gallery?'

'After all, he can't go anywhere,' Naylor observed when Watson-Smythe wavered. 'Without us he'll *never* get home.'

'All right.' He returned his gun to its shoulder holster. 'But don't think you're going to wriggle out of this, Corngold. Kidnapping's a pretty serious offence.'

Corngold's eyes twinkled. He pointed to a clock hung askew on the wall. 'Dinner's at nine. Don't be late.'

Wearily Naylor slumped in his armchair in his own living-room. He had spent an hour on Corngold's inertial navigator, enough to tell him that the gyros were precessing and the whole system would need to be re-tuned. It would be a day's work at least and he had decided to make a fresh start tomorrow. If he couldn't put the device in order they would all have to travel back to Earth in Naylor's habitat – as an MI19 officer Watson-Smythe had the power to require his co-operation over that. At the moment the agent was in his bedroom, bringing his duty log up to date.

The business with the navigator had brought home anew to Naylor the desirability of inventing some different type of homing mechanism. He was becoming irritated that the problem was so intractable, and felt a fresh, if frustrating, urge to get to grips with it.

Remembering that he had left the vodor lecture unfinished, he switched on the machine again, listening closely to the evenly-intoned words, even though he knew them almost by heart.

'The question of *personal* identity was raised by Locke, and later occupied the attentions of Hume and Butler. Latterly the so-called "theorem of universal iden-tity" has gained some prominence. In this theorem, personal identity (or *self-identity*) is defined as *having knowledge* of one's identity, a statement which also serves to define consciousness. Conscious beings are said to differ from inanimate objects only in that they have knowledge of their identity, while inani-mate objects, though possessing their own identity, have no knowledge of it.

'To be conscious, however, means to be able to perceive. But in order to perceive there must be an "identification" between the subject (self-identity, or consciousness) and the perceived object. Therefore there is a paradoxical "sharing" of identity between subject and object, similar, perhaps, to the exchange of identity once posited between electrons. This reasoning leads to the concept of a "universal identity" according to which all identity, both of conscious beings and of inanimate objects, belongs to the same universal transcendental identity, or "self". This conclusion is a recurring one in the history of human thought, known at various times as "the infinite self", "the transcendental self" and "the universal self" of Vedantic teachings. "I am you," the mystic will proclaim, however impudently, meaning that the same basic identity is shared by everyone.

'Such conceptions are not admitted by the empirical materialist philosophers, who subject them to the most withering criticism. To the empiricist, every occasion is unique; therefore its identity is unique. Hume declared that he could not even dscover self-identity in himself; introspection yielded only a stream of objects in the form of percepts; a "person" is therefore a "bundle" of percepts. Neither can the fact that two entities may share a logical identity in any way compromise their basic separateness, since logic itself is not admitted as having any *a priori* foundation.

'The modern British school rejects the concept of identity altogether as a mere verbalism, without objective application. Even the notion of electron identity exchange is now accepted to be a mathematical fiction, having been largely superseded by the concept of "unique velocity" which is incorporated in the Harkham velocitator. It is still applied, however, to a few quantum mechanical problems for which no other mathematical tools exist.'

Naylor rose and went to the window, gazing out at the blazing spiral galaxy which was visible over the humped shape of Corngold's habitat. 'Ah, the famous question of identity,' he murmured.

He knew why, the question continued to perplex him. It was because of the thespitron. The thespitron, with its unexpected tricks and properties, had blurred his feeling of self-identity, just as the identity of electrons had been blurred by the twentieth-century quantum equations. And at the same time, the thoughts occurring to him attacked materialist empiricism at its weakest point: the very same question of identity.

There came to him again the image of the categories of identity, proceeding and permutating down a dark, immensely long corridor. He felt dizzy, elated. Here, in his habitat living-room, his domain was small but complete; he and the thespitron reproduced between them, on a minute scale, the ancient mystical image of created universe and observing source, of phenomenon and noumenon; even without him here to watch it, the thespitron was the transcendental machine concrctised, a microcosm to reflect the macrocosm, a private universe of discourse, a mirror of infinity in a veneered cabinet.

Could the characters and worlds within the thespitron, shadows though they were, be said to possess *reality?* The properties of matter itself could be reduced to purely logical definitions, heretical though the operation was from the point of view of empiricism. The entities generated by the machine, obeying those same logical definitions, could never know that they lacked concrete substance.

Was there identity in the universe? Was that *all* there was?

Now he understood what had made him include a communication facility in the thespitron; why he had further felt impelled to talk to Frank Nayland, his near-double. He had identified himself with Nayland; he had tried to enlighten him as to the nature of his fictional world, prompted by some irrational notion that, by confronting him, he could somehow prod Nayland into having a consciousness of his own.

Who am I? Naylor wondered. Does my identity, my consciousness, belong to myself, or does it belong to this – he made a gesture taking in all that lay beyond the walls of the habitat – to infinity?

Sitting down again, he switched on the thespitron.

Naylor's sense of having duplicated the logical development of the universe was further heightened by the inclusion of the 'credible sequence' button. This optional control engaged circuits which performed, in fact, no more than the last stage of the plotting process, arranging that the machine's presentations, in terms of construction, settings and event structure, were consonant, if not quite with the real world, at least with a dramatist's imitation of it.

With the button disengaged, however, the criterion of mundane credibility vanished. The thespitron proceeded to construct odd, abbreviated worlds, sometimes from only a small number of dramatic elements. Worlds in which processes, once begun, were apt to continue for ever, without interruption or exhaustion; in which actions, once embarked upon, became a binding force upon the actor, requiring permanent reiteration.

The world of Frank Nayland, private investigator, was one of these: a world put together from the bare components of the Hollywood thriller *genre*, bereft of any wider background, moving according to an obsessive, abstract logic. A compact world with only a small repertoire of events; the terse fictional world of the private dick, a world in which rain was unceasing.

Summoning up Nayland from store, Naylor watched him pursue his investigations, his gaberdine raincoat permanently damp, rain dripping from the brim of his slouch hat. So absorbed did he become in the dick's adventures that he failed to notice the entry of Watson-Smythe until the MI19 officer tapped him on the shoulder.

'It's nine o'clock,' Watson-Smythe said. 'Time we were calling on Corngold.'

'Oh, yes.' Naylor rose, rubbing his eyes. He left the thespitron running as they went through the connecting tunnel, tapping on Corngold's door before going in.

A measure of camaraderie had grown up during the hour they had spent with the artist earlier. Naylor had come to look on him more as an eccentric rascal than a real villain, and even Watson-Smythe had mollified his hostility a little. He had still tried to persuade Betty Cooper, the maid allegedly abducted from the home of Lady Cadogan (from whom Corngold had also stolen a valuable antique bracelet), to move in with them pending the journey back to Earth, but so great was Corngold's hold over her (the hold of a sadist, Watson-Smythe said) that she would obey only him.

There was no sign of the promised dinner party. Corngold stood before his easel, legs astraddle, while Betty posed in the nude, sitting demurely on a chair. Though still a sullen frump, Naylor thought that when naked she had some redeeming features; her body tended to flop, and was pale and too fleshy, but it was pleasantly substantial, in a trollopy sort of way.

Corngold turned his head. 'Well?' he glared.

Watson-Smythe coughed. 'You invited us to dinner, I seem to remember.'

'Did I? Oh.' Corngold himself didn't seem to remember. He continued plying the paint on to the canvas, a square palette of mingled colour in his other hand. Naylor was fascinated. The man was an artist after all. His concentration, his raptness, were there, divided between the canvas and the living girl.

Naylor moved a few paces so he could get a glimpse of the portrait. But he did not see what he had expected. Instead of a nude, Corngold had painted an automobile.

Corngold looked at him, his eyes twinkling with mirth. 'Well, it's how I see her, you see.'

Naylor was baffled. He could not see how in any way the picture could represent Betty, not even as a metaphor. The auto was sleek and flashy, covered with glittering trim; quite the opposite of Betty's qualities, in fact.

He strolled to the other end of the egg-shaped room, glancing at the stacked canvases. Corngold had a bit of a following, he believed, among some of the avant-garde. Naylor took no interest in art, but even he could see the fellow was talented. The paintings were individualistic, many of them in bright but cleverly-toned colours.

Corngold laid down his brush and moved aside the easel, gesturing to Betty to rise and dress. 'Dinner, then,' he said, in the tone of one whose hospitality may be presumed upon. 'Frankly I'd hoped you two would have got tired of hanging around by now and cleared off.'

'That would have left you in a bit of a spot,' Naylor said. 'You have no way of finding your way home.'

'So what? Who the hell wants to go to Earth anyway. I've got everything I need here – eh?' Corngold winked at him obscenely, and, to the extreme embarrassment of both Naylor and Watson-Smythe, stuck his finger in Betty's vulva, wiggling it vigorously. Betty became the picture of humiliation, looking distressfully this way and that. But she made no move to draw back.

Naylor bristled. 'I *say!*' he protested heatedly. 'You *are* British, aren't you?'

Corngold's manner became suddenly aggressive. He withdrew his finger, whereupon Betty turned and snatched for her clothes. 'And why shouldn't I be?' he challenged.

'Well, dammit, no proper Englishman would treat a woman this way!'

There was a pause. Corngold gave a peculiar open-mouthed grin which grew broader and broader as he looked first at Betty and then back and forth between Naylor and Watson-Smythe.

'Fuck me, I must be a Welshman!'

'Perhaps the best thing *would* be to leave you here, Corngold,' Watson-Smythe commented, his tone one of coldest disapproval. 'It might be the punishment you deserve.'

'Do it, then! You'd never have got to me at all, you bastards, if I'd found a way to turn off the fucking beacon.'

'It can't be done,' Naylor informed him. It would be typical of such a character, he thought, not to know that. The beacon signal was imprinted on every velocitator manufactured, as a legal requirement. Otherwise habitats would never be able to vector in on one another.

Corngold grunted, and dragged the board table to the centre of the room. Around it he arranged the three chairs his dwelling boasted, and with a casual gesture invited his guests to sit down.

'What's all this "Corngold", anyway?' he demanded as they took their places. 'Have I agreed that I am Corngold? Establish the identity of the culprit – that's the first thing in law!'

'I am satisfied that you are Walter Corngold,' Watson-Smythe said smoothly.

Corngold banged on the tabletop, shouting. 'Supposition, supposition! Establish the identity!'

He laughed, then turned to Betty, who was clothed now and stood by in the attitude of a waitress. 'Well, let's eat. Indian curry suit you? How do you like it? Mine's good and hot.'

While Corngold discussed the details of the meal Betty went to the matter-bank and returned with a large flagon of bright red wine and four glasses. Corngold sloshed out the wine, indicating to her that she should knock hers straight back. As soon as she had done so he emptied his own glass, instantly refilling it.

'One good hot vindaloo, one lamb biriani and a lamb korma,' he instructed curtly.

Betty moved back to the matter-bank and twisted dials. Spicy aromas filled the room as she transferred bowls of food from the delivery transom to a tray. Naylor turned to Corngold.

'You can't seriously contemplate spending the rest of your life in this habitat? Cut off from humanity?'

'Humanity can go jump in the lake.' Corngold jerked his thumb towards the great nothingness that lay beyond the local galaxy. 'Anyway, who says I'm habitat-bound? You forget there are other races, other worlds. As a matter of fact I have a pretty good set-up here. I've discovered a simply fascinating civilisation on a planet of a nearby star. Here, let me show you.'

Rising, he pushed aside a pile of cardboard cartons to reveal the habitat's control board. A small golden ring of stars appeared, glowing like a bracelet, as he switched on an opal-surfaced viewscreen.

Corngold pointed out the largest of the stars. 'This is the place. A really inventive life-form, not hard to get to know, really, and with the most extraordinary technology. I commute there regularly.'

'And yet you always bring your habitat back out here again?' Naylor remarked. 'You must love solitude.'

'I do love it indeed, but you misunderstand me. The habitat stays here. I commute to Zordem by means of a clever little gadget the natives gave me.'

Heavily he sat down at the table, licking his lips. His visitors tried to ask him more about these revelations, their curiosity intensely aroused; but when the food was served he became deaf to all their questions.

Taking up a whole spoonful of the pungent-smelling curry Betty served him, and without even tempering it with rice, he rolled it thoughtfully round his mouth. Then suddenly he spluttered and spat it all out.

'This isn't vindaloo, you shitty-arsed cow! It's fucking Madras!'

With a roar Corngold picked up the bowl and flung it at Betty, missing her and hitting the wall. The brown muck made a dribbling trail down the yellow.

'You must excuse my common-law wife,' he said to Naylor, his expression turning from fury to politeness. 'Unfortunately she is a completely useless pig.'

'But I don't dare dial vindaloo,' Betty protested in a whining, tearful voice. 'The bank's been going funny again. On vindaloo –'

'Get me my dinner!' Corngold's bellow cut off her explanations. Submissively she returned to the machine, operating it again. As she turned the knobs an acrid blue smoke rose from the matter-bank, coming not from the transom but from the seams of the casing.

Naylor, with a glance at Watson-Smythe, started to his feet with the intention of beating a retreat to his own habitat and casting off with all haste. But Corngold sprang up with a cry of exasperation, marched over to the ailing bank and gave it a hefty kick, at which the smoke stopped.

'It's always giving trouble,' he exclaimed gruffly as he rejoined them. 'That's what comes of buying second-hand junk.'

'You do realise, don't you,' Watson-Smythe said, in a tone Naylor found admirably calm and even, 'that that thing can go off like a nuclear bomb?'

'So can my arse after one of these curries. Ah, here it comes. Better be right this time.'

Corngold's vindaloo was *very* hot. The sweat started out on his forehead as he ate it, grunting and groaning, deep in concentration. He was a man of lusty nature, Naylor decided, carrying his enjoyment of life to the limit. Afterwards he sat panting like a dog, calling for more wine and swallowing it in grateful gulps.

Then, the meal over, Corngold became expansive. With a wealth of boastful detail he began to describe his contacts with the inhabitants of the planet Zordem.

'Their whole science is based on the idea of a certain kind of ray,' he explained. 'They call them *zom* rays. They have some quite remarkable effects. Let me show you, for instance –'

He opened one of the egg-shaped room's four doors, disclosing a cupboard whose shelves contained several unfamiliar objects. Corngold picked one up. It was smooth, rounded in shape with a flat underside, easily held in one hand, and about three times as long as it was broad. He carried it to the viewscreen and slapped it against the side of the casing, where it stuck as if by suckers.

On the screen, the ring of stars vanished. In its place was intergalactic space, and in the foreground a long, fully-equipped spaceship of impressive size, the ring-like protuberance about her middle indicating the massiveness of her velocitator armature. They all recognised her as a Royal Navy cruiser, one of several on permanent patrol.

'Rule Britannia!' crowed Corngold. 'It's the *Prince Andrew*, ostensibly seeing that we habitat travellers don't mistreat the natives. But really, of course, having a go at a second British Empire. I should ko-ko.'

'It's no joking matter,' Watson-Smythe said sternly. 'There have been quite a few incidents. I dare say your relations with Zordem will come under scrutiny in good time, Corngold.'

'Is she close?' Naylor asked.

'No, she's quite a way off,' Corngold said, taking a look at a meter. 'Roughly a googol olbers.'

'Your gadget can see *that* far? But good God – how do you find a single object at that distance?'

'The Zordems put a trace on her the day I arrived. To make me feel at home, I suppose. Don't ask me how. They did it with zom rays!'

Naylor was stunned. 'Then *these* are the people who are masters of infinity!' he breathed.

Corngold sighed, strolled back to the table and sat down placing his bare, fat arms among the empty dishes. He wiped up a trace of curry sauce with his finger and licked it. Then he looked up at Naylor.

'You really are a clown,' he said. 'Masters of infinity! That's a lot of crap newspaper talk. The Zordems are nowhere into infinity, any more than we are. If you're going to talk about *infinity*, well then, the whole spread anyone's gone from Earth, or anywhere else for that matter, is no more than a dot. Okay, build a velocitator armature a light year across and ride it for a billion years. You've still only gone the length of a dot on the face of infinity. That's what infinity means, isn't it? That however far you go it's still endless? For Crissake,' he ended scathingly, 'you ought to know that.'

'Just the same, you've misled us with this talk of being stranded,' Watson-Smythe accused him. 'With equipment like this you can obviously find your way to anywhere.'

'Afraid not. This gadget gives the range but not the direction. And even the range is limited to about fifty googol olbers. The Zordems have hit on a lot of angles we've missed, but they're not that much in advance of us overall.'

'Still, it must be based on a completely new principle,' Naylor said intensely. 'Don't you see, Corngold? This might give us what everybody's been looking for – a reliable homing device! It might *even*,' he added shyly, 'mean a reduction in sentence for you.'

He stopped, blushing at the emerald malevolence that brimmed for a moment from Corngold's eyes. If he were honest, he was beginning to find the man frightening. There was something dangerous, something solid and immovable about him. His knowledge of an alien technology, and his obvious intelligence which came through despite his outrageous behaviour, had dispelled the earlier impression of him as an amusing crank. All Watson-Smythe's trained smoothness had failed to make the slightest dent in his self-confidence; Betty remained his slave, and Naylor privately doubted whether the charge of abduction could be made to stick. There was something ritualistic in Corngold's treatment of her, and in her corresponding misery. It looked to Naylor as though they were matched souls.

'I thought I had dropped plenty of hints,' Corngold emphasised, 'that I don't really want to come back to Earth. Betty and I want nothing more than to remain here, thank you.'

Watson-Smythe smiled. 'I'm afraid the law isn't subject to your whims, Corngold.'

'No?' Corngold's expression was bland. He raised his eyebrows. 'I thought

I might be able to bribe you. How would you both like to screw Betty here? She's all right in her way – just lies there like a piece of putty and lets you do which and whatever to her.'

Watson-Smythe snorted.

'What is it you want, then?' Corngold asked in sudden annoyance. 'The fucking bracelet? Here – take it!' He went to the mattress on the floor, lifted it and took a gold ornament from underneath, flinging it at Watson-Smythe. 'It's a piece of sodding crap anyway – I only took it because Betty had a fancy for it.'

Watson-Smythe picked up the bracelet, examined it briefly, then wrapped it in a handkerchief and tucked it away in an inside pocket. 'Thanks for the evidence.'

Corngold sighed again, resignedly. He reached for the flagon of wine and drained the dregs, finishing with a belch.

'Well, it's not the end of the world. I expect Betty will be glad to see London again. But before you retire for the night, gentlemen, let me answer your earlier question – how I make the transition between here and Zordem. It's quite simple, really – done by zom rays again, but a different brand this time.'

He went to the cupboard and brought out something looking like a large hologram plate camera, equipped with a hooded shutter about a foot on the side. 'This is really a most astonishing gadget,' he said. 'It accomplishes long-distance travel without the use of a vehicle. I believe essentially the forces it employs may not be dissimilar to those of the velocitator – but instead of moving the generator, they move whatever the zom rays are trained on. All you do is line it up with wherever you want to go and step into the beam – provided you have a device at the other end to de-translate your velocity, that is. Neat, isn't it? The speed is fast enough to push you right through walls as though they weren't there.'

'Why, it's a matter transmitter!' Naylor exclaimed.

'As good as.'

Already Watson-Smythe had guessed his danger and was reaching for his gun. But Corngold was too quick for him. He trained the camera-like device on the agent and pressed a lever. The black frontal plate flickered, exactly as if a shutter had operated – as indeed one probably had. Watson-Smythe vanished.

Naylor staggered back aghast. '*Christ!* You've murdered him!'

'Yes! For trying to disturb our domestic harmony!'

Naylor stuttered: 'You've gone too far this time, Corngold. You won't get away with this … too far.'

Scared and flustered, he scrambled for the exit. He scampered through the tunnel, slammed shut the outer doors and disengaged the clutches so that the two habitats drifted apart. Then, slamming shut the inner door, he rushed to the control board.

*

In the egg-shaped room, Corngold had quickly set up the Zordem projector on a tripod. He aligned the instrument carefully, focusing it through the wall, on to the intruding habitat a few yards away. He opened the shutter for an instant. Naylor and his habitat were away, projected out into the matterless lake.

A faint voice came from the communicator on the nearly-buried control board. 'I'm falling, Corngold. Help me!'

'I'll help you,' Corngold crowed, grinning his peculiar open-mouthed grin. 'I'll help you fall some more!'

He opened the shutter again, uttering as he did so a wild, delighted cry: '*FUCK OFF!* ...' Naylor was accelerated by some further trillions of light years per second, carried by the irresistible force of zom rays.

Corngold turned to Betty. 'Well, that's him out of the way,' he exclaimed with satisfaction. 'Bring on the booze!'

Pale and obedient, Betty withdrew a flagon of cerise fluid and two glasses from the matter-bank. She poured a full measure for Corngold, a smaller one for herself, and sat crouching on the couch, sipping it.

'We'll move on from here pretty soon,' Corngold murmured. 'If they could find us, others can.'

He tuned the opal-glowing viewscreen into the lake and surveyed the unrelieved emptiness, drinking his wine with gusto.

Corngold's mocking 'Fuck off' was the last message Naylor's habitat received from the world of materiality, whether by way of artificial communication, electromagnetic energy, gravitational attraction or indeed any other emanation. These signposts, normally informing space of direction, distance and dimension, were now left far behind.

There had been no time to engage the velocitator and now it was too late. Corngold had had the jump on them from the start. At the first discharge of the Zordem projector Naylor's speedometer had registered c^{413} and his velocitator unit did not have the capacity to cancel such a velocity even though the lake's shore, in the first few moments, had still been accessible. At the second discharge the meter registered c^{826} and unencumbered, total space had swallowed him up. He was now surrounded by nothing but complete and utter darkness.

Within the walls of the habitat, however, his domain was small but complete. He had, in the thespitron, an entire universe of discourse; a universe which, though nearly lacking in objective mass, conformed to the familiar laws of drama and logic, and on the display screen of which, at this moment, Frank Nayland was pursuing his endless life. Naylor's mind became filled yet again with his vision of the long dark corridor down which the logical identities eternally passed, permutating themselves into concretisation. Who was to say that out here, removed from the constraints of external matter, the laws of identity might not find a freedom that otherwise was impossible? Might, indeed, produce reality out of thought?

'The famous question of identity,' he muttered feverishly, and sat down before the flickering thespitron, wondering how it might be made to guide him, if not to his own world, at least to some world.

As the big black car swept to a stop at the intersection Frank Nayland emerged from the darkness and leaped for the rear door, wrenching it open and hustling himself inside. His gat was in his hand. He let them see it, leaning forward with his forearm propped over the top of the front seat.

Rainwater dripped from him on to the leather upholstery. Ahead, the red traffic lights shone blurrily through the falling rain, through the streaming sweep of the windscreen wipers.

Bogart peered round at Nayland, his face slack with fear.

'Let's take a walk,' Nayland said. 'I know a nice little place where we can talk things over.'

Bogart's hands gripped the steering-wheel convulsively. 'You know we can't leave here.'

'No … that's right,' Nayland said thoughtfully after a pause. 'You have to keep going. You have to keep running, driving-'

The engine of the car was ticking over. The lights had changed and Bogart started coughing asthmatically, jerking to and fro.

Stanwyck put her hand on his arm, a rare show of pity. 'Oh, why don't you let him go?' she said passionately to Nayland. 'He's done nothing to you.'

Nayland clambered out of the car and slammed the door after him. He stood on the kerb while the gears ground and the vehicle shot off into the night. He walked through the rain to where his own car was hidden in a culvert, and drove for a while until he spotted a phone booth.

Rain beat at the windows of the booth. Water dripped from his low-brimmed hat as Nayland dialled a number. While the tone rang he dug into his raincoat pocket, came up with a book of matches, flicked one alight and lit a cigarette with a cupped hand.

'Mr Naylor? Nayland here. This is my final report.'

A pause, while the client on the other end spoke anxiously. Finally Nayland resumed. 'You wanted to know about the couple in the car. Bogart is wanted for the snatch of the Heskin tiara from the mansion of Mrs Van der Loon. It was the Stanwyck woman – Mrs Van der Loon's paid companion – who got him into it, of course. The usual sad caper. But here's the rub: there's a fake set of Heskin rocks – or was. Mrs Van der Loon had a legal exchange of identity carried out between the real jewels and the paste set. A real cute switcheroo. It's the paste set that's genuine now, and Bogart is stuck with a pocketful of worthless rocks and a broad who's nothing but trouble.'

'Can that be done?' Naylor asked wonderingly.

'Sure. Identities are legally exchangeable.'

Staring at the thespitron screen, the stick-mike in his hand, Naylor was thinking frantically. He watched a plume of smoke drift up the side of Nayland's face, causing the dick to screw up one eye.

Something seemed to be happening to the thespitron. The image was becoming scratchy, the sound indistinct.

'Why does it never stop raining?' he demanded.

'No reason for it to stop.'

'But are you *real*?' Naylor insisted. 'Do you *exist*?'

Nayland looked straight at him out of the screen. The awareness in his eyes was unmistakable. 'This is *our* world, Mr Naylor. You can't come in. It's all a question of identity.'

'But it will work – you just said so,' Naylor said desperately. 'The switcheroo – the fake me and the real me –'

'Goodbye, Mr Naylor,' Nayland said heavily. He put down the phone.

Without Naylor as much as touching the controls, the thespitron ground to a halt. The picture dwindled and the screen went blank.

'Ah, the famous question of identity!' boomed the thespitron, and was silent.

Naylor fingered the restart button, but the set was dead. He fell back in his chair, realising his mistake. He realised how foolish had been his abandonment of the solid wisdom of materialist empiricism, how erroneous his sudden hysterical belief, based on fear, that logic and identity could be antecedent to matter, when in truth they were suppositions merely, derived from material relations. Deprived of the massy presence of numerous galaxies, signposts of reality, the thespitron had ceased to function.

The closing circles were getting smaller. Now there was only the shell of the habitat, analogue of a skull, and within it his own skull, that lonely fortress of identity. Naylor sat staring at a blank screen, wondering how long it would take for the light of self-knowledge to go out.

THE FALL OF CHRONOPOLIS

ONE

With a hollow booming sound the Third Time Fleet materialised on the windswept plain. Fifty ships of the line, the pride of the empire and every one built in the huge yards at Chronopolis, were suddenly arrayed on the dank savanna as if a small city had sprung abruptly into being in the wilderness. The impression was increased by the lights that shone within the ships, outlining their ranks of square windows in the dusk. A few fat drops of rain spattered on the scene; the atmosphere was moody, clouds were gathering in the racing sky, and soon there would be a storm.

Half an hour passed before a large porchlike door swung open at the base of the flagship and three men stepped on to the turf. Two were burly men in stiff maroon uniforms, displaying badges of rank on chest, sleeves, and hat. The third was a shrivelled, defeated figure who walked with eyes downcast, occasionally flicking a disinterested glance around him.

The trio paused on a small knoll a hundred yards from the nearest timeship. Commander Haight looked about him, taking pride in the sight. The ships were suggestive of two disparate forms: basically they looked like long office blocks built on a rectilinear plan, but the crude streamlining that helped them cruise through time meant that the storeys were arranged in steps, high at the stern and low at the bows. To the commander this was reminiscent of another, more ancient type of vessel: the hulls of wind-driven galleons that once – far beyond the empire's pastward frontier – had sailed Earth's seas.

'Good to get in the open air,' he muttered. 'It gets damned claustrophobic in the strat.'

'Yes, sir.' Colonel Anamander looked uncomfortable. He always hated this part of the proceedings. Usually he had the job of seeing to the disposal of the corpse and was spared the task today only because Haight felt like taking a walk outside.

Mixing with the erratic wind came a low-pitched whine from the surrounding timeships. That was the sound of their engines holding them steady in orthogonal time. Suddenly came a louder, skirling noise. The engineers were carrying out the repairs for which the fleet had made the stop.

What a desolate spot, Anamander thought. In this region of history the timeships always chose, if possible, an uninhabited region in which to beach themselves. The mutability of time was not something to be taken lightly.

The courier lifted his dispirited eyes to the face of the commander. He spoke in a hesitant, empty voice.

'Shall I die now?'

Haight nodded, his expression contemptuous and remote. 'You have performed your duty,' he intoned formally.

The courier's self-execution was a simple affair. It relied on the vagus nerve, by means of which the brain would signal the heart to stop. This nerve, aimed at the heart like a cocked gun, was the stock explanation of death by fright, grief, or depression, as well as by suggestion through a shaman or witch doctor. In his final briefing the courier had been trained to use this nerve voluntarily so as to carry out the order to kill himself once his task was done – an order that, in point of fact, could be said to be superfluous. The two officers watched now as he closed his eyes and mentally pronounced the hypnotically implanted trigger words. A spasm crossed his face. He doubled up, gasping, then collapsed limply to the ground.

Anamander moved a deferential foot or two away from the corpse. 'An unusually honoured courier, sir. Not many carry messages of such import.'

'Indeed not.'

Commander Haight continued to gaze on his fleet. 'This will be a testing time for us, Colonel. It looks like the beginning of a full-scale attack – perhaps even of an invasion. The empire will stand or fall by the efforts of men such as ourselves.'

'Strange that even his type should play a part in it,' Anamander mused, indicating the corpse. 'Somehow I can never avoid feeling sorry for them.'

'Don't waste your sympathy,' Haight told him. 'They are all criminals, condemned murderers and the like. They should be grateful for a last chance to serve the empire.'

'I wonder what they go through to make them so willing to die.'

Haight laughed humourlessly. 'As for that, it appears there's only one way to find out, and as you can see it's not a procedure to be recommended. Several times I've asked them, but they don't tell you anything that makes sense. In fact, they seem to lose the power of rational speech, more or less. You know, Colonel, I'm in a somewhat privileged position as regards these couriers. Until I speak the phrase releasing them from their hypnotic block they're unable to pronounce the key words triggering the nerve. What if I were to – I confess I've been tempted to keep one alive to see what would happen to him. He might come to his senses and be able to talk about it. Still, orders are orders.'

'There must be a reason for the procedure, apart from their being condemned anyway.'

'Quite so. Have you ever seen the strat with your naked eyes, Colonel?'

Anamander was startled. 'No, sir!'

'I did once – just a glimpse. Not enough to derange the senses – just the briefest glimpse. It was years ago. I was on the bridge when our main engine cut out for a moment after – well, never mind about all that. But there it is: I saw it, or almost saw it. Yet to this day I couldn't tell either you or myself exactly what it was I saw.'

'I've heard it leaves a mark on a man.'

'Yes, Colonel, it does. Don't ask me what sort of mark.'

Haight sniffed the air, then shivered slightly. The rain was falling faster.

'Let's get inside. We'll be drenched here.'

They crossed the turf and disappeared into the towering flagship. Half an hour later the whole fleet disappeared with a hollow *boom* that echoed around the empty plain. Shortly there came a crash of thunder and tumultuous rain soaked the savanna, pouring over the body of the courier who had died six centuries from home.

Colonel Anamander felt reassured with the thrum of the time-drive under his feet. They were building up speed, heading back into the past and traversing the planet's time-axis to bring them to the right location in both space and time: the continent of Amerik, Node 5.

As it moved, the fleet sprayed beta rays all around it into the temporal substratum – the strat, as chronmen called it. Electromagnetic energy could not travel through the strat, rendering communication difficult. The answer for short-range purposes was beta radiation, consisting of relativistic electrons moving slower than light. They did not penetrate far, but they sufficed for the timeships to keep contact with one another while in formation, as well as to maintain a limited radar watch.

Haight's orders were explicit. The hunt was on for the war craft that had violated the Imperial Millennium.

The enemy foray was well planned, as was evidenced by the failure of the Third Time Fleet to learn of it until the attackers had already passed to its rear. They had come in from the future at high speed, too fast for defensive time-blocks to be set up, and had only been detected by ground-based stations deep in historical territory. If the target was to alter past events – the usual strategy in a time-war – then the empire's chroncontinuity could be significantly interfered with.

It looked to Haight as if the assault could signal the beginning of the full-scale war with the Hegemony which the High Command believed to be inevitable. The Hegemony, existing futureward of the Age of Desolation, had long been the chief threat to the Chronotic Empire, and it was almost certain that the raiders had been dispatched from that quarter.

If their intention was to test out the empire's ability to defend itself, then Haight promised himself forcefully that they would be disappointed in the result. Like all chronmen he was fanatical in regard to his duty; service to the empire was the chronman's creed. He felt personally affronted, not only by the intrusion into imperial territory, but also by the attempt to alter the relationship of the past to the future, a right that belonged to no one but their Chronotic Majesties the Imperial Family of the House of Ixian.

Commander Haight mulled the matter over while keeping one eye on the scan screens. The bridge, as it was called by convention, was a large, elongated hemi-ellipsoid. The controllers sat elbow to elbow along its curved walls, the pilot section being situated in the nose of the ellipsoid whereas another line of manned consoles ran along its middle axis. At the moment, the size-contraction effect caused by the flagship's velocity through the strat was not pronounced enough to be noticeably dramatic. At top speed it would become so intense at the forward end of the ship that the pilots in the nose would be reduced to a height of inches, whereas the men in the rear would retain their normal size – an effect that gave the bridge a false impression of being drastically foreshortened.

The bridge crew numbered thirty-two men in all, not counting the cowled priest who moved among them dispensing pre-battle blessings and sprinkling holy wine. Commander Haight looked over the scene from the raised desk he shared with Colonel Anamander at the rear of the bridge. It had often amused Haight to think that, with the flagship undergoing full-speed test trials, a pilot who happened to glance back saw his commander as a massive titan hovering over him like an avenging angel.

A gong sounded. A scanman called out to him.

'We have a track, sir!'

'Follow it,' rumbled Haight.

There was a slight sense of nausea as the flagship, the whole fleet following suit, shifted direction in the multidimensional strat. It was succeeded by a series of sensations felt only in the gut, as if one were trapped in a system of high-speed elevators. Travelling through the strat was sometimes like riding a crazy, oscillating switchback. Geodesic eddies and undulations, which time-travelling vehicles were obliged to follow, were apt to occur in it.

Haight and Anamander both watched the big monitor screen. The representation of the strat it was bringing them was roiling and curling as they rode through the disturbed region. (Haight knew that such a region often spelled danger for imperial stability: it could mean that an established sequence in orthogonal time was undergoing mutation.) Then, slowly, it smoothed out and the sick feelings no longer assailed their guts.

A blurred formation of foreign timeships hove into view.

There were three of them on the screen, held unsteadily by the scattered light of beta radiation. They were recognisably ships of the Hegemony: inelegantly tall, wedge-shaped structures travelling edge-on.

The images flickered and then yawed, swinging around and changing shape like a moving display of geometric variations. The scope was picking up four-dimensional images of the ships as they altered direction.

'Projected destination?' barked Haight.

A voice answered him. 'Prior to course change, heading towards Node Seven, bearing seven-o-three on vertical axis.'

'Fire torps.'

Down below, gunnery released a standard set of five torpedoes, and they saw them flickering away on the screen. There was little hope of any of them making a strike. Strat torpedoes were heavy, clumsy weapons whose light-duty time-drives gave them little speed and little range.

'Shall we offer battle, sir?' Anamander asked in a low voice.

Haight pondered briefly and shook his head. 'They are on a homeward flight path after having completed their work. We need to find them on the ingoing flight before they've reached their target.'

The torpedoes faded away, lost in the strat. The Hegemonic warships eventually receded from view.

Haight gave the order to proceed pastward, traversing across the vertical time-axis. A hundred and fifty years deeper into historic territory he ordered the fleet to stand by; the flagship phased briefly into orthogonal time.

They hovered over a sunlit landscape. Down below, roads and rivers made a meandering pattern among the towns and villages that were dotted here and there across the patchwork of fields. The flagship's computer library was busy comparing the scene with the official encyclopaedia, but neither Haight nor Anamander needed its report to know the worst. The geography of the place simply did not correspond to the official record. In particular, the size-able city of Gerread was completely absent.

In orthogonal time the Hegemonic attack had already been successful.

Haight inspected the landscape carefully, looking for signs of recent devastation. There was none: it did not seem that Gerread had been removed by bomb or plague.

Instead, the Hegemonics must have used their most terrible weapon, of which the High Command had obtained some information but which they had never been absolutely sure existed: a time-distorter, capable of altering the fabric of time directly. Gerread had been simply ... annulled. All trace of it, past and future, had vanished.

It was a sobering thought that in all probability no one except those aboard the ships manoeuvring in the strat, and those in the special Achronal Archives at Chronopolis, had even heard of Gerread any more. Once again Haight experienced the familiar burden: the terrible responsibility of being a chronman.

The priest, having finished his asperges, retired to the rear of the bridge, where he learned the dreadful facts confronting Haight and Anamander. He began to pray in a sonorous, desperate mutter. The two officers shared his feeling of horror: Gerread and all its inhabitants had been swallowed, foundering like a ship, by the infinity of nonactual, merely potential time. That, at least, was how it was described technically. In church language it was the Gulf of Lost Souls.

Leaving behind it a clap of air, the flagship rephased into the substratum. Haight recalled the region of turbulence they had recently passed through. That, no doubt, had been connected with the new distortion in the orthogonal timeflow. But the battle was not yet lost. There was still strat time, and in strat time events did not vanish, once having taken place, but lingered for hours, days, sometimes months of subjective personal time. Nothing was irreversible.

They might yet snatch back those lost souls from perdition.

The fleet continued its traverse. This, Haight reminded himself, was but a preliminary exercise in how the coming time-war would be fought. Always the object would be to alter the adversary's history: reaching back and further back into the murky tale of mutated events, answering every move with a cancelling counter-move. And final victory would be achieved only when the history of one side was so completely distorted that the existential support for its fleets of timeships was removed. Even then they would continue to fight for a while, ghosts moving through the strat, never having been manufactured, manned by crews that had never been born. Then they would fade, sinking into nonactual, potential existence.

But it was some time before the warning gong sounded again and Hegemonic ships came up once more on the scope screen.

'Heading for Node Five,' the scanman informed him.

They counted the ships as they appeared blurrily on the screen. There were twelve.

'This is it,' Haight said. 'This is their incoming path. Get ready.'

Captain Mond Aton, officer commanding the *Smasher of Enemies*, had seen the Hegemonics' outgoing flight path on the scope screen of his own ship and had fully expected to enter battle. Only later, when the order to hold came from the flagship, did he realise that he had been impetuous. The homeward-bound ships would probably have refused to fight; and even if defeated, their destruction would solve nothing.

His own bridge was a miniature of Commander Haight's; it was manned by only seven men. Unlike the bigger, heavier ships that doubled as battleships and troop carriers, the *Smasher of Enemies* was a manoeuvrable, lightly manned, heavily armed destroyer. It had the speed to pursue, and elaborate chronphase equipment for accurate microsecond broadsides.

'Breaks your heart to see them go,' said the scanman, looking up from the screen, 'doesn't it, sir?'

Aton nodded. 'They haven't escaped us yet, Scanman. Those ships we see are already ghosts, though they don't know it.'

The wedge-shaped Hegemonics faded. Aton did not think too deeply about the paradoxes involved in what he had said. In the strat paradoxes were commonplace. And not only in the strat, either: since the rise of the Chronotic Empire every lowly citizen had been made aware of how contingent his existence was on the fickle mutability of time. Many were the millions who, having existed once (*once*, if that word were to be given a meaning outside time altogether), now ceased ever to have existed. Outside, that is, the roll of nonexisting citizens in the Achronal Archives, which contained more history that had disappeared than it did extant history.

Unless the Hegemonic attack could be stopped, many millions more would be added to that roll.

Aton turned to Lieutenant Krish.

'Hold the bridge for me. I'm going to make a quick check.'

As he left the bridge and walked through the galleries he could feel the tension building up in the ship. This would be his third sizeable engagement and on each of the others he had liked to visit each section under his command beforehand. It gave him a feeling of integrating the vessel into a tight fighting unit. And it would be a good half-hour, he told himself, before the fleet found its quarry.

He visited the gunnery-room, where tension was, of course, at the highest pitch – and no wonder. His glance swept around the computer terminals, of which the men themselves were in a sense mere appendages. In some ships gunnery was on the bridge itself, which at first sight seemed a logical arrangement, if cumbersome. But Aton preferred it this way, although he knew some captains did not.

After a few words of encouragement to his gunners he went deeper into the ship to the drive-room.

He paused outside the door at the sound of voices, then smiled to himself. Ensign Lankar, a keen young engineer but newly inducted into the Imperial Time Service, was loudly displaying his knowledge to a drive-room assistant in his charge.

'The time-drive is really based on the good old mass-energy equation,' Lankar was saying. 'E equals MC squared. Let's take one of the factors on the right-hand side of this equation: C squared. That's where time comes in. C is the velocity of light – the distance per time of an otherwise mass-less particle. So energy is really mass multiplied by time squared. But we can also write the equation this way: M equals E over C squared. This shows us that mass is a relationship between energy and time. So now we're getting somewhere: what happens if we disturb this relationship? We do this by forcing energetic particles to travel faster than light. And now we find that the equation doesn't balance any more: energy divided by the velocity of light squared no longer adds up to rest mass. But the equation *must* balance – it's a fundamental physical law. So what happens? The equation keeps the scales even by moving rest mass through time, to the same extent that the time factor is transgressed on the right-hand side.'

'But where does the strat come in, Ensign?'

'The strat is what time is made of, lad. If you move through time, that's what you have to move through.'

Ensign Lankar thumped the steel casings that bulged into the drive-room. 'And here's where it's all done. This is where we accelerate pi-mesons to anything between C and C squared. It's the most important part of the whole ship, and don't you forget it.'

Lankar's voice sounded incongruously young as he talked self-consciously down to his underling. 'M equals E over C squared,' he repeated. 'Notice that time is involved in both elements on the right-hand side. That's why pure energy can't be transmitted through the strat, only mass. So we have no radio communication with the High Command and have to use the couriers, poor devils.'

Both young men jumped up with embarrassment and saluted hastily as Aton entered. They had been seated on wooden benches well away from the main control desk, where the drive-room's senior staff were too busy for such idle talk.

'Everything in order?' Aton called gruffly, speaking over the high-pitched whine that always infected the drive-room.

The chief engineer looked up from his work. 'No problems, sir.'

Aton inspected the flickering dials briefly and went on his way. He paced the short galleries and corridors, speaking to a man here, an officer there. He was about to ascend a long ladder that would take him back to the bridge, passing by the gunnery-room, when a drone of voices caused him to pull up sharp.

It came from a nearby storeroom and had the sound of chanting. Aton felt himself stiffen. Then, dreading what he might find, he unfastened the clamps on the door and eased it quietly open.

The chanting came louder and he was able to distinguish some of the words. 'Lord of all the deep, if this be our moment for darkness … sear our souls with thy vengeance …'

He peered within. Six figures occupied the cell-like storeroom, having made space for themselves among the crates of chronphase spares. By the look of things this was their regular meeting place – the crates had been arranged to leave a neat cubbyhole that had a much-used appearance. All six wore normal uniforms, except that their caps had been replaced by black cloths that hung down over their ears. Five men were on their knees, heads bent and faces hidden in their arms, and they had their backs to Aton. The sixth stood before them leading the chant, a gold medallion hung about his neck, a black book in his hand. Aton recognised him as Sergeant Quelle, of gunnery. His lean sharp face bore the look of desperate rapture Aton would have expected from such a rite as this.

In the same moment that the startled Sergeant Quelle saw him, Aton pulled his pistol from his shoulder holster and flung the door wide open. He slammed a com switch on the corridor wall and bellowed for the ship guard. Then he moved into the confined space, towering over the kneeling figures, the heavy beam pistol sweeping over them all warningly.

White faces, shocked and guilty, turned to look at him. Sergeant Quelle backed away, slamming shut his book. He bore the look of a trapped rat.

'Traumatics!'

Aton spat out the word. The outlawed sect was known to have adherents in the Time Service – chronmen were, in fact, unusually prone to be affected by its heresies, for obvious reasons – but Aton had never dreamed he would find aboard his own ship not one heretic but a whole congregation. He felt shaken.

Booted, running feet rang on the metal decks. The com speaker on the wall outside the storeroom crackled.

'Are you all right, Captain?'

'Yes, Lieutenant,' he replied, recognising the voice from the bridge. 'Better send down Comforter Fegele.'

The guards clattered to the scene. Aton let them stare at it for a few moments. There was a strained silence.

'Better not do anything to us, Captain,' Quelle said in an impulsive, frightened voice. 'Your soul will go to the deep if you do!'

'Silence!' Aton was affronted by the continued blasphemy.

The ship's priest, Comforter Fegele arrived, pushing his way through the guards. As he saw the evidence before him, the six men standing half-sheepishly, half-defiantly, a gasp came from deep within his cowl. He swiftly made the sign of the circle, then raised his hand palm outward.

'Depart, Prince of Abominations,' he muttered in a hurried, feverish voice. 'Depart into the deeps of time, plague no more the servants of the Lord.'

The Traumatics immediately turned to him and made a curious sign with the fingers of their right hands, as though warding off a curse.

Quelle laughed fiercely. 'Don't *you* plague *us* with your exorcisms, priest!' But Comforter Fegele was already beginning an incantation of sacred names, at the same time producing a vase-like chalice from within the folds of his robe.

'Get them out of here and lock them in the cells!' ordered Aton angrily. 'Commander Haight can decide whether to charge them fleetside or back in Chronopolis.'

The guards hustled the heretics from the room, while the priest splashed consecrated wine everywhere, on the worshippers, on the crates, on the floor of the cubbyhole.

At that moment a deep-toned gong rang through the ship.

Lieutenant Hurse spoke from the bridge through the wall com. 'Message from the flagship, Captain. Enemy located on target-bound path.'

'I'll be with you presently,' Aton returned.

He made for the ladder, but suddenly Sergeant Quelle, who with the others was in the process of being handcuffed, burst free and lunged supplicatingly towards him.

'You need us, Captain. You need me, especially. Nobody can handle a gunnery comp like I do.'

Comforter Fegele hurled a handful of wine in his face. 'You have lent yourself to foul crimes and flaunted God's commandments ...'

Quelle appealed again to Aton. 'Let me do my duty, Captain. This is no time to cut down the ship's fighting power. Let me handle my comp.' He cringed. 'I don't want to sink into the strat ... without ...'

Suddenly Aton understood. The Traumatics believed that a certain ceremony could – or at least might – protect a soul if it was plunged naked into the strat, as, for instance, should the *Smasher of Enemies* be destroyed in the coming fight. That had no doubt been the purpose of the rite Aton had interrupted. It was all nonsense, of course, fanatical superstition; but Quelle, robbed of his imagined precaution, wanted to fight for his life and not sit out the battle helplessly.

And he was right about one thing. Quelle was an excellent gunner, the best the ship had. Without him the gunnery-room would be fighting below maximum efficiency.

Aton looked at the sergeant with open contempt. 'Very well. For the duration of the engagement.'

He glanced over the faces of the other prisoners and pointed to two others he recognised as also belonging to the gunnery crew. 'Release Sergeant Quelle and those two. They are to be rearrested once the invaders have been dealt with.'

Closely followed by Comforter Fegele, Aton turned from the scene and ascended the ladder to the bridge. The Hegemonic ships were already showing on the scope screen, relayed from the flagship's powerful beta scanners.

'We're closing, sir,' the scanman informed him.

It would not be long now.

But for the time being a lull fell over the proceedings, a lull during which the flagship was frantically busy assessing the situation, but in which the periphery ships, consisting in the main of destroyers like the *Smasher of Enemies*, were passive.

Aton waited for his orders, trying to fight down the feelings of shame that assaulted him. This was no time for emotion, but nevertheless that emotion was there.

Standing across the desk from him was Comforter Fegele (it was Church policy for the ship's priest to be present on the bridge during an action, ever ready to give moral support). The priest looked into the brooding face of the young officer. 'You are troubled,' he murmured.

Aton had been gazing at his own reflection in the metal of his desk. His even features, with their clear grey eyes and straight, finely chiselled nose, were distorted by the metal and seemed to stare back at him across tortured aeons.

'How long has this been going on aboard my ship?' he wondered quietly. 'Had you an intimation of it?'

'No. The Traumatic sect is notoriously good at keeping its presence secret. It disturbs you, no doubt, to discover such perversions.'

'I do find it hard to understand,' Aton admitted. 'Every man on board has sworn the same oath I have sworn. And that oath is to defend not only the empire but also the true faith. How can such men turn heretic?'

'The ways of religious delusion are indeed strange.'

'I confess, Comforter, that I am questioning my own judgment in permitting Sergeant Quelle and his co-conspirators to take part in this action. How can one trust heretics and traitors?'

'The odd thing is,' said the priest slowly, 'that their perversion is probably of a spiritual character only. It has been found that heretic chronmen are nevertheless loyal to the Time Service. That part of their oath remains sacred to them.'

A signal sounded on Aton's desk. A burry voice spoke from the annunciator.

'The following vessels will break off and engage the enemy. *Exorcist, Smasher of Enemies, Emperor's Fist, Incalculable* ...' Aton counted twelve names in all, the same number that made up the enemy's squadron. This was necessary, probably, if the Hegemonics were to be persuaded to stand and fight rather than to flee home without accomplishing their mission.

The *Smasher of Enemies* swung away from formation. The Hegemonics disappeared from the scope screen, then came back after a brief interval, even more blurrily, as the destroyer picked them up on her own less powerful radar.

The established procedures of attack swung into action. One of the bridge controllers was getting in touch with the rest of the attack squadron. At the same time beta contact beams sped ahead of their flight path, seeking out the enemy and offering negotiation.

Comforter Fegele retreated to one side and was heard muttering prayers and blessings, dipping his hand into his chalice occasionally and sprinkling a token amount of wine on to the deck.

As soon as they became aware of their pursuers the Hegemonics put on speed and went into evasion manoeuvres. The wedge-shaped ships, five times taller than they were broad or long, multiplied into a series of fading prismatic images, like a multiple exposure, as they changed direction. The pilot of the *Smasher of Enemies*, snuggled into the nose of the bridge, also put on a surge of velocity, taking them close to the maximum. Before Aton's eyes the forward end of the bridge diminished in size; the pilot became a midget, a boy-like figure, then a puppet no more than six inches high.

The flight of the Hegemonics failed to outdistance the ships of the Chronotic Empire, each of which was now picking out an adversary. The *Smasher of Enemies* vectored in on a dancing wedge. It was difficult, some-times, to sort out the flickering images from the wavering curves of the strat as they also showed up on the scope screen, but Aton never lost sight of it entirely. He issued a clipped order to the pilot.

The destroyer plunged forward in a new burst of speed until she overtook the Hegemonic craft and swung around to place herself directly in its path. The pilot rushed the ship back and forth, veering in close to the enemy and setting up a wash of discomfiting strat waves. In answer the Hegemonic darted away and tried to weave a path past the obstacle, but the pilot stuck close.

The beta operator depressed a switch and leaned forward to speak into a microphone. 'Hello, gunnery. You have contact.'

The tense voice of Sergeant Quelle sounded on the bridge and was relayed by beta ray to his counterpart on the Hegemonic war craft.

'Stand and fight; stand and fight,' he ground out in a gravelly tone. 'Here is our proposed location.' He repeated his words in the Hegemonic language, while at the same time a string of recorded co-ordinates was beeping out on the beta beam.

After a delay of only seconds came a terse answer: 'Agreed.'

The two ships sped away on nearly parallel courses, slowly diverging until they were both faint on each other's scopes.

The front of the bridge ballooned in size as they slowed down. The pilot leaned back, his hands lifting from the controls; the steering-board was now under the control of gunnery.

A curious but necessary tradition of collaboration existed among warring timeships. The self-powered torpedoes they carried, though deployed as a matter of course, were so slow and cumbersome, so much at the mercy of strat disturbances, as to be nearly useless. To be effective a warship needed to employ its heavy-duty beamers.

But because no pure energy could travel in the strat this meant phasing into orthogonal time. A timeship that stayed in its natural medium could neither fire on, nor be fired on by, another timeship. For that reason ships willing to join battle agreed on a rendezvous where each, by leaving the strat, made itself vulnerable to the other.

The tryst (as it was dubbed) had to be both precise and momentary: a point in time without duration. How long a warship lingered beyond that instant in passing time was entirely a matter of discretion, comprising a ratio between estimated survival time and the minimum time needed to locate the enemy and focus weapons upon him. The tendency was towards microseconds, during which each combatant discharged a massive broadside. That, very often, was the end of the battle. A heavily damaged ship would be reluctant to emerge again from the protection of the strat but would try to return home.

All of which explained the crucial importance of the gunnery crew, who made these calculations.

On his desk Captain Aton watched the countdown to emergence in orthogonal time. The suspense was almost unbearable, yet in a way the battle was a non-event – one could not keep track of it in time, since it was all over in a flash. There was only the aftermath, either triumphant or dreadful.

While the minutes and seconds ticked off, the gunnery crew would be priming their comps for those vital microseconds. The battle bracket itself, too small for human consciousness, would be handled by the comps. Afterwards would come the frantic damage assessment by the bridge, reports, if available, on damage inflicted on the enemy, and a decision as to whether or not to offer a second tryst.

Gunnery made an announcement: 'Entering ortho five seconds from *now*.'

The whole bridge waited in tense silence.

Then the *Smasher of Enemies* shook violently, reeled, and swayed as if spinning. Even without studying the damage board closely, Aton could see that something searing had penetrated her vitals.

He glanced up at the scope screen. The Hegemonic ship had reappeared there and was executing a peculiar-looking sideways manoeuvre. Its nearer wall was stained and bubbling.

Gunnery had scored a hit.

Voices came babbling into the bridge. Then, to his surprise, Aton glimpsed a second wedge shape hovering some distance away on the edge of the screen.

Sergeant Quelle's hoarse voice came through to him on his desk com. 'They tricked us, Captain! We were fired on by two ships together – caught in between 'em!'

Aton cursed. 'Evidently a new tactic,' he said wryly to Quelle. And a treacherous one: this sort of conduct was contrary to the unstated rules of temporal war.

He turned to listen to the damage reports. An energy beam had struck the destroyer's flank, penetrated its inner armour, and burned a swathe reaching as far as the drive-room. Luckily the damage in the latter was less than total: the drive was still operating, though the orthogonal field that maintained normal time inside the ship while it travelled the strat was weakened.

Next he turned his attention to news of the rest of the battle. About half the Chronotic timeships had so far engaged the enemy. On balance, events seemed to be going their way. Two Hegemonics had already been destroyed.

His lieutenant leaned towards him. 'It would be risky going into ortho again, Captain.'

Aton nodded, feeling the weight of responsibility. This was more than a skirmish: the existence of the city of Gerread depended on it, as well as the Chronotic control of a whole segment of history.

'I'm afraid we shall have to take that risk, Lieutenant. Those ships have to be stopped.'

His voice rose. 'Scanman, there are two enemy vessels in our vicinity. Range them both for gunnery.'

He contemplated how to take on two heavily armed Hegemonics at the same time. Somehow there must be a member of his own squadron without an adversary. Or had the Hegemonics adopted some complex chess-like formation in which their ships all covered one another?

A hint of a shudder passed through his mind at the thought that he might be seeing the first stage of a large, relentlessly unfolding Hegemonic plan.

He was about to speak to Sergeant Quelle again when a sudden movement on the scope screen attracted his attention. Among the wavering lines by which the screen represented the strat an indistinct shape was expanding swiftly.

A moment later the screen itself went blank and at the same time a horrifying explosion tore through the *Smasher of Enemies*. The destroyer shuddered for a second time. The nose tipped sharply downwards and the bridge caved in.

Before he deserted his desk Captain Aton verified that all com lines to the bridge were dead. Amid a hail of collapsing metal he fled from the room with the rest of his staff, helping them through the disintegrating door and leaving himself last of all.

He knew without any doubt what had happened. The flitting shape on the scope screen had been a strat torpedo which by a hundred-to-one chance had struck home. It was the sort of bad luck no chronman liked to think about.

By the look of things the torp could have hit the destroyer close to the impact point of the earlier Hegemonic energy beam. At any rate it appeared to have exploded inside the inner armour – within the ship herself – and had caused severe structural damage.

In short, the *Smasher of Enemies* was breaking up.

A frightening, tortured creaking sound came from all directions. Aton glanced around him at the twisted, heaving corridors. He grabbed the arm of his lieutenant.

'Get to the com room. If the beta transmitters are still functioning try to raise the fleet and request help.'

The lieutenant went off at a lope. Behind him, what was left of the bridge folded up like a tin can in response to the pressures of the ship's shifting girder frame. Its erstwhile crew moved closer to Aton as if for comfort. Up the corridor came the sound of shouting and a distant, pained groan.

Another, worse danger had occurred to Aton. It was possible that the *Smasher of Enemies* was now helpless; if so, one or both of the Hegemonic destroyers could move in close enough to fire more torpedoes at point-blank range. He seized another officer.

'See if you can get to the torp section. Tell them to fire on the standard pattern, once every two minutes.'

For the moment there was no knowing, of course, if the torp section had even survived the explosion. There was no knowing if any system in the stricken ship was still operational – except that there was obviously still some power flowing: the lights still burned.

Comforter Fegele was on his knees, praying for the survival of the ship – and, Aton thought cynically, of himself. Irreligiously he yanked the priest to his feet.

'The Lord's vengeance has fallen on our vessel,' Fegele babbled. 'This is the price of heresy.'

Aton pushed him away and pointed to a white-faced young ensign. 'Vuger, you come with me. The rest of you – get some rescue work organised.' He spoke harshly, aware that morale was dropping. 'There are bound to be a number of wounded. I want the situation stabilised for when we're ready to move.' With a last glance at Fegele he added, 'The souls of the dying need your ministrations, Comforter.'

He went scrambling down the twisted ladder towards the drive-room, with Ensign Vuger stepping down hastily above his head. As they went deep into the ship the evidence of the destroyer's own destruction became even more evident: walls that had bulged, then broken open like paper bags, lines and conduits that spewed everywhere like ravelled string.

But as they reached the bottom of the ladder and picked their way through the wreckage the lights dimmed momentarily and then burned more brightly than before. At the same time a nearby com speaker crackled. Aton mentally congratulated the repair crews; they had lost no time.

He paused by a speaker and managed to get through to gunnery. The voice that answered was not Quelle's or the gunnery officer's, but that of an ordinary crewman.

'We're blind, sir. And three of our beamers gone.'

'Where's Sergeant Quelle?' Aton demanded.

There was silence. Then, in a strangled voice, the crewman said, 'Deserted his post, sir.'

Aton left the com and pressed forward, motioning Ensign Vuger to follow.

They stepped over the bodies of two dead crewmen and into a scorched area where smoke drifted and the smell of hot metal was in the air. The bulkhead separating the drive-room from the rest of the ship seemed to have melted and only now had solidified. Within the drive-room itself there was fair calm, despite the destruction that had been wreaked. Aton saw the body of Ensign Lankar, who a short time before had been proudly displaying his knowledge of the time-drive, laid out neatly alongside one wall with several others.

To the searing effects of the Hegemonic energy beam had been added the punishment of the torpedo explosion. A gyro was stuttering and giving off a deep tremoring hum from behind the thick steel casings. Aton understood at once that the situation was very bad.

'Are we able to move?' he asked.

A young, officer, saluting hastily, shook his head. 'No chance, sir. It's as much as we can do to maintain ship's field.'

'What chance of phasing into ortho?'

The other looked doubtful. 'Perhaps. Do you want us to try?'

'No,' said Aton. It would do no good. Even if they managed to escape from the ship, without the requisite equipment to keep them phased most of the crew would be thrown back into the strat after a short period of time. And there was clearly no possibility of cruising to the nearest node, where ortho phasing could be made natural and permanent.

So it all depended on someone coming to their rescue.

How was Lieutenant Krish getting on in the com room?

He looked around for a com, found one that worked, and dialled. The com speaker crackled. A voice spoke through faintly, unintelligibly.

And then the floor rose under his feet. There was a *whoomph*, followed by a noise that vibrated on his eardrums to such an extent that he had the momentary impression of existing inside a deep, solid silence. Flung against the opposite wall, dazed, he watched in fascination as the floor and ceiling strained towards each other with a grating sound that made him think of giant bones breaking.

The blast of the explosion seemed to continue in a prolonged smashing and cracking. The collapse of the already weakened ship's skeleton – and timeships always suffered a good deal of physical stress in the strat – was accelerating.

Lieutenant Krish crawled towards him and helped him to his feet. 'Another torpedo,' Aton said breathlessly. 'I'm afraid we're finished.'

The movement of the ceiling towards the deck had ceased for the moment, but he did not think the drive-room would be habitable for long. He staggered to the instrument boards. An engineer joined him and they stared together at the flickering dials.

The engineer hammered his fist on the board in frustration. 'The ship field is breaking down,' he declared woodenly.

'How long will it hold?'

'I wouldn't give it another ten minutes.'

Aton went immediately to the com set and dialled a general alert. In a loud, firm voice he announced, 'This is the captain speaking. Take to the rafts. This is the captain speaking. Take to the rafts.'

He repeated the message several times, then turned to the stricken faces of the surviving drive-room crew. 'The ranking engineer will stay to do what he can to hold the field steady,' he ordered. The engineer nodded, and Aton told him, 'I will relieve you in five to ten minutes. The rest of you, get to a raft.'

Aton already knew that his own life was lost, but that hardly seemed to matter. It was his duty, now, to see that everyone still alive aboard the *Smasher of Enemies* made it to a life raft.

Before the ortho field failed. An almost impossible job.

The party advanced through the warped corridors, exploring the various departments and pulling survivors from the wreckage. The wounded they helped along or else carried on improvised stretchers. Aton knew that time was fast running out – even discounting yet a third torpedo strike, which, considering the evident helplessness of the vessel, seemed all too distinct a possibility.

When they came near to one of the ship's six life-raft stations Aton took Lieutenant Krish with him and set off towards the stern. There was no certainty that his order to abandon ship had reached all sections; he decided he would make one swift reconnaissance to ensure that the order was being carried out in a disciplined fashion, then return to the drive-room and take over there, giving the engineer a chance to reach the nearest raft.

Near Section 3 they heard a commotion that sounded even over the loud creaking of the tortured girder frame. Aton drew his beamer, signalling to Krish to do the same. They rounded a corner.

Sergeant Quelle, wearing one of the ship's only two protective suits, strode resolutely along the corridor. Behind him, like a swarm of bubbles in his wake, the heretics of the Traumatic sect ran in a chattering, terrified crowd.

Even through the suit's obscuring visor, designed to opaque itself once in the strat, Quelle's bulbous face displayed his determination to live at all costs. The gleaming brass armour totally encased his body; even if the ship field failed altogether the suit would keep him safe for a short while, maintaining a weak ortho field while its power pack lasted – long enough, in fact, to enable him to reach a life raft.

Aton and Krish straddled the corridor, blocking the Traumatic's path. 'Where are you going, Sergeant?' Aton demanded harshly.

Quelle's answer was a muffled growl. His followers, of whom he clearly did not regard himself as any kind of leader, clustered around him, eyeing Aton speculatively.

Quelle carried a crowbar with which, Aton guessed, he intended to smash the cage where the raft was kept. Aton fired a warning shot over their heads.

'Sergeant Quelle deserted his post and has stolen a protective suit. Get out of that suit, Sergeant. You'll take your turn like all the rest.'

And then, for the third, terrible time, an explosion smashed into the destroyer, hurling them all sideways. An ear-splitting rending noise told Aton that the stern of the ship was breaking away entirely.

Quelle, with what must have been desperate strength, was the first to recover, brass suit or not. His crowbar swung down on Aton's head. Encumbered as he was, the blow was clumsy and partly absorbed by Aton's uniform hat; nevertheless Aton slumped to the floor, barely conscious. Quelle aimed another blow at Lieutenant Krish, missed, then swept hastily on, followed by the mob.

Krish draped his captain's arm around his own shoulders and hauled him to his feet. 'Get to the drive-room, Lieutenant,' Aton mumbled. 'Relieve the engineer.'

'It's too late, sir. Can't you see what's happening? The field is already breaking up.'

Aton, fighting to remain aware, saw that he was right. A fog-like flickering was in the air. An almost overpowering vertigo assailed them both, and the walls – in fact everything solid – seemed to spin on themselves endlessly. All these signs were sure indications of an ortho field going bust.

Krish half-carried Aton along the corridor. The lights went out as the power finally failed, then the emergency lighting faithfully came on to replace them, each strip drawing on its own power pack to provide a dimmer, yellow glow.

And then, through everything, Aton heard horrifying screams. His ship was foundering, sinking into the depths of the strat. He was hearing the screams of men who were drowning in the Gulf of Lost Souls.

Like men plunged from air into the sea, these men were being plunged from their natural, rational time and into a medium that no man could experience and stay sane.

After a few yards Aton steadied himself and, though still groggy, disengaged himself from Krish's support. He leaned weakly against the wall.

'Leave me here, Lieutenant. Continue … do what you can.'

Krish took his arm again, but Aton drew away.

'You *must* let me help you, sir. There may be only seconds –'

'Surely you realise that I cannot leave the ship. Save yourself … and whomever else you can.' Seeing Krish's indecision, his tone hardened. 'That's an order, Lieutenant.' He waved his pistol. 'I have my own protection … against the strat.'

'Yes, sir.' Krish stiffened. He stepped back, clearly affected then snapped off a salute that Aton returned perfunctorily.

Then he turned on his heel and strode away.

Moments after he had gone the wavering ortho field deserted the stretch of corridor where Captain Aton was standing. The pistol, with which he had been meaning to shoot himself, dropped from his fingers. In a little over a second the field swayed back again, but in that second *Aton saw it*.

The strat. The temporal substratum.

The Gulf of Potential Time.

It was only a glimpse, but even a glimpse is too much. Fortunately, or perhaps not so, the returning ortho field saved him – saved him, among other things, from remaining conscious, for exposure to the strat does not bring merciful oblivion. With the return of passing time the glimpse of eternity became a mental shock of pathological proportions. Aton instantly fell unconscious.

At almost the same time two noncom chronmen, running desperately for the life raft, saw their captain lying there in the corridor. Without even thinking about it they each seized an arm and lugged him at speed towards Station 3.

When a field of orthogonal time (that is, of time as it can be understood by the human intellect) breaks down, it does not collapse all at once. Bubbles and fragments of it cling, eddying and drifting, for anything up to ten minutes.

One such bubble had attached itself to Station 3.

The scene at Station 3 was one of turmoil. Discipline had broken down in the face of horror, and about thirty men were fighting to get aboard the raft – even though, with an orderly embarkation, room could have been found for them all. On his arrival Lieutenant Krish tried to impose a sense of command. He was cut down by Sergeant Quelle, who had found a pistol beamer and held it awkwardly in his brass suit's mechanical claw.

Quelle had good reason for shooting the lieutenant. He was anxious that no one who knew his guilty secret, apart from his fellow Traumatics, should board the raft with him. He ensured that the Traumatics went aboard first, then entered the raft himself preparatory to casting off.

But among those who boarded in the final rush were the two noncoms carrying the unconscious form of Captain Aton. They themselves were not so lucky. They dropped Aton to the floor then bravely left the raft to assist some wounded men. Quelle indignantly clanked forward to rid himself of his potential accuser, but he was too late. In that moment others in the raft decided that they had lingered long enough and activated the escape sequence. The gates closed and the hum of the raft's own emergency ortho field filled the dim interior.

The last wisps of the ship field were now dissipating, and the shattered destroyer was wholly saturated by the strat. It ceased, in one sense, to have any material existence at all: matter cannot retain its properties without the vector of time to give it substance. As such, the life raft magically passed unimpeded through several walls and floated free.

It was the only raft to leave the *Smasher of Enemies*. All the others either were too damaged or else failed to energise in time. The survivors switched on the small scope and saw, by the light of the raft's feeble beta projector, the vague image of a tall Hegemonic warship looming over them. They cowered, fearing, but eventually the ship turned and receded beyond the scope's range.

Still wearing the protective suit, Sergeant Quelle fretted. He had felt it reasonably safe to kill in the confusion at Station 3, but here there would be witnesses who could not be silenced and bodies that could not be disposed of. He sweated inside the suit, glancing at Aton and hoping he would not recover.

The raft was transmitting, as a beacon, a rotating beta beam. Otherwise there was nothing they could do. They settled down and waited, for life or a fate worse than death.

TWO

Node One: Chronopolis, mistress of the Chronotic Empire, seat of the Imperial Government of His Chronotic Majesty Philipium Ixian I, and the location of that repository of imperial wisdom, the *Imperator*.

Chronopolis was complex and sprawling. In the morning light (the sun had risen to that angle which most accentuated the city's panoply of splendour) her towers, arches, and minarets sparkled and flashed, casting long shadows that fell sharply across the various quarters housing her polyglot population – across the Hevenian quarter, with its characteristically arcaded architecture; across the more rigidly styled Barek quarter; and so on. For people of every nation and of every period in the mighty time-spanning empire flocked to Chronopolis.

The incredibly massive, intricate palace that occupied the centre of the eternal city was well placed, for both practical and aesthetic reasons. Like a spider at the centre of a vast web, it cast out tentacles in all directions so that it was hard to say where it left off and the rest of the city began. This enmeshment was functional as well as descriptive: the palace merged gradually into the city in the form of government departments, military offices, and church institutions – the three pillars of any state. The residence of His Eminence the Arch-Cardinal Reamoir also lay within the palace grounds, so that all strands, spiritual as well as political, were drawn into the hands of His Chronotic Majesty. And visible from the upper reaches of the palace, from where one could overlook the entire city, were the massive shipyards beyond the outskirts of Chronopolis, busy now as never before.

On this day of Imdara in the fifth month of year 204 (as measured from the pastward buffer known as the Stop Barrier – the zero point in imperial reckoning) the activities proceeding in the imperial palace were too numerous to list. The business of attending to the affairs of the thousand-year imperium went on – all under the gaze, if they so desired, of those members of the Ixian dynasty who were domiciled there – in the thousands of chambers, halls, lecture-rooms, salons, and chapels. As they did on every other day, except for the specified holy days of observance.

Of these activities, not least in importance was the education of the next generation of rulers. In one of the domestic wings Brother Mundan, one of a dozen appointed tutors, wrestled with the problem of steeping a class of young Ixians – some of them quite closely related to the emperor – in the traditions of the dynasty.

Even his brown cassock and curtailed cowl, even all the majesty of the Church that lay behind him (the Church, of course, accepting the responsibility for all serious education) was sometimes insufficient to curb the irreverence of these youngsters, who were apt to place themselves above normal values even in matters of religion. Luckily the Church placed great reliance on repetition as a method of teaching, and this generally enabled Mundan to bludgeon his charges into submission. Indeed, it would have been difficult to instil the present lesson, 'The Foundation of Empire', with its mixture of history, abstract physics and religious dogma, by any other means. Brother Mundan was repeating it to the present class for at least the twelfth time.

'And to what,' he intoned, 'do we owe the existence of the empire?'

After a pause Prince Kir, cousin to the emperor, rose. 'To the intervention of God, Brother.'

Munden nodded. 'Correct, Your Highness. Once, time stretched unchanging from the interminable past to the interminable future, or at least it changed only slowly due to natural movements in the temporal substratum or to time-storms. There was no empire and no true religion. There was *religion*, of a sort, but it was superstition, such as some of the futureward heathens hold to. Then God acted so as to redeem mankind. At what is now called Node Six, in the city of Umbul, capital of the present province of Revere, He chose as His appointed messenger San Hevatar, a scientist working in the laboratories of the ruling Ixian family – of *your* family, Highnesses.'

Mundan's gaze settled on one who, instead of attending closely, was more interested in exchanging whispers with a neighbour.

'Princess Nulea, what are the three things that God revealed to San Hevatar?'

The girl started and jumped up. With glazed eyes she chanted the answers she had long learned by rote.

'One: the mutability of time, Brother Mandan. Two: the means of travelling through time. Three: the nature of the soul.'

'Thank you, that is correct. Through His messenger San Hevatar, God has taught us that time is mutable. He has taught us how to travel through time. And He has taught us that the nature of the soul is to persist in eternity.'

He rapped the lectern to pique their interest. 'The first of these truths shows us the possibility of the Church's mission. The second truth shows us how the mission may be accomplished. And the third truth shows us *why* it should be accomplished.'

His voice became challenging. 'And why should the Church work to accomplish its mission under the protection and banner of the Chronotic Empire?' Brother Mundan's dark eyes flashed. This point in the lesson touched the fires in his own breast.

Once again Prince Kir proved the most apt of his pupils. 'Because time does not die, Brother Mundan. Because the soul cannot leave the body.'

'Yes, Highness, that is so,' Mundan said with a slight frown. The answer was probably lost on the densest of those present. 'The Church works to bring the true faith to all men, past, present, and future – to *establish God's kingdom on Earth*. Even though we die we continue to exist in the past, because the past does not vanish. The Church seeks to transform our past lives and bring God into our souls.

'Let us take in turn each of the three truths revealed by San Hevatar. First: that time is mutable. This means simply that even the past may be changed because in absolute terms there is no past, just as there is no unique present. Orthogonal time is but the surface of the bottomless ocean of potential time, or the temporal substratum: the hidden dimension of eternity in which all things co-exist without progression from past to future. Prior to the foundation of the empire the past could change without man's knowledge or will, due to time-storms or natural mutations, just as the wind can change direction. Now, thanks to the grace of God, the past and the future can be controlled and altered by conscious intervention.'

This intervention took the form, of course, of the Historical Office, which undertook to edit and restructure history by manipulation of key events, and of the imperial time-fleets, which in the last resort enforced the imperial writ. To Brother Mundan this seemed entirely proper and right.

He proceeded to the second God-given truth, writing some equations on the blackboard.

'These equations describe the operation of moving mass through time. You should already be familiar with them from your physics lessons, so here we will concern ourselves with the structure of orthogonal time, which is of great importance for the stability of the empire.

'Time is composed of a wave structure. The nodes of the wave travel at intervals of approximately one hundred and seventy years and are of great interest to the time-traveller since they comprise "rest points" in the tensioning of the Chronotic energy field. This is of crucial importance in the business of time-travel, because matter can be transported from one node to another and will remain in place without any further expenditure of energy. On the other hand if matter is transported to a time between nodes, or conversely is taken from between nodes and is deposited somewhere else, it will not persist in its new location without a continuous expenditure of energy, usually accomplished by means of a device called an orthophase. This is the reason why nearly all Chronotic intercourse takes place from node to node. The seven nodes covered by the span of the empire form, as it were, the seven continents or provinces of the empire, while the intervening periods comprise a series of hinterlands, benevolently governed but rarely seeing a time-ship except in time of rebellion or by order of the Historical Office.

'In ordinary life, of course, none of this is of any consequence, since the nodes are invisible to us.'

'*Why* are there nodes, Brother Mundan?' asked Prince Kir seriously.

Mundan frowned again. 'We may take it as part of God's wisdom, Highness, though technically it is, as I say, the wave structure of time. The nodes give the empire an absolute standard of time-measurement – for the movement of the nodes is absolute, not relative. We are fortunate enough to live in Node One. Today, for instance, is Imdara of the fifth month, and tomorrow will be Juno of the fifth month. When tomorrow comes it would be possible for us to travel back in a time-machine to today, Imdara – but Node One will not be here. It will have moved on, to Juno. Thus nodal time, as apart from historical time, is the time the empire uses to conduct its business. The clocks of the time-fleets measure nodal time.

'Imagine what chaos would reign if we tried to govern a time-travelling empire where time was uniform, not gathered into nodes. If it were a simple matter – say, for a man to travel into tomorrow and meet *himself* there – why, antinomies and paradoxes would abound in such confusion that no order could survive. Time itself, perhaps, would break down and the whole world would sink into the substratum. That is why God, in His great wisdom, has so arranged the universe that the natural period *between* nodes is greater than the span of a man's life, so that he will not meet himself. And it is to prevent the harmful accumulation of paradoxes that it is forbidden to travel into internodal time, except in the emperor's name.'

Princess Nulea giggled. 'Narcis doesn't think so!'

'Silence!' Brother Mundan's face became an angry red. He was well aware that certain members of the imperial household did not consider themselves bound by the laws that restrained the rest of society. But he would brook no mention of Prince Narcis's unspeakable perversion here.

Princess Nulea lowered her eyes. 'Sorry, Brother Mundan,' she murmured, smirking.

'I have a question, Brother Mundan,' another young prince interrupted. 'What happens to a timeship if it phases into orthogonal time *between* nodes, but has a malfunctioning orthophase or runs out of power?'

Mundan had been asked that question before by this very class. He was convinced the questioner was doing it because he knew it distressed him.

'In that case,' he said, fighting to keep his voice calm, 'the ship will remain in phase for a short time. Then it will out-phase automatically and sink into the substratum, together with every soul on board.'

He turned, as much so as to hide his face as anything, and wrote on the blackboard the additional formulas which, together with the derivations from the mass-energy equation, described the nodal system associated wit time's forward momentum.

Then, once he was sure he had recovered his composure, he faced the class again.

'Now we come to the question of the soul,' he said quietly. 'The empire itself, if bereft of religion, could subsist on the first two truths alone, though it would not be the empire we know. Knowledge of the soul is the empire's spiritual meaning, as expressed by Holy Church.'

He paused to bring home the seriousness of the third truth, almost daring them to cheek him further. But they did not. They knew that on this subject he was fanatical. Any jeering concerning the existence of the soul would be reported straight to Arch-Cardinal Reamoir.

'Prior to the revelations received by San Hevatar it was even possible for atheists to deny that the soul exists at all. Once time-travel had been demonstrated, however, the existence of the soul became indisputable.

'Why? Because time-travel proved that the past does not vanish when our awareness leaves it; the past continues to exist. And that raises the following question: what of that awareness? Must that not also continue to exist in the past even though, paradoxically, we are not "aware" of it? And what happens to that consciousness of ours at death? It cannot be extinguished – for otherwise the past would vanish.

'There is only one way to resolve the riddle, and it is this: the soul experiences itself as a moving moment of time beginning with conception and ending with death. At death the soul travels back in time to the moment of conception to live its life through again exactly as before. This repetition continues eternally; thus is a man's past kept alive.

'From this proposition the existence of the soul is proved.

'This means that we have sat here in this room, hearing this lecture at this moment of time, countless times before, and will do so countless times again.'

With a sense of dignity Brother Mundan opened a book of Holy Scripture and began to read the words written by none other than San Hevatar.

'"There is the body and there is the soul. The body belongs to orthogonal time. But the soul, being spiritual, is eternal; yet it does not persist beyond its appointed period in time. On meeting the end of that period it travels back to the beginning, and experiences its life anew. Thus the soul has the God-given power to travel through time.

'"And why does the soul not remember the life it has already lived? It is because of death trauma, which wipes clean all the soul's memories ..."'

*

It sometimes seemed to Chief Archivist Illus Ton Mayar that the Achronal Archives, which he administered, had taken on an existence all of their own and had begun to separate from the rest of the universe. Many of the staff no longer ventured into the outside world. Mayar understood their feelings: men whose working hours were spent in cataloguing time's mutations were apt to feel that the world was insubstantial. Here, in this subterranean cluster of vaults and bunkers, could be found a refuge from Chronotic instability.

The Achronal Archives were, in essence, a record of deleted time. Whenever an event was altered – whether by natural causes, or by order of the Historical Office, or by act of war – the consequences spread up and down historical time making the adjustment complete in all directions. Only the existence of the archives made such changes detectable. Protected by powerful time-buffers, the vaults were impenetrable to the powerful rectifying vibrations that echoed through the strat. Thus the records that were kept on every facet of the empire remained intact and could be compared with time as it currently stood.

It was a record of ghosts. Millions of men, women, and children, entire cities, nations, and cultures, that now had never existed, were stored in the archival computers. Research into these vanished communities could be a fascinating experience, but to undertake it one had to be a staff member. Not even the universities were allowed such information – there was a theory that it would weaken the fabric of time, and besides, it might reflect on the permanence of the empire.

And there were times when Archivist Mayar himself wished that he did not have to know.

In the sepulchral dimness of Vault 5 the humming note of the computer was almost menacing. The bank of winking indicator lights seemed to be spelling out a mocking message of doom.

The operator's voice was sombre as he handed Mayar a thick print-out sheaf. 'The results have been double-checked, sir. There isn't any doubt about it – we knew almost straight away.'

The section had been carrying out what was known as an Anomalous Population Check. The Archives' Current State Bank was continuously matched, as a matter of course, with a similar information bank – unprotected by time-buffers – on the surface. When they failed to match, an Anomalous Population Check was immediately undertaken so as to map out any unauthorised changes in time.

Mayar barely glanced at the print-out before handing it back. 'I shall have to inform the emperor,' he said heavily. That meant a visit to the palace – never a prospect he relished.

As if to accentuate the blow, Mayar had that morning received indirect confirmation from another source. Units of the Third Time Fleet had arrived in the capital, badly damaged from an engagement with the enemy. Mayar had heard that the Third Time Fleet had been beaten and forced to withdraw, and he was willing to bet that the consequence of that battle was staring at him now. Gerread, a city of some importance in Node 5 (it had been a fair-sized town even in Node 4), had been elided from history, and the souls of its inhabitants (as theory would have it) dispersed into the formless dimensions of the strat like drops of rain in the ocean.

At least they had not suffered the fate of chronmen who, when their ships were destroyed, sank as conscious entities down into the gulf.

Without another word he left the operator and went through a double door leading to a long, low corridor. From all around him as he walked up the corridor came the muted sound of work going on in the surrounding chambers. Once, he passed another archivist, garbed in a white smock like himself, and muttered a perfunctory greeting. He avoided meeting the fellow's eyes, for the stricken look he knew he was apt to find there was becoming more pronounced among his staff lately. He was becoming concerned to know which way the growing cult of despairing isolationism in the archives would turn.

Once in his own quarters, he discarded his white gown and took the hundred-foot elevator to the surface.

As he passed through the shaded frontage of the surface building the bright sunlight hit him like a staggering blow, making him slightly dizzy. He entered the emblazoned coach that was waiting and instructed the chauffeur to take him to the palace.

The sights and sounds of Chronopolis washed over him as they drove through the streets. It all seemed slightly unreal. Did any of this really exist? Could anything that was liable to vanish from time be said to have substance? The familiar dreamlike sensation all achronal archivists were prone to came over him and he found himself wishing he were back in his quiet, cool vaults.

Once, to get some fresh air, he opened one of the coach windows, but instantly he was invaded by a low-key roaring that hung over this part of the city. Glancing overhead, he saw a drifting pall of smoke. Both the noise and the smoke came from the shipyards some miles away, where the tremendous armada that was to conquer the Hegemony was now nearing completion.

With a frown of distaste he closed the window again.

The coach travelled through the great arcaded entrance of the towering palace. Mayar was met in the reception chambers by Commander Trevurm, one of the emperor's select team of aides and advisers.

Calmly he gave him the news. Trevurm listened with head bent, then nodded.

'We already know of it. Commander Haight is here. He came in with ships of the Third Fleet this morning. They fought the Hegemonic raiders who did this.' He paused. 'How far does the mutation extend? Have you carried out a mapping?'

'We have, Commander. The elision covers everything related to the founding and sustaining of the city that was known as Gerread. There is no replacement.'

'No alternative city?'

'None.'

Trevurm sighed. 'This kind of thing is hard to grasp. You come and tell me there was a city called Gerread, which I have never heard of, and I have to believe you.'

'Before it was eliminated you had heard of it,' Mayar said, feeling how inadequate words were to express time's mysterious movements. 'Only last month you and I were speaking to its governor … or rather … I was speaking …'

'I cannot recall it.'

'Naturally not. It never happened. The meeting vanished along with the city, along with its governor.' And yet I am here and *I* met Governor Kerrebad and *I* remember it, Mayar thought wildly.

He turned his mind to more practical considerations. 'Has the emperor been told?' he asked.

Trevurm shook his head. 'Not yet. But it cannot be delayed further.'

He rose to his feet. 'I would prefer it if the news came from you,' he said. 'Commander Haight's interview with His Majesty will no doubt be uncomfortable enough without his having to bear the tidings as well.'

Mayar acquiesced and followed the commander deeper into the gorgeous palace. They passed through executive sections, through social sections where nobles and their guests relaxed with their various expensive entertainments. Finally they were in the inner sanctum. Mayar was obliged to wait while Commander Trevurm disappeared for a few minutes, after which they were admitted into the presence.

In a modest-sized room whose walls were of dark, panelled oak carved into curious patterns, His Majesty the Emperor Philipium I sat at one end of a long gleaming table of polished mahogany.

He was not an imposing figure: merely a tired old man sitting hunched and shrivelled at the corner of a table. His eyes had a deadness to them such as is brought on by continual fatigue or by a too-prolonged effort. The only touch of distinction to his grey face was a short pointed beard that was much faded. His costume, too, was modest and unregal: a tunic and breeches that were colourless and shiny with much use.

The two who entered bowed low. They could not help but notice that the emperor's right arm shook visibly. He suffered from the trembling palsy, which Mayar knew to be due to degenerative changes in the ganglia at the base of the cerebrum. The disease was incurable and grew chronic with advanced age.

They then turned to bow, less deferentially, to the second occupant of the room, who hovered like a shadow in the corner. In contrast to His Majesty, Arch-Cardinal Reamoir wore the most sumptuous of ecclesiastical garments. His floor-length cope was trimmed with purple fur and boasted orphreys richly patterned in gold and variously dyed tussore silk. Spun gold figured, too, in the coif which covered his head and which was decorated with the symbols of the Church.

The aloof prelate accepted their bow with a casual blessing.

'And what is this bad news I have been warned to expect?' the emperor inquired in a dry voice.

Briefly and concisely, Mayar gave him the facts. The old man's face sagged. At the same time, a look of puzzlement crossed his features.

Mayar knew that look. It happened every time someone was told of events or things that had been removed from the stream of time. Automatically one tried to remember what had gone, however much one knew that it was impossible.

With the emperor, puzzlement was soon replaced by muted rage at the realisation that an ungodly enemy had succeeded in altering even his memories. 'This is bad,' he said shakily. 'This is very bad.'

Arch-Cardinal Reamoir moved forward silently. A hand stole from beneath his cope and squeezed the emperor's shoulder comfortingly. Philipium reached up and patted the hand.

'Your Majesty will recall,' Mayar continued, 'that this is the second such attack. The first was not entirely successful, for it only modified the history of the coastal port of Marsel, and that not seriously. This, however, is an unmitigated disaster. We must presume that the enemy has now perfected his new weapon.'

'Yes! The time-distorter!' The emperor's face clearly showed his distress. 'Why does the Hegemony have such a device and we do *not* have it?' His right arm trembled more markedly, as it usually did under stress. And indeed, the enemy's possession of the time-distorter was frightening. When the Historical Office decided to change some aspect of history, months or years of preparation were needed to select some key event or combination of events whose alteration would produce the desired result. A big operation was usually required, entailing a staff of thousands to carry it out.

Yet apparently the distorter could mutate history simply by focusing some sort of energy that acted on the underlying temporal substratum. The threat to the empire was real and disturbing.

'God is testing us,' murmured Arch-Cardinal Reamoir smoothly.

'As always, you know best, old friend.' The emperor seemed to draw courage from anything Reamoir said. God forgive him for the thought, but Mayar simply could not see the arch-cardinal's influence as a healthy one.

'These indignities will cease once my invincible armada sets forth,' the emperor said, glancing up at Reamoir. 'The Hegemony will be part of the empire. The distorter will be ours.'

'Your Majesty,' Mayar said diffidently, 'a weapon as effective as the time-distorter must seriously be taken into account. There is very little defence against it, once its carrier ship has broken through into historical territory. I would go so far as to say that it is capable of destroying the empire itself.'

'*Archivist Mayar!*' Reamoir thundered, his face suddenly blazing. 'Take care what you say!'

'I said only that it is *capable* of destroying the empire,' Mayar replied defensively. 'I did not say that such an event could come about.' And if he did openly say it, he would be in serious trouble. The Two Things That God Will Not Do were as important a part of religious dogma as the Three Revelations of San Hevatar. The Two Things That God Will Not Do were that, once having given it, He would not take away the secret of time-travel from mankind; and that He would not allow the Chronotic Empire ever to perish.

It was dangerous to argue with the head of the Church. But Mayar, fearful of the calamity he saw hovering over them all, pressed on.

'What I say, Your Majesty, Your Eminence, is this: God has promised that the empire will not fall or be removed, but He has not promised that it will not meet with misfortune or be defeated in war. As Your Eminence will tell us –' he bowed his head again towards the arch-cardinal – 'the doctrine of free will means that even the mission of the Church may fail. God has left such matters in our hands, and we are fallible.'

He licked his lips and continued hurriedly. 'As chief archivist I am familiar with the changes of time. I know that their consequences can be dismaying and unexpected, and that precautions taken against them can prove to be futile. I do not think I am exaggerating when I say that the archives perform a function fundamental to the integrity of the empire. And I fear the distorter. I ask myself what degree of change the archives can accommodate. I believe they will break down altogether under the impact of the weapon.'

'And what do you propose we should do?' Philipium's eyes had lost their deadness now. They were glittering.

'It occurs to me that the Hegemony is carrying out these attacks because it feels itself threatened by us, Your Majesty. In my opinion we should seek a truce and abandon our plans for conquest – at least until we know more about the time-distorter.'

The emperor turned beady eyes on Commander Trevurm. 'And what is your opinion?'

Trevurm stroked his chin and sighed. 'There is much sense in what our friend says,' he admitted. 'The time-distorter brings an unknown factor into the equation.'

'So you both advise caution?'

'Yes, Your Majesty.'

'Have you both forgotten the mission of Holy Church?' said the arch-cardinal to Trevurm and Mayar, affecting a shocked tone. 'Your Majesty, we are doing God's bidding. The armada must do its work. The heathen must be converted by its power.'

'But at the risk of wreaking havoc with the structure of time?' Mayar protested.

Reamoir turned and spoke for the benefit of Philipium alone. 'What else should we do? Have we not tried to convert the Hegemony by peaceful persuasion? Our missionaries have gone forward in time, not only to the Hegemony but even beyond, to little avail. Many have been spurned and ejected back to their own time. Some have even been martyred. The pride and stubbornness of the future people is displeasing to God; only force remains. God will go with our armada; He is on our side. All will be well.'

'All will be well,' echoed Philipium. 'The armada must proceed. The only question to be answered is when. And that is a matter for the Military Council, not for amateurs.' He gestured irritably.

'I understand, Your Majesty,' Mayar said, feeling defeated.

The emperor rose from his chair and clutched at Reamoir, holding up his trembling right arm. 'My arm, see how it shakes,' he said, his voice hollow-sounding. 'Listen, my friend – I have had a vision in a dream. God has told me that if the Hegemony is subdued my affliction will vanish.'

'That indeed will be a miracle, sir.'

'Yes. God's message is clear. All will be well.' He turned to Mayar. 'And yet your forebodings are not without substance, Archivist. We are merely human and we can err. Even I am merely emperor, not *Imperator*. Come, we will consult a wiser being.'

Philipium tottered towards the door. Outside, attendants were waiting and accompanied them through the cloistered passages of the inner sanctum. From ahead came cheerful noises of talk and laughter, growing steadily louder until eventually a pair of large doors, quilted and padded with stuffed satin, drew open to admit them.

They entered the main inner chamber of the court.

Strictly speaking it was more than a chamber, being the size of a ballroom. Tastefully arranged here and there were couches, tables, and chairs. The arched recesses that skirted its circumference formed a motif that was repeated in the ribbed and curved formation of the ceiling. All in all, the effect was most pleasing and restful to the eye.

A favourite meeting place, the court chamber had a relaxed air and nobles and privileged persons from all parts and nodes of the empire came and went through its several entrances. The Ixian family predominated, of course, its members hailing from all periods of history – though in their case the term 'history' was practically redundant. The Ixian dynasty was fully mobile through time, being the only family permitted to intermarry with its descendants and ancestors.

One end of the court chamber was kept clear. Emperor Philipium I made towards it with tottering step, followed by the arch-cardinal, Mayar, and Commander Trevurm. A hush fell over the scene as his presence was noted, but then the chatter started up again.

One of his young daughters, Princess Mayora, approached him with a smile, but he brushed her aside and stood before the great panel, featureless and of a dull gold colour, that occupied that entire end of the chamber.

'*Imperator,*' he called in a weak husky voice, 'grant us an audience!'

After a pause the gold panel rumbled up to reveal a square-cut cavity. There was the whine of motors.

The machine they knew as the *Imperator* slid out on giant castors and stood in the vacant space as though surveying the chamber. A deep hum issued from within its body.

Even though he had seen it several times before, Mayar still could not prevent a sensation of awe as he beheld the huge machine. It towered over them like a miniature castle, with its odd crenellated towers, one at each corner, and its walls plated with matt greyish-black metal. It had a distinctly regal appearance entirely in keeping with its function. For though the *Imperator* was a machine – admittedly much more advanced and mysterious than a common computer – it was also, in some indefinable way, *alive*.

More than that, it was in principle the true titular head of the empire. Emperor Philipium I – like any emperor before or after him – held his position by proxy, as it were. The rationale behind this system was quite clear: the *Imperator* contained the distillation of the minds of all the Chronotic emperors, of whom there had been five before Philipium, as well as of many other members of the imperial dynasty whose wisdom seemed to merit it, this distillation being accomplished by a transfusion from the memory centres of their brains after death.

Not that the *Imperator* was merely a receptacle of their dead intelligences; it was much more. No one quite knew what went on inside the *Imperator*, or what it did with these borrowed personalities. They never emerged, that was certain; the *Imperator* had a nature of its own.

The origin of the machine was equally obscure to the outside world, being a state secret. San Hevatar was reputed, by legend, to have had a hand in its manufacture. Mayar, however – he was not privy to this state secret either – had received a very good indication from a member of the Ixian family itself, that there *was* no secret, that no one, not even the emperor, knew where the *Imperator* came from or how long it had been there.

The hum from within the machine grew deeper and the *Imperator* spoke in a full-bodied baritone that thrilled the hearer with its presence.

'You have summoned me?'

Philipium nodded, leaning on an attendant. 'Advise us on the matter we have been discussing.'

There was no need to explain further. Every room in the palace, as well as every department of government, was wired for sound for the *Imperator's* benefit. No one felt embarrassed by this state of affairs, since the machine had never been known to repeat anything it had heard.

The humming faded almost to inaudibility before the *Imperator* spoke again.

'What has been will be.'

The machine rolled back on its castors, disappearing into its private chamber. The gold panel slid down into place.

Mayar had expected nothing better from the interview. The *Imperator* undertook no executive function. While it was consulted occasionally, the cryptic nature of its pronouncements rendered it more in the style of an oracle. More than one emperor had spent days trying to puzzle out the meaning of its statements, only to have to ignore them in the end.

'*What has been will be*,' Philipium muttered feverishly. 'How do you interpret those words, Reamoir?'

'The *Imperator* understands the mysteries of time,' the arch-cardinal replied smoothly. 'It intimates that the victory of our invincible armada is foreordained.'

The emperor gave a grunt of satisfaction. 'The enterprise against the Hegemony must go ahead … all must be prepared to the utmost.' He lifted a shaking hand to his attendant. 'To my quarters. I must rest. Later I will receive Commander Haight.'

He moved off. Commander Trevurm bade Mayar good day and went about his business. The arch-cardinal, disdaining civilities, also drifted off.

Mayar allowed his gaze to wander over the court chamber. He was feeling dismal. He was about to make his way back to the archives when Princess Mayora rushed up to him.

'Chief Archivist, it is *so* long since we saw you here.'

Mayar smiled politely. 'Regretfully my stay must be short, Your Highness. I must return to the vaults.'

'Oh, nonsense. You can easily spare an hour or so. Come over here.' She seized him by the arm and led him towards a couch.

Disarmed by the young woman's charm, Mayar obeyed. Once seated, she turned and faced him directly.

'So what have you been talking to Father about?' she said breezily.

Mayar was embarrassed. 'With all respect, Your Highness –'

'Oh, yes, I know,' she interrupted with an impatient wave of her hand. 'State confidence. Still, I know what it was all about. Daddy's enterprise against the heathen.' She leaned closer, her eyes sparkling with excitement. 'Will there be great battles in the substratum? Awful mutations in time?'

'I fear there will, Your Highness,' Mayar said heavily.

She drew back in an expostulation of surprise. 'Well, don't sound so gloomy about it. Look over there – there's Captain Vrin.' She pointed out a tall chron officer in full dress uniform – resplendent tunic, plumed hat, and waist-high boots belled at the top – who was talking animatedly, surrounded by spellbound young women. 'He's in the Third Fleet. He's just come back from a battle at Node Five. Isn't it exciting?'

Mayar turned his head away, feeling that if he tried to speak his voice would choke him.

Noticing his reaction, Princess Mayora pouted in disappointment. 'Well, if you're going to be so serious about it you might as well go and talk to my brother Philipium.' she said. 'There he is over there.'

Mayar followed her gaze and located Philipium, the eldest of the emperor's sizeable brood. Aged about forty, he had already begun to resemble his father and sported the same type of beard. He was destined to become Emperor Philipium II, although the date of his coronation was not permitted to be made known to anyone in Node 1, particularly not to the present emperor. Gazing upon him, Mayar allowed his thoughts to dwell for a few moments on the perplexing intricacies of time such a situation presented. Futurewards of Node 1 – in the internodal hinterland – was a Philipium the Younger who was not emperor but who remained until his dying day merely the son of the emperor. Yet eventually Node 1 would travel onwards, past the death of Philipium I, and Philipium II would become emperor. The soul of Philipium the Elder would travel back in time to be reborn; but in *that* cycle of his eternally recurring life, the cycle succeeding the current one, he would not be emperor but merely the father of Emperor Philipium II.

Likewise Mayar, in the next cycle of his recurrent life, would find himself living in the internodal hinterland that Node 1 had left behind. He would be removed from the centre of the empire and so, he hoped, would find life a good deal more peaceful.

The eternally repeated rebirth of the soul into the same life was one of the few dogmas of the Church that had been scientifically proved. That, together with the nodal structure of time, provided the empire with a form of passing time that, so to speak, transcended ordinary sequential time. At the same time the system of nodes was extremely convenient for the average mind, such as that of Princess Mayora, who sat with him now. She was happily able to ignore the enigmas and paradoxes that time-travel entailed, leaving such troublesome matters to the theoreticians of the Historical Office, of the

Church's Order of Chronotic Casuistry, and of Mayar's own Achronal Archives.

Did these people surrounding Mayar have any idea what the mutability of time meant? It was quite obvious that Princess Mayora did not. Like nearly everyone else, she regarded the gorgeous palace in which she lived as permanent, secure, and unalterable. The Chronotic wars were centuries away. Mayar glanced despairingly at the ingeniously vaulted and domed ceiling. If only they could realise, he thought, that all this could be magicked away, could *never have been*.

Princess Mayora giggled. 'Oh, look! Here's Narcis!'

Into the chamber strolled two identical youths, their arms fondly about each other's necks. Looking closely at them, one could see them for Ixians. One could see in them, perhaps, what their father the emperor might have been in his youth: the oval face, the straight poetical nose. Here, however, their, lithe upright bearing, their unblemished skin turned Philipium's tottering figure into a travesty.

On looking even closer, one might discern that one of these apparently identical twins was in fact a few years older than the other. Their story needed no explication to Mayar. Narcis, youngest son of the emperor, a strange, wayward homosexual, had in defiance of all the laws of the empire travelled a few years into the future where he had met and fallen in love with *himself*. He had, moreover, persuaded his future self to return to Node 1 with him. The two now spent their time mooning about the palace together, flaunting their forbidden love for all to see.

Arch-Cardinal Reamoir, whenever he chanced to come upon them, would give them the sign of the curse, whereupon the two young Narcises would laugh with glee. But in the atmosphere of the Ixian dynasty their love affair was not nearly as shocking as it would have sounded outside. Ixians married only Ixians, to keep the imperial line pure. At first this had meant marriages that spanned centuries, a man marrying, perhaps, his great-great-great-grandniece. But gradually all distinctions became blurred. Marriages between brother and sister, parent and child, were no longer frowned on. The blood was what mattered.

And as for the crime of 'going double' – of consorting with one's future self – in a world where it was forbidden even to tell a man what lay in his future, well, young Ixians did not feel that Chronotic laws were made to be obeyed.

Princess Mayora waved to her double-brother. The Princes Narcis came towards them.

'Good day, Chief Archivist.' Narcis$_1$ greeted him with a smile.

'Good day to you, Your Highness.' As they came close Mayar could hear the faint whine of the orthophase that Narcis$_2$ wore on a belt at his waist to enable him to live outside his own time.

'Come and talk to the archivist,' Princess Mayora demanded. 'He appears to need cheering up.'

Narcis₁ gazed at Mayar with dreamy eyes while fondling the back of his double's neck. 'He is too old,' he said bluntly. 'Old people talk only of dreary things, of war and politics and religion. We live for love, do we not, Narcis?'

'Yes, Narcis.'

Smiling together, the two wandered away.

Meantime in another part of the palace's inner sanctum Narcis's other brother, Prince Vro Ixian, was busy receiving the report of Perlo Rolce, owner of the Rolce Detective Agency.

Prince Vro's apartments were gloomily lit and carelessly furnished. The cleaning staff was rarely allowed in and dust lay everywhere. To remind him of his great sorrow, one wall of the main room was taken up with a tridimensional hologram screen that gave a direct view into a mausoleum about a mile distant so that it seemed an extension of Vro's dwelling. The sarcophagus occupying the centre of the burial chamber gaped open, empty.

The burly detective sat stiffly in a straight-backed chair facing the prince, who stood in a curious stance at the other end of the room, head cocked and one hand resting negligently on a table. Three or four years older than Narcis, he had the same cast of face, but his eyes were more penetrating.

Rolce was used to Ixian peculiarities. This was not the first time he had been engaged by a member of the imperial household. He spoke directly, without prevarication.

'Your Highness, since our last meeting I have followed up the evidence suggesting that the Traumatic sect might have been involved in the affair. I can now confirm it categorically: it *was* the Traumatic sect who stole the body of Princess Veaa from its resting place.'

Vro looked pleadingly at the empty sarcophagus. 'But for what purpose?'

Rolce coughed before continuing. 'The motives for the crime are far from pleasant, Your Highness. The Traumatic sect, as you must know, is prone to bizarre practices. Rejecting the teachings of the Church, its members worship a god they call Hulmu and whom they deem to dwell in the uttermost depths of the strat. Hulmu, by their doctrines, feeds on the trauma that the soul experiences on separating from the body at death, but is usually robbed of his pleasure because the soul passes back in time and finds refuge in its body again. Therefore the sect practises certain rites, ending in human sacrifice, that they claim give the victim's soul to Hulmu.'

'What has this to do with my beloved Veaa?' said Vro harshly. 'She is dead already.'

'Your sister died of a brain haemorrhage, and later was embalmed by the Murkesen process, which leaves all the vital tissues intact,' the detective explained. 'Someone in the Traumatic sect apparently believes that these two factors together have left her soul in a state of suspension, and that it has not departed into the past.'

'You mean she is still *alive*?' Prince Vro asked in a shocked tone.

'No, Your Highness,' Rolce replied hurriedly. 'One should not pay heed to heretical theories.' Then, seeing Prince Vro's lips curl, he added, 'Even according to the Traumatics your sister is deceased. It is merely that her soul *is believed* to be still accessible to Hulmu. They hoped, by means of rites or medical experiments, to release her soul from its latent state and offer it to Hulmu. A personage of such exalted rank was, of course, a great prize to them.'

A low moan escaped Prince Vro's lips and his face expressed ashen horror. Then he turned away and began to give vent to strangled sobs, while Rolce sat impassively and stared at the nearby wall.

The private detective had come across many weird situations in the course of his work and the predicament of Prince Vro aroused no comment in his mind.

He knew that the prince had been desperately enamoured of his sister Princess Veaa. The emperor had even indicated that he would consent to a marriage between them. And then had come her sudden death. In an orgy of mourning Prince Vro had designed her mausoleum personally, placed her embalmed body in the sarcophagus with his own hands, and installed the direct-wire hologram to his private apartment so that he would never forget her.

Sadly, his misfortunes had increased still further. The embalmed body had been stolen from the mausoleum, for no explicable reason. Exhaustive police investigations had proved fruitless. Eventually Vro had called upon Rolce's services.

Rolce had wondered why the prince had not followed the example of his brother Narcis and travelled back in time to when Veaa was still alive (though that might, he reflected, entail complications of a personal nature). But the speculation was sterile. Vro seemed as deeply in love with the corpse as he had been with the living woman.

With difficulty the prince recovered his composure. 'And what has become of her now?'

Rolce frowned. 'At this point the affair becomes perplexing. I gained most of my information so far by infiltrating one of my men into a secret Traumatic cell. Unfortunately his guise was eventually penetrated and the fellow was murdered. I then used more direct methods to track down the cor – to track down the princess, and ascertained that she had been removed from Node One on an internodal liner. However –'

'They can do that?'

The detective nodded. 'The sect is very resourceful. It has good contacts in the internodal travel services.'

'I see,' muttered Vro. 'And how soon before my beloved Veaa is found?'

The other gave a worried sigh. 'The trail has petered out, Your Highness. Quite frankly I do not understand it. I have never come up against such a blank wall before. Even if the body had been disposed of in some way – and I seriously doubt that it has – the methods I have used should have given me some information about it. Everything that happens leaves a trace that the trained investigator can pick up.'

'What are you babbling about, Rolce?' Vro swung around and confronted the older man, hands on his hips. 'You are not doing your job! Is your fee not inducement enough?'

'It is not that, Your Highness!' the investigator protested. 'My entire agency – which is an organisation to be reckoned with – is engaged solely upon this one assignment. We have never failed yet. But something odd seems to have happened.'

For the first time Perlo Rolce displayed a degree of discomfiture. He shifted uneasily in his chair.

'At my headquarters we have the man who shipped out the body of Princess Veaa,' he said. 'We are certain we have not mistaken his identity. Earlier we picked up his thoughts on the subject with a field-effect device.'

'And?'

'He does not know anything about it any longer. He does not remember leaving Chronopolis on the requisite date.'

'His mind has been tampered with.'

'That might be the explanation if we relied on physical persuasion alone. He knows nothing of Princess Veaa, except vaguely as a one-time member of the imperial family. Yet we know for a fact that he had custody of the body for a considerable period of time.'

'Just what are you suggesting?'

The investigator looked, briefly, straight into Vro's eyes, something he had never done before. 'I do not know, Your Highness. I am a detective, not a Chronotician. But I am beginning to get the feeling that something outside my control has closed off the investigation.'

He hesitated before going on. 'The phenomenon is not unknown to me. Of late, there have been a number of such cases. Odd details that do not mesh together – a cause not producing the usual effect, or an effect not preceded by the usual cause. Only someone like myself, trained to notice details, would pick them up. In my belief the war with the Hegemony is beginning to touch us, even here at Node One. Time is under strain.'

The prince brooded on his words. 'It almost sounds as though you were looking for excuses,' he said in a surly tone.

'Your Highness, I assure you of my sincerity.'

'Well, are you implying you wish to leave off the assignment?'

'The Rolce Agency does not abandon assignments,' Rolce told him. 'There is one move still left to us. We have procured an orthophase and I am negotiating for the clandestine use of a time-travel unit.'

'I could have arranged that for you,' Vro interrupted in a mutter.

Rolce shrugged. 'One of my agents will phase himself into the past and carry out a surveillance of our prisoner at the time he hid and transported the body of Princess Veaa. If we find that he did not commit these acts – *as we know he did* – then it will demonstrate that time has mutated in some peculiar way, leaving loose ends.'

'In a very peculiar way,' Prince Vro agreed huffily. 'Are you not aware that a time-mutation leaves no loose ends and is generally undetectable after the event?'

'I am aware of it, Your Highness, but I must deal in facts.' He rose and handed the prince an envelope. 'Here is my written report of all information to date.'

'Thank you, my good fellow. Come and see me again soon.'

After the detective had gone the young prince stood for a long time with the envelope unopened in his hand, staring into space.

Defeat is never a pleasant thing to have to recount to one's master. Commander Haight's large, rugged face was stonily impassive as he answered the emperor's probing questions concerning the attempt to save Gerread.

At length Philipium I uttered a deep trembling sigh. 'No blame,' he said, to Haight's relief. 'The action was gallantly fought. Tonight the Military Council meets. We shall be discussing what action to take between now and the launching of the armada. There will be some, no doubt, who wish to abandon the enterprise and make peace overtures with the Hegemony.' He looked closely at the commander. 'How do you read the situation?'

'The armada must be launched as soon as possible, Your Majesty – much sooner than was originally planned. The time-distorter is a terrible weapon. I cannot guarantee the ability of the defensive forces to ward off every attack that might be made.'

'Can we not set up time-blocks?'

'Time-blocks cannot be kept in continuous operation without years of preparation, Your Majesty. And I am advised that the rearward Stop Barrier already consumes one-third of the imperial budget. Our only safeguard is to overwhelm the Hegemony without delay. Otherwise I can foresee disaster.'

The emperor grunted contemptuously. 'Don't tell me you're another who thinks the empire can fall.'

'Naturally not, Your Majesty,' replied Haight, taken aback by the suggestion. 'But serious damage can be wrought from which it would take centuries to recover. More to the point, the Hegemonics must know of the armada we have in preparation. It will form a prime target for their attentions. They will certainly try to destroy it before it is completed.'

This time it was the emperor's turn to be startled. 'They could penetrate even this far – to Node One?'

'Even that cannot be discounted, though it's unlikely in my view. They will try to attack it indirectly by wreaking such changes in our future that the effects will reach far back in time, delaying or preventing the construction of the armada in the first place. It could be done if their knowledge of Chronotic history is detailed enough.'

'And it probably is,' Philipium confirmed in a worried tone. 'I have heard there has been some intercourse between agents of the Hegemony and a dissident religious sect known as the Traumatics.' He shook his head in exasperation. His right hand began to tremble more noticeably.

'The assembling of the armada simply cannot be hastened,' he informed Haight. 'The project is already at full stretch; there are no more resources that can be put into it.'

'Your Majesty, if we leave matters as they stand at the moment, there is no saying how things will end.'

'You speak as though you were one of my ministers, instead of merely a commander in the Time Service,' Philipium said with a warning note of reproof.

'I beg Your Majesty's pardon. It is my concern over the situation that prompts me to speak so.'

'Everyone, it seems, has decided to be impudent today. Still, you have seen action at first hand. You know how things look at the frontier. What suggestions have you for strengthening the forward watch? We could,' he added as an afterthought, 'release some ships completed for the armada for that purpose.'

'That would help, Your Majesty, but the first priority must be to gain parity with the enemy over the matter of his new weapon. To that end I advocate a raid into Hegemonic territory with a force strong enough to overcome any local resistance, in an effort to capture a sample distorter.'

'Do you think that is a feasible operation?'

'Yes, if we have agents who can find out where a distorter is kept, so as to give us a target point. The Hegemony consists of one node only, which makes the matter simpler.'

The emperor opened a lacquered box and sniffed at a pinch of the reddish powder it contained. He was thoughtful. 'We do have agents in the Hegemony. Mostly among those whom our early missionaries converted to the true faith. Needless to say they are already at work on the business of the distorter, but messages are slow to reach us due to the inability to transmit through time.'

He inhaled more snuff. 'You will attend the meeting of the Military Council tonight. We will discuss this.'

'With great pleasure, Your Majesty.'

In the event Illus Ton Mayar delayed his departure from the palace for an hour or two. Princess Mayora was an insistent host, and despite his gloomy manner, she continued to inveigle him into conversation with the socialites who flitted in and out of the court chamber. He even spoke with Captain Vrin and heard from him a first-hand account of his part in the recent battle for Gerread – an account, he suspected, already polished with much retelling, even thought the battle-damaged timeships had arrived only a little before dawn.

But his nagging desire to return to his underground vaults eventually overcame the pleasure of social life. He was about to tender his farewells to the princess when a liveried servant approached him.

'His Highness the Prince Vro would speak with you, Archivist, if it is convenient,' the servant informed him.

Although couched in the politest terms, coming from a prince the message was an order. Puzzled, Mayar followed the servant and shortly came to Vro's morbid quarters.

The prince leaped up with alacrity when he entered. 'Ah,' he greeted, 'I tried to contact you at the archives, but they said you were here at the palace.'

Mayar glanced surreptitiously around the place, trying not to seem inquisitive. 'An audience with His Majesty your father,' he explained diffidently.

'More mutations, eh?' Vro gave him a querying, penetrating look.

'I'm afraid so.'

He relaxed a little. Prince Vro had always struck him as being the most intelligent of the imperial family. The business with the body of Princess Veaa was known to Mayar, of course ... but that was entirely a personal affair.

He tried to keep his eyes away from the wall-wide holocast of the vacant mausoleum. 'How may I serve Your Highness?' he asked.

'Ah, you come straight to the point. A man after my own heart.'

Holding nothing back, Prince Vro told him how he had hired the Rolce Detective Agency to hunt down Princess Veaa's body. He recounted, as well as he could, the conversation he had held with Rolce an hour before. When he came to speak of the peculiar difficulties and anomalies Rolce had been encountering, Mayar grew more and more agitated.

'Could time become dislocated in the way Rolce suspects?' he asked Mayar.

'From natural mutations – no,' Mayar told him. 'The natural movements of the substratum always smooth out cause-and-effect relationships in both directions. But in principle there's nothing to prevent dislocated phenomena arising through some sort of artificially applied distortion. Excuse me, sir, but may I be permitted to sit?'

Prince Vro nodded sympathetically. Mayar edged himself to the straight-backed chair Perlo Rolce had recently occupied. He felt weak and dizzy.

'A detective agency – of course!' he exclaimed, his voice hoarse with sudden understanding. 'It's logical. Only a detective would notice details on so small a scale. Even the Achronal Archives cannot keep track of everyday events.'

'But what does it all mean?'

'It means what Rolce says it means. That the war with the Hegemony is going badly. It's that damned distorter of theirs. Cracks are appearing in the order of things – little cracks, at first. Eventually they'll get bigger.'

'What an amusing prospect.'

Mayar looked at him sharply.

'Well, you might as well get used to the idea, Archivist. It's got to happen. Nothing can stop the war now. You have observed, of course, that my father the emperor is a religious maniac. Aided and abetted by that incredible bigot Reamoir, he is determined to hurl his armada at our descendants in the far future. I am even expected to command one of its squadrons myself!' Vro's lips twisted cynically. He moved away to gaze into the mausoleum. 'No doubt all will shortly come crashing about our ears. But all of this means nothing to me. I care only for saving my beloved Veaa.'

Mayar scarcely heard his last words. He passed a hand wearily across his brow. 'We are living in a dream,' he said in an exhausted voice. 'This world – it is all an illusion. Only the strat is real …'

'An interesting point of view.' Prince Vro turned to face him again.

'In my archives are records of nations, cultures, whole civilisations that have been removed from time,' Mayar said. 'Millions of people – mere figments, of whom we have a record only by a technical trick. How can something that vanishes and changes be real? That is why I say only the strat is real – and even then, what is the strat? We do not know. This time-travel: it is merely a way of moving from one part of a dream to another.'

'Your view of life comes close to my own,' Prince Vro told him softly. 'Nothing is real; no matter is of more significance than any other. That is what I tell myself whenever my intellect chides me for my obsession with my beloved Veaa.'

The prince handed Mayar a thick envelope. 'Since you are able to take Rolce's suspicions seriously, I want you to do some work for me. This is his report. I'll send him to you tomorrow to explain it personally.'

'Work, Your Highness?' Mayar accepted the envelope gingerly.

Vro nodded. 'With his investigations and the contents of your files, it should be possible to carry out a – what do you call it – a mapping, should it not? I want you to help Rolce locate the princess. If detective work in orthogonal time is not enough, then perhaps you can turn something up in strat time.'

When Mayar left Prince Vro and made to leave the palace, clutching the private investigator's report, his mind feverish, he chanced to pass by the audience chamber where he had earlier spoken with the emperor.

The huge frame of Commander Haight emerged from the chamber. Grim-faced, he swept by Mayar without a word.

After him came the emperor, leaning on the arm of an attendant. He stopped when he caught sight of Mayar, who bowed low.

'Still here, Archivist?'

'Your Majesty, there is a recommendation I would make.'

The notion had been in his mind for some months, but in the last half-hour it had jelled into a firm desire. Philipium frowned, not liking to be accosted so, but he signalled Mayar to continue.

'I am becoming increasingly concerned for the safety of the archives, Your Majesty. I have come to the conclusion that the present arrangements are unsatisfactory.'

Now Philipium became displeased. 'The time-buffers surrounding your vaults were installed at colossal expense,' he admonished. 'You approved them at the time. Now you tell me they are no good.'

'I feel that the situation is changing rapidly, Your Majesty. My new proposal will entail less expense. The buffers are satisfactory up to a point – but if the enemy should succeed in getting behind us, as it were, and attacking the year in which the buffers were erected, then they could be obviated and the archives would be rendered useless for their purpose.'

Philipium's grey face lost its anger as, with eyes downcast, he considered the point. 'So?'

'The only really foolproof way of making the archives safe from orthogonal mutations is to locate them in the strat. This could not be done before, due to the communications problem – it's necessary to have continuous computer contact with the records of the Imperial Register, so as to detect anomalies, and there was no way to do this. The technical problem has now been solved. We can float at anchor in the strat while connected by cable to the offices of the registrar.'

'By *cable*?'

'The technique is a new one known as graduated phasing, Your Majesty. The Achronal Archives should then be proof against any orthogonal changes.'

'Very well, I approve. I will issue an authorisation.'

The secretary in the emperor's retinue immediately made a note of the proceedings. Mayar bowed low and left.

Philipium retired to his private quarters, dismissed the retinue except for one personal servant, and sent for his favourite comforter. With a hoarse, deep-seated sigh he sank into a comfortable couch and accepted a dose of the medicine that quieted his shaking a little.

The comforter arrived. This was Philipium's favourite relaxation. An atmosphere of peace and silence, the lights shaded to rest his aching eyes.

The comforter sat to one side of the emperor so as to be out of his line of vision. He opened the book he carried and in a gentle, soothing voice began to read.

'There is the body, and there is the soul. The body belongs to orthogonal time. But the soul, being spiritual, is eternal; yet it does not persist beyond its appointed period in time …'

Elsewhere $Narcis_1$ and $Narcis_2$ disported on a couch that was more luxurious than their father's and surrounded by orchids, while the atmosphere of the boudoir was pervaded by sweet perfumes.

They looked into each other's eyes, smiling and sated. 'One day soon something strange will happen,' $Narcis_2$ said in a sad, dreamy voice. 'Something very, very melancholy.'

'What is that, dearest?' $Narcis_1$ murmured.

'*He* will come and steal you from me. Like a thief in the night. The third one.'

Briefly there dawned in $Narcis_1$'s eyes the realisation of what the other was talking about – the day, barely a year ahead, when by natural ageing they would reach the date when he had secretly appeared in his future self's bedroom and seduced him. It was a paradox he had never really bothered to work out for himself.

'Yes, I shall have a visitor,' he said wonderingly. 'He will enchant me and entice me away. Away into the past!'

'Don't talk like that! I shall be left all alone!' $Narcis_2$ covered his face with his hands. 'Oh, I hate him! I hate him!'

$Narcis_1$ gazed at him with teasing, imagining eyes.

THREE

The Seekers, the Pointers, the Pursuers, all were present. The Choosing could go ahead.

The ceremony was in the apartment of a rich member of the sect. One of the elegant rooms had been converted into a temple. The altar, containing a representation of the Impossible Shape (an abstract of warped planes, said to echo the form of Hulmu), was lit by shaded cressets.

All knelt, the ceremonial black cloths draped over their heads, save the vicar, who stood facing the assembly, wearing the Medallion of Projection, which showed a gold miniature of a holocast projector. On his head was a low flat-topped hat. Upon this hat he placed the black Book of Hulmu to allow the vibrations of its words to flow down into him.

The orisons began. 'Lord of all the deep, perceive us and know that we thy servants act out our parts …'

The chanting grew louder. The vicar feverishly muttered an incantation, known only to sect members of his own rank, which acted on a hypnotically planted subconscious command. Almost immediately he went into a trance.

He spoke with the voice of Hulmu.

It was a harsh, twanging voice, quite unlike his own or that of any other human being.

'*Are my Seekers present?*'

'We are present, Lord!' cried one section of the congregation.

'*Are my Pointers present?*'

'We are present, Lord!' chanted another group.

'*Are my Pursuers present?*'

The remainder of the gathering spoke up. 'We are present, Lord!'

'*Then let my Pointers choose.*'

Abruptly the glazed, empty look went out of the vicar's eyes. He removed the black book from his head.

'All right, let's get on with it,' he said conversationally in his normal tone.

The tension went out of the meeting. They removed their black headcloths. The gathering was suddenly informal.

The Pointers huddled together. One of them pulled a cord. A curtain swished aside, revealing a complete set of Chronopolis's massive street directory.

A sect member with a self-absorbed face thoughtfully selected a volume.

Another snatched it from him, bent back the covers, and flung the book to the floor so that it splayed its leaves on the tiles.

Yet another picked it up and smoothed out the pages that fortune, through this procedure, had selected. He stared at the ceiling while allowing his fingers to roam at random over the paper.

Everyone watched in silence as his fingers slowed to a stop.

'Eighty-nine Kell Street,' he read out. 'Precinct E-Fourteen. Inpriss Sorce, female.'

'Inpriss Sorce,' someone said, savouring the name. They all started wondering what she was like: young or old, pretty or plain; what her fear index was.

'The Pursuer team will begin operations tomorrow at nine,' the vicar intoned.

'Inpriss Sorce.' All the Pursuers began murmuring the name to themselves with a growing sense of pleasure.

They were glad the victim was a woman.

Inpriss Sorce was thirty years old. She had a neat, slightly melancholy face with light-brown eyes, and an average figure. She lived in a two-room apartment and worked as a clerk for Noble Cryonics, a firm that did a great deal of work for the government.

Once she had held a better-paid job with the Historical Office, but had lost it when a jealous comforter cast aspersions on her piety. The post she held now, though it reduced her station in life, did not require vetting by the Church. It did, however, entail living in a poorer part of the city. Also, most of her friends from the Historical Office now wanted little to do with her, so she was, for the time being, lonely.

She had come home from work and was wondering what to do with the evening when the Pursuers paid their call.

The casers had already been at work some hours before. One of them met Rol Stryne and Fee Velen as they arrived at the entrance to the apartment block. Briefly he explained the layout of Inpriss Sorce's small dwelling. The window in the living-room gave access to a fire escape.

'Very good,' said Stryne. 'Give us half an hour.'

Velen carried a large tool-box which he lugged awkwardly as they mounted the stairs. On the third floor Stryne found the right door and knocked on it. When it opened, they both pushed their way inside.

Inpriss Sorce was carried back by their onrush. 'What – what do you want?' she demanded shrilly.

Their eyes flicked around the small apartment. Stryne looked at Inpriss, studying her face, his gaze roving up and down her body. He liked what he saw and was feeling a warm glow of anticipation.

Hulmu had chosen well. It was going to be good; Hulmu would be entertained.

The girl retreated to the far wall and put her hand to her throat. 'What do you want?' she repeated in a whisper. She had seen the expression in their eyes. 'Just tell me what you want.'

'This is the most important day of your life, lady,' Stryne told her. 'You're going to experience … what you never experienced before.'

They both took the black cloths from their pockets and draped them over their skulls.

Inpriss shrank back in horror. 'Oh, God! No! No!' She let out a weak scream, but before she could finish it they had seized her and Velen had clapped a hand over her mouth. She was trembling and almost unresisting as they carried her to a table from which Stryne swept cups and books. They placed her on it. Stryne took stout cord which he looped around the legs of the table and, using specially prescribed knots, caught her wrists and ankles.

When Velen took his hand from her mouth she no longer screamed. They rarely did; the appearance of the infamous Traumatic sect was calculated to inspire helpless terror. Instead she began to pray in a trembling, sobbing voice.

'It's no good praying to your God like that,' Stryne said conversationally. 'He doesn't exist, it's all a con. Before we've finished here you'll be praying to Hulmu, the authentic god who created us by projecting us on to the screen of reality.' He liked to engage the sacrificial victims in a dialogue, to establish a rapport with them.

Humming meditatively – a nervous habit that came over him at moments like this – he noted her carrying satchel lying on a chair. Caressingly he opened it and inspected the contents. Small personal effects, identification papers, a voucher, for a bank account, money, and a few letters.

He placed the satchel on a ledge near the window.

They opened the tool-box and began taking out their equipment.

The girl ceased praying and lay gasping with fright. Stryne waved a meter near her head. Her fear index was high – nearly eighty. That was good.

'How are you going to do it?' she asked them. '*Please tell me how you're going to do it!*'

'Mmmmmm … There are so many ways. The knife, inserted slowly? The Terrible Vibrator? The Exit by Burning?' He showed her the various instruments one by one.

Her head had raised itself off the tabletop, straining, to look. Now it sank back again. Her face collapsed into despair.

Velen set up a hologram screen and a laser projector. The screen hovered slantwise over the girl like a descending wing. Velen flicked a switch; the screen came to life. The Impossible Shape of Hulmu gyrated and twisted hypnotically against a background of shifting moiré patterns. Stryne and Velen knelt on either side of the girl, watching her face, their backs to the screen.

'Hearken to Hulmu!' declared Stryne.

And the first of the ceremonies began.

Inpriss went into a slight trance brought on by the holo projection. In this state the words and responses from Stryne and Velen penetrated deep into her consciousness.

'You are to be sacrificed to Hulmu,' Stryne told her. 'Your soul will not return through time to your body; you will never live again, as others do. You will belong to Hulmu. He will take you with him deep into the strat.'

'Hulmu will take you with him,' reiterated Velen in a singsong voice.

'You must pray to Hulmu,' Stryne whispered in her ear. 'You belong to him now.'

While they intoned the rituals Velen switched on more of their apparatus. Devices gave out strange buzzes and clicks that grated on the nerves; alien whines filled the air. Stryne applied a prong to the girl's body and began delivering pain in intermittent, increasing amounts. Everything was designed so as to enhance the trauma, and Inpriss Sorce was now catalytic with terror.

She came out of the trance with a start and he let her see the Exit by Burning device ready for use in his hands. Her eyes widened and her face sagged. Her mouth opened but her voice was too paralysed to scream.

There came a knock on the outer door.

Stryne and Velen looked at each other. 'We'd better see what it is,' Stryne said.

They left the room, closing the door behind them, and paused. Stryne opened the door to the corridor.

The caser was there. 'You timed it nicely,' Stryne said to him.

They stood there, not speaking. Stryne bent his ear to the inner door. There was a scuffling from inside. Then he heard the window open.

A minute later they entered the room. Inpriss Sorce was gone. She had slipped the special knots Stryne had tied and escaped by the fire escape. With satisfaction he saw that she had shown the presence of mind to snatch up her satchel so that she would not be without resources.

'We made a good start,' he breathed.

The pursuit was in progress.

FOUR

For some weeks Captain Aton had been forced to wear military prison garb. Now, on the day that his court-martial was due, the guards brought him his full duty uniform. He dressed slowly and carefully, but had no mirror in which to check his appearance.

The walls of his cell were made of grey metal, which reminded him of the starkly functional interior of the destroyer class of timeship in which he had served prior to his arrest. He missed the deep vibration of the time-drive, and even more so the sense of discipline and purpose that went with active service. Instead, his solitude was broken only by the shouts and clangings that made up the daily life of the prison. It depressed him to know that he was in company with deserters and various other malefactors. Occupying cells in his block were some religious offenders – members of the Traumatic sect – and Aton would hear their calls to Hulmu echoing through the night.

The Traumatic sect. That struck a chord in Aton's mind. A puzzled frown crossed his face as he tried to recollect why, but the answer eluded him.

He heard footsteps. The door of the cell grated open to reveal two burly guards and his defence counsel, a nervous young lieutenant.

Aton was already on his feet. At a signal from one of the guards he stepped into the passage.

'The court is convened, Captain,' the lieutenant said with a diffident cough. 'Shall we?'

They walked towards the court block ahead of the guards. Despite his predicament, Aton found time to feel some sympathy for his counsel, who was embarrassed at being in the company of a doomed man.

'We might have a chance,' the lieutenant said. 'The field-effect reading is in our favour. I shall argue incapacity.'

Aton nodded, but he knew that the hearing would go the same way that the earlier investigation had.

Gates swung and clanged as they were let out of the penitentiary area of the prison. An elevator took them further up the building and without further preamble they were admitted into the courtroom.

Aton was to be judged by a tribunal of three retired commanders. One glance at their seamed faces told him that they felt about the matter much as he would in their place: that there was no excuse for cowardice.

The prosecutor, an older and more practised man than Aton's counsel, turned suavely to regard the accused before reading out the charge.

'Captain Mond Aton, serving in His Chronotic Majesty's Third Time Fleet under Commander Veel Ark Haight, it is laid against you that on the eleventh day of cycle four-eight-five, fleet-time, you were guilty of cowardice and gross dereliction of duty in that, the vessel under your command being crippled by enemy action, you abandoned your ship the *Smasher of Enemies* ahead of your men; and further that you fought with the men under your command so as to board a life raft, thus saving yourself at their expense. How do you plead?'

The young lieutenant stepped forward. 'Sirs, I wish to tender that Captain Aton is unfit to plead, being the victim of amnesia.'

'I plead not guilty,' Aton contradicted firmly. 'I do not believe I am capable of the acts described.'

A faint sneer came to the prosecutor's lips. 'He does not believe he is capable!'

With a despairing shrug the counsel for the defence stepped back to his place.

Inexorably the prosecution proceeded to call witnesses. And so Aton was forced to experience what he had already experienced at the preliminary hearings. First to be called was Sergeant Quelle, his chief gunnery noncom. With blank bemusement he heard him recount how he, Aton, a beamer in each hand, had killed all who stood in his way in his haste to leave the foundering *Smasher of Enemies*. Occasionally Quelle glanced his way with what seemed to him a spiteful, fearful look. At those moments a double image flashed into Aton's mind: he seemed to see Quelle's face distended and made bulbous as if seen through a magnifying glass or through the visor of a strat suit. But the picture faded as soon as it was born, and he put it down to imagination.

Seven other witnesses, all crewmen from the *Smasher of Enemies*, followed Quelle. All repeated his tale, pausing sometimes to glare accusingly at their captain. They named the men and officers they had seen Aton gun down, and told how they had succeeded in disarming him only once the life raft was floating free in the strat and the *Smasher of Enemies* had broken up. Then, after an agonising delay, they had eventually been located and picked up by the flagship. Aton had been arrested and sent to Chronopolis.

Of all this Aton remembered practically nothing. He could recall some details of the battle with the Hegemonics, in a confused kind of way, but it all had the aspects of a dream. As for the events Quelle and the others spoke of, it was just a blank to him. The only thing he could remember was coming to and finding that life raft 3 was being hauled inboard the *Lamp of Faith*, Commander Haight's flagship.

Could he really have murdered, among others, Lieutenant Krish? Could

he have fallen prey to such animal panic, in the grip of some mental derangement, perhaps? If so, the derangement was still affecting him, for everything
seemed still possessed of a dreamlike quality. He simply could not reconcile
what was happening with his own image of himself, with his love of the Time
Service, and with his loyalty to the empire.

The prosecutor conceded the floor to the defence. The young lieutenant
called his one and only witness.

'Major Batol,' he said to the slim officer who entered, 'what is your function in the Time Service?'

'I am a doctor and surgeon.'

'Do you recognise the accused?'

The major eyed Aton briefly and nodded.

'Will you please tell us the result of your examination of Captain Aton
earlier.'

Major Batol turned to the tribunal. 'I examined the captain with a field-
effect device. This is a device that responds to the "field effect", that is to say
the electrostatic nimbus that surrounds the human body and brain. By its
means it is possible to ascertain a person's mental state and even what he is
thinking, since thoughts and emotions leak into the field. The technique may
be likened to eavesdropping on the operation of a computer by picking up its
incidental electromagnetic transmissions –'

'Yes, you may spare us the explanations,' the head of the tribunal said
sourly. 'Come to the point.'

'Captain Aton has total amnesia of the period under question,' Major Batol
informed them.

'And what would be a likely cause of such amnesia?' asked the defence
counsel.

'It is almost certainly traumatic in origin,' the major said. 'Remember that
the destroyer was foundering into the strat. Anyone who happened, for only
a moment, to see the strat with his bare eyes would undergo trauma sufficient to account for amnesia of this type.'

'Thank you, Major.'

The prosecutor was quick to come forward. 'Major Batol, would you say
that a man suffering from the trauma you describe would be capable of purposeful action, such as fighting his way aboard a life raft?'

'It is highly unlikely that he would be capable of any action whatsoever,
certainly not of an integrated kind.'

'And is there any evidence to say *at what point* in the proceedings this
experience of Captain Aton's took place? Ten minutes before he entered the
life raft? Five minutes before? *Or only a moment before?*'

'None. Traumatic amnesia can obliterate the events leading up to the
trauma as well as those following it.'

'Thank you very much, Major.'

When the time came for him to sum up his case, Aton's counsel did the best he could. He began by speaking of Aton's excellent service record and of his three previous engagements, for one of which he had received a commendation. He stressed the fact of Aton's amnesia, trying to suggest that this threw something of a mystery over the whole affair.

'It is odd,' he said, 'that Captain Aton should be unable to make any reply to the accusations that are made against him. Finally-' he confronted the tribunal, his face white – 'I request that the witnesses for the prosecution should themselves undergo a field-effect test!'

The prosecutor jumped to his feet. 'The prosecution objects to that remark! The defence is imputing perjury in my witnesses!'

The tribunal chief shifted in his seat and looked grim. 'Use of the field-effect device is not recognised in civil law, and this tribunal takes its cue from the civil establishment where the laws of evidence are concerned,' he said to the defending lieutenant. 'Although we were prepared to listen to the opinion of Major Batol, in law the amnesia of your client has not itself been established. Your request is denied.'

That, Aton knew, had been the counsel's last desperate fling. The tribunal spent little time deliberating its decision. When the commanders returned from the inner chamber, the tribunal head looked at Aton with no hint of compassion.

'Captain Mond Aton, we find you guilty. The evidence of eight independent witnesses can hardly be gainsaid. As for the effort by the defence to suggest your actions were the result of a personality change, and thereby to mitigate your guilt, that argument cannot be accepted. Even if true, it remains that an officer named Captain Aton committed the offences, and an officer named Captain Aton stands before us now. Personality changes are not admitted in an officer of the Time Service.'

He paused before coming to his grave conclusion. 'Your sentence is the only one that can be expected. From here you will be taken to the laboratories of the Courier Department, where you will perform your last service to the empire. And may God restore your soul.'

As he was led away, Aton passed by Sergeant Quelle who was sitting in the anteroom alongside the others who had given evidence against him. They all – Quelle especially – looked at him with glittering eyes. They could not hide their triumph.

'Most unusual,' murmured the technician.

He was sitting casually across from Aton in the briefing-room. 'I think this is the first time I've had to deal with someone of your calibre,' he said. 'Mostly we get common murderers, thieves, petty traitors – scum like that.'

He eyed Aton with unveiled curiosity. His manner was relaxed and he seemed to think of his job as a mildly interesting technical exercise instead of as the bizarre method of execution which it was to be for Aton.

'I'm supposed to teach you as much as you need to know to perform your task properly,' the technician resumed, 'but as a chronman yourself you hardly need to be told very much, of course.'

'All chronmen fear the strat,' Aton said emptily. 'It surrounds us. We never forget that.'

'Are you afraid?'

'Yes.'

The other nodded. 'You're right to be. It is fearful. This business is worse for you than it is for some criminal of low intelligence, I can see that. Still, we all have our job to do.'

He doesn't pity me, Aton thought. He has no sympathy for me at all. He's probably processed hundreds of men – it doesn't mean anything to him any more.

The technician came around the table and placed a headset over Aton's cranium. He felt electrodes prodding his scalp. The other retreated back to his chair and glanced at tracer dials, making entries on a sheet of paper.

'Good,' he announced. 'Your cephalic responses are adequate – we'd expect them to be, wouldn't we? Some of the dimmer types get out of this business by not having the alertness to be able to target themselves once we put them through. So it's the gas chamber for them.'

'How soon?' grated Aton.

'Hm?'

'*When do I go through?*'

'Oh –' the technician glanced at his watch – 'in about an hour.'

Aton steeled his nerves to face the coming ordeal. He had been languishing for nearly a week since his trial, waiting for his name to be called. Despite that the department dispatched a daily stream of messages to the distant time-fleets it never seemed to run short of couriers.

He reminded himself that he had been in the strat before – millions of times, in fact. Everybody had. Only nobody remembered it. When the body died, the soul, robbed of the body's existential support, found itself in the strat. That was what caused death trauma – the bedazzlement of the soul when faced by potential time. But because it had nowhere to exist apart from the body, and even though shock reduced it to a state midway between unconsciousness and a dreamlike trance, it hurried back along its time-track, experiencing its life in reverse at a tremendously speeded-up rate like a video-tape on rewind, until it reached the moment of conception. At which point it began to live again.

Thus Aton's imminent punishment would be something like the experience of death, except that not simply his soul but his body too was to be catapulted into the strat, and except that he would be pumped full of dugs to keep him conscious even under the impact of unspeakable trauma. An unconscious courier would be no good; he would not be able to guide himself towards his destination.

While the technician continued marking his papers, Aton began to speak in a low, haunted voice.

'Scientists have debated whether the strat really exists as an independent continuum,' he murmured, 'or whether it is only an apparency our own machines have created; merely the result of that crucial act of accelerating pi-mesons faster than light. In the Time Service we are accustomed to thinking of the strat as an ocean, with orthogonal time as its surface ... but perhaps the strat is only the world itself, scrambled and twisted because one no longer obeys its laws.'

The other man looked up, fascinated to hear this talk from one of the couriers. It was an unusual reaction; commonly three men or more were needed to hold them down.

'The Church has an answer to that, at any rate,' he pointed out to Aton. 'The strat is real, but not as real as the world of actual time.'

'Yes ... the Church has an answer for everything,' Aton replied, only slightly cynically. 'The strat is the Holy Ghost, connecting God with the world. In the Time Service one inclines to take a more pragmatic view. Now that I am to be exposed unprotected to what chronmen fear most, it's not surprising if my mind dwells on what its true nature might be.'

'Your collected state of mind is, if I may say so, admirable,' the technician admitted. 'In your place, however, I would not be disposed to take the teachings of the Church so lightly. A comforter will be at hand at your dispatch to offer final consolation. Need I point out that the view you have just put forward – that the strat does not exist apart from the visible world – denies the Holy Ghost and is tantamount to materialistic atheism?'

A mocking smile played around the technician's mouth and Aton realised the man was toying with him. He remained silent.

'In any case,' the technician continued after a pause, 'the strat would appear to be what you called it just now: an ocean of potential time. For one thing, it has depth. It's some years since the Church forbade any further deep-diving expeditions, but no doubt you know what happened to the earlier ones. The pressure of potential time gets stronger the deeper you go. Some of the ships had their ortho fields crushed.'

Aton shuddered slightly.

'Do you resent what's happening to you?' the technician asked.

Aton shook his head, shrugging. 'They say that I am a coward and a murderer. I don't know if it's true or not. But if it is, then this is just ... for an officer.' If he truly thought that he had committed those crimes, then he would almost have welcomed the punishment as a chance to redeem himself.

The technician rose. 'Over here, please.'

A high-backed chair with dangling straps stood on the other side of the room. The two guards pinned Aton's arms to his sides and forced him into it. The straps passed across his chest and over his thighs and forearms.

'When your mission is accomplished you are instructed to die,' the technician said softly. 'The method will be the simple and direct one of vagal inhibition. To that end we will now implant a trigger word with which, at the appropriate time, you can excite your own vagus nerve and stop your heart.'

A needle pricked Aton's arm. A coloured disc began to rotate in front of his eyes, attracting his gaze and holding it even against his will. A voice murmured soothingly in his ear.

Presently Aton fell asleep.

VOM.

When he awoke the word lay somewhere in his mind like a dead weight. He was vaguely aware of it, but he was unable to speak it, either aloud or mentally. That would not be possible until a certain phrase, spoken by a voice he would recognise when he heard it, released the word from its confinement.

The coloured disc wheeled away. In its place was put a more elaborate piece of apparatus that included, on the end of a flexible cable, what looked like the helmet of a diving-suit without a face-plate.

The technician glanced at his watch again and became more animated. 'Time presses on. The dispatches you are to carry have already arrived. Now then. There are two reasons why we have to use live couriers to communicate with the time-fleets, and why those couriers have to be expendable. In the early days we tried other means – fast launches and one-man boats. But the time-drive is too bulky and expensive for such an application, especially if it is to have sufficient speed. So we evolved the method that will propel you. A massive generator will build up tremendous potential; that energy will be used to catapult you through the strat at high speed – much faster even than a battleship can move – and will give you sufficient momentum to reach your destination.

'At first this method was tried out on unmanned missiles and even men in strat suits, but they would not do. The missiles got lost without a hand to guide them through the strat's turbulence. A strat suit falls down on several counts: it's bulky and so raises the energy requirement, its batteries would be able to maintain an ortho field only over short journeys anyway, and in any case using a strat suit defeats the whole object of the exercise because a courier needs to see the strat with his own eyes. It might work if we could include a scan screen such as a timeship has, but the weight of that would be prohibitive.

'You will have *some* equipment with you, which will help you steer yourself towards your target. But what all this means is that for a while you're going not just to *see* but to *live* in nonsequential strat time: in four-dimensional and five-dimensional time. No one can tell you what that will be like. Nevertheless we have to train you as well as we can so you'll be able to carry out your task.'

The diving-helmet was lifted over Aton's head to rest on his shoulders on a harness of foam rubber. He was in darkness. The technician's voice came to him again, tinnily through the tiny earphones.

'The purpose of this apparatus is to familiarise you, however inadequately, with what you will see immediately on entering the strat. It's a mock-up, of course, since we cannot reproduce the real thing. The important thing for you to learn is how to keep your direction. Remember that reaching your destination is the only way you can ever leave the strat, and therefore *the only way you can ever die*. This, I assure you, will become your most vital concern.'

Suddenly Aton was assailed by an explosion of sense impressions. So meaningless were they that they seemed to be pulling each of his eyes in separate direction. He closed his eyes for a few moments, but when he opened them again the barrage had increased in intensity. A steady bleeping sound was in his ears.

He felt as though he was swaying back and forth.

Eventually he began to glimpse recognisable shapes that emerged out of the welter of images and just as quickly vanished again. At this point the technician's voice entered again and in persuasive tones provided a running commentary.

The ordeal continued for about half an hour. The technician taught him how to know when he had changed direction from his appointed course and how to correct it with the equipment he would be given. At last the helmet was lifted from his head and the restricting straps unfastened. Somewhat disoriented, Aton rose.

'Well, you seem to have got the hang of it,' the technician announced.

'Half an hour's training? You really think that is enough?' Aton asked in a blurred voice.

'Perfectly. Your mission is not too *difficult*. Merely harrowing.'

Aton was trying to form an idea that had just occurred to him. 'Why … do we have to die?'

The other looked at him, puzzled. 'You are condemned men.'

'I know that. But why such an elaborate method? Oh, I know the practical reason for the hypnotic conditioning: men of the Time Service should not have to dirty their hands by executing condemned criminals. So the criminals have to do it themselves. But why are you so careful to ensure that the couriers should die *after only one trip*? Why not use them again? It seems to me that their usefulness is not finished.'

The technician looked thoughtful and withdrawn. 'There is no doubt, a reason,' he murmured. 'Frankly, I do not know what it is. But everything has a reason. I never heard of anyone going into the strat twice.'

'The fleet commanders have strict orders not to allow a courier to live after arrival, not even for a few hours. Why? What would be the harm?'

'An act of mercy, perhaps.' The technician glanced up at a winking light on the wall. 'It's time to fit you out.'

A section of wall slid aside. Aton, the two guards at his back, followed the technician into a narrow circular tunnel that sloped sharply downward. They emerged after a few minutes into a place totally unlike the clinical briefing-room Aton had just left. It was a large area with walls of flat, grey metal. A heavy droning hum came from an incredible array of equipment that took up the further end of the space.

The power of the droning sound struck right into Aton's bones. He gazed briefly at a large circular metal hatch that was clamped to the far wall with bolts and fitted with view windows. Then he was being tugged to one side where white-coated men eyed him speculatively.

A hoarse shout made him look to the other end of the room. A bizarrely accoutred figure was being dragged struggling towards the metal hatch. The man wore what appeared to be a tray, or small control board, extending outwards from his waist. His face was obscured by a rubber breathing-mask, and his body was criss-crossed with straps. Alongside the trio of prisoner and guards, contrasting with their exertions, paced the calm figure of a comforter, sprinkling holy wine from an aspersorium.

The muffled shouts grew more desperate as the disc of steel swung open. With practised skill the courier was eased inside and the hatch bolts screwed tight.

'That's more commonly the manner of their exit,' the technician remarked to Aton. 'I may say I find it a pleasure to be dealing with someone who has more nerve.'

Aton ignored the praise. The humming sound swelled, grew to climactic proportions, then ended in a noise like a prolonged lightning strike, accompanied by a vivid flash from within the dispatch chamber.

A singing silence followed. For some moments the air was charged with energy.

The technicians began to equip Aton for his journey. First the dispatch case was strapped to his chest. Then came the tray-like control panel, fastened around his waist so as to bring its knobs within easy reach of his hands.

During the session under the simulator Aton had been told that he would be aware of his proper course by reason of something mysteriously described as 'like a wind blowing in your face'. This wind represented his initial momentum. The control tray was a device acting like a rudder; it would enable him to guide himself along his course like a speedboat.

He felt the prick of hypodermic needles as stimulative drugs were pumped into his veins. An oxygen mask and earphones were added.

The comforter appeared by his side and began to murmur words he could scarcely hear. He felt the cold touch of drops of wine. He was ready.

The steel hatch swung open.

As he was propelled unresistingly towards the hatch and glimpsed the narrow rivet-studded chamber it guarded, a fog seemed to dissipate from his mind. Suddenly, and for the first time, he understood clearly and vividly just what was happening to him.

And he understood why!

His amnesia lifted like a curtain. He recalled the terrible events on board the *Smasher of Enemies*: his discovery of heresy within his command, the repeated savage hammer blows sustained by the ship, and Sergeant Quelle in a strat suit striding along surrounded by fellow heretics.

The rest was plain. Who had put him aboard the life raft he did not know – his memory ended some time before that – but evidently the heretics had reached the raft too. They must have suffered agony to realise that once they were rescued Aton could denounce them, and his subsequent amnesia must have seemed almost miraculous to them. They had taken full advantage of it, bringing their false charges against him so as to rid themselves of a potential accuser. A desperate, daring manoeuvre.

And what had caused Aton's loss of memory? *A glimpse of the strat.*

Would he recognise it a second time?

He turned, about to say something even as he realised that it was too late now to offer the truth. But he was given no time to speak. They bundled him through the circular hatch and swiftly screwed it up behind him.

He stood in a replica of the standard octagonal execution chamber. Death seemed to seep visibly into the cramped space from the leaden walls, which gave the appearance of being several feet thick. There was a peculiar tension in the air he had experienced only once before: when he had helped to remove the protective shields from an operating time-drive to effect emergency repairs.

A face peered in at him through the view window, distorted and blurred by the immensely thick plate. As the powerful generators swung into action a drumming noise assailed Aton, making the walls vibrate. The noise built up, deafening him. Despite the oxygen mask a feeling of suffocation seized him. He felt as though he had been seized by a giant hand that squeezed, squeezed, squeezed –

And then a numbing blow hit him on all sides at once and the chamber vanished. He had the impression of being shot forward at tremendous speed as though out of the mouth of a cannon.

Utter darkness. Blinding light. Which was it?

It was neither. It was whirlpools of the inconceivable. It was visions which the eye accepted but which the brain found unrecognisable: reality without the sanity that made reality real. The brain reacted to these visions with terror and dwindled in on itself to seek refuge in death or unconsciousness. Such sanctuary was denied Aton, however. The drugs that coursed in his blood pre-empted the closing down of the mind and condemned it to full alertness.

Yet alongside this jarring shock was a start of recognition. He *remembered* it now. This was what he had seen for a bare instant aboard the *Smasher of Enemies*.

Aton went reeling and spinning on a five-dimensional geodesic. There was no point of comparison to the space or time that he knew. The wind of the strat blew against his face like a cloying mist composed of ghostly pseudo-events, and whenever it ceased or lessened, his hands went instinctively to the control knobs at his waist.

But this phase, in which his mind still clung to its allegiance to passing time, lasted only seconds. Then the continuum of the strat seeped into his every cell and time ceased.

Eternity began, and Aton's sanity disintegrated.

Luckily one did not need to be sane to accomplish one's mission. One needed to know that there was an escape, that one could die. One needed to know that failure would mean to sink endlessly into the strat.

Therein lay the cunning of the courier system. Neither the senses nor the intellect could understand the environment in which they found themselves, but some primeval instinct enabled the mind to find a direction. The courier strove with all his being to reach the distant receiving station where he would be permitted to stop his heart.

Until that goal was attained, Aton lived in a world that was timeless. He could not measure the duration of his journey either in seconds or in centuries, because there *was* no duration. There could be no such thing as duration without a before and an after, and in this state nothing preceded and nothing followed. He skirled and spun. He went through titanic processes where five-dimensional objects menaced him as though they were living beings, but nothing began and nothing ended.

After a while his brain seemed to revive and to attempt to recover its old mode of perception. It was, he realised, beginning to come to terms with the five-dimensional strat and to abstract three-dimensional worlds from it.

Captain Mond Aton lived his life over again, beginning with conception and ending with his being sealed into the dispatch chamber at Chronopolis. After that, everything was just a vague shadow.

The illusion – could it be called an illusion? – was absolutely real. Every incident, every pleasure, every pain, and every effort exercised his soul anew. And not merely once. His life became like a film strip and was run through hundreds, thousands, millions of times over. The continued, reiterated experience became unbearable.

Interspersed with this continual re-enactment were other experiences that were more or less intelligible. At first he thought he had somehow been dumped back into orthogonal time in a different body and a different life. But soon he realised that the dreamlike episodes that so much resembled events in the real world were phantoms: mock-ups located in the strat. The strat was eternity. And eternity, as he had learned at training college, was the storehouse of potentialities. Somewhere in this vast insubstantial ocean were mock-ups of everything existing in orthogonal time, as well as of every fictitious variation of what existed. And also there were mock-ups of that which did not exist but which could be thrown up into the world like flotsam on a beach by some convulsion of the strat.

After enduring all this for millenniums, or microseconds, an odd feeling of strength came over Aton. The strat was no longer so strange to him. It was as if *he himself* was transforming into a five-dimensional being. He was able to look down on his life as an entirety and give his attention to any part of it.

Sequential time would seem, after this, flat and narrow. But his fingers still moved over the steering controls. His mind still strove to release itself in the only way possible.

His target, a fleet of timeships, loomed ahead of him. Protected by their own orthogonal time-fields they stood out clearly as glowing solid bodies surrounded by the swirling strat. Aton's earphones were beeping as he came within range of the homing signal.

Then he whirled around as something darted in suddenly from one side. It was the image of a man, which he saw sometimes as a three-dimensional figure and sometimes as a four-dimensional extension. The man was burly, bedecked like a stage magician in a flowing cloak and coloured hose. In place of eyes his sockets were filled with glittering, flashing jawels. He grinned wolfishly at Aton, at same time directing a bazooka-like tube from which issued a billowing exudation.

The purple mist struck Aton like a physical force. He felt his whole body vibrate; he veered aside to avoid the attack.

The intruder lunged at him again. Hissing, the bazooka tube went into action for a second time, and Aton saw that what it actually did was to distort the substance of the strat. With alarm he felt himself being sucked into the turbulence; he worked his rudder controls frantically.

Then both the apparition and the strat fled. He stood limply in a steel-clad chamber identical to the one he had left an eternity ago, and a loud humming noise filled his ears.

Just before the grinning jewel-eyed man had pounced Aton had recognised the galleon-like battle wagon that was to receive him. As irony would have it, the ship was Commander Haight's *Lamp of Faith*.

FIVE

Exhausted with fear and fatigue, Inpriss Sorce collapsed with a sigh on to a rickety couch. She pushed straggled hair out of her eyes and looked around the cheap, dismal room she had just rented.

The two weeks since she had escaped from Chronopolis had nearly driven her insane.

It was lucky she had taken the satchel containing money and bank cards from her apartment in Kell Street, otherwise she would have been completely helpless. Her one thought had been to flee as far away as possible. Everyone knew that once the Traumatic sect had chosen someone for sacrifice they would do everything possible to track the victim down and complete the rite.

Briefly it had occurred to her to go to the police with her story, but she had heard of people who had done that … only to be sacrificed by Traumatics inside the police force once they were taken into protective custody. The vision of some stone cell from which she could not escape filled her with claustrophobic panic.

No. The only answer was flight. To hide, to become too small to be noticed.

Only it was so difficult! This was already her third hiding place since quitting the eternal city, and the third time she had changed her name. The first move had been to a town barely fifty miles from Chronopolis, and for a few hours her eagerness to be safe had fooled her into thinking that she *was* safe. Then, coming home to her new apartment, she had spotted the two men who had tortured her, walking down the street and glancing up at the houses one by one.

And so she had had to leave, after only one day. But that had not been the end of it. She had left Amerik and gone to Affra, but they had followed. By good chance she had caught glimpses of them several times and so had been warned – in the jetliner passenger lounge and hanging around the transit and accommodation centres. And so finally, not caring about the expense, she had taken several jetliner trips in quick succession, zigzagging about the globe to shake off pursuit before retreating here to an old, out-of-the-way city in the middle of Worldmass.

Besides the two men she knew – Stryne and Velen, they had called each other – how many others she would not recognise had kept watch for her and hunted her down using all the methods that could be used to find a person? By now she had become afraid of everyone and everything.

She wondered if it was possible to live with terror indefinitely.

Idly her thoughts turned to the Church. Could a comforter help her? But churches would be dangerous places to approach. The sect could be watching. As it was, for the first time she felt some relief. Virov was well off the main routes and this tiny room, in a back street away from the main thoroughfares, had a closed-in, cupboard-like feeling. The narrow window admitted no direct sunlight at any time of the day and that, too, gave her a perverse feeling of safety, as if it was a room the world could not see.

She would get a job, would survive somehow. She would make no friends for years to come.

She opened the window and relaxed with the sound of the breeze and with Virov's quaint, well-melded odours.

Then she heard a nervous, tuneless humming from the other side of the door. Mmmmmmmmmm …

With a fear-stricken cry she flung herself against the door, trying with her body to hold it closed. Her slight frame was far from sufficient to resist the force that pushed it open from the other side.

The feral-faced Stryne moved into the room, followed by Velen.

'Nice to see you, Inpriss. Let's carry on where we left off, shall we?'

For an hour they enjoyed themselves with her, going through the ceremonies slowly. The hologram screen pounded out a sensuous, sinister mood, showing Hulmu in a playful aspect and filling the room with weird light. They went through the litanies that reminded Inpriss Sorce of what awaited her soul in the depths of the strat, where Hulmu would use her for his own purposes, and they urged her to forsake and vilify the false god of the Church.

After the Sporting of Shocks, where mild electric currents were applied to various parts of the body at random, they decided to carry out the Ritual of Mounting. First Stryne had intercourse with her and then Velen, while they both chanted the Offering of Orgasm.

Panting and sighing with satisfaction, they paused for a while, looking down at the glazy-eyed woman.

'That's enough for here,' Stryne said. 'They want to finish the rituals in the local temple.'

'We have to move her?'

Stryne nodded.

Velen frowned petulantly. 'Why didn't you tell me before? I thought this was going to be our show.'

Stryne shrugged. 'They have some special equipment they want to use. It will be spicy. Come on, help me get her ready.'

'Now listen, lady,' Stryne said when they had dressed her and put her on her feet, 'we're going to take a short walk. Act normal and don't try to scream for help, because we'll only use a narco-spray on you and get you there any-way.' He shoved her satchel into her hand. 'Right, let's move.'

Velen had finished packing their equipment into his tool-box. They went down the wooden stairs and out on to the street, which was overhung with tall silent houses and wound down a steep incline.

Inpriss walked as if in a dream. The air was heavy. Virov was a city totally unlike Chronopolis. Thick scents cloyed along its antique streets and alleys: the smell of coffee, of spices, of exotic blossoms. In other circumstances she would have liked it here.

Perhaps she could commit suicide, she thought wildly. Killing herself would be one way of saving herself from whatever horrible thing it was the Traumatics would do to her soul at death. Would she have the opportunity? But then she remembered that if she succeeded in dying free from their attentions, her soul would travel back in time and she would live her life again.

Would it end with this same nightmare? A curious thought occurred to her. If the Traumatics gave her soul to Hulmu she would not repeat. Inpriss Sorce would vanish from ordinary time. Did that mean that the Traumatics had never before, in her previous repetitions, threatened her? She tried to imagine what kind of life stretched ahead of her without their intervention.

Or had they always chosen her for a victim? And had she always cheated them by committing suicide? The eternal recurrence of this nightmare was, in itself, a horrible thing to contemplate.

They emerged on to one of the town's main concourses, close to the bazaar, and walked past open-fronted shops, many of them selling handmade wares. The street was quite crowded. Stryne and Velen stuck close to her, one en each side. Stryne nudged her warningly whenever she faltered.

Suddenly a commotion erupted from a side street. A gang of brawling youths swayed and spilled on to the sidewalk. Inpriss felt herself jostled and pushed roughly aside. A bottle narrowly missed her face and thudded on the head of a ginger-haired young man who was punching someone else in the stomach.

Stryne clutched at her with a snarl, and then, with a feeling of wonder-ment, Inpriss realised that she had been separated from her captors. Bewildered, unable to make sense out of the noise and confusion, she strug-gled through a tangle of violent bodies. Something struck her a blow on the face.

Uncertainly she stood for a moment on the edge of the crowd. She caught a glimpse of Velen trying to ward off blows from an acned thug.

Then she ran and, unable to believe her freedom but exulting in it, ran and ran without pause.

*

The Internodal travel official was a pinch-faced man wearing a short peaked cap. He was circumspect when Inpriss tendered her application and read it slowly while rapping his fingers on the desk.

'The travel quotas have been cut down, citizeness,' he told her coldly, 'due to the hostilities.' He peered closer at the form. ' "Reason for journey: migration." You intend to live in Revere?'

'Yes.'

'Why?'

'I just –' Inpriss wrung her hands. She hadn't known it would be like this.

She had got out of Virov in disguise, buying a ticket on a charabanc, and had tried to settle in a smaller town a few hundred miles away. But the Traumatic sect had caught up with her again!

For the third time she had escaped, again by a lucky accident. Her tormentors hadn't known there was a back way out of the house, through a door hidden by a curtain. A few minutes after their arrival they had left her alone for a moment to carry in a box. She had slipped away.

To escape three times! It seemed miraculous to Inpriss. Perhaps God was helping her, she thought, but she couldn't depend on miracles. It had become plain that the Traumatics could find her in any part of the world. Only one other recourse was open: to flee into the future and hope that the Traumatics could not, or would not, pursue her down the centuries. She had returned to Chronopolis with the intention of boarding a chronliner.

But it was dangerous and more difficult than she had anticipated. To obtain a permit to leave Node 1 she had to use her real name. And the official was proving obstructive.

'I *have* to leave,' she pleaded desperately. 'There are some people I have to get away from!'

The official looked at her expectantly.

She fumbled in her satchel. 'Look, this is all I have, except for the fare. Five hundred notes. I'll land in Revere with nothing.'

She laid the money on his desk. The official coughed, then began shuffling his papers, tidying up the desk. When he had finished, the money had magically vanished.

'It's not really in order … but I think I can stretch a point for a charmer like you.' He winked at her, his manner suddenly cheery and patronising in a way that filled her with disgust.

He filled out her travel permit and she hurried to the offices of Buick Chronways, one of the three commercial enterprises that had imperial charters for internodal services. There was a chronliner due to leave in a few hours, and she spent the remaining time walking the streets, keeping always to busy places.

It was dark by the time she went to the big terminus. As she passed through the barriers and set off down the long boarding ramp she could see the chronliner towering up out of its well. It had none of the grey-clad grimness of the military vessels of even greater size. Though of the same general design, it was covered name brightwork and along the flank of its upper storey the name *Buick* stood out in flowing, graceful letters.

With a rush of hope, feeling the press of the crowd around her, she moved towards the humming timeship.

SIX

The crew of the receiving chamber took Aton out of it quickly, silently, and efficiently.

They entered wearing strat suits, because the chamber was always partially energised in readiness for any couriers that might be en route. Once through the, hatch Aton was relieved of his equipment: the tray like rudder control, the oxygen mask, and the earphones. The dispatch case they left strapped to him. No one could handle that but the commander whose duty it was to accept all messages from a courier personally.

Aton, meantime, stood staring blankly with arms akimbo, not speaking, not moving.

Two ensigns came up to either side of him and took a light grip of his upper arms. A door slid open. They urged him forward. They were used to this detail. For a while newly arrived couriers were quite helpless, were scarcely able to keep their balance, bumped into walls, could not find their way through doors.

Dimly Aton sensed all around him the regular activity of the gigantic flagship, which was much bigger than the destroyers he was familiar with.

Steadily they mounted through the pile of decks and storeys, riding on elevators and moving corridors. The chronmen they passed flicked one glance at Aton, then looked away. Everyone was embarrassed to stare at a man who had just died, and was about to die again.

Aton's consciousness seemed to have retreated a long way from his perceptions, as though in using his senses he was looking the wrong way through a telescope. At the same time everything had a curiously flat, two-dimensional appearance to him. In the strat his mind had begun to accustom itself to four-dimensional, even five-dimensional figures. By comparison the three-dimensional world was weirdly listless, a series of simplified cartoons drawn on paper. No depth. Sounds, too, were flat and empty, without resonance.

He was feeling an urge to leave this paper world. To complete the process that had begun with his being discharged from the dispatch chamber.

To die.

They came to the officers' quarters in the upper reaches of the timeship. Aton recognised hints of comfort that would have been out of place aboard his own *Smasher of Enemies* or even aboard most battleships. Then they went through some double doors into an area displaying real, though modest, luxury, such as would not be found anywhere in the Time Service except in one of the great flagships.

It was Commander Haight's private suite. They halted before a walnut door carved with simple designs. The ensigns knocked, entered, saluted, and departed. Aton faced his former commanding officer.

Haight, sitting at a mahogany table, looked at him gloomily, broodingly. From a replayer in a corner came quiet, moody music, viols and trombones convoluting a web of melancholy calm.

Standing near Haight was a man Aton knew as Colonel Anamander. Like Haight he had the granite impassivity common to many senior officers in the Time Service, but his features were more amenable, slightly less uncompromising.

Haight lifted a hand in a half-hearted gesture. 'Later, Colonel.'

'Yes, sir.' Anamander skirted around Aton and exited.

The commander rose and approached Aton, who stared straight ahead, the muscles of his face slack. As if he were an inanimate object Haight unstrapped the dispatch case from his chest and carried it to the table.

Before opening it he glanced up at Aton again and suddenly his eyes narrowed in recognition.

'Captain Aton, is it not?'

After a long pause Aton forced his larynx into action. 'Sir,' he croaked feebly.

'Captain Aton,' Haight repeated sourly to himself. 'An extraordinary case. One that surprised and distressed me a good deal. I have wondered if you would end up here.'

Aton found his voice. 'Am I to terminate my life now, sir?' He waited expectantly for Haight to pronounce the releasing words.

'Wait until I am ready,' snapped the commander. He eyed Aton calculatingly, then sat down and broke the seals on the dispatch case.

For what seemed like a long time he studied the papers he found within, and outwardly became oblivious of Aton's presence. The viols and trombones pursued each other unendingly through winding, cloying themes, and listening to the music, Aton found himself drifting back to a seemingly stratlike state. There was no before or after. The intricate melody hung on the air like a perfume and Aton stood stock-still in an eternal moment, unable to locate the transition between one note and another.

Commander Haight jutted out his lower lip as he finished studying the papers. He laid them aside, frowning. Then he leaned back in his chair. His grey eyes settled on Aton's face, concentrating there with an almost obsessive interest.

'The dispatches originate from the emperor himself,' he announced gruffly. 'The raid into Hegemonic territory is to take place. And the *Lamp of Faith*, no less, is to conduct the mission. That, surely, is a measure of its importance.'

Aton said nothing and Haight continued, his eyes never leaving the other's face. 'Do you realise how successful the Hegemonics' attacks have been over the past week or two? Cities and regions eliminated or mutated. At Node Five the entire continent of Australos was altered. It is now peopled by tribes of Stone Age aborigines. Even worse, there are numerous cases of causal discontinuity. You know what that can do to the fabric of time. The work of the Historical Office is being set at naught. And all due to the Hegemonics' new weapon, the time-distorter. Once our scientists had called such a device impossible. Now –' He spread his hands.

His gaze became heavy, penetrating. 'Speak, Captain Aton,' he said in a deep voice. 'Tell me what it is like in the strat.'

Aton blinked and stuttered. 'It is – it is –'

He fell silent.

Haight nodded. 'I know that it is beyond description. And yet something could be described. Words are never entirely useless. Try to collect your thoughts. To remember. Take possession of yourself once again. Speak, Captain.'

Aton struggled, then said, 'Sir, should I terminate my existence now?'

'Ah, you wish to obey your orders and escape this realm. And it is my beholden duty to see that you do. Yet I could not tell you how many times I have been tempted to forget my duty at these moments. There is a comforter at the Imperial Palace – Brother Mundan is his name – whose father fell into the strat some years ago, following a collision between timeships. Mundan cannot forget the strat since then. He dreams of it, has nightmares about it, tries to imagine what the Gulf of Lost Souls is like. After a lifetime in the service I am filled with a similar curiosity.'

The drift of Haight's speech came through only faintly to Aton.

'Most of the couriers who stand before me are, of course, low types,' the commander continued. 'Mentally degenerate, hopeless cases. But you, I tell myself, are of different mettle. Despite your astonishing dereliction, you are presumably a disciplined officer. Given time, you might recover your senses. You might be able to answer my questions.'

He lumbered to his feet, walked around the polished table, and stood close to Aton, peering straight into his eyes. 'On this occasion I think I will commit a dereliction of my own. At such a time – for in my opinion the raid has little chance of succeeding, it is suicide – a small peccancy will go unnoticed. No, Captain Aton, you are not to die now. You are to live, to recover, and perhaps to tell me what you have experienced.' He turned and pressed a button.

'This is Captain Aton,' he said to the two batmen who entered at his summons. 'See that he is made comfortable in the guest bedroom. But do not allow him to leave this suite.'

Blood was pounding in Aton's veins as he was led away. This turn of events went entirely against his indoctrination. He felt his nerves falling apart as the death wish, thwarted of its expectation, began to burn up his brain.

Planning the raid occupied Commander Haight and his staff for a whole day.

The information contained in Aton's dispatch was less precise than might have been hoped for. The base from which the Hegemonics carried out their attacks when using the distorter was named, but there was very little guidance as to where on the base it was kept or on what would be found there.

To raid an operational military base was a requirement of no mean order, which was the reason why the Lamp of Faith had been selected even at the risk of losing the flagship. It had the speed, the firepower, and could carry a sufficient number of fighting men to hold the base for a short while.

For there was even more at stake than the increasingly unstable situation within the empire. The Historical Office was determined to acquire a sample of the time-distorter before the Hegemonics, overwhelmed by the might of the armada, decided to destroy it. Possession of the distorter, or rather of the principle by which it worked, opened up limitless possibilities for the easy restructuring of history.

Aton, meanwhile, spent the time lying on his bed and staring at the ceiling. Gradually his mind began to clear. Little by little he felt as though he was being reinserted into the world of orthogonal time. But he still behaved like a robot or a zombie. The batmen brought him meals; he ate nothing. They asked if he wanted anything; he made no answer.

He felt as though his body was made of dead flesh, his mind of dead thoughts.

Eventually Commander Haight walked into his room unannounced. 'Well, how are you feeling?' he demanded gruffly.

Aton was silent.

Haight walked over to him and peered down. He poked Aton in the chest, as though making sure he was still alive. He grunted.

'I'm no psychologist. God knows what those hypnotic commands will do to you while I'm fouling up the programme. Still, even that should be interesting to watch.' Haight sighed. 'You know, I'm curious to know why couriers *have* to die. Something of a mystery surrounds it. The instructions are very strict – I'll be in serious trouble if this business gets back to Chronopolis – but nobody will tell you the reason. As far as I'm able to ascertain, it's a Church secret.'

He paused thoughtfully. 'I'm tired of seeing you in that convict's garb. Let's go the whole hog.' Turning his head he let out a bellow.

'Sturp!'

Instantly one of the batmen appeared. 'Sir?'

'Go and fetch a captain's uniform somewhere, to fit Aton here.' He threw himself into a deep chair. 'Maybe it will help you get your bearings,' he remarked, 'if the cloth of the service doesn't unnerve you. Tell me, do you feel any disgrace over what you did?'

'Did?'

'Shooting down your own men! Deserting your ship!' Haight was in an aggressive mood. His face went slightly purple as he roared the accusations at Aton.

'No, sir.' He strove to recall the events he should feel ashamed of, but for the moment could not.

Haight leaned forward earnestly. 'The strat,' he urged. 'Try to describe it now.'

Aton looked up at the ceiling. His mouth opened and closed. He licked his lips.

'One sees one's life, not as a process, but as an object,' he said. 'Something that can be picked up, handled, re-moulded like a piece of clay.'

Haight laughed shortly.

'Would you like to die?' he asked after a moment.

'Yes.'

'*Why?*'

'When you have lived through your life millions, billions of times in every detail, the purpose of living is exhausted. There is nothing left that's new. One wants only to forget, to find oblivion; that way, if one must live again, one will not realise it's for the billionth time. It will seem new.'

'Death is the only positive experience remaining?'

'One has been cheated. Death is an event; once begun it should be completed. Mine was only partial death. It yearns to be complete. I must die naturally, so as to forget.'

Haight mulled over his words. 'Mm. It seems that our couriers are more fortunate, after all, than the poor chronmen who drown in eternity when their ships go down.' He shot Aton a look of contempt. 'What is the strat? How would you describe it?'

'It is a place of terror.'

With a slightly bleary look Haight climbed to his feet. 'Don't be too sure you've seen the last of it. We move out in an hour. I'm going to get some rest till then.'

The big man padded away. Aton had remained motionless throughout the exchange. He continued to stare at the ceiling, where by some projective trick of the imagination various incidents of his life were being played out before his eyes.

Big as a city block, the step-storeyed *Lamp of Faith* moved through the eternal geodesics of the strat like a glimmering shadow. Riding in support were three escort ships of the destroyer class, designated as expendable in Commander Haight's despairingly realistic battle plan.

Beyond Node 7 the formation hurtled into the no-man's-land separating the empire from the Hegemony: a great uninhabited wilderness of over a hundred years' duration. Once the squadron was futureward of the imperial forward alert posts, the destroyers shot ahead of the larger flagship. It was here, where the entire Earth was a radioactive desert, that the Hegemony's beta-radar stations would probably pick them up.

Given sufficient warning the Hegemonics might try to set up time-blocks. These installations, though costly and requiring effort and skill, could bring a timeship travelling in excess of a certain velocity to a savage halt, precipitating it into orthogonal time where it was vulnerable. For this reason a timeship usually moved cautiously if it was suspected that a block was being attempted. Yet the *Lamp of Faith* needed to move fast to arrive at its target with any chance of success.

On the bridge, Commander Haight did not allow himself the luxury of personal feelings. His fatalistic gloom was relegated to the closed corners of his mind as he brought the full force of his attention to bear on the operation in hand.

He had already received the precombat blessings of the Church. The comforter still moved about the bridge asperging each man in turn. As he traversed the room from end to end his cowled figure changed size dramatically due to velocity contraction. In the nose of the ellipsoid he was barely a foot tall.

A gong sounded. The scanman spoke.

'Enemy approaching. Two items.'

Presently the louvred wedge shapes of the Hegemonic ships appeared on the swirling strat screen. They hovered and turned close by the flagship looking like prismatically cascading towers, showering images of themselves as they kept pace.

'Release torpedoes,' ordered Haight automatically.

The torpedoes trundled away without hitting their targets.

'They are offering tryst, sir,' the beta operator informed him.

'Ignore.'

The second beta operator spoke up urgently. 'Sir, I think *Incalculable* has gone ortho!'

'Full speed astern!' roared Haight.

Their stomachs lurched as the *Lamp of Faith* decelerated fiercely. The nose of the bridge ballooned in size; the pilot was near normal, height.

The three destroyers had been strung out ahead of the flagship in a staggered echelon. *Incalculable*, the leading vessel, had clearly run into a time-block.

Although the destroyer had probably been annihilated by now, in an instantly withering barrage of fire, the success of his ploy occasioned Commander Haight a grim satisfaction. The two remaining destroyers – *Song of Might* and *Infuriator* – had, like the *Lamp of Faith*, managed to check their speed in time. Slowly the depleted formation cruised through the block region. Instruments on the bridge flicked and pinged as they registered the blocking field, which was designed to retard the c-plus velocity of pi-mesons in a moving ship's time-drive, thus preventing the passage through time.

The steady thrum of the time-drive changed to a lower pitch. Even at their present speed, too slow for its relativistic field to be efficacious, the block had a damping effect.

Then they were suddenly through it and were picking up speed again.

And now they had passed beyond the Century of Waste and were into the territory of the Hegemony. Their journey now would be short. The Hegemony, unlike the empire, comprised only one node – did not extend over the entire Earth's surface, in fact. Indeed, as far as was known, only the empire imposed its authority on other centuries. No similar grand design had been detected anywhere in the future.

In terms of history, the Hegemony began at the fringes of the Century of Waste and continued for about a hundred years up to its domestic node, and for a similar period after that. By the time of the succeeding node (Node 10 by imperial reckoning) it appeared to have changed its political character and no longer called itself the Hegemony. What it would call itself after receiving the empire's attentions was, at this point, a matter of speculation.

'Several enemy vessels converging,' said the scanman.

'Ignore.'

They would be subject to a considerable number of interception attempts from now on. The pilot was busy tracking the *Lamp of Faith* through the multidimensional continuum in a preplanned zigzag. The manoeuvre had two purposes: to render more difficult any further stopping exercises by means of time-block and to disguise the ultimate target.

The screen operator tried to get them a glimpse of what chronmen called 'the surface' – the orthogonal time-scape they were invisibly skimming through. This was occasionally possible by adroit handling of the scanning equipment. But on this occasion the strat defeated him. The roiling, multidimensional geodesics, the rapid course changes, turned the surface of reality, even though he managed to focus the instruments in that direction, into a senseless collage without one recognisable shard.

More important was the abstract metering that told them where they were. In the bowels of the ship was a device of extraordinary subtlety: an inertial navigator capable of noting and computing shifts of position on a six-dimensional scale. Without this gadget to make a timeship free of reliance on surface-based reference points, the operation of warships would have been quite impracticable.

As the minutes ticked by tension in the bridge became almost unbearable. Haight accepted readiness reports from all sections. Gunnery, commando, technical teams, were all pent up and waiting to go.

Wedge ships flew around them thick and fast. By now the Hegemonics knew that something was up. The Time Service had already carried out a few retaliatory raids on their bases and cities, but generally had been too busy trying to defend imperial history. The appearance of the mighty battle-wagon flagship on their territory probably came as an unpleasant surprise.

And, the nature of the strat being what it was, they had little chance to prepare. Warnings could not go ahead of them any faster than the *Lamp of Faith* itself travelled; even if the Hegemony used the courier system, which was doubtful, they would not have installed the expensive catapult apparatus midway between nodes. And they could not attack the intruders until they emerged into ortho.

A thought occurred to Haight. From the defenders' point of view he was now travelling on the incoming, attacking flight path. If the raid was to be successful and the *Lamp of Faith* to return home again, then somewhere in the strat must already be the outgoing homeward flight path with the flagship hurtling along it. That was one of the paradoxes of this business: that the strat contained every chronman's future, even though he himself could not determine what that future would be. Only in orthogonal time, and at the very nodes themselves, was time regarded as determinate.

'Base Ogop in scanner range!' announced the scanman excitedly.

Haight sounded the alerting klaxons. The elements of the operation were now coming to a climax. One of the beta operators, in touch, but barely, with the destroyer vanguard, was babbling reports and figures.

'*Song of Might* and *Infuriator* due for ortho in one minute five seconds. Our approach due in three minutes –'

Another operator broke into Haight's attention. 'Twelve Hegemonic ships harassing formation.'

Haight licked his lips. Down below the commandos and technical teams were pouring into their exit bays. The word for them to go would have to come from him. But first the approaching enemy ships, as well as Base Ogop's, defensive armament needed to be dealt with.

'How much weight have they got?'

The operator was studying his blips with a frown, glancing occasionally at the big strat screen. 'Three at least are of the Hegemonic Tower class. Most of the others look like the Ranger class.'

'Going ortho!' yelled the destroyers' linkman. The vicarious excitement of their exploit was upon him.

A sudden silence fell upon the bridge.

These were probably the most crucial few seconds of the whole enterprise. The destroyers *Song of Might* and *Infuriator* did have one advantage: they were not engaging in a tryst. They were emerging from the strat without warning and it would take the pursuing Hegemonic ships seconds or minutes to realise what had happened and follow suit. In that time the destroyers had to silence Base Ogop's guns, prevent any ships there from phasing into the strat, or at least do as much of all that as possible to soften up the approach for the *Lamp of Faith*.

'Report?' demanded Haight impatiently.

The linkman was intent upon his earphones. '*Infuriator's* drive crippled, severely holed, but armament intact. *Song of Might* undamaged.' He strained to hear what was being said. 'Base defences inoperable … five warships grounded … two got away.'

It was much better than he had feared. He nodded brusquely. 'Right. We're going in.'

A minute later the great ship phased into materialisation on the main yard of Base Ogop.

Every window on the exterior of the huge battle wagon tuned to transparency. The crew could see the shattered base all around them.

Haight surveyed the scene on the bridge's main monitor screen. They were parked on a yard perhaps half a mile in extent. Ringing it were buildings in a foreign, exotic style, some of them burning, others dashed to the ground. Nearer at hand were the wrecks of column-like timeships, either tumbled across the concrete or sagging and smoking.

Towering above it all was the mighty *Lamp of Faith*, vaster and more powerful than any timeship the Hegemony had built. It had crushed smaller vessels, trucks, and machinery beneath it as it settled its full weight on to the yard. With its rows and tiers of windows it would have looked in place lining the street of any major city, except for its beam projectors and torpedo tubes.

Scanning the environs, Haight spotted the *Infuriator* lying propped athwart a blockhouse, exactly like one building thrown on top of another. Further off, beyond the other side of the base, the *Song of Might* hovered in the air in a standoff position so as to provide the flagship with covering fire.

Haight picked up a microphone and sent his voice haranguing throughout the ship. At ground level, the port porches opened. Combat chronmen and technicians' surged through to take possession of Base Ogop, hurrying away from the timeship before the anticipated assault from the strat met it.

Less than half a minute later Hegemonic craft began to flick into existence. Within microseconds heavy-duty energy beams had been focused on them and they either exploded into flame or fled back into the strat to lick their wounds.

Colonel Anamander looked at the commander, his lips curling. A time-ship standing in orthogonal time had every advantage over one trying to attack it from the strat. It was not a tryst situation where each party was prevented by the rules of war from phasing out of the strat earlier than his antagonist and so pre-empting the appointed moment. This was like shooting ducks out of the air. They had simply to sit still and watch for ships to appear, focusing and firing before the enemy had a chance to do likewise.

Very soon the Hegemonics gave up the unequal fight. They were leaving it now for Base Ogop to be relieved by slower air and land forces.

Haight imagined those forces would start arriving in ten to twenty minutes. He reckoned on being able to hold the base for up to an hour. In that time the sample distorter would have to be found.

Reports began coming in. Fighting with the base staff. The technical teams going over the damaged ships, examining the workshops, questioning prisoners for some knowledge of the coveted weapon.

He controlled his impatience and sat stolidly, as if made of stone.

Fifteen minutes later radar reported strike aircraft converging from three directions. The *Lamp of Faith* lifted off the shipyard and hovered at two thousand feet. As the aircraft approached at supersonic speed their courses were tracked and plotted. At almost the same instant that the timeship released missiles to down them, the strike planes fired their own missiles. Those hurtling towards the *Lamp of Faith* were licked out of the sky by energy beams. The flagship's own projectiles found their targets. Somewhere beyond the horizon the attacking planes rained down in fragments.

There was a lull. Occasionally surveillance craft screamed overhead at a height of miles. Haight let them go. The time-ship could stave off any amount of missile attack. The real fight would begin when the enemy brought in their own energy beamers.

So far the technical teams had discovered nothing. Haight was becoming worried. Half an hour after their landing, huge vehicles appeared over the horizon, moving swiftly forward on what was probably an air-cushion principle. Large-aperture beamer orifices were plainly visible. Behind them came troop-carriers carrying, he estimated, thousands of men with full equipment.

He put the *Lamp of Faith* down on the ground again to lower its profile.

The blue flashes of high-energy beams began to criss-cross one another like swords. Molten metal ran down the sides of the *Lamp of Faith* as the beams slowly ate into the structure of the ship.

Then the exchange died down as the flagship's weapons put the Hegemonic beams out of action. But the respite could only be temporary. More and more projectors would be brought up until the ship's resources – and those of the two destroyers – were beaten down.

As it was, the *Infuriator* had been silenced and the *Song of Might* had only one projector operating. Haight gave orders for any survivors on the grounded ship to come aboard the flagship. *Song of Might* he sent back into the strat for its own protection.

'If we stay any longer, sir,' Colonel Anamander reminded him, 'we may not get away.'

He was referring to the possibility that the Hegemonics might be able to erect a time-block to prevent their escape pastward.

'My orders are perfectly explicit, Colonel,' Haight told him. 'We are to stay *until the distorter is found*, whatever that might mean.'

'Even if it means losing the *Lamp of Faith*?' Anamander seemed to find the notion incredible.

But Haight merely shrugged sardonically. 'Yes … so what if we do? We are all expendable.' His gaze flicked around him, as though he were able to look through walls and see his command in all its entirety. 'What of the *Lamp of Faith* – do you imagine the empire cannot manage without it? The Invincible Armada will include a thousand ships as good as this one.'

The ship lifted off again and drifted beyond Base Ogop's boundary to attack a concentration of projectors that was building up there. But it was forced to retreat. So many of its own beams were out of action that it was being outgunned, and while it left its central position, Hegemonic troops poured into the base to fight it out with the chron commandos.

The officer in charge of the technical teams spoke to Haight over a vidcom. His face was haggard with desperation.

'There's no distorter on the base, sir. We've been through everything.'

Haight cursed. 'There *has* to be one!' he snarled.

'Sir –'

The *Lamp of Faith* lurched. One corner of the ship hit the concrete with a huge crunching sound. Moments later the whole mass slammed down as the lifting engines cut out and the great vessel rocked from side to side.

'Should we phase out, sir?' questioned Colonel Anamander in a low voice.

'What did I just tell you, Colonel?' Haight growled. 'We don't leave until we are successful, and that comes from the emperor himself.'

Captain Mond Aton had been largely unaware of events taking place outside the small bedroom where he lay. But he felt the sudden lurch followed by the impact, and knew that the ship was losing power.

The knowledge provoked only slight interest in him. The batman had brought him a passably fitting uniform. He had donned it and inspected himself in a full length mirror.

For a moment it had made him think he was back aboard the *Smasher of Enemies*. Things had started clicking into place in his mind.

The room shifted in perspective and suddenly acquired depth. It glowed with new colour. He was no longer in an insubstantial two-dimensional world. He could understand his surroundings again.

Now he lay quietly, considering the remarkable situation he was in.

After a while other distant noises began to intrude into his consciousness. The hissing of energy beams biting deeper into the ship. The spit of beam pistols closer by.

He rose and went into the main lounge. As he did so, Commander Haight burst in and slammed the door behind him, a gun in his hand.

'What's happened?' Aton asked calmly.

Servants hurried into the room. Haight waved them away. He stepped to the large mahogany table and opened a panel in its top, turning a dial-like device this way and that.

Then he sat down at the table, his pistol pointing at the door, his free hand near the device, toying with a switch.

'We couldn't find a distorter,' he rumbled. 'Now the Hegemonics are all around us. The power has failed and our beams are gone. There's fighting inside the ship.'

'Is that a destruct device?' Aton asked, eyeing the switch.

Haight nodded. 'The one on the bridge doesn't work. A long time ago I had an additional one installed here.'

'Then what are you waiting for?' Aton inquired pointedly.

The commander grunted. 'The Hegemonics have offered a truce! It seems they want to talk to us, so I've agreed. Might as well hear what they have to say.'

'They are coming here?'

'Where else?'

Aton took a seat at the other end of the room. For some minutes they waited in silence.

At length there was the sound of footsteps and the door opened. Colonel Anamander entered. He surveyed the room and raised his eyebrows at Haight, who nodded.

Into the room came two tall slim men. They wore brocaded garments of yellow cloth that accentuated their slimness and gave them a formal elegance. The most striking feature of their apparel was their headgear: cylindrical hats over a foot high, surmounted by curved lips that projected forward for several inches.

Commander Haight kept his gun trained on them. 'Forgive me if I do not rise to make a proper greeting,' he said in a gravelly tone. 'Announce yourselves.'

One of the two stepped forward. He looked at Haight with none of the rancour that was evident in Haight's own expression.

'I am Minister Ortok Cray, and I am a member of the Ruling Council of

Saleem, which is, as you know, the faction which has hegemony in the federation you know as the Hegemony. And this –' he gestured to his companion '– is Minister Wirith Freeling, of the same council.'

Haight did not show his considerable surprise. 'I am privileged indeed,' he murmured. 'I am Commander Haight, a loyal servant of His Chronotic Majesty Philipium the First.'

Minister Ortok Cray glanced at Aton as if expecting to be introduced to him also. 'I can assure you that there is no need to threaten us with your weapons,' he told Haight. 'It is not our intention to trick you or even to capture your ship. It is our wish that, after making the necessary repairs for which we shall offer every assistance, you should return to Chronopolis and convey our sentiments to your master.'

The Hegemonic spoke with a drawling accent. Haight, however, used to the variegated dialects and languages of the empire, scarcely noticed its strangeness.

'Sentiments?'

Minister Wirith Freeling made an expansive gesture. 'I don't know if you are aware of how difficult communication between our two civilisations is made by religious differences. To a large extent our cultures are ignorant of each other – by far the greater ignorance, however, is on *your* side.'

Commander Haight was proud of, rather than insulted by, this ignorance. 'It is no part of our habits to pander to heathens.'

Ortok Cray sighed. 'But in the present circumstances, surely some intercourse would be advisable? As it is, the empire appears not even to know the elementary facts of the Hegemony's history.'

Commander Haight's opinion was that, once the Invincible Armada was launched, any conversation between the two would be extremely one-sided. It was true, of course, that no real study of Hegemonic culture had been undertaken, and such cultural contact as there had been had consisted of proselytising Church missionaries. He could not see that it was in the least important. But he laid down his gun.

'Come to the point.'

'We wish to end the war and come to an understanding based on co-existence.'

'Hah! You fear the armada.'

'Indeed. But do you not also have much to fear?' The mildness disappeared from Ortok Cray's face and Haight found himself confronting two men of steely determination.

'We have shown that we are ready to risk all to defend ourselves,' the Hegemonic leader continued. 'You know what the time-distorter can do. It is a weapon so terrible that, if it is employed without restraint, then the user stands in as much danger as the victim. That, no doubt, is why you have not made use of it against us. But our situation is so desperate that we will stop at nothing.'

Aton spoke up from the other side of the room. 'You had expected *us* to use the distorter?'

Haight glared at him in displeasure for the interruption. Ortok Cray turned to regard the young captain.

'It is, after all, an invention of the Chronotic Empire,' he said. 'Our acquisition of it is quite recent.'

'And just how *did* you acquire the distorter?' Haight grated. He and Anamander exchanged puzzled glances.

'That, naturally, I cannot tell you. The important thing is that we have it and will continue to use it. Furthermore, so far we have used it only at low power and with small aperture. If driven to it we will pull out all the stops. In no circumstances will we surrender. But we would prefer to live in peace. Surely you can see that this struggle is going to be a calamity for us both?'

'And you, of course, try to place the blame for the conflict squarely on us. That, I'm afraid, won't do. Long before the armada was thought of the empire was suffering from your armed incursions, your attempts to interfere with imperial chron integrity –'

'And we were suffering from the impudence of your missionaries,' retorted Wirith Freeling hotly. 'You evidently do not appreciate what your religious aggressiveness means to us. And apart from that, there was always your patent desire to see us as a part of your territories.'

Haight shrugged gloomily. 'Your intransigent attitude towards the true faith renders it a duty to bring you the light of the Church.'

'We have our own religion, the religion of the Risen Christos! We want none of your – of your –' Freeling was sputtering with indignant rage.

Ortok Cray raised a hand. 'Patience,' he murmured to his colleague. 'This is not the time for quarrels and recriminations. This is the time for explanation.'

He turned to face Haight once more. 'You complain of our earlier attempts to interfere with Chronotic history. But I wonder if you realise the reason behind those attempts? Our endeavours to make our case plain to your government at Chronopolis have always been thwarted, since your Church refuses to accept our representatives there.'

'Well, now I am your prisoner and you can say what you like.'

'Precisely. The point at issue concerns the Century of Waste. Our cultures are separated by a period of a hundred years when the Earth is uninhabitable. The origin of this is presumably known to you.'

'Some war in the hinterland of Node Seven,' said Haight reflectively. 'Node Seven is the empire's frontier. We have not yet consolidated ourselves in the stretch of time succeeding it. Indeed, it may be left for that to be accomplished by the natural advance of the node.'

'That's right: a war which left the Earth desolate. In point of fact this was established in orthogonal time well before time-travel was introduced at what you call, I believe, Node Six. But do you not see what this means? *During that war mankind was wiped out*. History came to an end at that point until, by some random movement in the strat, there was a historical mutation that led to the invention of time-travel. The future Earth was then colonised by migrants from the past. Thus it transpires that time-travel is the instrument of mankind's survival.'

'So? All this is recognised. Time-travel came as a gift from God, to redeem mankind from its own destruction. That is the entire basis of the true faith and the justification for the Chronotic Empire. You have told me nothing new.'

'Except that we do not regard the invention of time-travel as an act of God, but never mind about that. Do you not see the implications? The annihilation of mankind took place before the Chronotic Empire had begun to establish itself throughout time. The course of history was quite different then. The migration to the future took place when the empire began to expand – and more particularly when the Church of San Hevatar established itself as the one true church. Do you now see what I am getting at?'

Haight merely frowned, but the truth struck Aton forcibly. 'You are refugees!'

Ortok Cray nodded. 'We, or rather our ancestors, were religious dissidents who were driven out of the empire in the early days. We established ourselves here, beyond the empire's reach – at that time. Hence our proud independence and our dislike of your Church.'

'None of this explains your impudent forays into our territory,' complained Haight broodingly. 'If you wished to be left alone, why did you draw our attention to you?'

'Because the empire's hold on the structure of history is increasing,' Ortok Cray reminded him. 'We have every reason to fear the Historical Office. If nothing is done now, then in about fifty years' time the Hegemony will disappear from history.'

'How do you know that?' Aton said, puzzled, and ignoring his lack of entitlement to join in the discussion.

'Time is not static,' pointed out the Hegemonic minister. 'The nodes proceed forward at a steady rate, overtaking events that are already established in the future. If the node contains some Chronotic mutation or has been altered in some way, then events ahead of it will also change as it approaches. And this means that the Chronotic Empire, even while maintaining its fixed rear at the Stop Barrier, will continue to grow into the future – quite apart from further conquests by timeships. At the moment the events leading to the disastrous war that wiped out mankind are still intact. But Node Seven is already encroaching on them and eventually will overtake them. The Historical Office, naturally, will want to delete this war. There will be no general destruction, no Century of Waste.'

'A change we should all applaud, surely,' Aton commented. 'To annul such a terrible happening does not seem at all bad.'

'*We want the war to be fixed in time for ever.*'

They were all taken aback by the ferocity of the minister's words.

'If there is no war,' Ortok Cray continued quietly, 'if the Earth is not depopulated, then the disciples of the Risen Christos can have found nowhere to settle themselves on fleeing the persecutions of your Church – or, at best, can only have been absorbed into a more friendly population, whatever that population might be. The future will have a new, completely different history. The Hegemony will never have come into existence at all.'

Commander Haight came to his feet and paced the lounge, frowning. 'Once time-travel becomes an established fact of life such temporal upheavals become inevitable,' he commented. 'Only the continued existence of the empire is absolutely guaranteed. Yes, I can see that you have good cause to fear us.'

'We do not agree that the continued existence of the empire is a certainty,' Wirith Freeling snapped. 'The empire is contingent, like all other things existing in time. That *time-travel* cannot vanish, once having been invented, is true, no doubt, but not the empire. Time-travel came before the empire.'

'The two are indissolubly linked.'

'Let us not argue theology,' Ortok Cray put in. 'You have your religion, we have ours. We believe we can destroy your empire, even though we destroy ourselves in doing so. These are our demands: the Chronotic Empire must limit itself in time and must not intrude into the period containing the annihilatory war. You have a thousand years, be content with that. Let Node Seven continue without you, do not extend your authority beyond its current generation.'

Haight stopped short and looked at the two Hegemonics with controlled fury. 'Do you expect His Chronotic Majesty to agree to terms like that?'

'We wish him to examine the situation and to recognise the delicacy of our own position. Also, that the present course will destroy us both.'

'Then I will not answer you, since the answer belongs to His Majesty.'

Minister Ortok Cray acknowledged this with an inclining of his head.

'We would welcome a meeting between our respective representatives,' he said. 'Some arrangement tolerable to us both would be better than total war. If your side is willing to take part in talks, send a timeship broadcasting an appropriate message.'

'I will convey your requirements.' Haight's tone was sardonic, almost sarcastic.

'Then we thank you. Please let us know if you need anything to make your ship timeworthy. I think we can expect you to be on your way in, let us say, ten hours?'

Haight nodded. Ministers Ortok Cray and Wirith Freeling made some parting gesture that was strange to him, and swept sedately from the room.

When they had gone, Commander Haight stroked his chin for a few moments, then looked thoughtfully at Aton.

'I can see allowing you to wear the emperor's uniform has done the trick,' he said slowly. 'You are a veritable model of rationality.'

As Aton made no reply, Haight turned to Anamander. 'Well, our enterprise has come to a surprising conclusion, eh, Colonel?'

Seating himself at the table, he carefully deactivated the *Lamp of Faith*'s emergency self-destruct.

SEVEN

'It's hard to say what it is, or what it's like,' Aton muttered. 'There are really no words to describe it. All the words of our language refer to three-dimensional, orthogonal time.'

'Are the experiences still in your memory? Are they vivid?'

'Yes, but they tend to fade, to become … recast so as to resemble ordinary experiences. Such as what you might see on a strat screen.'

Commander Haight sighed deeply. 'That figures. A strat screen interprets the substratum in terms of sensory criteria. One might well expect the brain's memory banks to do the same.'

They were heading back towards Chronopolis, Node 1, accompanied by the *Song of Might*, and were already deep inside the empire's historical territory. Haight had been kept busy, first attending to repairs to the *Lamp of Faith* and then negotiating a homeward course, the journey to the frontier being under escort by a squadron of Hegemonic Tower-class ships. But the moment he had been able to take a rest from his duties he had hurried to his quarters to question Aton closely on the nature of the strat.

'Nothing has a single nature,' Aton said. 'Everything merges into everything else; there are a billion aspects to everything. Nothing exists as an object; all is flux and motion.'

'Hmmm.' Haight listened carefully to the words, fixing his gaze on Aton's face. It was as if he was trying to find in Aton's steady eyes some glimpse of what those eyes had seen.

He was somewhat disappointed by the results of his experiment. Aton's descriptions had been fairly lucid but resembled technical descriptions such as one might find in textbooks. They did not convey the *essence* of the experience.

Aton's return to normalcy was also something of a disappointment to him. He turned, stretched his weary limbs, then stepped to the cocktail bar and poured himself a stiff slug of gin. After brief hesitation he poured one for Aton too and pushed it across to him.

'I have not had my money's worth,' he said with a grim smile. 'Interfering with your hypnotic instructions should at least, I would have thought, have produced some interesting psychological disorder. But here you are as healthy as apple pie.' He reflected before knocking back his gin. 'Perhaps next time I should try an ordinary criminal type who will have no mental discipline.'

Aton had a question of his own. 'Commander, do you think the representations the Hegemonics have made to us will influence policy in Chronopolis?' His face wore a worried frown.

Haight looked at him in surprise. 'Don't be a fool, Captain. The emperor's will is inviolable.'

'But, sir –'

'I would probably not even bother to deliver such pathetic pleas,' Haight told him irritably, 'had not the Hegemonics inadvertently given us such valuable information at the same time. My orders were to seize the distorter or to sacrifice the mission in the attempt. But that business about its origins is most peculiar, don't you think? One can only think that there is high treason in the realm. The historical background to the Hegemony too, should prove most useful, though I should think the point about the advance of Node Seven is something the Historical Office is already alive to.' He gave a loud, braying laugh. 'See how invincible is the empire! No wonder the Hegemonics are in a panic. There's no way they can win!'

'In that case, would it not be advisable to hold back the armada, and gain our ends by subtler means?'

'That would not end the provocations of the Hegemony. It would only give them more time to work their mischief. And besides, the Church has declared the enterprise a holy crusade. The Church being infallible, its edicts cannot be reversed.'

Aton became depressed as he realised the inevitability of what Haight said.

'I shall report the full conversation to the emperor personally,' Haight mused. 'It will make little difference. Of greater interest is the news that the Hegemonics spring from our own dissidents. That, too, offers possibilities of eliminating the Hegemonics by tracking down these dissidents *before* they flee – though where time-travel's concerned such a course of action is not guaranteed to be effective. In any case I doubt that it will be considered.'

'Why not?'

'The Church wants converted souls, not annihilated souls. The purpose of the armada is to save men, not to destroy them.'

Aton brought himself to attention, aware of the import of what he was about to say.

'I agree with the Hegemonics, sir. The only important thing is that the war should be brought to a stop. We are headed on a course of mutual disaster.'

Haight, in the act of filling his glass again, glanced up sharply. 'You are way out of line, Captain. You have forgotten your role. *You have performed your duty.*'

As he performed the trigger phrase lifting the hypnotic block on the implanted death urge, Aton went dizzy. Something inside his mind struggled madly for expression. But he clamped down on it. There was a mental convulsion, a struggle. Then calm.

'What happened?' asked Haight softly.

Aton had closed his eyes. He opened them. 'You were supposed to keep me alive for not more than an hour. I've been here for more than three days. The death command has lost its force.'

'A hypnotic command should be permanent.'

'The hypnotic component is not a command, only a suggestion. It depends for its force on immersion in the strat. That experience is three days old.'

Haight nodded. 'I thought this might happen.' He toyed with his tumbler, his expression becoming curious. 'You know, men have been pulled out of the strat after falling into it, and they don't recover. Though there have been some cases I couldn't speak for, taken into the care of the Church to spend the rest of their days in monasteries. Poor devils.'

'This is the second time I've been in the strat. I saw it for the first time when the *Smasher of Enemies* went down.'

'You think that might have acclimatised you, eh?'

'Possibly, sir.' Haight's obsession with the strat, Aton saw, was a growing one. For his part, he was eager to return to the former subject of conversation.

'Sir, we must try to make the emperor understand the seriousness of the situation. *The war must be brought to a stop.*'

'*We* must? Did you not just now hear me pronounce sentence of death on you? Or are you trying to save your skin?'

'I am not trying to save my skin. It is your doing that the normal procedure has … misfired. But I am still willing to submit to execution, if you will grant me one last wish.' Aton spoke evenly, with increasing urgency.

'And what is that?'

'Let me be present at the interview with the emperor. Let me put the Hegemonics' case as they would wish it to be put. Frankly I do not think that you will do so.'

'You accuse me of misrepresentation?'

'Sir, I believe the empire is in danger, deadly danger. Yon understand the havoc that can be wreaked, by the time-distorter – and we have not even seen it used at full power yet! – but your instinct is that of a warrior: to fight, to defeat the enemy. Yet to take a detached view, the Hegemonic cause has some slight justice in it. The issues at stake are not worth the strain we will be putting on the structure of time.'

Haight took a step towards Aton, dangerous emotions chasing themselves across his face. 'You want to sell out to the enemy!'

'We *must* reach an accommodation with the Hegemonics! Or else the empire itself may be destroyed!'

The commander stared at him incredulously. 'Hah! So you really think the empire can be brought down! Why, the empire's resources are inexhaustible! Other powers in time have at the best but one node to draw on. The empire has seven! That means seven times the industrial might, and seven times the manpower, of any enemy we might face. And our strength will grow.' He shook his head. 'No, the empire cannot be defeated.'

'You speak of orthogonal time. I have seen the strat. You have not. All we have can be wiped away in the blink of an eye.'

'You add heresy to your crimes,' Haight said with increasing virulence.

'Is that your only response – to take refuge in doctrine?' Aton replied, in a voice thick with disappointment. 'It is clear that with you for a messenger the emperor can gain no clear idea of what the Hegemonics intend.'

Haight sneered, looking him up and down. 'Who are you to lecture me?' he retorted. 'Your offers and arguments are all tricks to help yourself! Let *me* tell *you* something-something of service! True, even emperors can make foolish mistakes. What is Philipium but a foolish old man? But that is not important. Something more surrounds the Ixians and welds the empire together. That something is *service* – the ideal of service to the empire! Men give their lives to this ideal, it is the empire's main strength. And what of you? What do you understand of this strength?' Haight's voice rose to a roar. 'You are a traitor, a criminal, a coward! But now you face *me*, a loyal servant of the empire!'

Aton stood pale-faced but erect while the commander raged. 'I had been undecided as to what to do with you,' Haight said more quietly, 'but now I think I will kill you anyway.'

Aton skipped back. His hand darted into his tunic and came out with a small hand beamer he had found in Haight's stateroom.

'I am set upon a course, Commander. I will not give up, at least until I have spoken with Colonel Anamander. Perhaps he agrees with me.'

'And perhaps he does not. It makes no difference, but in fact he does not.' Haight stared contemptuously at the beamer.

Aton was pointing the gun uncertainly at Haight. 'Keep your hands where I can see them, sir.'

'I need no gun. I have a weapon pointed directly at your heart: your own vagus nerve.'

Aton's eyes opened wide.

'Your information is probably incomplete,' Haight continued. 'You have conquered the compulsion to pronounce the trigger-word, evidently. But it is not necessary that you should pronounce it. It is only necessary that your nervous system should *hear* it. And I, as the receiving officer, know what the word is.'

Although his finger tightened on the stud of the beamer, Aton found that he could not, after all, fire on his commanding officer. He staggered back yet another step.

'*Vom*.' The word dropped from Haight's lips like a dose of poison.

And Aton's nervous system reacted instantly. Brain cell after brain cell fired in response to the signal, spreading the message in a web of pending death. Aton sought to clamp down on the impulse, to dampen it before it could reach the vagus nerve, sometimes called the suicide nerve because of its ability to initiate cardiac arrest on instructions from the brain.

His heart gave a convulsive leap and missed several beats. Aton staggered, the gun slipping from his fingers. He was vaguely aware of Haight looking on, half in satisfaction, half repelled.

Then the scene before him vanished, for a split second – a split second that was an eternity long. And so, for that same split second, did orthogonal time.

He was back in the strat, transposed there spontaneously by his nervous system somehow and experiencing its impossibilities all over again.

And when, almost immediately, he phased back into Haight's lounge, the cabin bore its former flat, two-dimensional appearance. But this time he was far from being mentally, incapacitated. He felt strangely young, strong, and omnipotent, as if he could fly while others were earthbound.

Vom. The word had no danger in it now. Its fearful virulence had been expunged from his mind.

'Wha – Did something happen just then?' Haight whispered. For a moment he had seemed to see Aton surrounded by an aura of near-invisible flame.

'Yes. Your word won't work against me either. I have rid myself of it.'

He paused. He still did not understand what was happening to him, at least not entirely. He only knew that it was surprising, incredible, and yet logical.

'Commander, you have wondered why the empire requires a time-courier to die. I think I can tell you.'

'Oh? Why?'

'It is because he becomes like a god.'

'A god.' Haight chuckled derisively. 'Well, you may have broken the psychological conditioning, but let's see how well you fare against hot energy.'

He had unflapped his waist holster and now he drew his clumsy-looking hand beamer, larger than the toy-like weapon Aton had discarded. With slow deliberation he clicked off the safety and aimed the orifice at Aton's chest.

Aton had time for a hasty valediction.

'Commander,' he gasped, '*I also am a loyal servant of the empire.*'

Then he seemed actually to see the dense microwave beam, made visible by its accompanying dull red tracer waves, advancing through space towards him.

And Commander Haight gave a hoarse cry. For Aton had vanished completely from his cabin. He had been plunged back into the strat.

As he fell through the unending plenum of potential time Aton wondered why – and how – his nervous system had rescued him. Had it been a survival response, an instinctive reaction against threatened death? Or had his subconscious mind, still obeying the suicide command in some perverse fashion, welcomed and anticipated that death, precipitating him into the strat through over-eagerness?

As to how his body had gained this power, he could only guess. Presumably it was connected with the unique combination of his recent experiences. How it was accomplished, considering the heavy equipment and intense energy that was normally required, he could not say. But one thing was sure. He was no longer as others were. He was a four-dimensional man, able to transpose spontaneously through time.

And no longer was he a despairing mote tossed about by the currents of the strat. This time he was not robbed of the sense of sequential time that was his brain's birthright; he carried his own weak ortho field with him. Because of this his mind maintained its natural rationality. His perceptions had learned to handle the supernal contents of the strat in a way that did not cause his ego to blow a fuse.

Previously the strat had engulfed him, and half-drowned him. That was why his consciousness had taken refuge in experiencing his life over and over: it had been the only familiar element in his surroundings. He could, if he wished, choose this refuge again, but he did not, because this time his consciousness was not overwhelmed and in his new condition, with his brain no longer scrambled by endless unintelligible monstrosities, the start took on an entirely different appearance.

Fire. That was the nearest he could come to describing it. He was in an ocean of eternal fire, whose flames consisted of the myriad half-creatures whose existence was, as yet, only potential. The flames blasted and trembled, whirled and rolled, swelled and receded.

This, he knew was not the strat as it was in reality; this was the interpretation his newly adjusted perceptions put upon it. The fire hurtled and withered everywhere; it was a five-dimensional sea that could not be understood any other way.

If he turned in a certain direction he could see what appeared to be a vast leaden wall. Upon it, as upon a huge mural, ran scenes of an amazing variety and richness. It was the surface of the strat. The realm of existential, orthogonal moving time from which Aton came. The real, solid world. And if he wished he could gaze upon this world and see what took place there.

But instead he was hurtling pastwards – pastwards, that is, in orthogonal terms – at a terrific rate, bent upon a mission that was only gradually becoming dear to him.

His trajectory, however, was to be interrupted. Suddenly, looming ahead of him, he saw a form that did not belong here. Like himself, it moved in a bubble of orthogonal time, but it was larger than he was. Much larger.

Briefly he recognised it as it swept past him: a step-tiered office block travelling taller end sternwards, the company name. *Buick* written hugely along its side in graceful silver script. It was an internodal chronliner.

He would have passed it by, but apparently the section of his nervous system that controlled his new-found powers had its own autonomic responses. As the ship's orthogonal bubble touched him he phased precipitately out of the strat and found himself in a new, unexpected situation.

He was standing, still in his captain's uniform, in the chronliner's main lounge.

Nervously Inpriss Sorce sipped her drink, her eyes flicking here and there around the lounge like the wary eyes of a bird.

She spent most of the time in the big lounge. There were always plenty of people there, and bright lights. She was short of sleep because she was reluctant to stay long alone in her cabin, where she feared unwelcome visitors. Instead she had learned to live on nervous energy. At the same time she knew that she would have to learn to break this habit when she reached Revere, where she would spend much time alone – hopefully safe and unobserved.

Captain Mond Aton noticed the frightened girl as soon as he took stock of his surroundings.

Surveying the spacious, well-appointed lounge, glancing at the faces of the passengers, he discovered that along with the ability to travel through time at will went another gift. Insight. Either his awareness or his senses had been heightened; he seemed able to guess instantly what thoughts and feelings lay behind the faces he saw. Human personality was an open book to him.

But even without this clarity of perception the young woman's condition would have been no secret. He recognised her look as that of a hunted animal. He had seen that particular look only once before in his life, and that had been on the face of a man with whom he had been slightly acquainted. At the time it had been a puzzle to him. Later the fellow had been found murdered in an imaginative, bizarre fashion that bore all the hallmarks of the Traumatic sect.

Cautiously he moved towards the girl and sat down at her table. A waiter approached. Having no money, he waved him away.

'Where are you bound?' he asked the girl. 'I haven't had a chance to ask you before.' She would not find the question strange: chronliners called at all nodes en route and they were now, he believed, somewhere between Nodes 4 and 5. The ship probably had two or three stops to make.

Her reaction, however, was far from reassuring. She shrank instinctively away from him. In her eyes Aton seemed to see the thought: Who is he? What does he want? Is he following me?

She's terrified of strangers, he realised.

Seeing that she was afraid to answer the question he let it pass; covering up her confusion with a stream of chitchat while he looked around the lounge, wondering who it was she was so badly frightened of.

He spoke of his experiences in the Time Service, talking in such a way that few responses were required of her. He felt her eyes on his face and gradually she seemed to relax a little. If his guess was correct it would be hard for her to trust anyone, but he hoped he might inspire just a little confidence.

To test out his theory he mentioned the time he had found Traumatics aboard his ship. She gasped. He sensed her body tense, go rigid.

'They are extremely unpleasant people,' he said.

She nodded dumbly.

'Listen,' he said gently. 'I think you ought to tell me what's worrying you.'

She looked away. 'Nothing's worrying me. What makes you think it is?'

'If you don't mind my saying so, it does show, enough for me to notice, at any rate. I've seen it before.' He paused. 'It's the Traumatic sect, isn't it?'

Her lower lip trembled. She nodded again.

'Have you really seen it happen before?'

'Only once. To a friend of mine.'

In a rush of words she told him everything. The three visitations, her desperate efforts to escape, to get lost. Finally her decision to migrate to another province of the empire.

He could see that it was a great relief to her to be able to tell someone. It also showed just how desperate she had become, for she could hardly imagine it was safe to talk to a stranger. Probably the uniform had helped. The Time Service was greatly esteemed. Few people knew that chronmen were perversely prone to the Traumatic heresy.

'So now you hope to settle in Revere?'

'Yes. In Umbul, probably.'

'Ah. The holy city.'

'I thought that perhaps – perhaps–'

'Yes, I see.' Her hopes were plain. She thought that perhaps the Traumatic sect stayed clear of Umbul, birthplace of San Hevatar, of the Church, and in fact of the whole Chronotic Empire.

He looked down sombrely at his hands folded neatly on his lap. 'Citizeness Sorce, I am sorry to have to tell you this but you have been doing everything the Traumatics want you to do. This is their play, part of their ritual. The sacrificial victim must not be killed outright but must be captured and allowed to escape in the nick of time – by luck or his own efforts, so he thinks. Then captured again, allowed to escape again, on and on. The purpose is to make the victim aware of his, or her, situation and of the fact that he is being hunted, so as to produce a particular psychological state. This continues until his will is entirely broken and he actually co-operates in the final ceremony.'

Inpriss Sorce's brown eyes widened pleadingly. 'Then I haven't shaken them off?'

'No.'

'Oh!'

Her hands flew about agitatedly. Aton thought she might be near a break-down. In that case the Traumatics would not be far behind her.

'Help me!' she cried. 'Somebody must help me!'

'I'll help you. Calm yourself.'

She gazed at Aton, studying his face. 'You will?'

'I hate these people as much as you do.'

'Is that why you're going to help me?'

'I'd help you anyway.' Aton's eyes narrowed as he saw a man enter the lounge and walk to the bar with a swaggering gait. His jaw clenched.

The man was Sergeant Quelle!

'Stay here and don't move,' he told Inpriss. 'I'll be back shortly.'

The gunnery noncom uttered a grunt of startlement, his sharp face becoming a grotesque mask of disbelief, when Aton joined him at the bar.

'What the hell are you doing here? I thought –'

'You thought I was safely dead,' Aton supplied. 'More to the point, what are *you* doing here?'

'Me? Why –' Quelle gave a weak, hysterical laugh. He was, Aton noticed, wearing civilian clothes. 'Just taking a spot of leave, Captain. Well-deserved leave. I'm on a cruise. I've got a medal now, you know. All of us have who got off the *Smasher of Enemies*. Except you, of course,' he added thoughtfully. He gulped down the drink he had, just bought, nearly choking on it, 'Did you get a reprieve, Captain?' he asked quaveringly. 'How did you get here?'

'Suffice it to say that I am here and that I can now remember all that took place on the *Smasher of Enemies*.' Aton watched the look of agony that appeared on Quelle's face. 'How many of your friends are with you?' he asked.

'Eh? I've no friends here, sir.'

'You're lying. I happen to know who it is you are pursuing.'

Quelle's glance flicked involuntarily to Inpriss Sorce, who sat watching anxiously from across the lounge. 'I don't know what you're talking about.'

Perhaps Quelle was alone after all, Aton thought. Perhaps he was merely shadowing Inpriss Sorce and others would take over when the ship reached Umbul. But the gunnery sergeant's shiftiness and deceit was so plain that nothing could be taken as certain.

'Are you going to turn me in, sir?' Quelle asked mildly, inspecting the bottles stacked against the bar.

'Yes.'

'Then why haven't you done it before?' Quelle turned to him, smirking. 'You know what I think, Captain? I think you're an escaped prisoner. I don't know how you did it, but the fact you're here shows you did. There's a courier dispatch chamber waiting for you in Chronopolis, isn't there? Maybe I should turn *you* in. Because whatever you say it's still your word against the testimony of *eight witnesses*.'

Aton stepped closer to the man. His hand darted inside Quelle's jacket. As he had expected he found a tiny beamer, small enough to fit into the palm of a hand.

No one around them had noticed his sudden movement. 'Let's go and see the security officer, Quelle.'

Quelle stood his ground for a moment. Then, at an insistent nudge from Aton he reluctantly preceded him towards the exit.

Although unfamiliar with the layout of the civilian time-ship, Aton found the security office without difficulty. Quelle made no attempt to escape or to move against him, and Aton reflected that the Traumatic had made a good point. Back in Chronopolis his own story would carry little weight. But that did not matter; somehow or other he would rescue Inpriss Sorce from the Traumatic sect's attentions.

In the security office was a middle-aged, long-jawed man in the blue uniform of the Buick line. Aton pushed Quelle in ahead of him.

'Officer, I am Captain Aton of the Third Time Fleet,' he announced. 'This is one of my men, Sergeant Quelle, whom I must ask you to place under close arrest. He is a criminal, a perjurer and a heretic, a member of the Traumatic sect, and he is currently engaged in hounding one of your passengers with intent to murder her.'

The officer looked from one man to the other, his face impassive. But behind that impassivity Aton caught feelings that were unsettling – recognition of Quelle, dismay at the whole proceeding.

'Serious charges,' said the officer. 'One moment, I'll call my men.'

He pressed a button. Almost immediately two security guards appeared at the door. Uneasy now, Aton turned to face them.

'He has my beamer,' Quelle said quickly.

A numbing, stinging shock struck Aton in the neck and spread down to his shoulders and arms. The beamer slipped from his nerveless grasp; his arms hung uselessly. He swung around clumsily and saw the security officer holding the numb-prong with which he had half-paralysed him.

The door slammed shut. All four men crowded around Aton, pushing him back. 'What on Earth happened?' the officer snarled at Quelle.

'He knows about me,' Quelle said in a surly tone. 'He's supposed to be dead; we thought we'd fixed him in Chronopolis. Hulmu help me, I nearly dropped when I saw him in the passenger lounge just now.'

'Does the girl know about you too?'

'I don't know.'

'You'd better stay out of her way. We can't let this get to the captain.'

Aton made a lunge for freedom, kicking with his feet, butting and shoving with his body. Before he could gain the door they had restrained him and held him in a corner where he panted in quiet fury.

Quelle swaggered in front of him. 'It's not only the Imperial Time Service that's host to the Cult of Hulmu, Captain. We Traumatics make much use of the internodal facilities.'

'What shall we do with him, Quelle?' the security officer asked.

'Maybe we could use him,' one of the guards said in a caressing voice, looking Aton over in a way that was incongruous coming from this burly, blue-jowled strong-arm man.

'Don't be a fool, he hasn't been pointed.'

'He's no problem,' Quelle said gleefully. 'He may have been my captain once, but the truth is that now he's a condemned convict who's escaped from the Courier Service. We can get rid of him without anybody asking questions.'

'Good. We'll put him through the garbage chute.'

Quelle cackled, eyeing Aton with undisguised hatred. 'I'm sorry about this, Captain, speaking as one chronman to another. But you see how it is – dog eat dog.' He darted a look at the security officer. 'I hate to do this to my own superior officer, you understand.'

'You traitor,' breathed Aton. 'You're worse than scum.'

'Don't you go saying that, now.' Quelle seemed genuinely hurt. 'I'm a good chronman. Religion is one thing, the Time Service is another. Why, as soon as my leave is finished I'll be riding out with His Chronotic Majesty's armada!'

One of the guards checked the corridor outside to ensure it was empty. The officer gave Aton another dose of the numb-prong so that he could give as little trouble as possible. Then they were dragging him along the passageway.

After a few yards they opened a grey-painted door and proceeded through narrow service passages, safe from the eyes of either passengers or crew.

Aton knew that for the moment attempts at resistance were useless, and bided his time. Presently, close against the outer wall of the ship, they came to an area littered with cardboard boxes and tubs of rubbish.

The mouth of a big cylindrical chute, with a covering lid clamped shut, projected from one wall and was accompanied by several large steel levers. The two guards gripped Aton's arms tight.

'You tried to put me in the strat once, Captain,' Quelle murmured. 'It's my turn now, I reckon.'

Aton struggled weakly. The security officer pulled on one lever; the chute's lid swung open. Aton was swung off his feet and inserted into the smelly cylinder, upon which the lid closed up over him to leave him for a moment in darkness, his feet pressing upon some further obstruction down in the chute.

Then this too, a second valve, slid open. He heard a clicking, grating noise and then the chute's hydraulic rams swept down on him, clearing the chute. He was pushed at speed through the ship's wall, through the limit of the containing orthogonal field, back into the strat.

Supernal fire burned all around him. Looking back, Aton saw the chronliner receding into the futureward – the plus-ward, in chronman's jargon – direction.

The fate of anyone else thrown into the strat would have been clear. They would sink deeper and deeper into mere potentiality, into the Gulf of Lost Souls. If, as a time-courier, he had failed to reach his target that would have been his fate too, once he lost momentum.

But now he had nothing to fear from such a horrendous ending – if ending it could be called. He could move through the strat at will, by the mere wish.

His intention was to return to the chronliner where he would continue his efforts to help the Traumatics' frightened quarry, the unfortunate Inpriss Sorce. When he willed himself to follow the timeship, however, another, deeper urge in him took over and instead he moved with accelerating speed minuswards – into the past and towards Chronopolis. His sojourn aboard the chronliner had, it seemed, been but an accidental interruption of his journey.

For it was slowly becoming clear to Aton that his subconscious mind, not his waking thoughts, was controlling his destiny. His subconscious mind had discovered, under duress, the secret of time-travel. And now it was sending him, at near-courier speed, on a mission *to save the empire*!

To one side the shimmering leaden wall of the ortho-world flashed by. He knew that he could phase himself into that world anywhere he liked, choosing any of the millions of locations and scenes that the endless screen presented.

But he passed them all by. Prompted by his inner urgings, he had a definite destination in mind.

Chronopolis. Node 1. The Imperial Palace.

After what seemed like a long time the majestic vision of the empire's administrative centre swung up before him. He sped closer, seeing it expand as upon a holo cinema screen. Then he phased himself into actual, orthogonal time.

EIGHT

Archivist Illus Ton Mayar, a slender wispy figure standing alongside the stocky detective Perlo Rolce, exhibited some awkwardness as he delivered his final report to Prince Vro Ixian.

When informed that the investigation he had ordered was complete, Vro had answered peevishly: 'It has taken you long enough!' and had turned his back on them to gaze into the holocast of the empty mausoleum.

'An undertaking of this kind *does take time*, Your Highness,' Mayar told him apologetically. 'It was with the greatest difficulty that I was able to include it in our work programme. The tragic events befalling the empire have practically overloaded the capacity of the archives.'

'Yes, all right. What have you to tell me?'

'Perlo Rolce's suspicion has been vindicated. The body of Princess Veaa has disappeared in a causal hiatus.'

'And what is that, exactly?'

'Put simply, a dislocation in time. A failure of cause and effect to match up. In practical terms, Princess Veaa was transported to Node Six and, presumably, hidden there. Later a crack in time appeared; all events leading up to a certain point – in the city of Umbul – were wiped away. Normally this would lead to the body still being back in Chronopolis, never having been removed. Instead the effect of the now-nonexistent cause remains: the body remains where it was hidden.'

'But with the trail leading to it eradicated,' Rolce put in.

Prince Vro nodded his understanding. 'All this would have seemed incredible only a short while ago. Now it seems commonplace.'

Mayar murmured in agreement. The attacks from the Hegemony had intensified. Not only were whole continents undergoing existential deformation but the empire now seemed riddled with cause-and-effect cracks, some of them large enough to present enormous administrative difficulties. Sometimes it seemed to Mayar, from his unique standpoint, that the structure of time was about to come crashing down like a shattered vase.

'It's like magic,' Vro said wonderingly. 'She's been spirited away with no one doing it.'

'That's what it amounts to, Your Highness,' Rolce said stiffly.

'Well.' Vro's voice became brisker. 'What can you do to find her?'

'The temporal discontinuity has been mapped, Your Highness.' Mayar produced a thick scroll and opened it, laying it on the table. It was so large that it covered the whole surface.

Vro stared perplexed at the chart, written in the esoteric Chronotic symbolism used by the Achronal Archives. Mayar explained that the vertical grid bars referred to time-units, though whether to minutes, days or months he did not say. He pointed out the jagged, wandering line that staggered through the neat layout like an earthquake crack.

'Here is the path taken by the discontinuity. Now, the issue revolves around Rolce's information that the body was secretly taken aboard the chronliner *Queen of Time*. Later this gilt-edged information was contradicted by the direct observation – and this has been verified by agents equipped with orthophases – that the body was *not* taken aboard. This anomaly suggests that time had mutated in a nonuniform way, leaving traces in the environment of both versions of history. Typical of a causal hiatus. The body is neither in Chronopolis, nor was it removed from Chronopolis. The perfect dilemma.

'Now what became of the princess during the *first* version? There are six stops where the *Queen of Time* could have off-loaded the body, presuming it was not discharged into the strat in transit. We reason that the body must have been taken off the ship before the hiatus occurred, otherwise it would still be here in Chronopolis and indeed might still be resting in the mausoleum; there would be no anomaly. On the other hand, it had probably been offboard for only a short time when the hiatus occurred. Transition from one resting place to another would seem to offer the most likely circumstance for the dislocation of the cause-and-effect relationship.'

Mayar paused to catch his breath. This argument had been worked out between himself and Rolce, and it had cost them considerable mental effort.

'Now look again at this discontinuity line,' he resumed. 'We find that it answers our deductions in every respect. It comes very close to intersecting the point in space and time when the chronliner was due to arrive at Umbul, Node Six. To be precise, it intersects Node Six just five hours after the *Queen of Time* docked.'

'Umbul,' breathed Vro. 'The Holy City.'

'We conclude that Umbul is where the princess was taken, and probably is where she still lies.'

'Archivist Mayar has even pinpointed the streets and buildings through which the discontinuity passed,' Rolce informed in a dry voice. 'It sounds incredible. Nothing, an investigator's void, and then, suddenly, clues begin again. The trail starts out of thin air.'

The prince rounded on him. 'You believe you can take up the trail again – in Umbul? You can find my beloved Veaa using your normal methods?'

'If our conclusions are correct, Your Highness, I feel every confidence.'

'Then you and I will both depart for Node Six, Rolce. I will order my private yacht to be readied tonight. Go, prepare yourself. Your instruments, your gadgets, whatever you will need. Can you manage it alone? Or do you need your agents?'

The detective shifted his feet. 'One or two men, perhaps.'

'Whatever you need. Go, now. Return as soon as you can.'

With a bow the detective departed. Prince Vro flung himself into a chair and lounged there, relaxed. For the first time in many months his manner was almost cheerful.

'Well, Archivist, I hear your establishment has been moved into the strat. A wise measure, perhaps.'

'It was deemed so, Your Highness.'

'And so how does it feel to visit the world of we mortals?'

Prince Vro's tone was amicably sardonic; in point of fact Mayar found the necessity for the visit far from pleasant and he longed to return to the safety of his vaults. His department's deployment into the strat had increased the sense of separation and isolation pervading the archives, and he had had to conquer a very considerable fear in order to make the trip to the Imperial Palace. Nothing but a command from a member of the imperial family was enough to persuade him to venture forth these days.

'It feels unsettling, Your Highness. The world is in a far from happy state. It has lost stability. Who can tell what will happen?'

'So you still feel it is all a dream, eh? Perhaps you feel you only wake from this dream when back in your archives.'

'Something like that.' Mayar licked his lips. 'Your Highness, since you are going to accompany Perlo Rolce in the search for Princess Veaa, let me entreat you to take care. The Traumatics are highly dangerous people. They are afraid of no one.'

Vro laughed. 'Why, I had thought you were well on the way to becoming one yourself!'

The archivist looked puzzled. 'I, Your Highness?'

'But of course! Surely you realise that all this gloomy talk of yours about time being a dream, and that only the strat is real, is part of the Traumatic heresy? That it conflicts with the doctrine of the Holy Trinity? You should be careful who you speak like that to. If Arch-Cardinal Reamoir were to –'

'I hadn't thought of it like that,' Mayar muttered uncomfortably.

'Probably, like me, you have no time for religion. And of course you avoided the misfortune of receiving a prince's education. I know every aspect of Church doctrine by heart; it was drummed into me from infancy.'

'My work is more scientific than religious,' Mayar admitted. 'I was brought up in the tradition of the Church, of course, but I cannot say I have made a study of heresies. It is not encouraged in a high official.'

'Just as well, or you would probably be too frightened to indulge in your present freedom of thought.' Vro swung a leg negligently from the arm of his chair. He seemed amused. 'You are definitely heretical. Compare your frame of mind with the Church's teaching on the Holy Trinity. God is the Father, the world of orthogonal time is the Son, and the strat is the Holy Ghost, by means of which the Father creates the Son. According to the Church the orthogonal world is real, palpable, actually existing, while the strat, or Holy Ghost, is less real because it is spiritual and potential. It's a sort of median between the real world and God, who transcends reality.'

'I know my catechism,' Mayar muttered, a trifle put out by the lecture. Vro, however, continued. He enjoyed such discussions; although he was privately an atheist, theology fascinated him.

'Your own beliefs come closer to those of the Traumatics,' he repeated to Mayar. 'The world is unreal, or relatively so, and the strat is real. According to them the world is created by Hulmu, their god who dwells in the deeps of the strat, and he creates it by projecting it on to a screen, exactly as in a cinema. Its entire purpose is to comprise a sort of picture show for him. That's why their emblem of the creation is a hologram projector and why one of their ceremonial names for Hulmu is "the Projector Operator".'

'Strange that an organisation with such horrible practices should support them with so philosophical a doctrine.'

'Oh, the cult of Hulmu is not new. It is at least as old as the Church. Some say it challenged the Church for supremacy in the early days.'

'You mean it sprang from an independent source?' Mayar frowned. 'I always thought it was founded by renegades.'

'The origin of the Traumatic sect isn't quite clear,' Prince Vro admitted. 'But the Church's own doctrine has been modified over the years. In the beginning it was somewhat closer to the Traumatic beliefs. God was deemed to dwell in the uttermost depths of the strat. The Holy Order of the Chronotic Knights even organised deep-diving expeditions to try to find God, but they all came to grief. Later the Church's theology became more sophisticated and now it is taught that God cannot be found in any direction accessible to a time-ship. Seeking for him by entering the deeps of time is regarded as a trap for the ignorant, for it harbours not God but the Evil One.'

'Hulmu.'

Vro nodded. 'Officially the Traumatics are devil-worshippers. Hulmu is identified with the Adversary. It's rather interesting that even the Church doesn't dismiss the sect as simple foolishness. In the Church's eyes Hulmu really exists, though he deludes his followers into believing him to be the creator.'

'Then the soul of Princess Veaa is in mortal danger,' mumbled Mayar, and instantly regretted his words.

Vro's face clouded over. 'Yes, Archivist,' he said softly. 'But I may yet save her. Like a knight of old, armed and ready, I shall go forth into the future!'

Aton materialised behind a pillar in the main court of the inner sanctum.

While vectoring in on the spot he had glimpsed the multitudinous activities of the palace. He had glimpsed Emperor Philipium himself, holding audience with nobles, ministers, civil servants, and military commanders.

The court itself had an air of tension and excitement, as though something was about to happen. Aton stepped into the open, looking about the sumptuous place with interest. There was much coming and going. All around him was the buzz of conversation.

Accustomed to a more austere life, Aton found the colour and luxury disconcerting. He was wondering how to achieve his object – an audience with the emperor – when an oval-faced young woman wearing the tiara of an Ixian princess caught him by the arm.

'Good evening, Captain. You're new here, aren't you?'

Hastily Aton bowed, frantically trying to place her from pictures he had seen of the imperial family. The trouble was that the family was so large. But he thought he recognised her as Princess Mayora, one of the emperor's own children.

'Are you going to be with the armada?' she asked, not giving him time to speak. 'But of course you are! A handsome fellow like you wouldn't let himself be left behind. Isn't it exciting? To fight for one's religion!' Her eyes sparkled.

Aton was about to frame a reply when a hush fell on the gathering. Through the padded doors came a procession; the emperor, noticeably tottering and with his right arm shaking visibly, was partly supported by servants. Behind him walked some of the dignitaries with whom he had recently been conferring. Close to the emperor, like an ever-present shadow, was Arch-Cardinal Reamoir, head of the Church. Something like triumph was on the arch-cardinal's face. Philipium's eyes, too, displayed a beady, unnatural brightness.

Everyone present bowed.

Philipium's weak, reedy voice rose to address the court. 'Our tribulations soon will be at an end,' he announced. 'All vessels of the armada have successfully finished their trials and are fully provisioned. In a few days the enterprise will begin!'

His words were greeted with cheering and applause. Philipium advanced through the great chamber, a path spontaneously appearing before him, until he faced the gold panel that took up a large section of one wall.

'*Imperator!* Grant us audience!'

The gold panel slid up. From out of the deep recess the massive machine-emperor slid out on its castors.

Aton stared, entranced. So this was the *Imperator*, the enigmatic construct that stood even higher than the emperor himself in the exercise of authority. And yet Aton had never heard of a single edict that had issued from it. In practical terms most people believed the *Imperator*'s power to be nominal only.

Philipium repeated his words to the humming machine. 'Give us your approval of this plan,' he added. 'Confirm its outcome, that our confidence may be justified.'

The humming sound emanating from the *Imperator* intensified and broadened, changing into a vibrant baritone voice.

'The enemy of the empire grows powerful. The struggle will ensue.'

Silence.

'Speak on, mighty *Imperator*!' Philipium urged. 'Grant us the wisdom of my fathers!'

This time a grating tone entered into the magnificent voice. It spoke falteringly, as if in distress.

'*The struggle will ensue!*'

'In your omniscience, grant us the boon of knowing that the outcome is certain, *Imperator*.'

But already the crenellated structure was retreating into its interior chamber. The gold panel slid down into place.

'Well, what do you make of that, Reamoir?' Philipium turned to his confessor, a frown on his narrow features.

'The *Imperator* is always cryptic, Majesty,' Reamoir murmured, 'but one thing is without doubt: it instructs us to continue with our plans.'

'Yes, that is so. That is so.'

Philipium was assisted to a throne, cushioned and moulded so as to give comfort to his weak frame, where he reclined, speaking occasionally to those who approached him.

The chatter of the court started up again.

Aton turned to Princess Mayora and in his urgency was nearly insubordinate enough to seize her by the arm. 'Your Highness, I must speak with your father. Will you help me?'

'What is this?' She smiled at him gaily. 'You have a petition? You are most importunate.' She leaned closer, becoming a shade more serious. 'Have a care. Father can be a crotchety old thing and is sometimes impatient with trifles.'

'This is no trifle, Your Highness. I cannot put the matter through the proper channels. But, as an officer of the Time Service I feel it my duty ...' He trailed off, realising the impossibility of explaining who he was and how he had got here. 'If you could help me into His Majesty's presence I will risk the rest myself,' he murmured.

Somewhat curious, she sauntered towards the throne, beckoning him to follow. As they came near, he heard the emperor talking to his eldest son, the future emperor Philipium II.

'Not two hours ago a courier arrived from the dispatching station at Barek – from Commander Haight, no less, who put in there en route to Chronopolis. He has returned without the distorter but with the offer of a truce from the Hegemonics. It seems they want to parley for peace. That's a good sign they know how hopeless their situation is.'

Philipium II laughed. It was a reedy, dry laugh. He had inherited his father's manner of speech, as he had much else about him. 'Rather late for that now!'

The emperor nodded with satisfaction. 'No doubt our retaliatory attacks have taught them what's in store for them. Also they must have gained some intelligence concerning the might of our armada.' He frowned. 'Haight discovered something about the distorter, too, but we shall have to wait until he arrives here for his full report.'

Aton and the princess were now mingling with the courtiers surrounding the throne. Boldly Aton stepped forward to confront the emperor and prince.

'Your Chronotic Majesty!' he said in a loud voice.

Both men turned to look at him. Philipium II appeared cold and supercilious, the emperor merely startled.

For one instant Aton looked into his ruler's tired, feverish eyes and knew that his mission stood no chance of success. Behind those eyes was … nothing. The emperor was dead inside. There was nothing but bigotry, prejudice, set patterns of thought. Even if Aton were to persuade him of the truth of his story, which seemed unlikely, nothing at this stage could possibly cause him to alter his decision.

Aton glanced from him to the younger Philipium, and again from him to Arch-Cardinal Reamoir, who was hovering as always by the emperor's side. As before he found that his new perceptions laid bare their inner natures. In Philipium II there was only a blind arrogance that was a sort of later version of his father's unctuous religious humility. And in Reamoir there was ambition of truly shocking proportions: ambition that was prepared to sacrifice whole worlds, to cheat, lie, and kill in the pursuit of personal and religious aims.

He stood, tongue-tied and white-faced, as the awful realisation struck him.

'What is it, young man?' Philipium said sharply. 'Who are you?'

'Captain Aton of the Third Time Fleet, Your Majesty.'

'Then you should be helping defend the frontier. On leave, are you? Why?'

'… The action for Gerread, Your Majesty,' Aton said after a momentary effort.

'Ah, yes. Take courage, young man. Eventually we shall regain Gerread, together with all the other possessions that have been lost since.'

An official slid through the circle and murmured something in the emperor's ear, who then turned and began a conversation with someone else. No one took any notice of Aton. His rude intrusion had been forgotten.

Princess Mayora accosted him as he slipped away. 'Well, I don't think much of that!'

'I suddenly realised how foolish my course of action was,' Aton said ruefully.

'Rather belatedly, don't you think?' The princess eyed him with growing inquisitiveness. 'What was your petition? Can I help?'

'I think not, Your Highness.'

Awkwardly aware of his bad manners, Aton made a perfunctory bow and walked stiffly away. He felt desolated. Here was the centre of the empire and everyone around him was hell-bent on destruction. Impending calamity was tolling like a great bell.

It seemed that his mission was impossible.

Or almost impossible.

Hours later the court chamber was deserted and in half darkness. A shadow slipped through that darkness, pausing and listening to the sleep of the huge palace.

At length Aton stopped before the dully gleaming gold sheet that hid the *Imperator*.

He had spent the intervening time wandering through the inner sanctum or just sitting brooding in one of the libraries. No one questioned his presence. It was assumed that anyone who had managed to enter the sanctum had a perfect right to be there.

'*Imperator*,' he called in a hoarse voice, afraid to speak too loudly in case he was heard from outside the chamber. 'A loyal servant seeks audience.'

He had no idea whether the machine-emperor would respond to any voice but Philipium's. But it was worth a try.

Nothing happened, and he called again. '*Imperator*. The empire is in danger!'

Miraculously the golden panel withdrew towards the ceiling. From the dark cave came the whine of an engine and the rumble of castors. The *Imperator* rolled majestically into view, a strange sheen playing over its matt surface. A scarcely visible light seemed to flicker between its four corner towers.

'*Who has dared approach?*'

The thrilling full-bodied voice, even though at low volume, filled the hall. The experience of facing the *Imperator* alone was strange and frightening. The machine radiated charisma. Aton, conscious of its majestic relationship with the empire, felt small and insignificant.

'I am Captain Mond Aton,' he announced. 'Late of the Third Time Fleet.'

The *Imperator* hummed and clicked. 'Sentenced to death for cowardice and dereliction of duty. Placed at the disposal of the Courier Service. Dispatched to the receipt of Commander Haight on the thirtieth day of the fifth month of this year.'

'The facts are as you state, *Imperator*. However I am still alive, as you can see.'

'Poor little tool of broken time …'

'*Imperator*, I have just returned from the Hegemony,' Aton said. He launched into his tale, describing Commander Haight's experiment, their meeting with the Hegemonic ministers, and his subsequent discovery of his new powers. Throughtout, the *Imperator* made no interruption except for the continuous humming that swelled and receded in volume.

Finally, with complete frankness, Aton related the intransigence of the emperor and of the advisers who surrounded him. 'You are mightier even than the emperor, *Imperator*,' he said. 'Command that the empire make peace. Draw back from this suicidal course.'

'All must be as it has been.'

Aton puzzled over the words. He had heard that the *Imperator* rarely expressed itself in plain speech.

'The enemy of the empire is the enemy of mankind,' said the *Imperator*. 'Fight, Aton. The power is yours alone.'

'*Imperator*, I do not understand you. Can you not explain what I am to do? Your meaning is not clear.'

'We live in dreams and walk in sleep. All that is real is unreal.'

Suddenly Aton heard footsteps behind him. Approaching out of the gloom came a young man wearing a short cloak of deep purple. The face was that of an Ixian, but unlike most of that brood, the eyes had a steady percipience and the man's whole bearing an uncharacteristic lack of vanity. As he came closer Aton recognised Prince Vro.

'An incredible story!' said the prince.

'You heard?'

'Forgive my eavesdropping,' the other said with a shrug. 'I merely happened to be passing. It was a scene I could not resist. Yes, I listened to every word.'

A rumble caused Aton to whirl around. The *Imperator* was withdrawing into its chamber. The golden panel closed and left them in silence.

'I must say I think you're wasting your time petitioning that machine in there,' the prince told him affably. 'Nobody has got any sense out of it, and in my opinion never will for the simple reason that our much-vaunted *Imperator* is quite insane.'

Aton must have looked shocked, for Prince Vro laughed softly. 'Well, is it any wonder, my friend? Infused with the brains of all the emperors! If my father is anything to go by, it must consist of lunacy piled on lunacy.'

He clapped Aton on the back. 'We are somewhat exposed here. I was on my way to supervise the readying of my time-yacht, in preparation for a certain romantic quest. Come with me. Afterwards we can talk in my quarters.'

With a last despairing look at the *Imperator*'s dwelling, Aton followed.

Prince Vro's chill and morbid apartment intensified still further Aton's feeling of desperation. While looking over the yacht the prince had explained his great loss to him, describing the steps he was taking to recover his beloved.

Yet despite the prince's bizarre preoccupation, Aton saw him for a man of rare intelligence by the standards of the Imperial Palace. It was a relief to be able to talk to him.

'Hmm. This certainly explains the rule about the disposal of couriers,' Vro remarked, lounging in an easy chair and dividing his attention between Aton and the empty sarcophagus in the wall hologram. 'Evidently people exposed to the strat are liable to develop a natural time-travelling ability. The Church wouldn't like that.'

'Then that means I'm not the first,' Aton pointed out. 'The phenomenon must already be known. Where are the others?'

'It is, no doubt, a closely guarded Church secret,' Vro said. 'Chronmen who are pulled out of the strat are generally put in the care of secluded monasteries and are never heard of again. Officially that's because they're mentally deranged. Now we know there's more to it, eh, Captain? We can be sure care is taken to see they never realise their powers. You'd better watch your step or you might find yourself forcibly enlisted as a monk.' Vro smiled faintly.

Aton reflected. 'Did you mean what you said about the *Imperator*?' he asked.

'Of course. It's a demented machine, no more. That's why it's only a figurehead. My father can't quite believe it's not rational, of course. He treats it as a totem and consults it from time to time. But it never says anything meaningful.'

'Then will *you* help me, Your Highness?' Aton pleaded earnestly. 'You, at least, seem to understand what the present situation will lead to. Can you not try to persuade your father?'

'I?' Prince Vro chuckled. 'Affairs of state are far from my interests.'

'But how can you ignore them at a time this?'

'I care only for my beloved Veaa,' Vro said, gazing pitifully into the mausoleum. 'Let the world perish, it's nothing to me.'

Aton sighed deeply.

'As for my father the emperor and his enterprise against the Hegemony,' Vro went on, 'that old lunatic could never be moved by anything I say to him anyway. I have not spoken to him for three years, yet he still expects me to command a wing of the armada! He will be disappointed. I shall not be here. I shall be away, into the future, to rescue my beloved and make her mine again!'

Without warning a change came over Vro's face. He leaped to his feet and appeared to be listening intently.

'What is it?' asked Aton in alarm.

'Can you not sense it?'

Aton became quiet and indeed did seem to sense something. A swelling that was inside him and outside him, in the air, in everything. Then he momentarily blacked out. When he came to, he was aware of a loss of consciousness lasting a split second.

Prince Vro went rushing about the room examining everything, peering into the mausoleum, studying his face in a mirror.

'What happened?' Aton asked in a subdued voice.

'That's the third time they've got through. Nothing's changed here anyway. But then, I wouldn't remember ... not unless the change was discontinuous, perhaps not even then.'

'The Hegemonics? They can strike even here?'

Vro nodded. 'Usually they are beaten off, occasionally they manage to focus their projector for a second or two. Chronopolis has undergone a few minor changes, so the Achronal Archives tell us. I wonder what it is this time.' His lips twisted wryly. 'It could be for the best. Maybe my father has had some sense mutated into him.'

This revelation of how hard the Hegemonics were attacking was the most depressing thing Aton had met with so far. He laid his chin on his hands, thinking deeply. At length he decided upon something which had been brewing in his mind, but which he had not dared to think about up until now.

'You can see why my father is so keen to get the armada under way,' Vro remarked. 'Much more of this and there won't be any empire left.'

'But once the armada is launched everything will get worse!' Aton protested. 'Both sides will let loose with everything they've got. The Hegemonics will use the time-distorter at full aperture!'

Vro did not seem interested. 'What are you going to do now, Captain? You ought to give it some thought. It's dangerous for you here. Once someone realises who you are they'll make short work of you.'

'I haven't stopped trying yet. The emperor won't listen to me. The *Imperator* won't. There's still someone left.'

'Who?'

'San Hevatar!'

Vro grunted. 'Him! What do you expect him to do?'

'I don't know. The whole empire springs from him. Perhaps he can change everything. Perhaps he could even suppress the invention of time-travel.'

'And wipe out the empire from the beginning?' Vro's voice was soft with awe.

There was a tight pain in Aton's chest. When he spoke, his tone was leaden. 'It sounds strange, doesn't it? I, a committed servant of the empire, talking of annulling the empire. The ultimate in treachery. But I can see no other way. It is not just the empire that's at stake now, it's mankind, perhaps time itself. Mad the *Imperator* may be, but one thing it said is true: the enemy of the empire is the enemy of mankind. Perhaps madmen – or mad machines – can see clearly what saner men cannot.'

'Your vision is certainly grandiose.'

'With no communication through time each node would live separately, undisturbed. There would be no Chronotic Empire, but neither would there be any time-distorter, any Chronotic war, any strain on the fabric of time. Who can say what will remain when it finally rents open?'

'And no Holy Church,' Vro reminded him. 'I wonder what San Hevatar will have to say to that.'

Aton turned to him. 'You tell me you are heading for Node Six in the morning, Highness. Have you room for me aboard your yacht? Can you drop me off in the hinterland?'

'I thought you could travel through time at will.'

'Not quite at will. I have already tried. It seems my nervous system only asserts the ability during an emergency, or under certain kinds of duress.'

'Well, it seems the least I can do,' Prince Vro murmured, 'to aid in the annihilation of the empire.'

NINE

The origin of the Chronotic Empire was, to some extent, obscured in the haze of recurrent time. It had taken place at a point in time that now lay between Node 5 and Node 6 – between Barek and Revere – about fifty years into the hinterland of Node 5. But two nodes had swept over the spot since the earth-shaking discovery attributed to San Hevatar. The empire had had three hundred years or more of nodal time, as apart from static historical or orthogonal time, in which to establish itself.

And during that nodal time the soul of San Hevatar had, of course, traversed his life several times, as had that of everyone around him. The world in which he lived had changed much in the course of those repetitions. The original San Hevatar would not have recognised it. Largely because of his own efforts, he was now born into a world where time-travel and the empire were already facts.

Most history books inferred that the Ixian family had already been the rulers of Umbul when San Hevatar placed the secret of time-travel at their disposal. Prince Vro told Aton, however, that he believed this to be a distortion of the truth. It was unlikely that the city of Umbul itself had existed in the beginning. As far as he could judge, the Ixians had not been kings or rulers, but the owners of a giant industrial and research conglomerate where San Hevatar had worked as a scientist. They had seized their chance to indulge their wildest ambitions, conquering past centuries, always moving pastward, where the technology was inferior to their own.

For his part San Hevatar had been a man with a vision. He had given a religious meaning to his discoveries and had found the past a fertile ground for his teachings. He had founded the Holy Church, thus giving the burgeoning Chronotic Empire a unifying culture.

Eventually the Ixians had realised that, once it was let loose on mankind, time-travel, which they had used so successfully, could also work against their interests. It would be particularly dangerous if time-travellers were to penetrate the empire's rear, travelling into the past beyond the empire's control and working changes there – changes which inevitably would influence the present in ways not planned by the Historical Office. They determined to fix a date in time beyond which time-travel could not be introduced. To this end the stupendous Stop Barrier had been built, consuming one-third of the imperial budget and rendering the past impenetrable to time-travellers. One day it would be moved back to bring yet more of history under the empire's control, but for the moment it remained both the pastward limit on the empire's expansion and its rearward protection.

Umbul, on the other hand, was much too close to the futureward frontier to be entirely safe from marauders from the future. A new imperial capital, Chronopolis, had been built close to the Stop Barrier, at what was designated Node 1 (although now another node, Node 0, lay between it and the barrier), protected by nearly the full extent of the empire.

So San Hevatar, prophet and God's special servant, now lived a life of relative quietude away from the mainstream of events. But he continued, in each repetition of his life, to make the crucial discovery of how to move mass through time, paradoxically even while the evidence of that discovery was all around him *before he had made it*. It was as if his inner being performed this act as a sacred rite: the central, essential rite of the Church.

Captain Aton meditated on all this as Prince Vro's yacht crossed Node 5. 'Where in San Hevatar's life cycle would you like to intervene?' Prince Vro asked him politely.

It would be no use approaching the prophet when he was an eager young man, Aton thought. Someone on the verge of a momentous discovery would hardly be persuaded to abandon it. Aton needed to talk to a man who had had time to reflect, who would be old enough to make a sober judgment.

'At about fifty years of age,' Aton requested.

'So late? That is a quarter of a century after the gift of time-travel. If your object is to annul the empire I would have thought, perhaps, a few decades earlier.'

'That is not really my object,' Aton said with a smile. 'It would, after all, be asking too much. But if San Hevatar were, perhaps, to appear at Chronopolis and speak against the war, then I am sure his word would carry more weight than that of all the emperors put together.'

'Maybe. If His Eminence Arch-Cardinal Reamoir does not declare him a heretic!' Vro laughed caustically.

The cabin of Prince Vro's yacht was not large (nearly all the vehicle's mass being taken up by its powerful drive unit) and with six passengers, three of whom were Perlo Rolce's assistants, Vro had been obliged to dispense with his crew and attend to both navigation and piloting himself. He typed some instructions into the yacht's computer and made adjustments in accordance with the figures it gave.

Rolce and his men, trying not to appear inquisitive, kept glancing at Aton surreptitiously. They could hardly believe what was happening.

The yacht slowed down as it approached Aton's target. Vro became fretful.

'I am at a loss to know where to phase into ortho,' he said. 'To tell the truth

I am reluctant to do so at all. As you know, civilian timeships are forbidden to materialise anywhere between nodes, and I am not keen to make myself conspicuous. I'm afraid I shall have to land you somewhere quiet, Captain, and that could put you many hundreds of miles from San Hevatar.'

A strange look came to Aton's face. 'There's no need to phase in at all,' he told Vro. 'Just open the cabin door and let me out.'

Perlo Rolce surged to his feet, his hard face displaying most uncharacteristic shock.

'Your Highness!' He and his staff plainly thought Aton was insane. Prince Vro waved him back. 'It's all right, Rolce. We know what we're doing.' But even he looked at Aton in a puzzled, doubting way.

'You're sure of this?' he asked.

'As sure as a swimmer knows he can enter the water.'

Vro went to a cupboard and took out a flat box-like gadget attached to a belt. 'You'd better take this orthophase.'

'Thank you, although I'm not sure I shall need it.'

Aton strapped the device around his waist. Returning to the pilot's seat, Prince Vro watched the computer countdown while glancing at a small strat screen. 'Right. We're about there.'

'You'd all better face the wall,' Aton advised. 'Open the door, Your Highness.'

Vro tapped out the safety sequence on the computer keyboard. With a hum the door slid open. Beyond it, outside the ortho field, the strat billowed and swirled.

Aton steeled himself and leaped right into it.

After the door had closed again the five men remaining in the cabin turned and stared after him, not speaking.

The Manse of San Hevatar lay in a great park in the southwest of the city of Umbul: a quieter, more sedate Umbul than it would be at Node 6 a hundred and twenty years hence. The park was dotted with shrines and religious monuments. The approach road that wound through the town was lined with churches, and that stretch of it that crossed the park was strewn every day with rose petals by order of the local bishop.

For all its magnificence the manse itself still bore traces of the research laboratory from which it had been converted. The limestone cupolas floated in places above rectilinear structures of glass and steel. An outhouse contained the powerful transformers, fed by underground cable, that had once provided energy for the scientists' experiments.

Like a ghost Aton observed all this as he approached from the strat. He phased into orthogonal time in a circular lobby, paved with mosaics, surrounded by balconies, and surmounted by a dome of frosted yellow glass.

The murmur of voices came from one side. Padding towards the sound,

Aton found himself peering through the open door of a chapel. Two figures knelt before the altar, one wearing the prophet's mitre permitted to San Hevatar alone. The other was an older man, perhaps seventy, a small bent figure with a wrinkled face and bushy eyebrows.

Aton could not hear the words of the prayer or service which San Hevatar was intoning with feverish intentness. The older man was acting as his assistant, speaking the responses and holding a chalice of holy wine into which the prophet dipped his fingers, anointing both himself and the other.

Presently their business was finished. Both men stood, San Hevatar straightening his voluminous cope, and came away from the altar. It was then that San Hevatar saw Aton. He strode towards him.

'An officer of the Time Service!' he said wonderingly. 'And may I ask how you got in here? No permissions were given for today, and I have been informed of no unwarranted intrusions.'

'I made my own way here, Your Holiness, I have journeyed through time to see you. I feel that the information I have is so important that you must hear it.'

San Hevatar looked about him. 'You came through time? I see no timeship. I still do not understand how you entered my manse unobserved.'

'I came by my own power, Your Holiness. My brain has learned to propel me through the substratum.'

San Hevatar's eyebrows rose. He indicated a door to his left. 'In here. We will talk.'

When Aton had finished, San Hevatar's expression changed not at all.

'Your power is not entirely unknown,' he murmured. 'It was at one time the Church's intention to create a body of time-travelling sainted knights. But the gift is unreliable. One cannot initiate it at will. Conversely one never knows when it will spontaneously show itself. It appears to answer to the subconscious mind, not to one's thinking self. In that respect it resembles other legendary powers of the saints, such as levitation, the ability to talk to animals, and so on.'

'That is what I have found, Your Holiness.'

'And that is why the Church has kept it a secret. Anything that cannot be controlled is dangerous. There is another reason also. You must beware, Captain.'

'Holiness?'

'All chronmen fear the strat. You may think you have conquered that fear because you believe yourself safe in it. You are not. Eventually your power will fail and the strat will claim you. You will drown in the Gulf of Lost Souls, as have others who thought they had become supermen.'

Already Aton was beginning to feel that he would be disappointed for the third time. Even in middle age San Hevatar's face was striking. Full, sensuous lips, large soulful eyes, and an appearance of enormous self-collectedness that was somehow selfish rather than benevolent. It was the face of a fanatic. Aton could already guess what was coming.

'Your Holiness, the matter I have touched upon. You must agree that the Church, the empire, everything that has been achieved stands to be destroyed if the war continues. Instruct your Church in the foolishness of this Armageddon. The emperor is a deeply religious man; he would obey any command that came from you.'

San Hevatar smirked ever so slightly. He turned and glanced at the aged assistant who also sat with him, as though sharing some private joke with him.

'Have you so little faith?' he said quietly. 'The Church, the empire cannot – *must not* – be destroyed. It is eternal. The armada is God's plan. The Evil One must be fought. Mankind must be saved.'

As he uttered the last words San Hevatar seemed to find speech increasingly difficult. To Aton's amazement he passed his hand over his eyes and seemed to be in distress, rocking to and fro.

'Fight the enemy of mankind, Captain Aton!' he gasped as though in a trance. 'Conquer his minion! All is not as it seems!'

Aton was fascinated to hear the prophet coming out with words almost identical to those of the *Imperator*. Then San Hevatar seemed to recover himself and become once more self-composed. He stood up.

'Your concern, though bordering on the heretical, is commendable,' he said smoothly, as though unaware of his words of a moment before. 'It deserves a reward. It would be possible for me to have your sentence of death commuted. We have a certain monastery where by means of special techniques your dangerous gift can be unlearned and your nervous system returned to normal. Of course, it would be necessary for you to pass the rest of your life in seclusion, as a monk. You know too much to be returned to public life.' He nodded. 'Spend the night here and think it over. Rilke will look after you.'

Suddenly Aton said, 'What do you know about a man with jewels for eyes?'

He did not know why the image had come to his mind so abruptly, but the prophet's mouth opened and his face went ashen.

'You have *met* him? Already?'

'Yes.'

San Hevatar's expression closed up. He reminded Aton of an insulted woman as he swept from the chamber, his long cope rustling.

The old man regarded Aton for long moments with tired eyes. 'My name's Dwight Rilke,' he said, standing and offering his hand. 'Come along with me, I'll find you a room.'

*

Aton had slept for a number of hours when he was awakened by the sound of the door opening. He sat up. At the same time, the light came on.

Dwight Rilke entered the room, looking stooped, defeated and very tired. 'Sorry if I'm disturbing you, Captain, but I want to talk to you,' he said. He found a chair and sat down close to Aton, then licked his lips before speaking again in a dry, ancient voice.

'Listen, I've been doing some hard thinking,' he said. His eyes, though tired, were almost unnaturally bright. 'San Hevatar isn't really capable of responding to what you've been saying, you know. He's too deep into his role … the whole weight of the empire is on him. I'm the one you should have been talking to, because I'm the one you've convinced.'

Aton felt a stir of interest. 'Just who *are* you?'

'Me? I was Hevatar's assistant, you know.'

'Yes, I can see that.'

'No, I'm not talking about this religious stuff. I *was* his assistant; his scientific assistant. We were on the project together.'

'*The* project?'

'Yes. Would you like to see it?' Rilke rose. 'Come on, I want to show it to you. You don't mind, do you?'

He waited while Aton quickly dressed. Then Aton followed him through the passages and courtyards of the still brightly lit manse. Cowled monks and comforters stood guard here and there, some wearing handguns strapped over their habits. Rilke ignored them all, however, and halted before a door apparently made of solid lead. He took a big iron key from beneath his cloak and inserted it in a keyhole. There was a loud click, and the door swung open.

'Here you are, this is where it all began.'

They entered what Aton, after, first taking in the profusion of heavy-duty equipment, realised was a high-energy physics research laboratory. This, he supposed with a feeling of awe, was the centrepoint of the whole empire.

Carefully Rilke closed the door behind them.

'So this is where San Hevatar discovered the secret of time-travel!' Aton breathed reverently.

'Him? He didn't discover it,' Rilke told him flatly. 'I did.'

Aton stared at him blankly. 'You?'

'Hevatar developed it, but I made the initial discovery.' Rilke's face softened, and he began to reminisce. 'We were a team. Hevatar was the leader, Absol Humbart and myself were his chief assistants. There was a lot more equipment in here in those days. There were particle accelerators, high-energy plasma chambers, and so forth. But we weren't even thinking of time-travel then. We never dreamed it was possible. We were investigating the nuclear binding force of baryons, that was all. One day I thought of a new way to isolate pi-mesons. When I set up the apparatus, by chance a surge gate malfunctioned and there was a sudden rush of power. Suddenly I found I had discovered a way to accelerate pi-mesons faster than light.'

The old man looked around the laboratory as if remembering. 'It was an accident, a million-to-one shot. From then on, Hevatar took over. Naturally he grabbed something like that with both hands, and he explored it from all angles. Before long he had discovered the most important consequence of the effect I had produced: that it could be used to move mass through time. From then on there was no stopping him. He takes all the credit for it now, of course, but none of it would have happened if I hadn't carried out that one experiment.'

'You must feel proud.'

'Do I? For a long time I did. But lately it frightens me. We get all the news here; we're privileged in that respect. History is being ripped apart. It's like seeing the end of the universe, but no one seems to realise that time itself can collapse and no one wants to stop it. I opened a real Pandora's box when I made that experiment. And when you came this afternoon I realised that everything had gone too far.'

'What happened to this other man – Absol Humbart? Is he dead?'

Rilke turned away and muttered something Aton could barely catch. 'We've spoken of him already. Let's not go into that.'

Aton reflected bitterly that of the only two people to share his view of the situation, one was too obsessed with his insane love for a corpse to care and the other was this weary old man.

'I'm glad that you at least agree with me,' he told Rilke. 'But there seems little we can do.'

'Isn't there? There's something *I* can do. Something I can try to do, at least. I can go back in time, prevent any of it from happening.'

'You can do that?'

Rilke led him to a large dull-brown cabinet that at first Aton had taken to be a cupboard. 'This is a functional time-machine. The very first, in fact.' He opened the door. Inside Aton saw seats, a control panel.

'You really think you stand a chance of influencing Hevatar's – or your own – younger self?'

Rilke's smile was wintry. 'Hevatar has never been influenced by anybody. As for myself, I was an eager young pup and I certainly wouldn't have passed up the chance to make a crucial discovery, not for anyone. Besides, there's something you need to understand. We didn't know the empire existed in those days. It's strange, isn't it? Time has changed such a lot. Past, present and future have all changed. But there's one thing the empire and Church are very careful to see doesn't change. They are careful to preserve the vital event that led to the creation of the empire. San Hevatar and myself were brought up under special conditions and weren't allowed to know that there already was time-travel. We worked for the same company, Monolith Industries, that presumably we had worked for before anything had altered. But not until we had unearthed that one secret of how the time-drive works was the truth gradually revealed to us.' He smiled. 'It was like coming out of a dream. In a way we'd known all along; there was plenty of evidence for it if we had cared to piece it together. But we never had. The answer is, of course, that we were psychologically constrained in some way.

'And that's why,' he finished briskly, 'my younger self would never believe me if I went to him with such a wild tale.'

'It's logical,' Aton commented. 'The Historical Office would want to avoid paradoxes in anything as important as that. But you mentioned another assistant, Absol Humbart. Presumably he was put through this procedure too?'

'Did I mention Absol Humbart? No, he wasn't there,' Rilke said vaguely. 'Maybe he was in the earlier repetitions.'

The point didn't seem worth pursuing. 'So what *do* you propose to do?' Aton asked.

The old man produced a heavy hand beamer from under his cloak. 'Kill myself,' he said simply. 'It's the only way. Kill the young Rilke before he makes that experiment in isolating pi-mesons, then none of this can happen. There'll be no empire, no Chronotic wars. The world will be as it was before time-travel was invented.'

'And how was that, do you think?'

'I don't know. Nobody seems to know any more.'

'Kill yourself,' Aton said woodenly. 'Are you really prepared to do that?'

'Somebody has to do something. I can't think of any other way, and besides I'm really responsible for what's happening.' His face creased. 'It's taken me six hours to reach this decision. Now I've taken it, I know what to do.'

'Paradoxes,' Aton murmured. 'If you kill your earlier self, then you'll no longer be alive to kill yourself.'

'We'll just have to let that sort itself out.' Rilke jutted out his jaw ruminatively.

'Why have you taken the trouble to tell me all this?'

'Piloting the machine is a two-man job. One to navigate, one to steer. If anything happens to me you'll still be able to get back, though. It's programmed to retrace its course automatically.'

'If you succeed,' Aton mused, 'there won't be any question of coming back. There'll be no time-travel. As a matter of fact, I probably won't exist. Few people now living will.'

'True. Well, what about it?'

Dwight Rilke's self-sacrifice did not surprise Aton or occasion any particular admiration in him. The issues at stake were so awesome that the fate of any individual shrank to insignificance. Rilke was clearly not aware, however, of the other side of the coin; if the world returned to its original state, humanity would become extinct in a few hundred years.

But, in fact, Aton was certain that the reversion would not be anything like as complete as the aged scientist imagined; otherwise he would not for a moment have contemplated letting Rilke carry out the scheme. Rilke's understanding of Chronotic mutations was evidently crude and simplistic. He did not realize that the original world had been so deeply erased that it could probably never reappear. Something else, resembling it in many features perhaps, would assemble itself out of the jumble the Chronotic Empire had made of time.

Which meant there was a good chance the annihilatory war that had made a desert of Earth would never take place. Mankind would survive even without time-travel.

'All right, I'll be your navigator,' he told Rilke. 'But it's your show.'

He followed Rilke into the narrow cabin and examined the controls. They were antiquated, but he recognised them as the forerunners of the timeship controls he was used to.

Rilke closed the door and busied himself preparing for the journey. The drive unit started up with a whine, and Aton realised it was more powerful than he had first thought.

He studied the navigator screen. Rilke, mumbling to himself, phased them into the strat.

The Umbul of Node 6 was a place of slender towers whose smooth walls, straddled at the base, curved up to end in knife-edge peaks. It was a place of boulevards and curiously intricate passages that wound around the base legs of the soaring buildings. Inpriss Sorce ran through these passages in blind panic.

She had been in Umbul for a day and a half, during which she had not slept. She had found nowhere to live, nowhere to earn money. She had been too busy running.

On the chronliner she had searched desperately for the handsome young Time Service officer who had promised to help her. He was nowhere to be found and she could think of only one explanation: the Traumatics had already murdered him. Neither had she seen the man he had left the passenger lounge with.

But the officer's warning was not lost on her. The Traumatics were playing cat-and-mouse with her. She could not escape them and they would kill her when they were ready.

When the chronliner docked she had fled into the city. She soon discovered there was nowhere she could go. As she stepped off the disembarkation ramp a man had emerged from the crowd and smiled at her.

It had been Rol Stryne!

She had run past him, but he hadn't tried to stop her. Since then either he or the other man, Velen, had seemed to appear everywhere.

Now her nerve had finally cracked. She ran up to strangers in the street. 'Help me, please help me!' But they shouldered off her hysterical pleas. Once or twice she mentioned the Traumatics, but that only made the response even more hostile. The Traumatics were a secret power, here in Umbul as elsewhere, and there was scarcely a citizen who would knowingly cross them.

Inpriss collapsed on to a bench, sobbing.

A man sat down beside her.

'You see, baby, it just isn't any good to fight it. Go along with it, it's better that way.'

She looked up open-mouthed into the lean, predatory face of Stryne.

'You just have to co-operate,' he told her soothingly. 'Then the hunt will be over.'

Suddenly she was like a rabbit hypnotised by a stoat. Her eyes were glazed. 'You want me to come with you willingly,' she said in a flat, empty voice. 'That's why you let me go before. Because I wasn't willing.'

'That's right, honey. You understand now.' He flashed a knowing glance at Velen, who was standing nearby, and made a signal to the helpers, who had been keeping track of the woman for them and were hovering in the background, to disperse.

She had broken and would obey them. Stryne knew how to recognise the signs. In a way he was slightly regretful it was ending so soon. Many victims kept up the chase for years. He knew of one, a man, who had been pursued for two decades before submitting.

'Hulmu is the only true reality, sweetheart. You'll find that out soon. You're going to him.'

She closed her eyes.

'Come on, Inpriss. Let's go.'

Meekly she rose and walked with the two men, clutching her satchel. She was in the grip of something she had never felt before: a resignation so strong it overpowered her. It wasn't as if they had broken her will. It was as if her will had changed, so that she agreed with what they were going to do to her, simply because she couldn't see any other future.

'You see, honey, by the time we get to this stage we're doing you a favour,' Stryne told her as they walked. 'Just imagine if we didn't sacrifice you for some reason or another. Every time your life repeated you'd have to go through all this again. But this way your life won't repeat. Your soul will go to Hulmu. You'll never have to endure the pursuit again.'

'Where are we going to do it?' Velen asked eagerly. 'Somewhere nice and quiet? We could hire a hotel room.'

'We have to go to the main temple,' Stryne informed him. 'The Minion himself is taking an interest in this case. He'll be watching.'

'The Minion? Wow!'

'Yes, he's one, Your Highness. I was right.'

In Prince Vro's suite in the discreet, extremely select Imperial Hotel a man was stretched out on the floor. The oblong plates of the field-effect device stood on either side of his head. Perlo Rolce fiddled with the device's knobs, watching a small screen with a greenish tint across which dim shapes flickered, while one of his men knelt by the prisoner holding a pain-prong.

Progress had been much quicker than even Vro had hoped. Rolce had started by visiting the street where Archivist Mayar believed the causal hiatus might have occurred. While using a map to help him look out the likely routes where the body might have been taken, he had noticed some activity an untrained person would not have observed. In his own words the place was 'crawling with snoopers'. Rolce had taken a chance and his men had performed a routine but efficient street kidnapping.

'Why should so many Traumatics be on the street?' Vro asked with a frown, sipping a liqueur.

'That's easily answered, Your Highness. This man's part of a pursuit operation. They are harrying some poor devil through the city till he drops.'

He nodded to his assistant to apply the prong again, repeating his question to the prisoner. The Traumatic gave a long gurgling scream and squirmed on the thick pile of the carpet, and Rolce kept watch on the screen, stroking his chin.

He had long found that a field-effect device coupled to long jolts of unbearable agony provided an almost foolproof method of interrogation. The subject might discipline his mind so as to prevent the answers the inquisitor sought from forming there, but pain broke down this discipline. While his attention was preoccupied with pain, images and information flooded into the body's electrostatic field automatically, quite against his will.

'He doesn't know anything about Princess Veaa,' Rolce declared at length. 'But he knows the address of their chief temple here in Umbul.'

'So what do you recommend now?'

'The princess might be in the temple, or nearby. At any rate someone there should know what has been done with her.' Rolce cogitated briefly. 'Our best bet is to act quickly and decisively, before the Traumatics have time to suspect anything amiss; the disappearance of one of their members, for instance, might alert them to trouble. I suggest a raid on the temple, perhaps assisted by the police or by members of the Imperial Guard stationed here. Even if the princess is not on the premises we are very near the end of the trail.'

Vro gestured floorwards. 'And what of him?'

'If the majordomo can be depended on to dispose of a corpse ...'

'Have no fear. The standards of service in this hotel know no limits.'

'In that case …' Rolce bent low, taking from his pocket a rubbery cylinder which he applied to the prisoner's head. The struggling Traumatic went limp as the weapon turned his brain to jelly.

'Now, Your Highness, I propose that we make our move with the least possible delay.'

Inpriss Sorce was privileged to be sacrificed with full ceremony upon the altar of Hulmu, in the Umbul Temple itself.

She stared as if hypnotised at the representation of Hulmu's Impossible Shape. Here it was not an abstract sculpture but a hologram mobile that writhed and twisted. Stryne noticed her fascination and seized her chin in his hand to forcibly avert her gaze. If one stared at it too long one's eyes began to move independently of one another and sometimes did not right themselves for up to an hour.

As the accredited pursuers, Stryne and Velen had the right to perform the ceremony with no other Traumatics present. A camera had been set up so that the Minion, founder and leader of the Traumatic sect, could watch from another part of the temple.

'Do you believe in Hulmu now, honey?' Stryne asked Inpriss.

'Yes,' she said weakly. And she did. Evil as powerful as theirs could not be founded only on imagination. Something real had to exist behind it.

'He does exist, you know,' Stryne assured her. 'The God of the Church, *he* doesn't exist. We are all Hulmu's creatures. He projected us on to the screen of time, so he could watch us. Mmmmmm.'

The two men moved about the room adjusting the various apparatuses it contained. 'Strip off, Inpriss,' Stryne said.

Obediently she removed her clothes.

'Fine. OK, lie down on the altar.' His voice became caressing.

They began the ceremonies, going through the Compounding of Villainies, the Plot and Counterplot, the Scriptwriter's Diversion. To indulge themselves, though it was not obligatory, they both performed the Ritual of Mounting for the second time, offering up the orgasms to Hulmu as before. Sex and death always went well together.

The devices around them hummed and clicked, many of them performing symbolic functions secret to the sect. Eventually, at their prompting, Inpriss began to speak the responses herself. This was most important. The victim's co-operation had to be genuine.

Stryne and Velen knew that Inpriss had reached a stage of resignation quite divorced from reality: a state that was almost euphoria. If they did their job properly this would be followed by a return to cold realism, a new appreciation of the horror of her position. That was what made the euphoria so useful: the subsequent mental agony was that much greater.

Velen flicked a switch. A chill, urgent vibration undulated through the room. It acted on Inpriss Sorce like cold water. Her eyes widened and came into focus. There came a pause in the Traumatics' chanting.

'What will happen to me when my soul is in the gulf?' she asked in a quivering voice.

'You will be Hulmu's to terrify and torture as he pleases.' Stryne's voice was harsh and brutal.

Suddenly she was shaking all over, her naked limbs knocking uncontrollably against the altar table, and Stryne knew she was ready – in the state of terror required by the ritual. One that would multiply the natural death trauma a hundredfold.

To verify it he consulted one of the monitoring instruments that were arranged around the altar. Her fear index had passed the hundred mark.

Yet he knew that her obedience remained unconditional; her mind had given up believing in any kind of escape.

Finally he switched on an apparatus resembling a miniature radar set. From its concave scanner bowl a mauve effulgence crossed the room and bathed Inpriss Sorce in a pale flickering aura.

This device was probably the most essential of the sect's secrets. The method of its manufacture had been imparted by the Minion himself, who was said to have received it direct from Hulmu. The gadget ensured that during the death trauma the soul would be detached altogether from the body it had clung to for so long. No longer would Inpriss Sorce return to the beginning of her life and live again. She would sink bewildered into potential time, to be seized by Hulmu and enjoyed by him.

Stryne nodded to Velen. They had already decided to accomplish Inpriss's exit by means of slowly penetrating knives. They picked up the long shining weapons.

'Arch your back. Lift your body upwards,' he ordered.

Inpriss obeyed. Her belly and breasts strained up off the table to meet the downpointing knife points.

Slowly the knives descended.

In the prototype time-machine Aton and Dwight Rilke spoke little to each other until they approached the end of their journey. Rilke was meticulous about the final vectoring in. He knew to the minute where he wanted to go.

The laboratory they emerged into was the same one they had left, but less tidy, better equipped, and obviously a place of work rather than a carefully preserved museum. Its sole occupant sat at a workbench with his back to them, poring over some papers and oblivious of their arrival.

Aton viewed this on the time-machine's external vidscreen. Rilke picked up his beamer. He was trembling and there was perspiration on his wrinkled face.

'You're afraid,' Aton said quietly.

The other nodded. 'Not for me. For *him*.'

'How do you see your past self? Is he like someone else? Or is he still *you*?'

Rilke did not answer the question. 'You stay in here, Captain,' he said. 'This is something I ought to do, nobody else.' He paused, then opened a fascia panel beneath the control board. Another beamer was in the small compartment.

'He has a gun too,' he told Aton. 'One shooting lead slugs. Maybe he'll kill me instead. If so, you'd better finish it. Think you can?'

'If I have to.'

Rilke opened the sheet metal door and stepped out. Hearing the sound, the young Rilke turned. Aton saw a steady-eyed young man in his thirties who was less confused than most would have been by the sudden appearance of the bulky cabinet.

'Who are you?' he said sharply after a long time. 'How did you get here?'

The elder Rilke was close to collapsing with the emotion of the moment. 'I am your elder self, Dwight,' he cried in a shaking voice. 'And I'm here to kill you!'

The other looked startled and then, surprisingly, laughed. 'You lunatic!' He leaned over and held down a switch. 'Security? I have an intruder.' Then he turned back to the old man. 'Now why should you want to kill me?'

'Because in a few years you are going to discover something that will turn the world inside out. Look at me, Dwight, don't you recognise me?'

Aton was wondering why Rilke was prolonging the scene instead of getting it over with. Then he understood. Rilke could not bear to see his younger self die in ignorance. He had too much respect for himself.

And that self-respect was liable to prove fatal to his intentions. The young Rilke was astute. He glanced from Rilke to the time-machine as if prepared to take the old man's words seriously. Then he suddenly stood and crossed to one of the cupboards lining the walls of the laboratory and produced from there a hand weapon made of a bluish metal.

Old Rilke, who had kept his beamer out of sight up to now, pointed it and fired. From his shaking hand the beam went wide. The younger man dodged out of the way, turned, pointed, and fired his own gun.

Two loud bangs shattered the air of the laboratory. There was no visible beam but something whanged off some metal support struts. Old Rilke, it seemed, hadn't been hit. He took his beamer in both hands and held down the beam on continuous – a rarely used ploy since it exhausted the power pack. Before it faded the dull red ray scythed across the younger man, who toppled to the floor.

Aton came to the open door of the time-machine. Rilke let fall his beamer. His face sagged.

'It's done!' he said hoarsely. 'It's done!'

Aton stared with interest at the living paradox.

And then what life there was in Rilke's eyes went out. He collapsed to the floor as if every string holding his body together had been cut. With amazing rapidity the flesh began to dry up and shrivel. In little more than a minute nothing remained but a skeleton covered with parchment-like skin.

The paradox was resolved. If the time element was taken out it was a simple suicide.

In moments the security men would be here. Aton gazed around himself once more, marvelling at his continued existence. Then he moved back to the control board.

Experimentally he depressed the automatic retrack stud.

The drive unit started up with a whine and instantly phased the time-machine into the strat.

He sat passively while it carried him back to the starting point, his thoughts subdued. Through the still-open door he could see the naked strat and the conjunction of that with the orthogonal interior of the cramped cabin was one of the oddest things he had ever seen. It occurred to him that there was a way he could control, to a limited extent, his time-travelling ability. He could take a timeship into the strat, open one of its ports, and jump out to go where he pleased – if his subconscious did not take over for him. He could jump out now if he liked. But he decided to see the thing through, and after a while closed the door. From time to time he did some navigational checking to make sure the automatic pilot wasn't being blown off course by Chronotic vagaries, but everything seemed to be functioning normally.

When the machine phased back into orthogonal time San Hevatar was standing in the laboratory looking pensive. Aton stepped calmly out of the cabinet.

'Where have you been?' San Hevatar asked sombrely.

'Trying to straighten out time,' Aton said with a cynical twist of his lips, dispensing with the customary deferences. 'Your assistant Rilke suddenly became one of *my* disciples and thought he could cancel out everything that happened since you and he worked together. But he was wrong.'

Concisely he related what had taken place. San Hevatar was not in the least embarrassed by the disclosure that it had been Rilke who discovered the basic principle behind the time-drive. He merely remarked that for purposes of religious mythology it was better that he, founder of the Church, should be the man to take the credit and that he, in his humility, should attribute it to a direct revelation from God.

'I suspected it would turn out like this,' Aton finished. 'That's one tenet of the Church that's apparently true. Once invented, time-travel stays invented. Rilke's sacrifice was unavailing because paradoxes don't alter anything.'

San Hevatar nodded thoughtfully. 'I always considered that the Historical Office's protective attitude towards the crucial God-given event is unnecessary. Chronotic history is much too ravelled to be undone so easily. The very fact of time-travel weakens from the outset the unique relationship between cause and effect, even when movement is only from node to node. So now, we have time-travel without its ever being invented. Truly wondrous.'

'And truly disastrous,' Aton said. 'Rilke couldn't wipe out the empire, but the Hegemony can. And probably mankind with it.'

The prophet was staring at Aton with a terrible burning intensity. '*You are he!*' he gasped abruptly. 'You are the one! I know you!' He passed a hand across his eyes and swayed as though suffering from dizziness.

'What are you talking about?' Aton demanded harshly.

'Forget my small deceptions,' San Hevatar said with a weary smile. 'Despite those, I am still a prophet of God and occasionally I see through the veil.' His voice became dreamy. 'You are our hope, Aton. You are God's champion, His sword, to fight the enemy of Church and empire.'

A dizziness came over Aton also as he heard the unexpected words. Then, from deep within his mind, he seemed to feel an urgency, a summons. He struggled against the feeling and tried to frame a reply to San Hevatar.

But it was no use. The subconscious part of his nervous system was asserting itself again.

Aton phased into the strat.

He went hurtling futureward – plusward, in chronman's language. All around him flamed and roared the supernal fire of the strat. As he went, that fire burned into him and he realised that his personal ortho field was down. He was soaking up transcendental energies, was becoming multidimensional in his nature and powers.

Because he was fused with this fire, because he maintained no subjective sense of passing time, the journey to his new destination involved no duration. He was vaguely aware that he was skimming at tremendous speed close under the silvery lead screen of orthogonal time. The events on the screen raced past him in a blur of motion.

Then the screen swayed as he slowed down and approached a certain location on it. He found himself looking into a room in a tall building in Node 6. Two men, one lean and feral, the other pudgy and bland, stood over a naked woman who lay on a cloth-draped table, her back arched. In their hands were gleaming daggers which they were bringing down slowly and deliberately towards her white body. All around stood humming, clicking, droning instruments.

Coming closer, Aton knew where he had seen the woman before. She was Inpriss Sorce.

He phased into orthogonal time.

To the two Traumatics it seemed as if he had emerged from the Impossible Shape of Hulmu, for he materialised between it and the altar. They stumbled back with cries of fear, convinced for a moment that their god had appeared to them. Aton was surrounded by a shining halo of iridescent colours. The energies with which he was saturated pulsed and flashed as he moved.

Then they regathered their courage, and, deciding in their confusion that Aton was after all but human, moved in to attack with daggers extended.

A dazzling cloud of pure power, like a charge of ball lightning, shot from Aton's chest and enveloped Stryne, who fell dead.

Velen halted in his stride and stood looking stupid, the knife held awkwardly in his hand. His attention wandered perplexedly between Stryne and Aton. A second power charge soared towards him and he died soundlessly.

Aton stepped softly to the girl. She still lay quivering with back arched, eyes closed, little grunts of exertion coming from her throat as she awaited the knife thrusts. As gently as he could, he put an arm under her shoulders, raised her to a sitting position, and told her to open her eyes.

She looked at him blankly. 'You're safe now,' he said. But it was plain she was in deep shock. Someone who had been subjected to her experience could remain a psychiatric case for years.

He put his hand to her brow. Subtle powers flowed from his palm into her brain. He could sense her every thought, every crevice and receptacle of her mind. Into those hollows he sent healing influences as his thoughts flowed into hers.

Eventually she stopped shivering and became normally alert and calm. 'Thank you,' she said.

'Get dressed. We're leaving.'

While she hurriedly pulled on her garments he prowled around the room, contemptuously knocking over the still-active items of equipment. When he came to the holo camera he cursed himself for not having noticed it before, but disconnected its lead.

He knew that he was at the back of the building and on the third floor. He opened the door and peered out. Glancing back to make sure she was ready, he signalled her to follow him. Together they ventured into the corridor.

On either side were doors, from some of which came the sound of murmurs or muffled chanting. Aton led Inpriss to a staircase. Confident of his ability to deal with all comers, he set off down it, leading her by the hand.

On the second floor a door opened a few yards along the corridor and a bony-faced figure wearing a preoccupied look stepped out. Aton pulled up sharply at the sight of him.

'Sergeant Quelle!'

Quelle looked up, jerked out of his reverie, and plainly could not believe his eyes. His lips mumbled something inaudible. He seemed rooted to the spot. Then, with an inarticulate cry, he turned and tried to claw his way back through the doorway.

Aton raised his free hand and pointed with his index finger. From the finger issued a tight, brilliantly white ray that struck Quelle on the back of the skull. Along the ray passed images: a succession of images at the rate of billions per second. A few of them were marginally visible to Aton and Inpriss, rushing along the narrow beam like a superfast comic strip.

The heretical sergeant fell headlong to the floor, his brain overloaded and burned out by the unnaturally high rate of impressions that had been forced into it.

More Traumatics crowded the doorway in answer to Quelle's cry of alarm. Aton released more power balls in their direction, feeling exultant in his newly acquired might. Inpriss simply watched, her disbelief totally suspended by everything she had been through.

Again he led her down the stairway, but now the building was coming to life. He heard the sound of running feet, of doors opening and slamming.

Aton was puzzled. Could all this activity be on account of him? Not, he reasoned, unless they had been observed by remote, which could not have been by means of the camera in the altar room or they would have been intercepted before now.

One floor further down his question was answered. Here the staircase descended to a lobby opening out from the building's hotel-like front entrance, whose doors had been forced. The lobby was filled with the toques, plumes and grim faces of the Imperial Guard. The temple was being raided.

The guardsmen spread out through the building, trotting past the two fugitives as they mounted the stairs. The captain of the invading force put a bullhorn to his lips.

'*The building is surrounded. There is no escape. Come down and surrender to the forces of the law.*'

As soon as they appeared Aton and Inpriss were seized and hustled urgently down to the lobby. Aton found himself face to face with Prince Vro Ixian, who was accompanied by the stocky Perlo Rolce.

The prince, enwrapped in a purple cloak, presented a picture of youthful hauteur. He raised his eyebrows on seeing Aton.

'But that the question might provoke a lengthy answer,' he said, 'I would ask what you are doing here.'

'Highness, the lady with me is one of the Traumatics' victims,' Aton replied. 'I beseech you to guarantee her safety. She has suffered much at their hands.' In a lower voice he murmured: 'She needs careful handling.'

Vro gestured impatiently to the guardsmen who held the two in their grip. 'It's all right, they are no Traumatics. Release them.'

Inpriss immediately curtsied, apparently overawed by the presence of royalty. Vro acknowledged her with a just-perceptible movement of her head, but his eyes softened.

'Did they abduct you too, my dear? Never fear, you are under the protection of the House of Ixian now. This nest of villains will be cleaned out. Here, let my officer take care of you.'

He called over the Captain of the Guard. As Inpriss was led away, she looked back imploringly at Aton. He smiled and nodded to her, trying to reassure her.

Prince Vro turned back to Aton. He could not help but notice a change in him since he had last seen him. There was something godlike about the handsome young officer. His eyes were stern and flashing; his whole being seemed charged with life and energy.

'We are here looking for my beloved Veaa,' he told Aton. 'I would appreciate your assistance. Have you acquainted yourself with the layout of this den?'

'I'm sorry to disappoint you. I arrived here only in the last few minutes. But I have killed three Traumatics in that time.'

'Easy,' Prince Vro objected, 'I want them alive.'

They walked together up the staircase and through the house. Aton watched as Vro's detective and his assistants questioned the Traumatics who were brought to them, using a combination of torture and field-effect device. Most were eliminated after a minute or two; Rolce did not become interested until he interrogated one of the two women to be found.

She was a tough-faced woman of about fifty whose ragged hair bore streaks of grey. 'She knows something.' Roice announced as she lay between the plates of the device. 'I'm getting images.'

Vro peered close. On the monochrome screen flickered the shadowy spectre of a young girl in a coffin. 'Veaa!' he cried in a choked voice.

'The prong, long and hard!' snapped Rolce.

The female Traumatic screamed and drew in breaths in hard noisy gasps. 'I'll talk!' she begged. 'I'll talk!'

'Let her talk!' commanded Prince Vro.

'That's not necessary, Your Highness. Information is more reliable when obtained by field effect.'

'Let her talk!' roared Vro. He leaned close. 'You know of Princess Veaa. Was her body brought here?'

'Ye-e-e-s.' The woman's lips twisted lasciviously. 'An imperial princess! The Minion thought her soul might be retrievable. That it was suspended in the strat.'

'And was it?'

'No! She was good and dead. Properly dead. Her soul had gone back to the beginning, like everyone else's.' Her face registered disgust.

'So what did you do … with the body?'

'Kept it. For a trophy.'

'Is it here in the temple?'

'No.'

'Then where?'

'Don't know.' She shrugged. 'In the city somewhere.'

Rolce ascertained that she was telling the truth. And as more interrogatees were put under the device, Vro grew more and more fretful. Many of them knew of Princess Veaa. But no one seemed to know where she had been taken.

'Don't despair, Your Highness,' Rolce comforted him. 'She's been here, that's certain. It's a routine matter to trace her from here on.'

Aron decided to explore the temple and left them to it. It was fairly quiet now, but the Imperial Guard would have their work cut out to winkle out everyone in a building so large. There were probably a hundred hiding places. Aton made his way upstairs towards the area where he had found Inpriss. Perhaps, he thought vaguely, he could find what Prince Vro was looking for.

He opened all doors he came to as he went. He saw altar rooms, store-rooms filled with enigmatic equipment, rooms for mysterious purposes. In some of the rooms people huddled in corners and stared at him fearfully. He did not envy them; the Church was not kind to heretics.

Venturing down a deserted corridor he heard a strange mewing sound from behind a door. Aton hesitated, then opened the door slowly and slid inside.

Standing with its back to him was a fat, shabby, slope-shouldered figure holding in pudgy hands a mirror-like object whose surface crawled and shimmered with unrecognisable shapes. The mewing seemed to be an expression of pleasure or amusement as the man gazed into the roiling surface.

At Aton's entrance he put down the mirror and turned to face him. Aton confronted a being straight out of a nightmare, a nightmare he had endured only recently.

The man with jewels for eyes!

The crystal-filled sockets flashed and glittered in a multitude of colours. The face was pudgy and covered with a film of sweat. The slobbery mouth was agape with mirth.

'Come in, Captain Aton, and close the door!' welcomed the creature, its voice giggly and cheerful. 'I have been waiting for you!'

Aton felt an urge to retreat, to get away. 'Who – what – are you?'

'I? Do you not know? I am Hulmu's Minion, chief of all his worshippers!'

'But you are not human.'

'Not human? Indeed I am! A little extended, perhaps, but that is because

I am Hulmu's pet, his little favourite. Like you, I am familiar with the strat. I have been all the way down to Hulmu, to let him sport with me. From time to time he gives me little presents and gadgets. He gave me these eyes, all the better to see in the strat with.'

'Hulmu is real?' Aton became aware of a peculiar offensive odour the Minion gave off.

'Oh, indeed! Do not doubt it. He gave me the time-distorter, all the better to wreak havoc with.'

'The distorter? It comes from *you*?'

'Correct. Surprised?' The Minion lolled his head disclaimingly. 'I don't use it much myself,' he drawled. 'I have an arrangement with the Hegemonics – purely out of the goodness of my heart, of course. When they want to raid the empire, I lend it to them. Afterwards I take it back for safekeeping. They tried to keep it for themselves once. They still don't know how I got it back!' He chortled.

'There is only one?'

'Only one. It's enough.'

'Why don't they try to make another?'

'Can't. They might have tried to analyse it, I dare say. No human being will ever make a gadget like my time-distorter. Only Hulmu is clever enough for that.'

'But why? Why should you want to destroy the empire?'

'Why not? It's all part of Hulmu's plot and counterplot. He is the script-writer, is he not? He projects us, does he not?' The Minion's giggles became hysterical. 'How does it feel to have an audience?'

Aton felt dirtied by this creature's presence. Surely, he thought, the Traumatics' creed cannot be literally true. When he compared this giggling monster with the sedateness and calm reason of the Church …

The Minion seemed to read his mind. 'Oh, the cult of Hulmu is very old. A little bit older than the Church, even. I should know, I started it! Before I became Hulmu's Minion I was Absol Humbart! But those other fools, San Hevatar and Dwight Rilke, rejected Hulmu, the genuine creator. They founded their silly church.'

Grinning, the Minion came towards him with tiny mincing steps. Aton determined to destroy the loathsome creature if he could. He ejected energy from his body, sending rays and waves against the shambling figure. The Minion laughed. His own body began to pulse, shedding sparkling rainbows all around. He seemed to regard it as a game. Their contest filled the room with fantastic forms of light, but neither was hurt in any way.

'I was wiser. I gave myself to Hulmu. He gives me my little toys, and I help him to get what he needs – souls in death trauma!'

They both left off wasting energy in firework displays. Suddenly the sound of booted feet came from further along the corridor. The Imperial Guard were on their way.

'Come, friend Aton,' the Minion hissed. 'Come to Hulmu!'

With surprising agility he bounded forward and seized Aton in his arms. Fetid breath wafted across Aton's face, but before he could react, the Minion had phased into the strat, *taking Aton with him.*

The Minion was amazingly strong. Aton could not break loose from his embrace. Down they sank, spiralling and plummeting, down, down, down. The four-dimensional screen of orthogonal time was left behind. Left behind, too, were the upper reaches of the strat where what was potential already bore some resemblance to what was actual. They went down, down, into the deeps where potentiality had less and less prospect of becoming actuality – that is, of materialising on to the orthogonal world – and had less and less in common with its forms. The pressure was frightful. They sank into gloomy six-dimensional regions where nameless things lurked and waited in the murk. Aton felt brooding hatred as they passed by; the potential quasi-beings sensed that he and the Minion came from the upper world and experienced a writhing envy.

The descent was timeless and Aton seemed temporarily to lose the will to free himself. Then he began to feel the presence of a vast overpowering intelligence.

Hulmu!

Hulmu was something impossible. A six-dimensional, nonexistent shape that lashed and danced in all directions in frantic convolutions. He was lord of this region; all bowed to him.

A voice he could almost smell spoke in Aton's mind.

'Know me and surrender your being.'

In that instant it came home to Aton with a certainty and conviction he could not analyse who the enemy was that had been spoken of by the *Imperator* and San Hevatar.

The enemy of the empire was not the Hegemony. It was not even the Traumatic sect, or the Minion.

It was Hulmu.

He could not define the ultimate evil that was Hulmu. He only saw, as if in a vision, that the struggle was relentless and would continue until victory was gained by one side or the other.

With newly regained strength Aton lashed out. The Minion sought to restrain him, but he broke free and soared upwards like a bubble, out of the reach of Hulmu's lashing tentacles. Other powers snatched at him but he knew he was safe.

Up, up, up.

TEN

Aton was semi-conscious for the latter part of his ascent to the realm of materiality. He did not fully recover until he had already phased into ortho.

His subconscious mind had brought him to familiar territory. He was standing in the deserted court chamber of the Imperial Palace's inner sanctum, Node 1. It was night and the chamber was only dimly lit.

Silence prevailed everywhere.

After some moments he saw a lone figure seated on a couch and stepped closer.

It was Inpriss Sorce.

'Inpriss?'

She looked up. 'You're back!'

'How did you get here?'

'Prince Vro's men brought me. They said I'd be safe here in the palace. I'm under imperial protection.' A note of pride entered her voice as she said the last. She smiled. 'It's certainly a different type of life from what I'm used to.'

'But it can only have been minutes ago that I last saw you.'

A slightly wary look crossed her face. 'It's been nearly three days.'

Three days. Had he been that long in the gulf?

Shaken, he glanced at a wall clock and frowned.

'Where is everybody? Surely they don't retire this early?'

'They're all in the churches and chapels, praying. The armada has set out.'

So matters were coming to a climax. And his mission had failed.

Disconsolately he paced the great hall. He tried to imagine the pace of events beyond the bounds of the palace in the eternal city and throughout the mighty time-spanning empire. Did he fancy he heard the structure of time creaking like the timbers of a crippled ship?

Unexpectedly there came the whirring of motors. The *Imperator* rolled out from its hidden compartment and towered over the man and the woman.

'My servant, Captain Aton,' the resonant voice murmured.

'*Imperator.*'

'It was a stirring sight, Captain. Powerful timeships, seemingly without number, coming one by one up the procession ramp to be presented to the people and blessed by the Arch-Cardinal Reamoir, before phasing into the strat. Now the three main wings are joining formation from the nodes where they were built. Very soon the Hegemony should feel their presence. If it does at all …'

'May God go with them, *Imperator*,' Aton replied dully.

'If it does at all,' repeated the *Imperator* fatalistically. 'The Hegemony is also gathering all its forces. It knows the last card has been called. For the past few days it has been using the time-distorter at full aperture.'

'*Imperator*,' Aton said eagerly, though it now seemed rather late for this information, 'the time-distorter belongs to the Traumatic sect and was given to them by the being they call Hulmu.'

The machine-emperor's continuous hum undulated thoughtfully. 'Orthogonal time is breaking up, Captain. If you were to journey through the empire now you would not recognise it. For the past two days it has been impossible to phase into Nodes Three and Four.'

Aton was aghast. '*What?*'

'Nothing intelligible exists there. Orthogonal time has become totally deranged in the area. The strat is like an ocean in many respects, Captain Aton. The features we call the nodes are the regularly spaced ripples on the surface that hold the orthogonal world together. But there can be deeper waves that can overthrow everything. Tidal waves that tear the world of reality apart.'

Aton noted that the *Imperator* spoke more lucidly than on an earlier occasion. But if it had recovered its sanity it had done so belatedly. The picture it drew was frightening.

'What will happen?'

'What has happened will happen.'

Back to cryptic utterances, Aton thought in disgust.

Inpriss had crept forward to join them. She looked up overawed at the *Imperator*, which she could only have known as a semi-legendary ultimate authority. Her hand touched Aton's sleeve as if seeking comfort.

Aton happened to glance to his right and with bulging eyes saw the east wall curve inward as though it were a wall of water. In seconds the heaving structure righted itself and stood rigid, but he knew the signs of spatio-temporal deformation.

'Are we under attack?' he asked sharply.

'The whole empire is under attack. Time is under attack.'

Those were the last words the *Imperator* spoke before the great darkness descended on them all and expunged them from reality.

They returned still carrying the memory of their previous existence. 'What happened?' said Aton.

'The empire was annihilated,' said the *Imperator*, 'and then put back.'

The entirety of the strain being put upon orthogonal time had been steadily building up into a wide-scale wave motion originating deep in the substratum. Eventually it had climaxed in a sort of tidal wave. The Chronotic Empire, and everything associated with it, was swept away.

But the giant time-storm was by no means over. On the contrary, the oscillations were building up and becoming more violent. As the wave entered the second half of its cycle the empire reappeared, almost exactly as when the wave had overtaken it.

But not quite.

There were innumerable small changes. And the difference between these and normal Chronotic mutations was that the inhabitants of the empire were aware of them.

Prince Vro Ixian had at last achieved his heart's desire. Following leads found in the Traumatics' temple in Umbul, the detective Perlo Rolce had traced the body of Princess Veaa to a rundown house in the outskirts of the city. Prince Vro, arming himself and taking only Rolce with him, entered the house and found it uninhabited.

Methodically he went through the dwelling room by room. In the second floor back he discovered a chamber draped in white silk. An open coffin of pinewood lay on a dais, and in the coffin, as beautiful as a pale rose, was the embalmed corpse of the young princess.

'My dearest, my beloved Veaa!' Vro swept towards the coffin.

And in that moment the tidal wave of potential time overcame the material world and swept everything away. The world came back in what, to the actors in it, could have been only an instant. But Vro was aware of the hiatus and understood what it implied.

In the coffin Princess Veaa opened her eyes, moved her head, and slowly sat up.

Vro gave a wild cry. 'Veaa!' he shrieked.

'Vro!' Her shriek was no less mortified.

The two stared at each other in utter horror.

In the court chamber everything was more or less as before. Inpriss Sorce clung tightly to Aton.

'Will it happen again?' Aton asked.

'The wave has but receded for a moment. The turbulence is still building up. When it returns there will be no reprieve. All will dissolve … permanently.'

The *Imperator* clicked and hummed. Suddenly there was a muted whine, and a part of its matted surface opened. Aton saw a tiny room within, illuminated, its walls padded.

'Get inside, quickly,' the *Imperator* ordered.

The command's urgent tone brooked no inquiry. Hastily Aton and Inpriss crowded into the small space. The door closed up behind them.

The rolling geodesics of the substratum, summoned up from the deeps, had hit a resonance that nothing could withstand. As the mighty preponderance of Chronotic potentiality smashed against the empire for the second time, the edifice that had been built up with such care was not temporarily annulled merely, but torn apart, and the materiality of the fragments dissipated beyond recovery. The screen of orthogonal time was, itself, ripped to shreds.

Seconds before this happened the *Imperator* had phased into the strat. Aton, reading the move on a small instrument panel with which the tiny cabin was provided, was only mildly surprised to learn that the machine-emperor possessed this ability. He heard the strained drone of the modest drive unit as it battled against the dangerous turbulences.

Where was the *Imperator* taking them?

So it had happened. The one thing uniquely feared by achronal archivists had finally come to pass.

Phased permanently into the strat, the Achronal Archives were the one department of Chronopolis's administration to survive. The archivists now saw the fullest justification of their cult of isolationism. The emotionally shattered men and women prowled around the vaults, touching one another for comfort, caressing the humming casings that contained the computer store of all that had taken place in the vanished Chronotic Empire.

All around them lay nothing but the strat. *There was no orthogonal time.* The time-storm, of unprecedented proportions, had eliminated it, and potentiality reigned supreme. There was no actuality, except for this one little isolated bubble.

The in-turned atmosphere of the sepulchral establishment, always noticeable, now intensified by the minute. Chief Archivist Illus Ton Mayar knew that in short order it would develop into group insanity. But he did not think that any of them would live to see that happen. Very soon the archives would melt into the strat like sugar in water. Their existential support – the whole material background from which they had sprung – had been taken away. They persisted now only by virtue of strat time, which did not match one-for-one with orthogonal time.

Mayar was sitting alone in his private room when there was a hammering on the door and an excited shout from one of the senior archivists.

'There's something approaching through the strat.'

Mayar hurried to investigate. He arrived at the loading bay just in time to see the imposing bulk of the *Imperator* materialise there.

All present fell to their knees. A door in the side of the *Imperator* clicked open and a man and a woman, the man dressed as a captain of the Time Service, stepped out.

Mayar watched the apparition with astonishment. 'God be praised!' he managed to say. But he still did not dare to hope.

The man and the woman stepped towards him, but before he could speak again the *Imperator* had once more vanished.

And in the Invincible Armada, swaying its way through the disturbed and roiling strat, there also dawned the realisation of the empire's destruction.

Prince Philipium, Grand Admiral of the Armada, enthroned in the majestic bridge in the titanic flagship *God's Imposer*, froze as though paralysed. His face was almost green with shock.

There could be no mistake. From all parts of the huge armada the message was the same. The instruments revealed that the concept of order and religion which everyone on board was sworn to serve was irrevocably gone.

To the commanders surrounding Prince Philipium the news brought varied emotions. Sick anger, sinking fear, stony grimness, defiant hatred.

'We are ghosts!' uttered Prince Philipium in a voice hollow with grief. 'What can we do? The empire is vanquished!'

'Ghosts we may be, but we shall still live for a while,' growled Commander Haight. He tried to calculate how long it would be before the armada faded away and lost all vestige of materiality, now that it had no existential support. It could be hours or days.

'One thing is still left to us,' he urged. 'Revenge! Let us ensure that of the Hegemony, too, nothing remains!'

Exultant shouts greeted his words. Prince Philipium, his eyes staring but devoid of life, gave the orders.

The ghost armada moved forward only to find that its quest was needless. The Hegemony had gone down along with the empire. The ships that it had put into the strat, however, persisted like those of the armada itself. The two forces locked on to each other and began to battle. There was no question of phasing into ortho to fire their weapons – there was no orthogonal time any longer – and the strat torpedoes were too ineffective to satisfy their blood lust. Instead the ships sought to destroy each other by collision. The conflict raged on, fed by despair and hatred.

Aton found he could strike little cheer from the Chief Archivist and his assistants. They seemed unable to recognise that the existence they knew had, in fact, vanished and that they would shortly die. In what Aton found a morbid manner they preferred to go about their duties and spent as much time as possible lovingly going over recorded scenes of bygone days and endless lists of names, places, and events.

Neither was he able to answer any of their questions. But two hours later those scanning the surrounding strat reported that an object was again approaching.

For the second time the *Imperator* materialised into the loading bay.

'Aton, my servant!' it boomed.

Aton stood before it stiffly. 'I am here, *Imperator*.' Then he added, 'Where have you been?'

'Into the far future. My mind is clear now.'

The *Imperator* seemed larger, more powerful, more majestic than it ever had before. 'The time for your greatest service to the empire has arrived, Captain Aton.'

'I do not understand, *Imperator*. There is no empire.'

'What has been will be. If you are victorious.' The machine-emperor paused. 'The Minion thinks he has won. He has recovered the time-distorter from his Hegemonic tools and now plans to use it again for another purpose.'

'*Imperator!* What is there to talk about?' Mayar interrupted brokenly. 'All is gone!'

Impatiently Aton cautioned Mayar to keep silence. The *Imperator* hummed loudly. 'At present potential time, alike to primordial chaos, has drowned the world of real time,' it resumed. 'The Chronotic storm, however, is abating; soon orthogonal time will form again on the gulf's surface, like a skin forming on a liquid. If allowed to congeal without interference, it is impossible to say what that new world will be like. That is where the Minion intends to come in. He will use the time-distorter to project a world agreeable to Hulmu, his master. That must not be. You must fight him, Aton. You must take the distorter away from him.'

'But I don't think I can, *Imperator*,' Aton said. 'I have already learned to my cost that the Minion is strong.'

'With the help of religion, you can defeat him.'

Without warning a wide-angled beam of light shot out from the *Imperator* and bathed Aton. Immediately an extraordinary flood of thoughts and feelings flooded his mind, all connected with the religion in which he had been brought up. Prayers, catechisms and hymns such as he had been taught as a child seemed to sing in his brain.

The emotion engendered by this experience made him feel humble. Objectively, he recognised the use of a thought ray similar in principle to a field-effect device, except that it worked in reverse. The *Imperator* was reminding him of his religious training. But why?

'The Minion approaches. Come.'

Once more the door to the inner chamber in the machine's metal side opened. Aton hesitated.

Then he entered. The *Imperator* phased into the strat and went speeding down, seeming to know where to go. After what felt like a long wait, Aton became aware that it had killed its velocity and was idling. The door opened, and through it he could see the strat, spreading and convoluting before his tortured eyes.

The message was clear. He ventured into the strat.

He saw the Minion almost immediately, soaring up from the deep, carrying the big tube-like device Aton had seen once before. As Aton came closer he saw the jewel eyes flash and glint through the supernal fire that surrounded them both. The Minion's mouth was agape and raucous laughter issued from it.

'Ha ha ha! You want my little toy! Oh, no! This time Hulmu will have *you*!'

Aton moved in to the attack.

The Minion pointed the tube. Vapours gushed forth and Aton felt himself being wafted away, his four-dimensional form deformed and eroded. With difficulty he evaded the vapours, and then he closed with the Minion and wrestled bodily with him.

The Minion had more than one shape! Limbs and extruberances shot out from him in all the directions of the five-dimensional space in which they fought. Aton found himself encaged in a living organism of roots, limbs, and branches.

He himself was not without resource. With a supreme effort he caused every cell of his body to discharge the transcendent energy it had gained by immersion in the strat. There was a sort of explosion, an uncoiling of the immaterial continuum, and he was free.

But he was weakened. And then, before he could take stock of himself, he was imprisoned once more.

This time he seemed to be transfixed or encaged in brilliantly coloured glass or crystal. There was a sudden shift, and then he knew he had been transferred to a similar, but second prison.

He was inside the Minion's eyes, being flashed alternately from one to the other!

Laughingly the Minion ejected him and hovered jeering. His ability to alter him in size gave Aton a real appreciation of the greater power of his enemy. He began to despair.

'Hee hee hee! First I will reform the world, and then I will take you down again to Hulmu, poor little captain!'

Tenaciously Aton circled, and then moved in again.

Through his brain was running a prayer, one he had known since he was a child. Something within him was urging him to say this prayer aloud, and when he came near the Minion again, he sent the vibrations of the words spearing into the strat.

'Holy Father, bringer of comfort, deliver us from the enemy of time.'

That was all, but surprisingly the Minion recoiled as if in horror. Aton pursued him, speaking the prayer over and over again.

'Holy Father, bringer of comfort, deliver us from the enemy of time. Holy Father, bringer of comfort, deliver us from the enemy of time.'

The Minion shrieked with pain. He flashed out and writhed in a million illusory shapes, running the full gamut of his evil energies in an uncontrolled spasm. The prayer seemed to reduce him to a condition akin to the effect of nerve gas on a normal nervous system. Aton dived in and seized the time-distorter. The Minion struggled briefly to retrieve it, then fell back.

Then the Minion suddenly fell headlong into the gulf at extraordinary speed. 'Hulmu! I have failed you again! Ohhhhhh ...'

And Aton had carried out the orders of the *Imperator*.

The *God's Imposer* was junked.

The huge ship had run head-on into countless enemy vessels. Smaller craft it had swatted like flies. But finally the total of those collisions had proved crippling. The twisted and shattered hulls of upwards of a dozen Hegemonic vessels were embedded in the *God's Imposer*, and the giant drive units now were silent.

'The ortho field won't last long, sir!' gasped an ensign. 'It's down in parts of the ship already.'

'Then kill yourself, you little fool, like the others are doing,' growled Commander Haight. 'Me, I'm not hanging around like a trapped rat.'

And in fact the bridge was littered with suicides, including Prince Philipium. No one had bothered to use the ship's many life rafts or strat suits. But Commander Haight was not on the bridge. He was down in the guts of the ship, just within its outer wall. And the ensign was stationed at one of the ports that, had the armada succeeded, would have been pouring troops on to the ground.

'There's something I've always wanted to experience,' Haight grated out, 'and now I'm going to. Open the port, Ensign.'

'But, sir!'

'You heard me, you young squirt. It's an order. *Get that port open!*'

Trembling, the ensign turned his back to the port and operated a series of switches. The port whined slowly open, dilating iris-fashion. The safety cover went up.

Pressing his forearm against his eyes so that he would not be struck unconscious and fall to the deck, Commander Haight flung himself at a run into the strat.

'To understand what has happened,' said the *Imperator* to Aton, Inpriss Sorce, and the assembled archivists, 'it is necessary to understand the nature of time and the origin of Church and empire.

'Orthogonal time is reality. But reality cannot continue to subsist by itself. Like every structure in the universe it requires a certain kind of feedback on itself to remain steady. It requires something against which to rest itself, to react upon, otherwise, if it simply existed in a void, it would soon collapse into nothing.

'This something is the temporal substratum. The strat is, if you like, aberrated reality; it provides the feedback that keeps real time stable, or relatively so. As such, it is potential, not actual, and less than real.

'The deeper one goes, the less like reality the strat is. In the uttermost depths are forms of quasi-existence inconceivable for us! And they are only there at all because somewhere – in orthogonal time – is the authentic existence from which they are degraded.

'The quasi-beings in these depths have a terrible hunger for authentic existence. But they are unable to emerge into it because they are too far removed from its nature. Some of them, however, are immensely powerful in their own realm; such a one is Hulmu.

'He is the enemy of mankind.'

'I had thought Hulmu was just a superstition on the part of the Traumatic sect,' Mayar said hesitantly. 'I hadn't even believed the Church when it identified him with the Evil One.'

'He is genuine and we have been fighting him for countless aeons. The empire is much older, in terms of eternity, than you think.'

The *Imperator* hummed meditatively. 'Until the discovery of time-travel the existential world was safe from such monsters. There was no possibility of their touching orthogonal time. Then, in some unique accident of history, a man called Dwight Rilke hit on a flaw in the structure of the world. He discovered that there was a way whereby matter could be moved through time.

'From that instant the universe of actuality was in danger. And that danger manifested almost immediately. During the early experiments there was an unfortunate accident whereby one of the assistants fell headlong into the temporal substratum. This man was Absol Humbart, later the Minion. He was caught by Hulmu, who realised that the weakening of orthogonal time offered him an opportunity to claw his way up and become real. But still it was not easy. In order to gain a foothold Hulmu needed first to acquire sufficient reality, in order to transfer himself to the surface.

'For this Absol Humbart promised souls! If Hulmu could devour enough souls that had lived in orthogonal time, then he could erupt into our world and establish himself there, satisfying his enormous hunger to become real!

'But the driblets he has been given are not nearly enough. His strategy has only one object – *to be able to absorb the death trauma of mankind, past, present, and future!* Only by devouring every man, woman, and child who ever lived, or will live, can Hulmu gain the wherewithal to climb out of his pit, claim the Earth and eventually, perhaps, the galaxy. To this end he and the Minion scheme, trying to create a situation that will bring about the death of humanity in special circumstances. If the Minion could have employed the time-distorter just as orthogonal time was reforming, he might have achieved this. The distorter is an instrument no man could have conceived of; its construction requires the powers of a god.'

The *Imperator* paused to allow them to digest its words.

'You say we have fought this beast for aeons,' called a brave archivist, 'but the empire itself has not existed that long.'

Something resembling a laugh issued from the machine. 'The empire has risen, fallen, and risen again, countless times. All that will be has been, again and again and again. Always, at this point, we have managed to foil Hulmu; always we have managed to resurrect the empire by the same means that he destroyed it. The process has, I estimate, gone through the cycle one billion times.

'But I have not completed my tale. How did the empire arise? It was no accident. Of those involved in so rashly presenting mankind with time-travel one, San Hevatar, saw the danger. He knew that the evil Traumatic sect had to be countered. He founded the Church to fight Hulmu. He designed the rituals of the Church as a weapon and a bastion against Hulmu. That is why, Aton, your prayer was so effective against the Minion; it is especially constructed to contain vibrations he cannot endure. If it were not for the Church, all might have fallen victims to Hulmu by now.'

'You say this,' pointed out Aton seriously, 'but the San Hevatar I have met did not strike me as being aware of it.'

'He was not. Perhaps the first time around he was. But now, after so many changes and resurrections, we move through our parts as if in a dream. Did you know that you must fight the Minion? Even I did not know, I only remembered flashes, like San Hevatar. Most of the time I am completely insane, as your friend Prince Vro tells you. I am insane, and know only these lucid periods when the empire has vanished. Then I travel into the far future to visit the civilisations there, and everything becomes clear.'

'The future people,' Inpriss objected, 'why don't *they* help us to fight Hulmu?'

'They cannot, and in any case they do not believe in Hulmu. They know only that the secret of time-travel is the most dangerous secret in the universe, that if it is not controlled it can destroy time. That is why they want the empire continually to rise and fall in its war with the Hegemony; it is history's warning to mankind. There are no Chronotic empires in future ages; men are too afraid. But if the example of the empire were not before them then they might forget and begin to tamper with time.'

'And you,' said Aton. 'Who are you? *What* are you?'

'I am the oldest part of the empire. I began life as an administrative computer in the physics laboratories of Monolith Industries. I took part in the
original discoveries concerning pi-mesons. When the struggle with the Minion began I played a leading part in it. Gradually I was extended and increased
my intelligence. Now I and the Minion are the main actors in the drama. He
has an advantage because he is coached by Hulmu. With every cycle he grows
stronger. We, too, must grow stronger, Aton! I could not tell you often how
you often have fought the Minion!'

'One billion times,' Aton said dryly.

'No, not so. No one could be expected to endure that for so long. Every so
often fate changes the champion who challenges him. Once it was Commander Haight; now he has been relieved of the duty and knows nothing of
it. Next time it may be you, or it may be another. I cannot tell. But someone
always arises with sufficient power to struggle against him. And always I am
here to see that he does so. Eventually, perhaps, I will have evolved sufficiently to play the role myself.'

The *Imperator*'s hum grew louder. 'You must understand that of the world
as it was before the empire arose nothing remains. Even the calendar is different. Dwight Rilke's discovery was made in the twenty-fourth century of
their era; and the Stop Barrier was eventually placed in what was their fif-
teenth century, before a technological society had even developed.'

'You speak of resurrecting the empire,' said Mayar, still puzzled, 'but how
can that be? How can it possibly be accomplished?'

'In the same way that the Minion hoped to accomplish a world fit for
Hulmu to live in. We have Hulmu's time-distorter. Hulmu misled the Minion
when he represented himself as the creator and projector of the images on
the screen of time; he is not that, merely an impotent spectator. Nevertheless
his time-distorter can, to an extent, achieve creation.'

The *Imperator* rolled forward and stood over those present in an almost
menacing fashion. 'The strat, just before the film of orthogonal time forms, is
like a supersaturated solution waiting to be seeded. The time-distorter is
designed to feed vibrations into that solution, and from those vibrations a
world will grow. Here we have all the components to recreate the empire. We
have the Achronal Archives with their detailed knowledge of the empire. The
rituals of the Church themselves are the basis whereby the essence of the empire
can be restored; San Hevatar intended them that way. We have the time-
distorter to project all this on to the newly forming orthogonal world, and we
have myself, *Imperator*, to operate it!'

With a small sharp explosion a section of the *Imperator* fell away to reveal
a neat concavity. 'Long ago I equipped myself for this task. Fit the distorter
into this space. Jack into me the output leads from your archival computers.
Quickly, there is little time! I will re-create all the original conditions, the

starting point from which the empire will burgeon! All will be foreordained! The war with Humlu must continue eternally!'

Inpriss Sorce gave a little cry. 'Must I go through it all again?' she quavered.

'There may be variations,' the resonant voice said in a near-whisper. 'Perhaps next time you will live in peace. Perhaps, too, some other officer of the Time Service, not Captain Mond Aton, will become familiar with the strat and be called upon to fight the Minion. Only one thing is certain; if the empire falls and cannot be reformed, then mankind falls to Hulmu, and monsters crawl out of the deeps of potential time to claim the Earth.'

While the machine spoke, the archivists were busy doing its bidding; the *Imperator*'s word was law.

And when at last the time-distorter was triggered and mighty energies began issuing from its mouth, and when at the same time they all began to fade out of existence, Aton, holding Inpriss's hand, felt in the depths of his being that this was not the end, that he would be called on, once more, to be a servant of the empire, and that the war, truly was, eternal.

ELEVEN

'These pi-mesons certainly are tricky fellers,' said Dwight Rilke.

'Tricky as hell,' agreed Humbart.

Rilke threw down his pencil and leaned back. Vague thoughts and ideas drifted through his mind, all related to the main problem: how to isolate pi-mesons in a stable state, for long enough and in sufficient quantity to do something with them.

His gaze fell on the computer across the room. Its unusual bulk was due to the fact that it incorporated its own compact nuclear power unit as insurance against the erratic electricity supply. The civil disturbances were becoming more pronounced of late and the computer did most of the administrative work for the branch.

Rilke had decided on a nickname for the machine, because of the imperious way it delivered data.

He would call it *Imperator*.

The door opened. One of the staff girls came in with a sheaf of reports.

'Thank you, Miss Sorce,' Absol Humbart said.

If you've enjoyed these books and would
like to read more, you'll find literally thousands
of classic Science Fiction & Fantasy titles
through the **SF Gateway**

✳

*For the new home of
Science Fiction & Fantasy . . .*

✳

*For the most comprehensive collection
of classic SF on the internet . . .*

✳

Visit the SF Gateway

www.sfgateway.com

Barrington J. Bayley (1937–2008)

Barrington J. Bayley was born in Birmingham and began writing science fiction in his early teens. After serving in the RAF, he took up freelance writing on features, serials and picture strips, mostly in the juvenile field, before returning to straight SF. He was a regular contributor to the influential *New Worlds* magazine and an early voice in the New Wave movement.